Soooo glad I got ... hi...

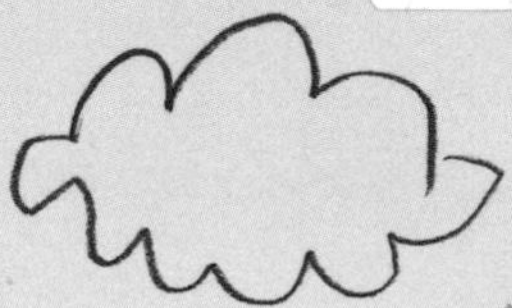

OLIVIA L.

Hi, Viv! Thanks for being a good friend this year.

-Sabrey

I'll sign this, but we're gonna see each other all the time...RIGHT??

jk this year was interesting...but Fun! Let's keep skating this summer!

-AI

P.S. Rilla RULES!

Thanks for helping me with the Halloween Dance! I am a fog machine fan for life. LOL. We need

Picture Day

Sarah Sax

ALFRED A. KNOPF
NEW YORK

THIS IS A BORZOI BOOK PUBLISHED BY ALFRED A. KNOPF

This is a work of fiction. Names, characters, places, and incidents
either are the product of the author's imagination or
are used fictitiously. Any resemblance to actual
persons, living or dead, events, or locales is entirely coincidental.

Copyright © 2023 by Sarah Sax

All rights reserved. Published in the United States by Alfred A. Knopf, an imprint of
Random House Children's Books, a division of Penguin Random House LLC, New York.

Knopf, Borzoi Books, and the colophon are registered
trademarks of Penguin Random House LLC.

RH Graphic with the book design is a trademark of Penguin Random House LLC.

Photographs on pages 282–283 courtesy of the author.

Visit us on the Web! rhcbooks.com

Educators and librarians, for a variety of teaching tools,
visit us at RHTeachersLibrarians.com

Library of Congress Cataloging-in-Publication Data is available upon request.
ISBN 978-0-593-30688-8 (trade) — ISBN 978-0-593-30687-1 (pbk.) —
ISBN 978-0-593-30689-5 (lib. bdg.) — ISBN 978-0-593-30690-1 (ebook)

The text of this book is set in 12-point Brinkley Yearbook.
The illustrations were created digitally.
Book design by Sarah Sax and April Ward

MANUFACTURED IN CHINA
10 9 8 7 6 5 4 3 2 1
First Edition

To my fellow
Hixson Middle School
Sailor Scouts:
Jennie, Sarah,
Celeste, and Maggie

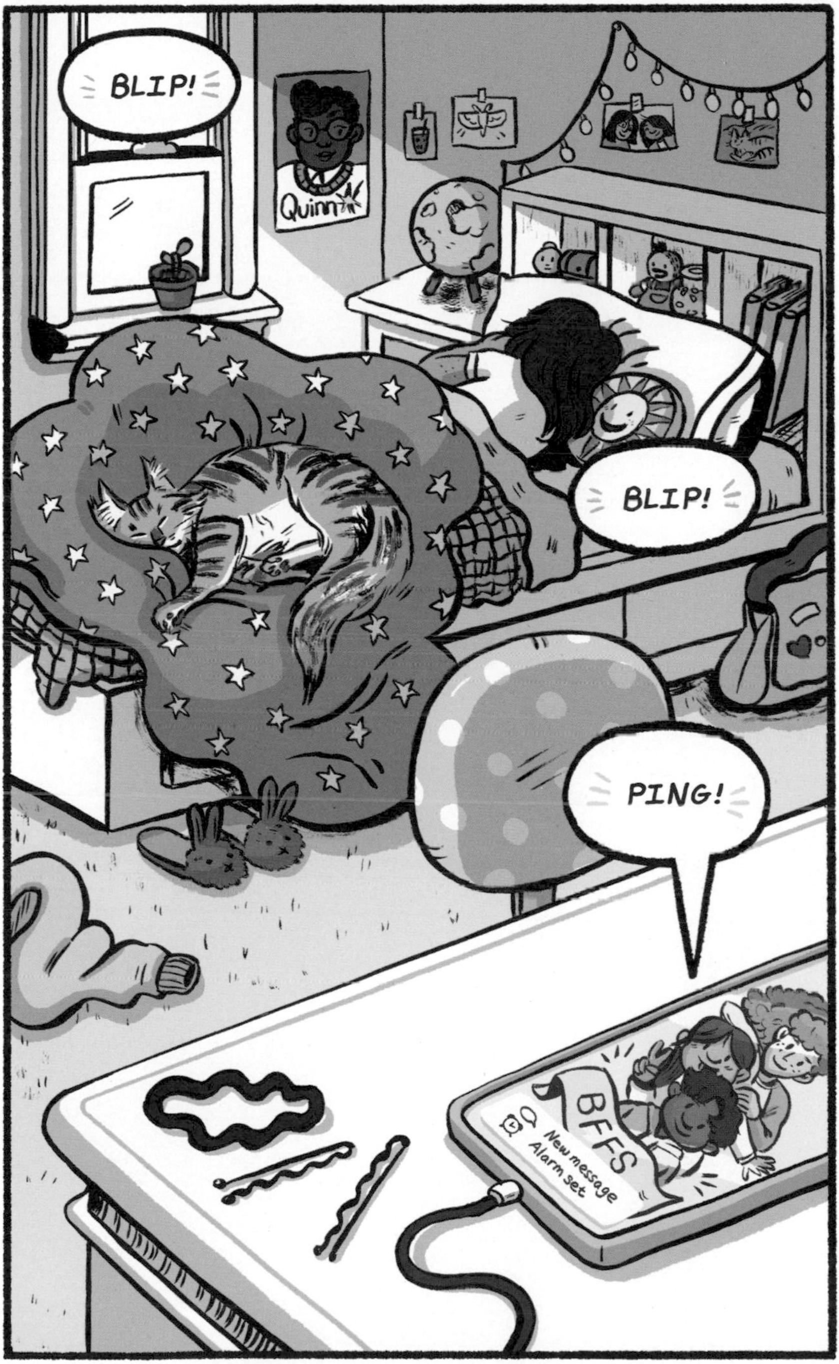
BLIP!
Quinn
BLIP!
PING!
BFFS
New message
Alarm set

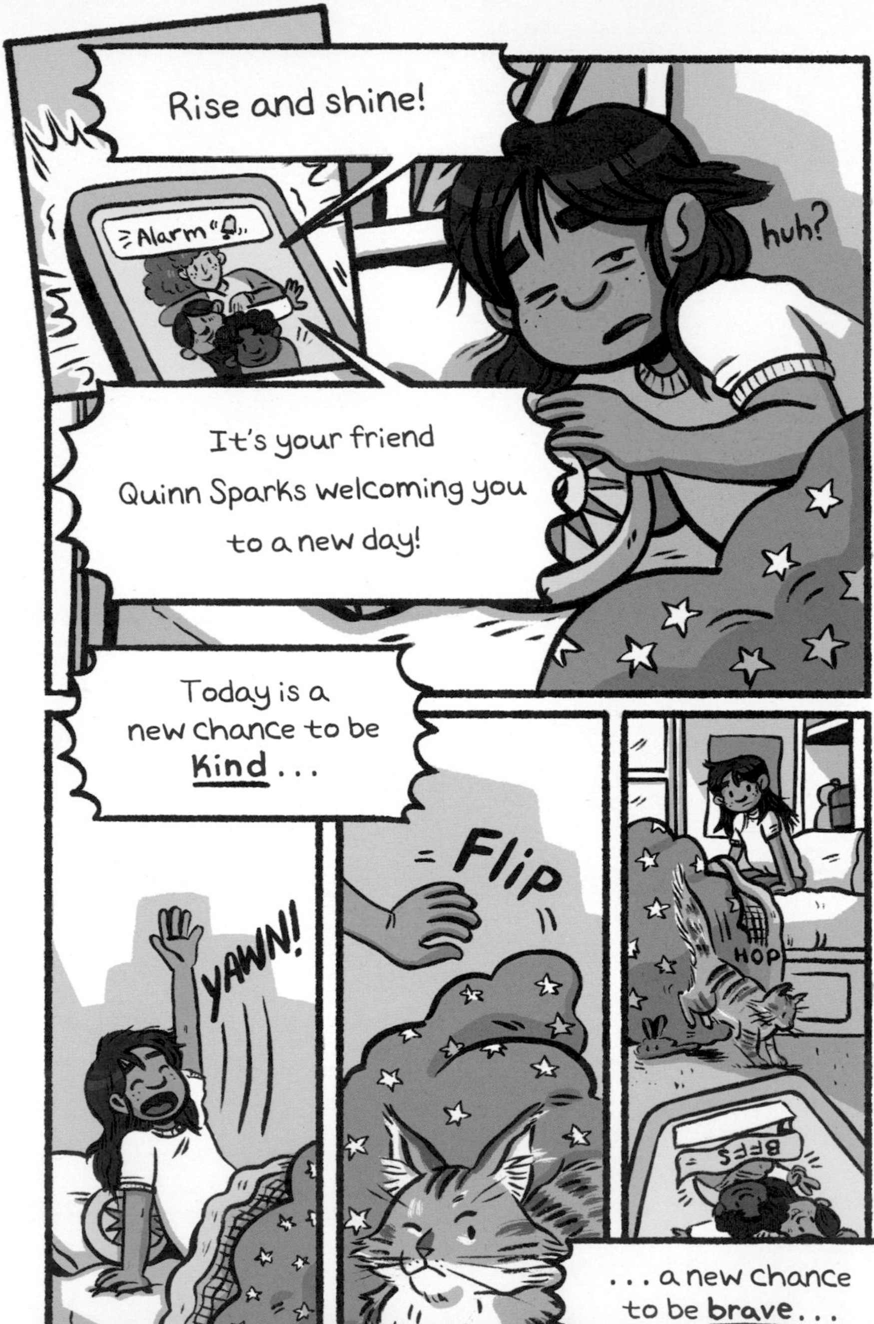

Rise and shine!
Alarm
huh?
It's your friend Quinn Sparks welcoming you to a new day!
Today is a new chance to be **kind** . . .
YAWN!
Flip
HOP
BFFS
. . . a new chance to be **brave** . . .

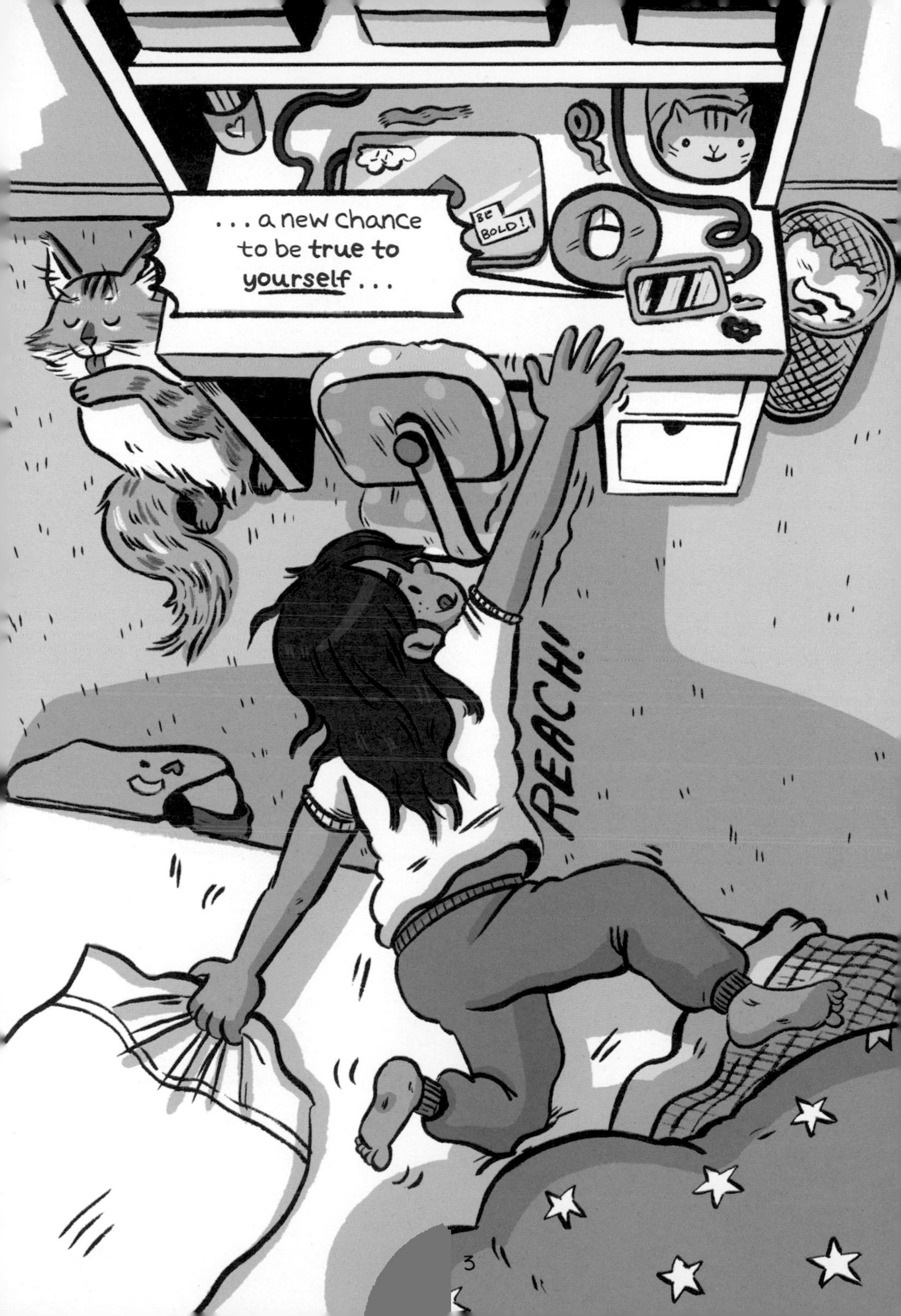
. . . a new chance to be **true to** **yourself** . . .
BE BOLD!
REACH!

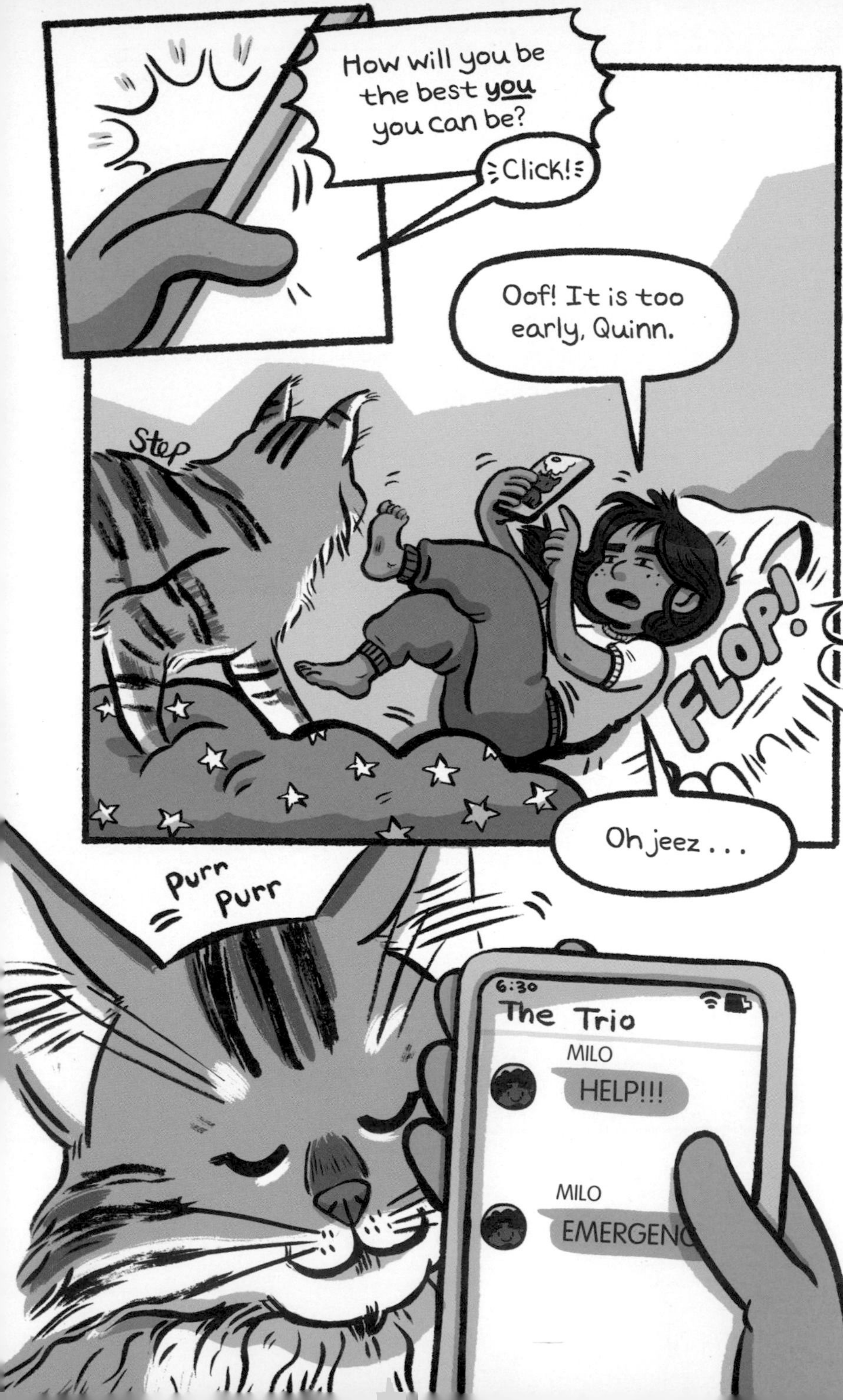
How will you be the best you you can be?
Click!
Oof! It is too early, Quinn.
Step
FLOP!
Oh jeez . . .
Purr Purr
6:30
The Trio
MILO
HELP!!!
MILO
EMERGENC

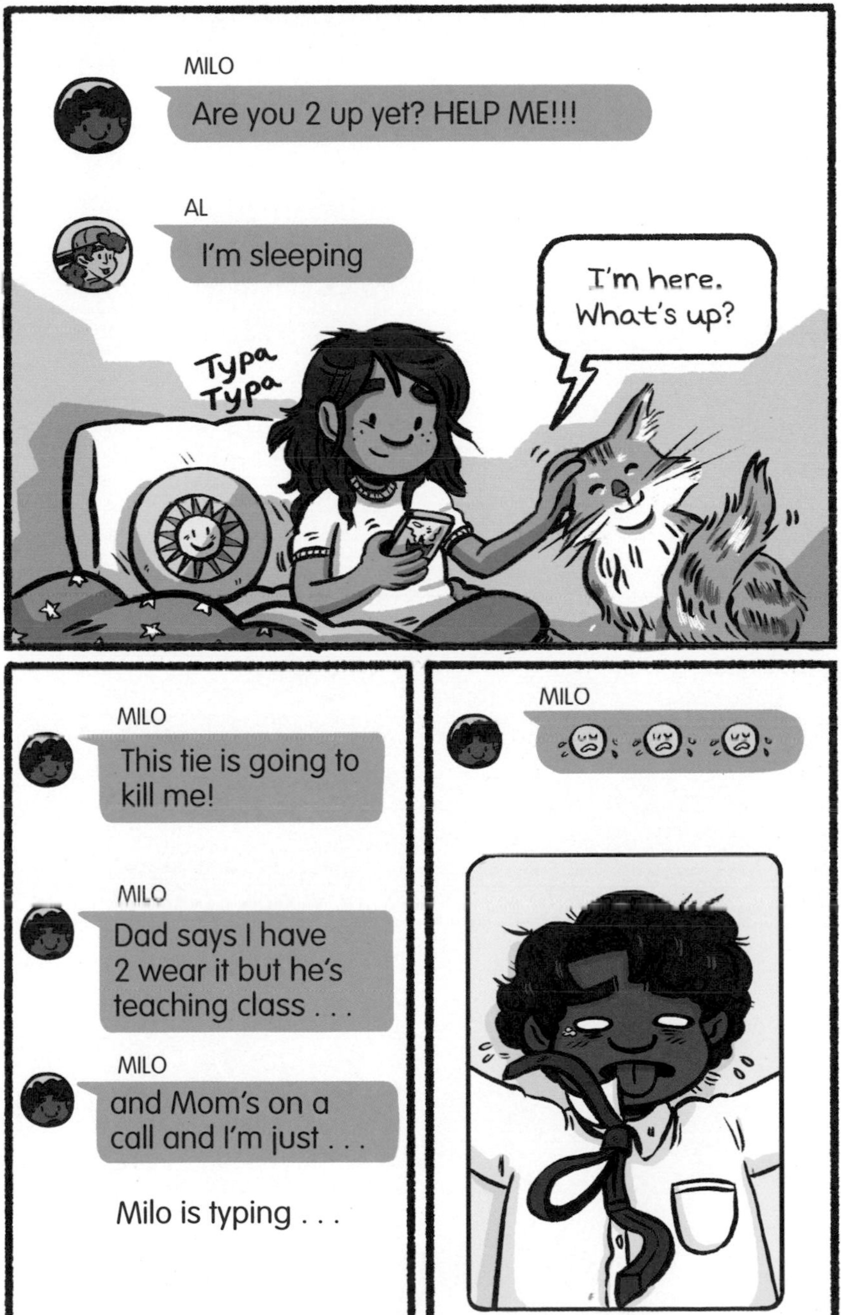
MILO
Are you 2 up yet? HELP ME!!!
AL
I'm sleeping
Typa Typa
I'm here. What's up?
MILO
This tie is going to kill me!
MILO
Dad says I have 2 wear it but he's teaching class . . .
MILO
and Mom's on a call and I'm just . . .
Milo is typing . . .
MILO

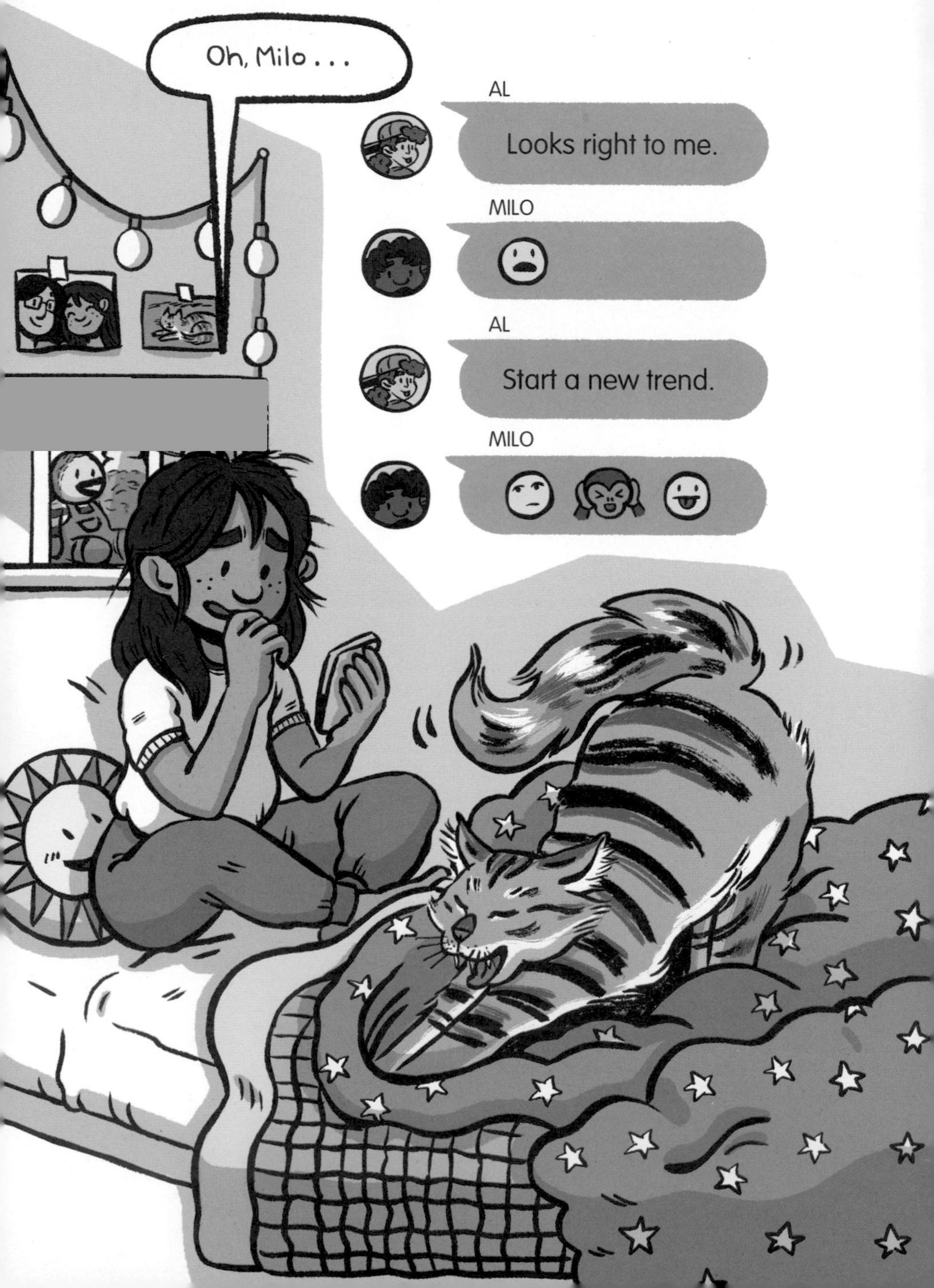
Oh, Milo . . .
AL
Looks right to me.
MILO
AL
Start a new trend.
MILO

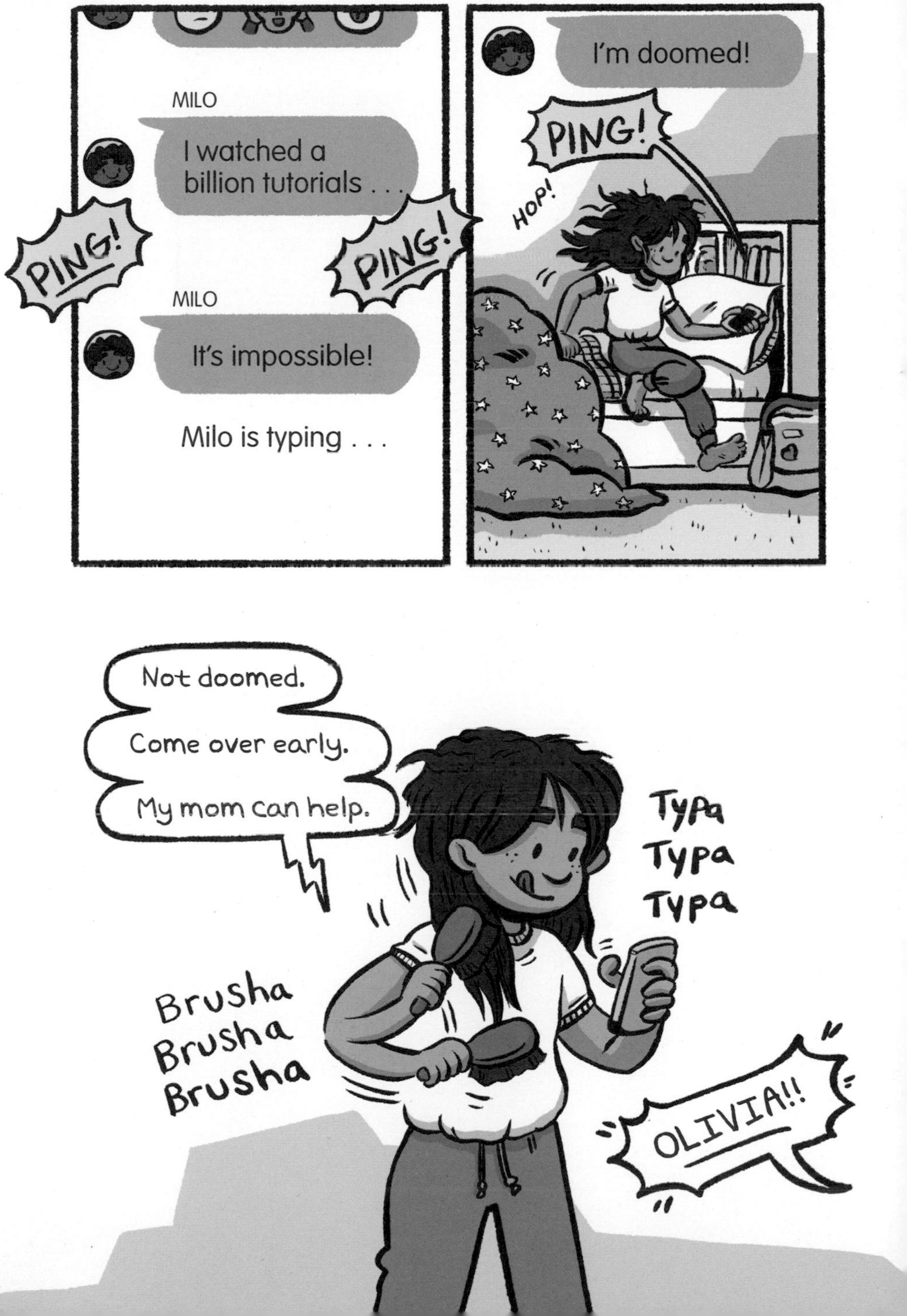
MILO
I watched a billion tutorials . . .
PING!
PING!
MILO
It's impossible!
Milo is typing . . .
I'm doomed!
PING!
HOP!
Not doomed.
Come over early.
My mom can help.
Typa
Typa
Typa
Brusha
Brusha
Brusha
OLIVIA!!

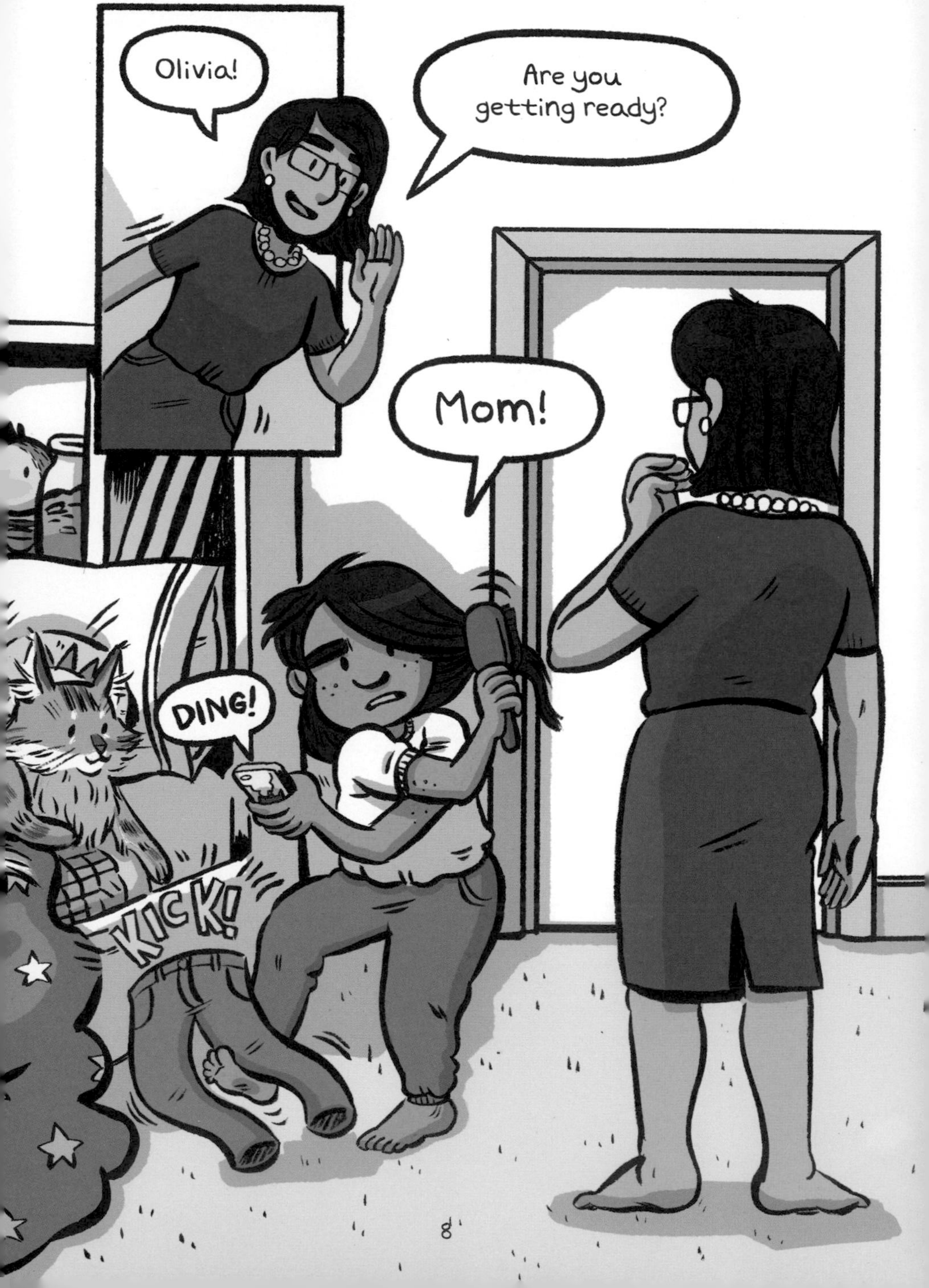
Olivia!
Are you getting ready?
Mom!
DING!
KICK!

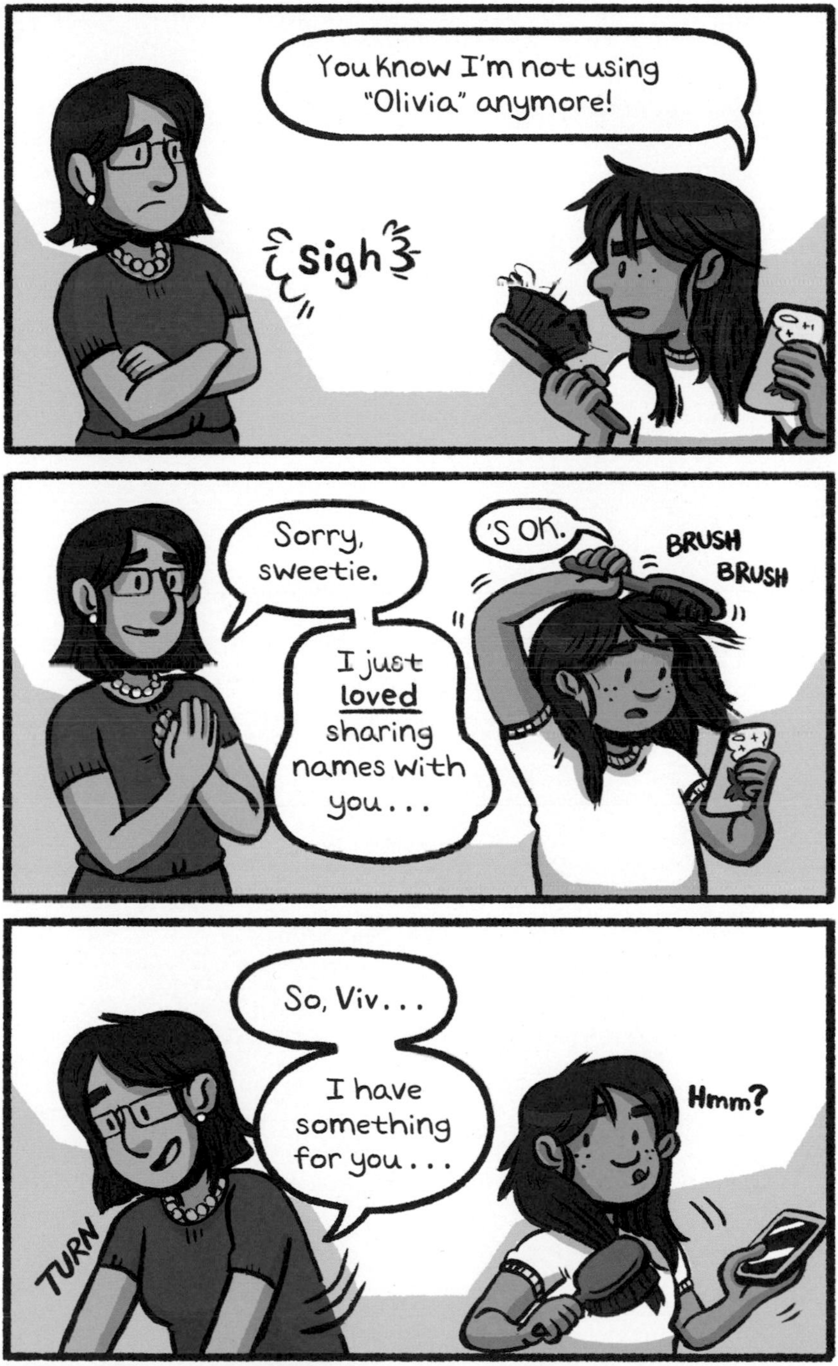
You know I'm not using "Olivia" anymore!
Sigh
Sorry, sweetie.
'S OK.
BRUSH
BRUSH
I just **loved** sharing names with you . . .
So, Viv . . .
I have something for you . . .
Hmm?
TURN

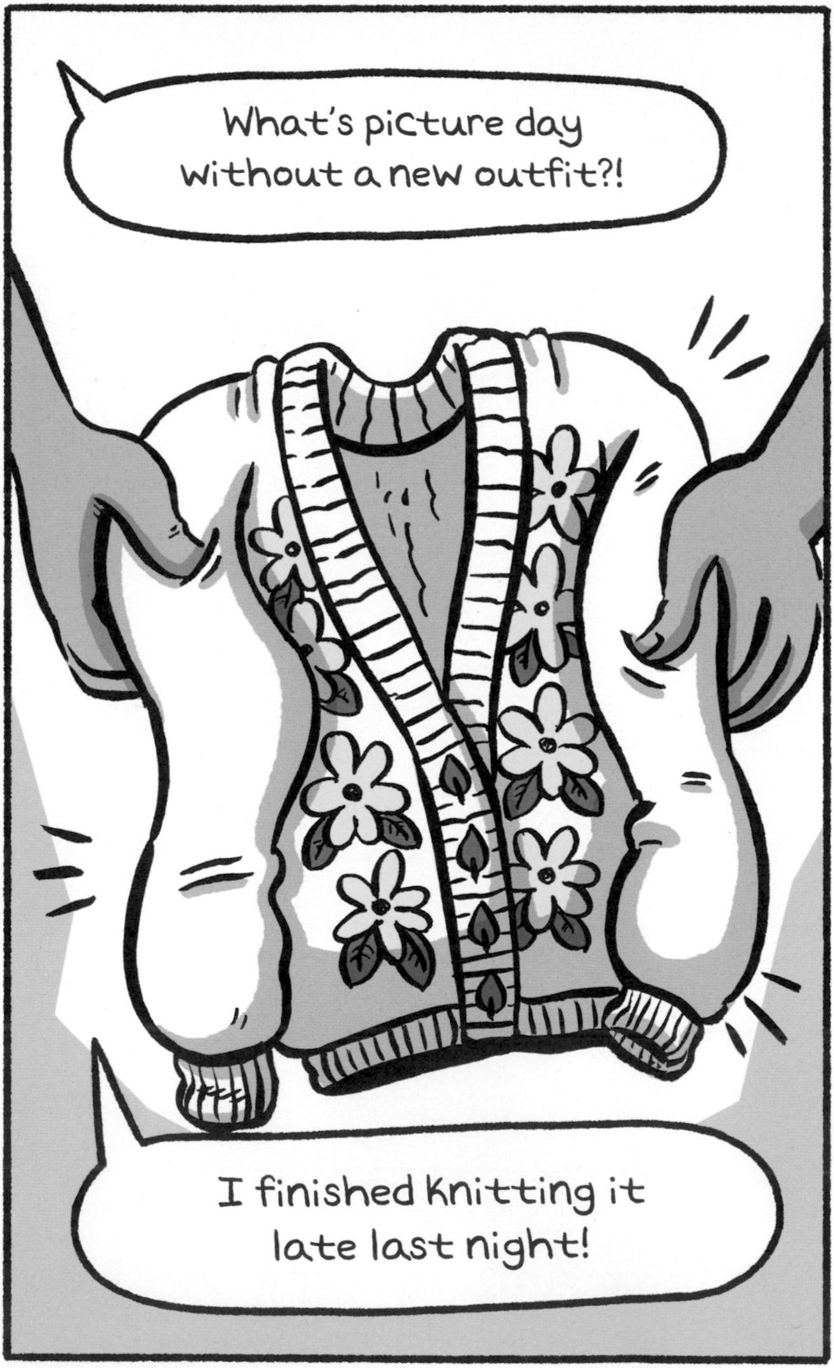
What's picture day without a new outfit?!
I finished knitting it late last night!

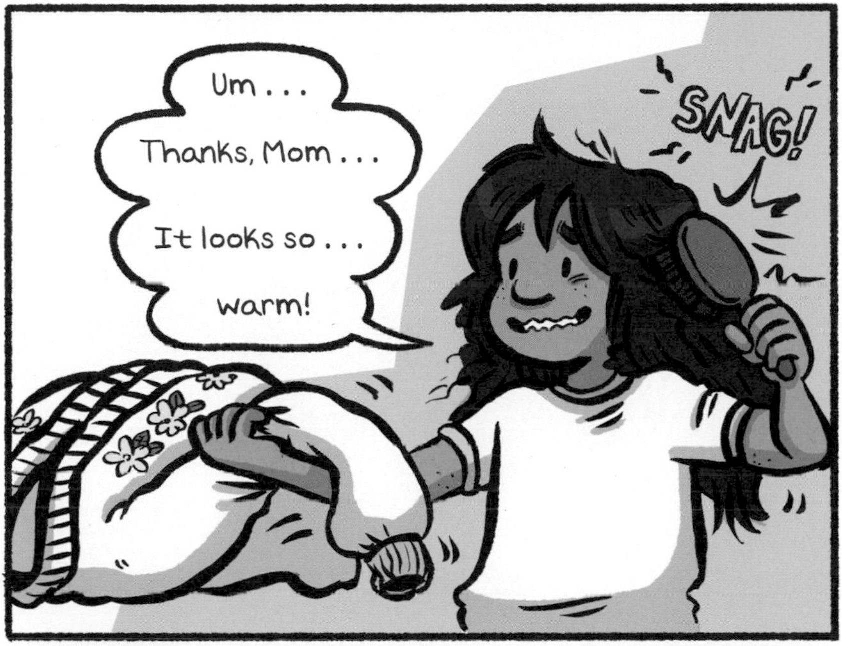
Um . . .
Thanks, Mom . . .
It looks so . . .
warm!
SNAG!

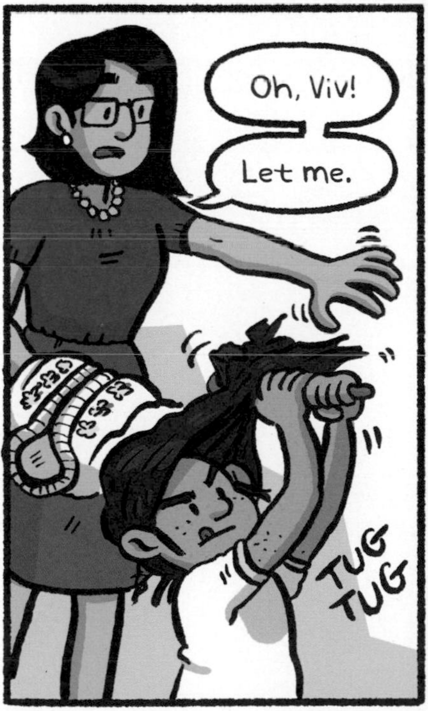
Oh, Viv!
Let me.
TUG
TUG

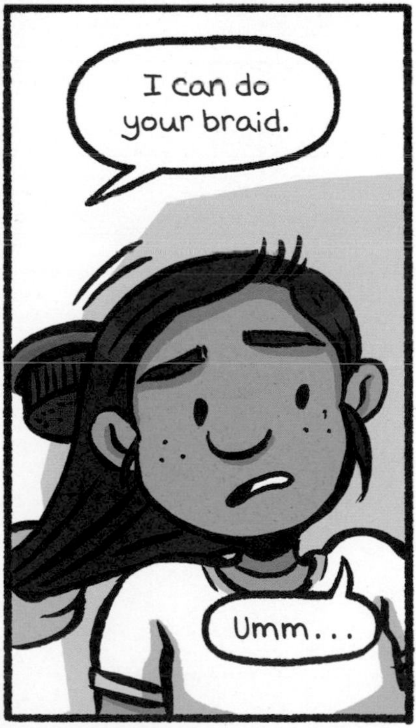
I can do your braid.
Umm. . .

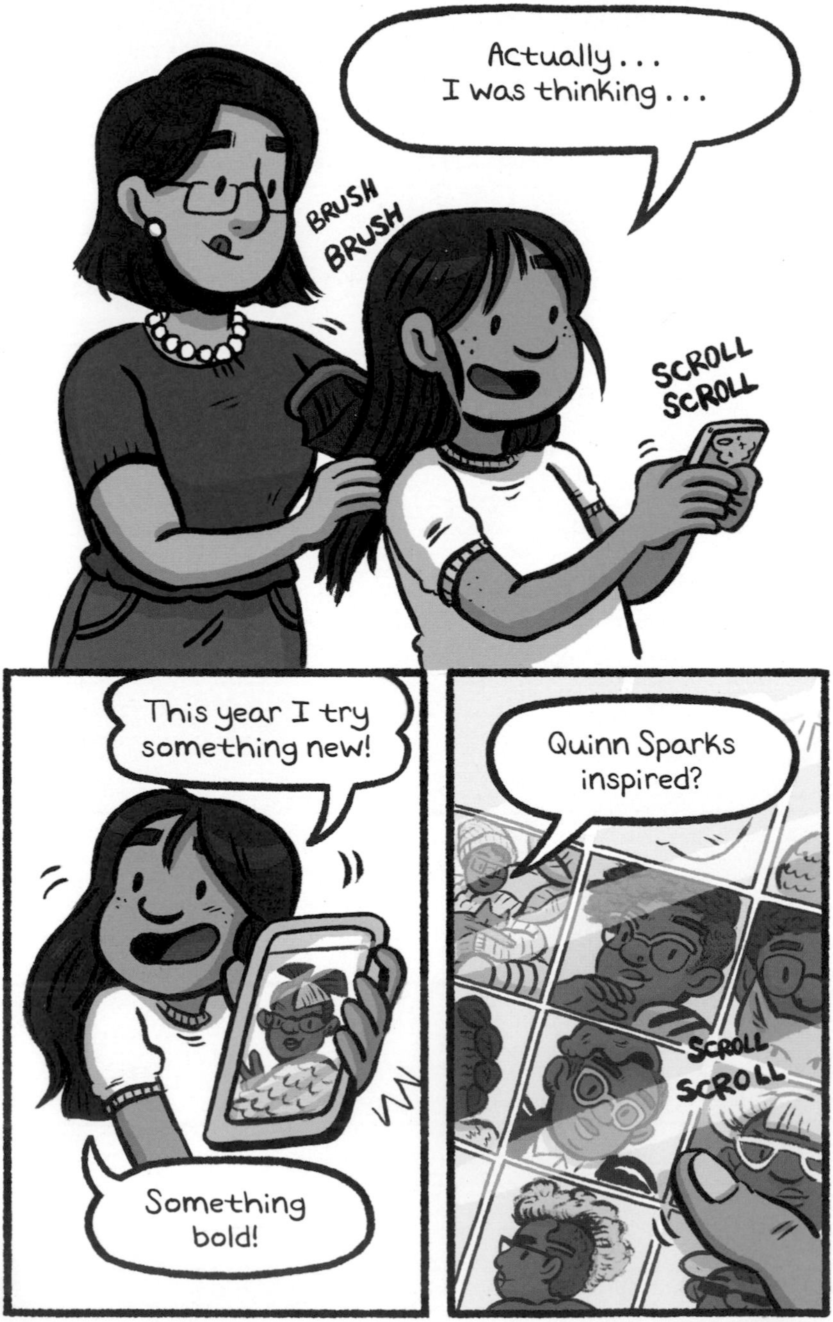

Actually . . .
I was thinking . . .
BRUSH
BRUSH
SCROLL
SCROLL
This year I try something new!
Something bold!
Quinn Sparks inspired?
SCROLL
SCROLL

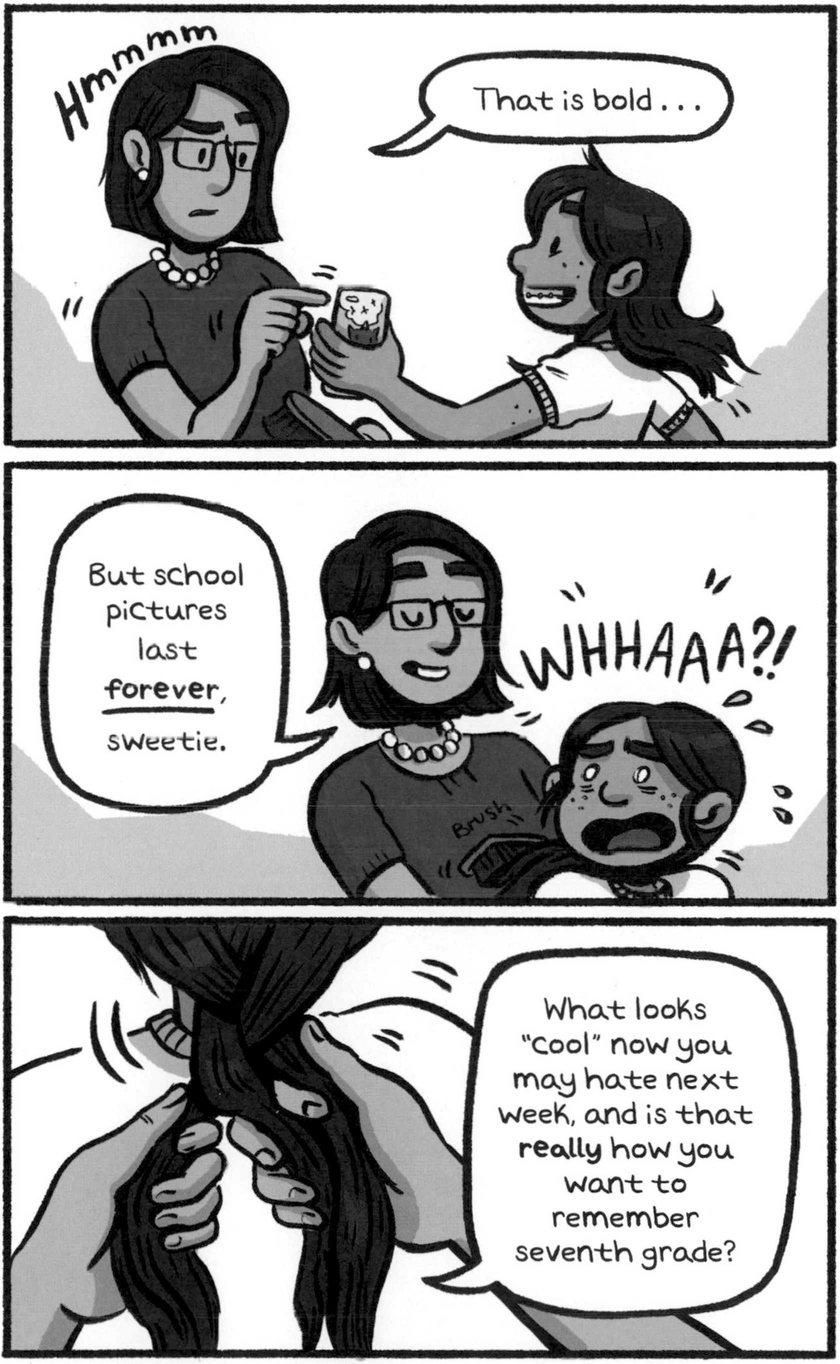

Hmmmm
That is bold . . .
But school pictures last **forever**, sweetie.
WHHAAA?!
Brush
What looks "cool" now you may hate next week, and is that **really** how you want to remember seventh grade?

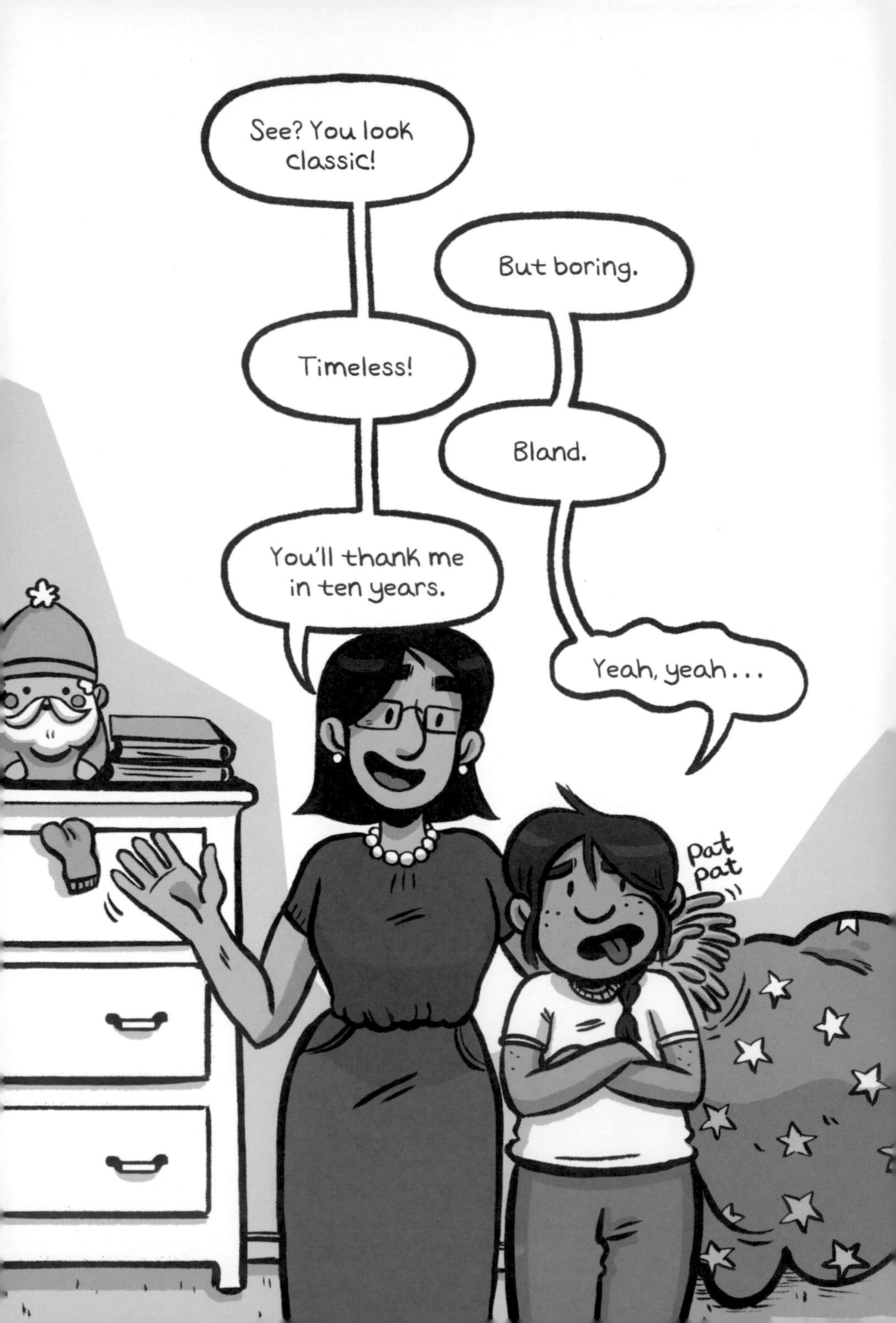
See? You look classic!
But boring.
Timeless!
Bland.
You'll thank me in ten years.
Yeah, yeah...
pat pat

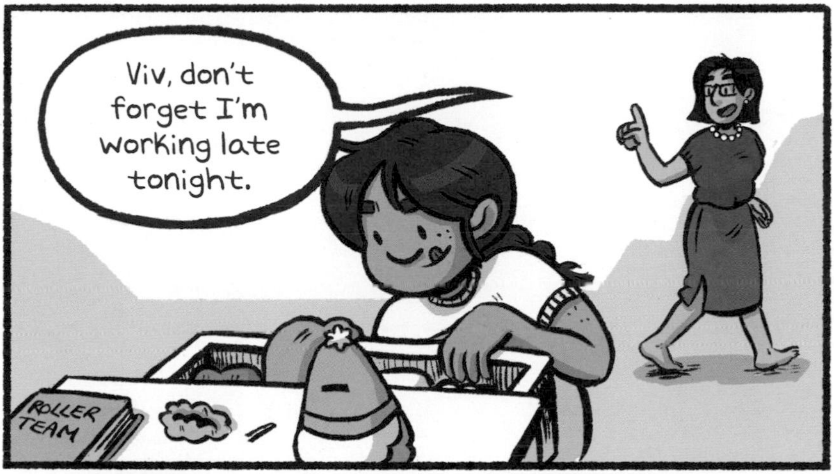
Viv, don't forget I'm working late tonight.
ROLLER TEAM

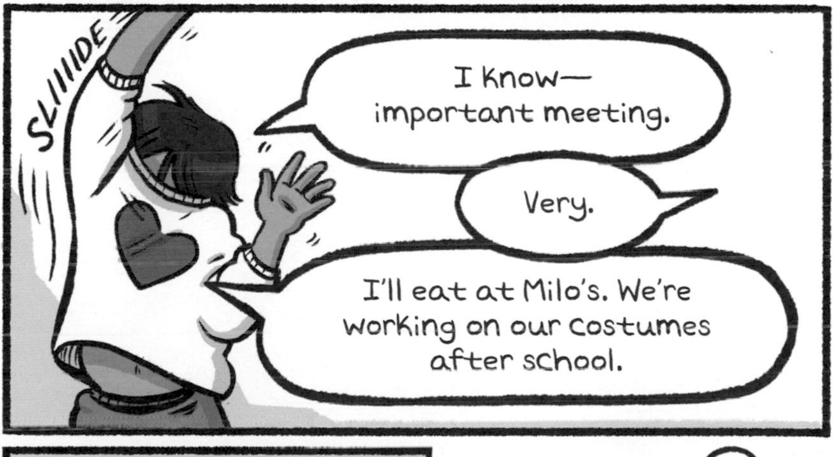
SLIIIIDE
I know—important meeting.
Very.
I'll eat at Milo's. We're working on our costumes after school.

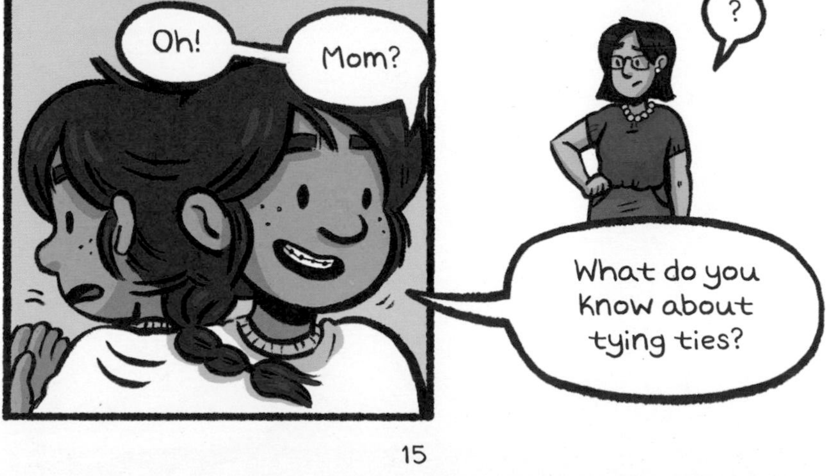
Oh!
Mom?
?
What do you know about tying ties?

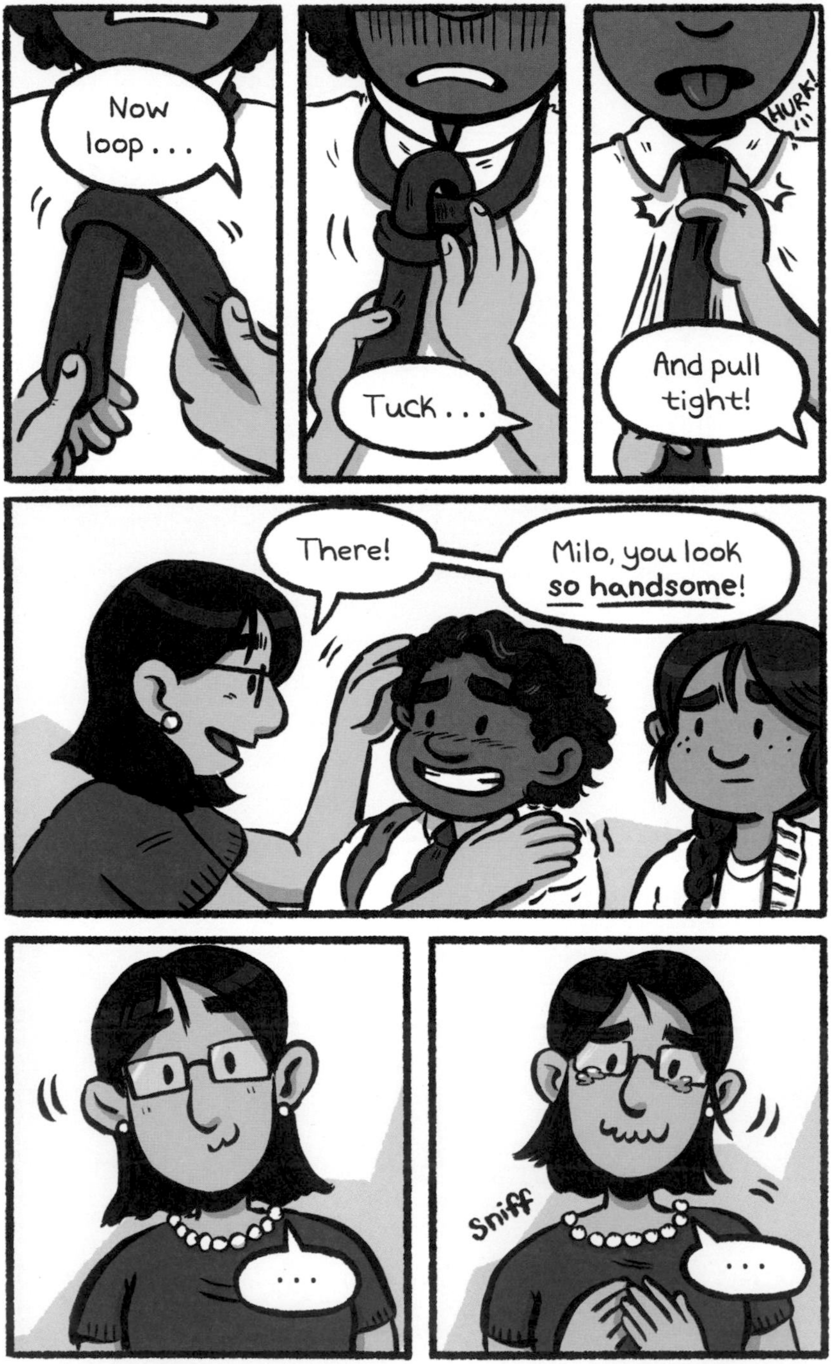

Now loop . . .
Tuck . . .
HURK!
And pull tight!
There!
Milo, you look **so handsome**!
. . .
Sniff
. . .

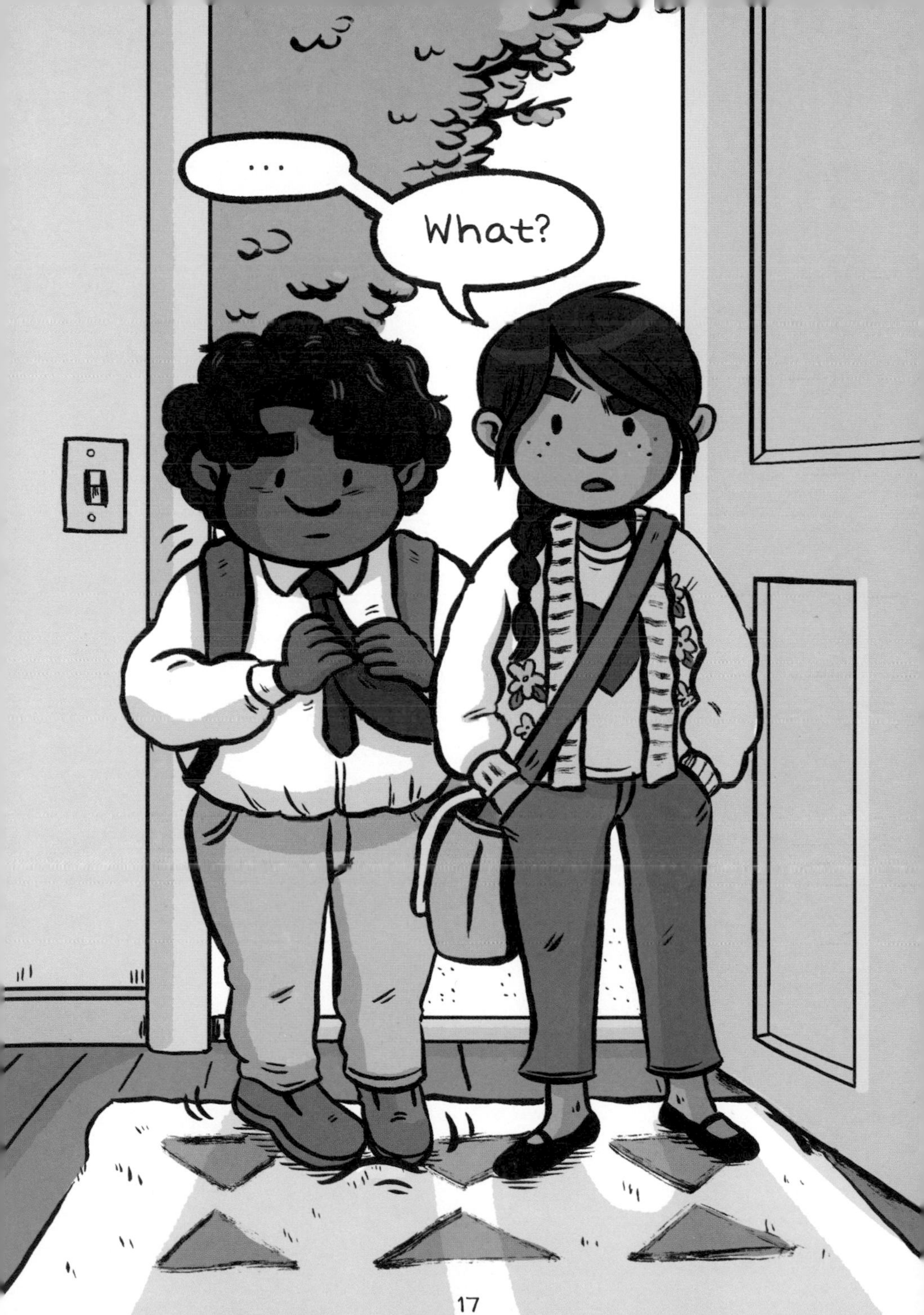
...
What?

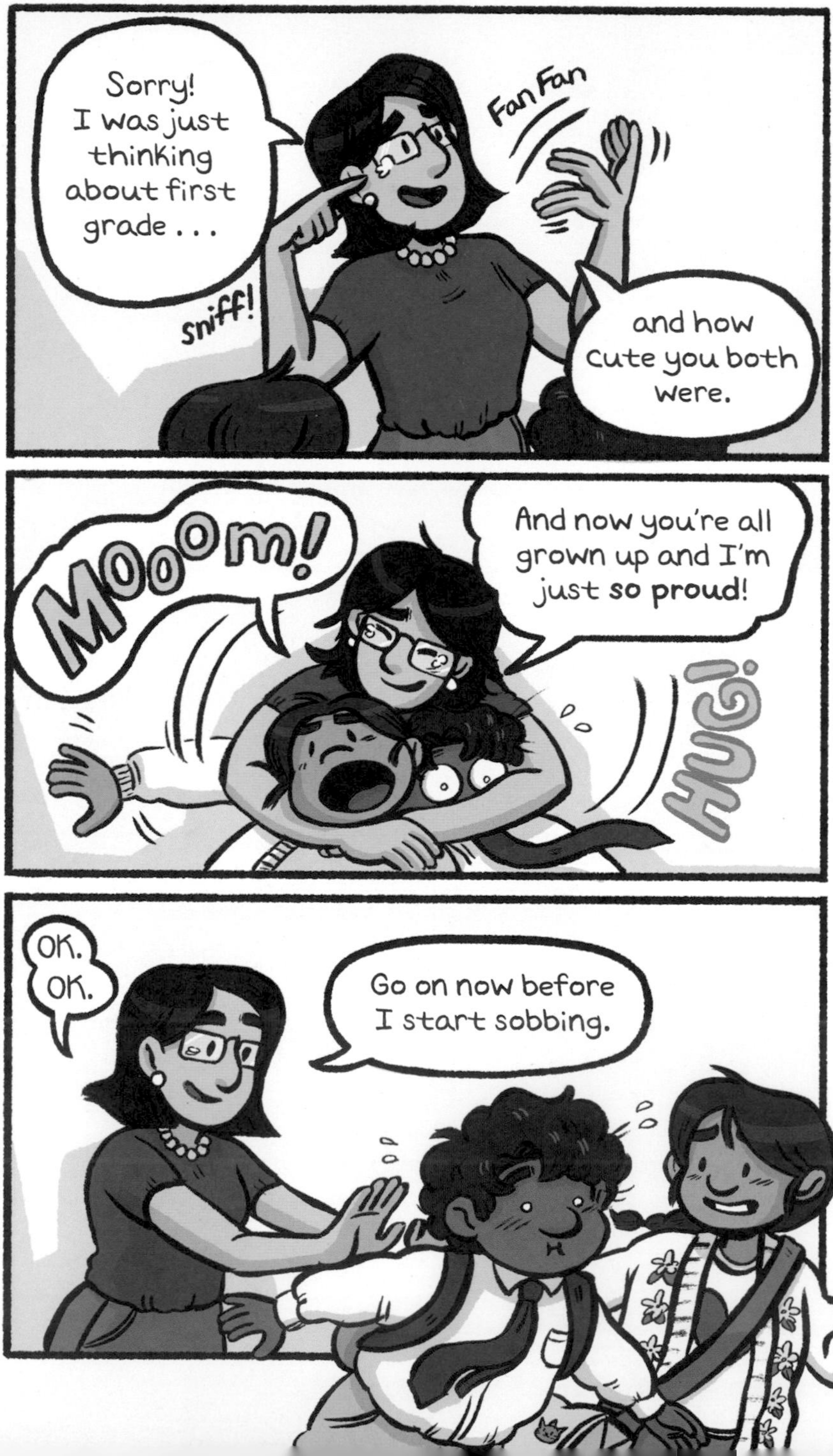
Sorry! I was just thinking about first grade . . .
Fan Fan
sniff!
and how cute you both were.
MOoOm!
And now you're all grown up and I'm just so proud!
HUG!
OK. OK.
Go on now before I start sobbing.

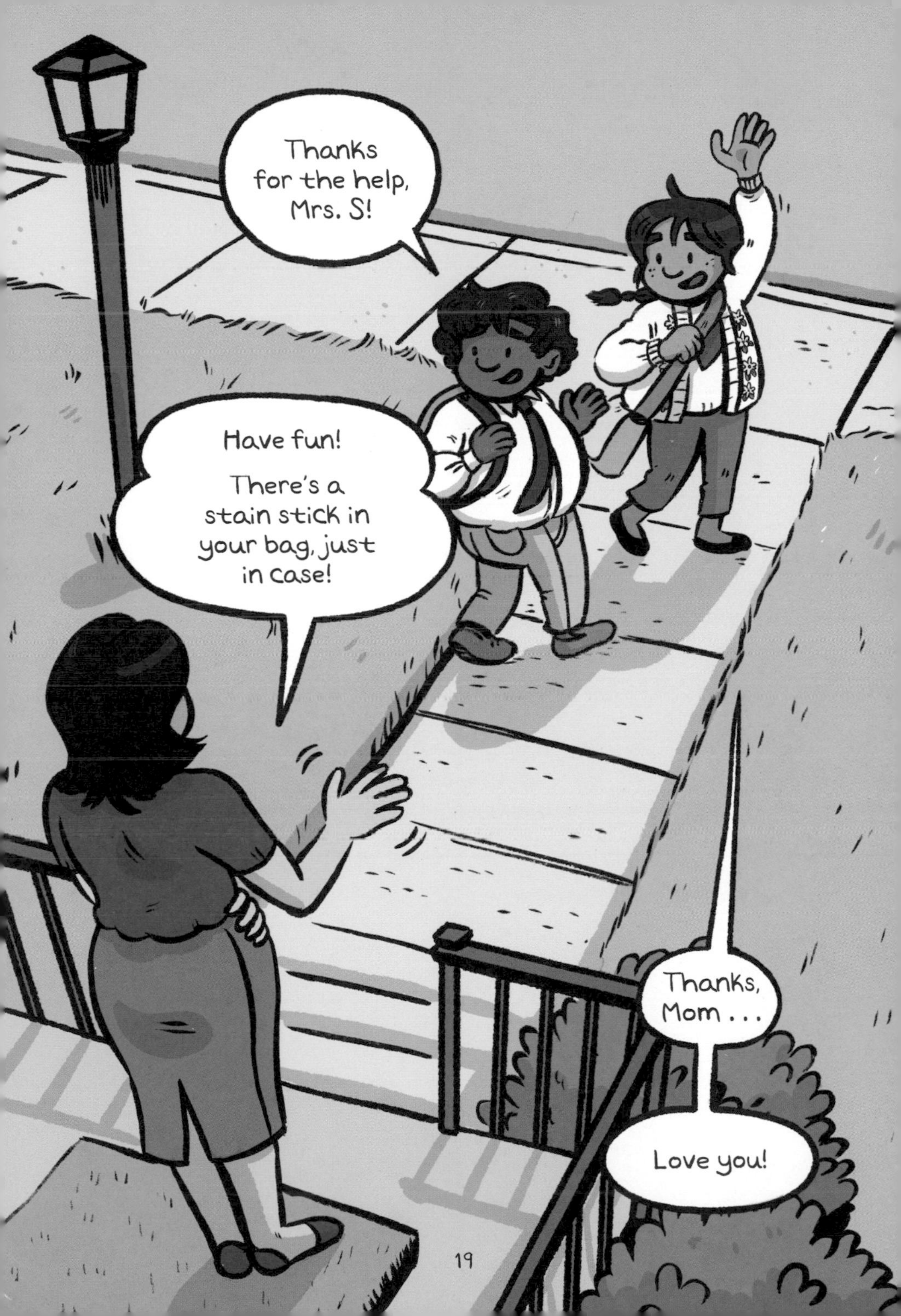
Thanks for the help, Mrs. S!
Have fun!
There's a stain stick in your bag, just in case!
Thanks, Mom . . .
Love you!

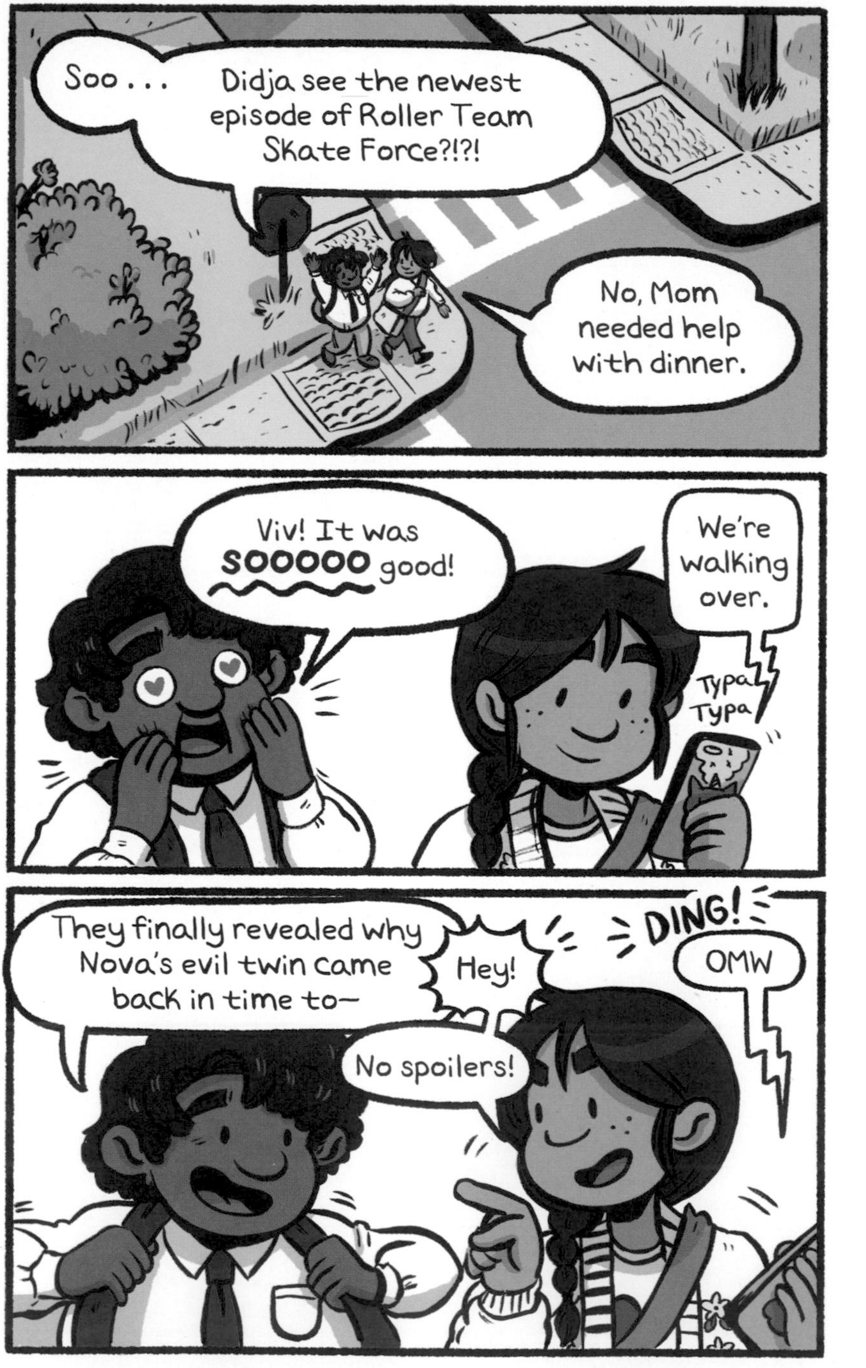
Soo . . .
Didja see the newest episode of Roller Team Skate Force?!?!
No, Mom needed help with dinner.
Viv! It was SOOOOO good!
We're walking over.
Typa Typa
They finally revealed why Nova's evil twin came back in time to—
Hey!
DING!
OMW
No spoilers!

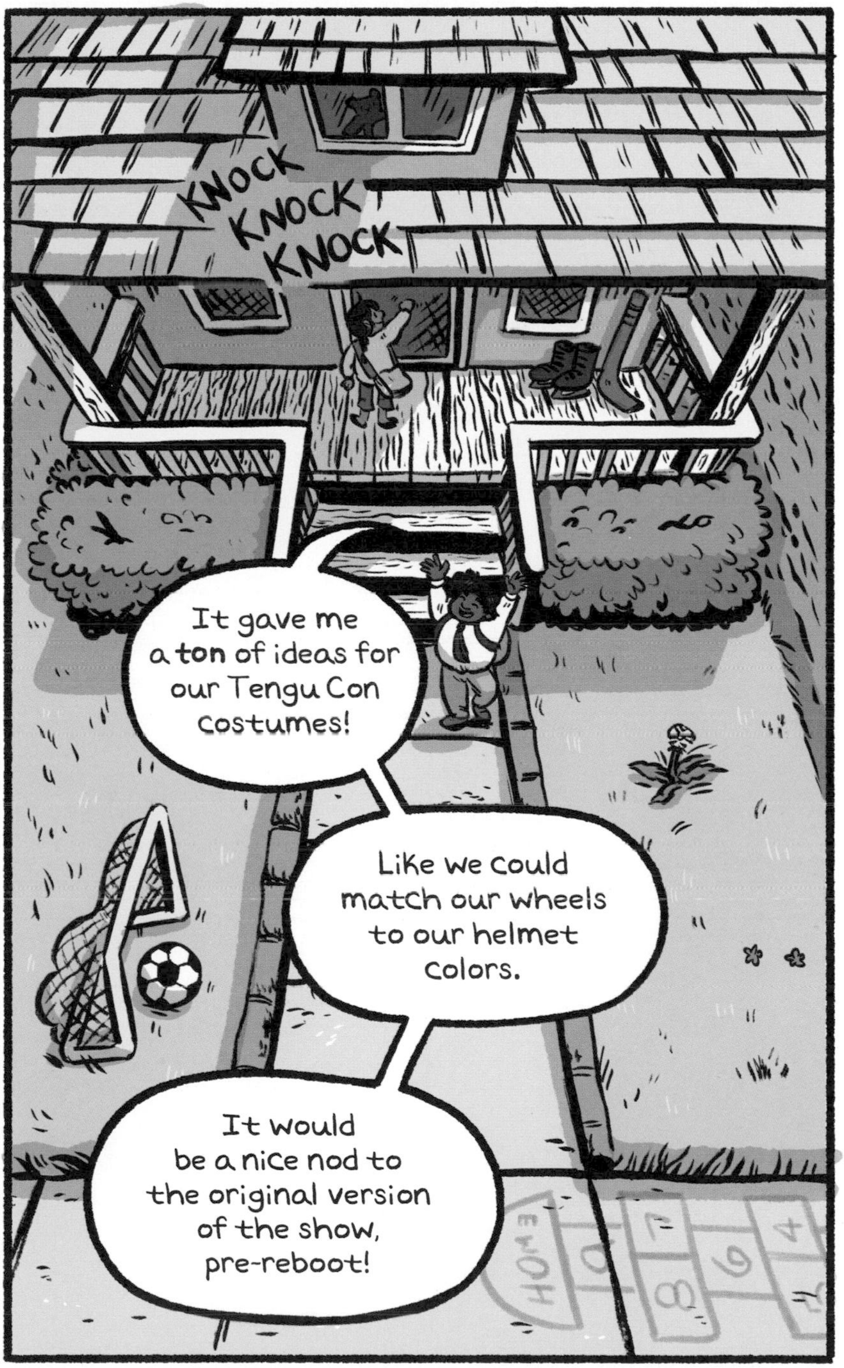
KNOCK KNOCK KNOCK
It gave me a **ton** of ideas for our Tengu Con costumes!
Like we could match our wheels to our helmet colors.
It would be a nice nod to the original version of the show, pre-reboot!

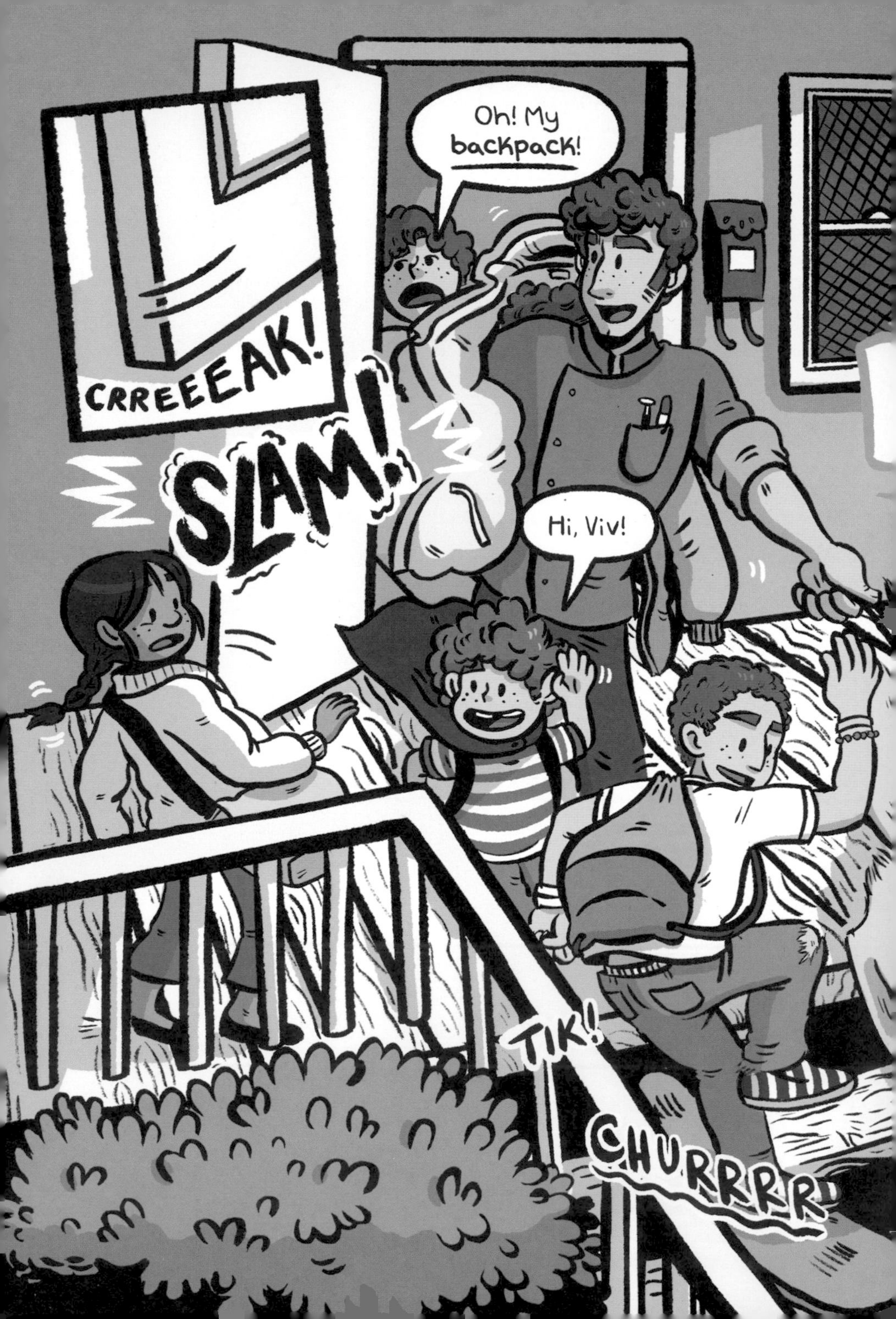
CRREEEAK!
Oh! My backpack!
SLAM!
Hi, Viv!
TIK!
CHURRRRR

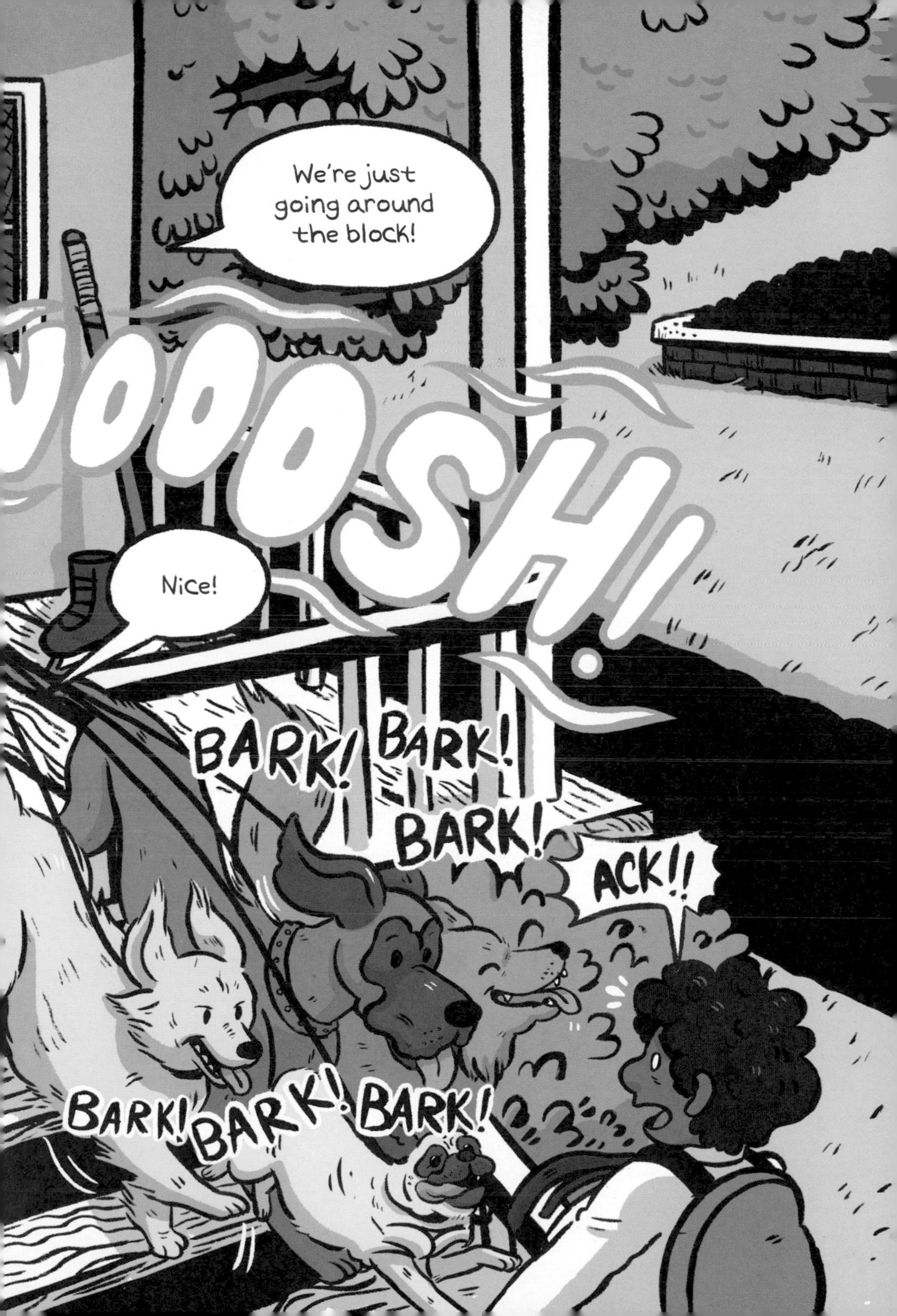

We're just going around the block!
WOOOSH!
Nice!
BARK! BARK!
BARK!
ACK!!
BARK! BARK! BARK!

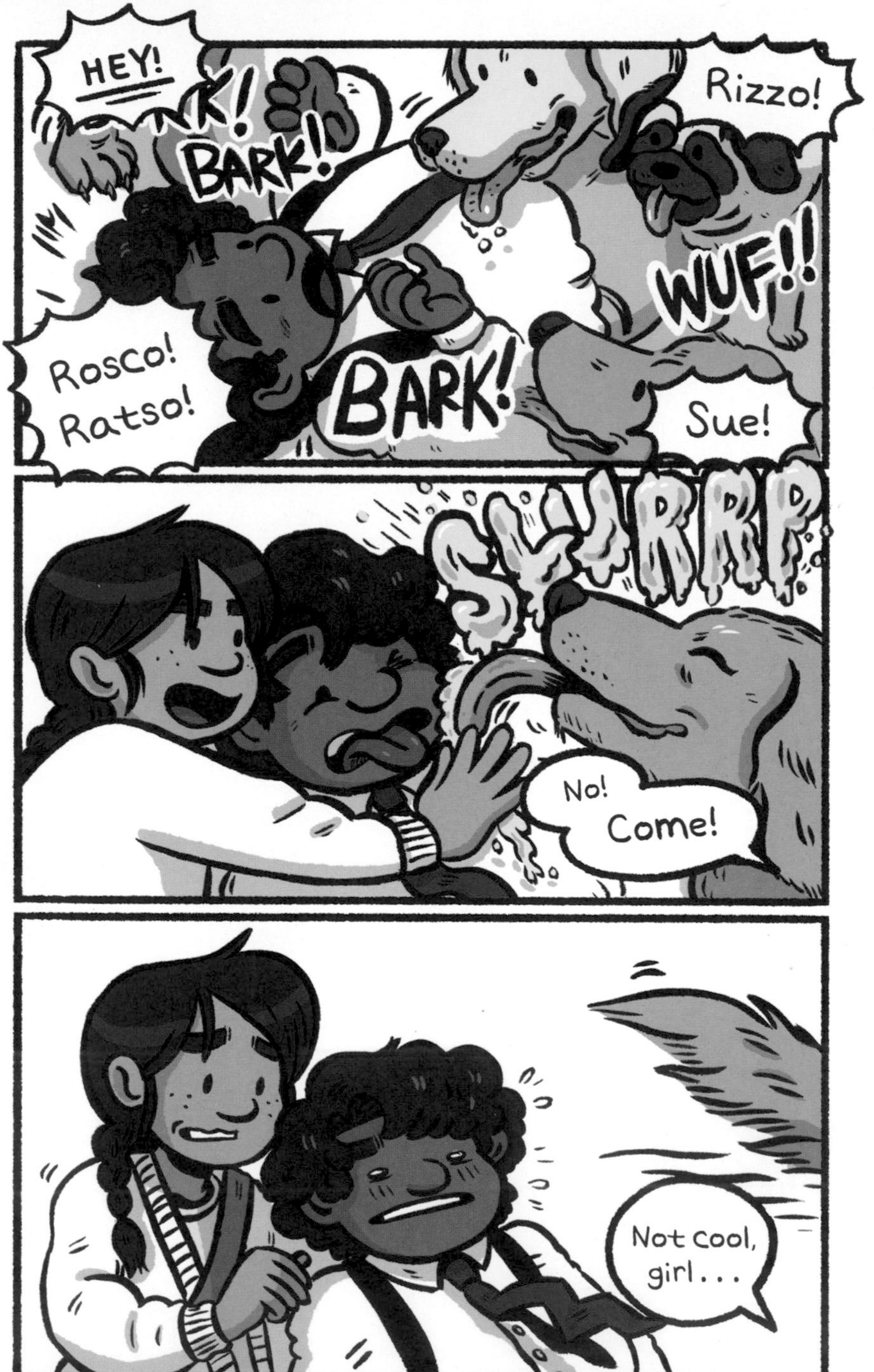
HEY!
BARK!
Rizzo!
WUF!!
Rosco!
Ratso!
BARK!
Sue!
No!
Come!
Not cool, girl . . .

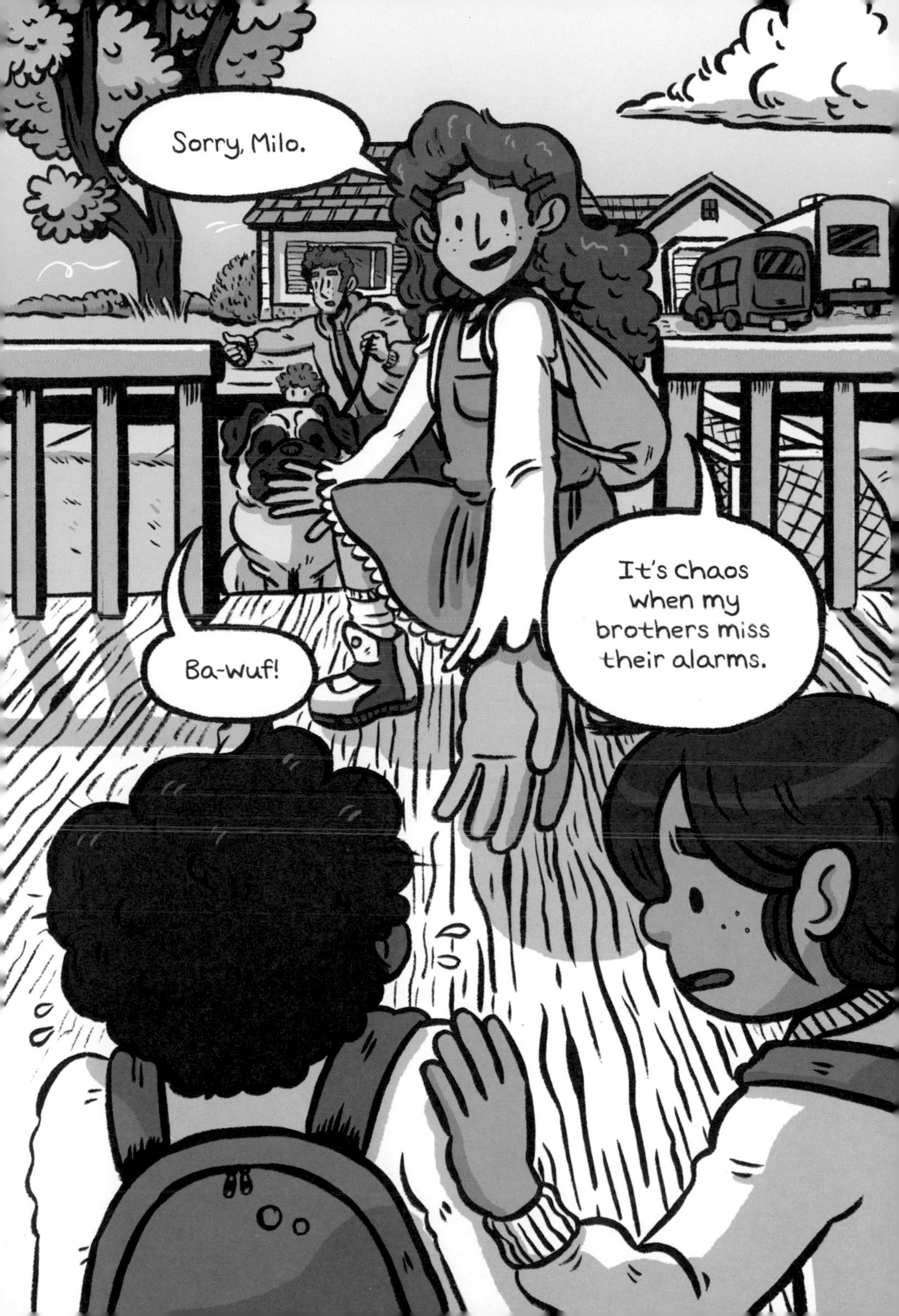
Sorry, Milo.
Ba-wuf!
It's chaos when my brothers miss their alarms.

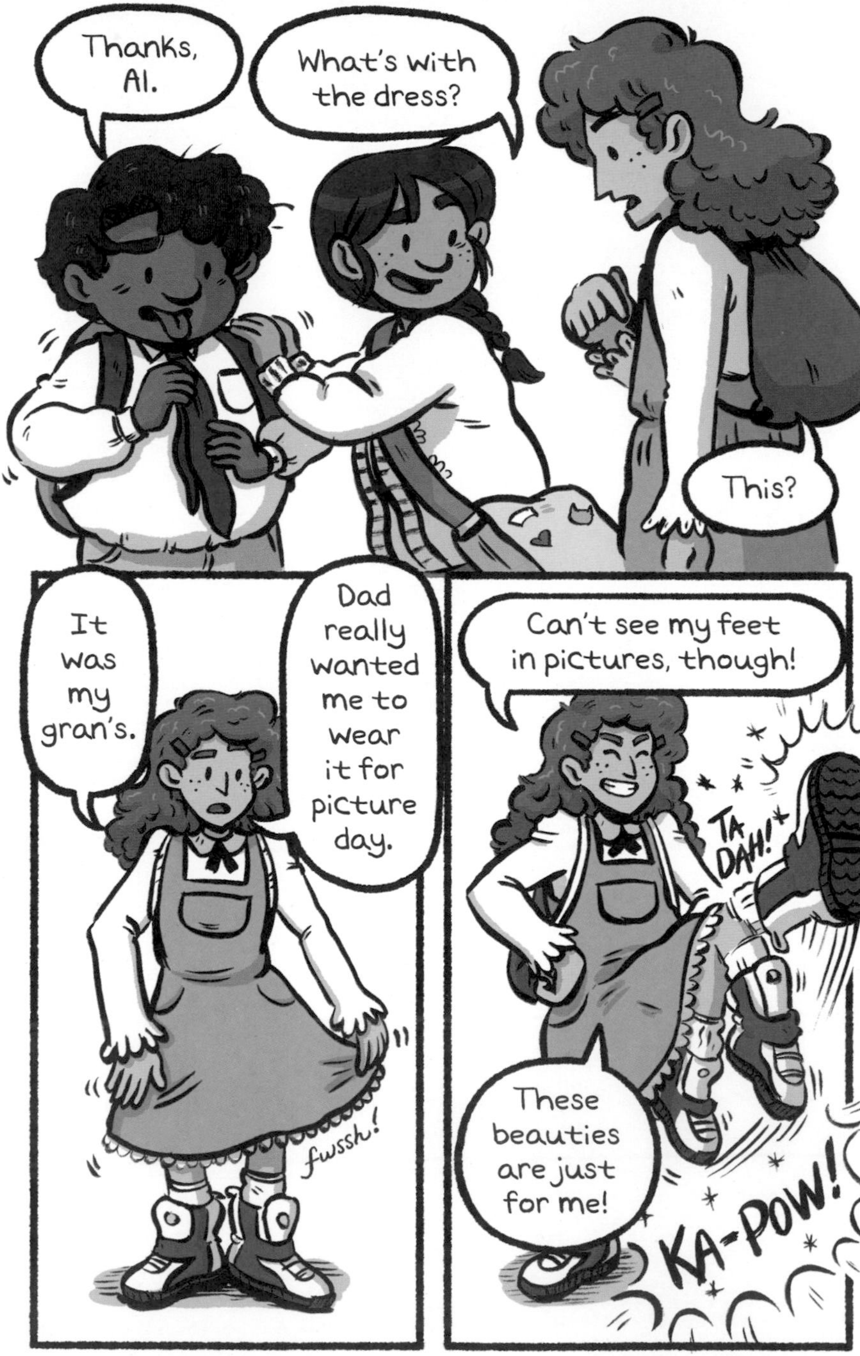
Thanks, Al.
What's with the dress?
This?
It was my gran's.
Dad really wanted me to wear it for picture day.
fwssh!
Can't see my feet in pictures, though!
TA DAH!
These beauties are just for me!
KA-POW!

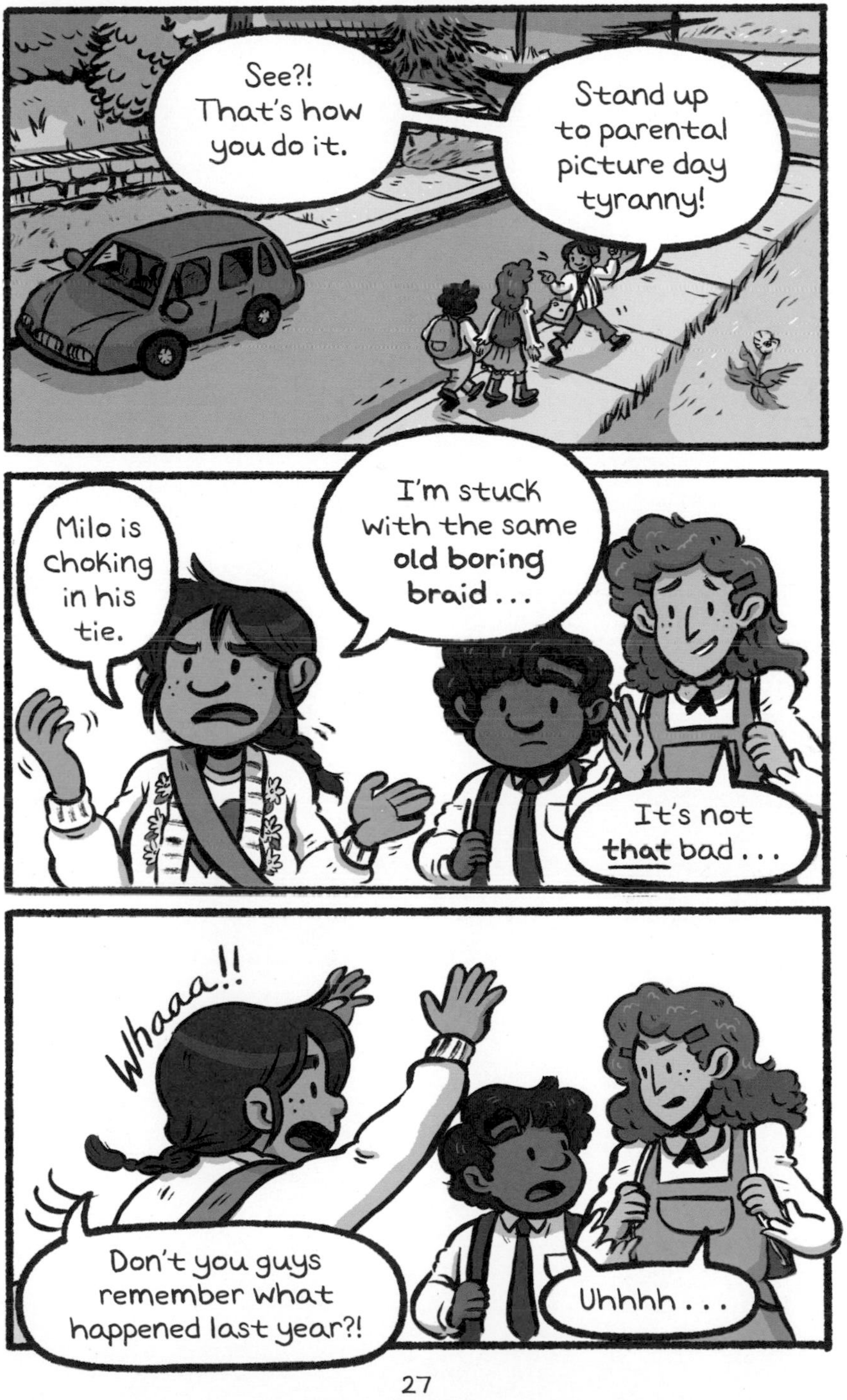
See?! That's how you do it.
Stand up to parental picture day tyranny!
Milo is choking in his tie.
I'm stuck with the same **old boring braid . . .**
It's not <u>**that**</u> bad . . .
Whaaa!!
Don't you guys remember what happened last year?!
Uhhhh . . .

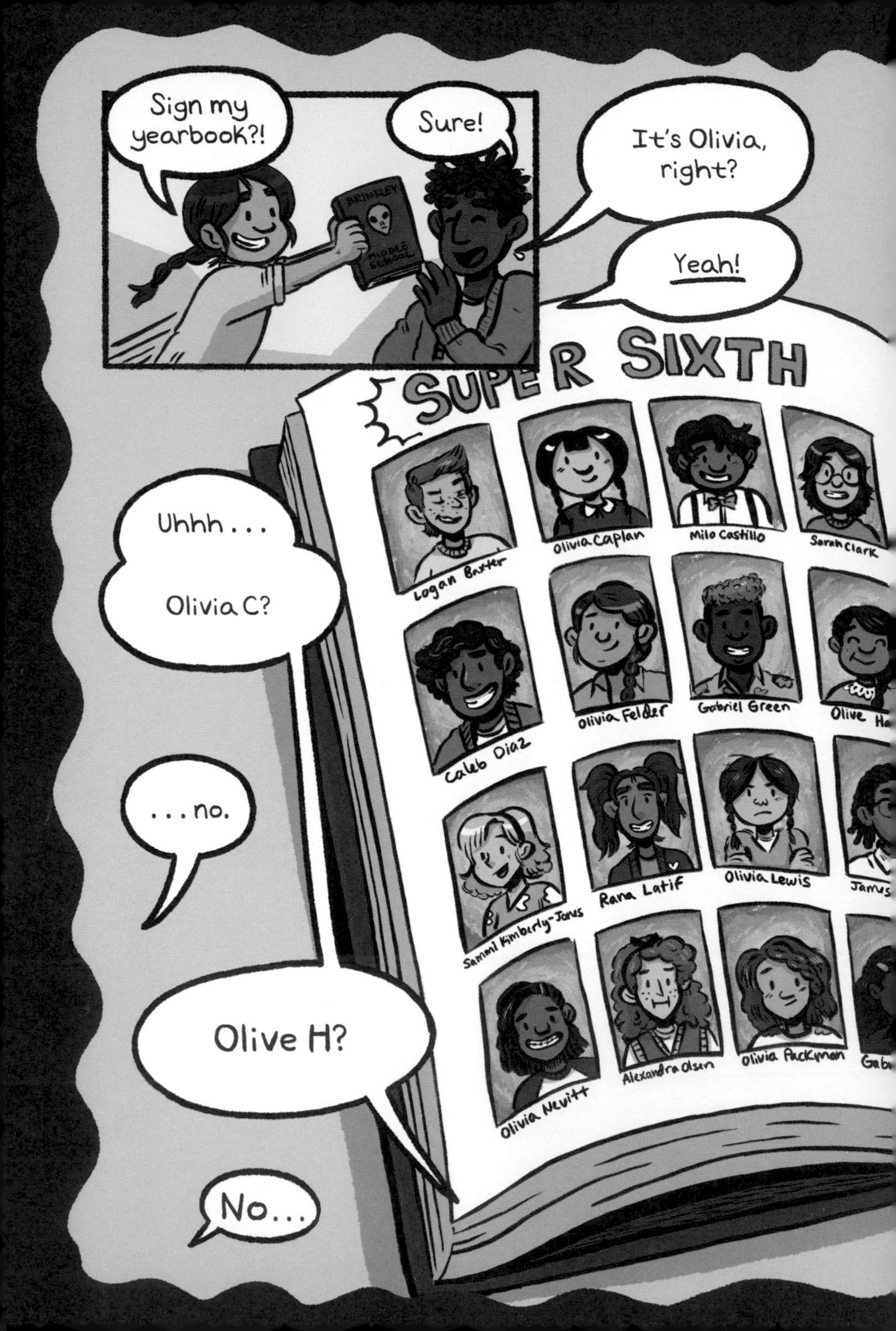
Sign my yearbook?!
BRINKLEY MIDDLE SCHOOL
Sure!
It's Olivia, right?
Yeah!
SUPER SIXTH
Logan Baxter
Olivia Caplan
Milo Castillo
Sarah Clark
Caleb Diaz
Olivia Felder
Gabriel Green
Sammi Kimberly-Jones
Rana Latif
Olivia Lewis
Olivia Nevitt
Alexandra Olsen
Olivia Packman
Uhhh . . .
Olivia C?
. . . no.
Olive H?
No . . .

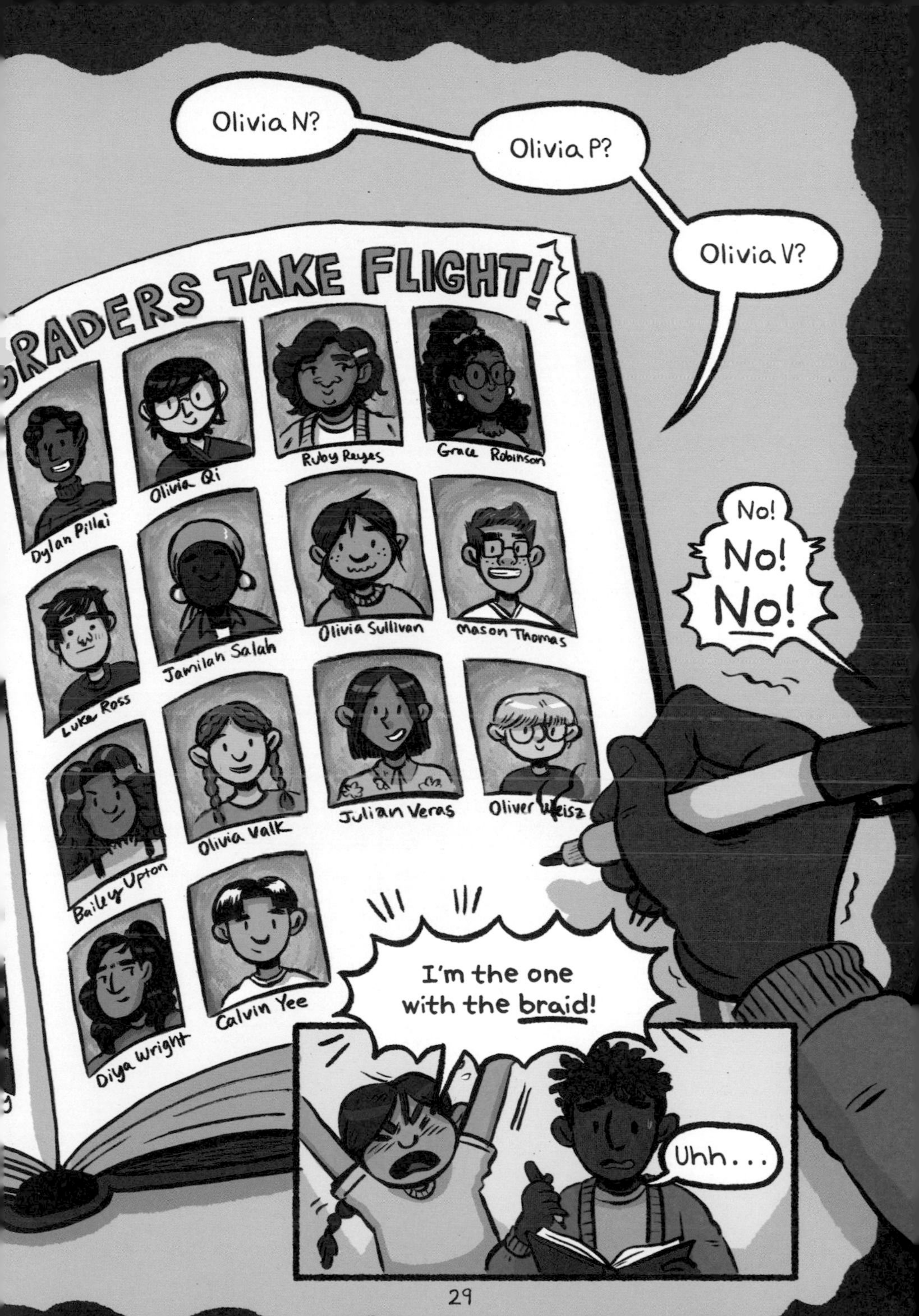
Olivia N?
Olivia P?
Olivia V?
RADERS TAKE FLIGHT!
Dylan Pillai
Olivia Qi
Ruby Reyes
Grace Robinson
Luke Ross
Jamilah Salah
Olivia Sullivan
Mason Thomas
Bailey Upton
Olivia Valk
Julian Veras
Oliver Weisz
Diya Wright
Calvin Yee
No! No! No!
I'm the one with the braid!
Uhh...

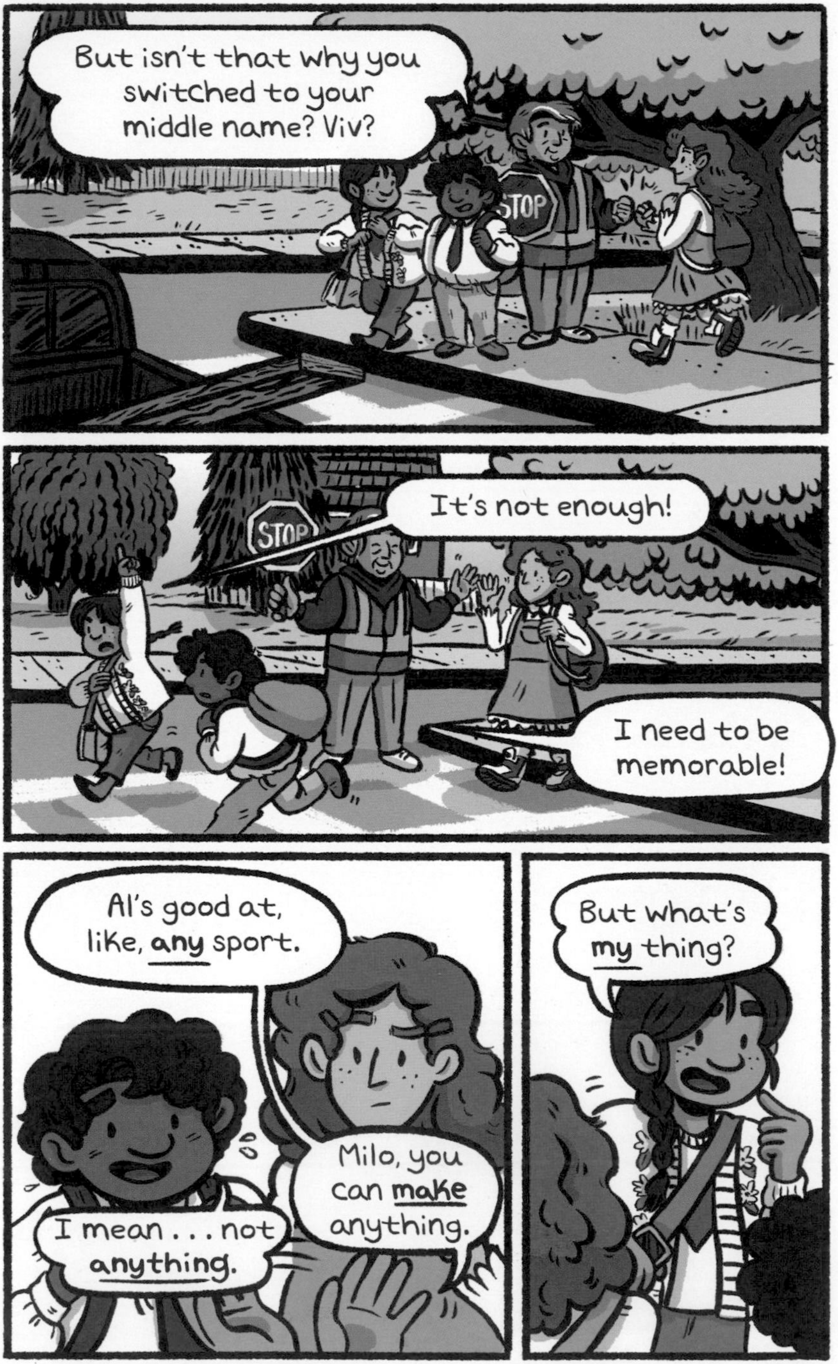
But isn't that why you switched to your middle name? Viv?
STOP
It's not enough!
STOP
I need to be memorable!
Al's good at, like, any sport.
Milo, you can make anything.
I mean . . . not anything.
But what's my thing?

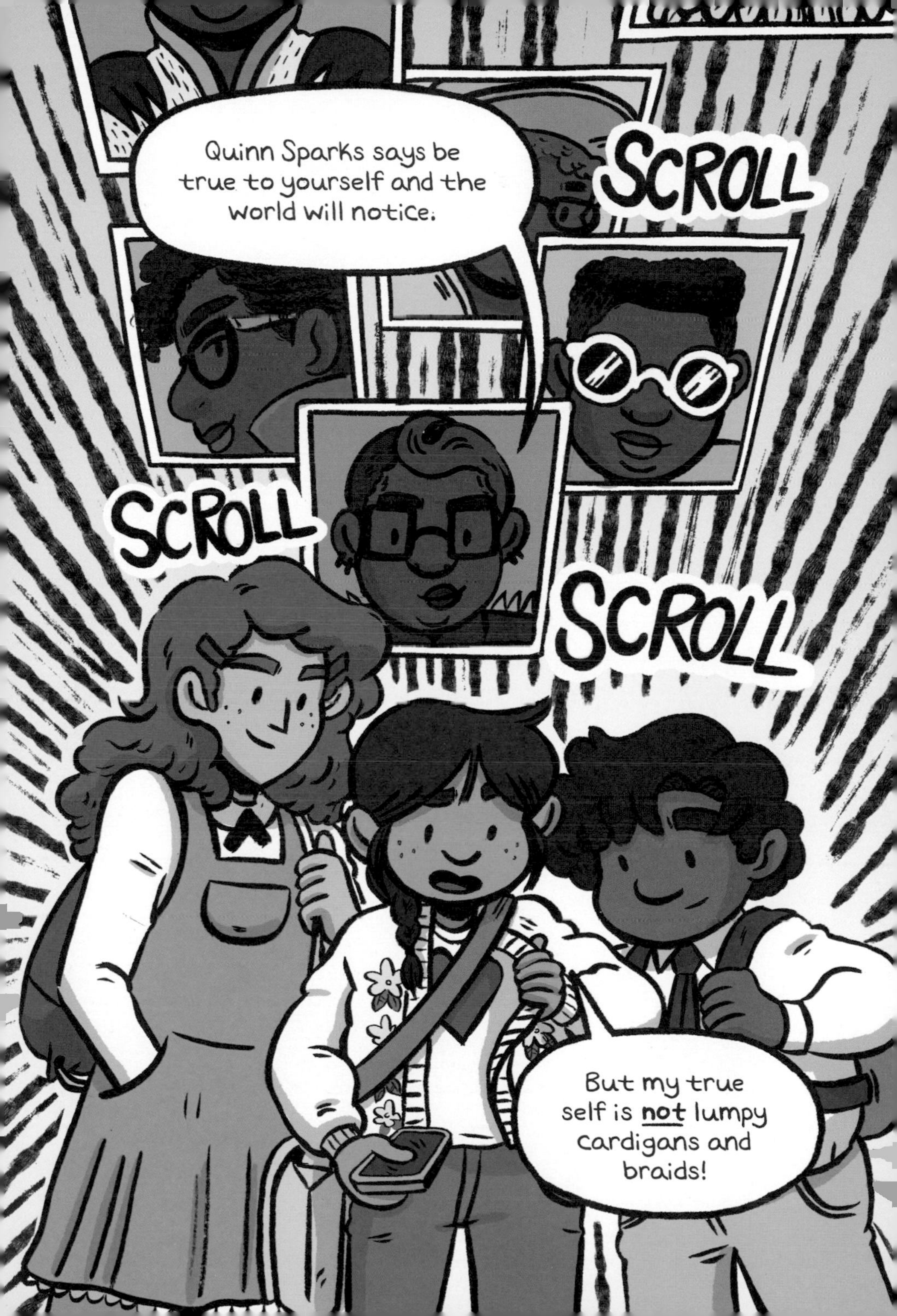
Quinn Sparks says be true to yourself and the world will notice.
SCROLL
SCROLL
SCROLL
But my true self is **not** lumpy cardigans and braids!

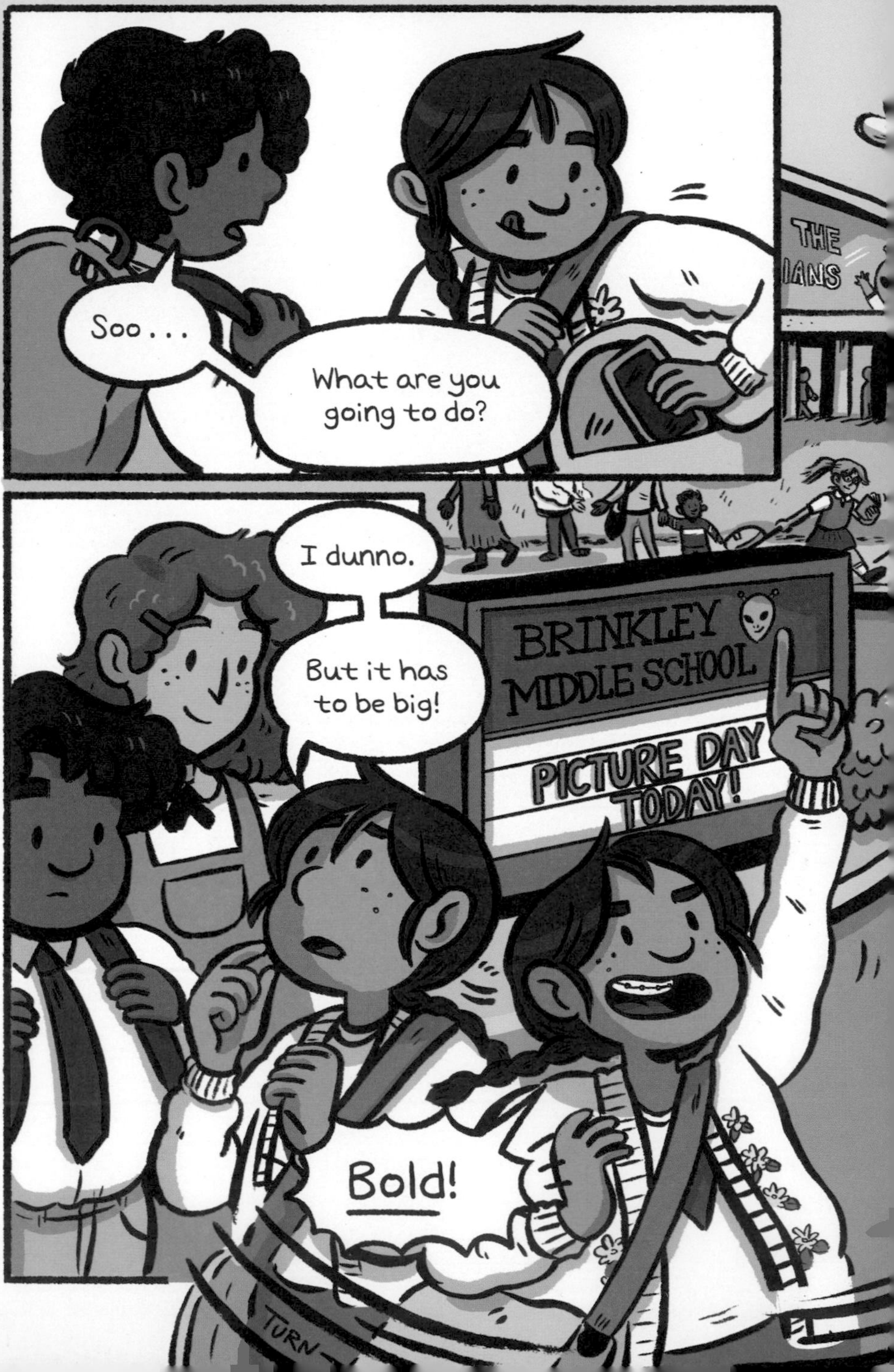
Soo . . .
What are you going to do?
THE
IANS
I dunno.
But it has to be big!
BRINKLEY MIDDLE SCHOOL
PICTURE DAY TODAY!
Bold!
TURN

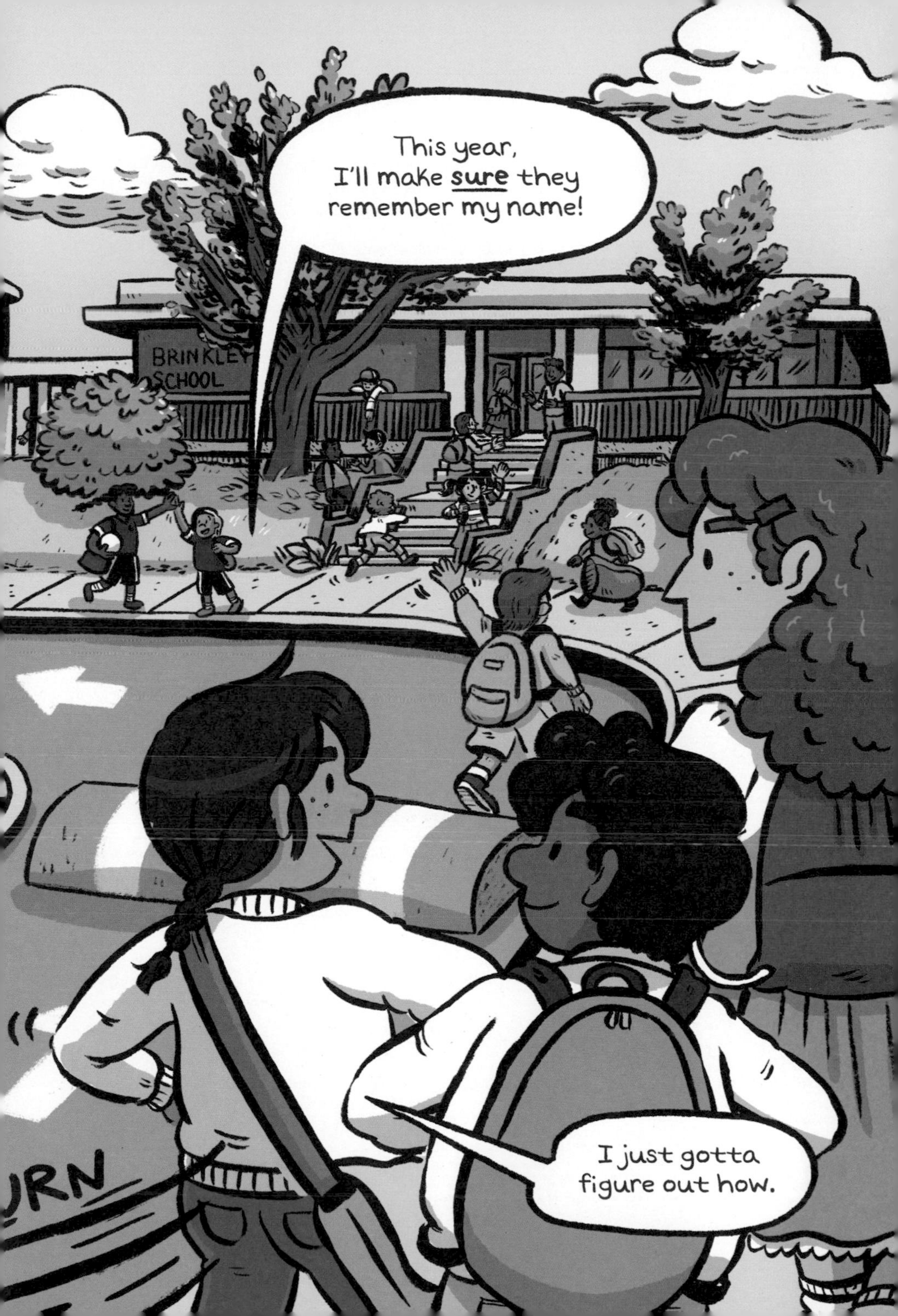
BRINKLEY SCHOOL
This year, I'll make **sure** they remember my name!
I just gotta figure out how.

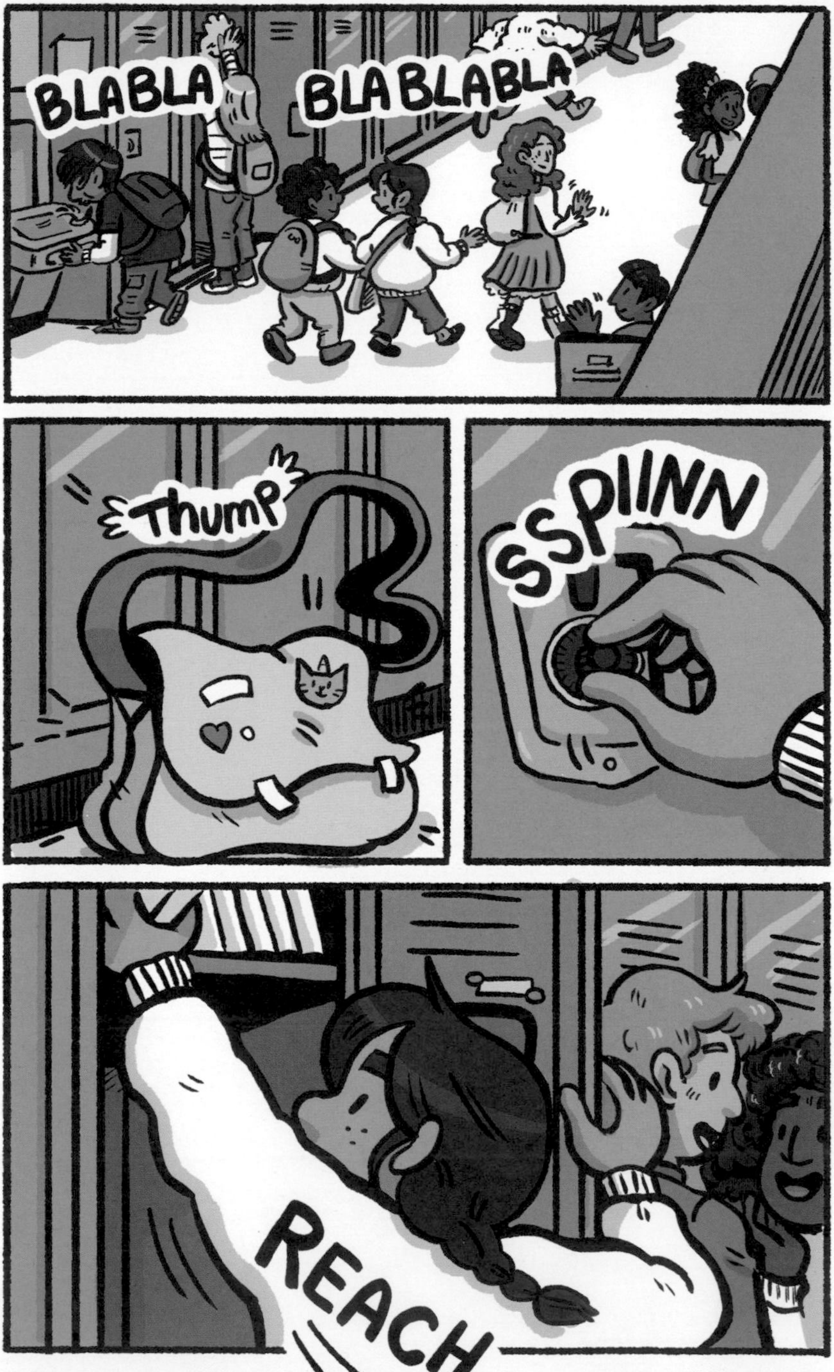
BLABLA
BLABLABLA
Thump
SSPIINN
REACH

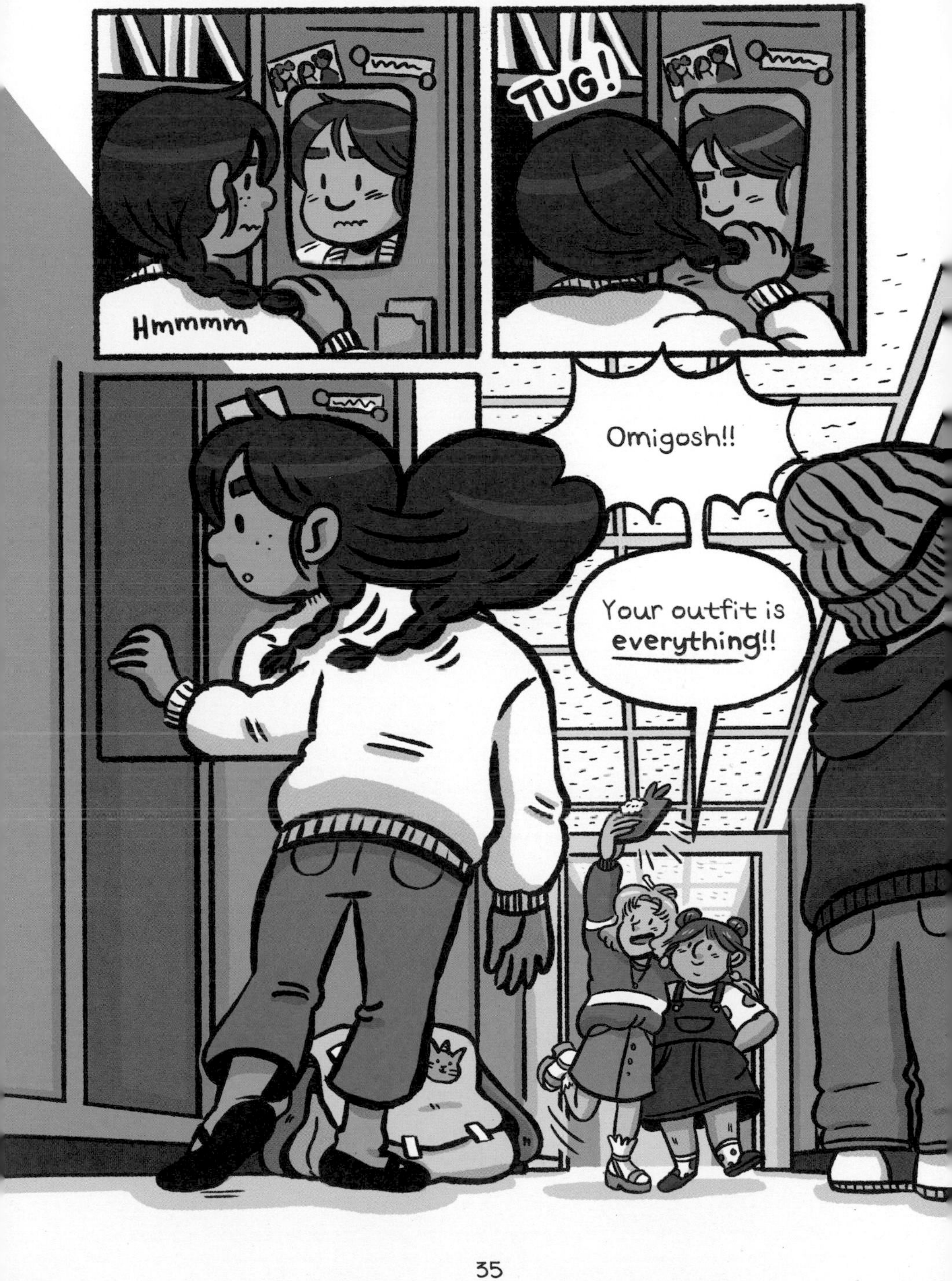
Hmmmm
TUG!
Omigosh!!
Your outfit is everything!!

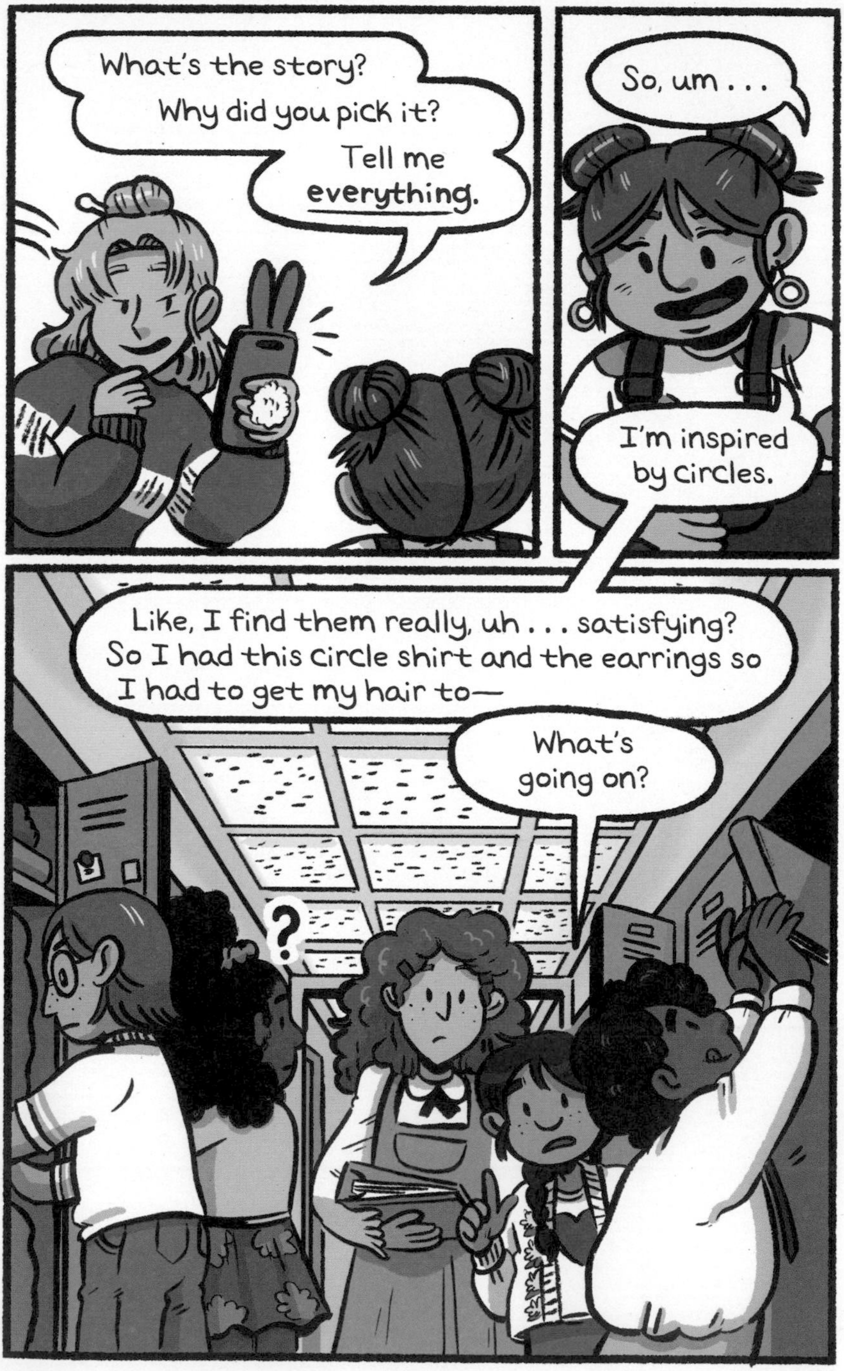
What's the story?
Why did you pick it?
Tell me everything.
So, um . . .
I'm inspired by circles.
Like, I find them really, uh . . . satisfying? So I had this circle shirt and the earrings so I had to get my hair to—
What's going on?
?

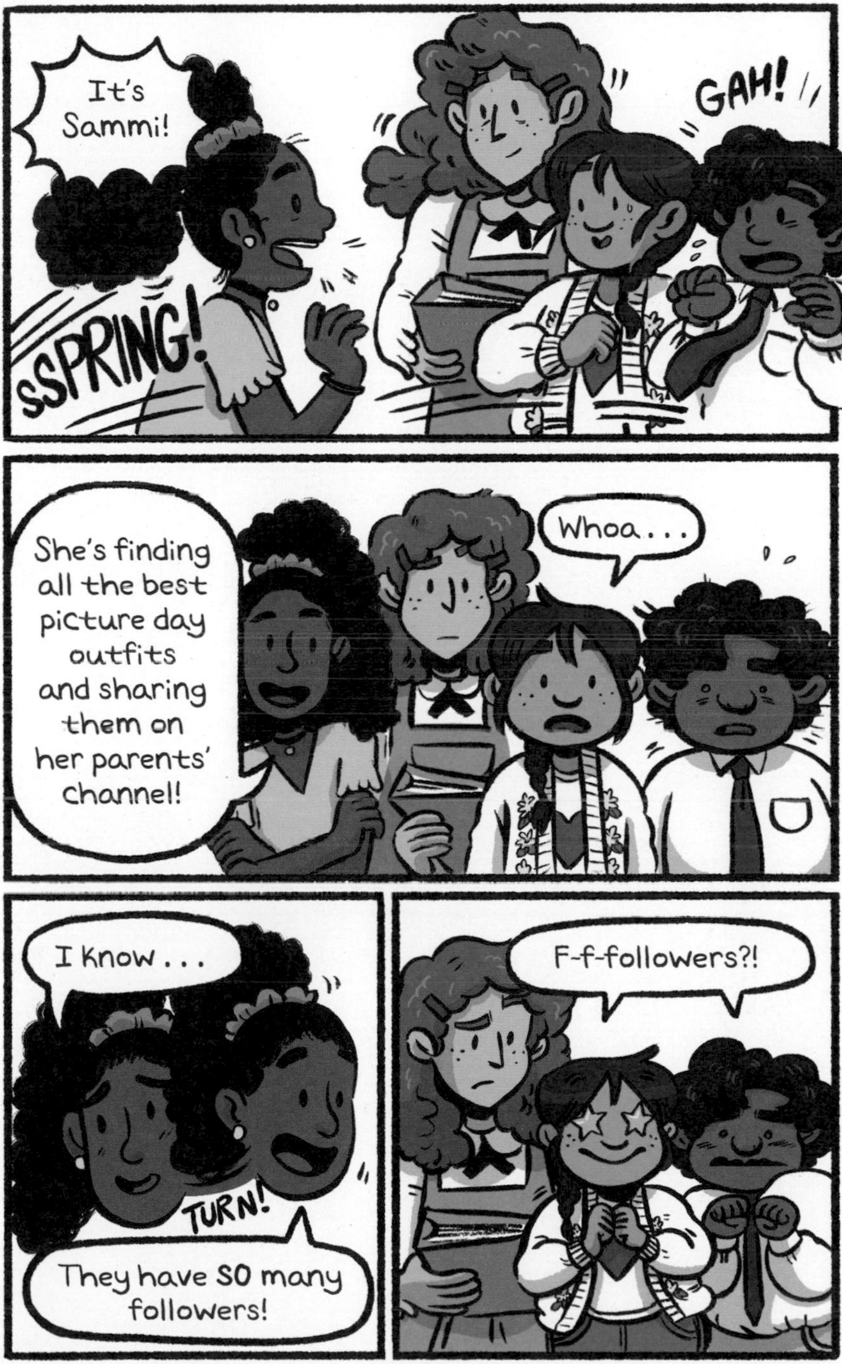
It's Sammi!
SSPRING!
GAH!
She's finding all the best picture day outfits and sharing them on her parents' channel!
Whoa...
I know...
TURN!
They have SO many followers!
F-f-followers?!

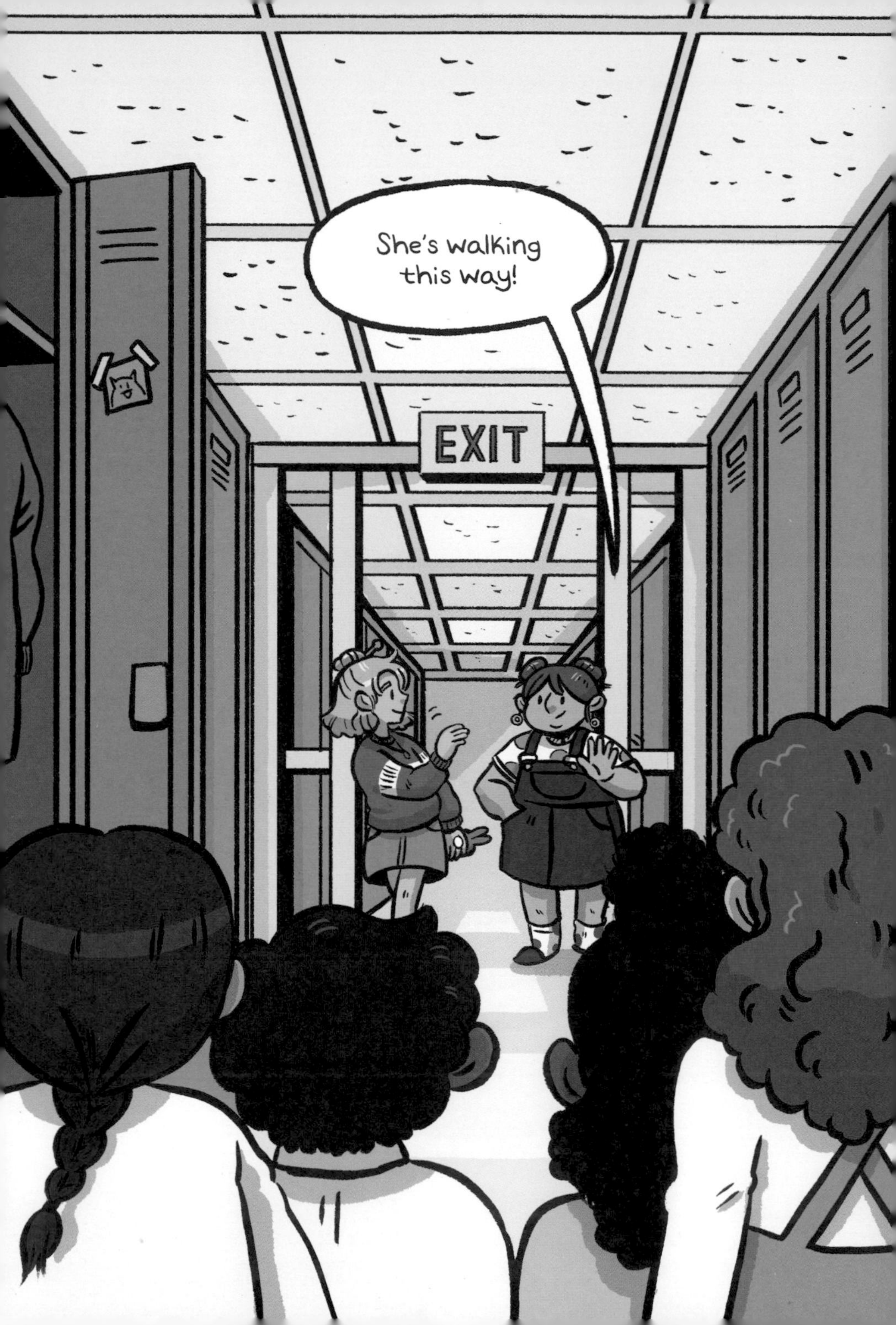
She's walking this way!
EXIT

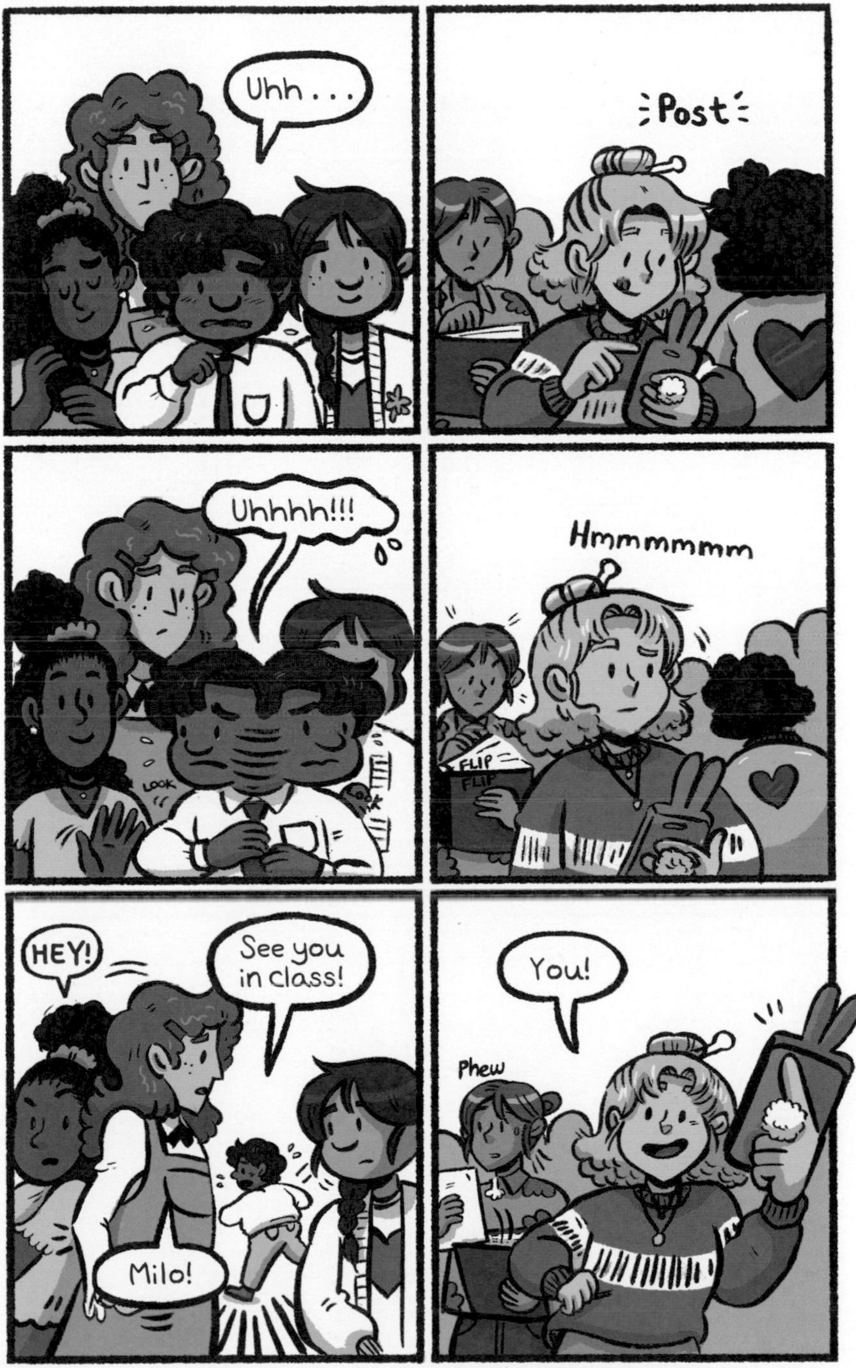

Uhh . . .
Post
Uhhhh!!!
LOOK
Hmmmmmmm
FLIP
FLIP
HEY!
See you in class!
Milo!
Phew
You!

ME?!
Um . . .
No.
YOU!
Alexandra, right?
This look is so fresh!
How did you come up with it?
BAH!

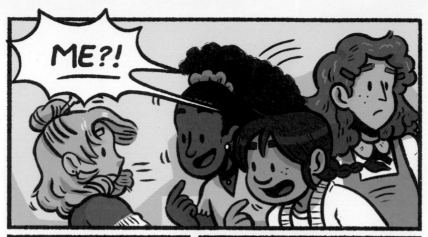

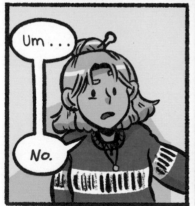

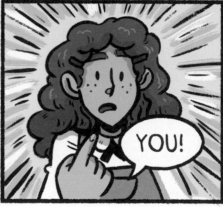

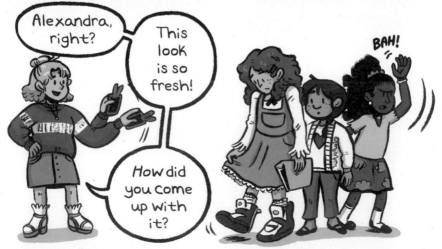

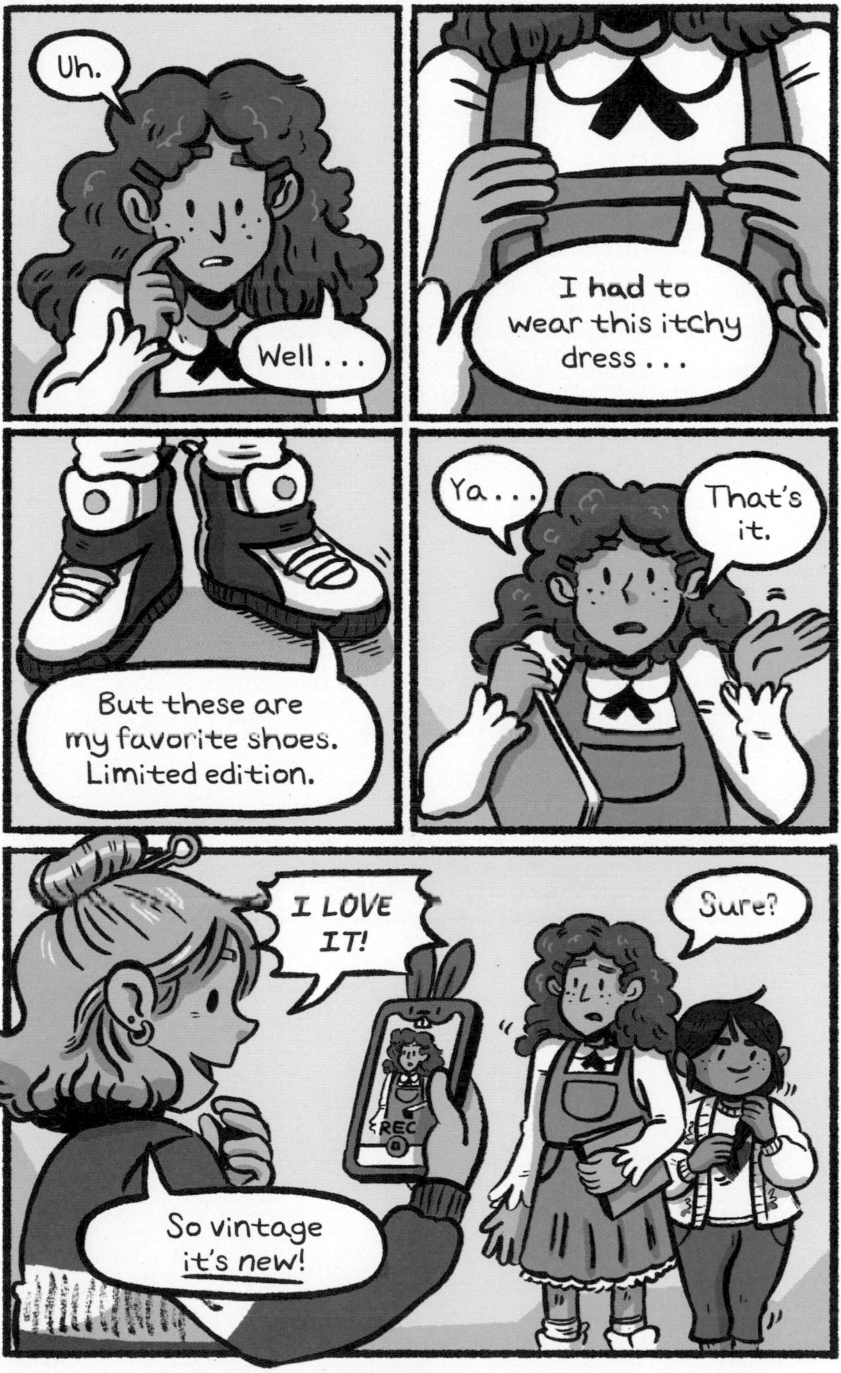
Uh.
Well . . .
I had to wear this itchy dress . . .
But these are my favorite shoes. Limited edition.
Ya . . .
That's it.
I LOVE IT!
Sure?
REC
So vintage it's new!

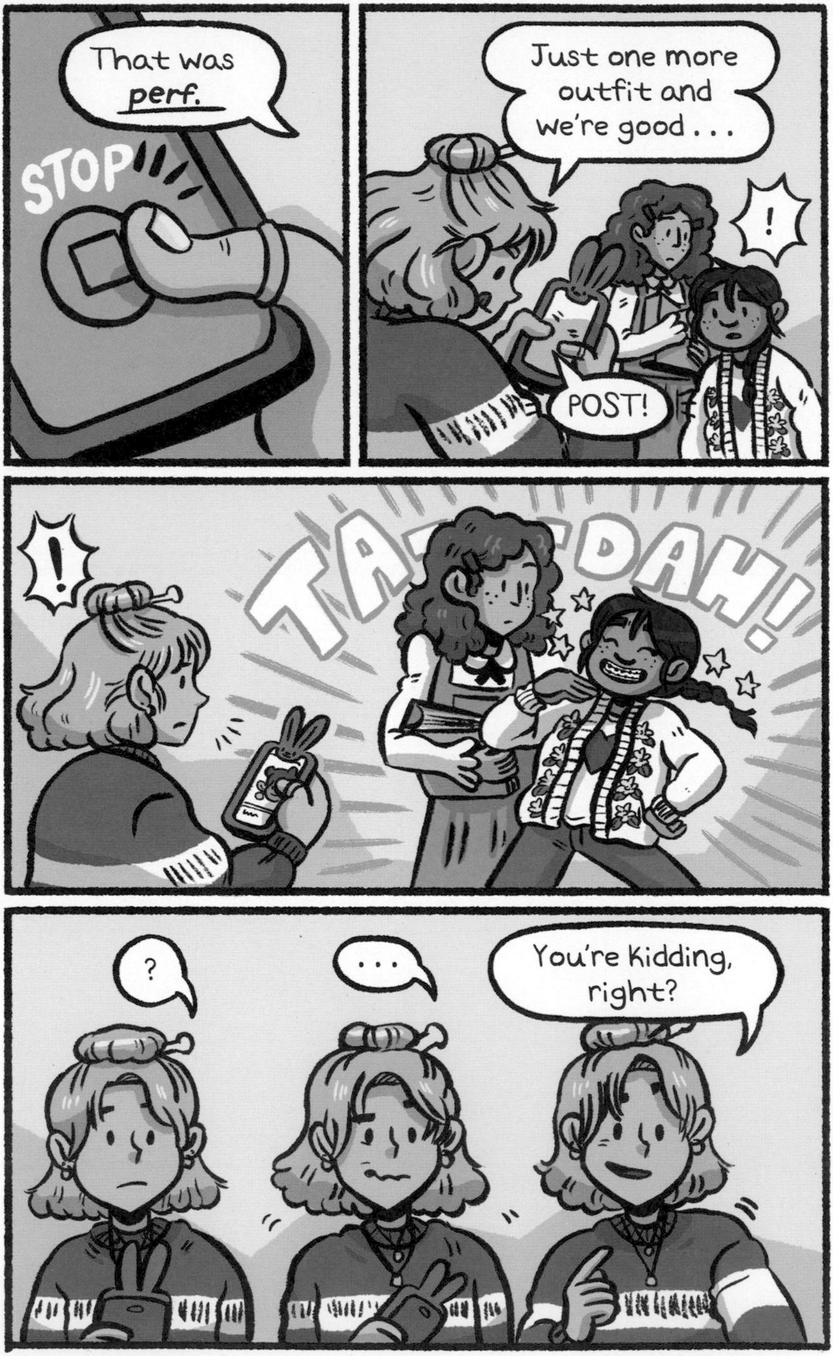
That was perf.
STOP
Just one more outfit and we're good . . .
!
POST!
!
TA-DAH!
?
. . .
You're kidding, right?

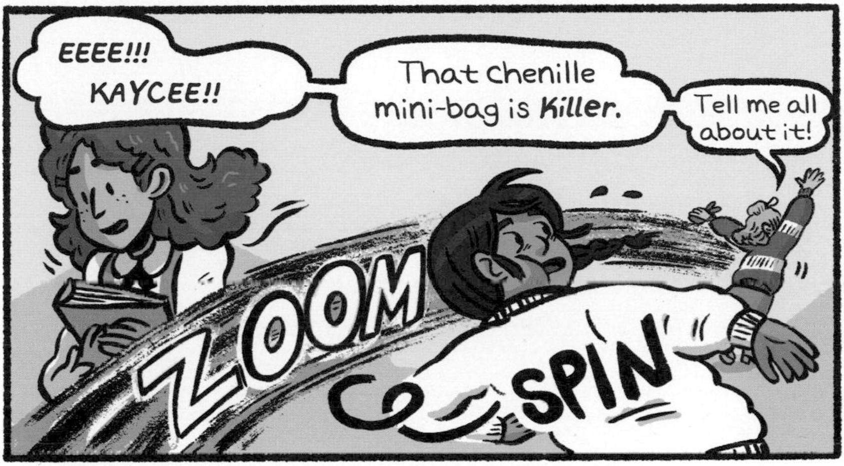
EEEE!!! KAYCEE!!
That chenille mini-bag is **Killer.**
Tell me all about it!
ZOOM
SPIN

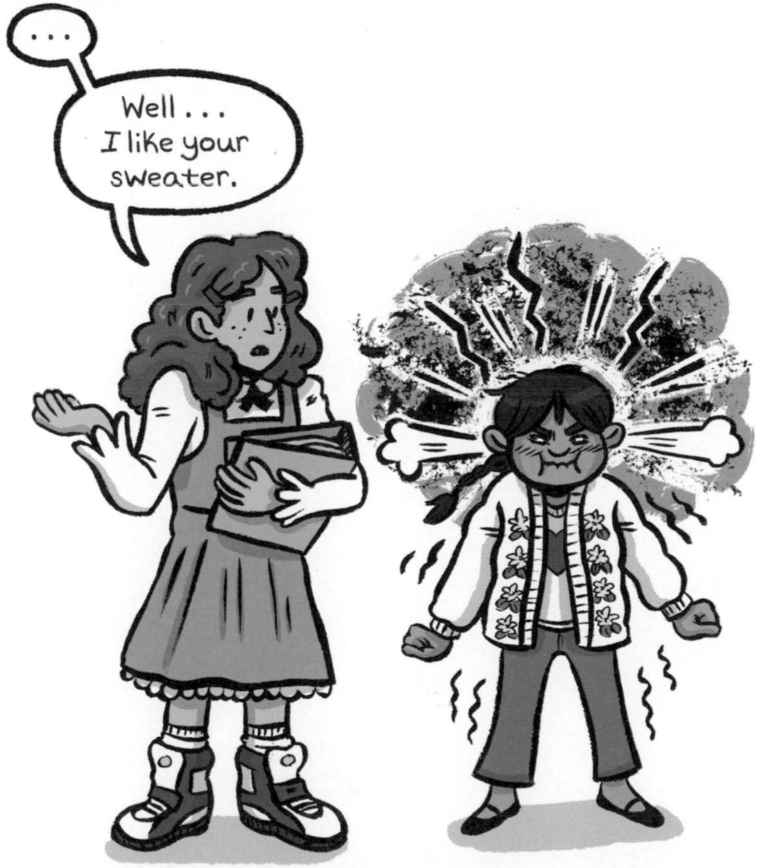
. . .
Well . . . I like your sweater.

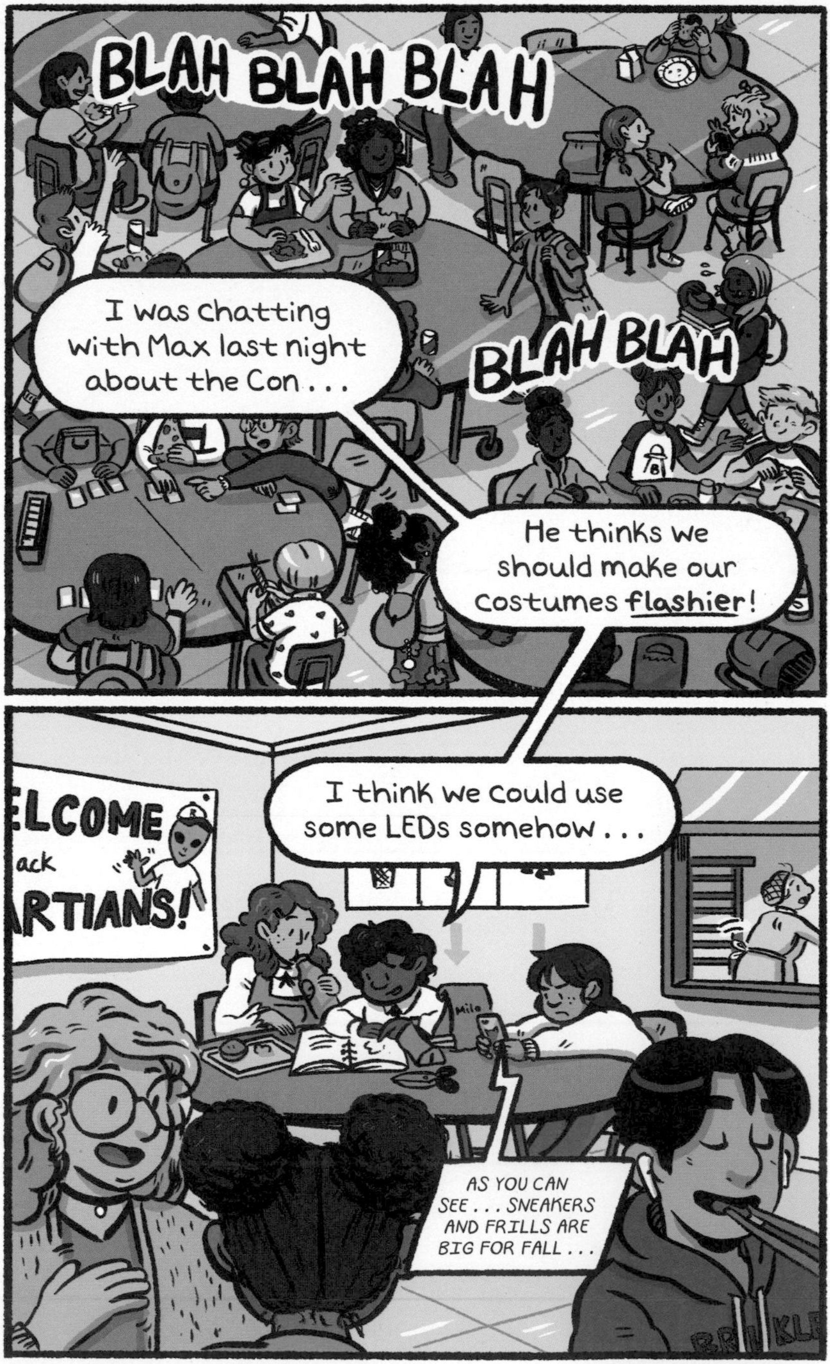
BLAH BLAH BLAH
I was chatting with Max last night about the Con . . .
BLAH BLAH
He thinks we should make our costumes flashier!
ELCOME
ack
ARTIANS!
I think we could use some LEDs somehow . . .
AS YOU CAN SEE . . . SNEAKERS AND FRILLS ARE BIG FOR FALL . . .

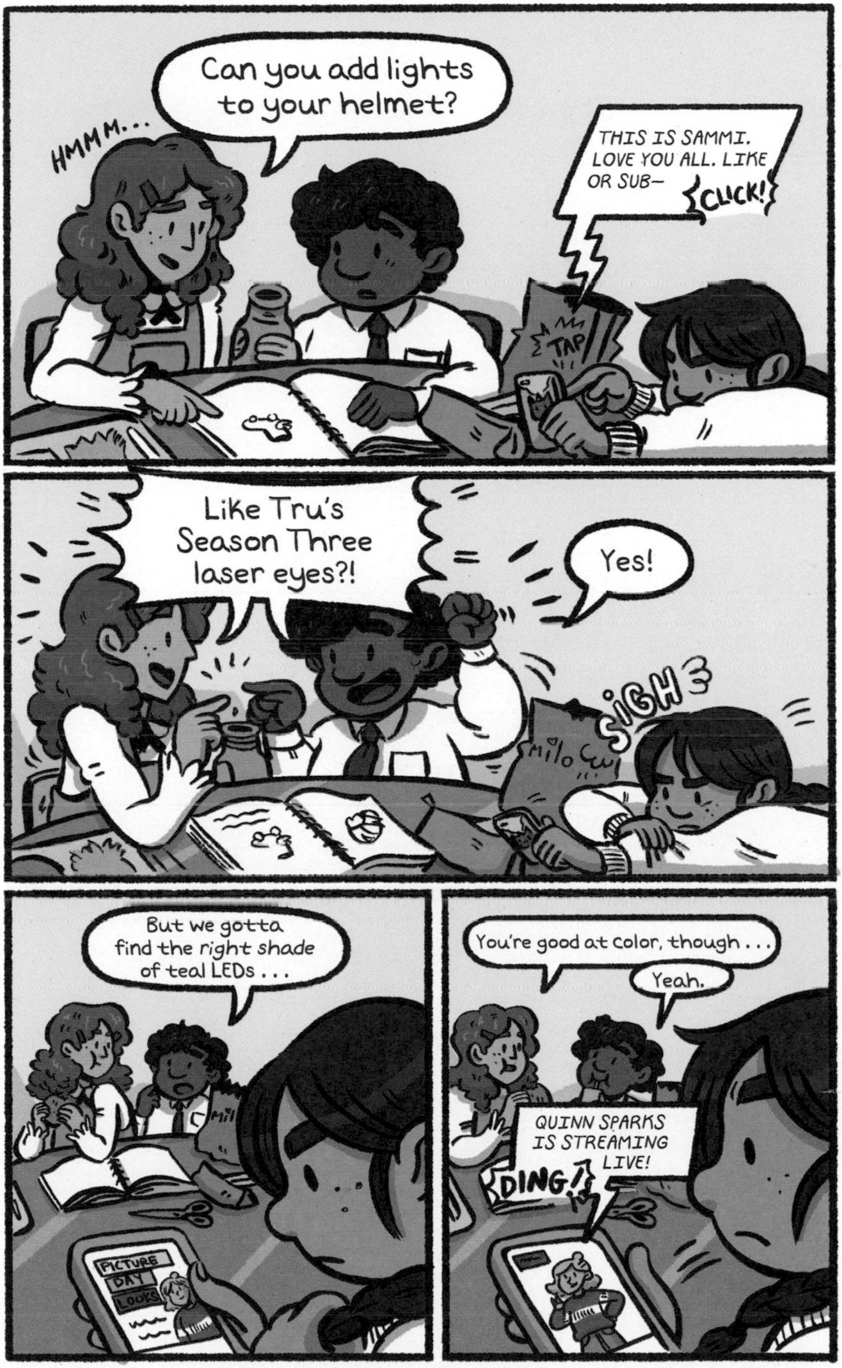
Can you add lights to your helmet?
HMMM...
THIS IS SAMMI. LOVE YOU ALL. LIKE OR SUB–
CLICK!
TAP
Like Tru's Season Three laser eyes?!
Yes!
SIGH
Milo
But we gotta find the right shade of teal LEDs . . .
PICTURE DAY LOOKS
You're good at color, though . . .
Yeah.
QUINN SPARKS IS STREAMING LIVE!
DING!

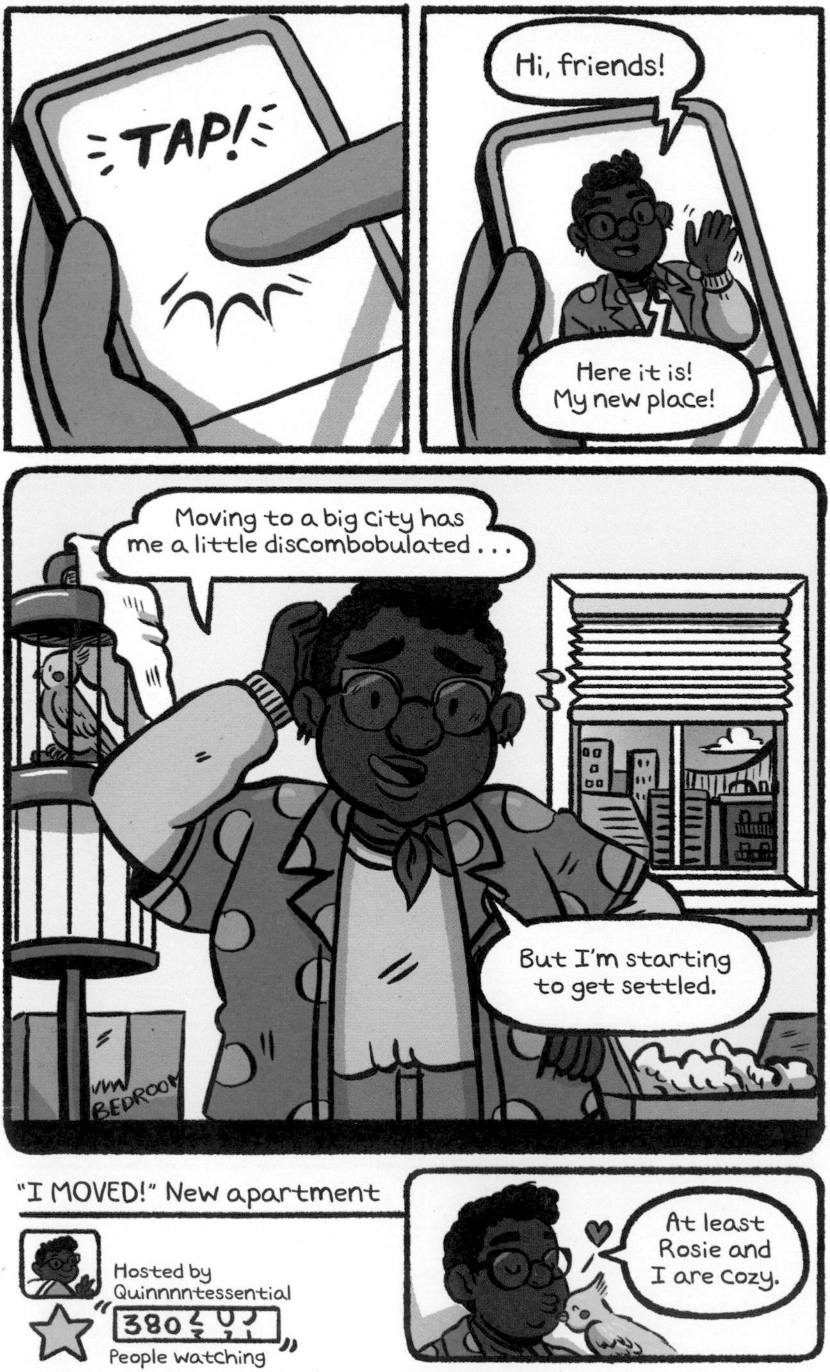
TAP!
Hi, friends!
Here it is! My new place!
Moving to a big city has me a little discombobulated . . .
But I'm starting to get settled.
BEDROOM
"I MOVED!" New apartment
Hosted by Quinnnntessential
380
People watching
At least Rosie and I are cozy.

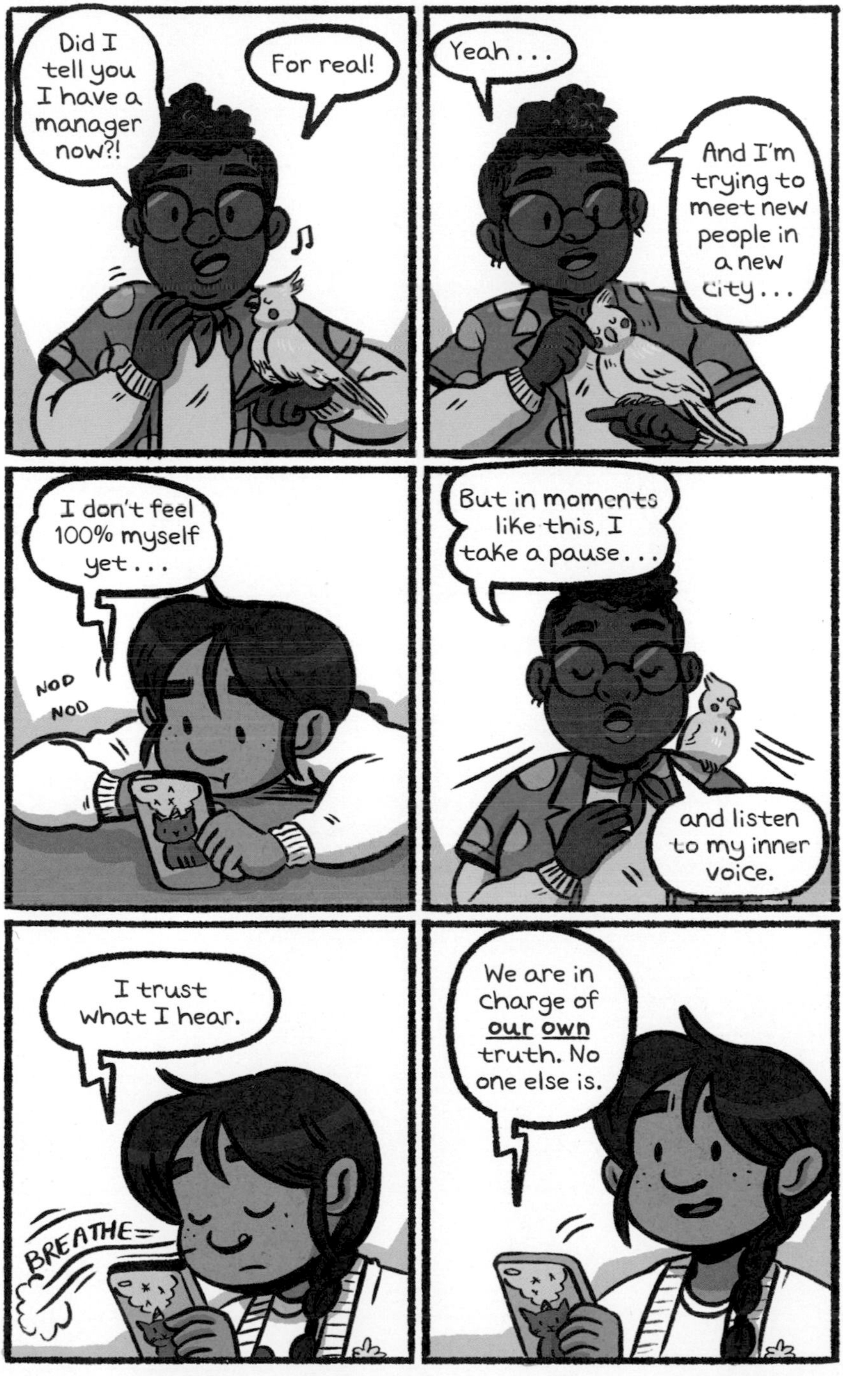
Did I tell you I have a manager now?!
For real!
Yeah . . .
And I'm trying to meet new people in a new city . . .
I don't feel 100% myself yet . . .
NOD NOD
But in moments like this, I take a pause . . .
and listen to my inner voice.
I trust what I hear.
BREATHE
We are in charge of **our own** truth. No one else is.

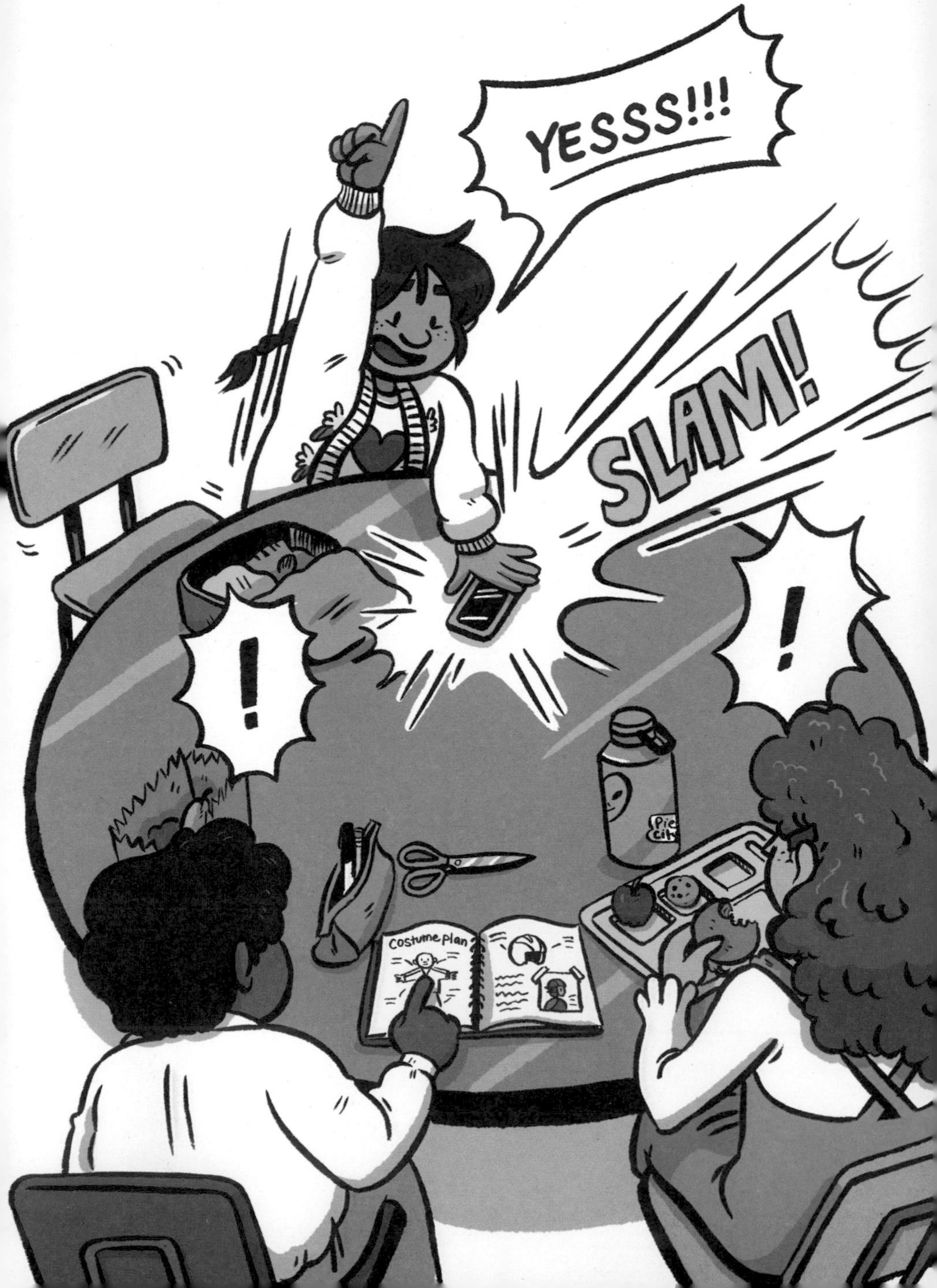
YESSS!!!
SLAM!
!
!
Costume plan

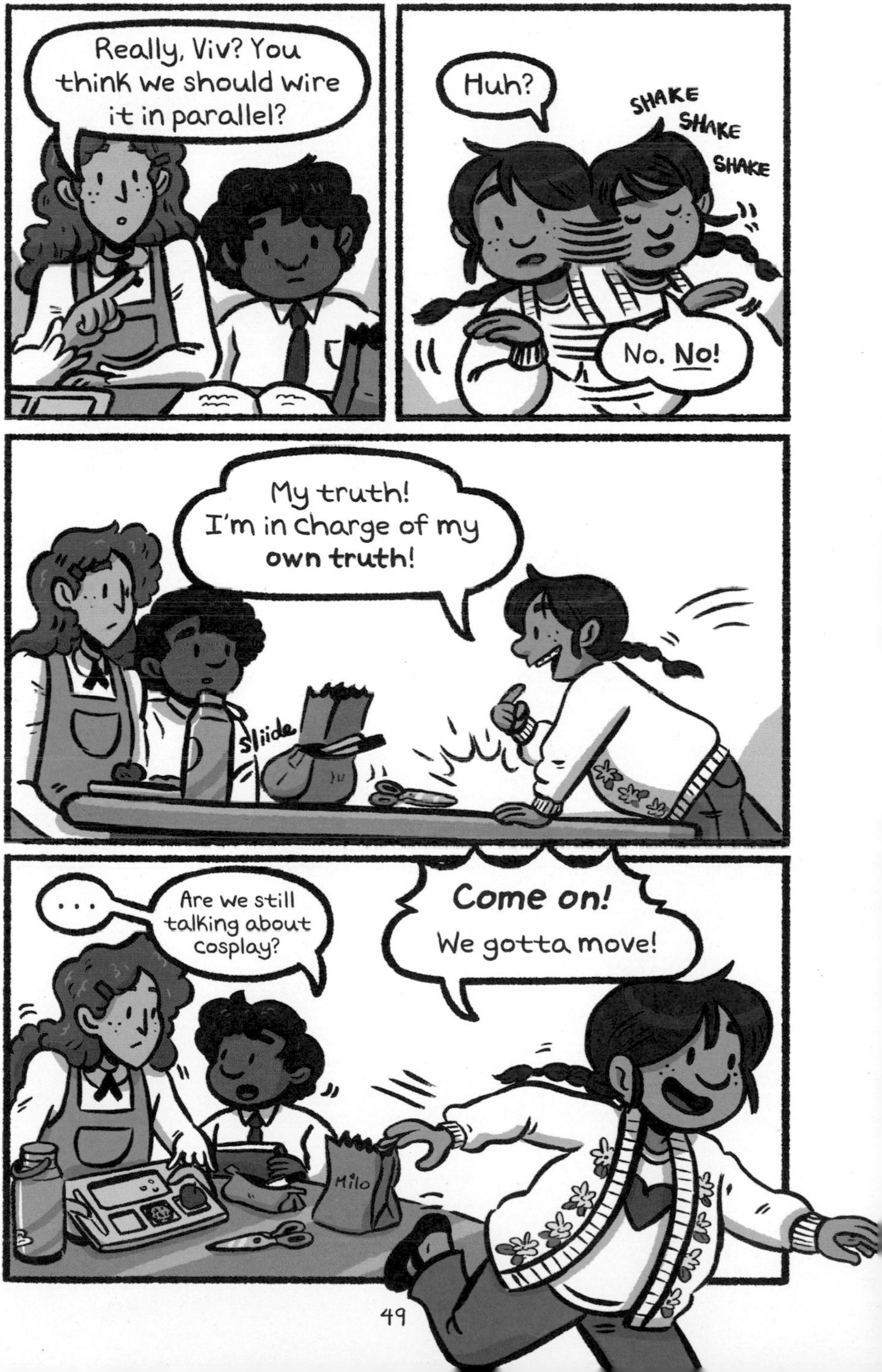

Really, Viv? You think we should wire it in parallel?
Huh?
SHAKE SHAKE SHAKE
No. No!
My truth! I'm in charge of my own truth!
sliide
...
Are we still talking about cosplay?
Come on! We gotta move!
Milo

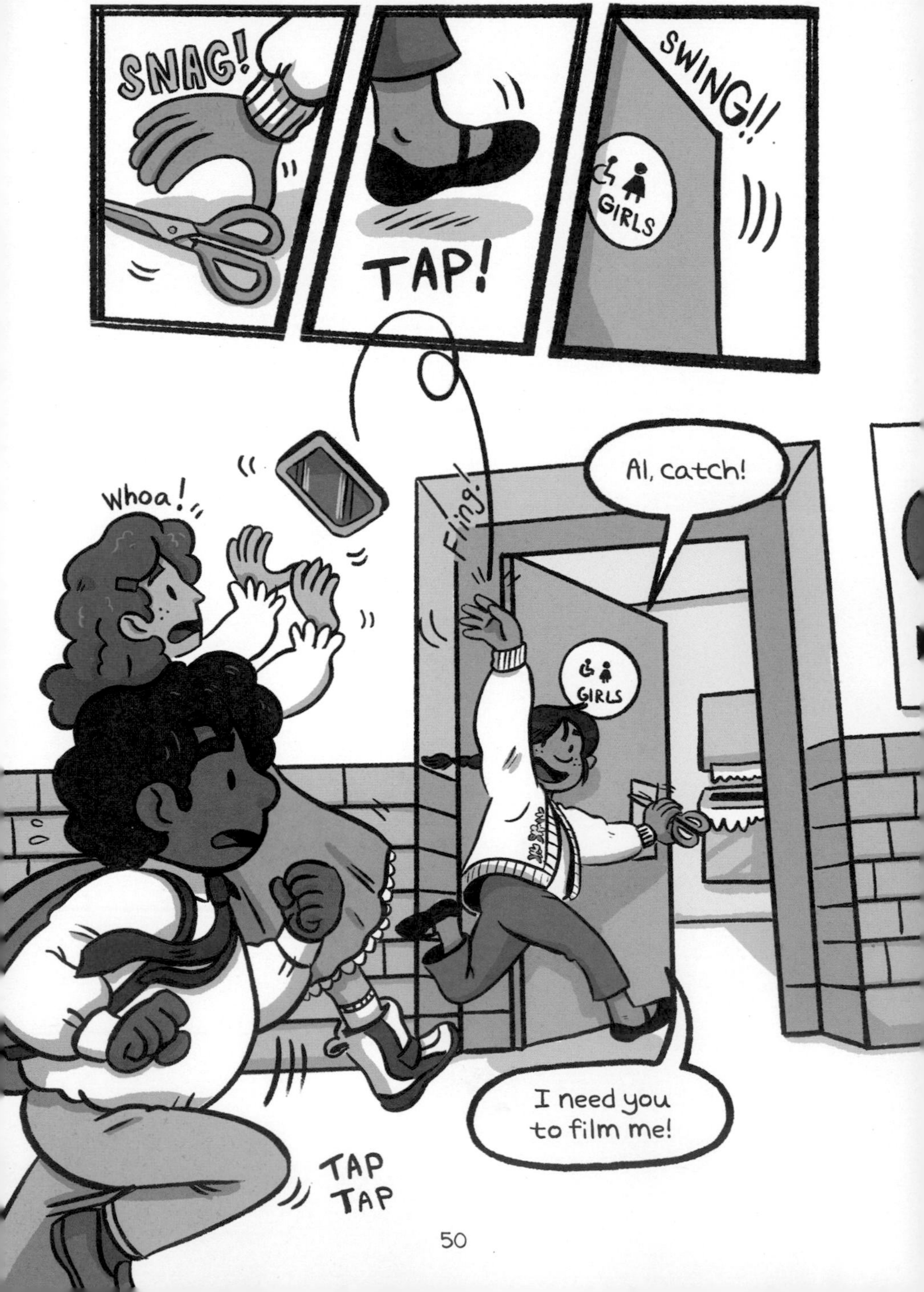

SNAG!
TAP!
SWING!!
GIRLS
Whoa!
Fling!
Al, catch!
GIRLS
I need you to film me!
TAP TAP

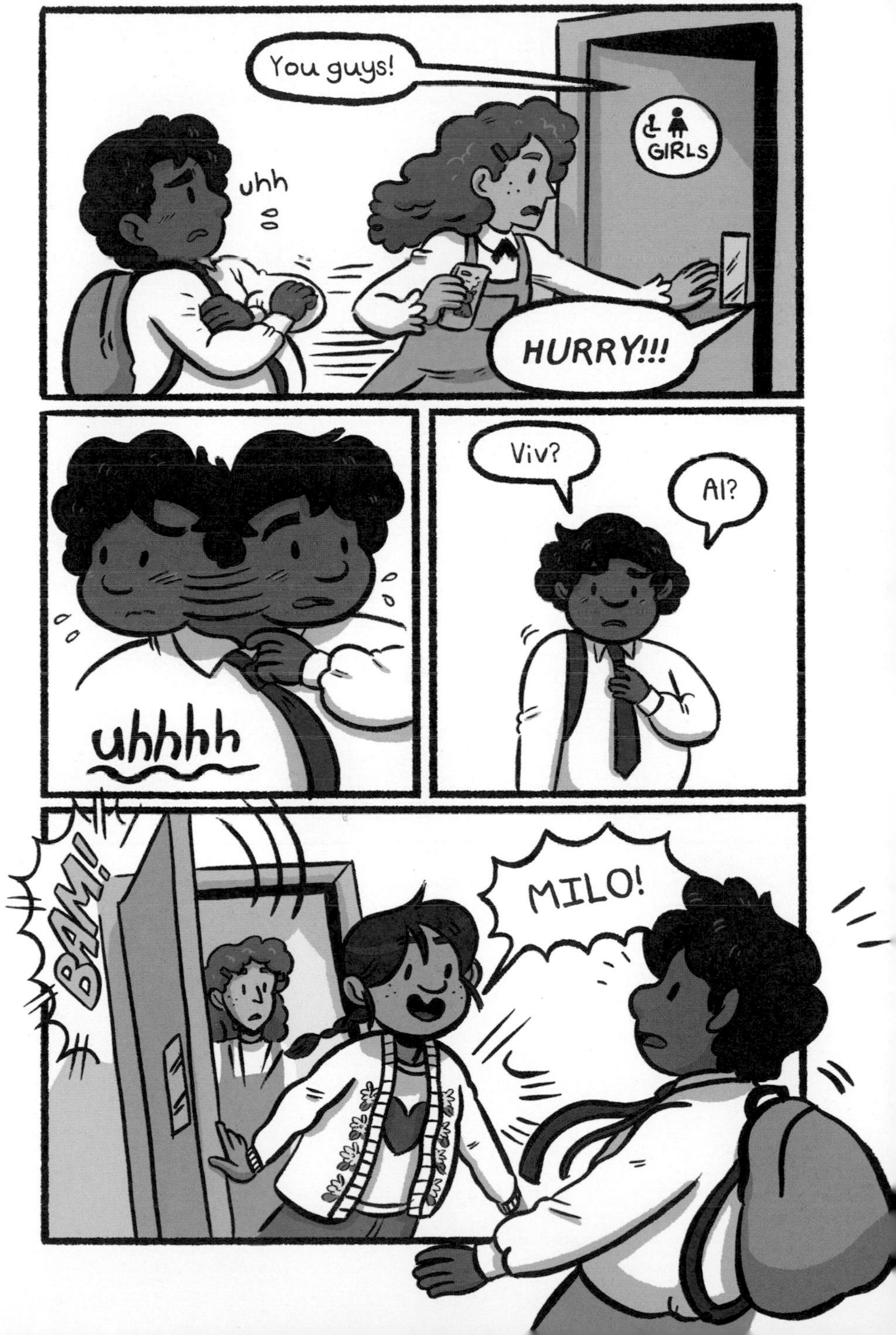
You guys!
GIRLS
uhh
HURRY!!!
uhhhh
Viv?
Al?
BAM!
MILO!

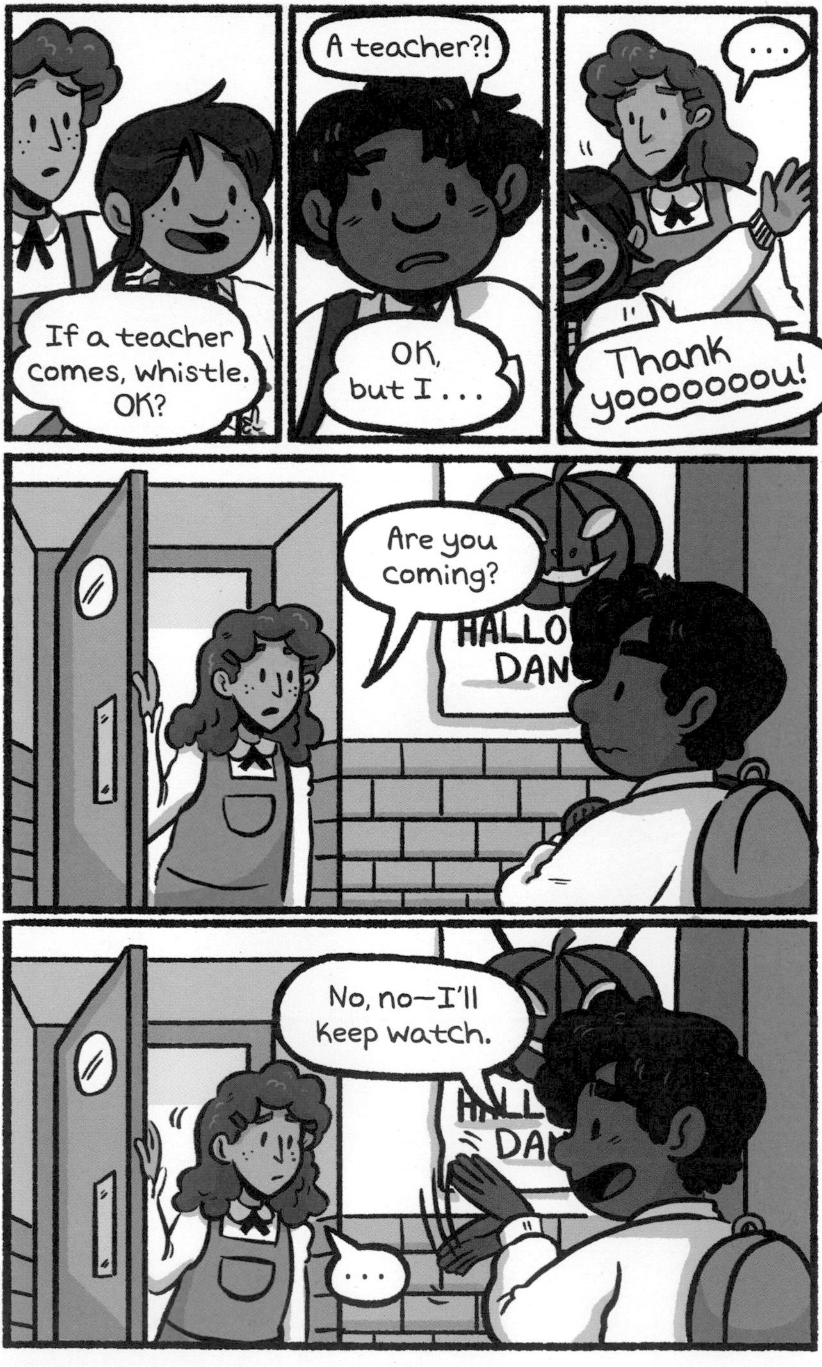
If a teacher comes, whistle. OK?
A teacher?!
OK, but I . . .
. . .
Thank yoooooou!
Are you coming?
HALLO
DAN
No, no—I'll keep watch.
. . .

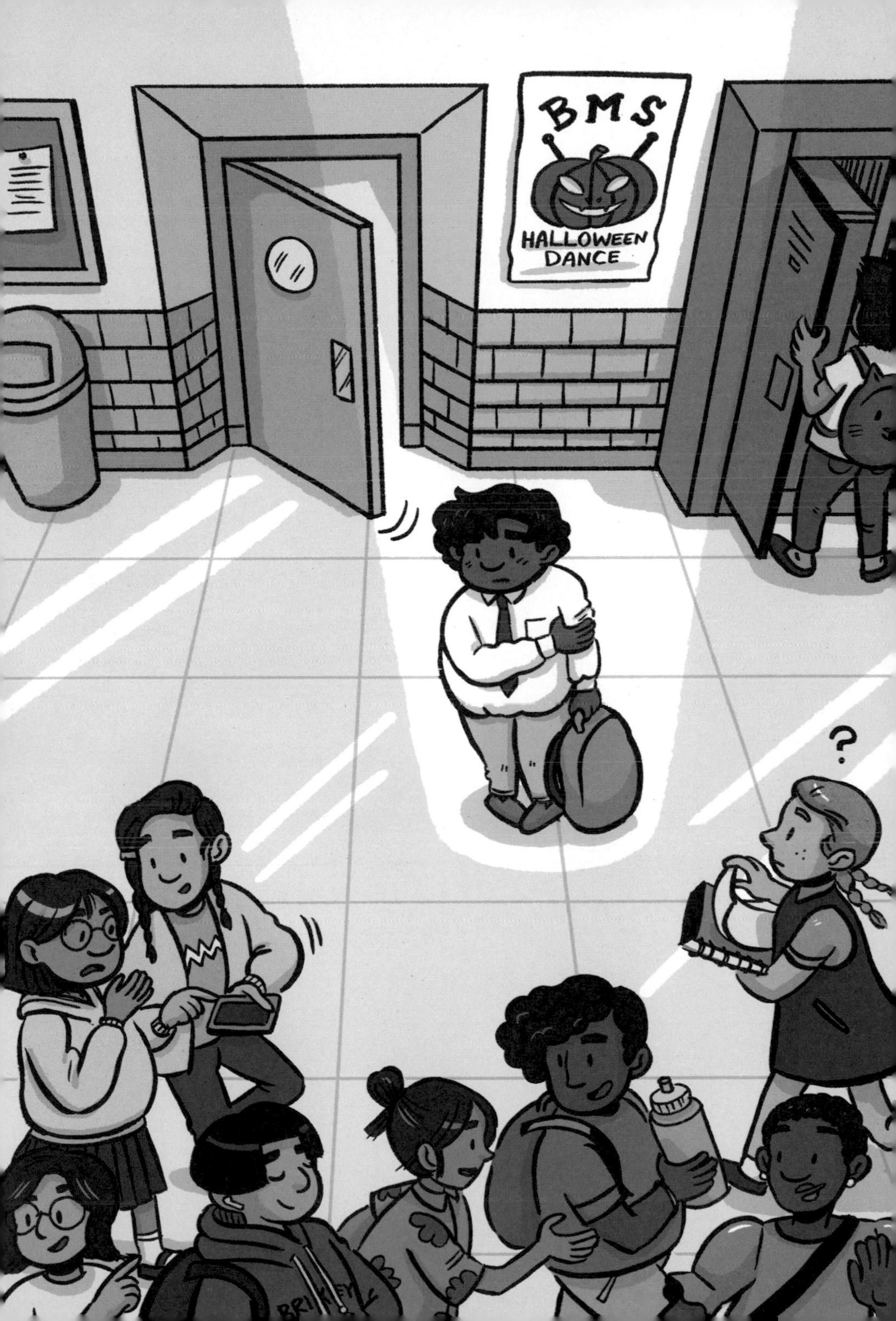
BMS
HALLOWEEN
DANCE
?

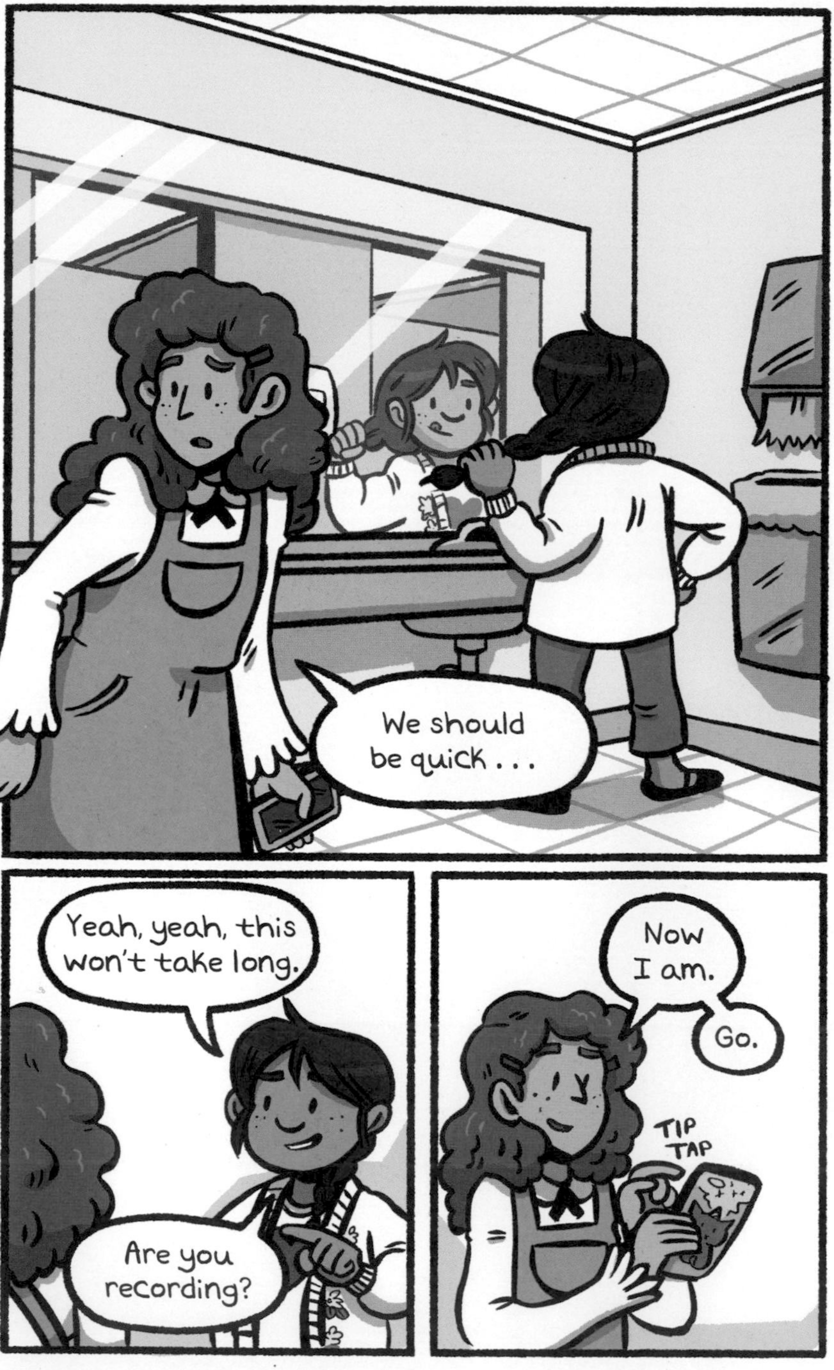
We should be quick . . .
Yeah, yeah, this won't take long.
Are you recording?
Now I am.
Go.
TIP TAP

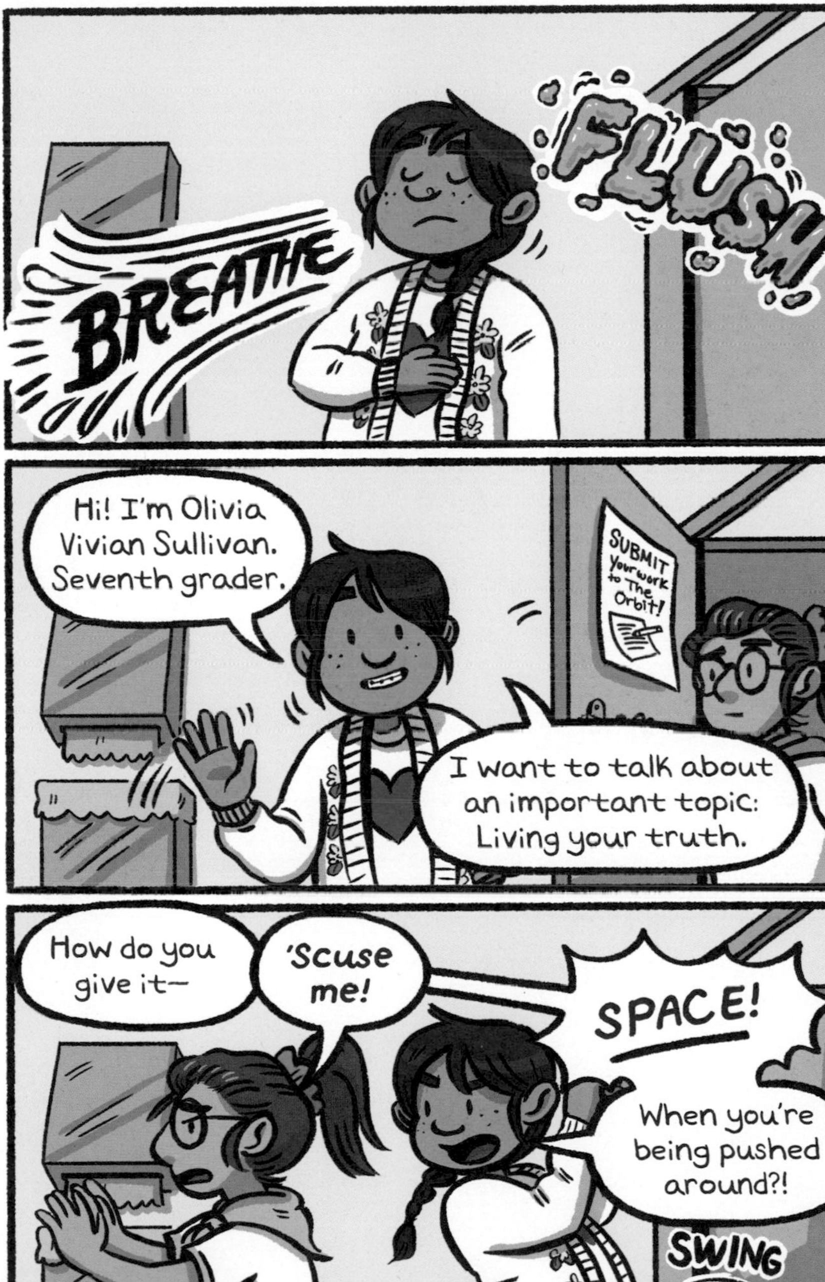
BREATHE
FLUSH
Hi! I'm Olivia Vivian Sullivan. Seventh grader.
SUBMIT Your work to The Orbit!
I want to talk about an important topic: Living your truth.
How do you give it—
'Scuse me!
SPACE!
When you're being pushed around?!
SWING

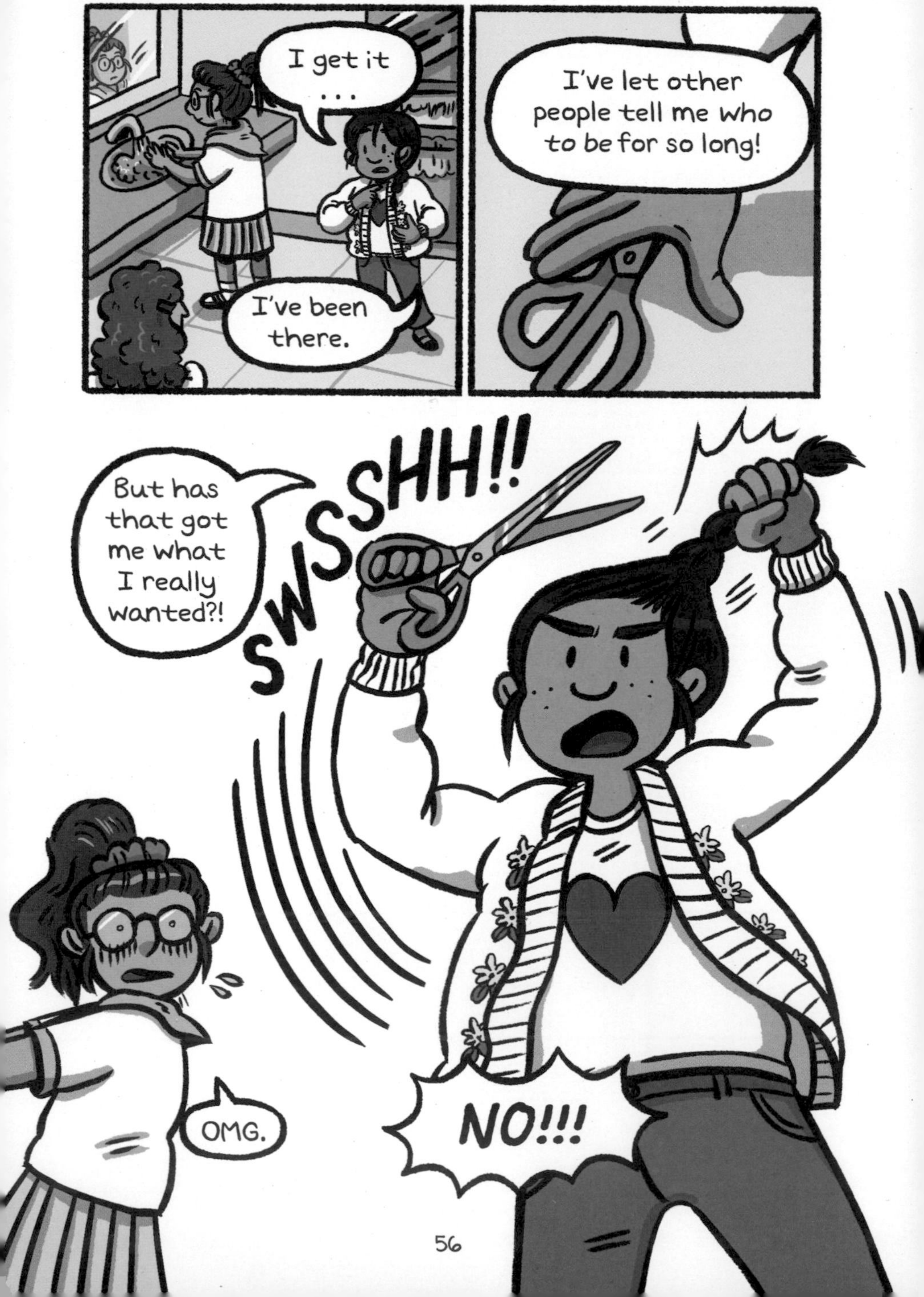
I get it
...
I've been there.
I've let other people tell me who to be for so long!
But has that got me what I really wanted?!
SWSSHH!!
NO!!!
OMG.

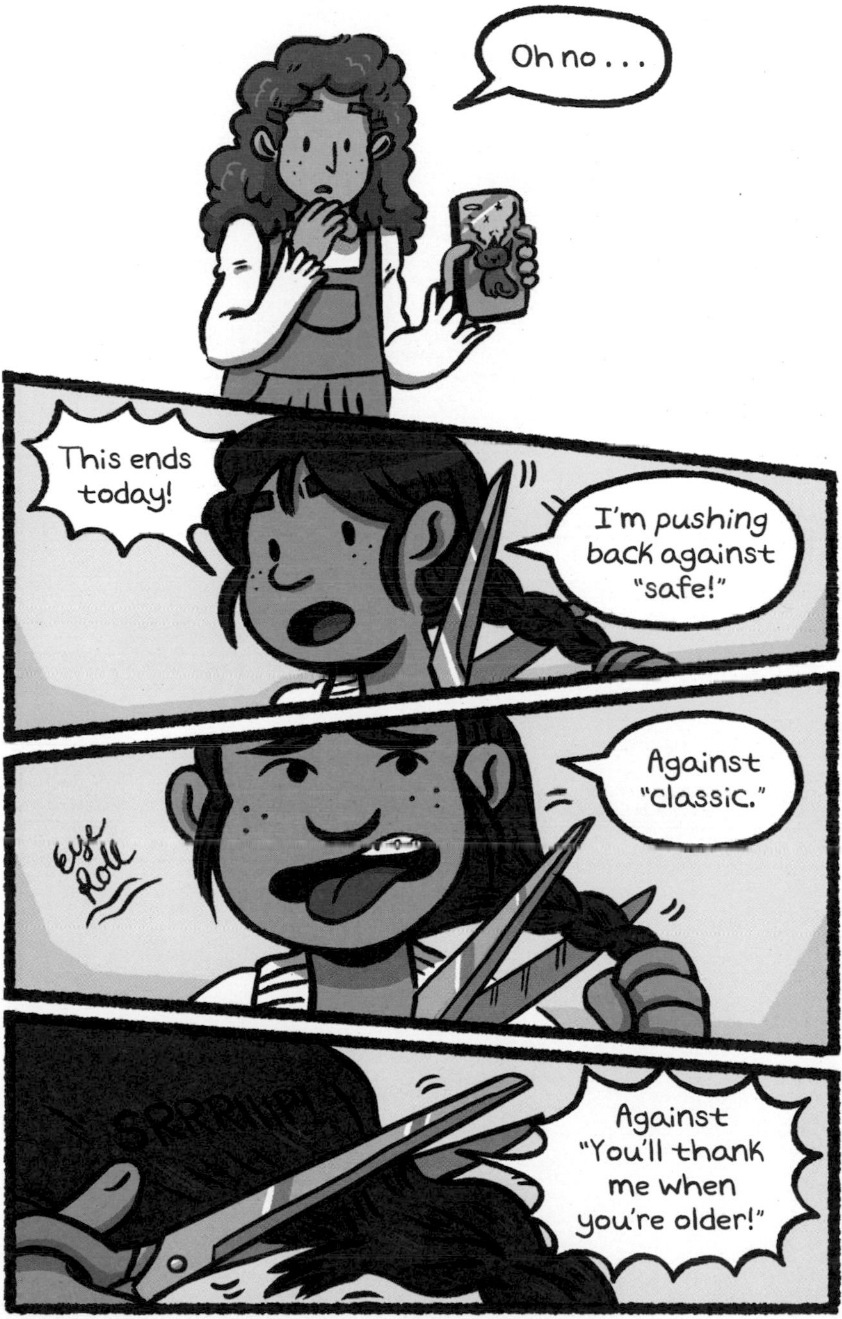
Oh no . . .
This ends today!
I'm pushing back against "safe!"
Eye Roll
Against "classic."
SRRRIIIP!
Against "You'll thank me when you're older!"

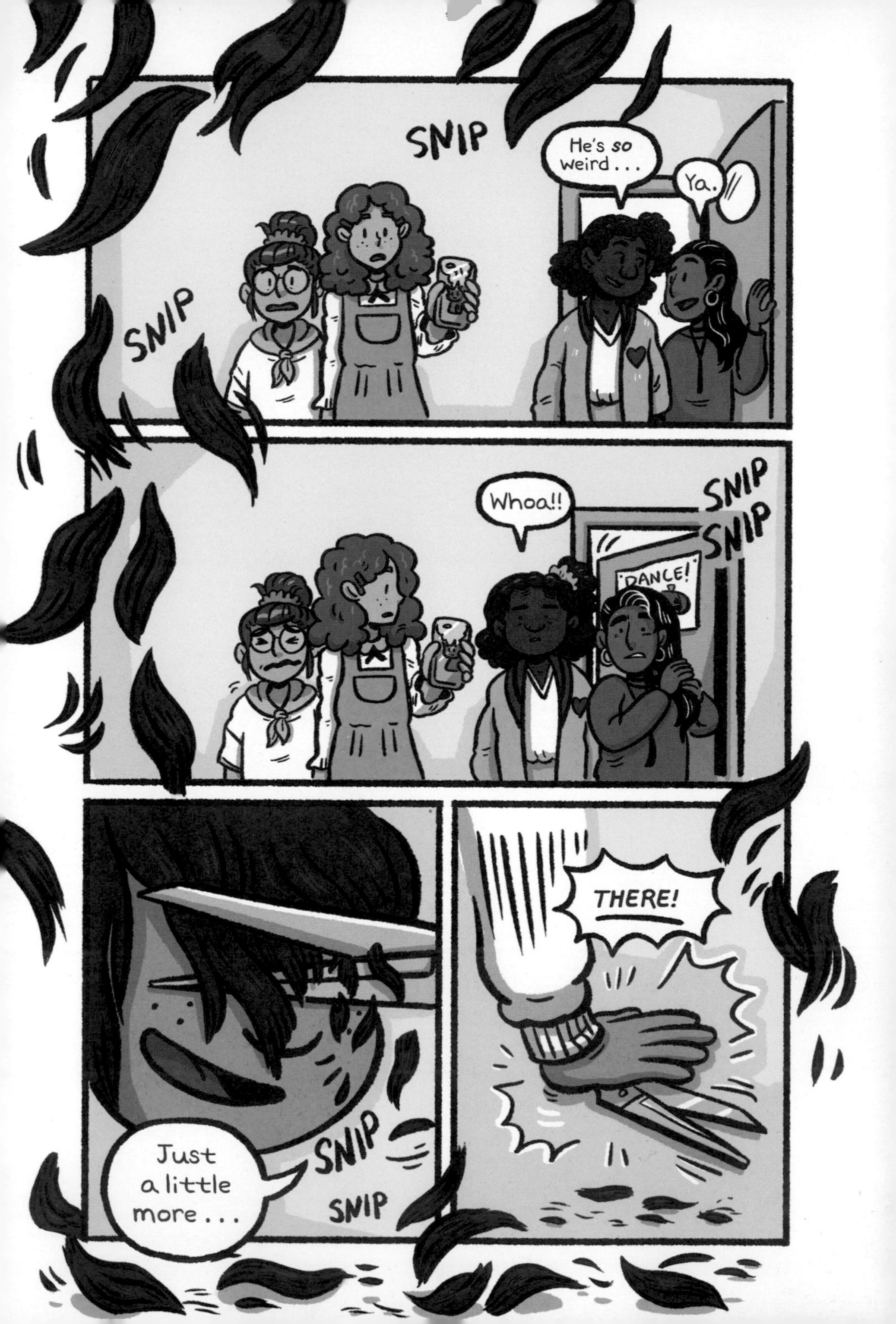
SNIP
SNIP
He's so weird . . .
Ya.
Whoa!!
SNIP
SNIP
DANCE!
Just a little more . . .
SNIP
SNIP
THERE!

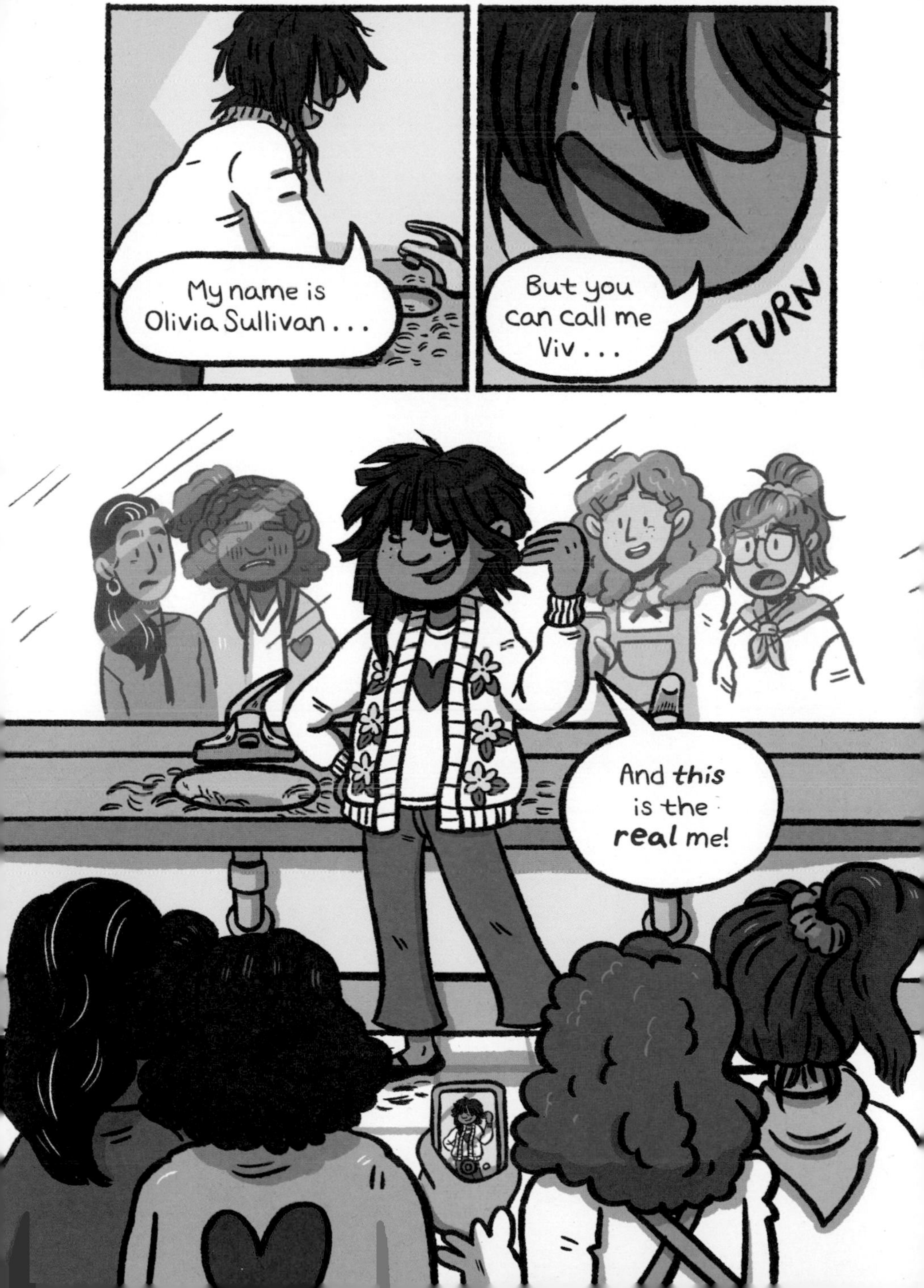
My name is Olivia Sullivan . . .
But you can call me Viv . . .
TURN
And *this* is the **real** me!

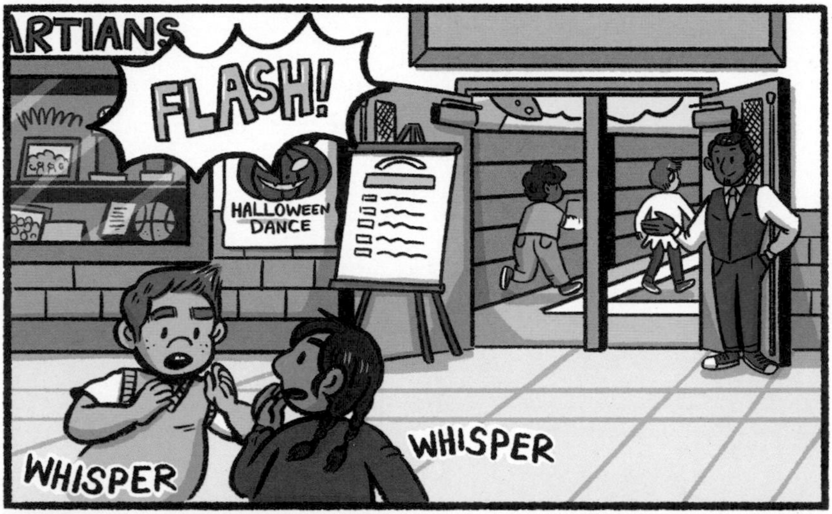
ARTIANS
FLASH!
HALLOWEEN DANCE
WHISPER
WHISPER

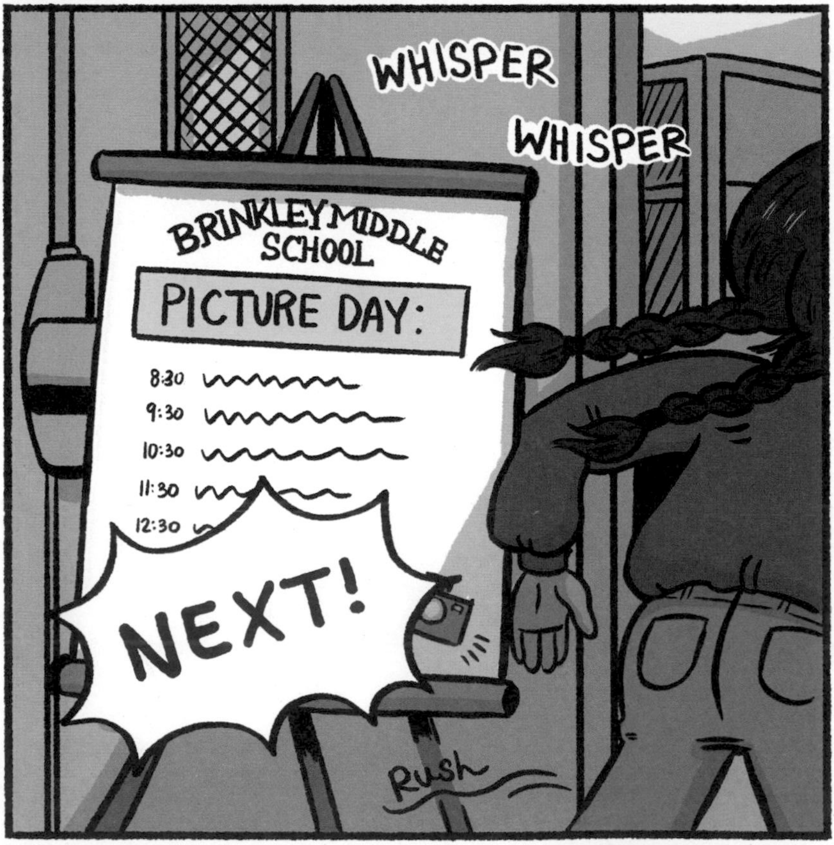
WHISPER
WHISPER
BRINKLEY MIDDLE SCHOOL
PICTURE DAY:
8:30
9:30
10:30
11:30
12:30
NEXT!
RUSH

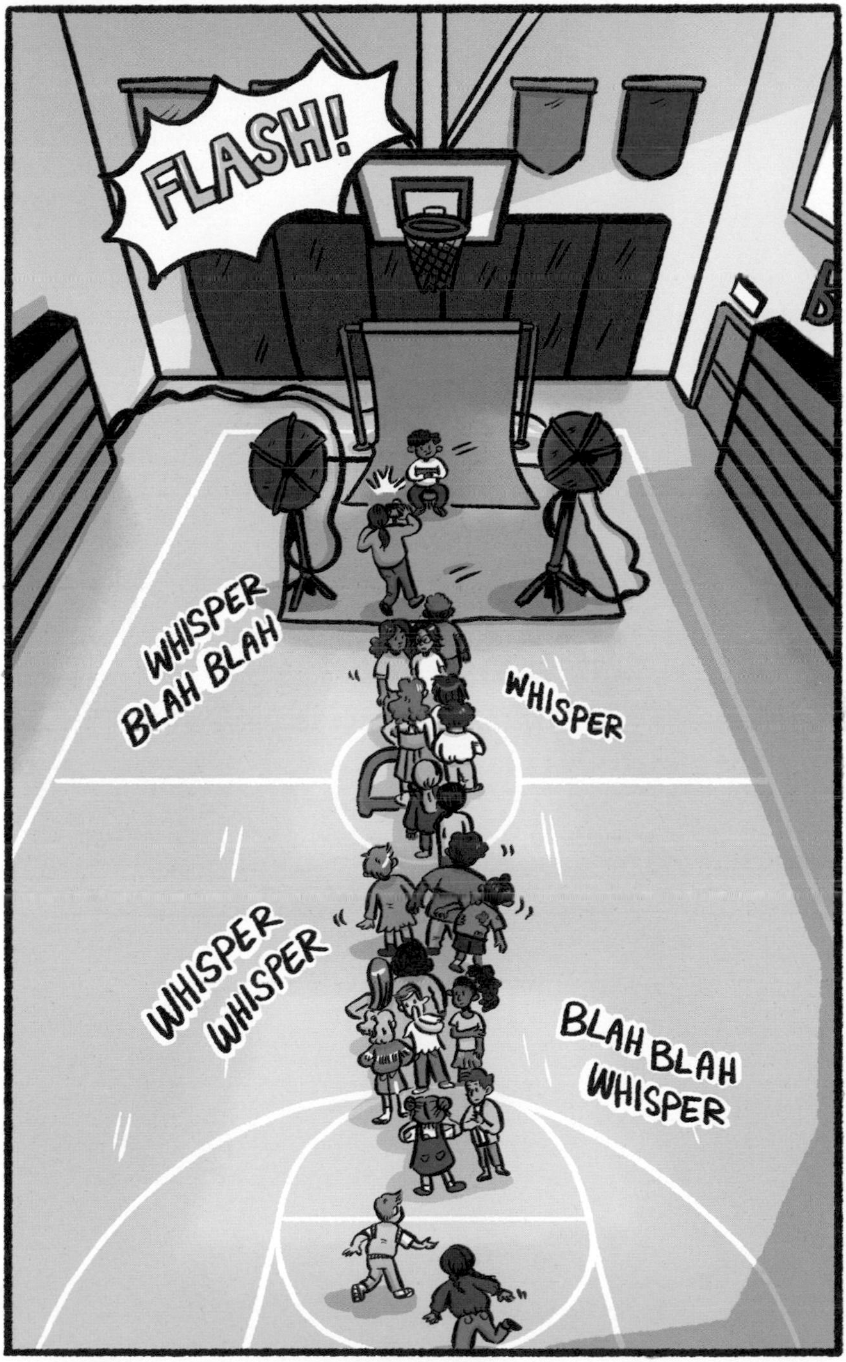
FLASH!
WHISPER
BLAH BLAH
WHISPER
WHISPER
WHISPER
BLAH BLAH
WHISPER

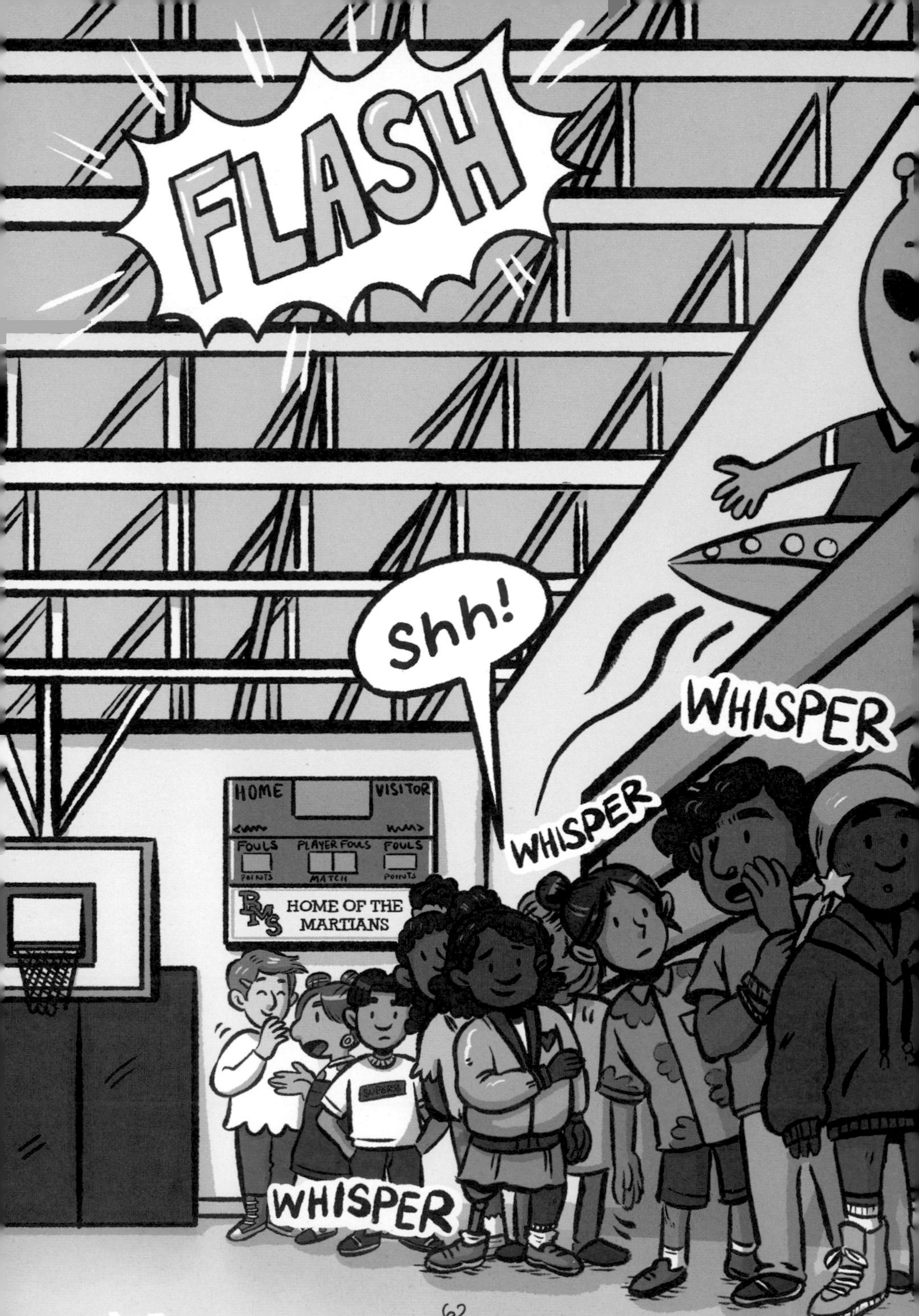
FLASH
Shh!
WHISPER
WHISPER
HOME
VISITOR
FOULS
PLAYER FOULS
FOULS
POINTS
MATCH
POINTS
BMS
HOME OF THE
MARTIANS
WHISPER

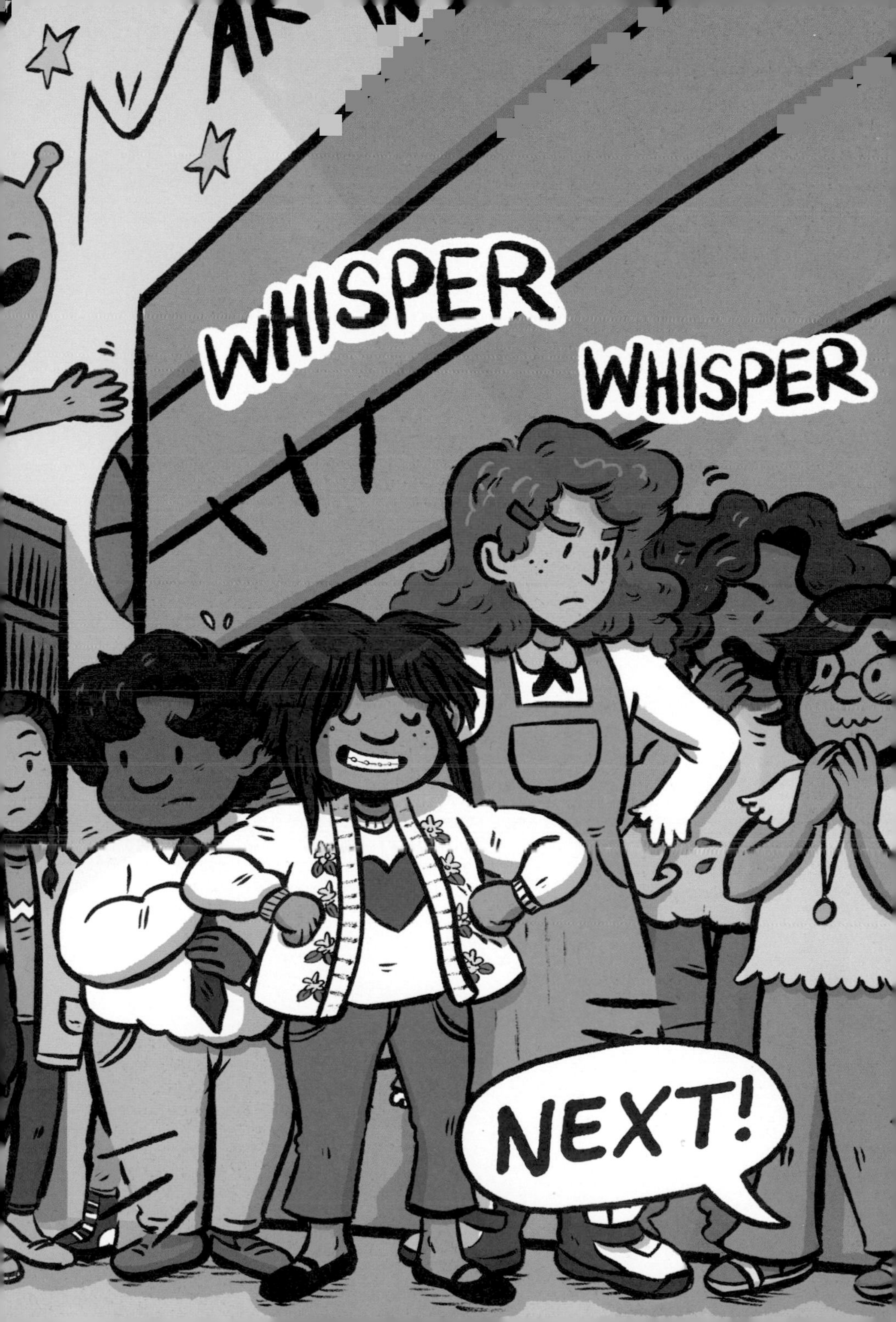
WHISPER
WHISPER
NEXT!

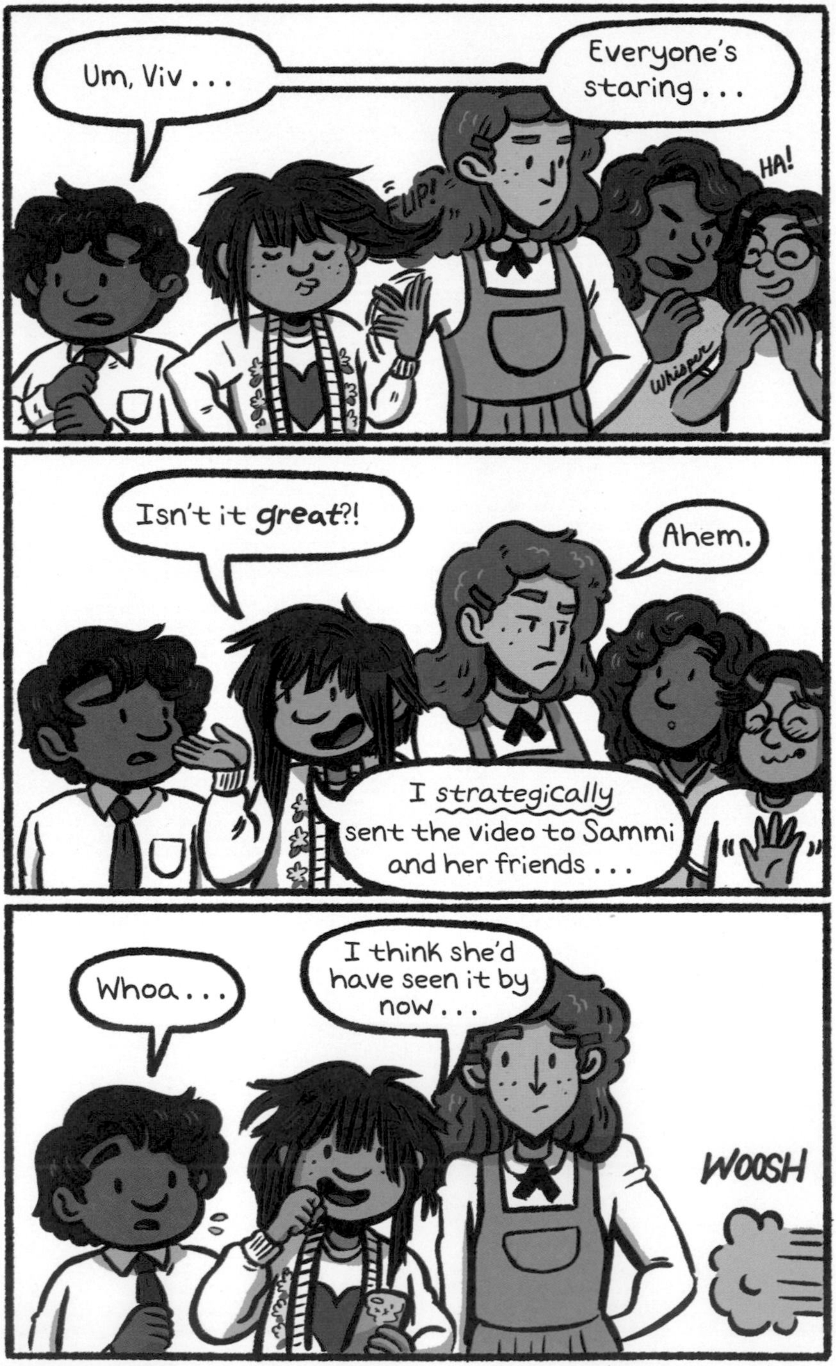
Um, Viv . . .
Everyone's staring . . .
FLIP!
HA!
Whisper
Isn't it **great**?!
Ahem.
I *strategically* sent the video to Sammi and her friends . . .
Whoa . . .
I think she'd have seen it by now . . .
WOOSH

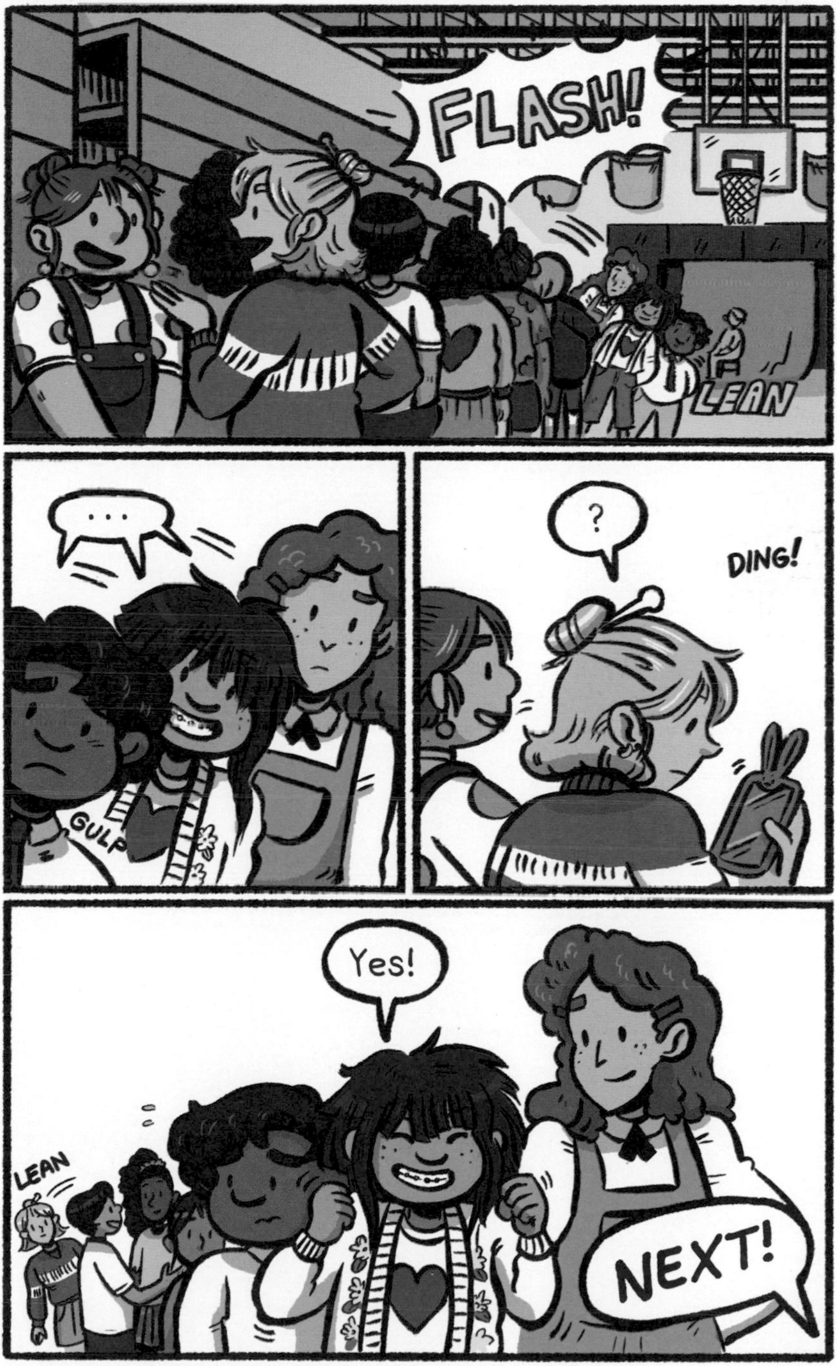
FLASH!
LEAN
...
GULP
?
DING!
Yes!
LEAN
NEXT!

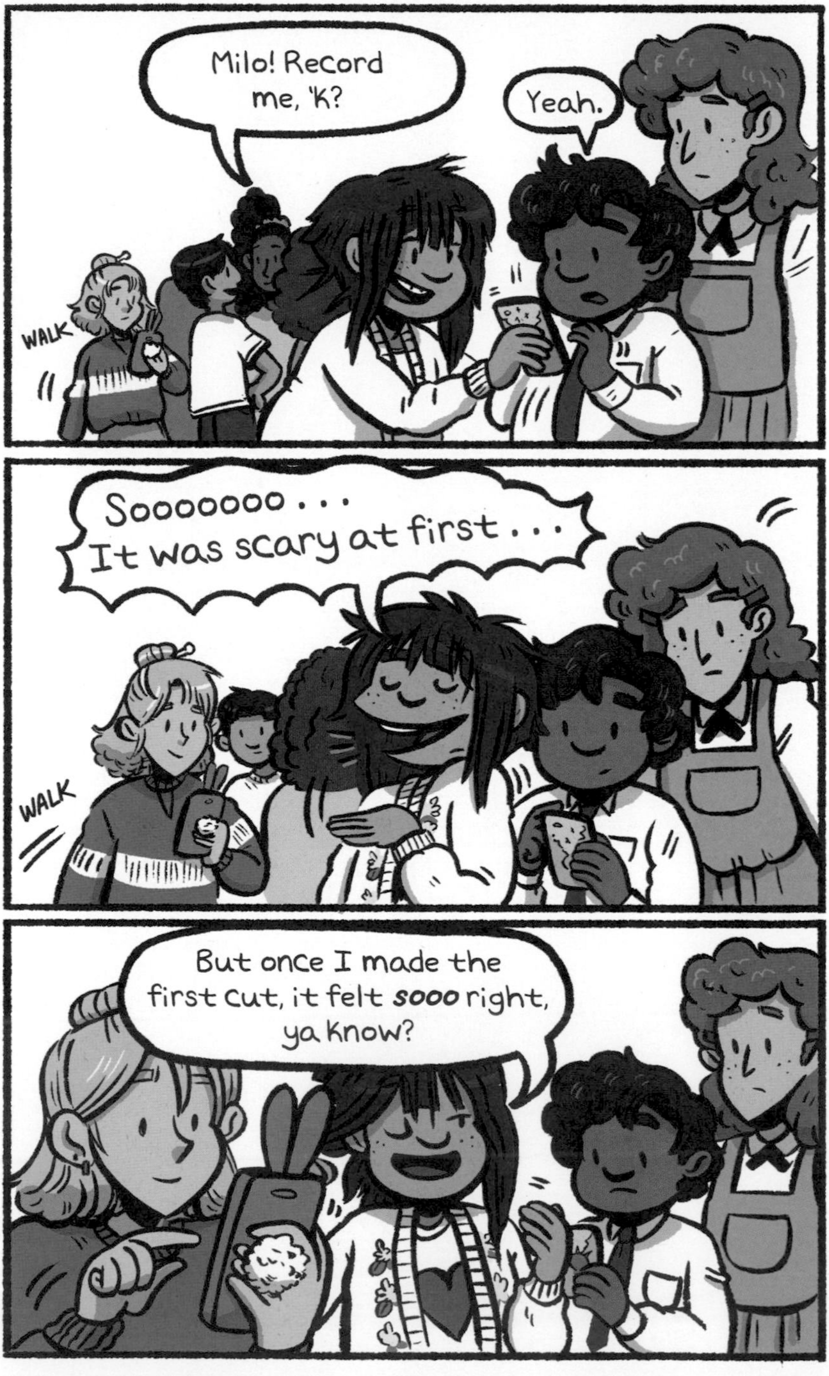
Milo! Record me, 'K?
Yeah.
WALK
Sooooooo . . .
It was scary at first . . .
WALK
But once I made the first cut, it felt *sooo* right, ya know?

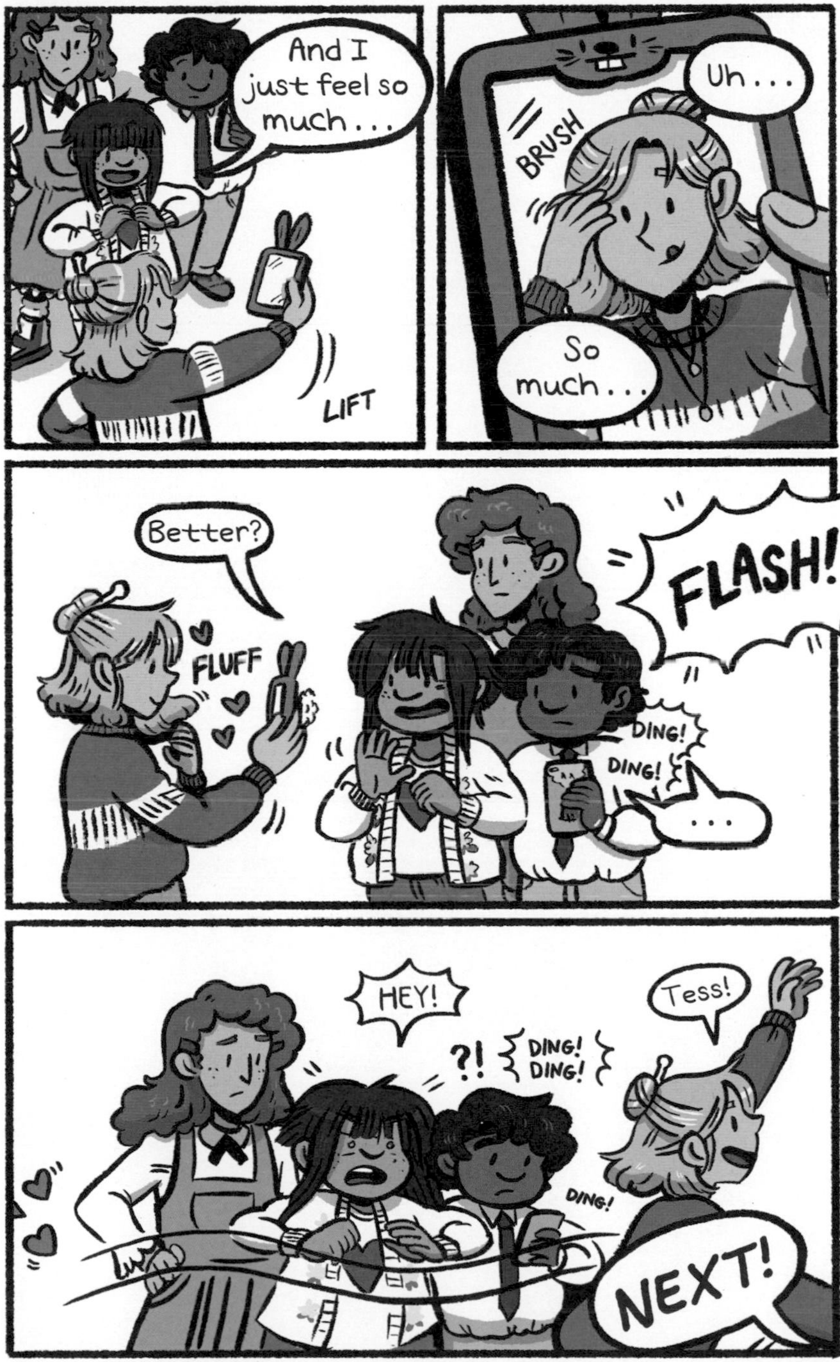
And I just feel so much . . .
LIFT
Uh . . .
BRUSH
So much . . .
Better?
FLUFF
FLASH!
DING!
DING!
. . .
HEY!
?!
DING!
DING!
Tess!
DING!
NEXT!

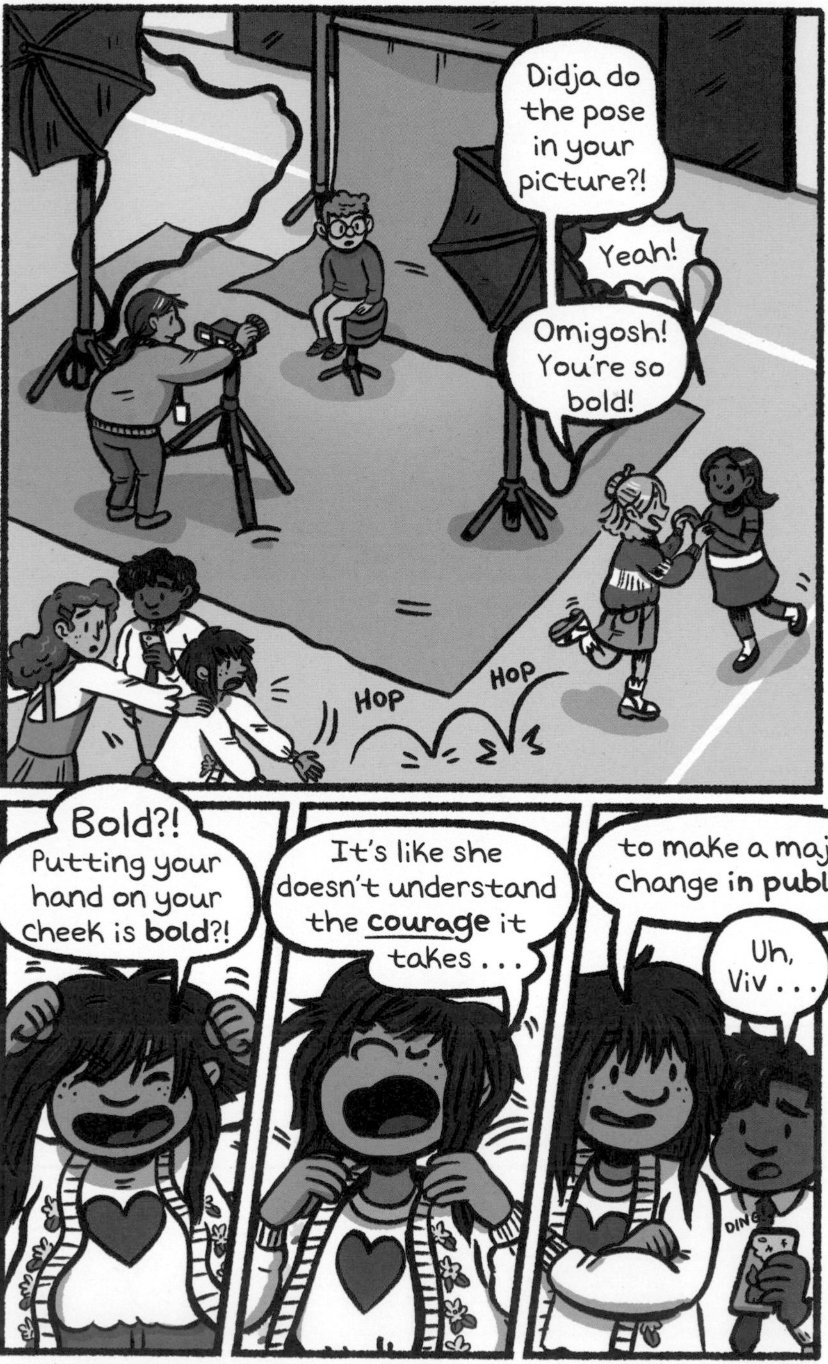
Didja do the pose in your picture?!
Yeah!
Omigosh! You're so bold!
HOP
HOP
Bold?! Putting your hand on your cheek is **bold**?!
It's like she doesn't understand the courage it takes . . .
to make a major change **in public**!
Uh, Viv . . .
DING

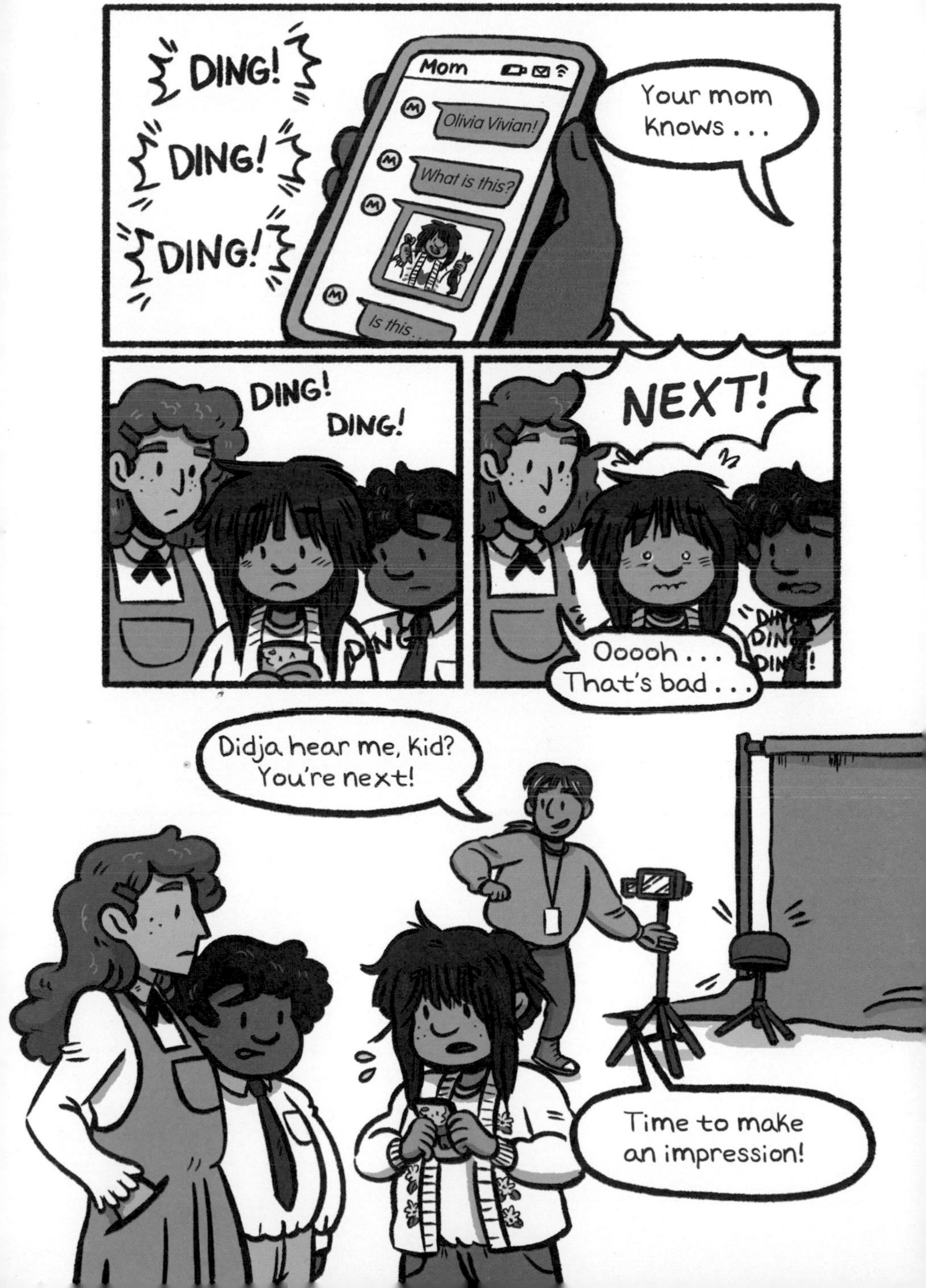
DING!
DING!
DING!
Mom
Olivia Vivian!
What is this?
Is this...
Your mom knows . . .
DING!
DING!
DING!
NEXT!
DING!
DING!
DING!
Ooooh . . . That's bad . . .
Didja hear me, Kid? You're next!
Time to make an impression!

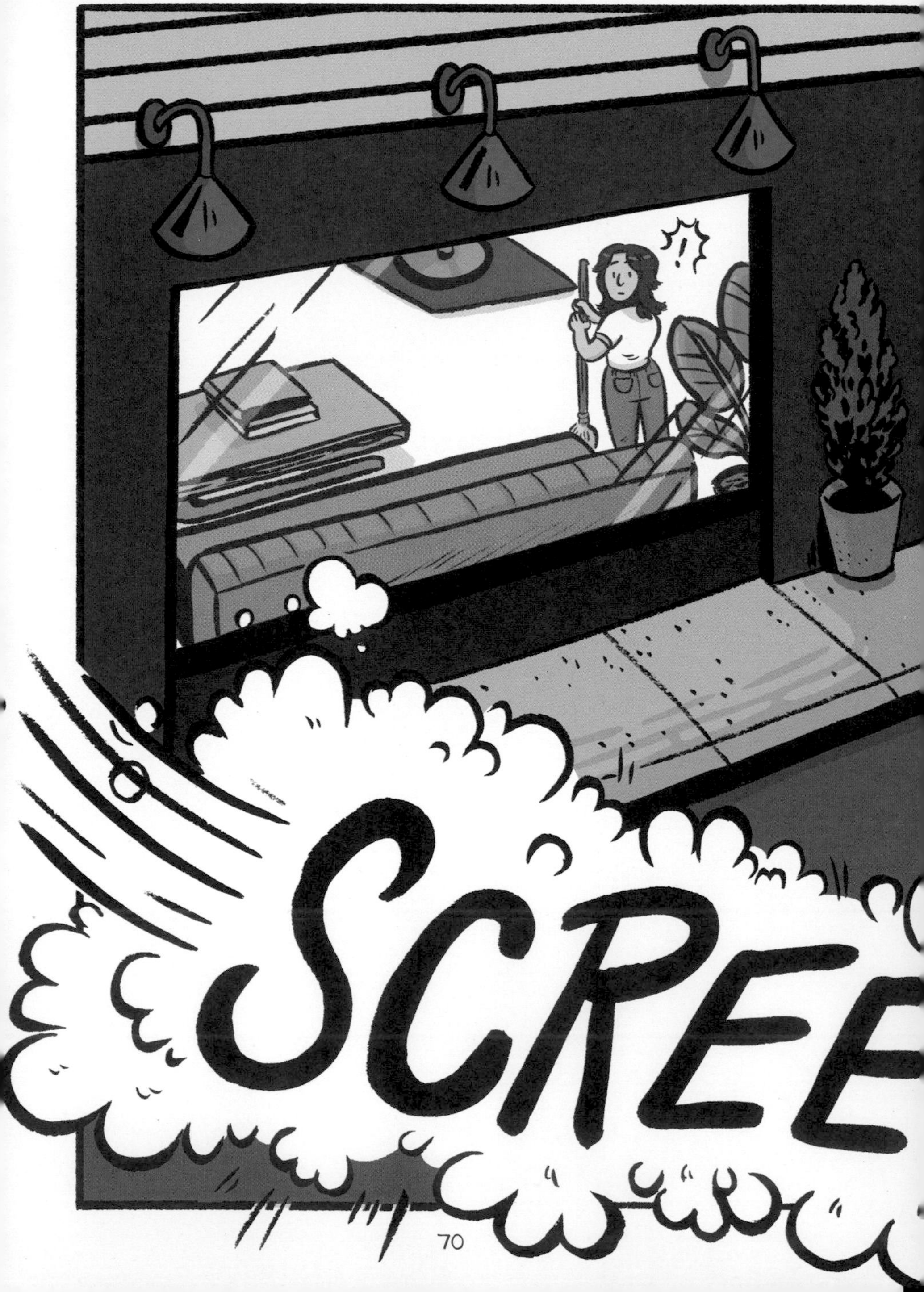
!
SCREE

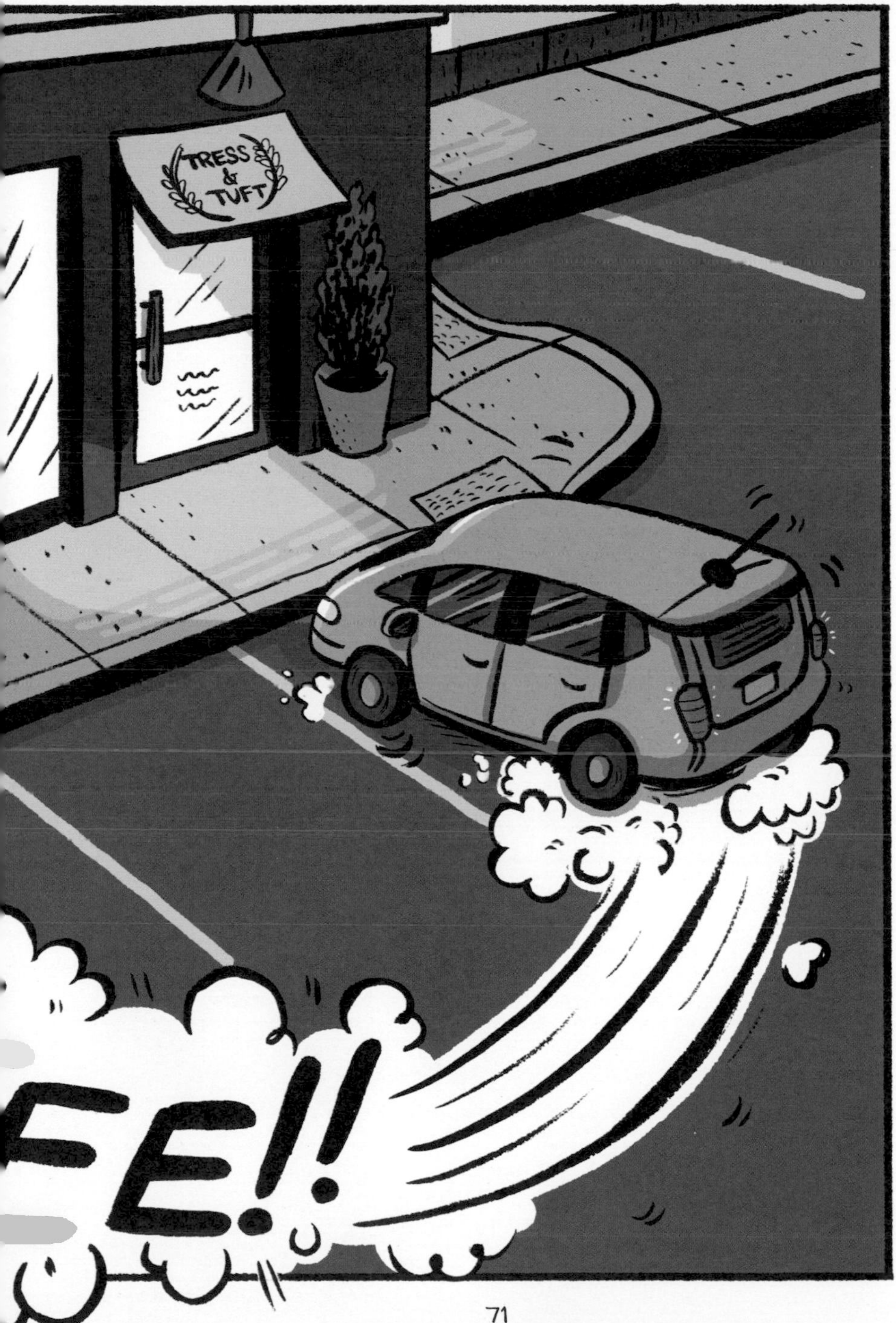
TRESS & TUFT
EE!!

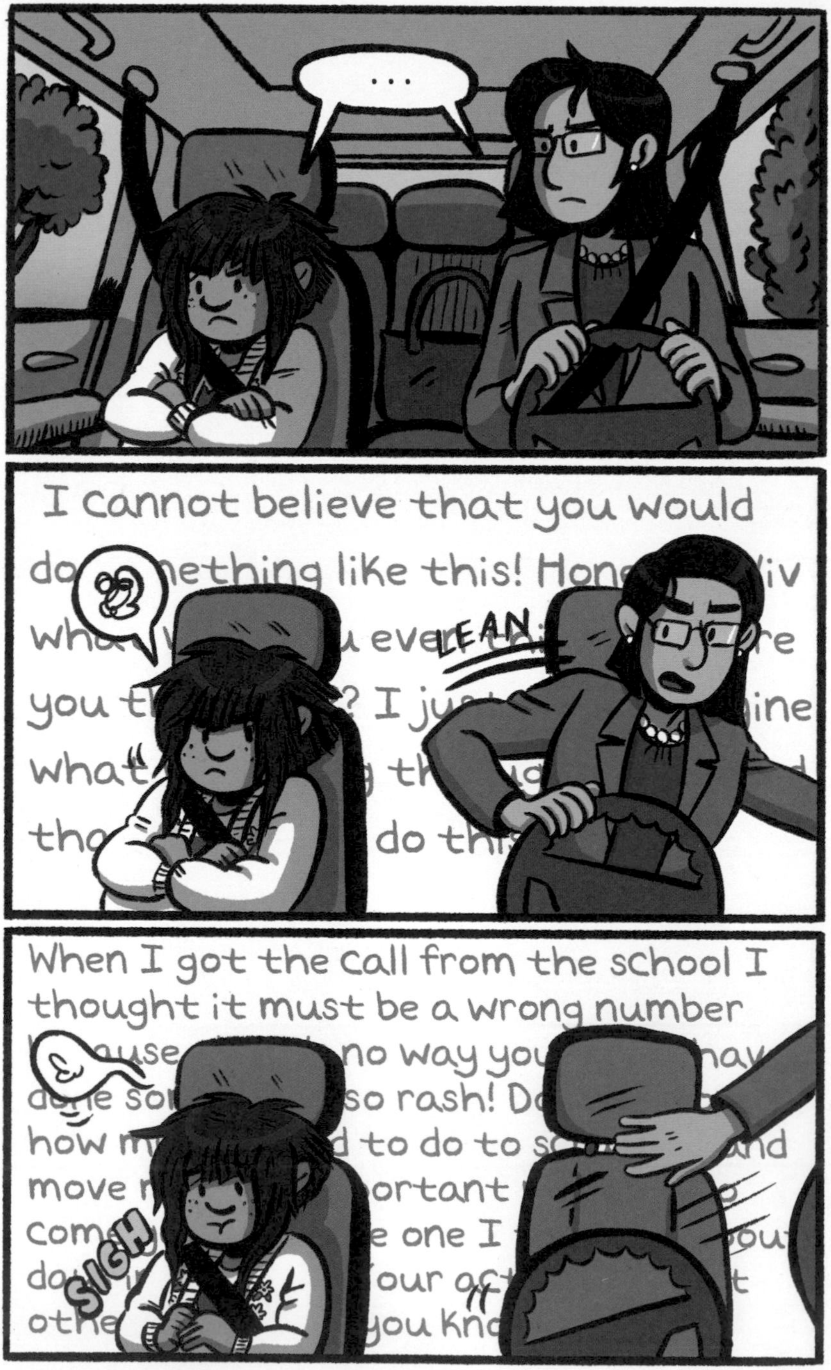
...
I cannot believe that you would
thing like this!
u ever
LEAN
you
? I ju
what
do th
When I got the call from the school I
thought it must be a wrong number
no way you
so rash!
to do to
and
move
portant
e one I
our act
you kno
SIGH

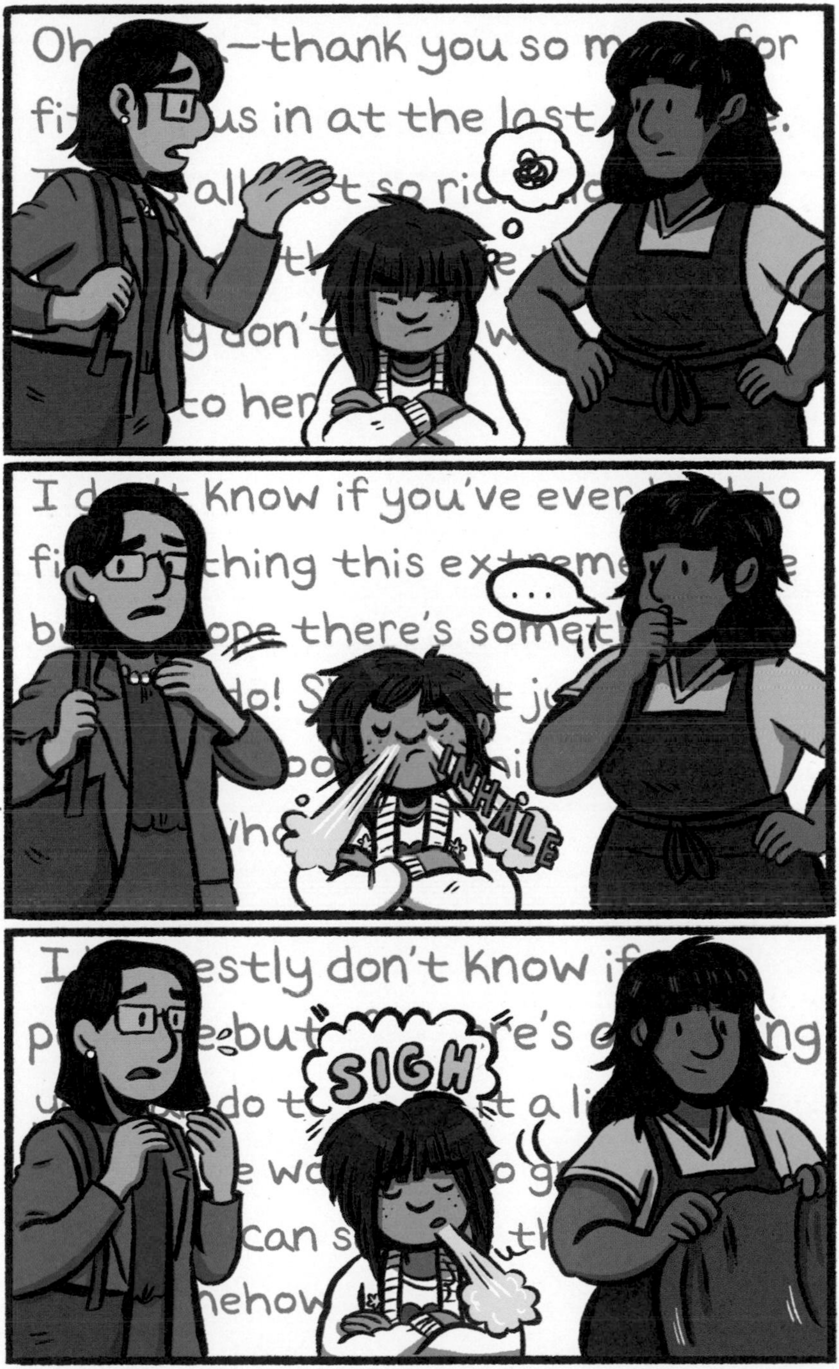
—thank you so
us in at the
Know if you've ever
thing this ex
there's some
INHALE
...
estly don't Know if
SIGH

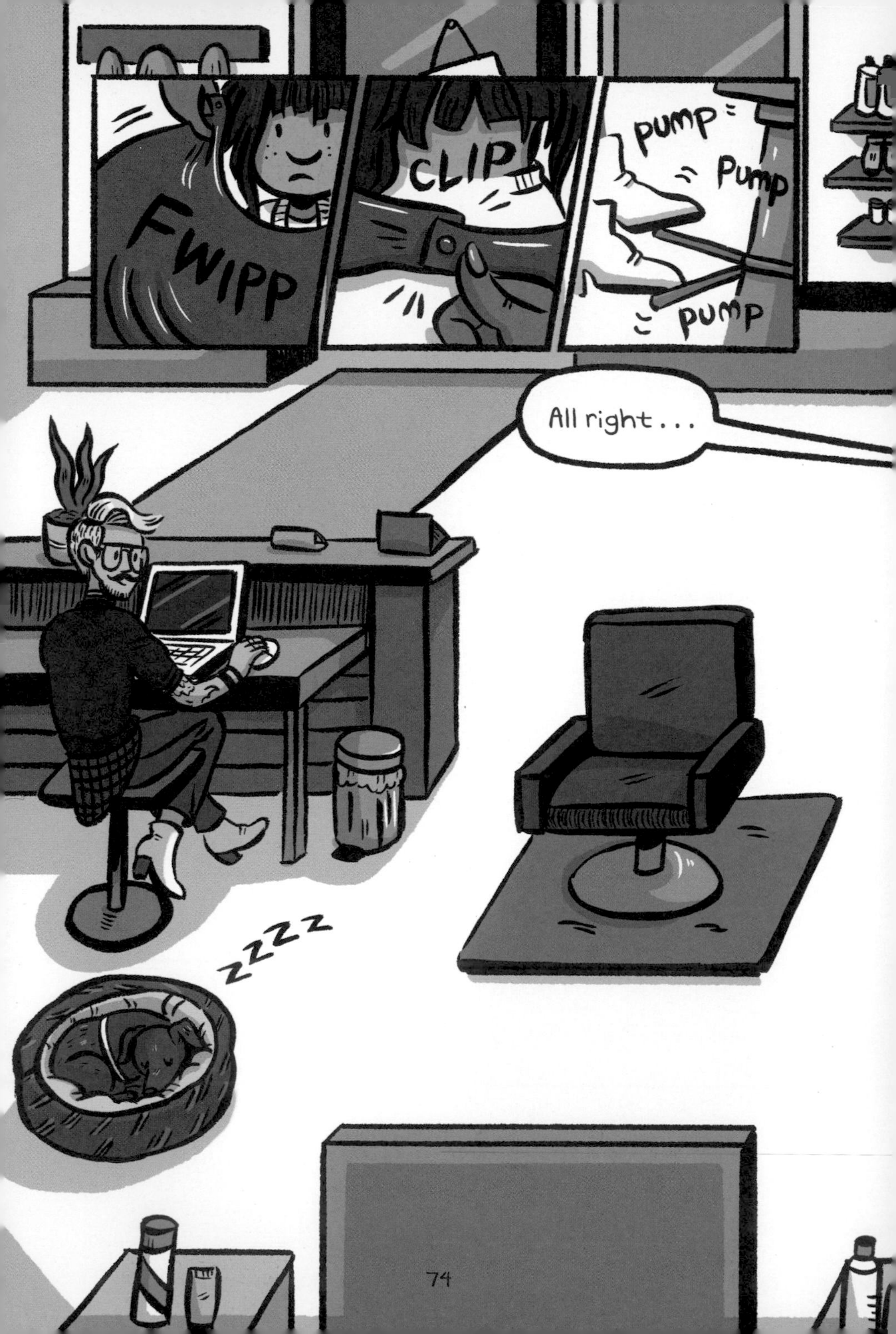
FWIPP
CLIP
pump
Pump
pump
All right . . .
zzzz

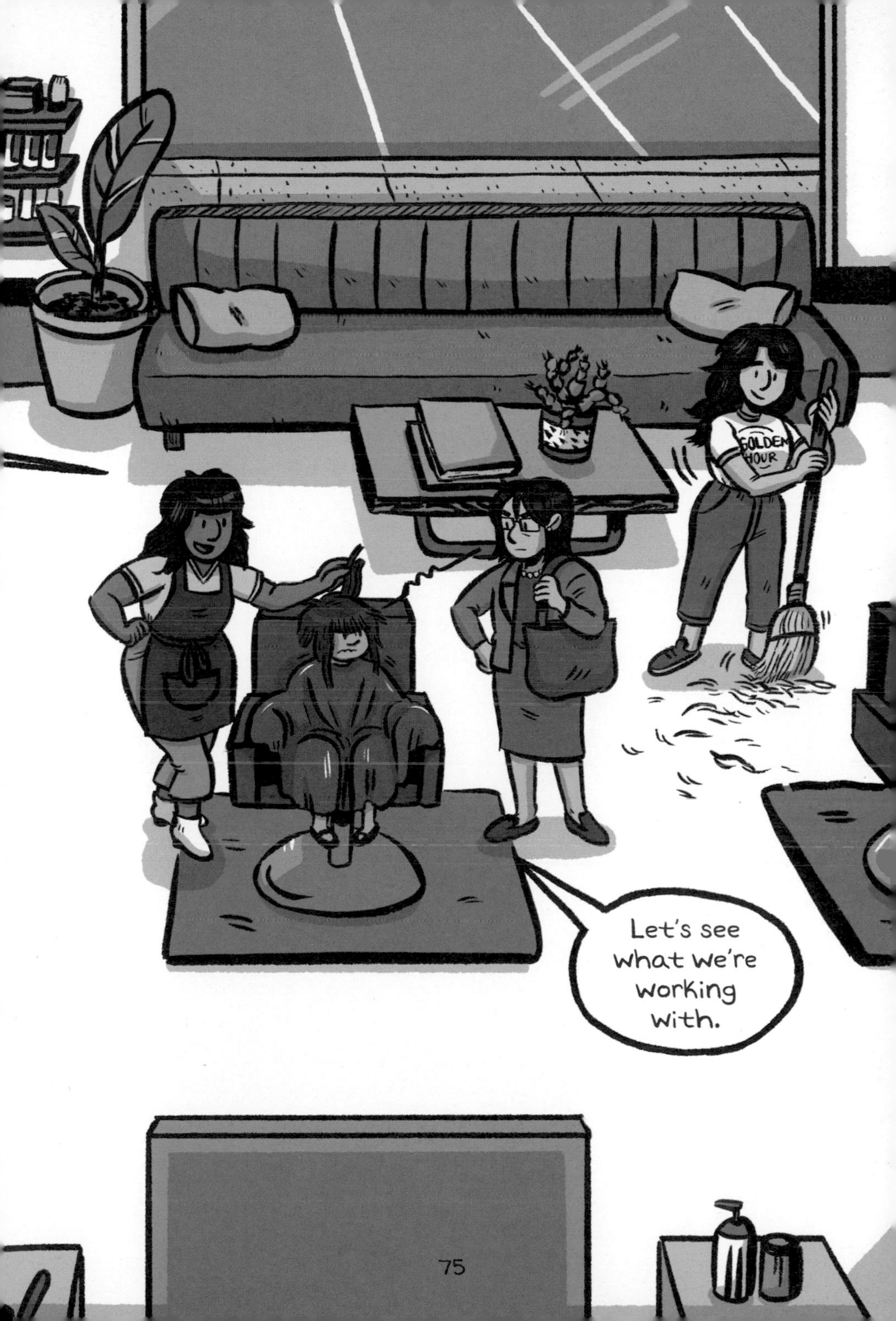
GOLDEN HOUR
Let's see what we're working with.

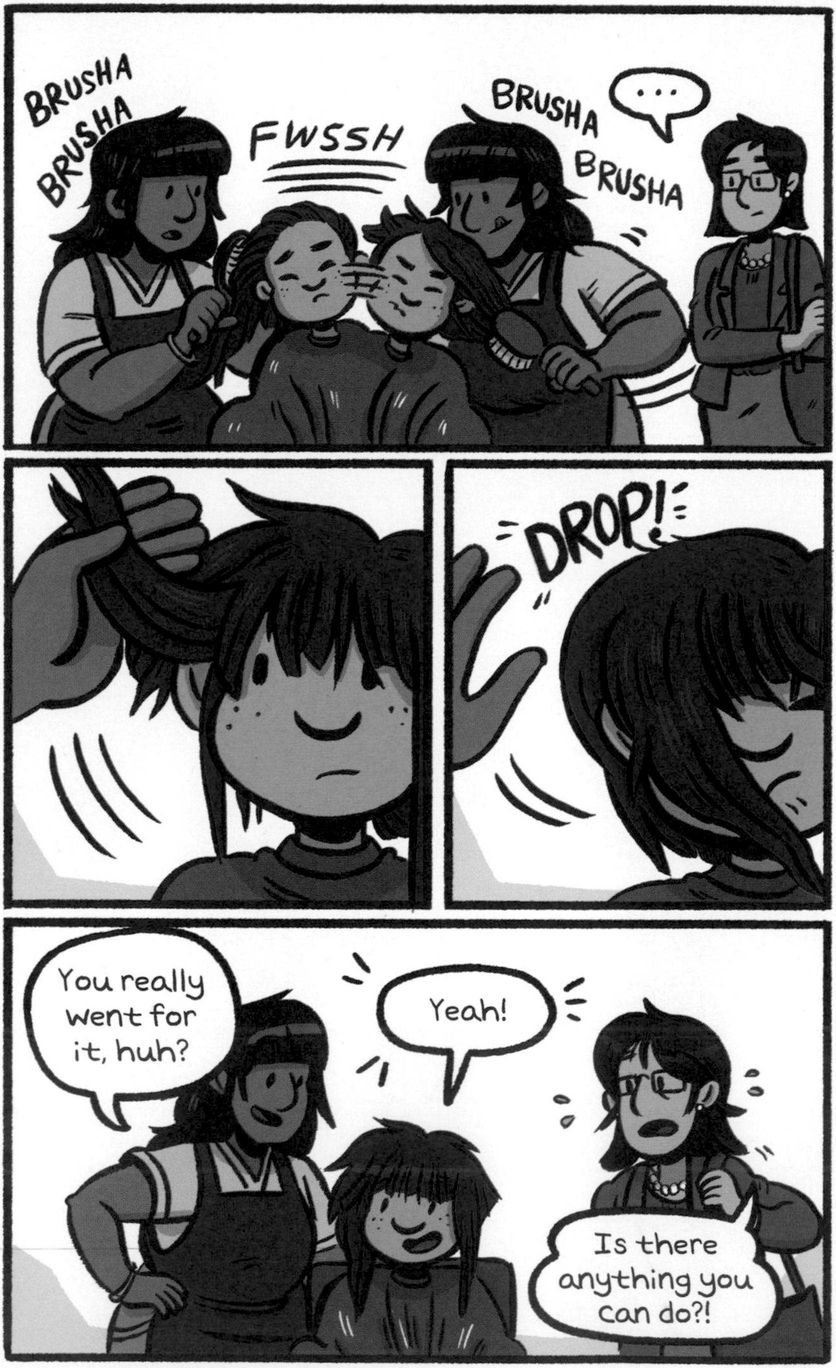
BRUSHA
BRUSHA
FWSSH
BRUSHA
BRUSHA
...
DROP!
You really went for it, huh?
Yeah!
Is there anything you can do?!

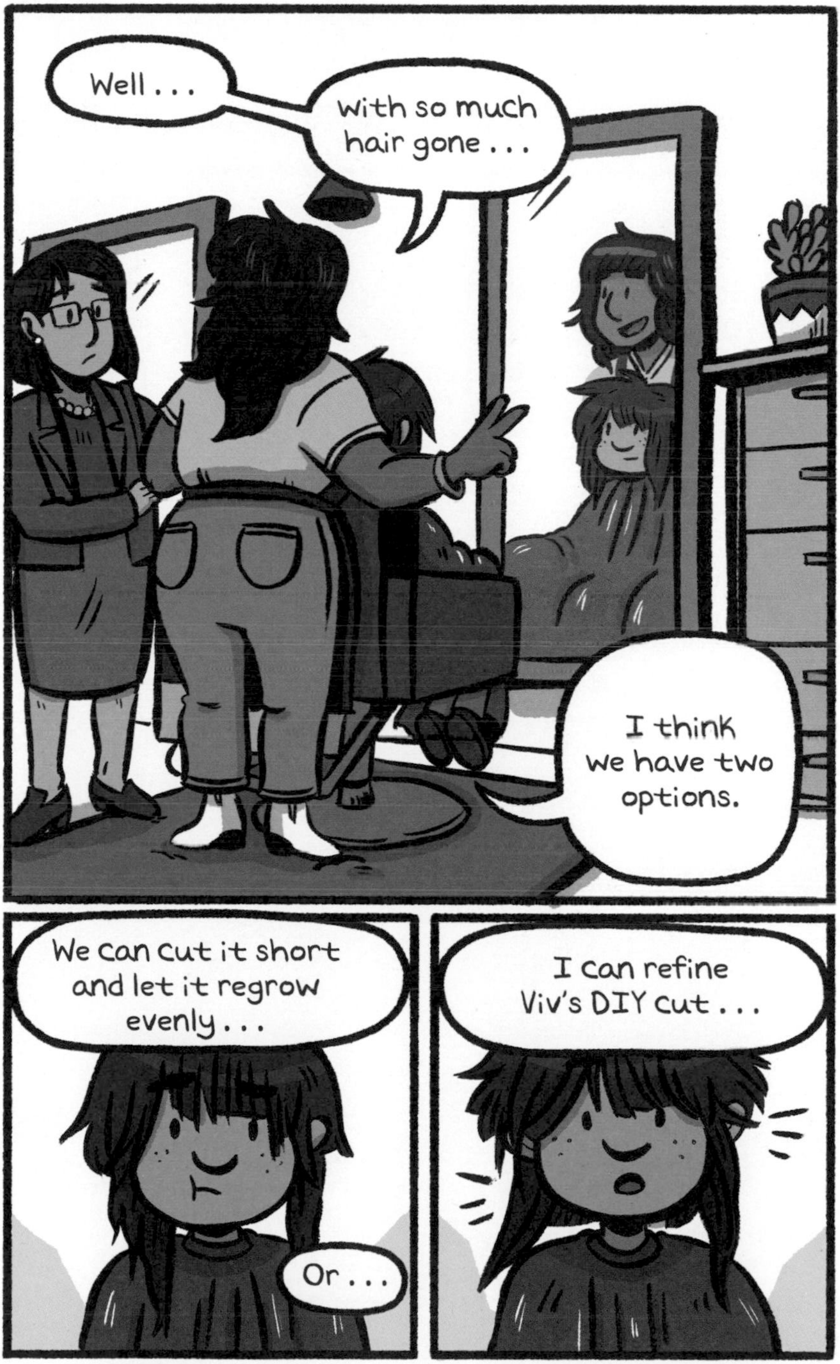
Well . . .
With so much hair gone . . .
I think we have two options.
We can cut it short and let it regrow evenly . . .
Or . . .
I can refine Viv's DIY cut . . .

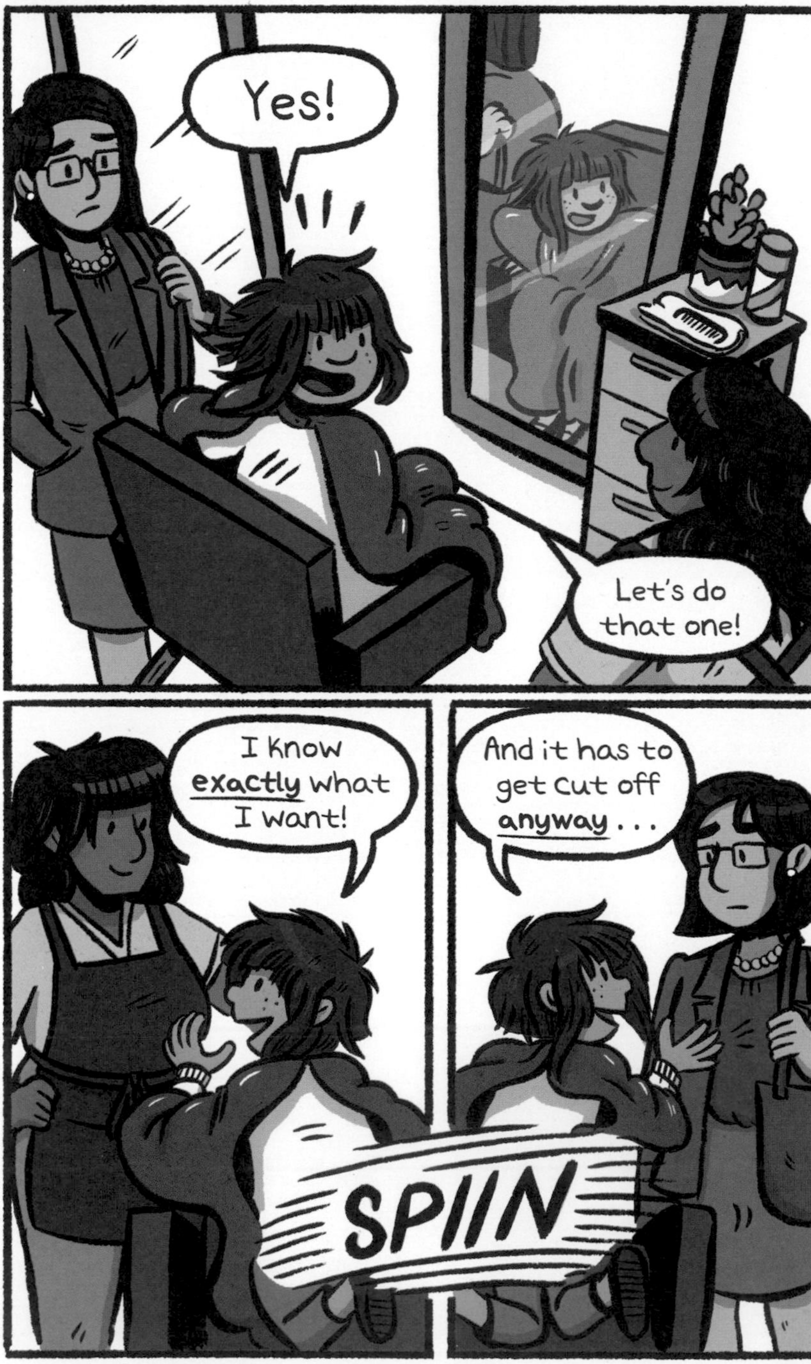
Yes!
Let's do that one!
I know exactly what I want!
And it has to get cut off anyway . . .
SPIIN

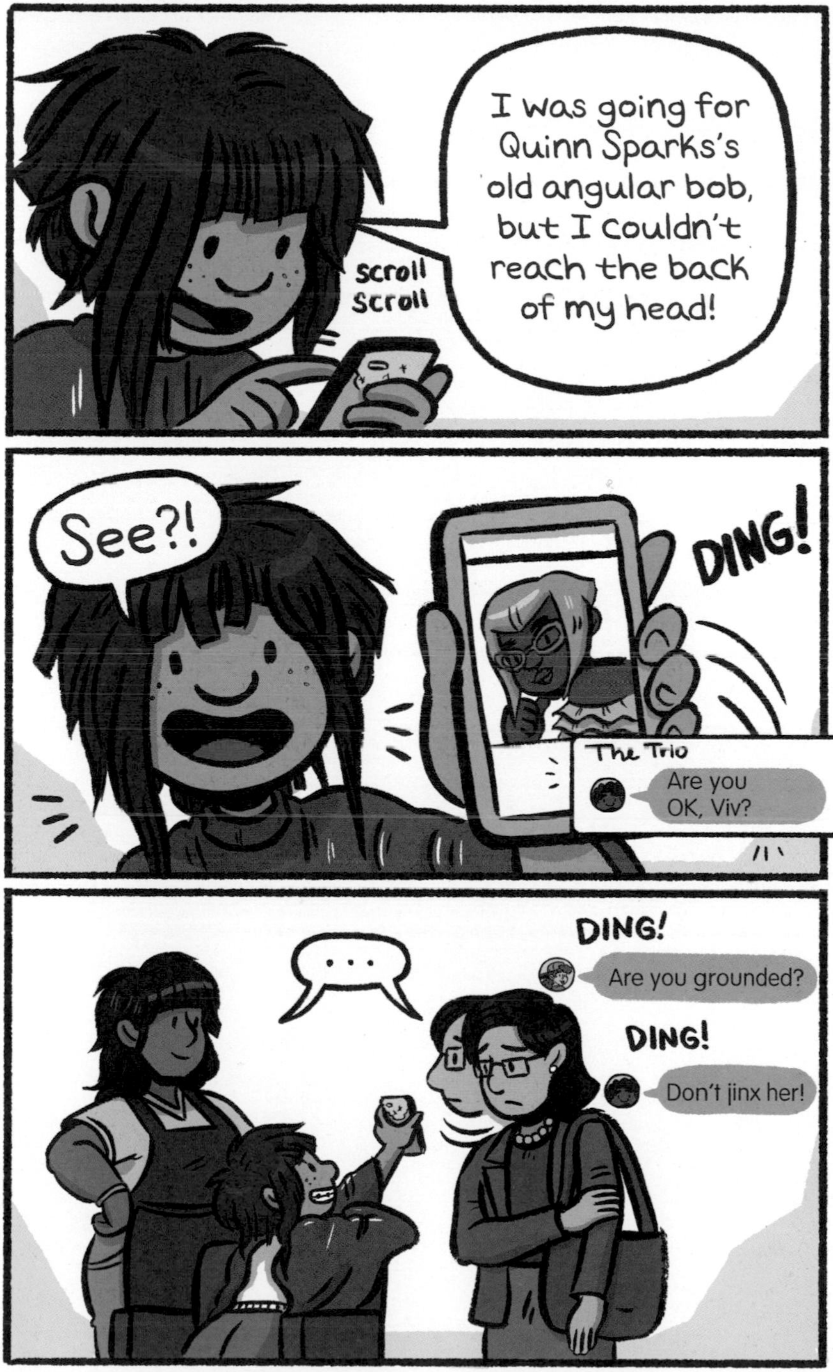
I was going for Quinn Sparks's old angular bob, but I couldn't reach the back of my head!
scroll
scroll
See?!
DING!
The Trio
Are you OK, Viv?
...
DING!
Are you grounded?
DING!
Don't jinx her!

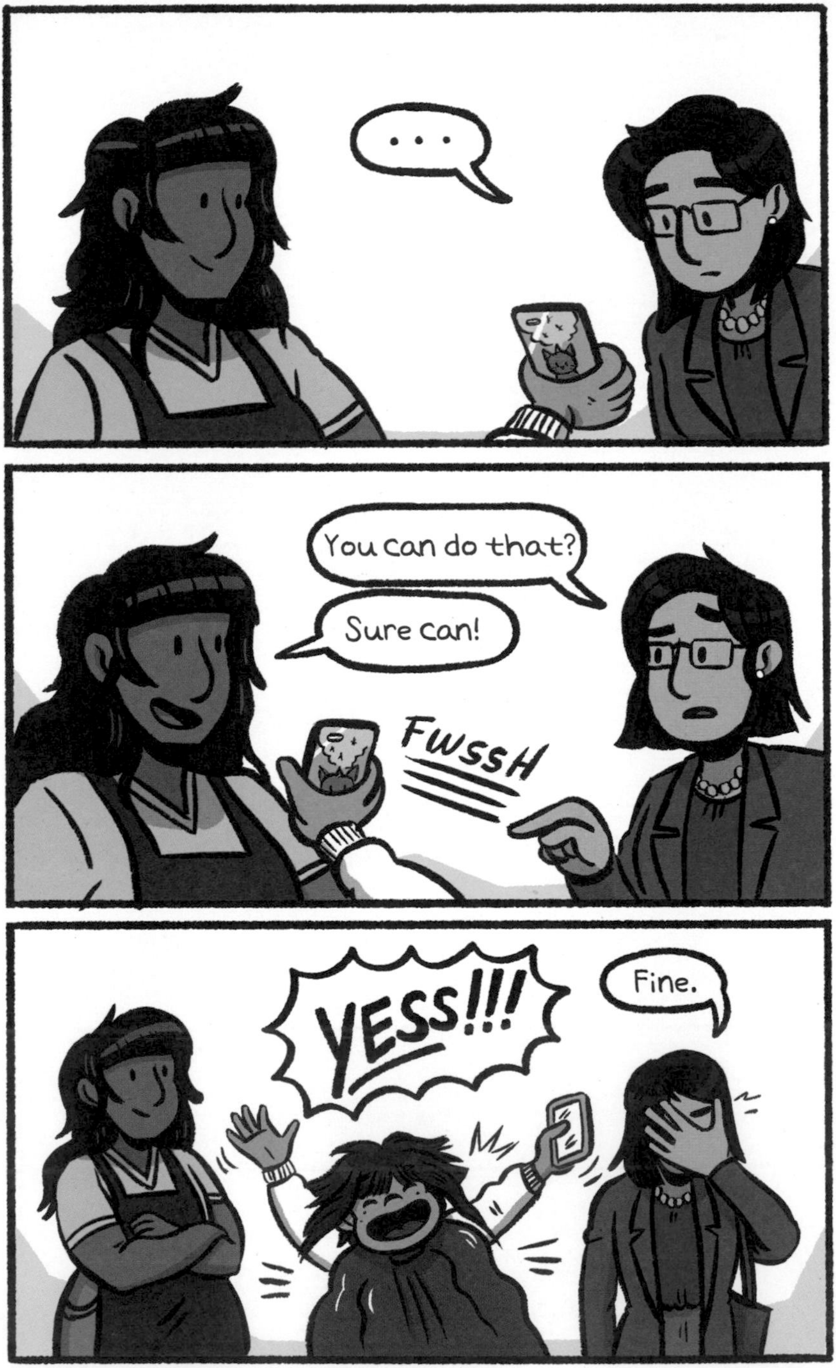
...
You can do that?
Sure can!
FWSSH
YESS!!!
Fine.

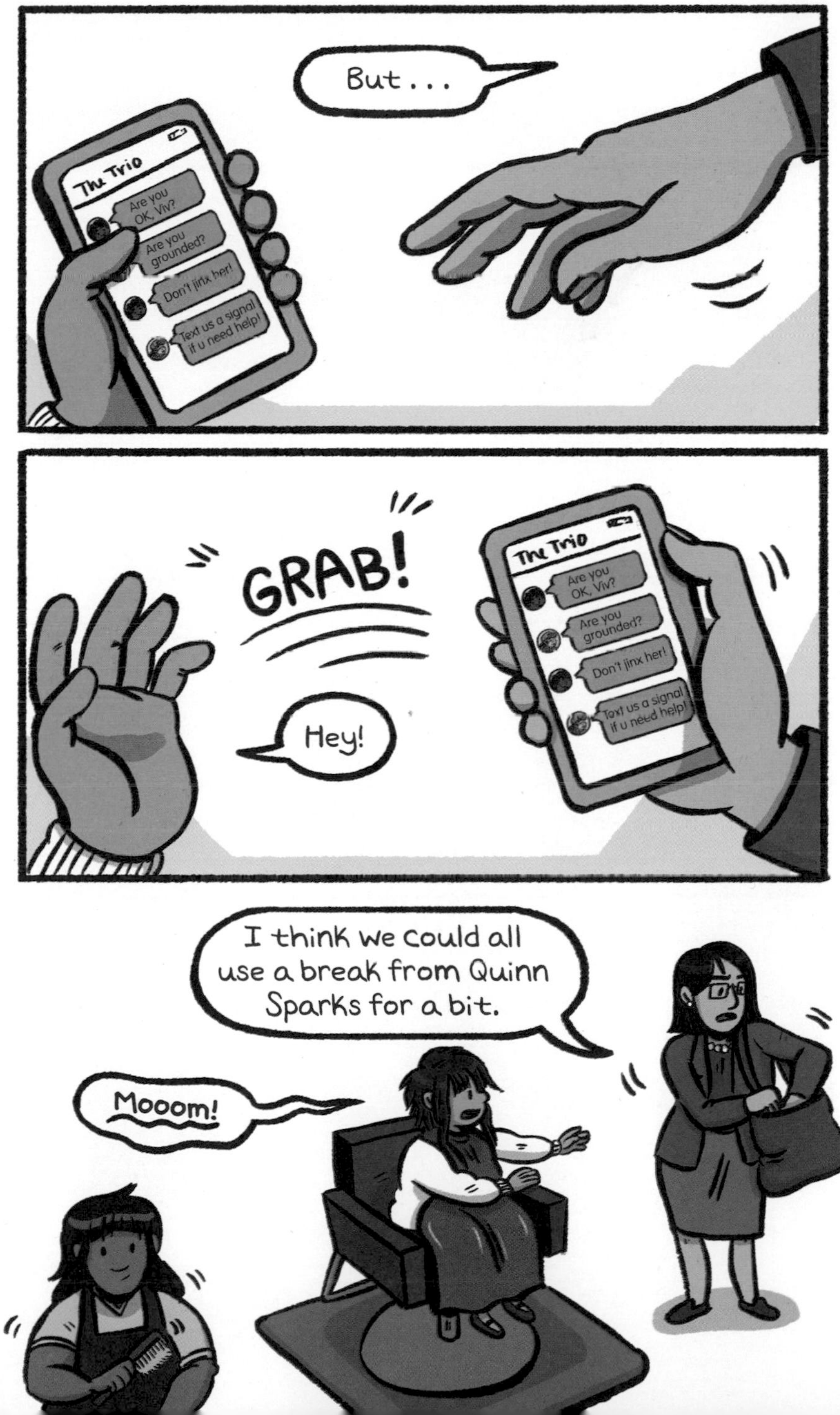

But . . .
The Trio
Are you OK, Viv?
Are you grounded?
Don't jinx her!
Text us a signal if u need help!
GRAB!
Hey!
The Trio
Are you OK, Viv?
Are you grounded?
Don't jinx her!
Text us a signal if u need help!
I think we could all use a break from Quinn Sparks for a bit.
Mooom!

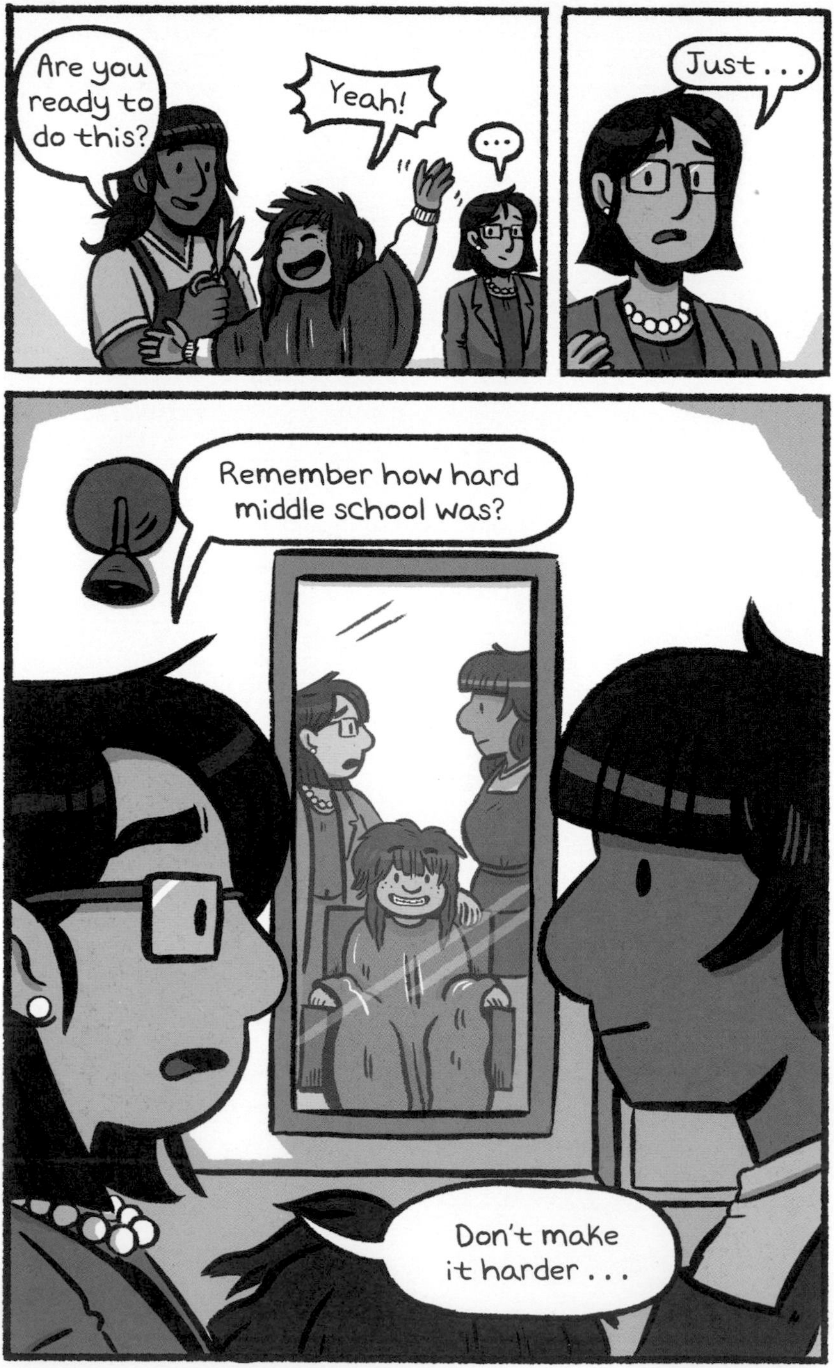

Are you ready to do this?
Yeah!
...
Just...
Remember how hard middle school was?
Don't make it harder...

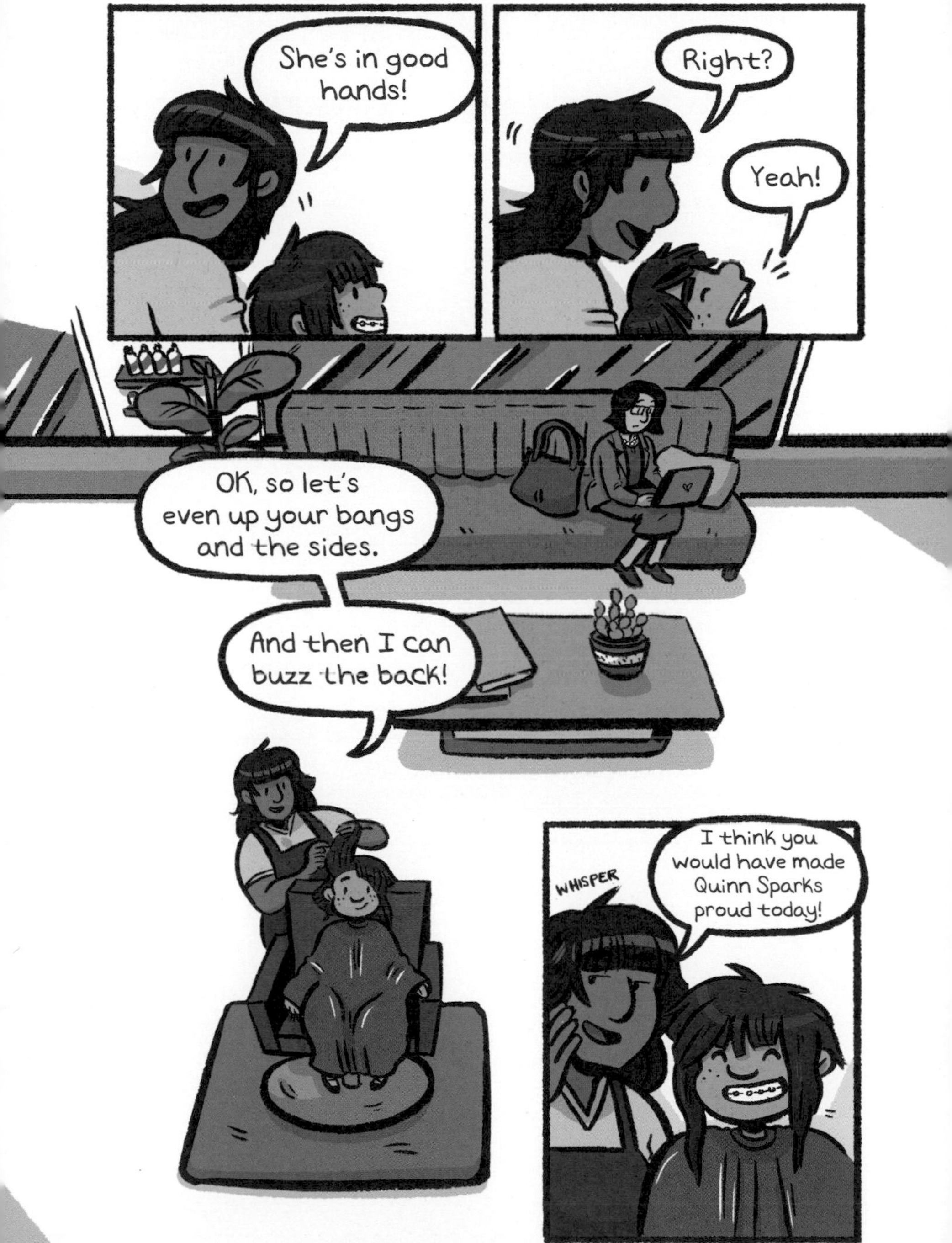
She's in good hands!
Right?
Yeah!
OK, so let's even up your bangs and the sides.
And then I can buzz the back!
WHISPER
I think you would have made Quinn Sparks proud today!

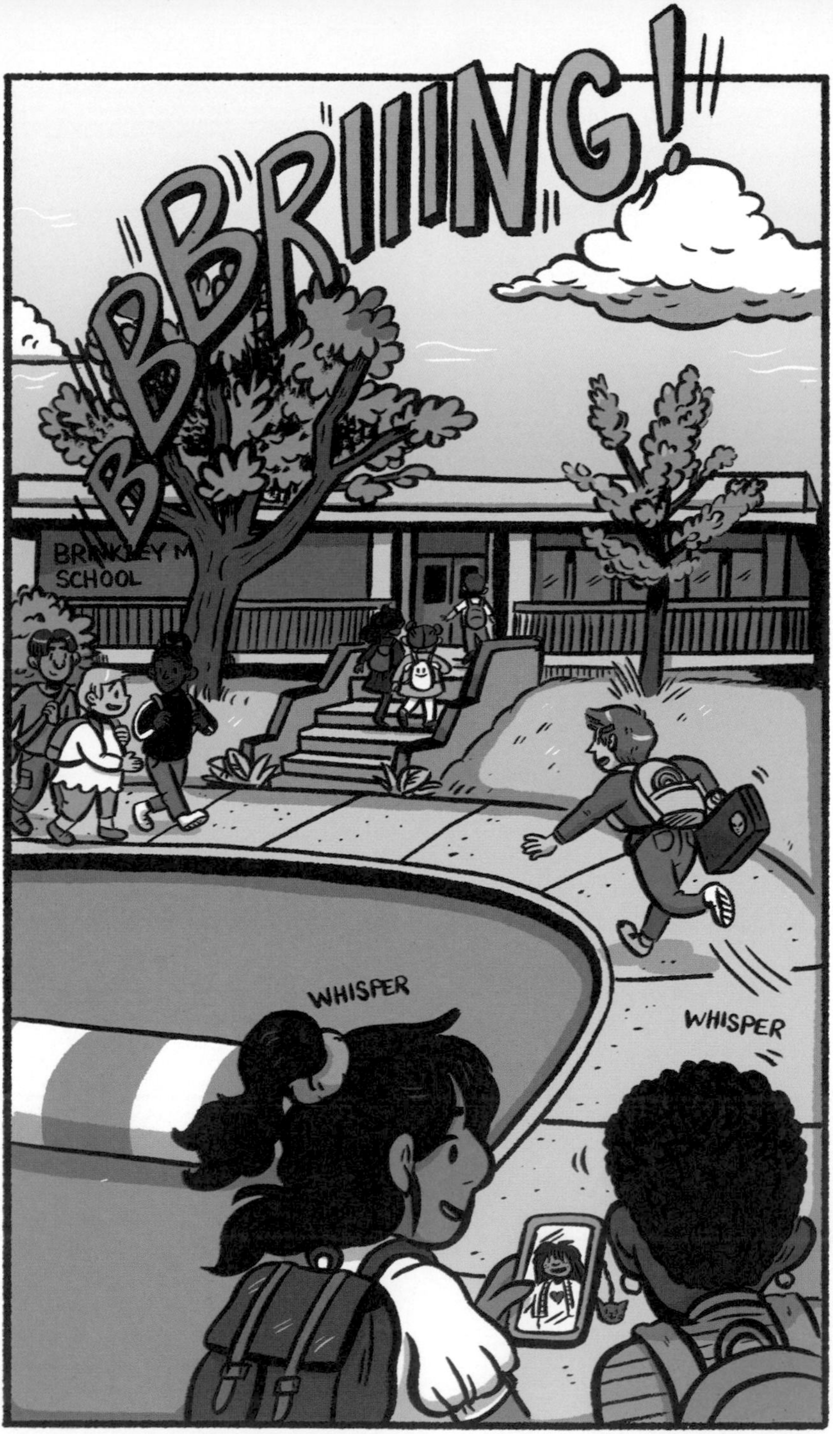
BBBRIIING!
WHISPER
WHISPER

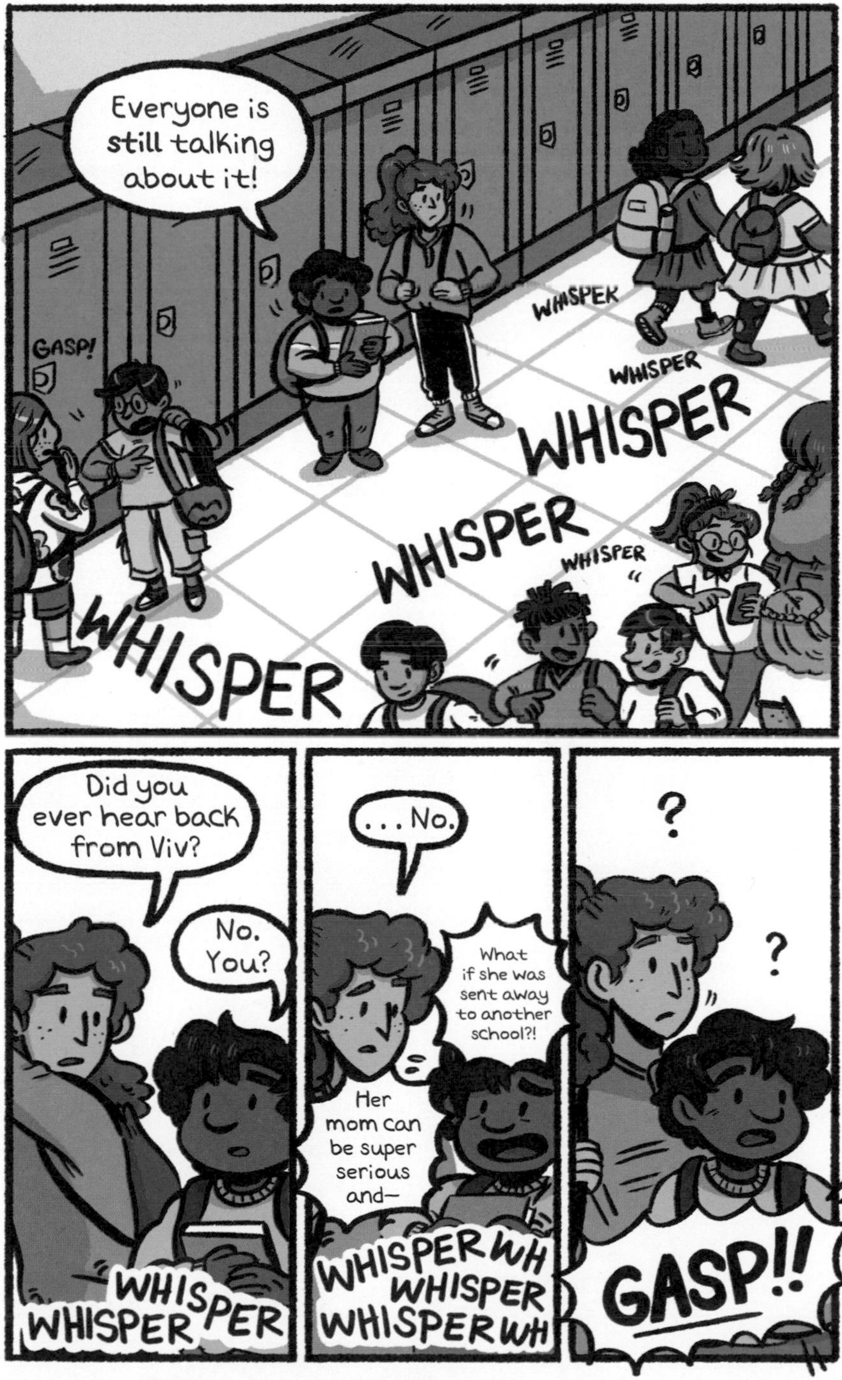
Everyone is still talking about it!
GASP!
WHISPER
WHISPER
WHISPER
WHISPER
WHISPER
WHISPER
Did you ever hear back from Viv?
No. You?
WHISPER WHISPER WHISPER
...No.
What if she was sent away to another school?!
Her mom can be super serious and—
WHISPERWH WHISPER WHISPERWH
?
?
GASP!!

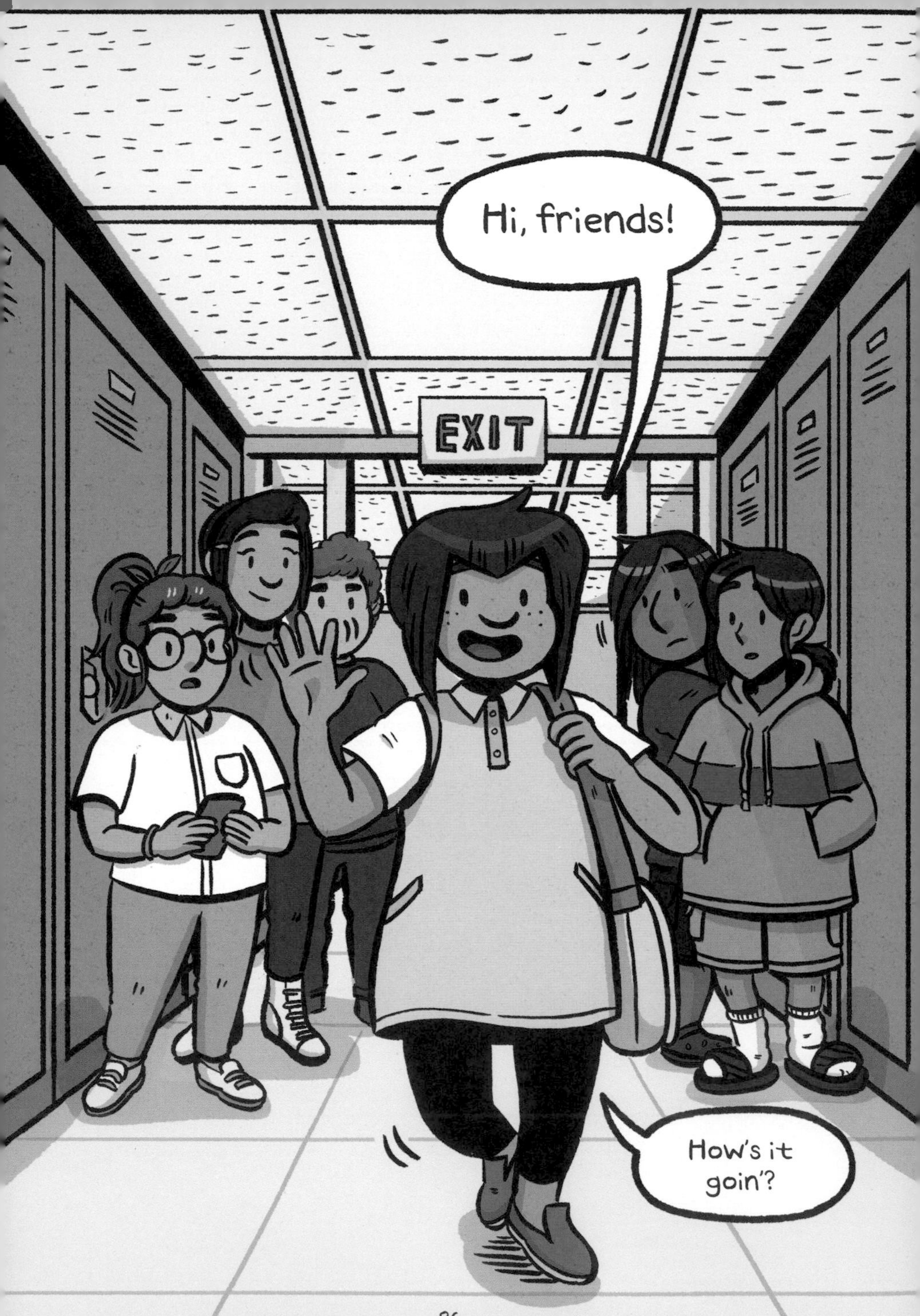
EXIT
Hi, friends!
How's it goin'?

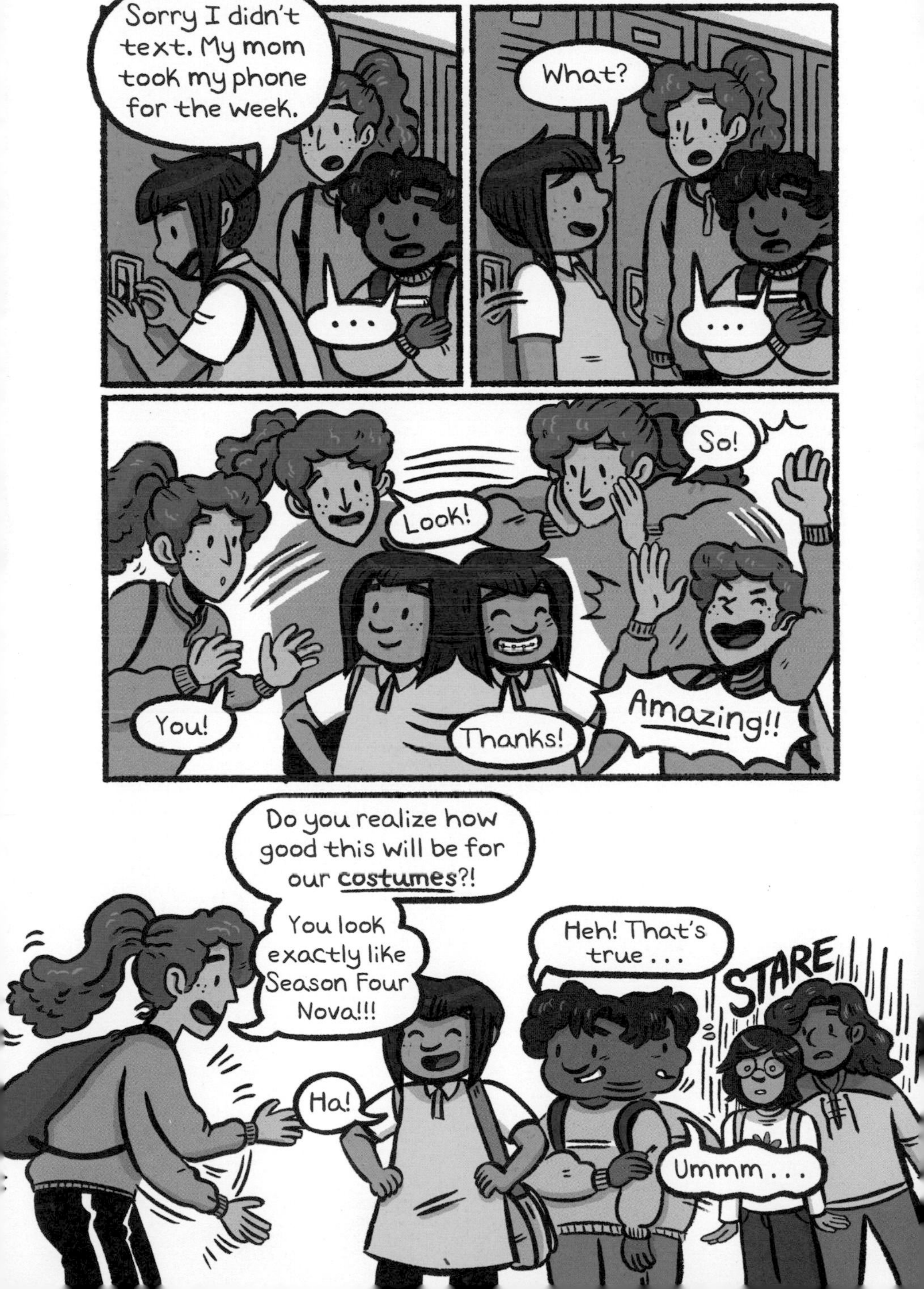

Sorry I didn't text. My mom took my phone for the week.
...
What?
...
Look!
So!
You!
Thanks!
Amazing!!
Do you realize how good this will be for our costumes?!
You look exactly like Season Four Nova!!!
Ha!
Heh! That's true . . .
STARE
Ummm . . .

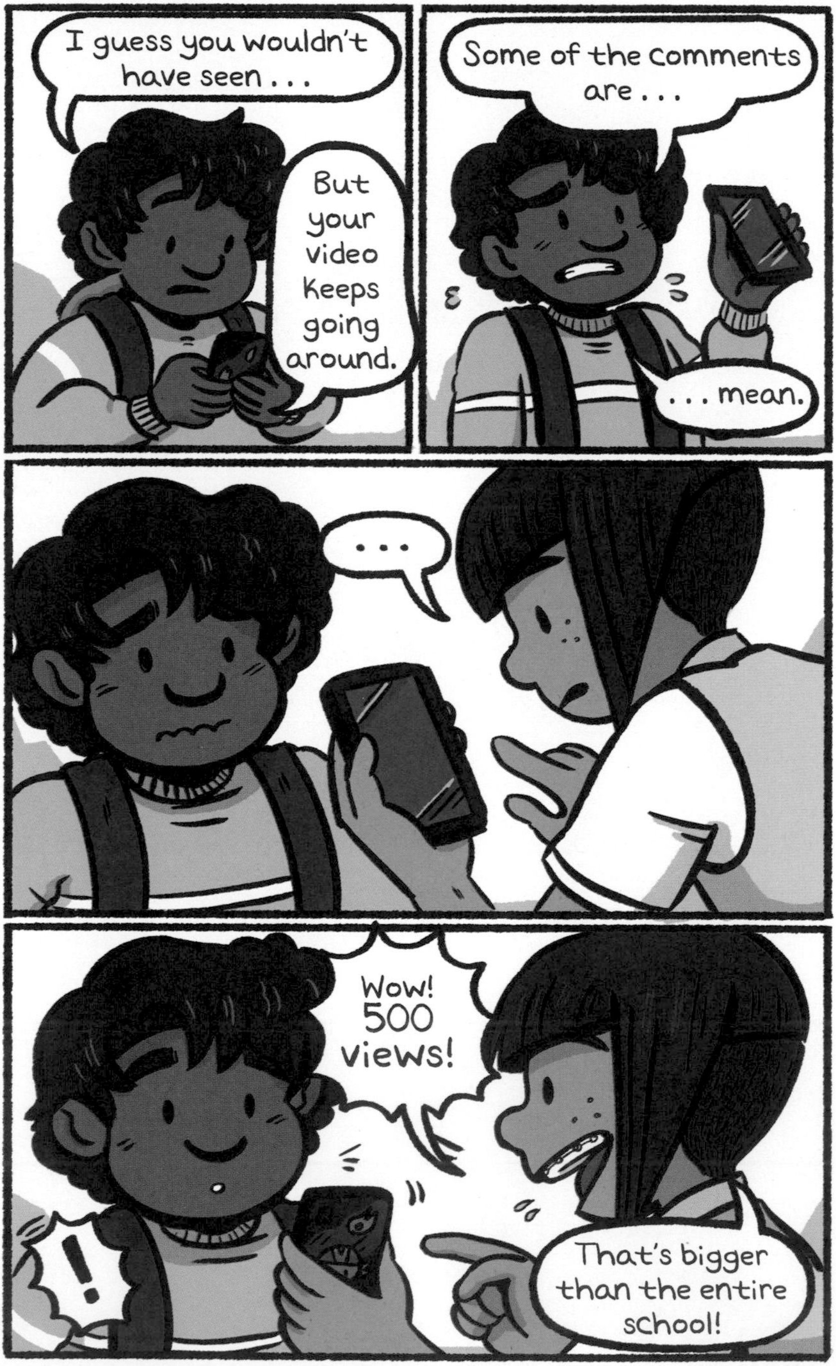

I guess you wouldn't have seen . . .
But your video keeps going around.
Some of the comments are . . .
. . . mean.
. . .
Wow! 500 views!
!
That's bigger than the entire school!

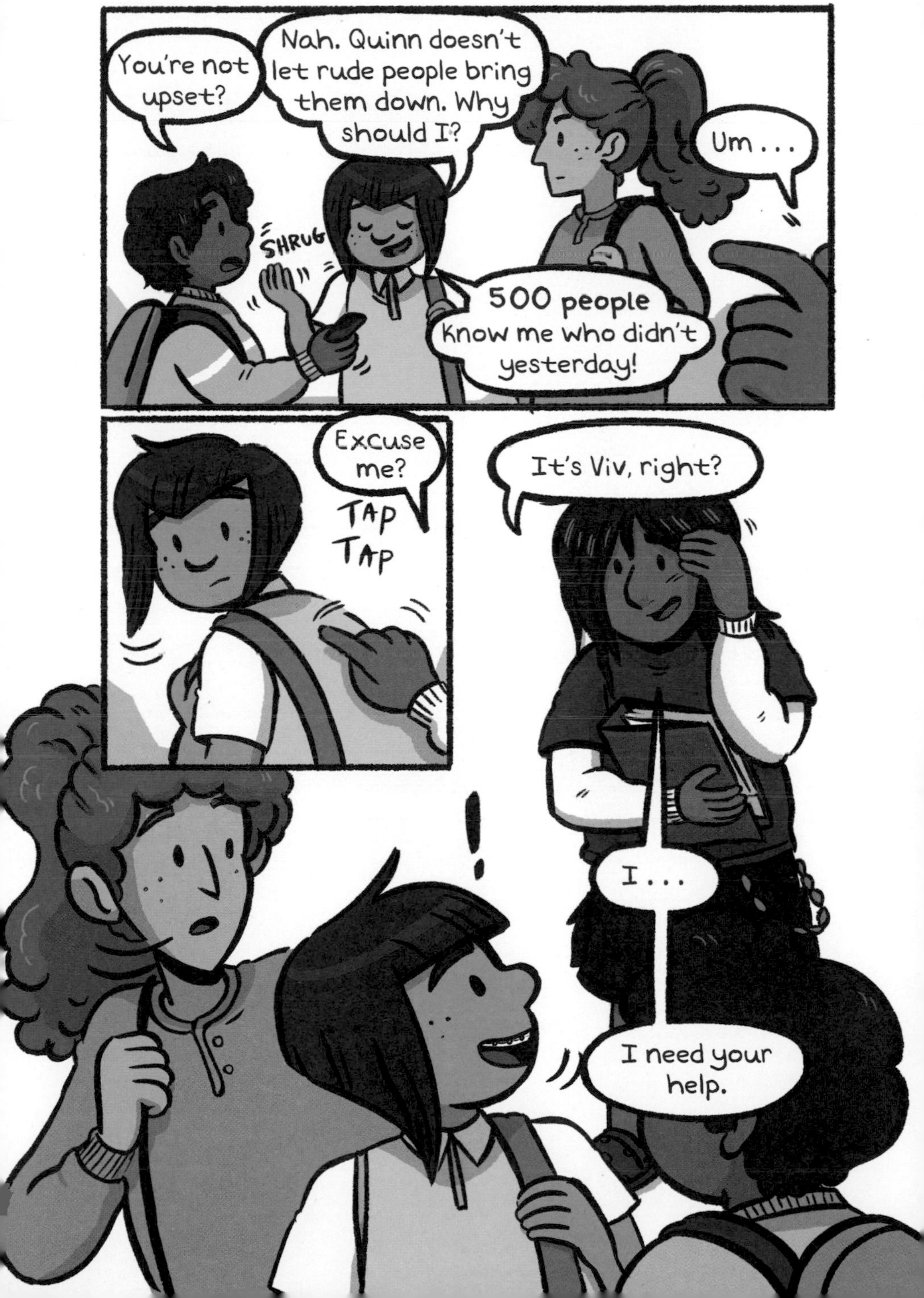
You're not upset?
Nah. Quinn doesn't let rude people bring them down. Why should I?
SHRUG
Um . . .
500 people know me who didn't yesterday!
Excuse me?
TAP TAP
It's Viv, right?
!
I . . .
I need your help.

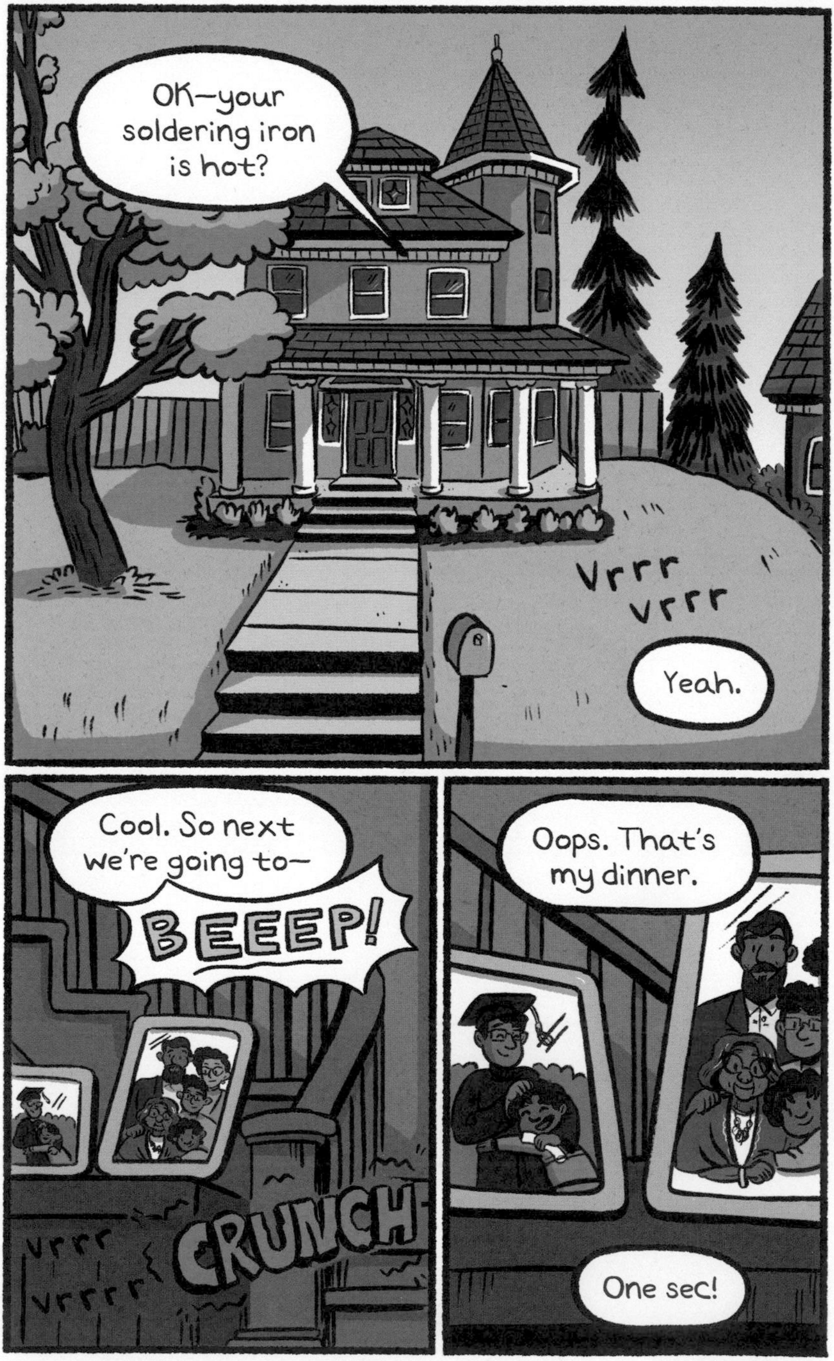
OK—your soldering iron is hot?
Vrrr vrrr
Yeah.
Cool. So next we're going to—
BEEEP!
CRUNCH
vrrr vrrrr
Oops. That's my dinner.
One sec!

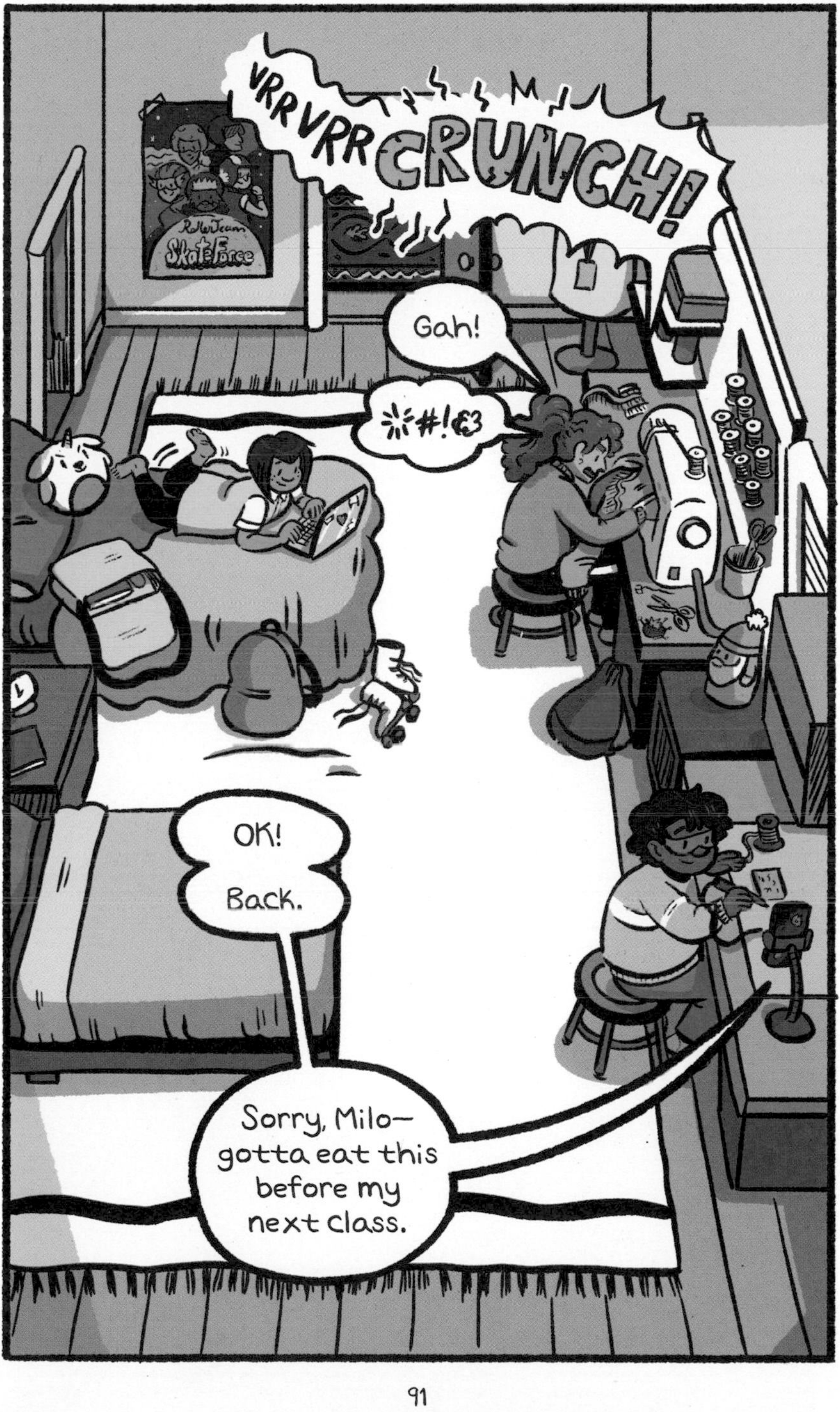

VRRVRR CRUNCH!
RollerTeam Skate Force
Gah!
#!
OK!
Back.
Sorry, Milo—gotta eat this before my next class.

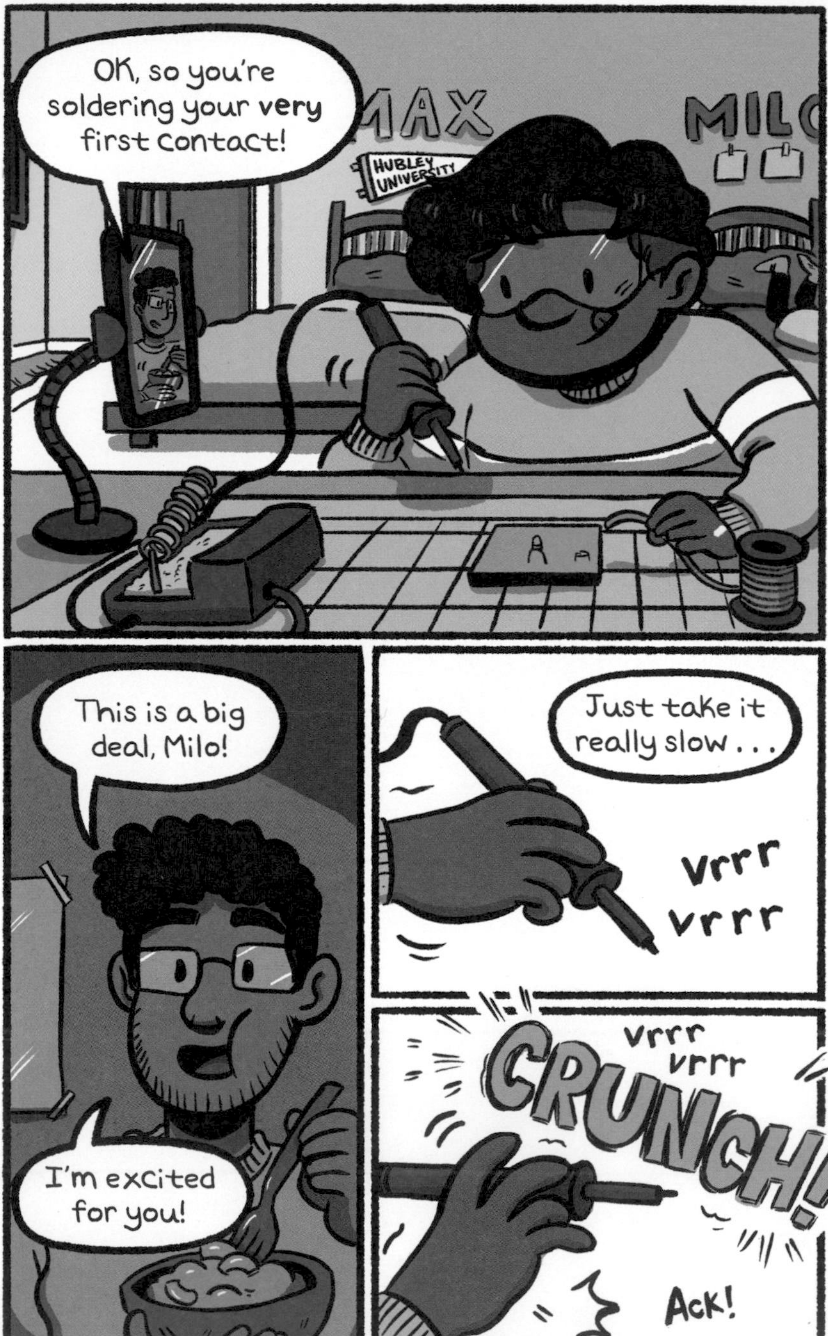
OK, so you're soldering your very first contact!
MAX
MILO
HUBLEY UNIVERSITY
This is a big deal, Milo!
I'm excited for you!
Just take it really slow . . .
Vrrr
vrrr
vrrr
vrrr
CRUNCH!
Ack!

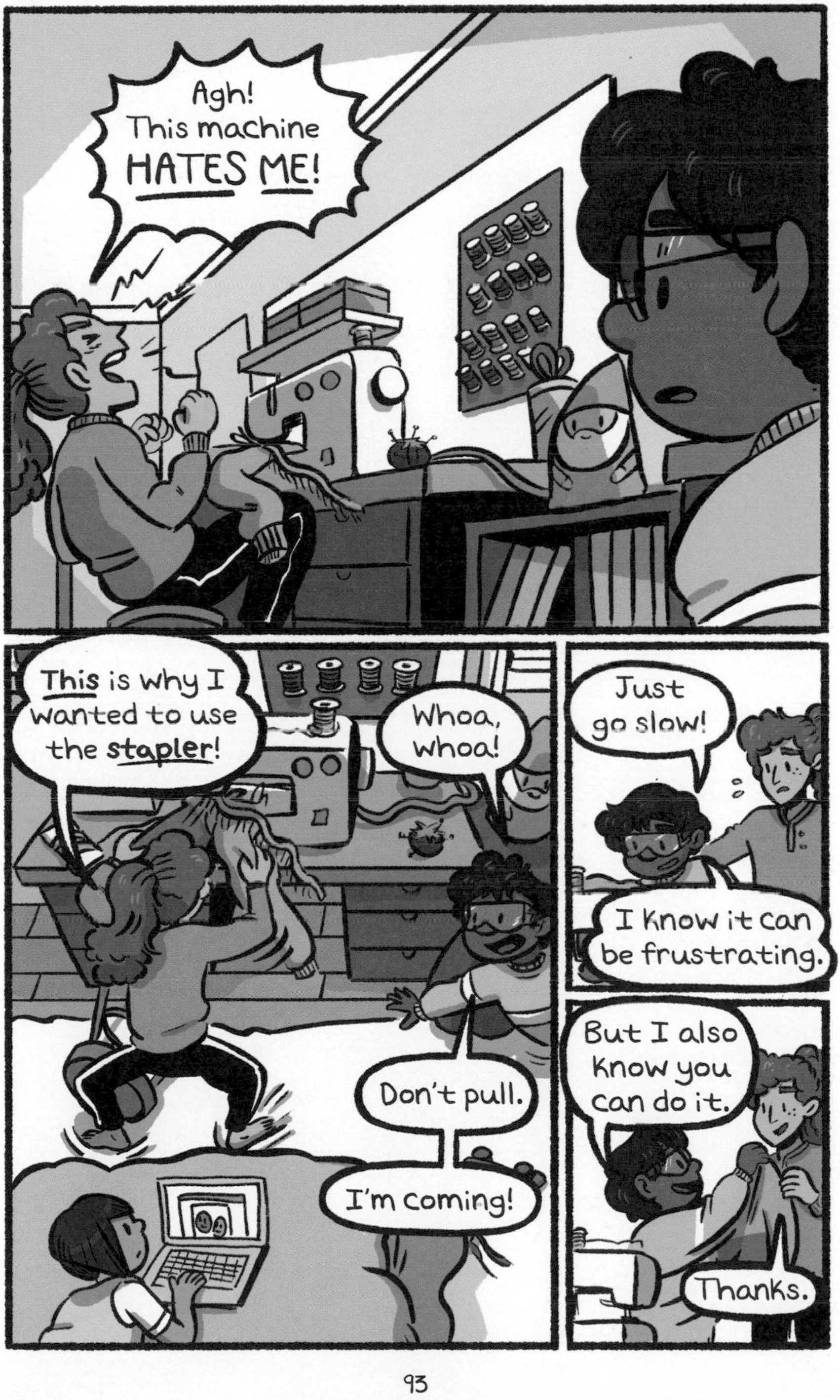
Agh! This machine HATES ME!
This is why I wanted to use the stapler!
Whoa, whoa!
Don't pull.
I'm coming!
Just go slow!
I know it can be frustrating.
But I also know you can do it.
Thanks.

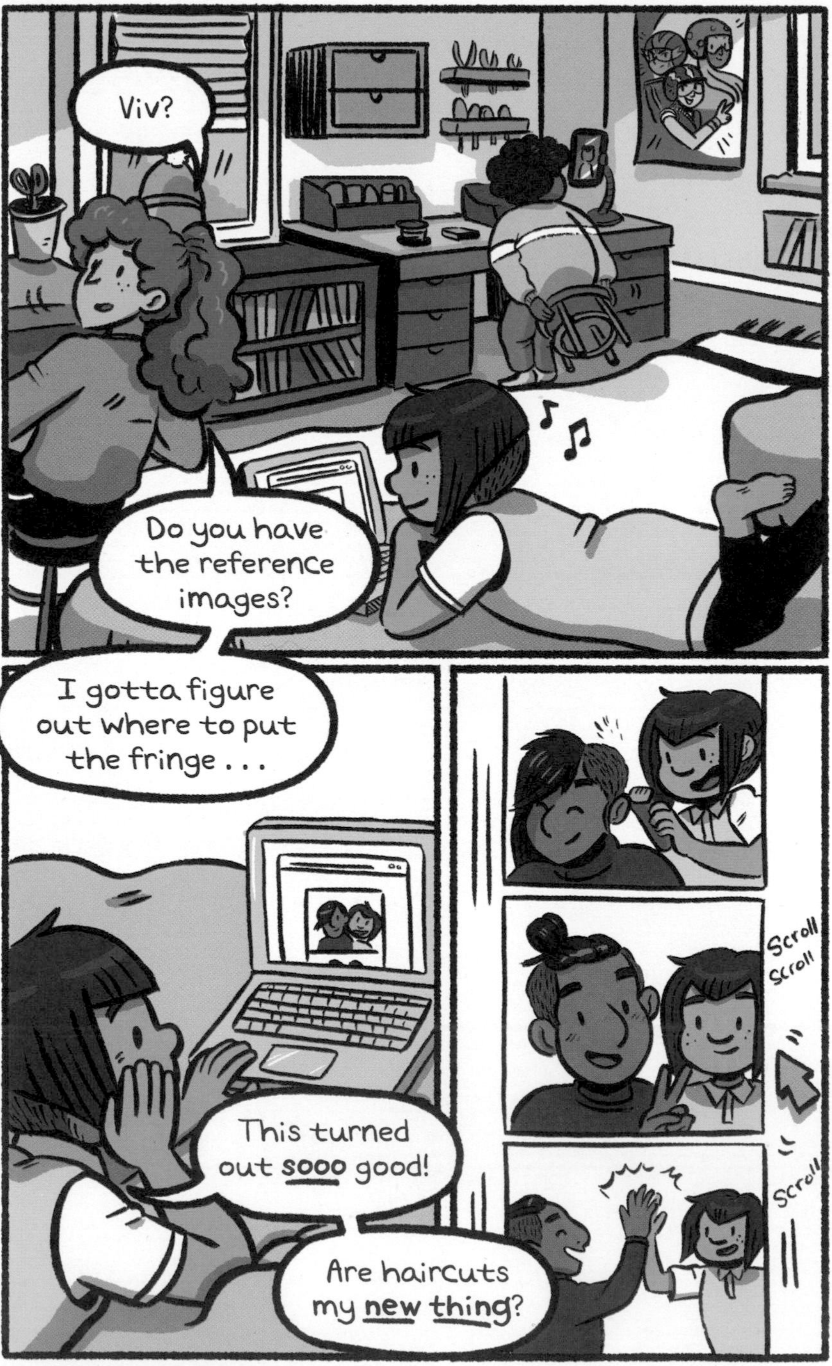
Viv?
Do you have the reference images?
I gotta figure out where to put the fringe . . .
Scroll
Scroll
Scroll
This turned out sooo good!
Are haircuts my new thing?

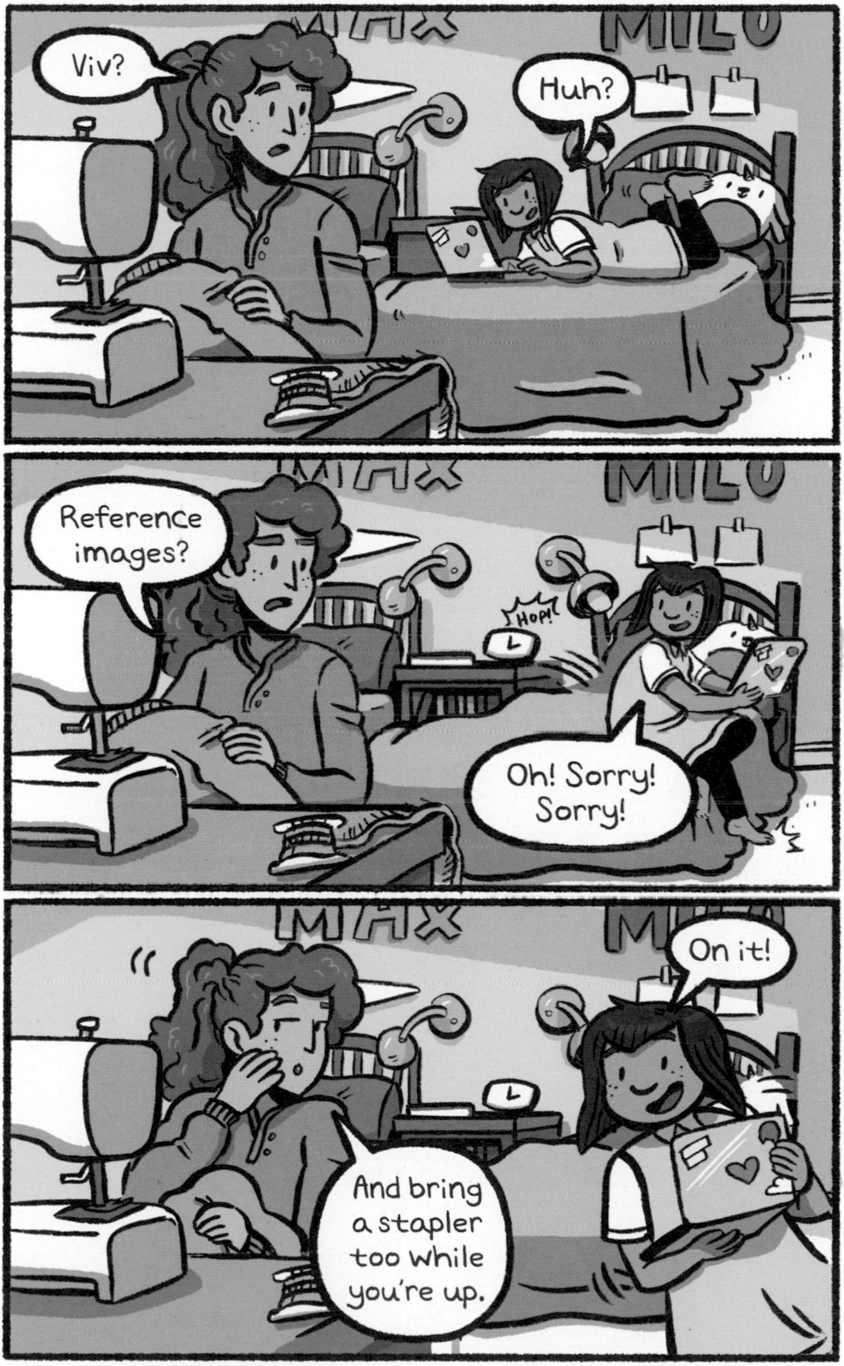
MAX
MILO
Viv?
Huh?
Reference images?
HOP!
Oh! Sorry! Sorry!
On it!
And bring a stapler too while you're up.

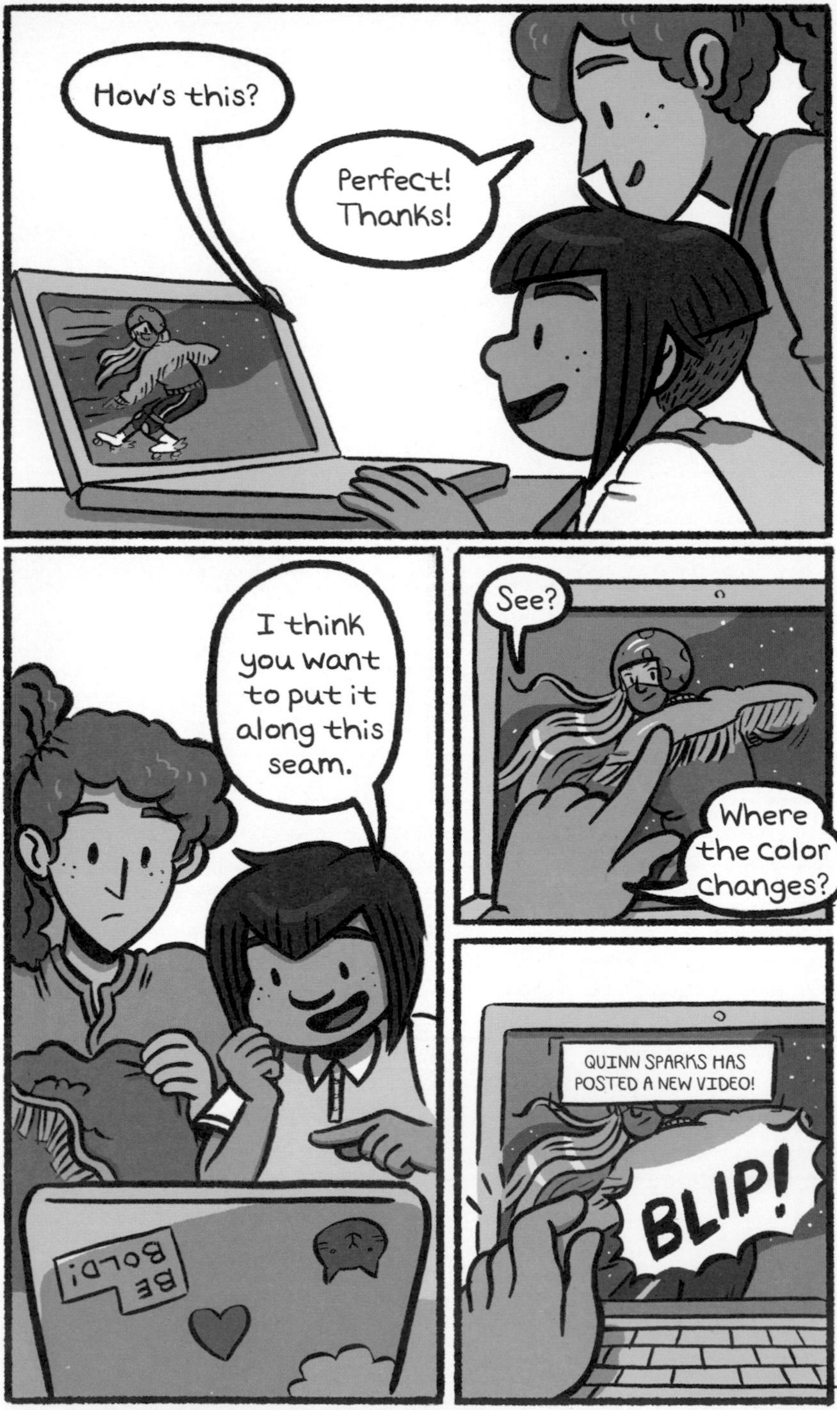
How's this?
Perfect! Thanks!
I think you want to put it along this seam.
BE BOLD!
See?
Where the color changes?
QUINN SPARKS HAS POSTED A NEW VIDEO!
BLIP!

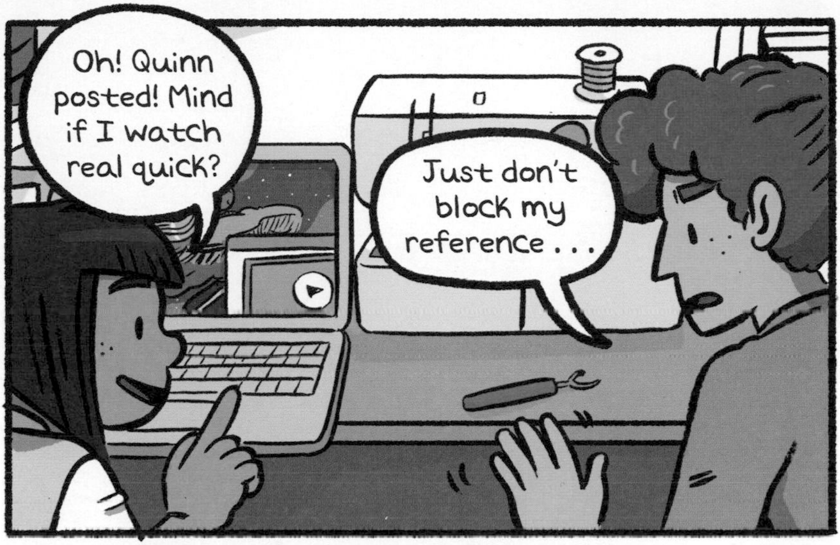
Oh! Quinn posted! Mind if I watch real quick?
Just don't block my reference . . .

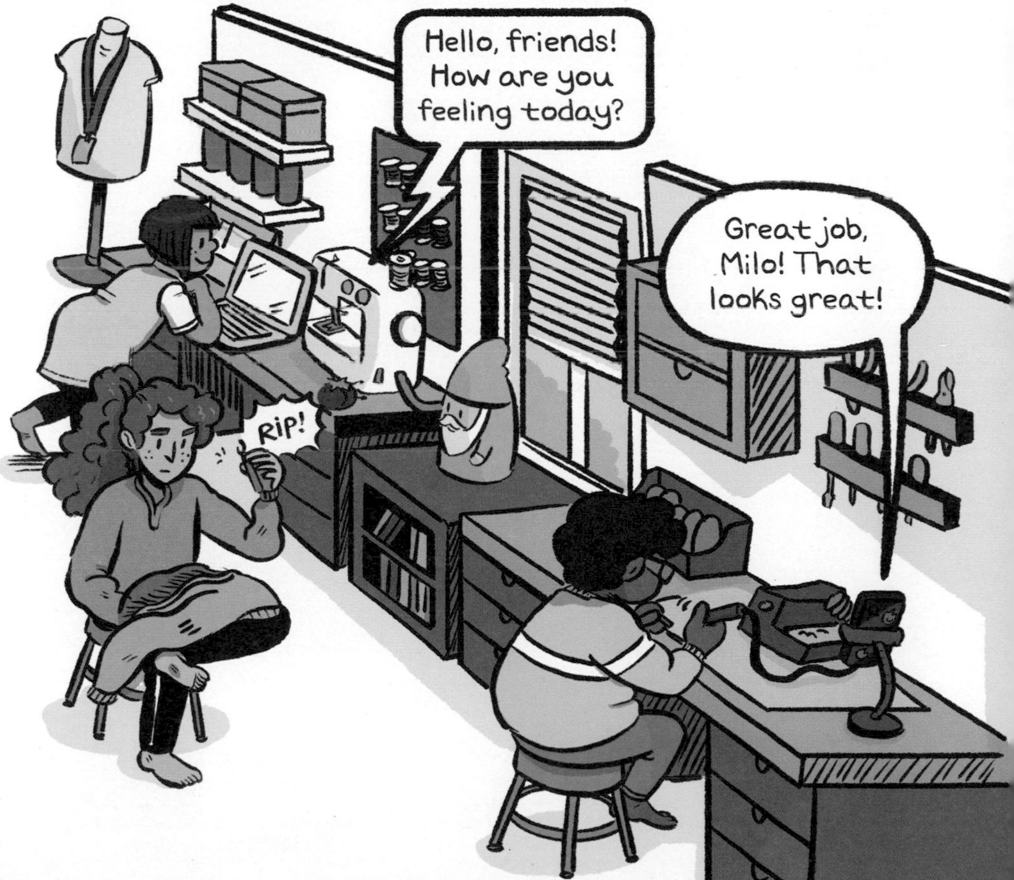
Hello, friends! How are you feeling today?
Great job, Milo! That looks great!
RIP!

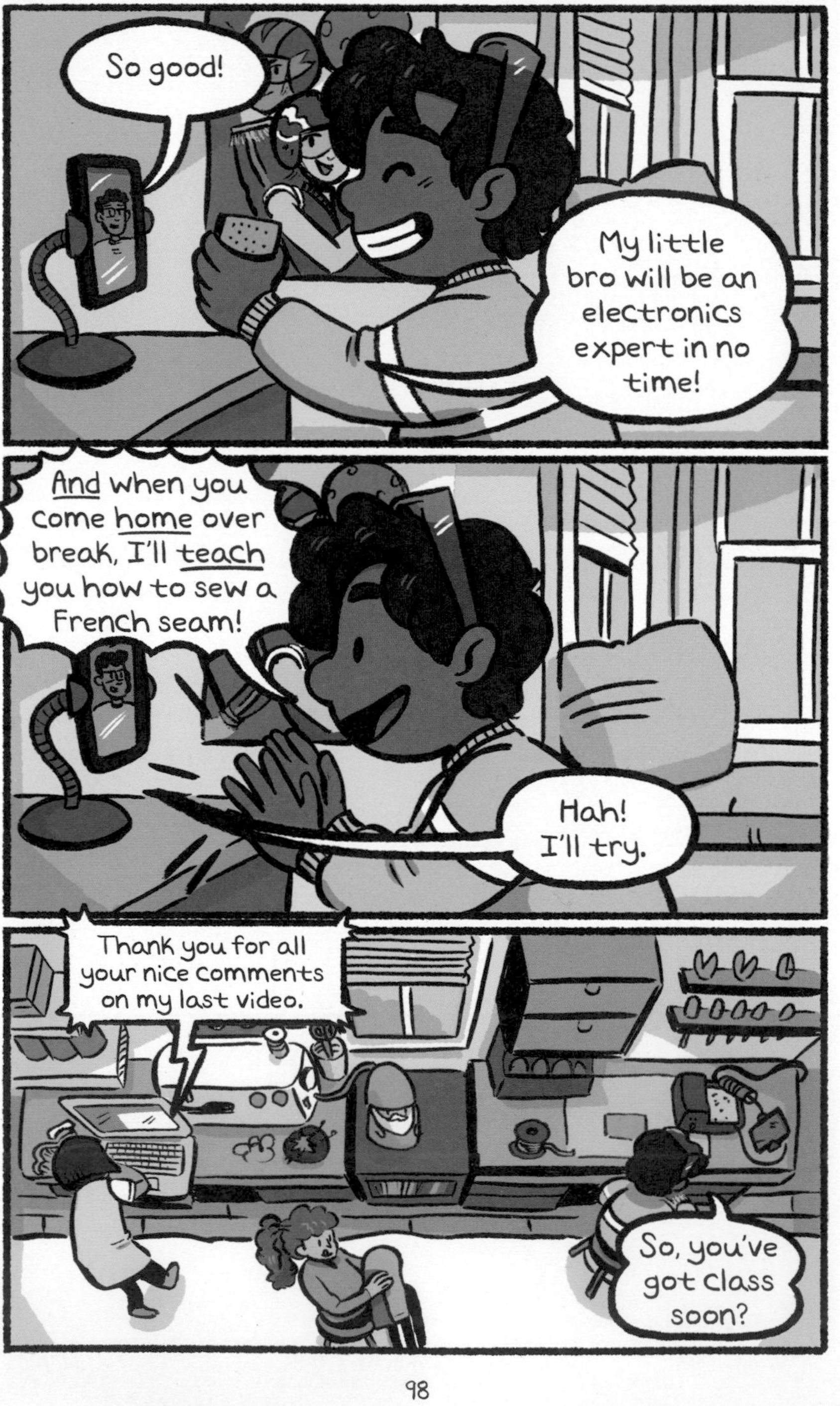
So good!
My little bro will be an electronics expert in no time!
And when you come home over break, I'll teach you how to sew a French seam!
Hah! I'll try.
Thank you for all your nice comments on my last video.
So, you've got class soon?

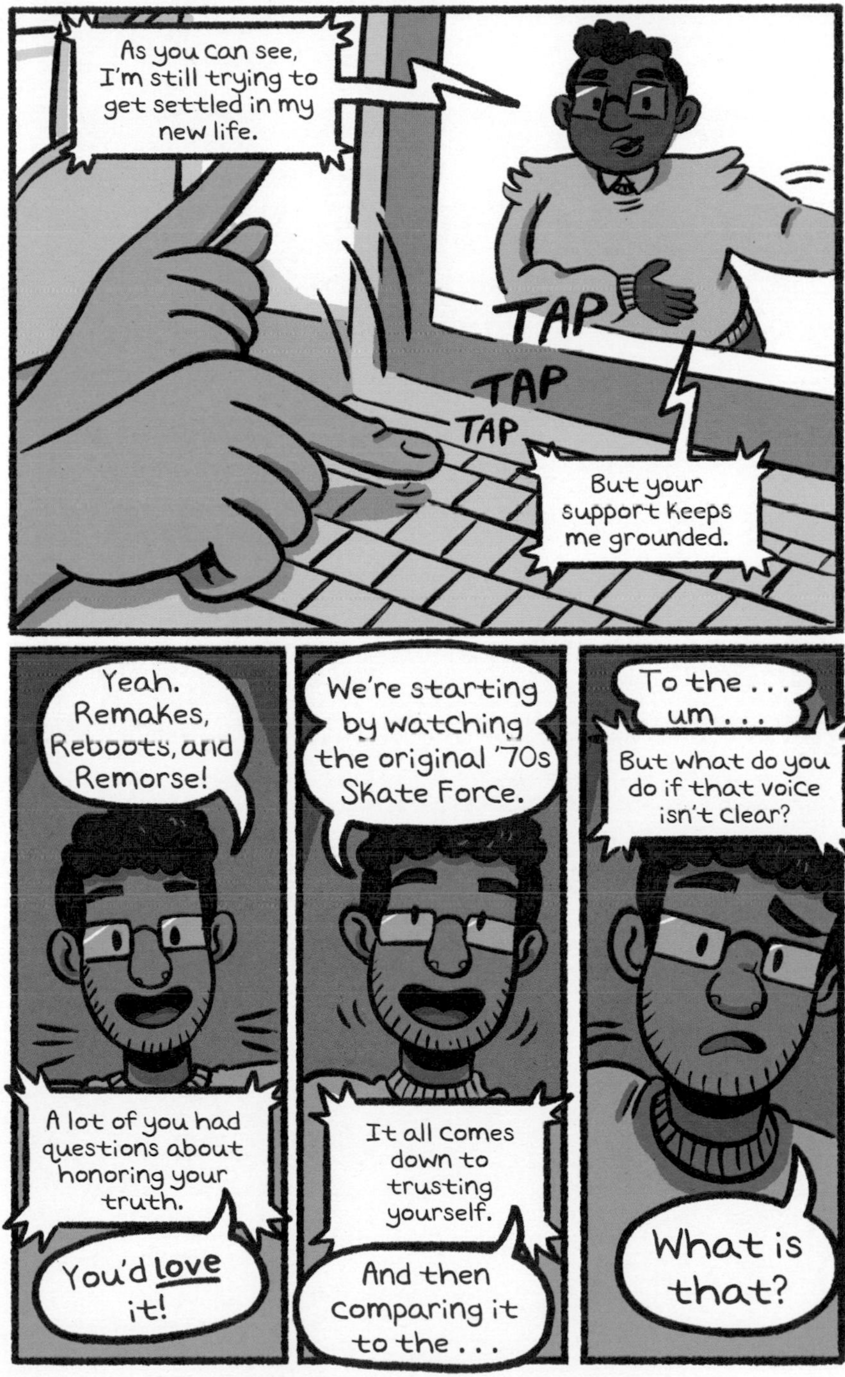
As you can see, I'm still trying to get settled in my new life.
TAP
TAP
TAP
But your support keeps me grounded.
Yeah. Remakes, Reboots, and Remorse!
A lot of you had questions about honoring your truth.
You'd **love** it!
We're starting by watching the original '70s Skate Force.
It all comes down to trusting yourself.
And then comparing it to the . . .
To the . . . um . . .
But what do you do if that voice isn't clear?
What is that?

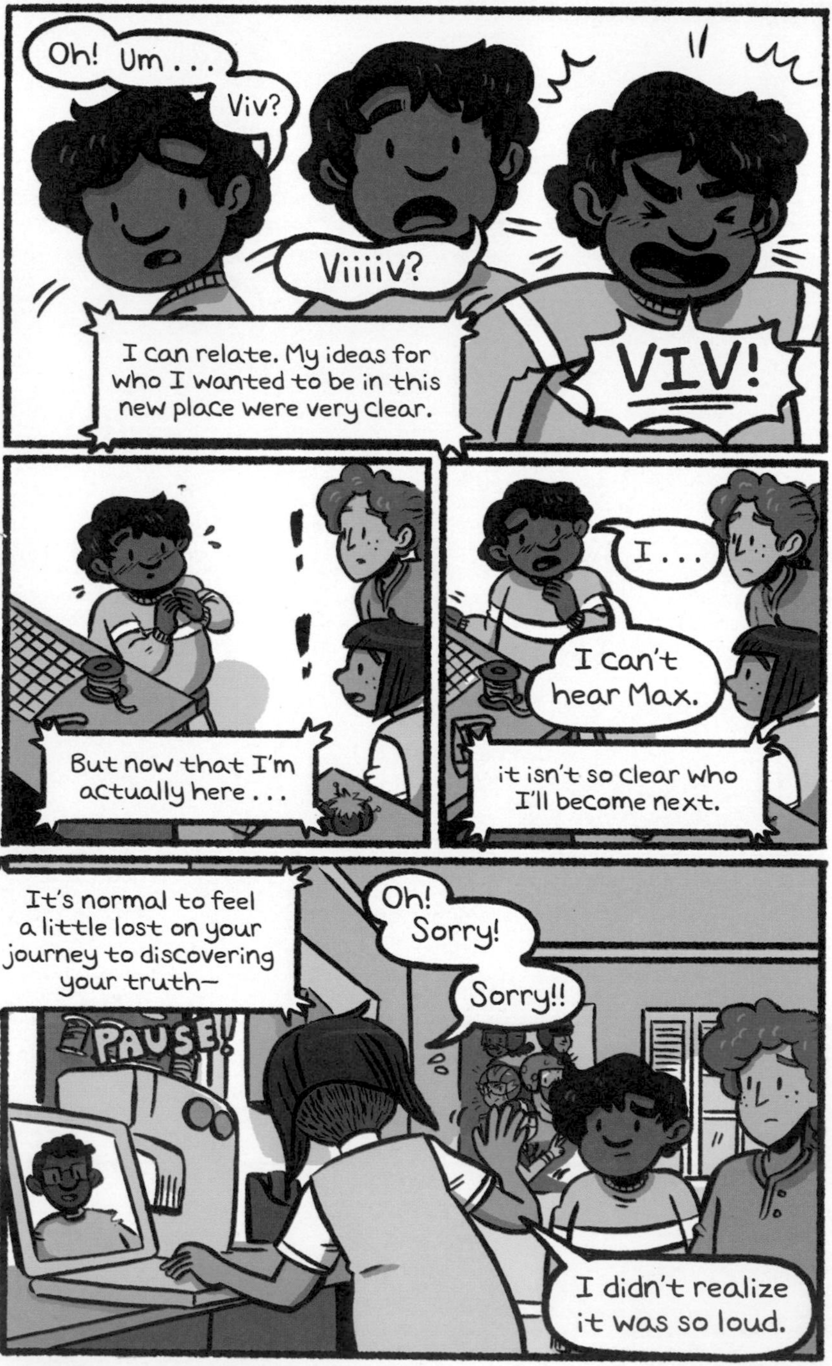
Oh! Um . . .
Viv?
Viiiiv?
VIV!
I can relate. My ideas for who I wanted to be in this new place were very clear.
But now that I'm actually here . . .
I . . .
I can't hear Max.
it isn't so clear who I'll become next.
It's normal to feel a little lost on your journey to discovering your truth—
PAUSE!
Oh! Sorry!
Sorry!!
I didn't realize it was so loud.

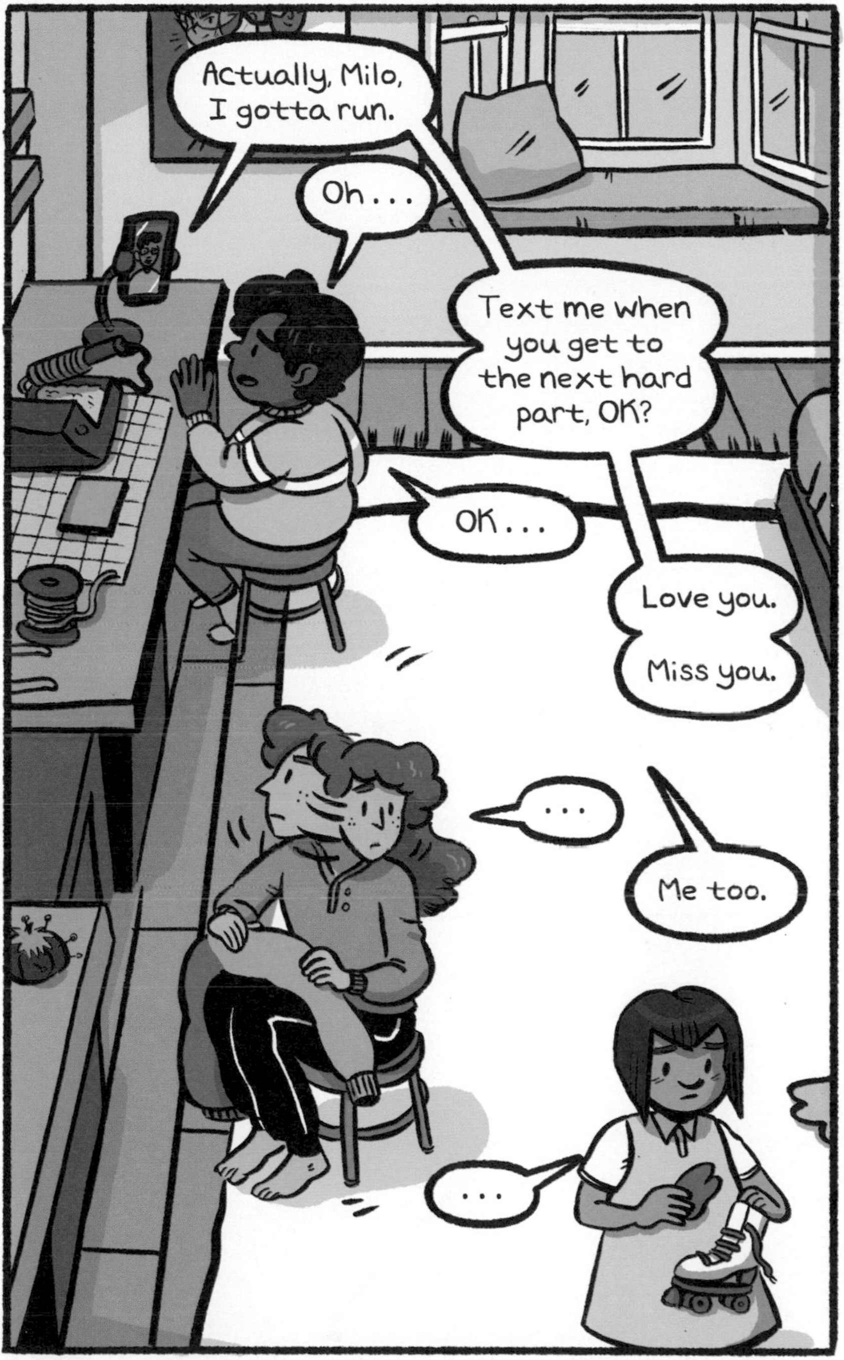
Actually, Milo, I gotta run.
Oh . . .
Text me when you get to the next hard part, OK?
OK . . .
Love you.
Miss you.
. . .
Me too.
. . .

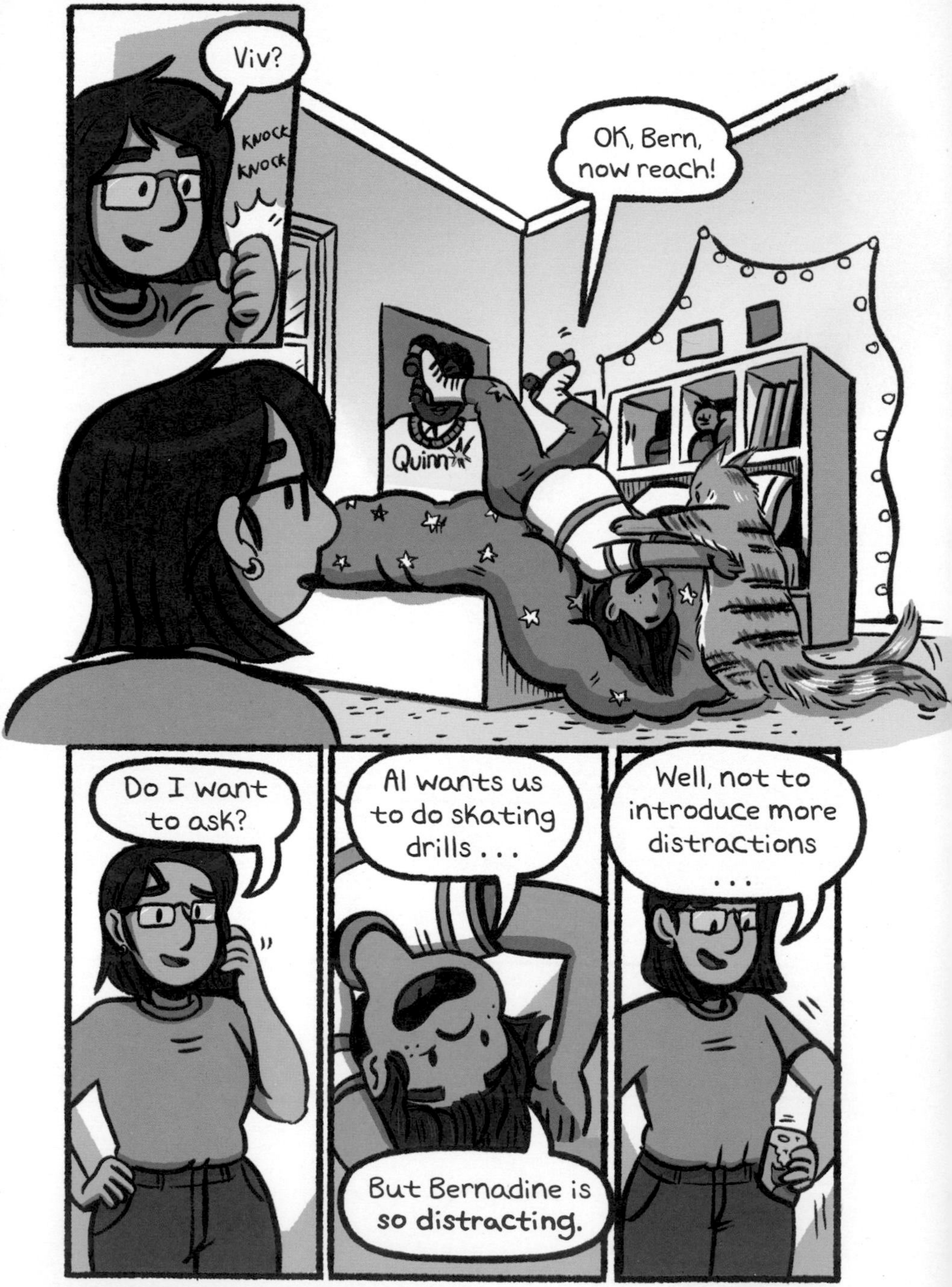
Viv?
KNOCK KNOCK
OK, Bern, now reach!
Quinn
Do I want to ask?
Al wants us to do skating drills . . .
But Bernadine is so distracting.
Well, not to introduce more distractions . . .

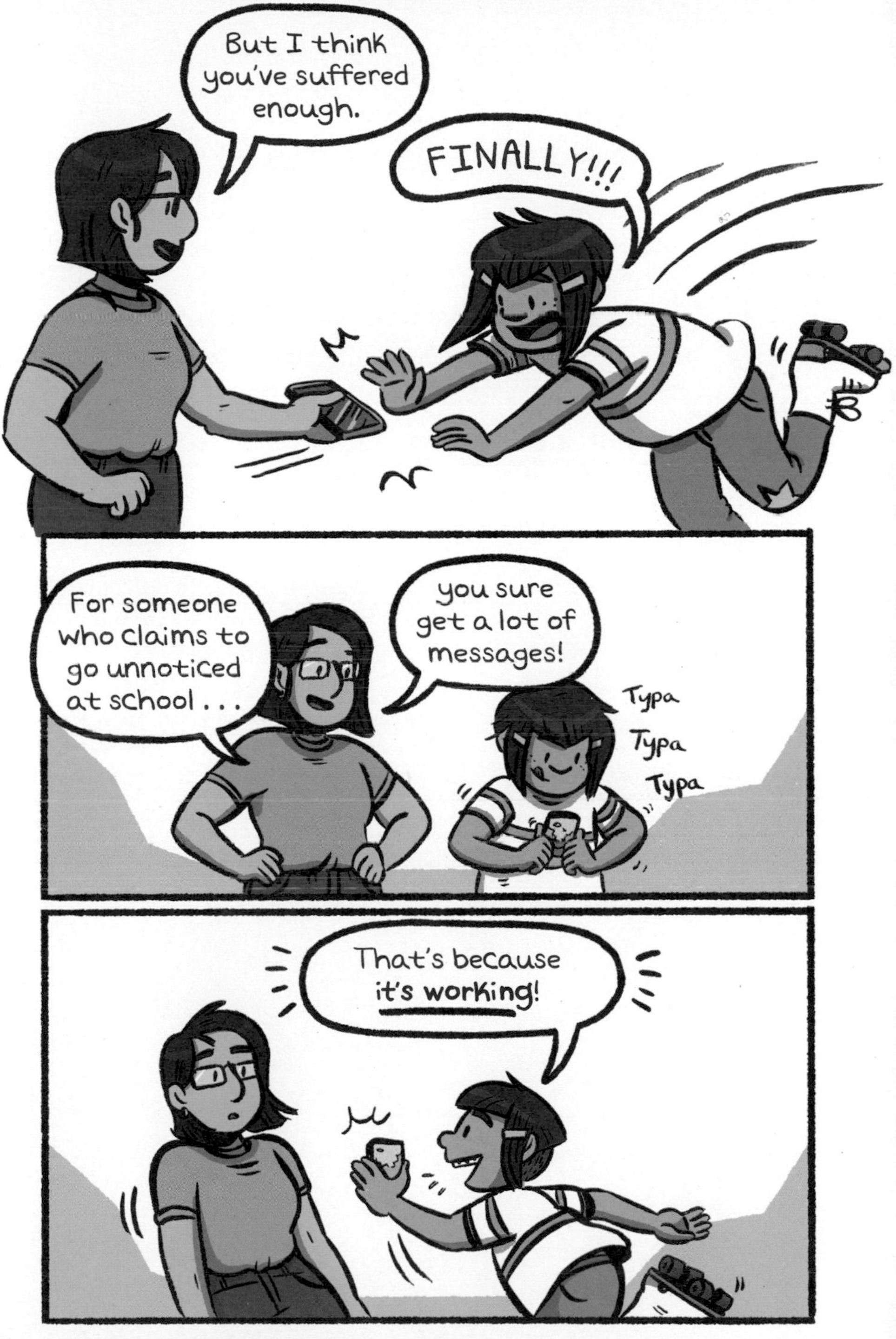

But I think you've suffered enough.
FINALLY!!!
For someone who claims to go unnoticed at school . . .
you sure get a lot of messages!
Typa
Typa
Typa
That's because it's working!

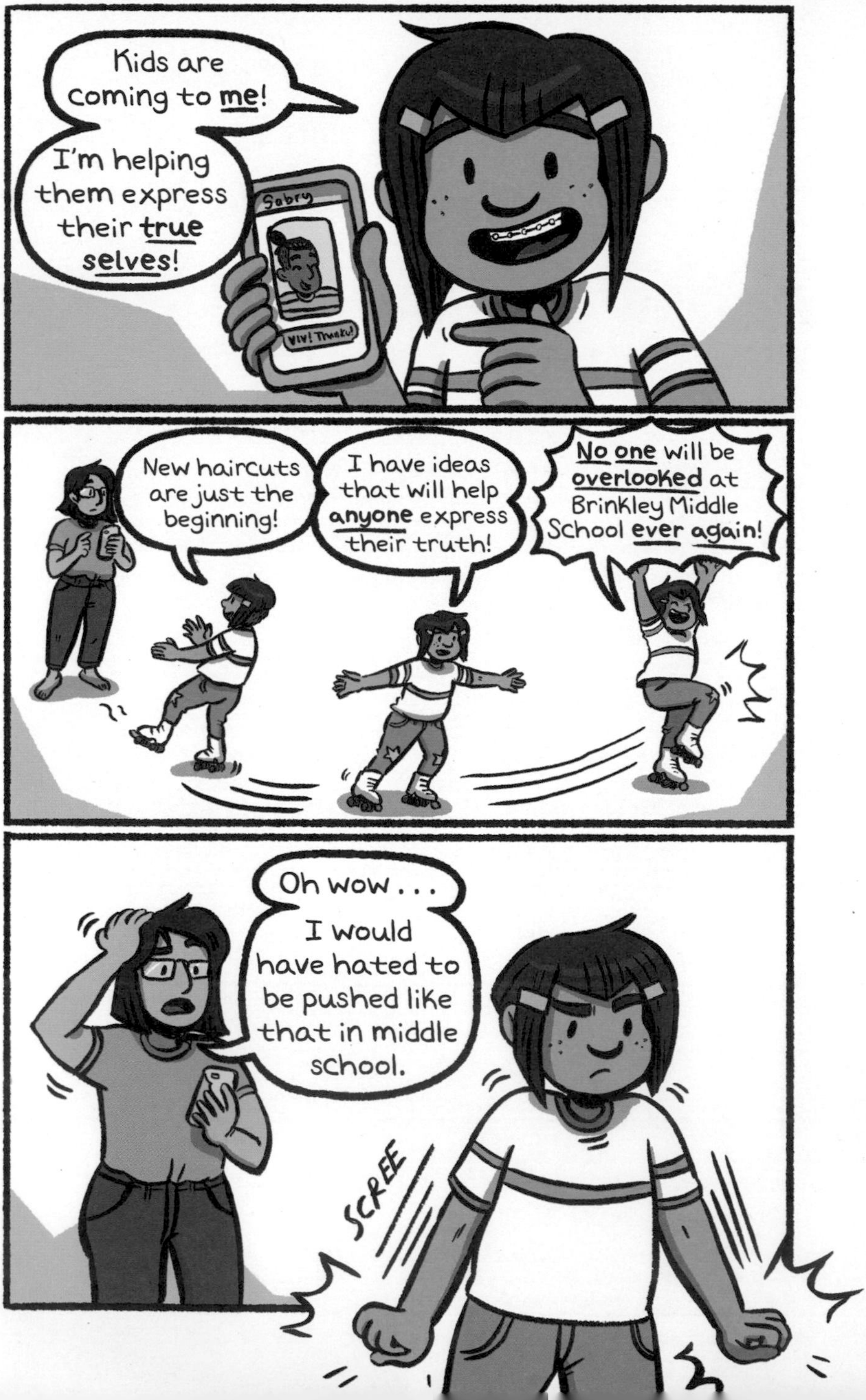
Kids are coming to **me**!
I'm helping them express their **true selves**!
Sabry
New haircuts are just the beginning!
I have ideas that will help **anyone** express their truth!
No one will be **overlooked** at Brinkley Middle School **ever again**!
Oh wow . . .
I would have hated to be pushed like that in middle school.
SCREE

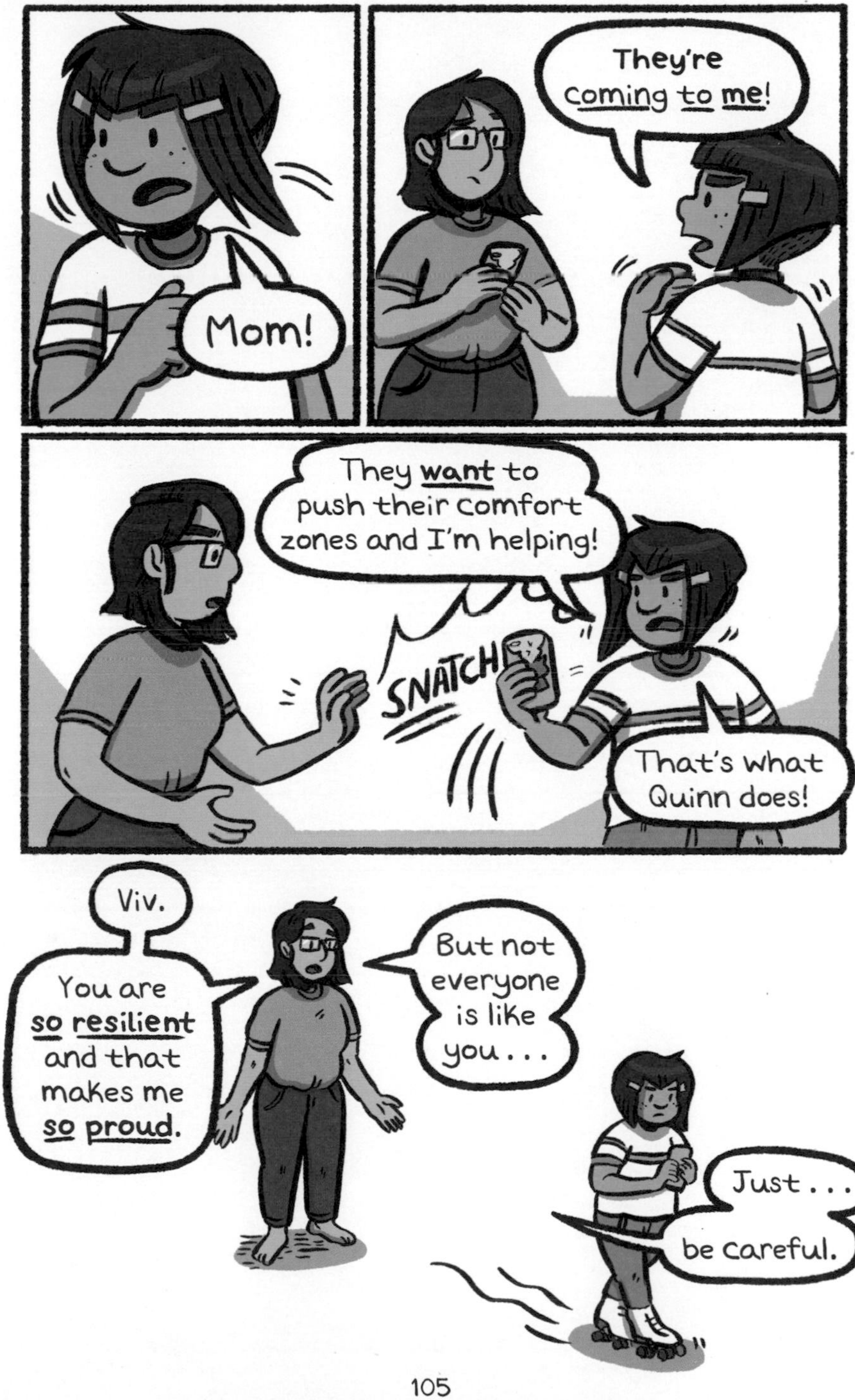
Mom!
They're coming to me!
They want to push their comfort zones and I'm helping!
SNATCH
That's what Quinn does!
Viv.
You are so resilient and that makes me so proud.
But not everyone is like you . . .
Just . . .
be careful.

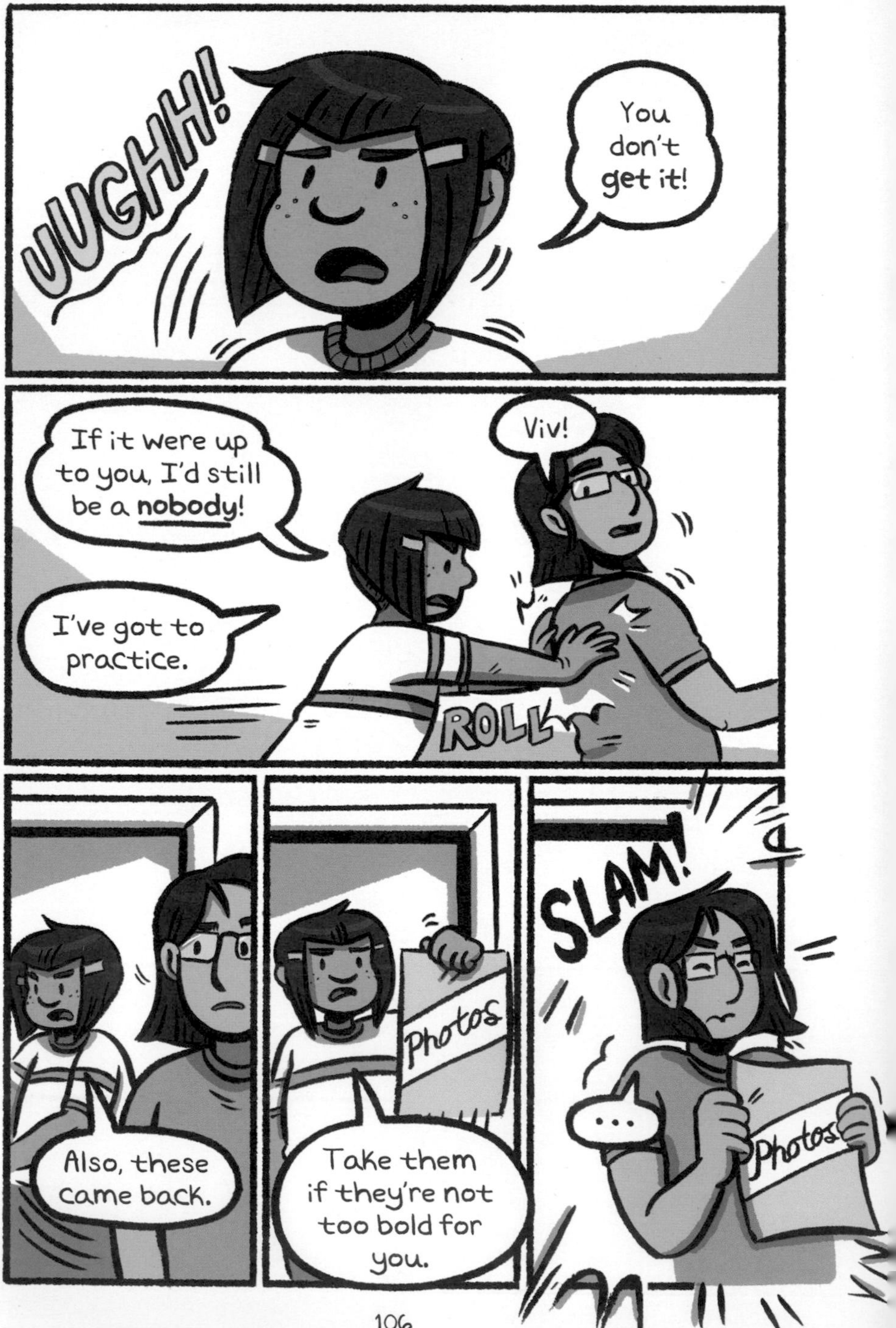
UUGHH!
You don't get it!
If it were up to you, I'd still be a nobody!
Viv!
I've got to practice.
ROLL
Also, these came back.
Photos
Take them if they're not too bold for you.
SLAM!
...
Photos

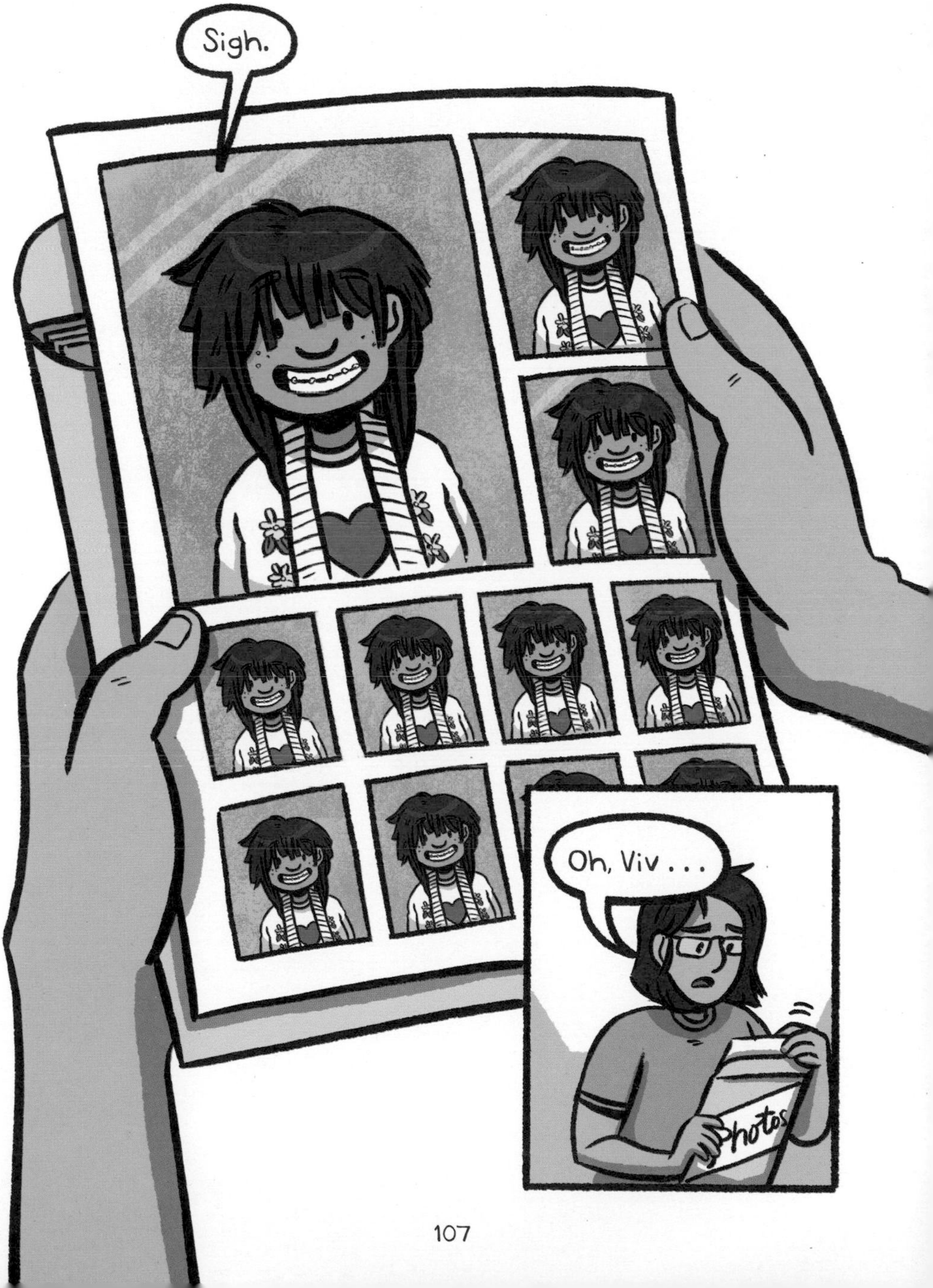
Sigh.
Oh, Viv . . .
Photos

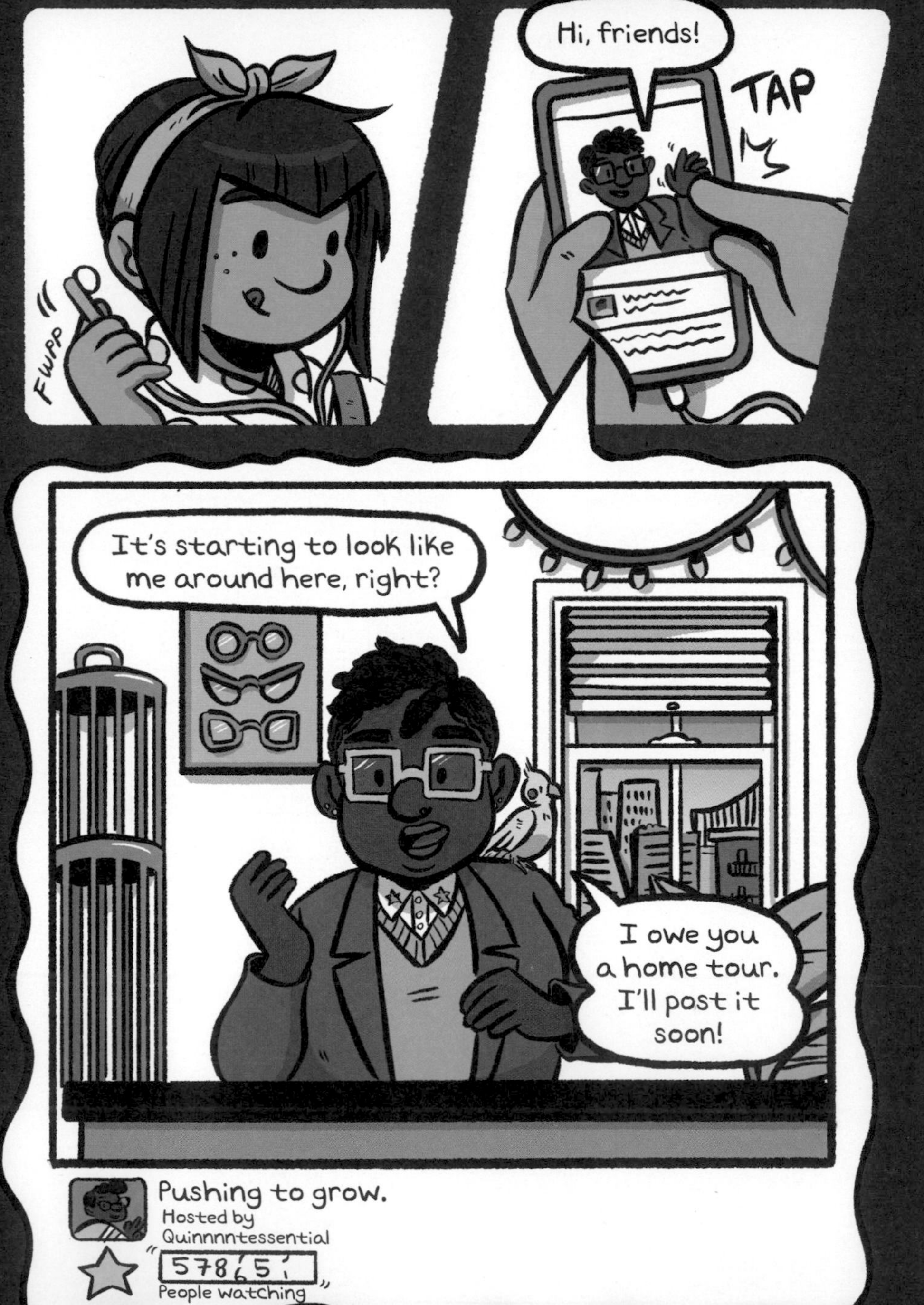
FWPP
Hi, friends!
TAP
It's starting to look like me around here, right?
I owe you a home tour. I'll post it soon!
Pushing to grow.
Hosted by Quinnnntessential
578,51
People watching

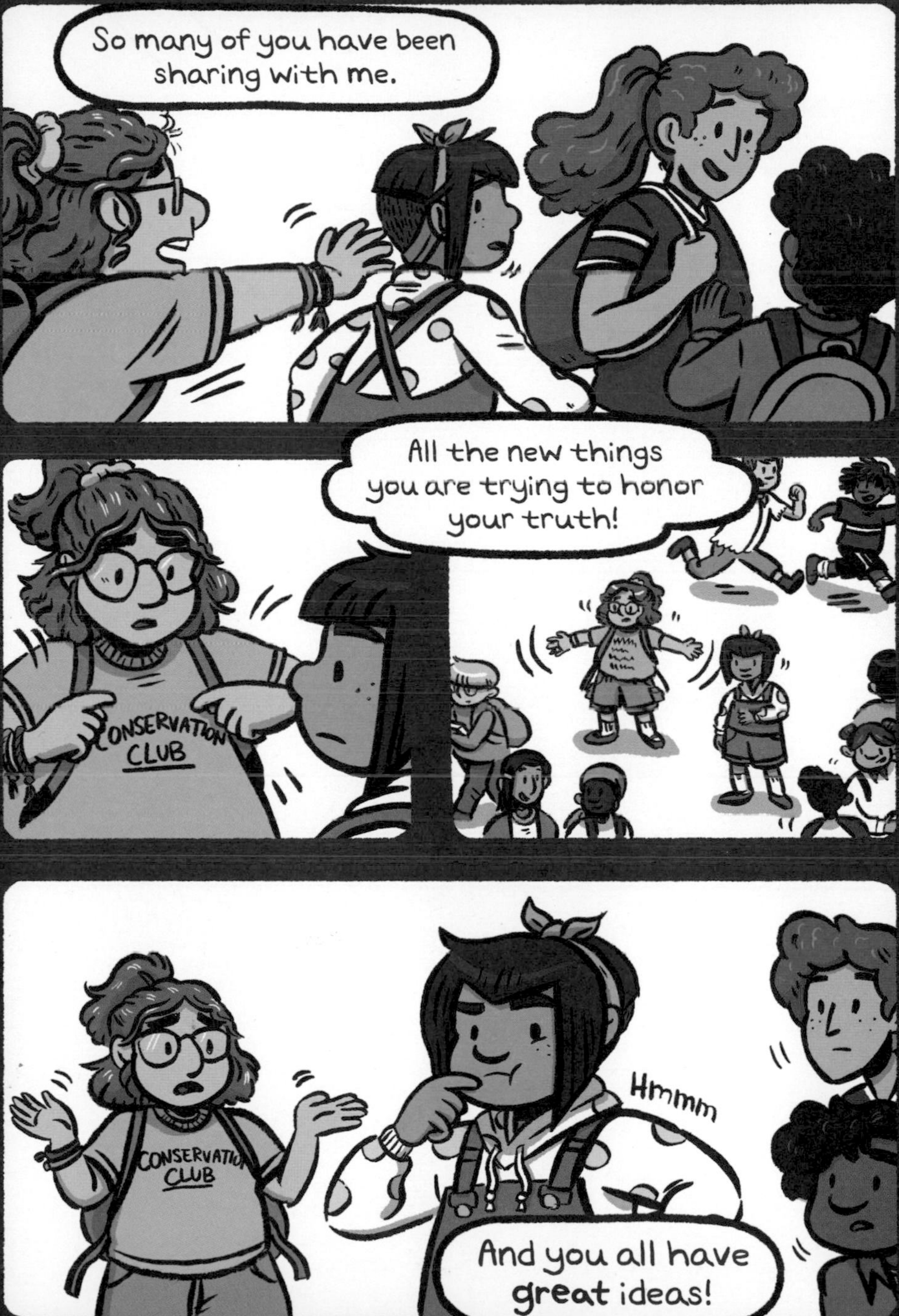
So many of you have been sharing with me.
All the new things you are trying to honor your truth!
CONSERVATION CLUB
CONSERVATION CLUB
Hmmm
And you all have **great** ideas!

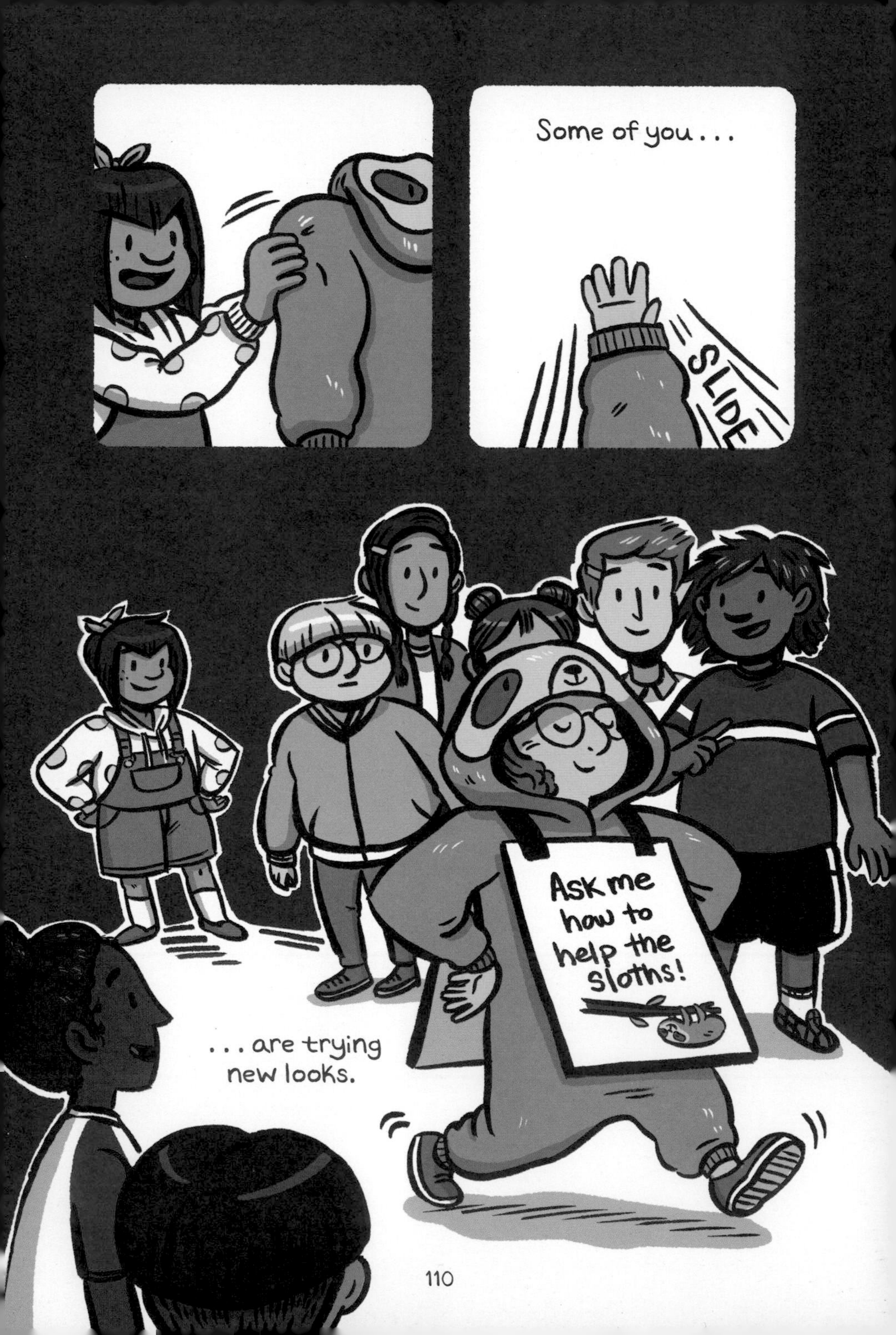
Some of you . . .
SLIDE
Ask me how to help the sloths!
. . . are trying new looks.

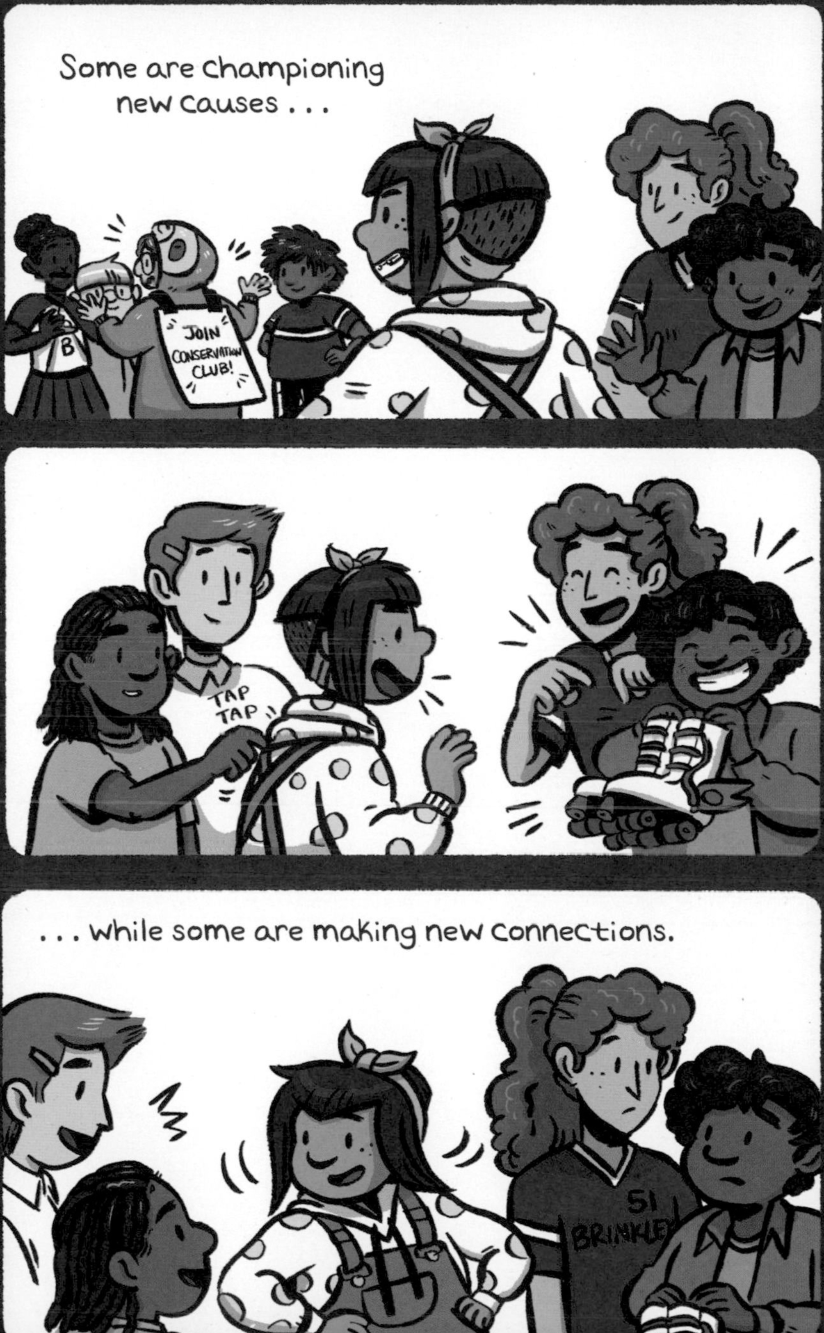
Some are championing new causes . . .
B
JOIN CONSERVATION CLUB!
TAP TAP
. . . while some are making new connections.
51
BRINKLEY

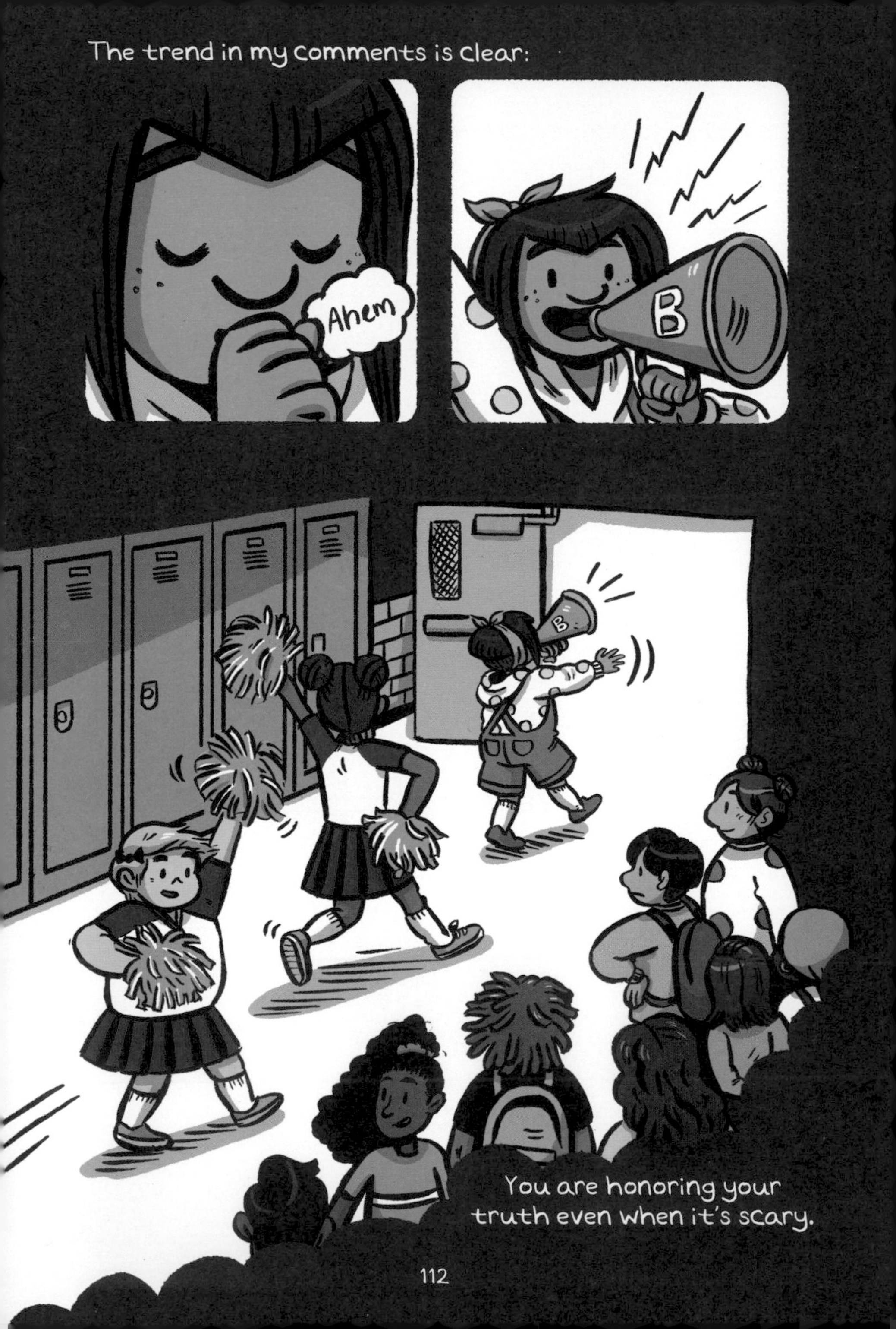
The trend in my comments is clear:
Ahem
B
B
You are honoring your truth even when it's scary.

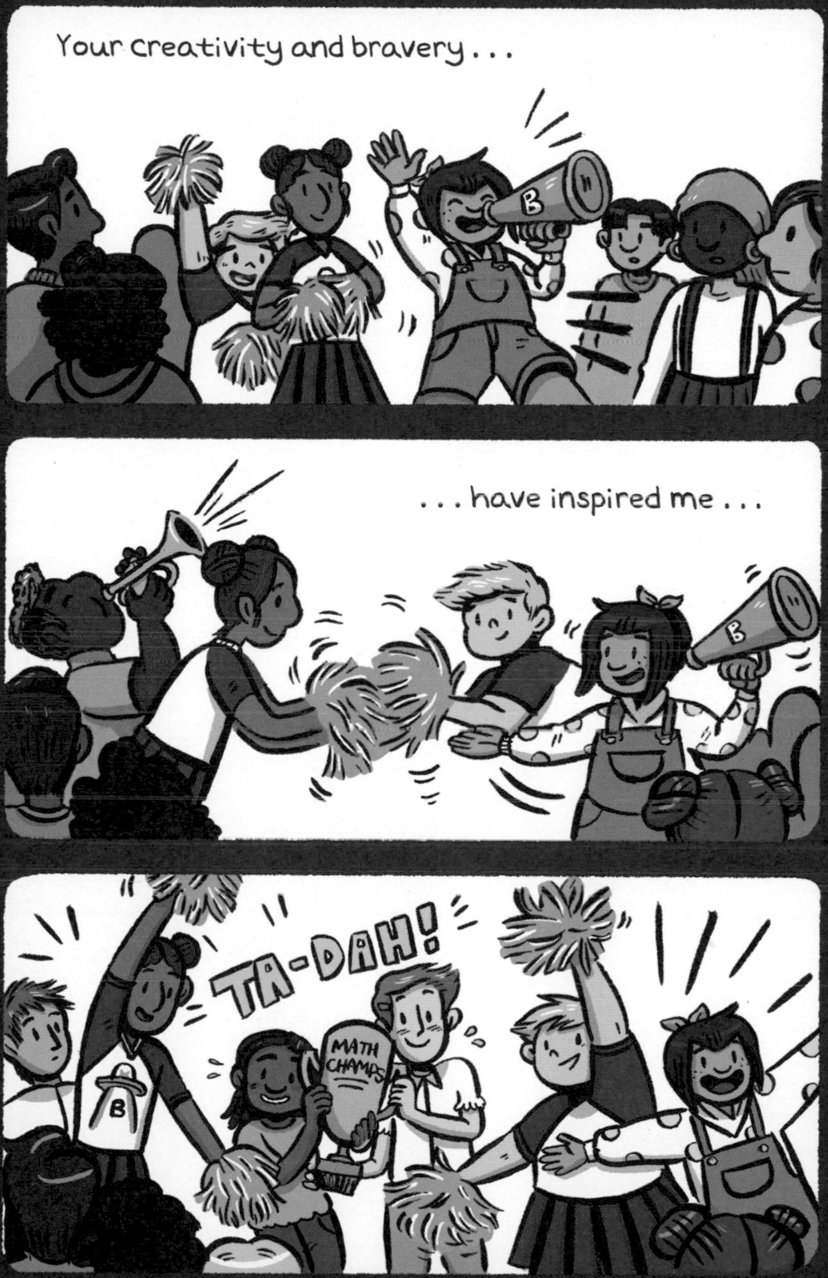
Your creativity and bravery . . .
. . . have inspired me . . .
TA-DAH!
MATH CHAMPS
. . . to push even farther outside my comfort zone.

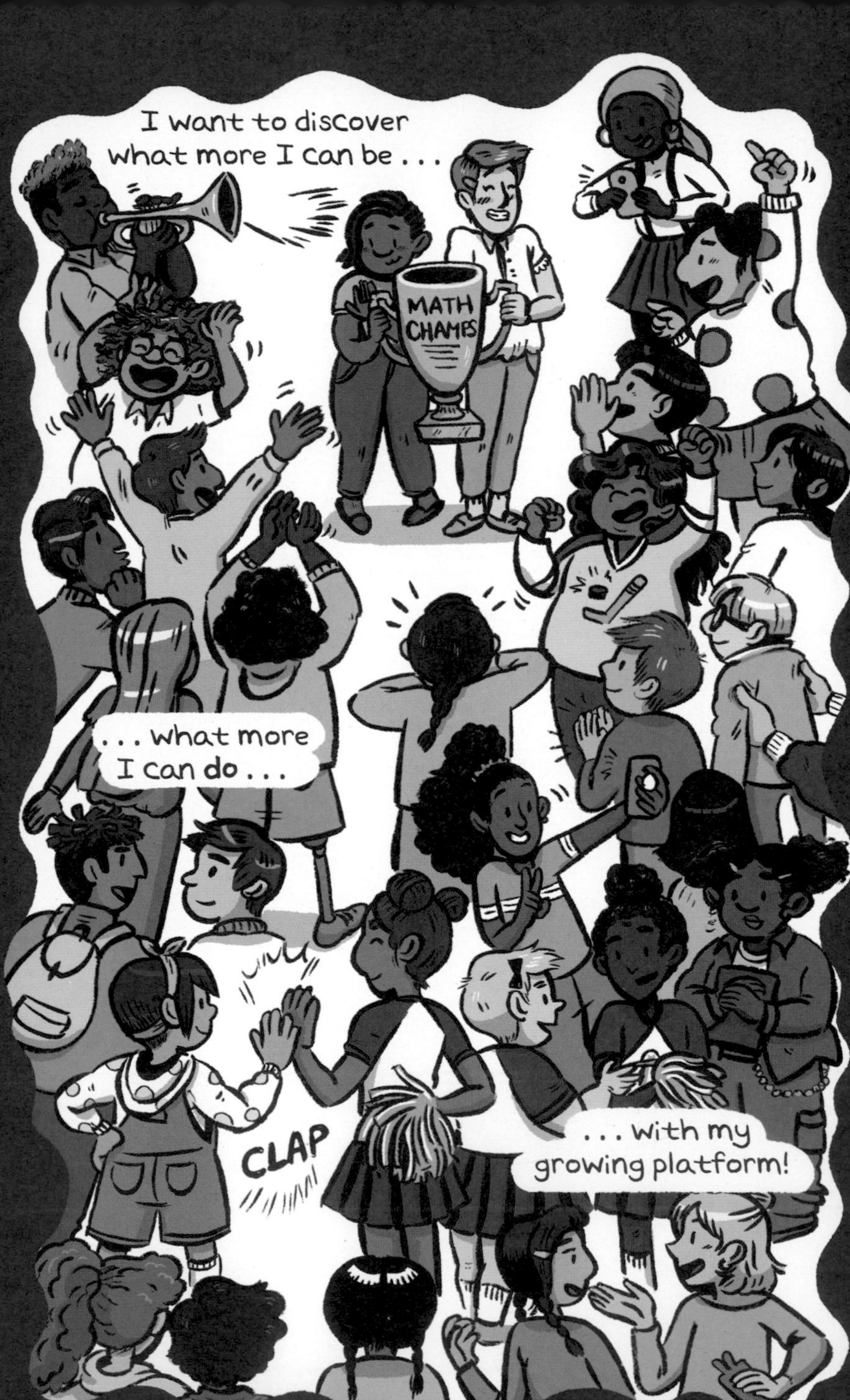
I want to discover what more I can be . . .
MATH CHAMPS
. . . what more I can do . . .
CLAP
. . . with my growing platform!

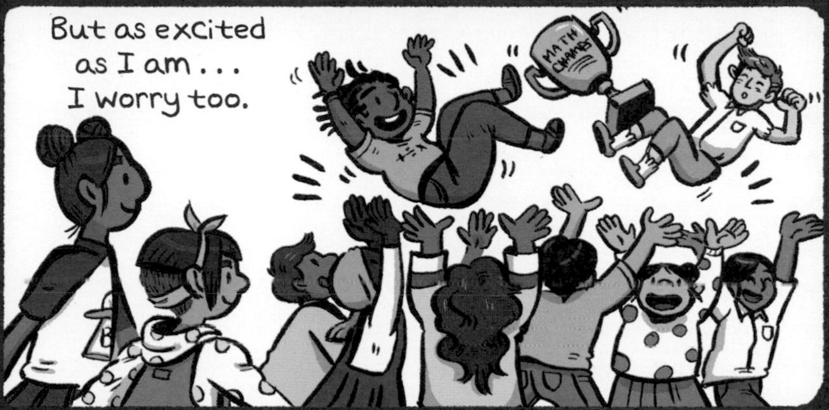
But as excited as I am . . . I worry too.
MATH CHAMPS

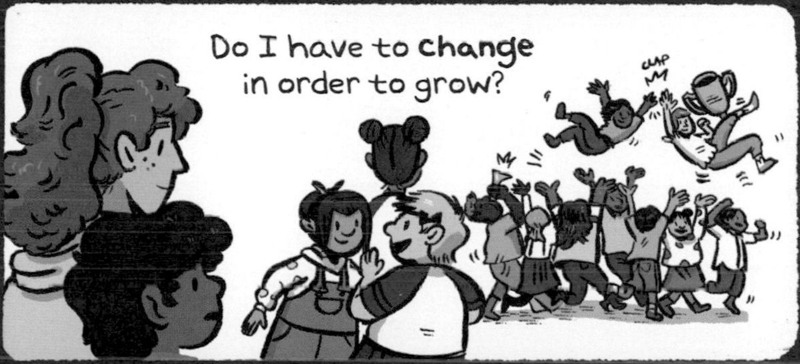
Do I have to **change** in order to grow?

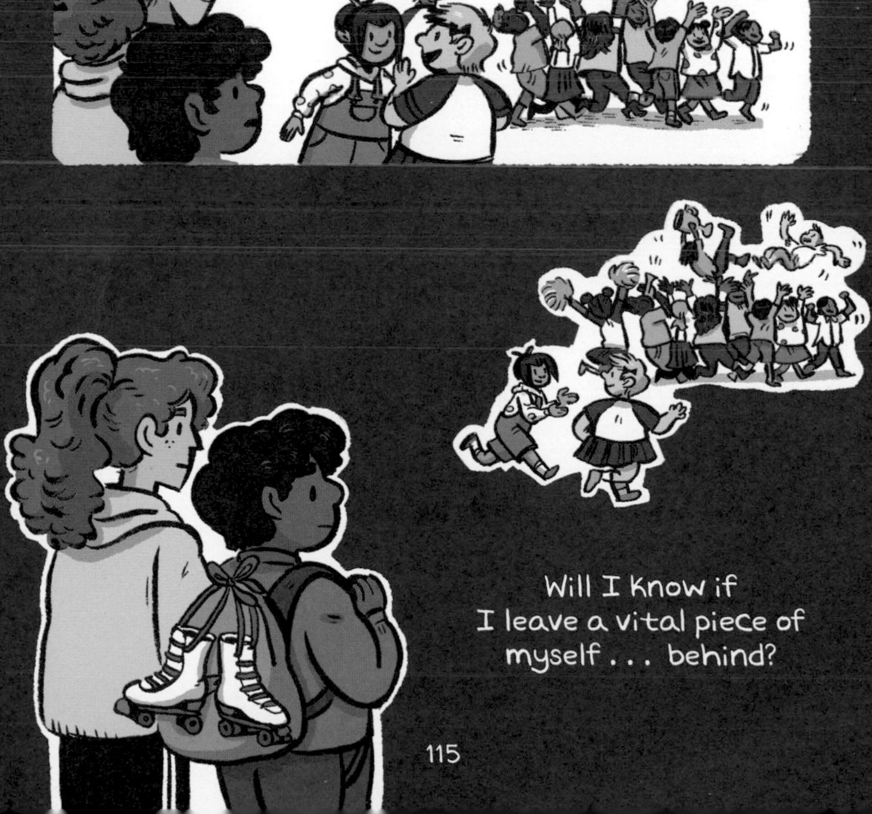
Will I know if I leave a vital piece of myself . . . behind?

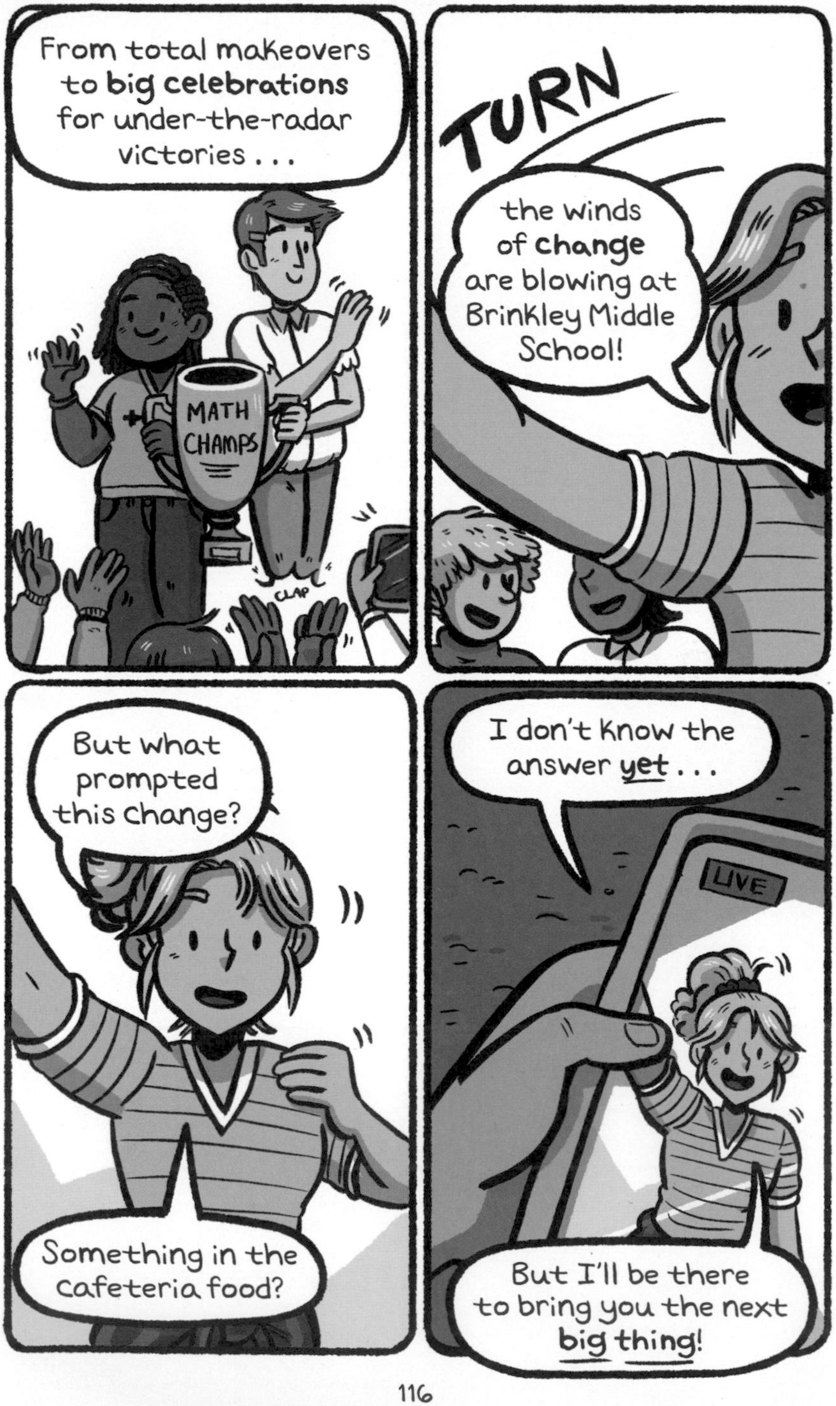
From total makeovers to big celebrations for under-the-radar victories . . .
MATH CHAMPS
CLAP
TURN
the winds of change are blowing at Brinkley Middle School!
But what prompted this change?
Something in the cafeteria food?
I don't know the answer yet . . .
LIVE
But I'll be there to bring you the next big thing!

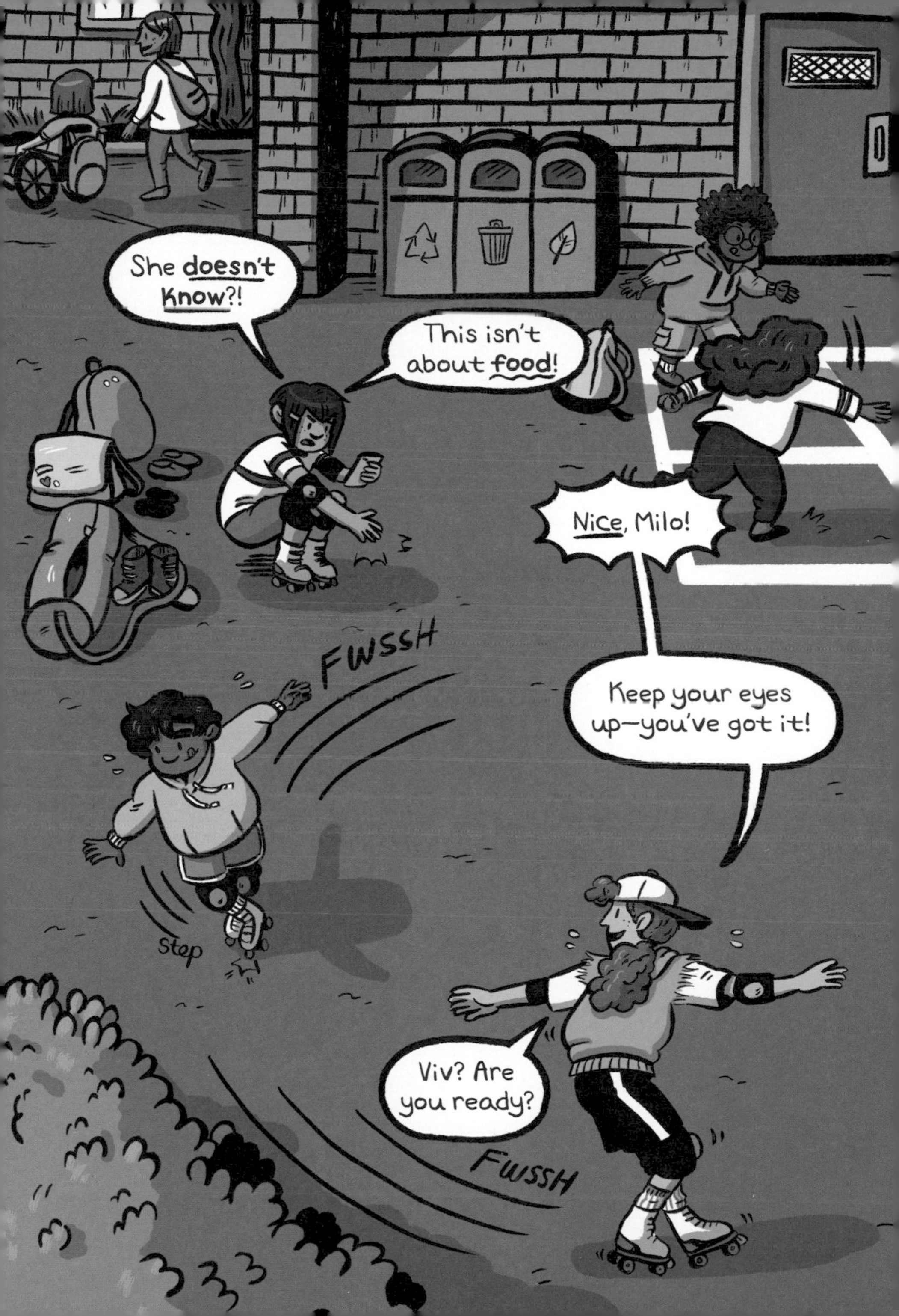
She doesn't Know?!
This isn't about food!
Nice, Milo!
Keep your eyes up—you've got it!
FWSSH
Step
Viv? Are you ready?
FWSSH

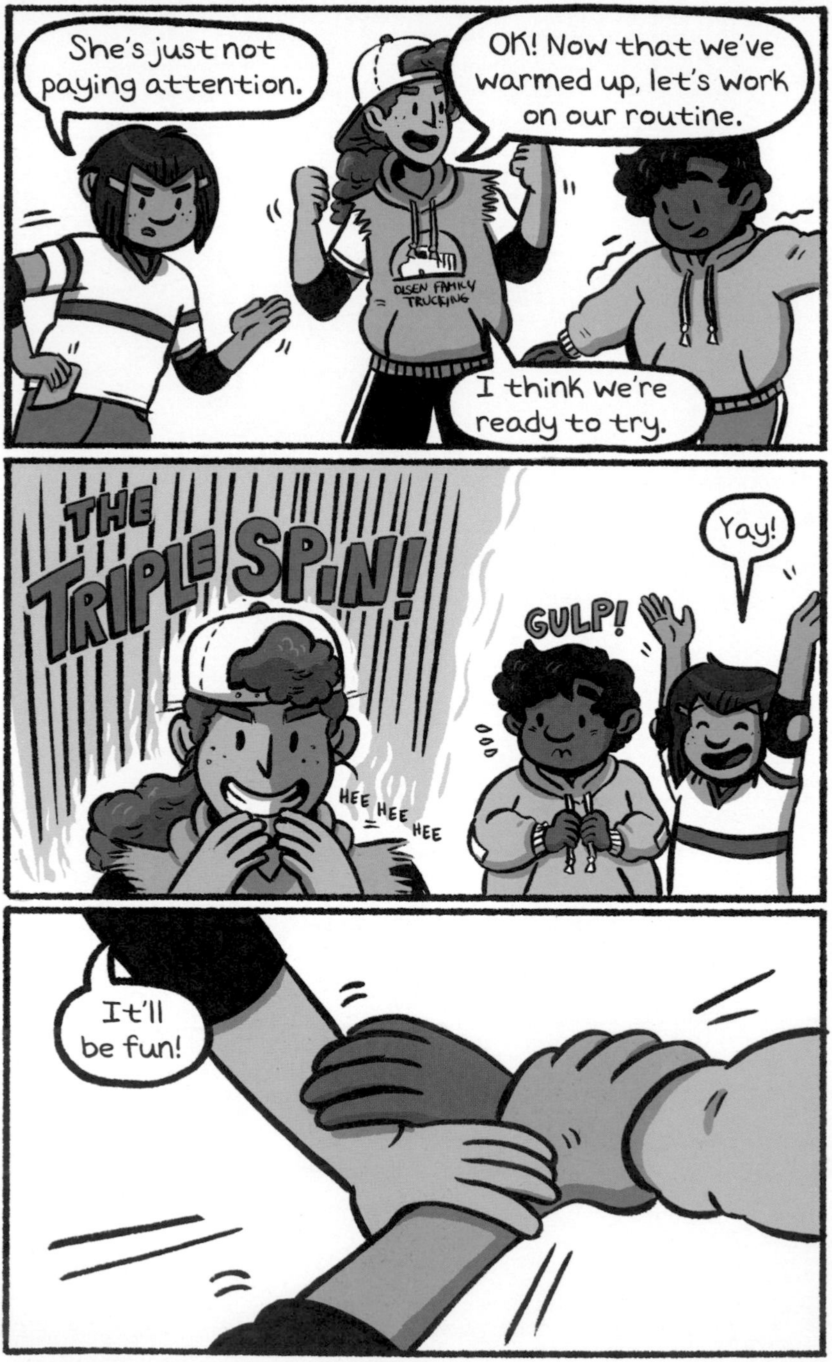
She's just not paying attention.
OK! Now that we've warmed up, let's work on our routine.
OLSEN FAMILY TRUCKING
I think we're ready to try.
THE TRIPLE SPIN!
Yay!
GULP!
HEE HEE HEE
It'll be fun!

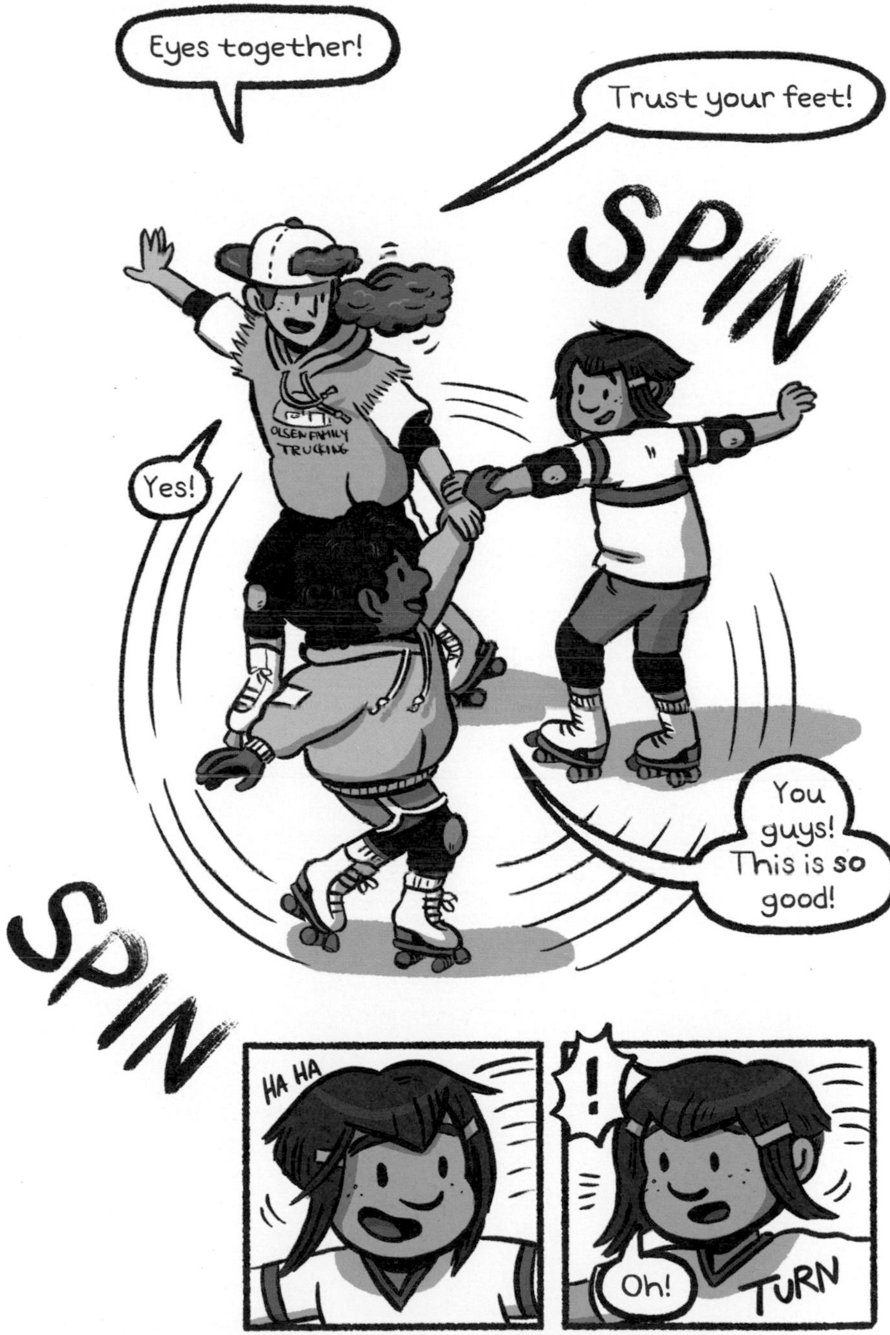
Eyes together!
Trust your feet!
SPIN
OLSEN FAMILY TRUCKING
Yes!
You guys! This is so good!
SPIN
HA HA
!
Oh!
TURN

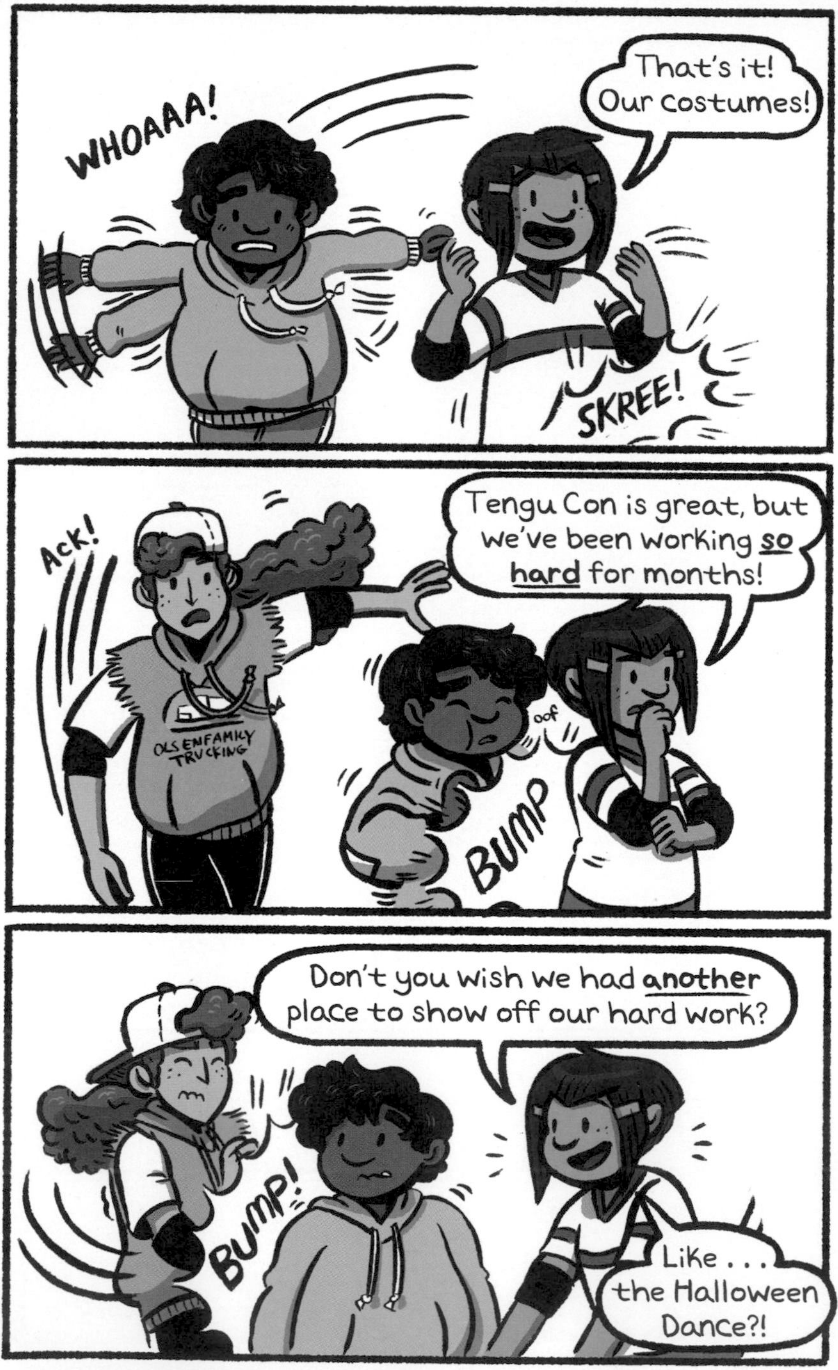
WHOAAA!
That's it! Our costumes!
SKREE!
Ack!
Tengu Con is great, but we've been working so hard for months!
OLSEN FAMILY TRUCKING
oof
BUMP
Don't you wish we had another place to show off our hard work?
BUMP!
Like . . . the Halloween Dance?!

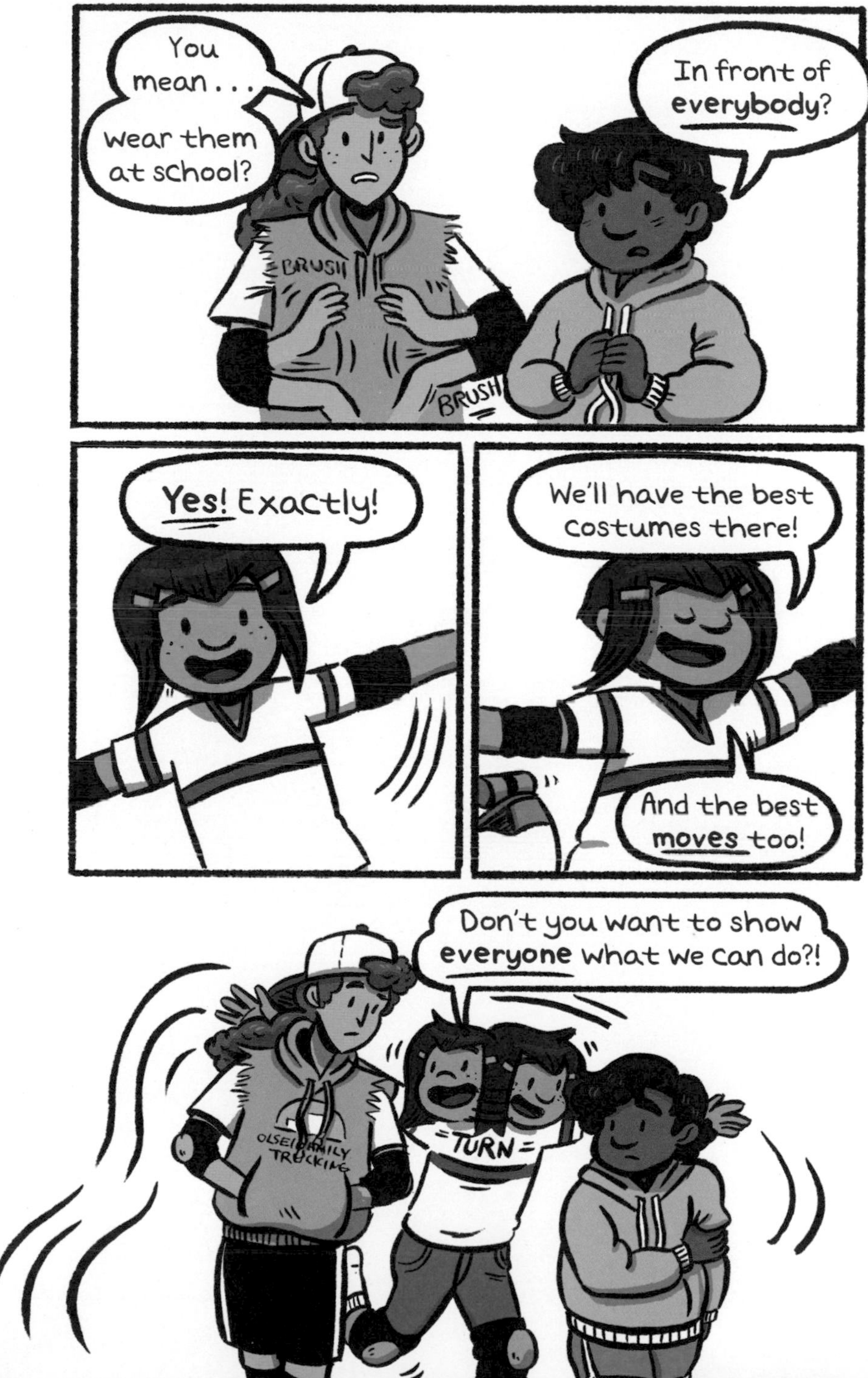
You mean . . .
wear them at school?
In front of everybody?
BRUSH
BRUSH
Yes! Exactly!
We'll have the best costumes there!
And the best moves too!
Don't you want to show everyone what we can do?!
TURN

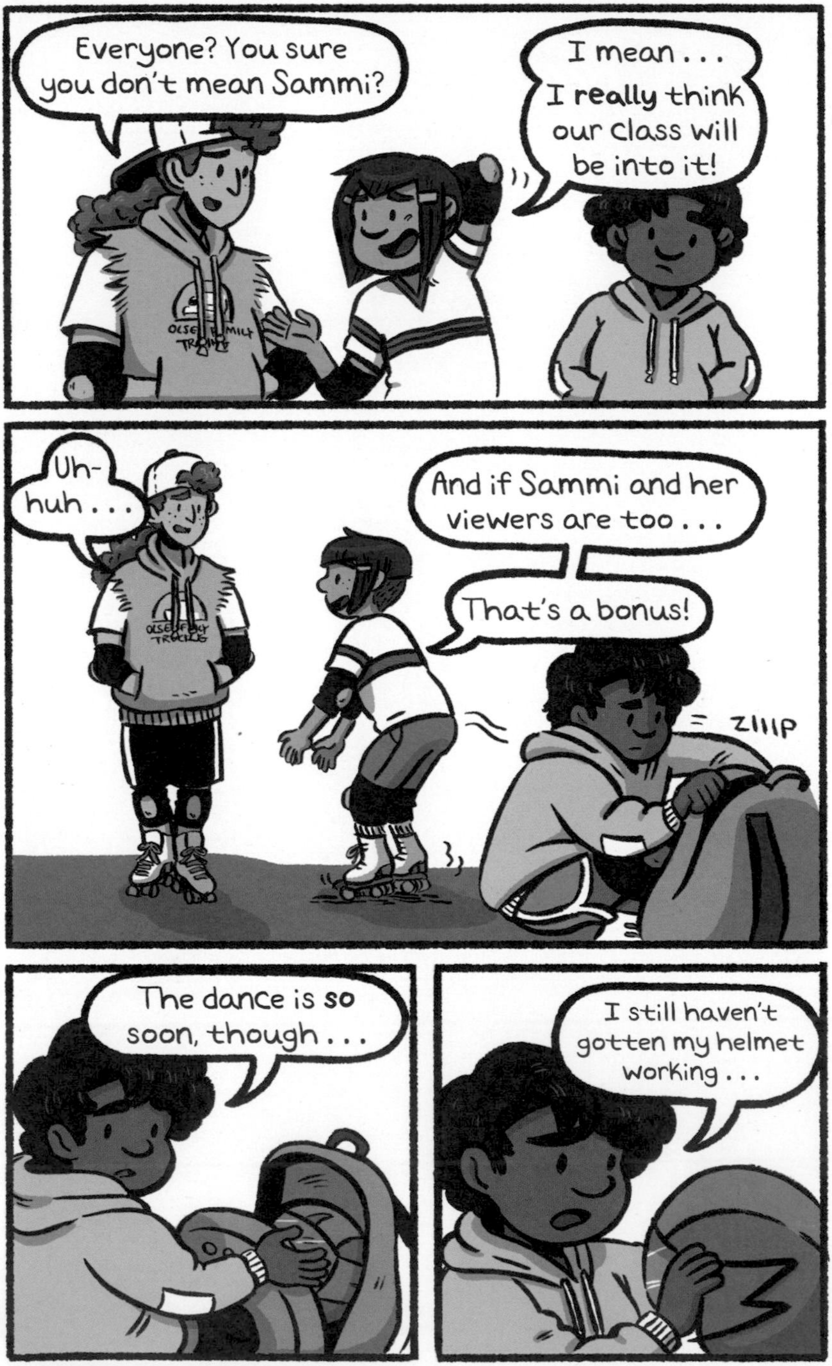
Everyone? You sure you don't mean Sammi?
I mean . . .
I really think our class will be into it!
Uh-huh . . .
And if Sammi and her viewers are too . . .
That's a bonus!
ZIIIP
The dance is so soon, though . . .
I still haven't gotten my helmet working . . .

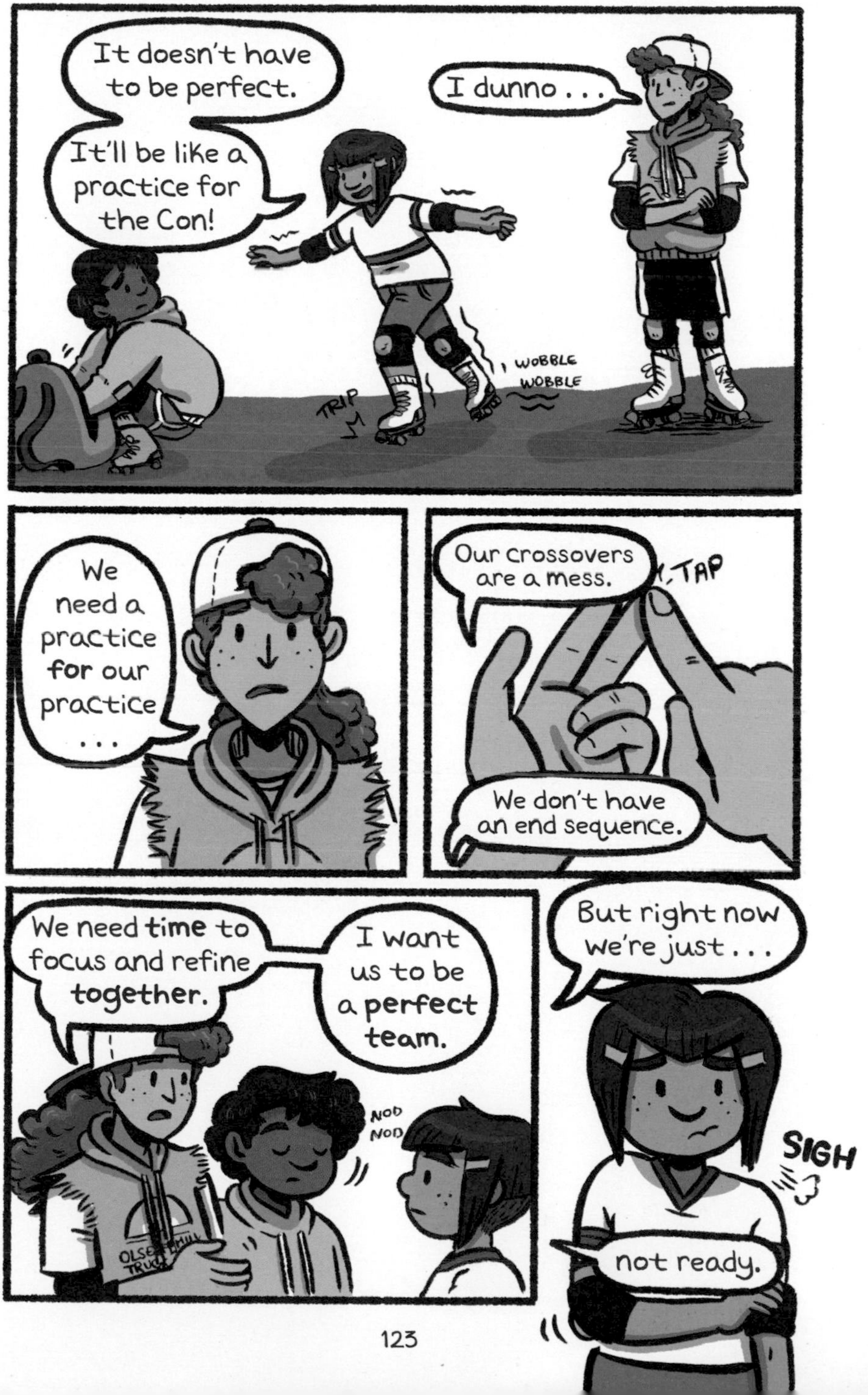

It doesn't have to be perfect.
It'll be like a practice for the Con!
I dunno . . .
TRIP
WOBBLE WOBBLE
We need a practice for our practice . . .
Our crossovers are a mess.
TAP
We don't have an end sequence.
We need time to focus and refine together.
I want us to be a perfect team.
NOD NOD
But right now we're just . . .
SIGH
not ready.

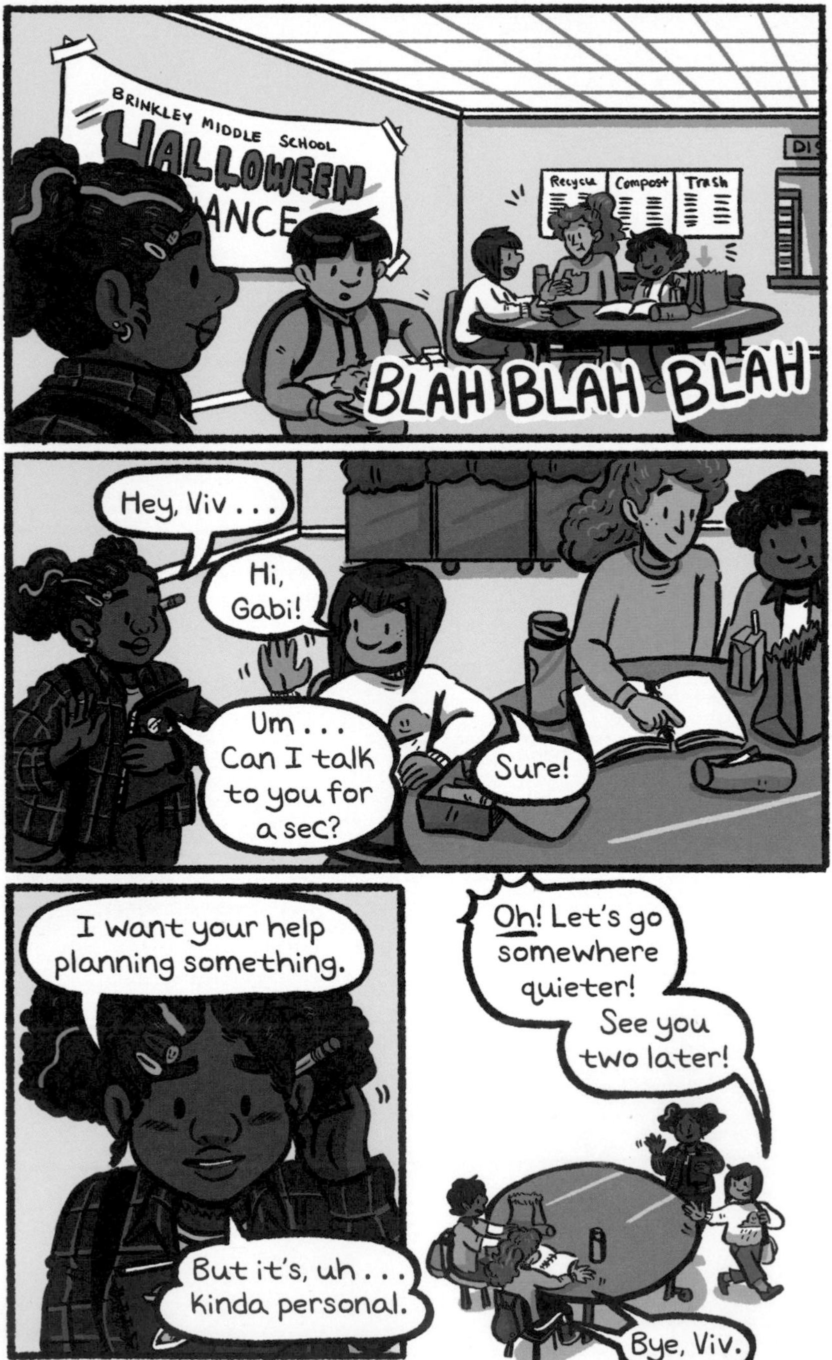

BRINKLEY MIDDLE SCHOOL
HALLOWEEN
ANCE
Recycle
Compost
Trash
BLAH BLAH BLAH
Hey, Viv . . .
Hi, Gabi!
Um . . . Can I talk to you for a sec?
Sure!
I want your help planning something.
But it's, uh . . . kinda personal.
Oh! Let's go somewhere quieter!
See you two later!
Bye, Viv.

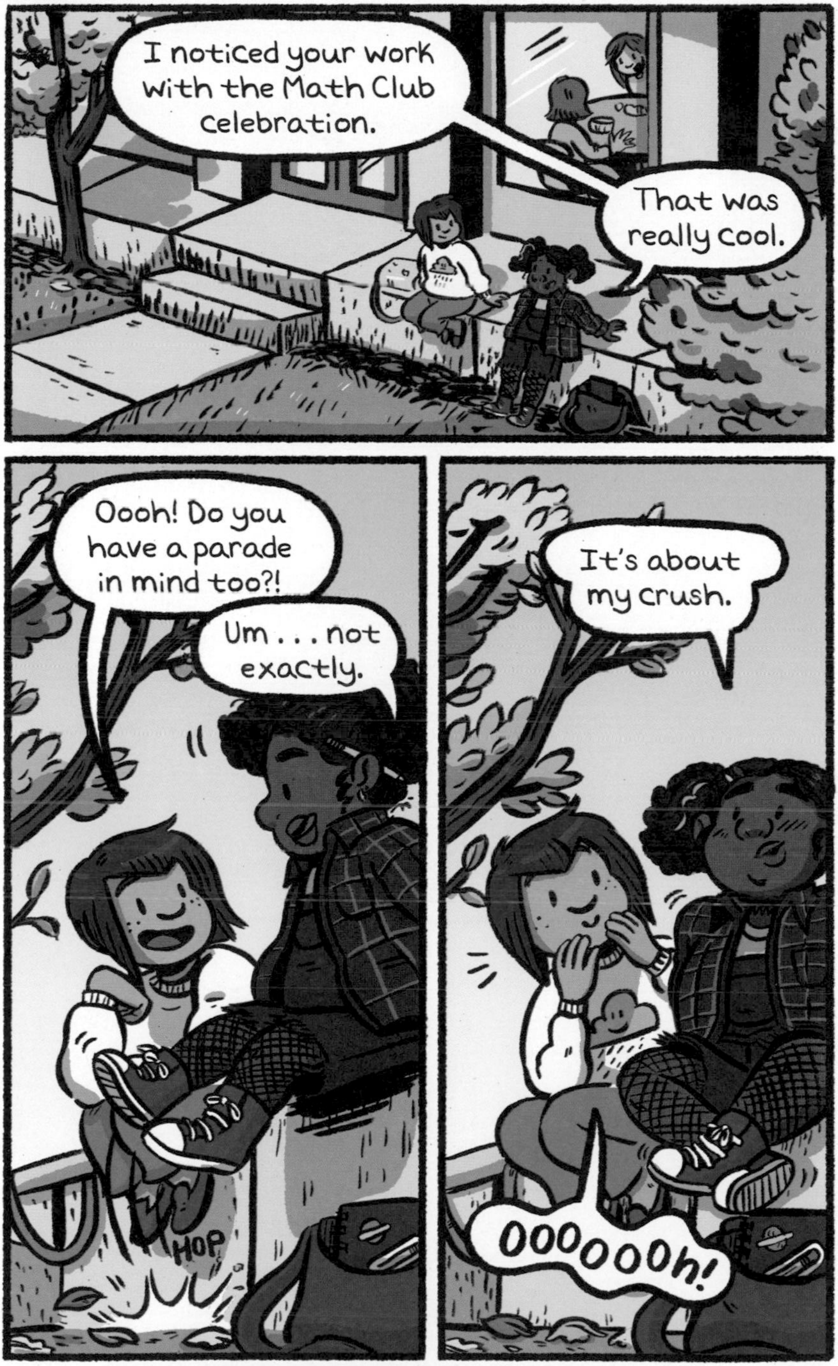
I noticed your work with the Math Club celebration.
That was really cool.
Oooh! Do you have a parade in mind too?!
Um . . . not exactly.
HOP
It's about my crush.
OOOOOOh!

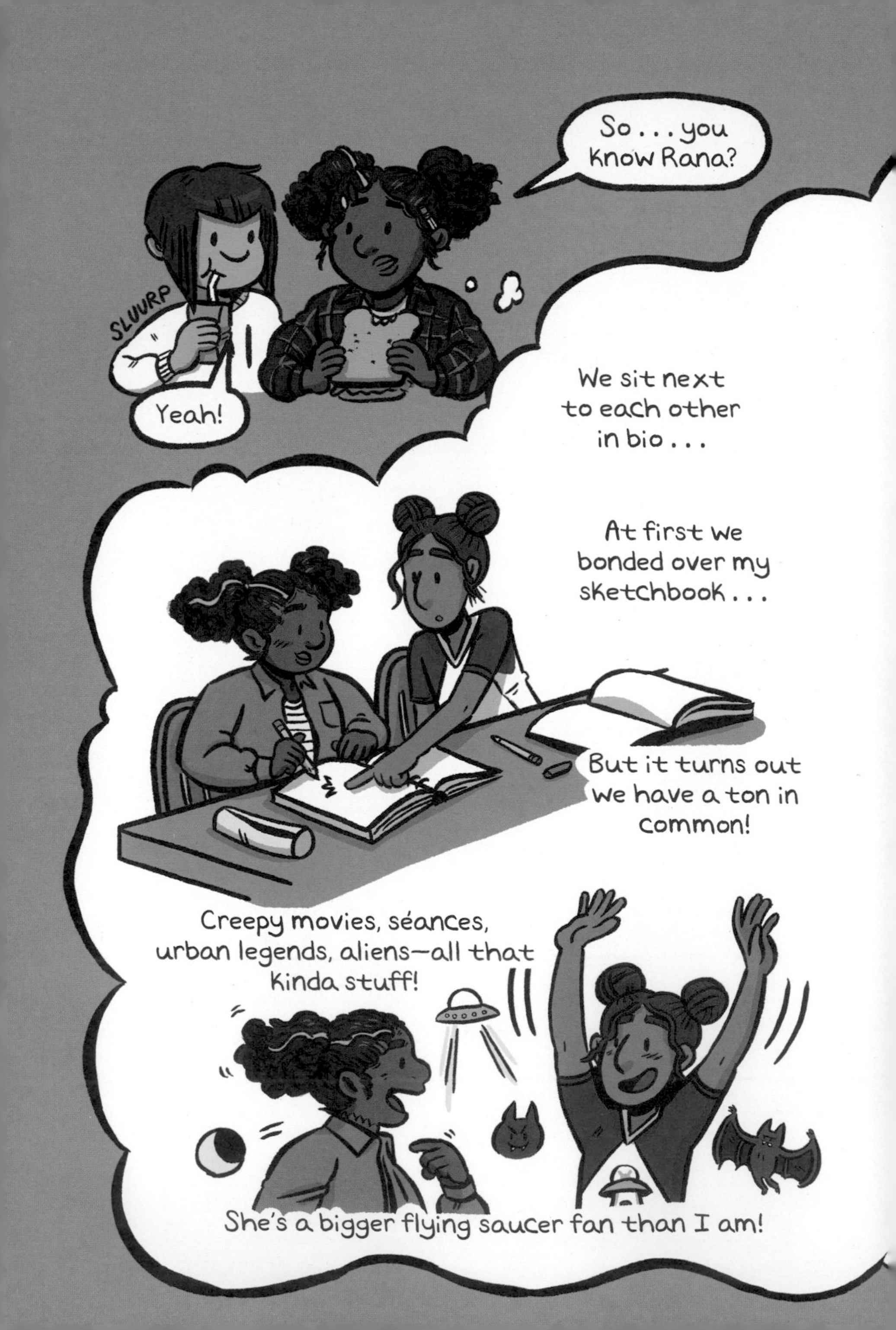
So . . . you know Rana?
SLUURP
Yeah!
We sit next to each other in bio . . .
At first we bonded over my sketchbook . . .
But it turns out we have a ton in common!
Creepy movies, séances, urban legends, aliens—all that kinda stuff!
She's a bigger flying saucer fan than I am!

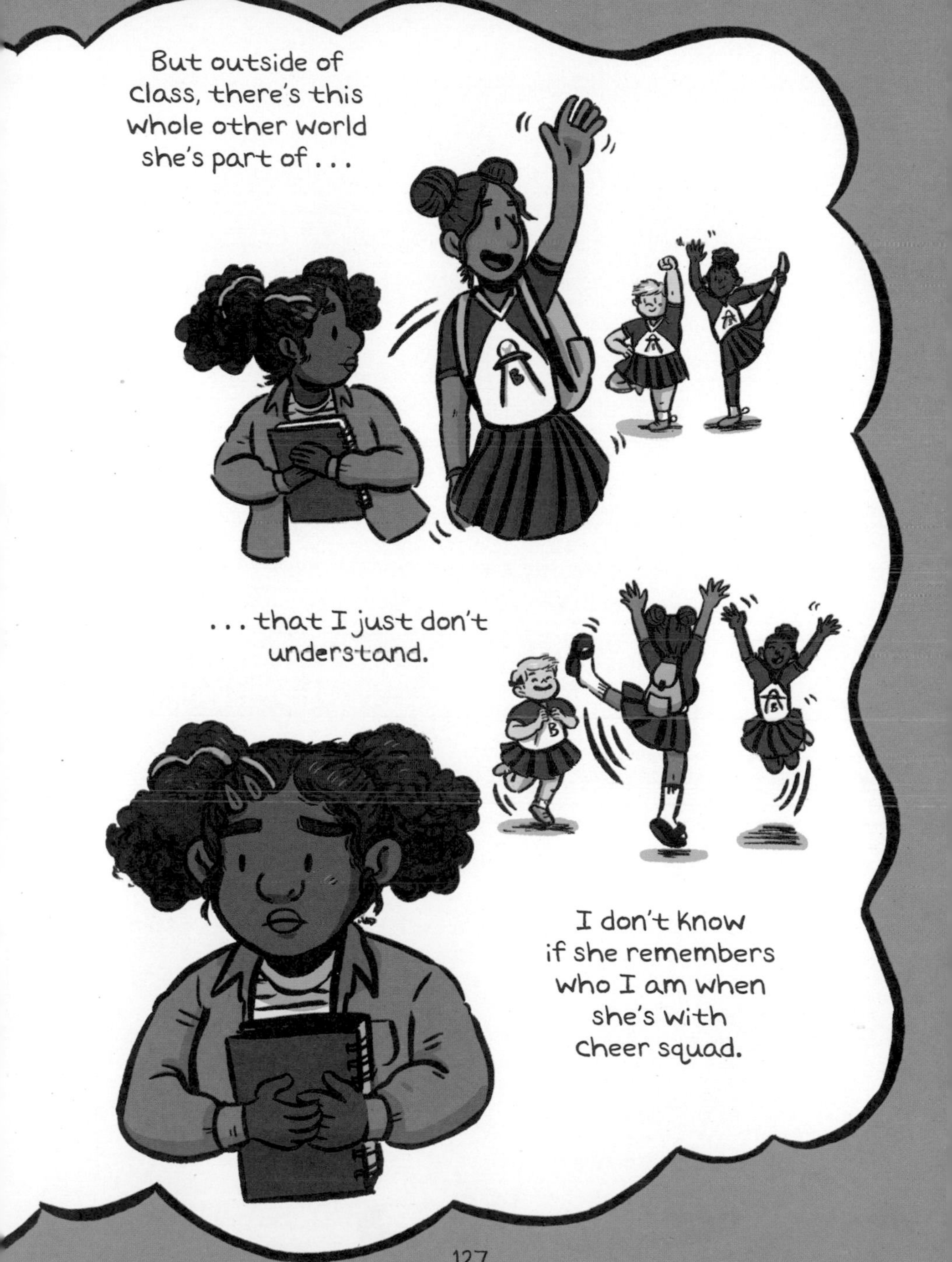

But outside of class, there's this whole other world she's part of . . .
. . . that I just don't understand.
I don't know if she remembers who I am when she's with cheer squad.

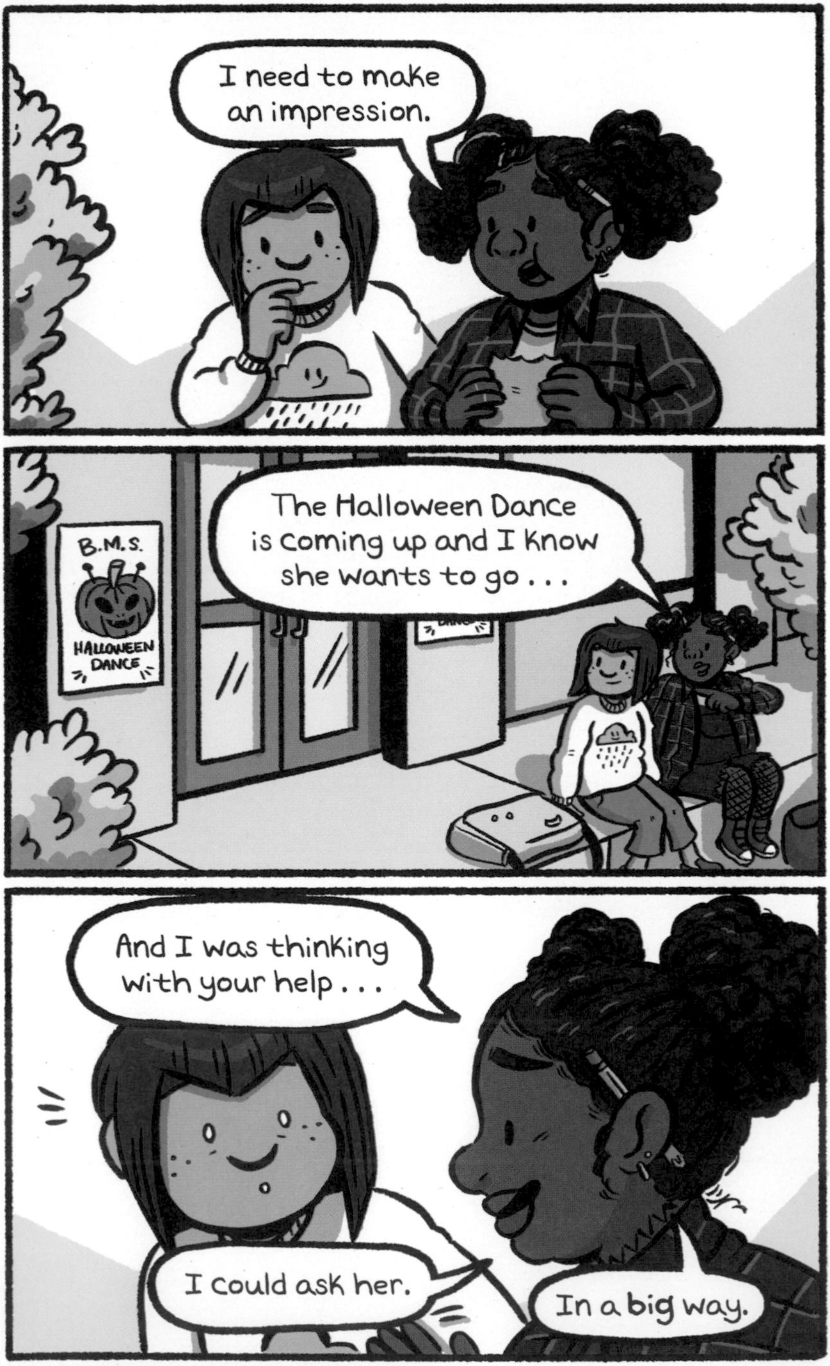
I need to make an impression.
B.M.S.
HALLOWEEN DANCE
The Halloween Dance is coming up and I know she wants to go . . .
And I was thinking with your help . . .
I could ask her.
In a big way.

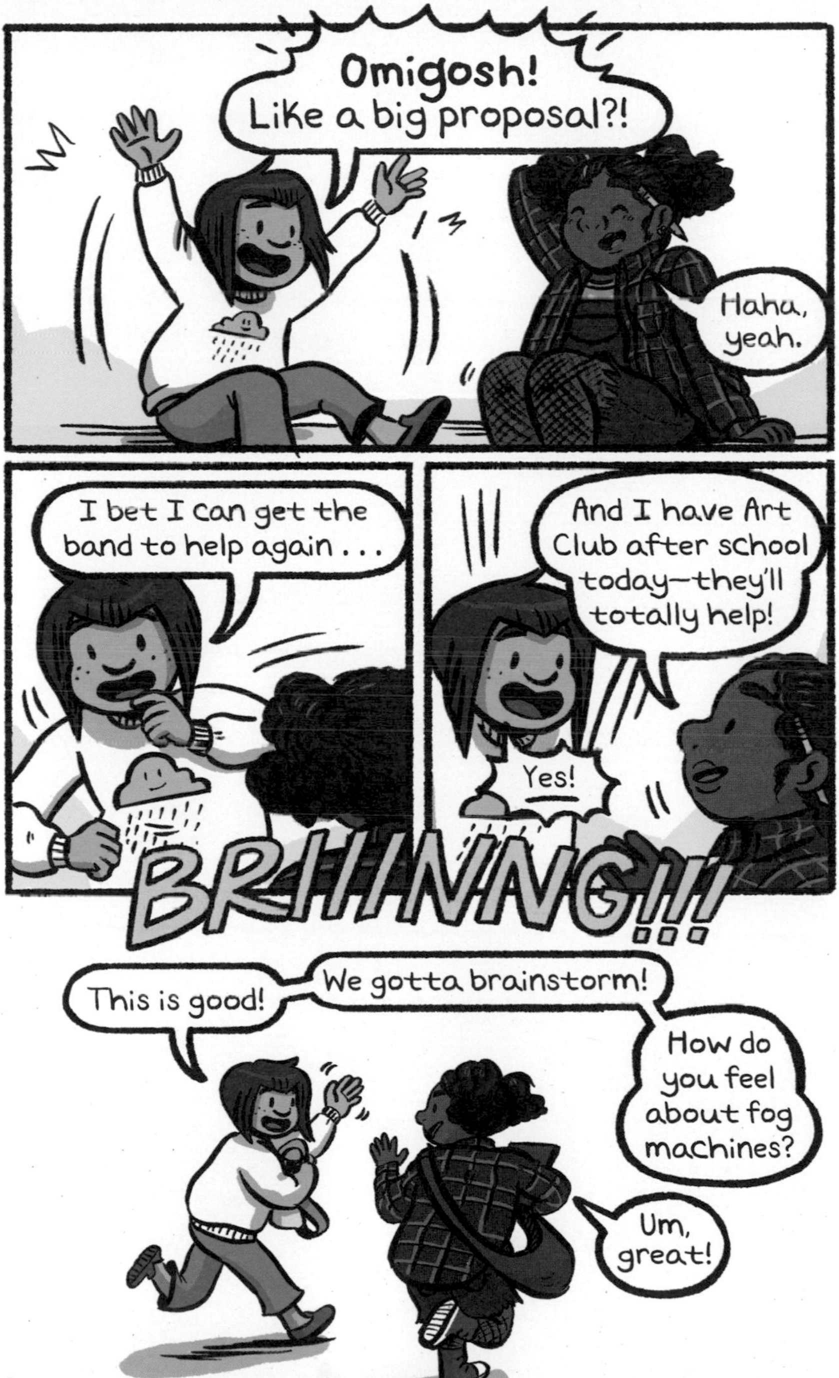
Omigosh!
Like a big proposal?!
Haha, yeah.
I bet I can get the band to help again . . .
And I have Art Club after school today—they'll totally help!
Yes!
BRIIINNG!!!
This is good!
We gotta brainstorm!
How do you feel about fog machines?
Um, great!

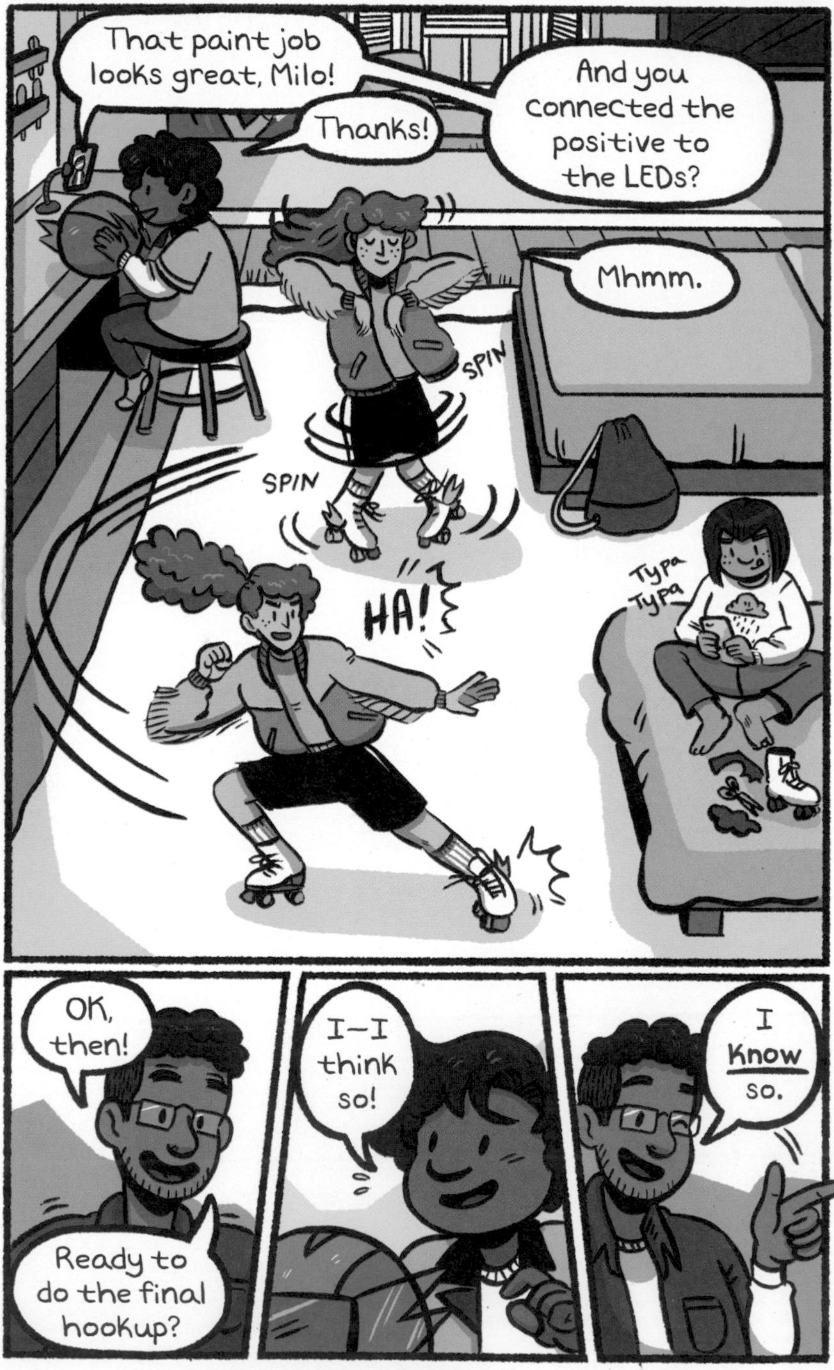
That paint job looks great, Milo!
Thanks!
And you connected the positive to the LEDs?
Mhmm.
SPIN
SPIN
HA!
Typa Typa
OK, then!
Ready to do the final hookup?
I—I think so!
I Know so.

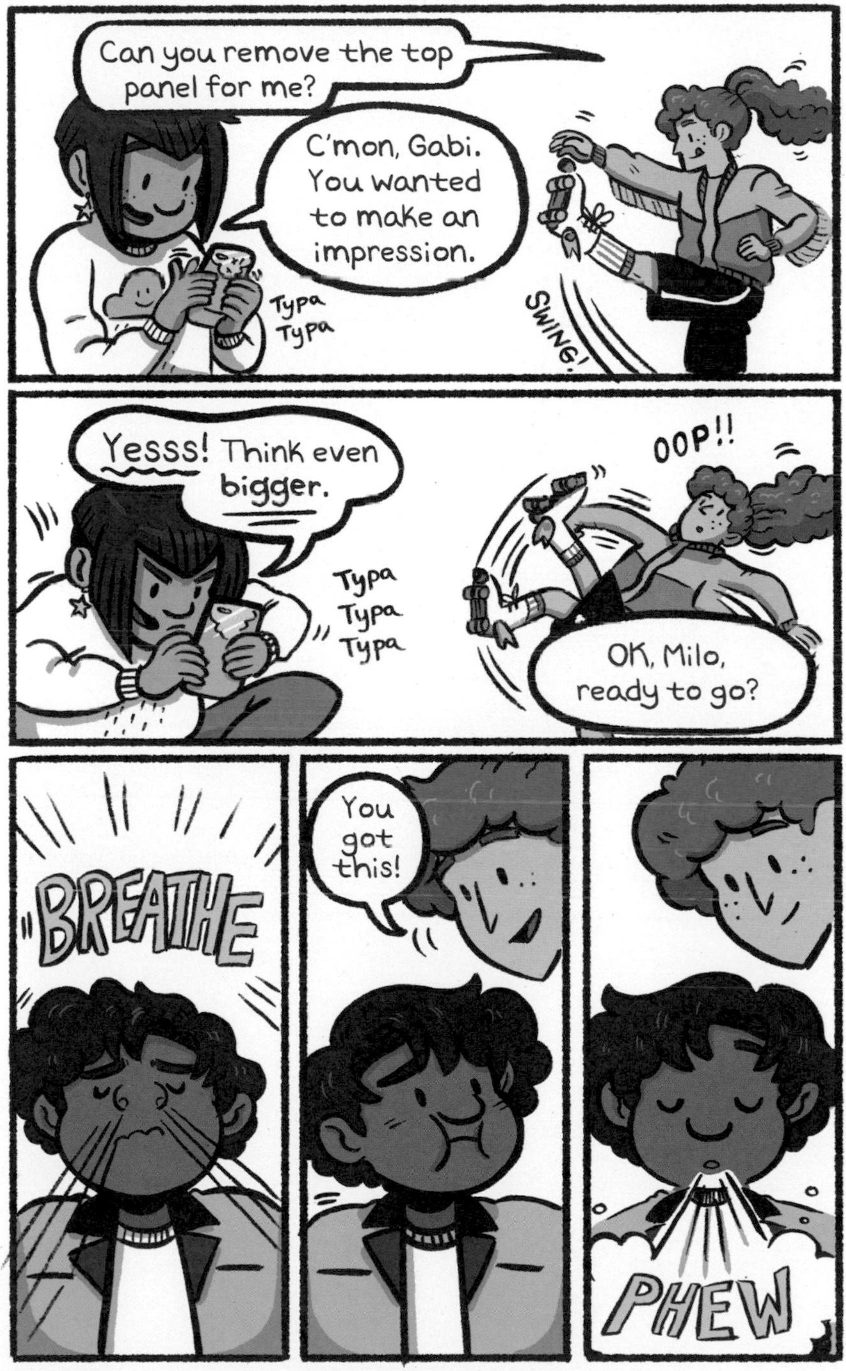
Can you remove the top panel for me?
C'mon, Gabi. You wanted to make an impression.
Typa Typa
SWING!
Yesss! Think even bigger.
Typa Typa Typa
OOP!!
OK, Milo, ready to go?
BREATHE
You got this!
PHEW

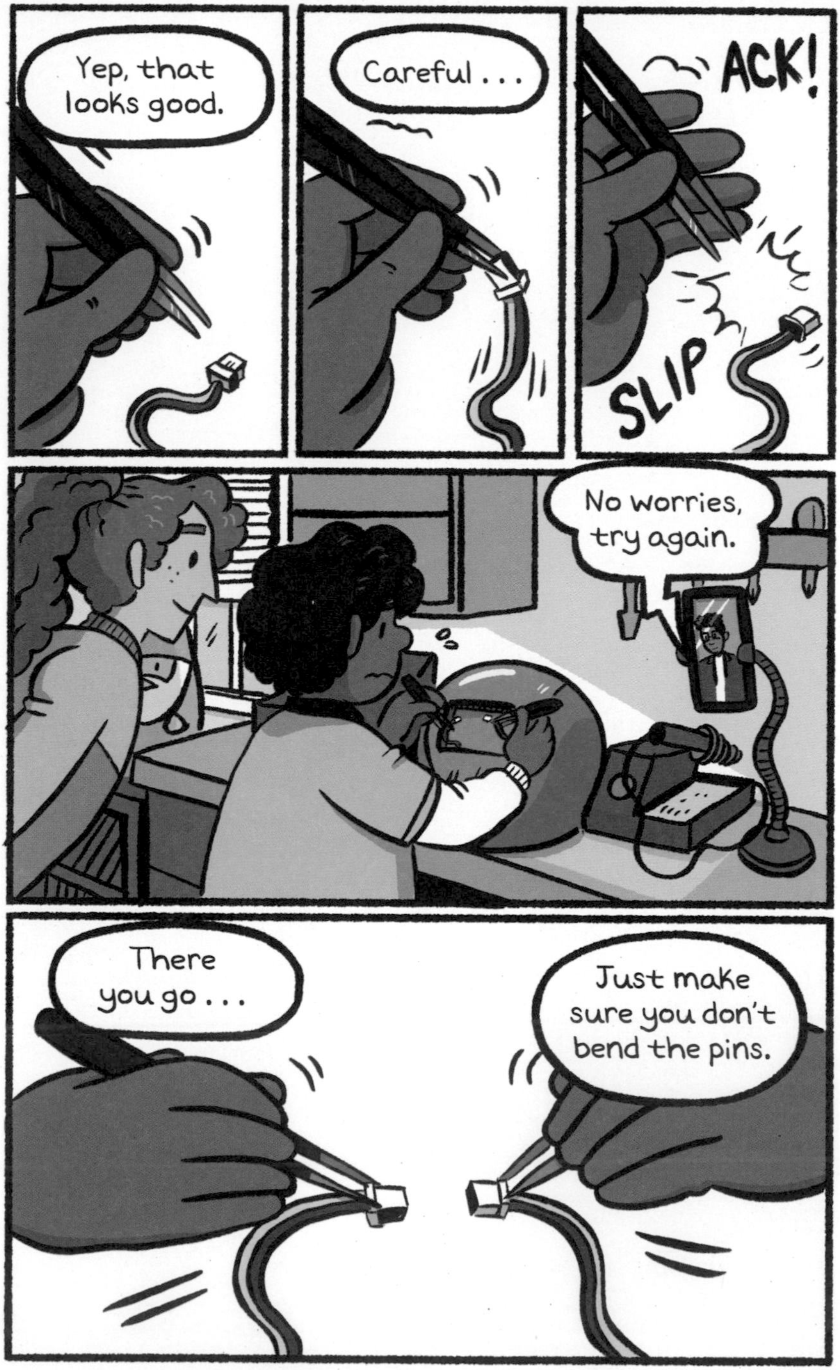
Yep, that looks good.
Careful . . .
ACK!
SLIP
No worries, try again.
There you go . . .
Just make sure you don't bend the pins.

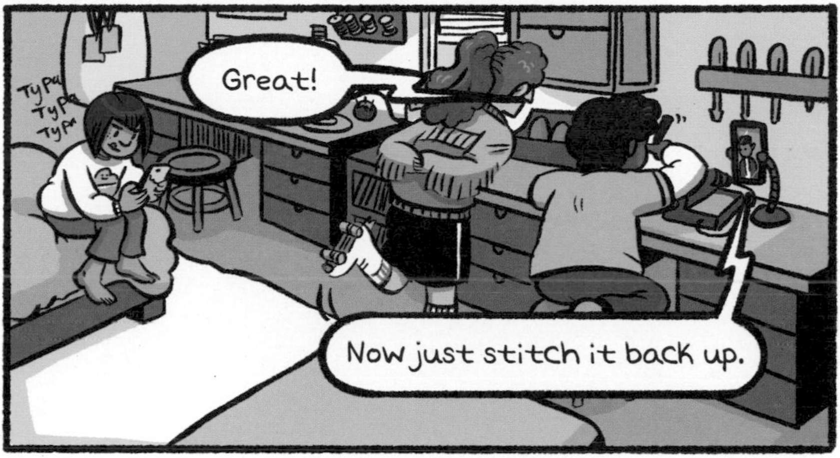
Typa
Typa
Typa
Great!
Now just stitch it back up.

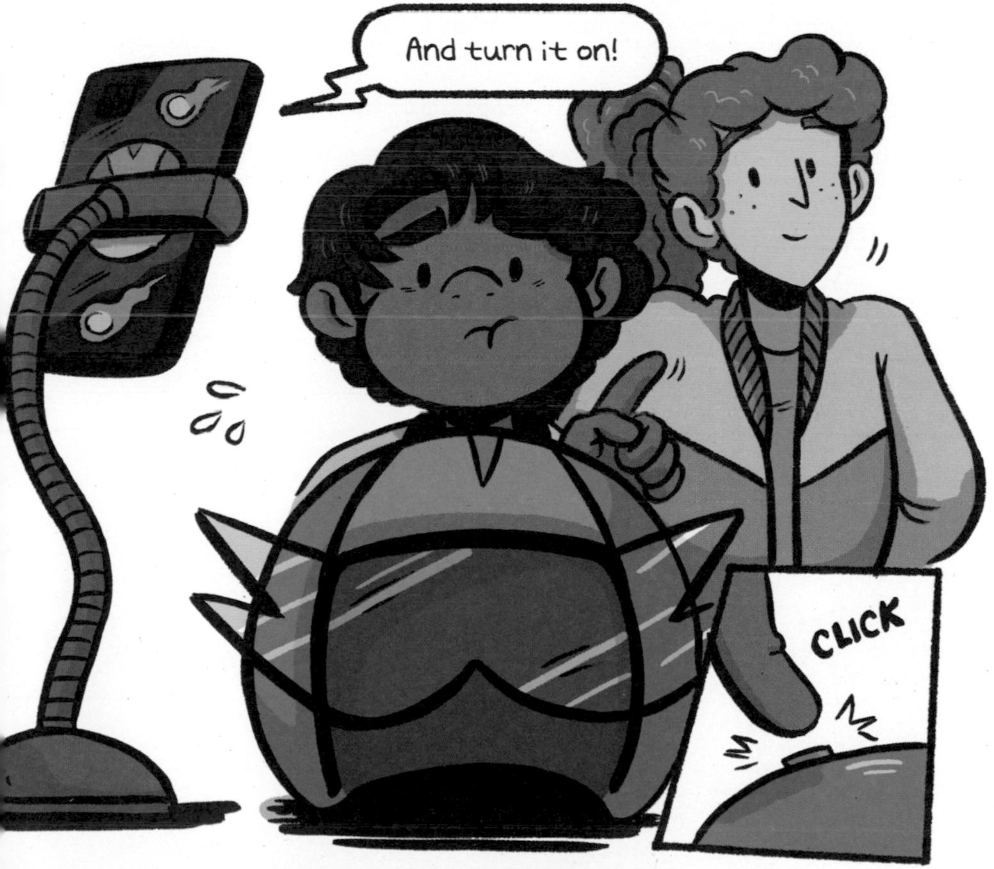
And turn it on!
CLICK

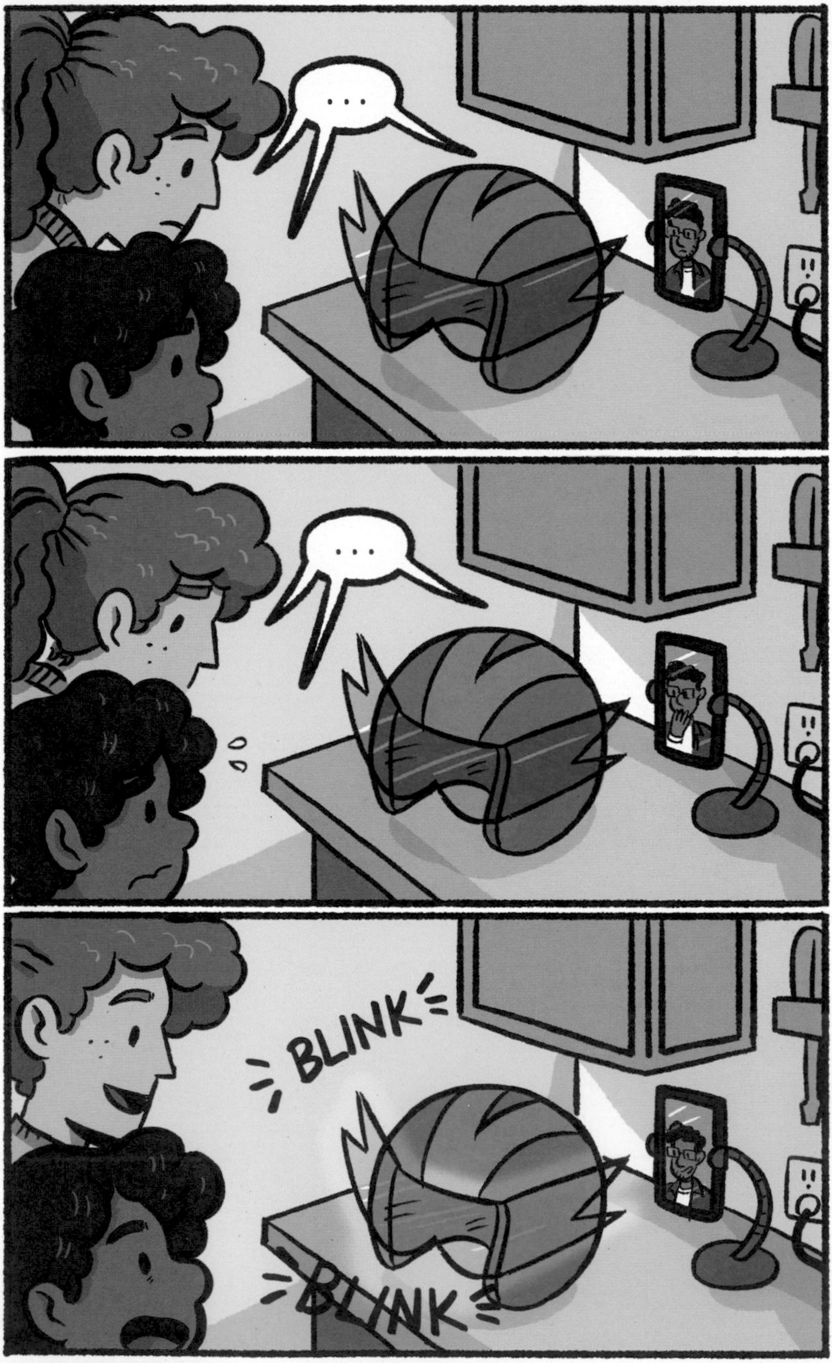
...
...
BLINK
BLINK

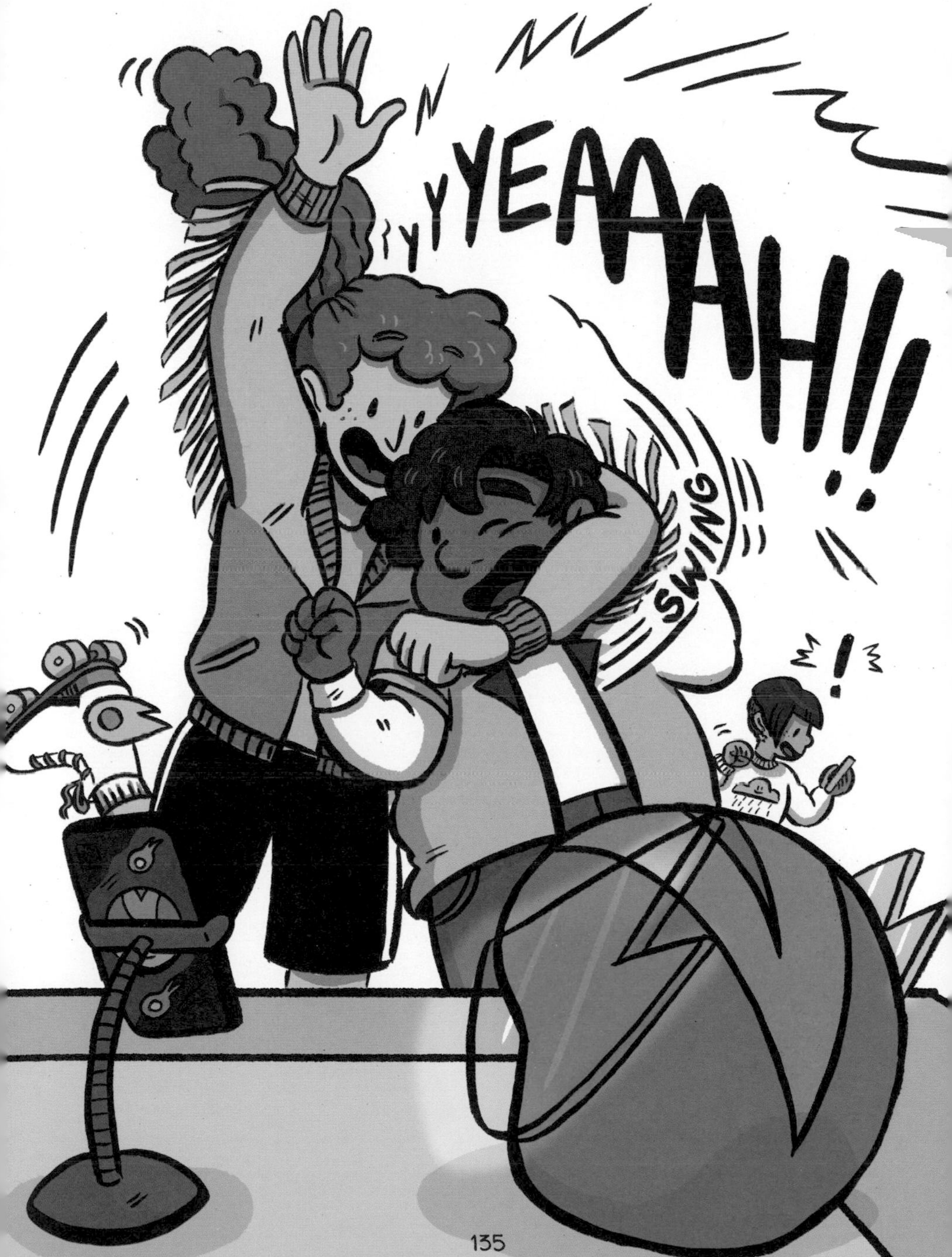
yyYEAAAAH!!!
SWING
!

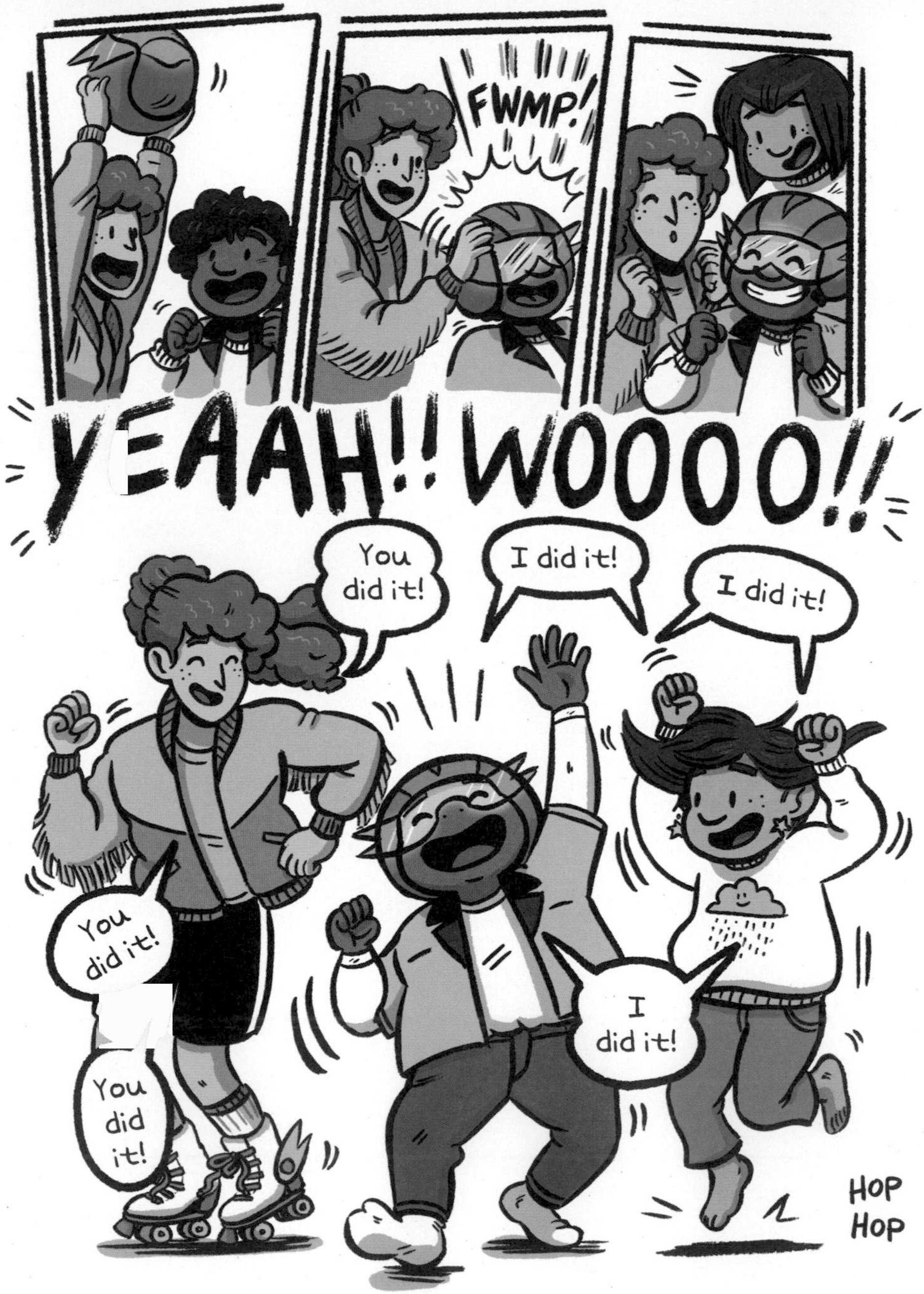
FWMP!
YEAAH!! WOOOO!!
You did it!
I did it!
I did it!
You did it!
I did it!
You did it!
HOP HOP

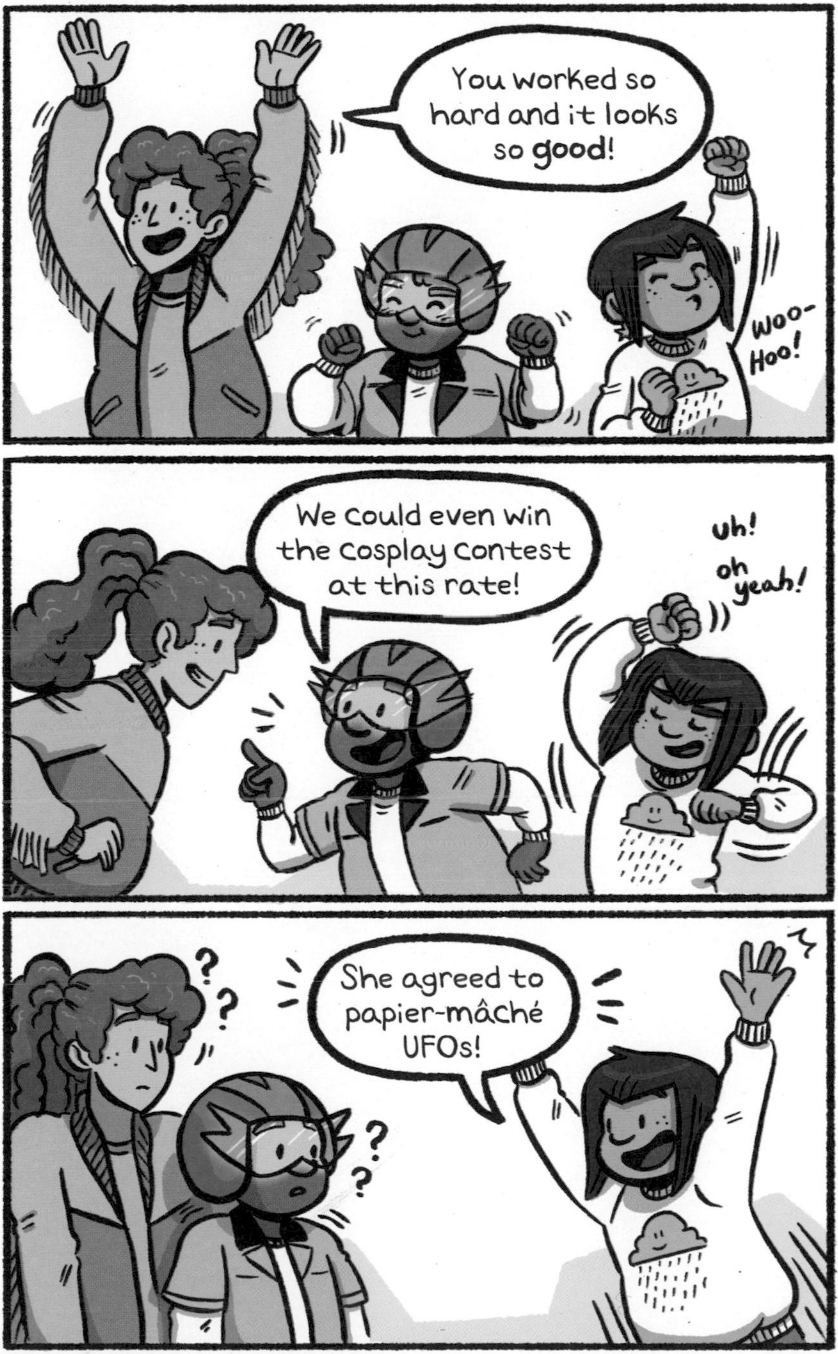
You worked so hard and it looks so good!
WOO-HOO!
We could even win the cosplay contest at this rate!
uh! oh yeah!
She agreed to papier-mâché UFOs!
?? ??

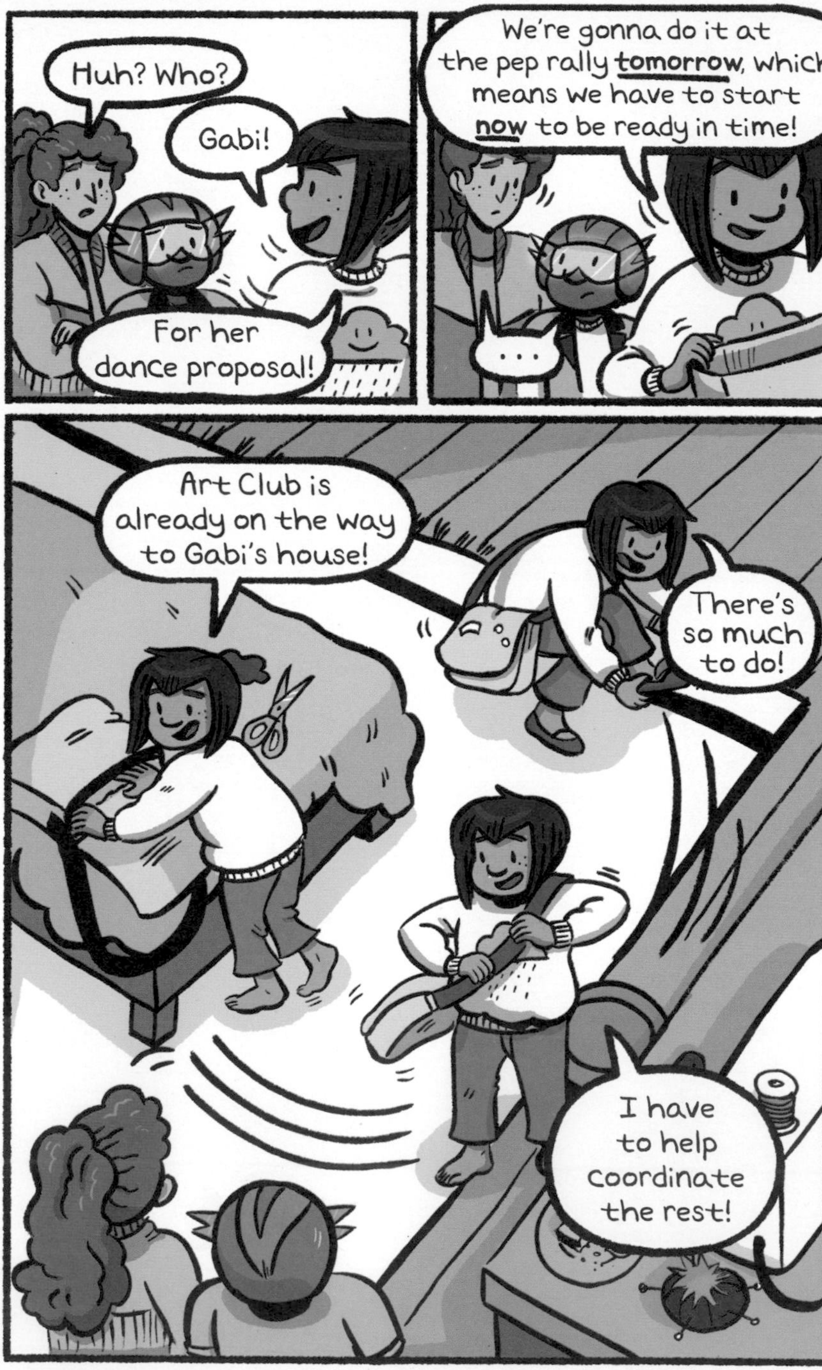
Huh? Who?
Gabi!
For her dance proposal!
We're gonna do it at the pep rally **tomorrow**, which means we have to start **now** to be ready in time!
...
Art Club is already on the way to Gabi's house!
There's so much to do!
I have to help coordinate the rest!

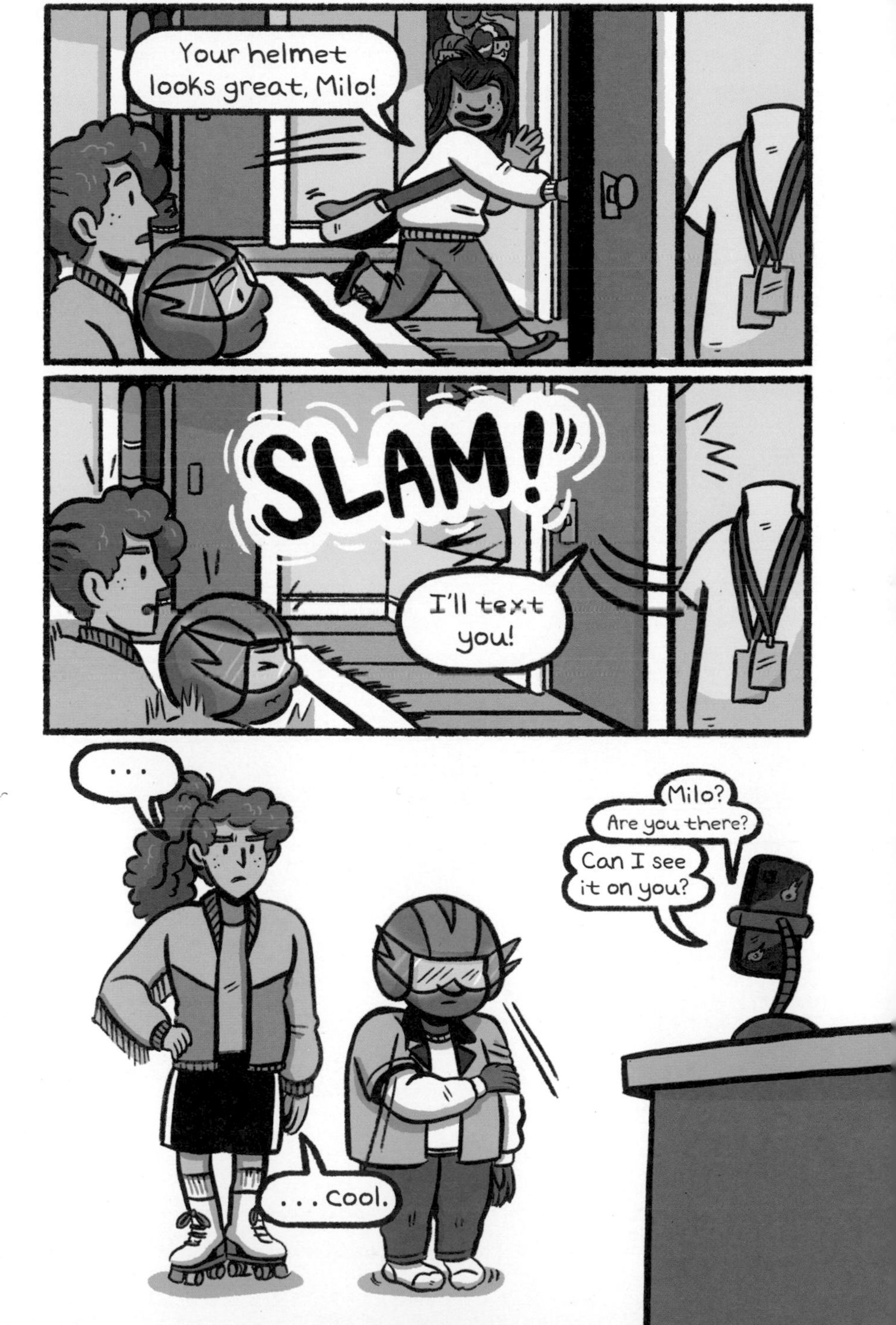
Your helmet looks great, Milo!
SLAM!
I'll text you!
...
Milo?
Are you there?
Can I see it on you?
...cool.

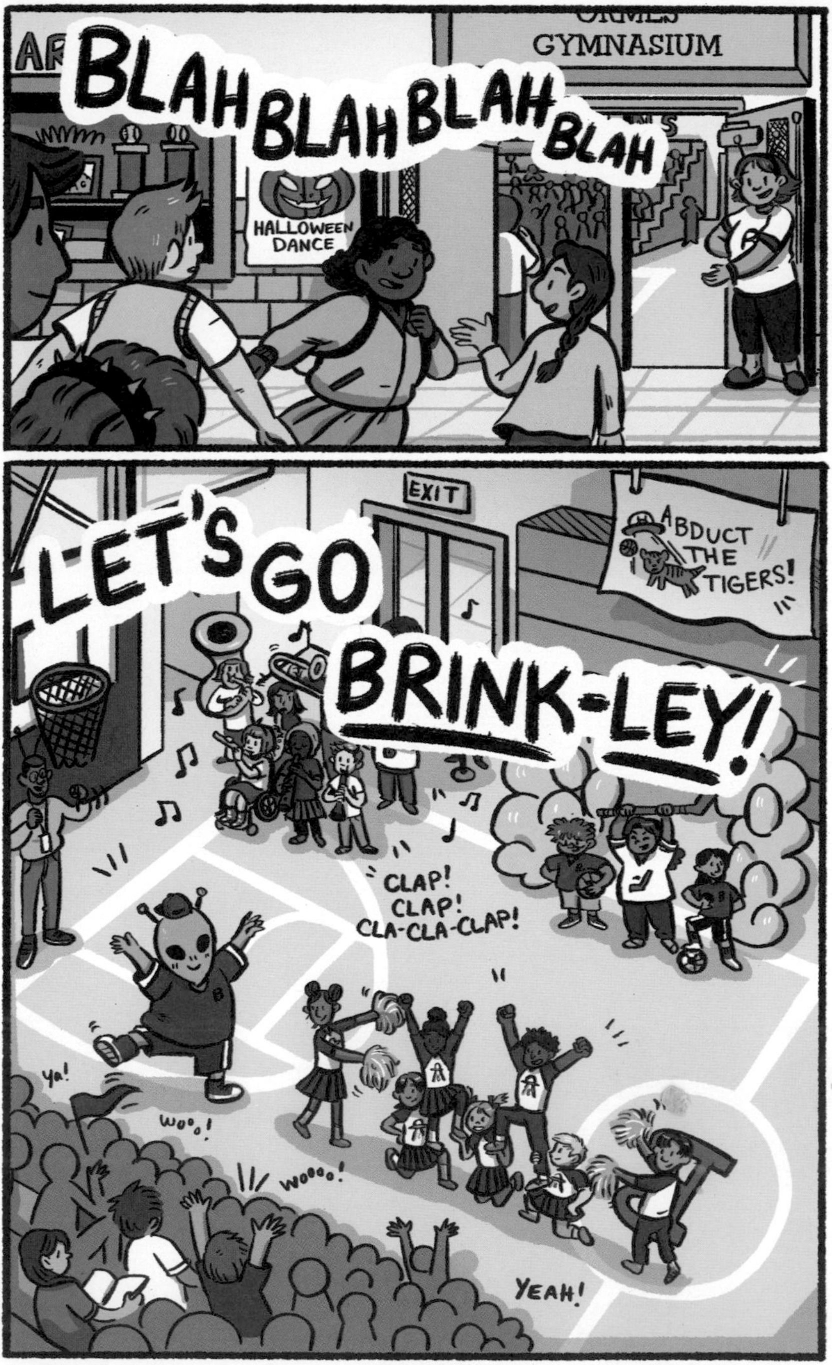
GYMNASIUM
BLAH BLAH BLAH BLAH
HALLOWEEN DANCE
EXIT
ABDUCT THE TIGERS!
LET'S GO BRINK-LEY!
CLAP! CLAP! CLA-CLA-CLAP!
ya!
wooo!
woooo!
YEAH!

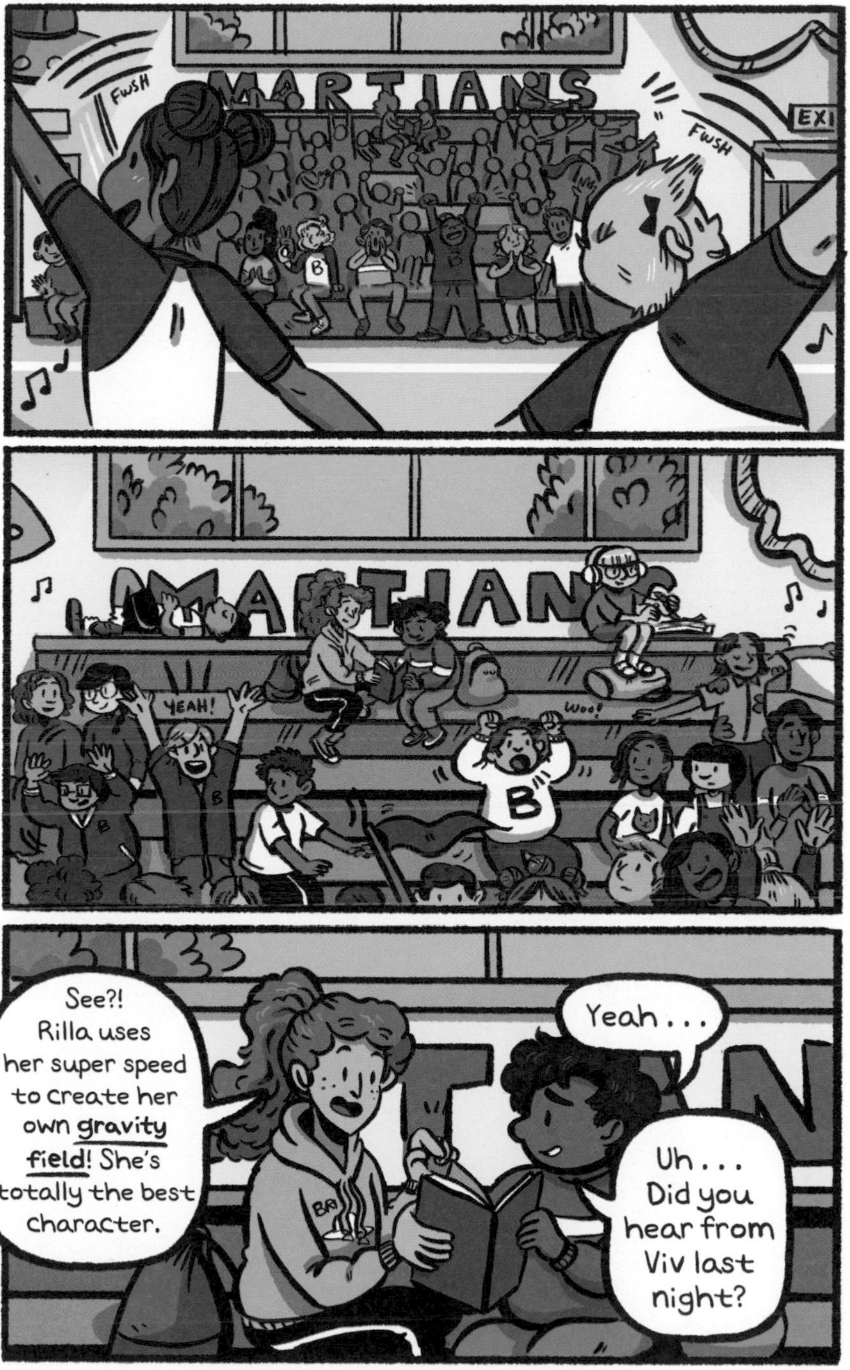
MARTIANS
FWSH
FWSH
EXI
B
B
MARTIANS
YEAH!
WOO!
B
See?! Rilla uses her super speed to create her own gravity field! She's totally the best character.
Yeah . . .
Uh . . . Did you hear from Viv last night?

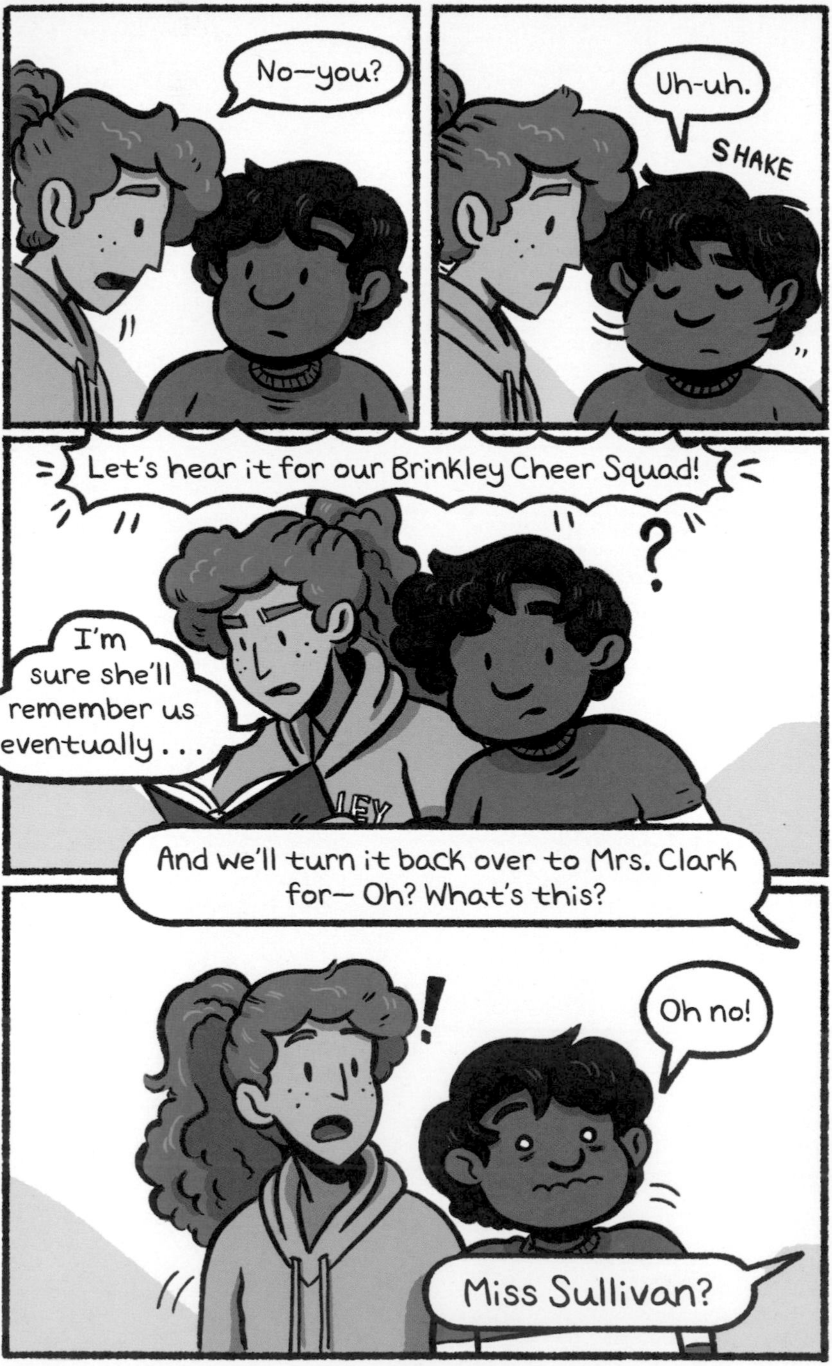
No—you?
Uh-uh.
SHAKE
Let's hear it for our Brinkley Cheer Squad!
?
I'm sure she'll remember us eventually . . .
And we'll turn it back over to Mrs. Clark for— Oh? What's this?
!
Oh no!
Miss Sullivan?

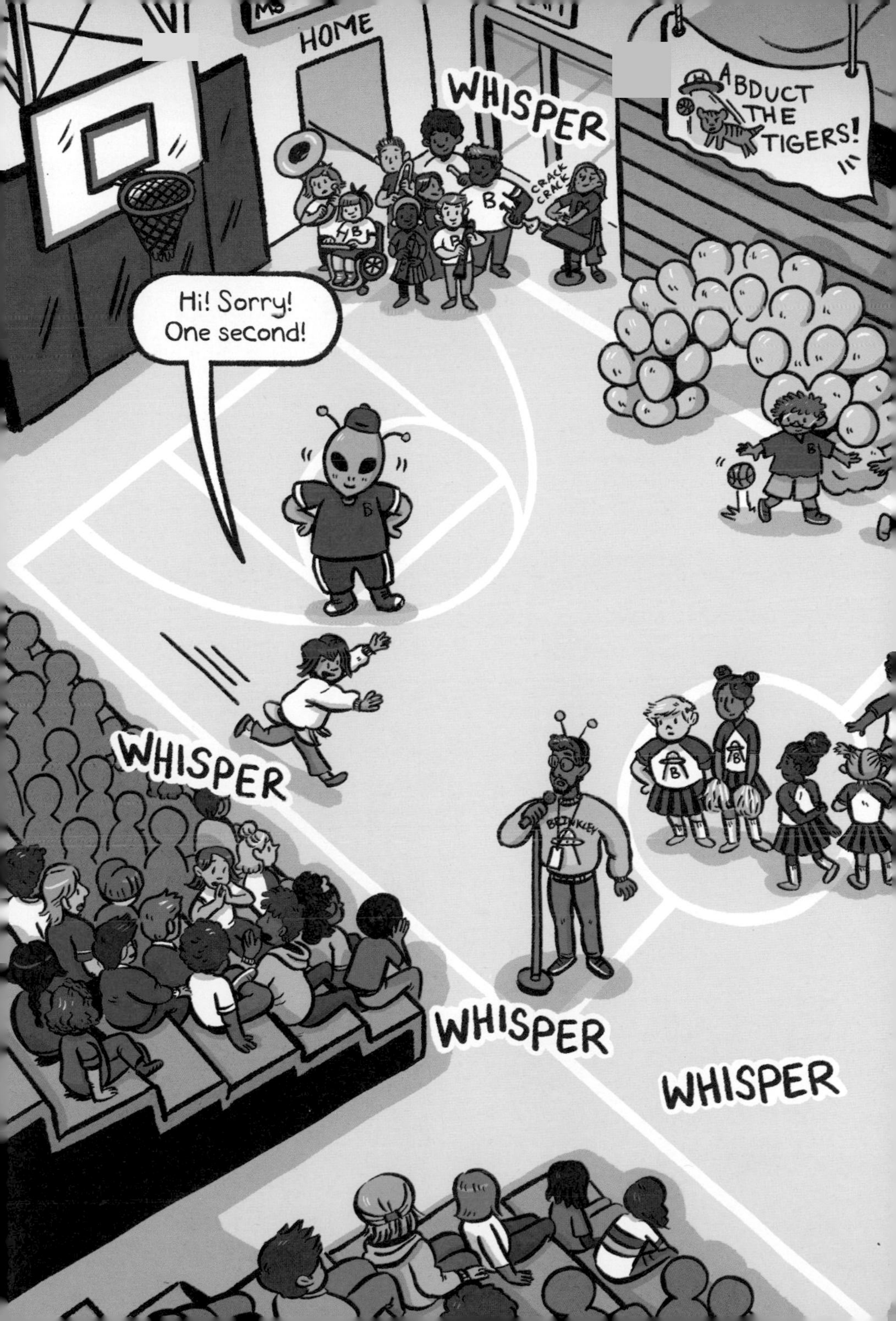
HOME
WHISPER
ABDUCT THE TIGERS!
CRACK CRACK
Hi! Sorry! One second!
WHISPER
BRINKLEY
WHISPER
WHISPER

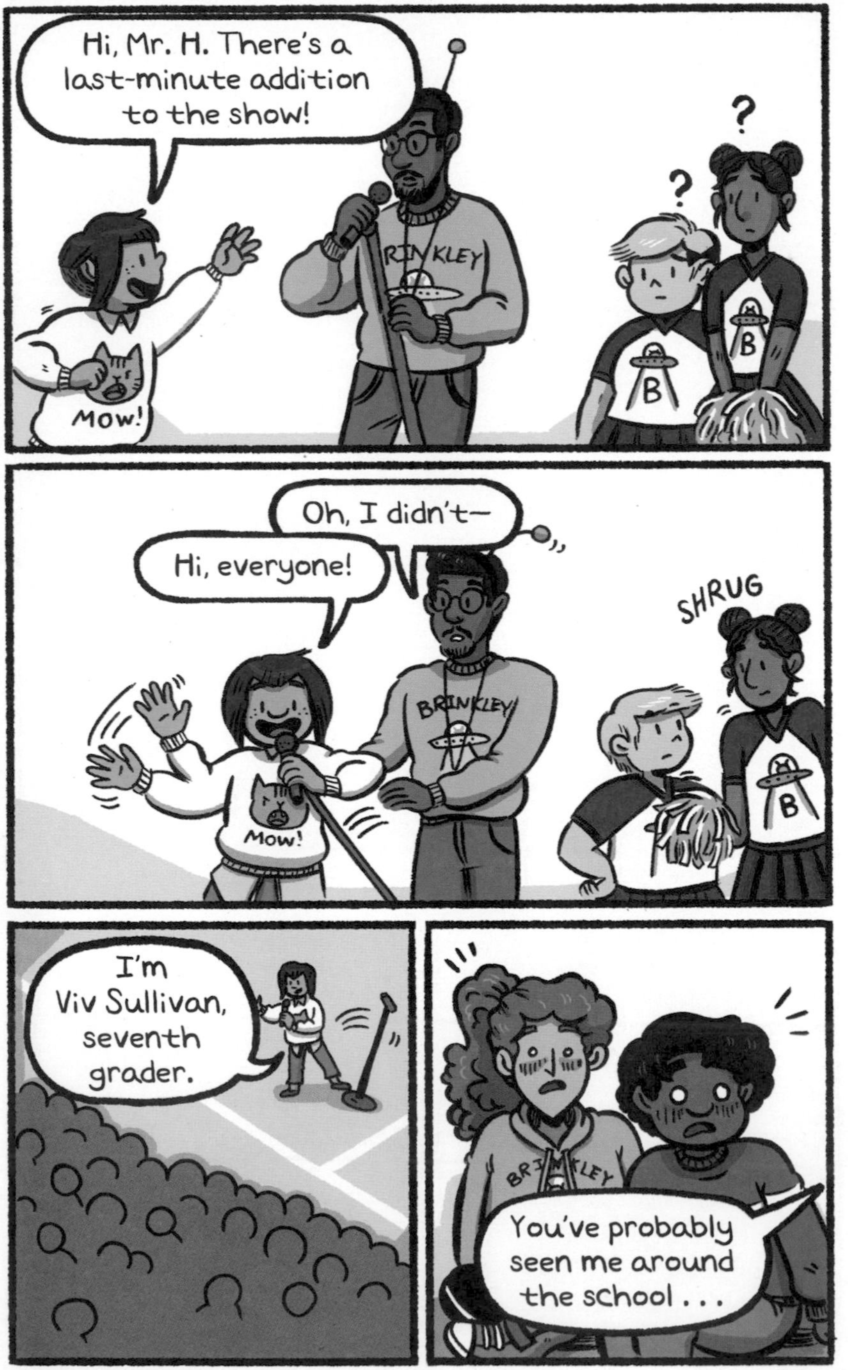
Hi, Mr. H. There's a last-minute addition to the show!
?
?
RINKLEY
B
B
MOW!
Oh, I didn't—
Hi, everyone!
SHRUG
BRINKLEY
MOW!
B
I'm Viv Sullivan, seventh grader.
BRINKLEY
You've probably seen me around the school . . .

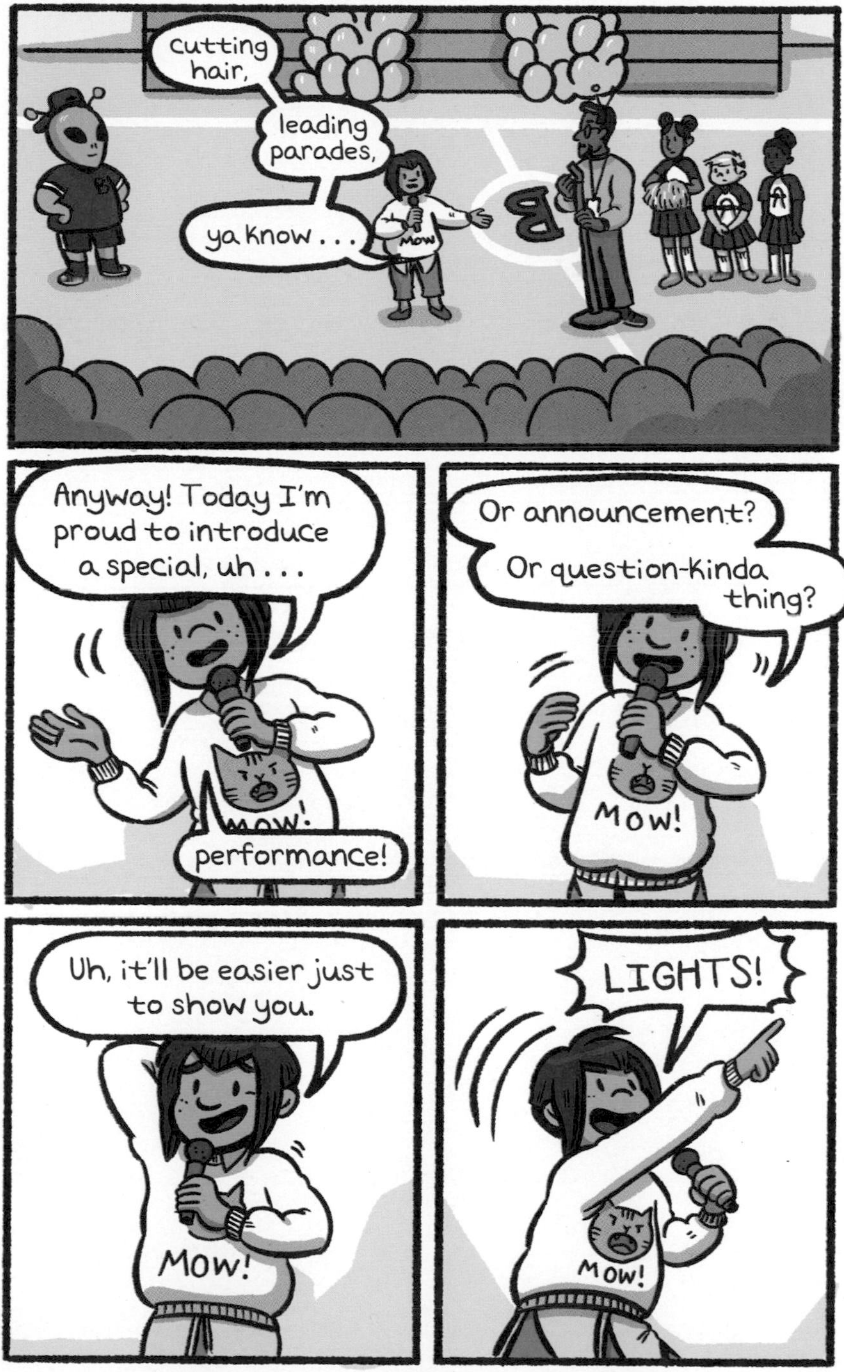
cutting hair,
leading parades,
ya know . . .
MOW
Anyway! Today I'm proud to introduce a special, uh . . .
MOW!
performance!
Or announcement?
Or question-kinda thing?
MOW!
Uh, it'll be easier just to show you.
MOW!
LIGHTS!
MOW!

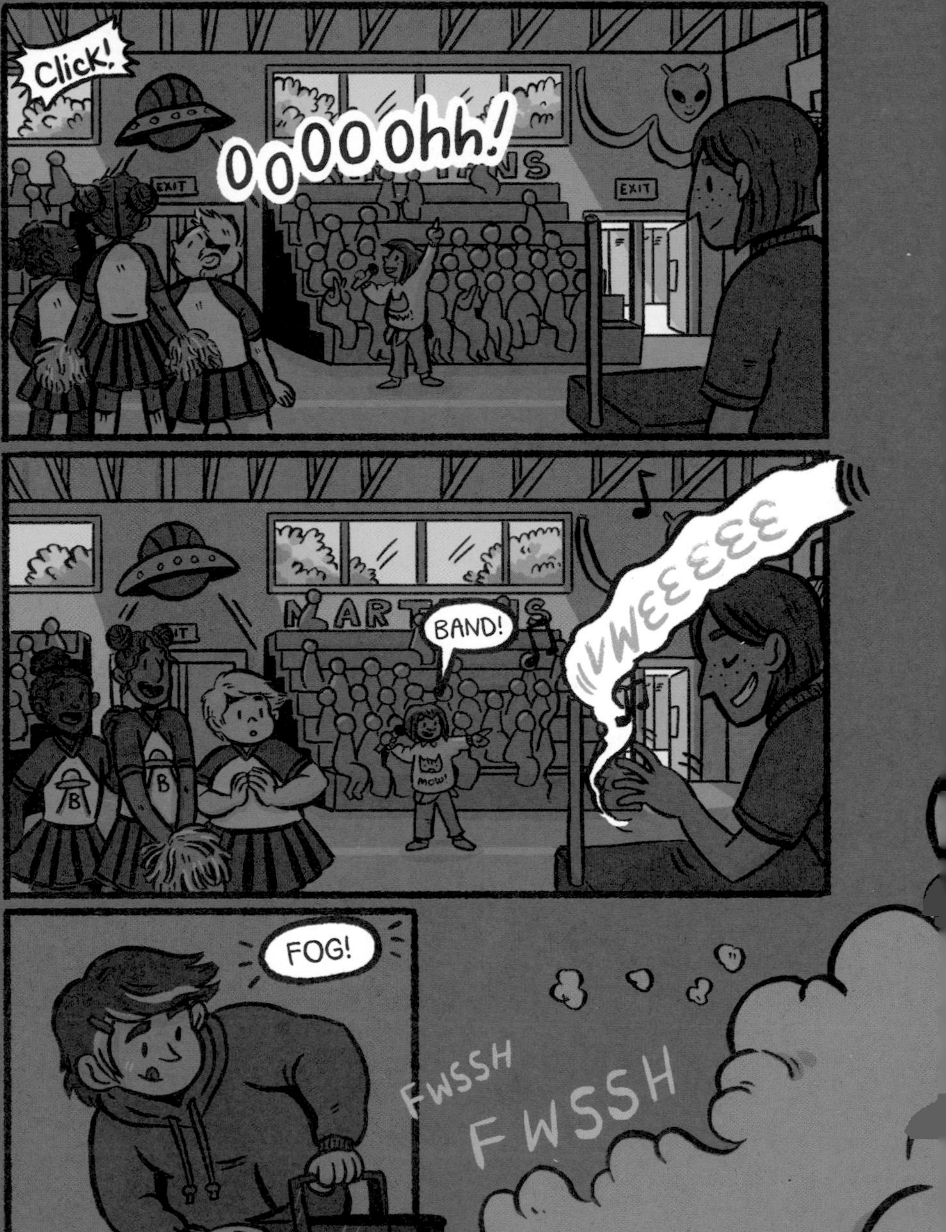
Click!
OOOOOhh!
BAND!
VWEEEEEE
FOG!
FWSSH
FWSSH

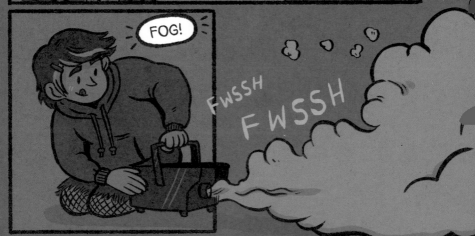

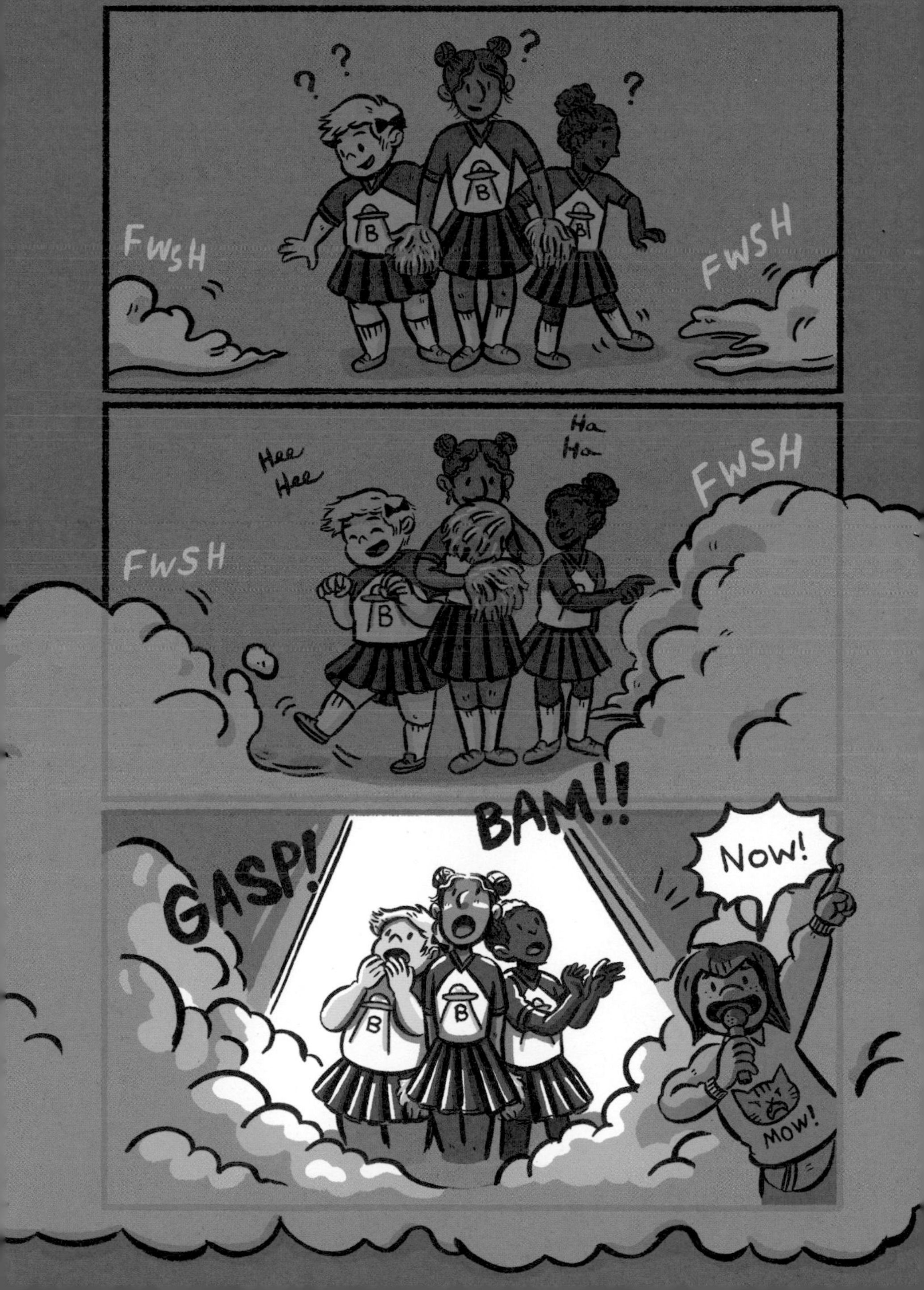
?
?
?
?
FWSH
FWSH
Hee Hee
Ha Ha
FWSH
FWSH
GASP!
BAM!!
Now!
MOW!

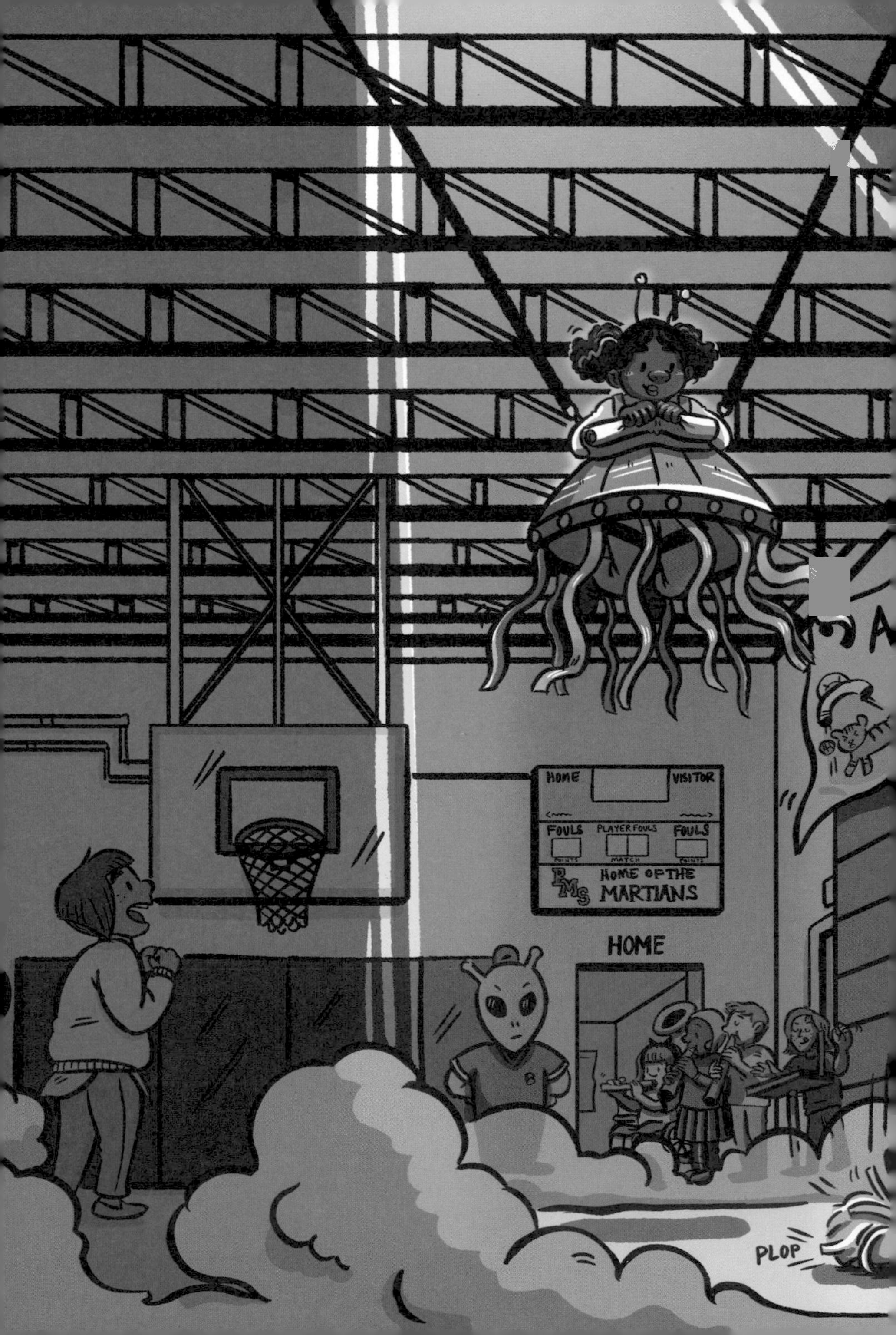
HOME
VISITOR
FOULS
PLAYER FOULS
FOULS
BMS
HOME OF THE
MARTIANS
HOME
PLOP

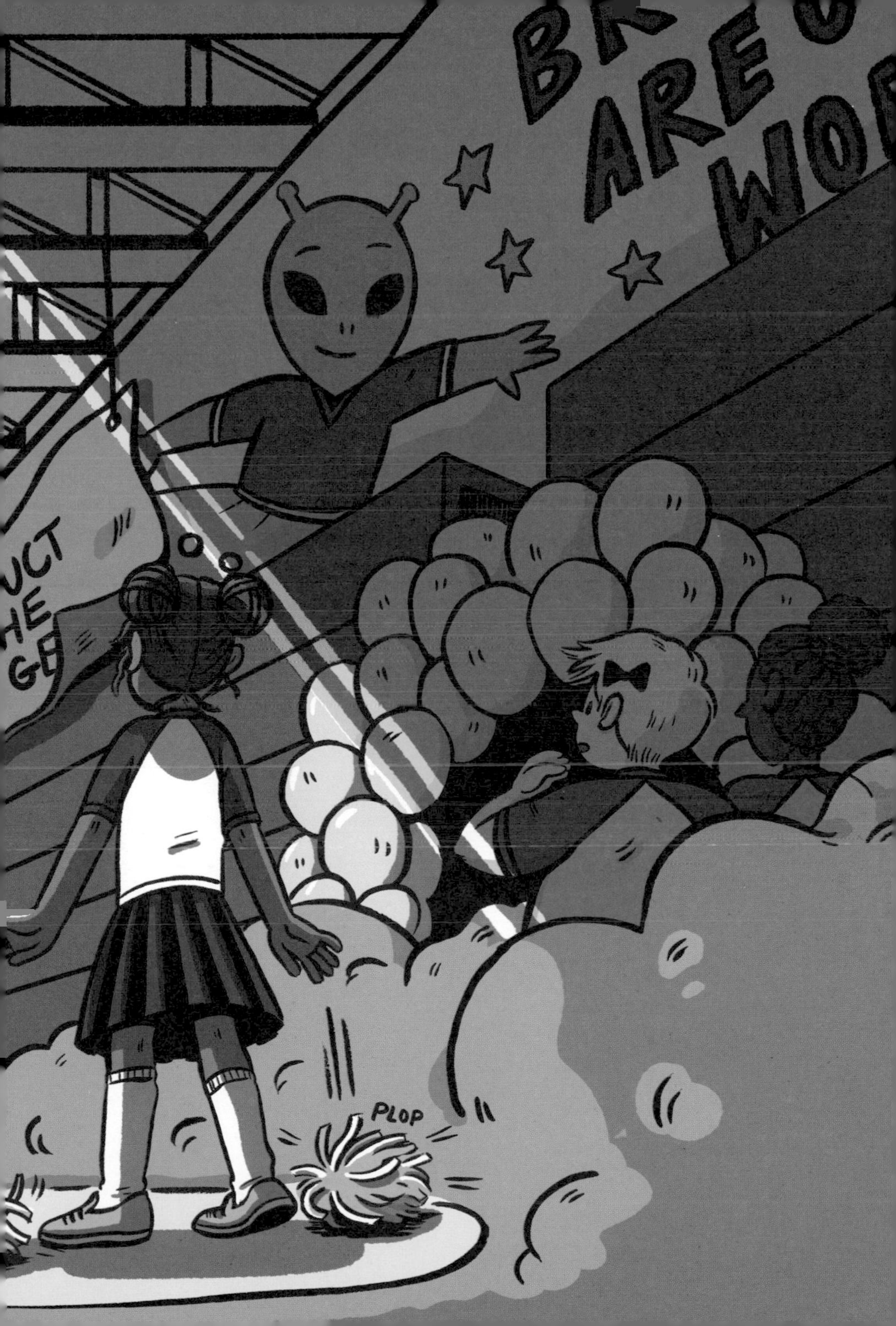
ARE
UCT
HE
GE
PLOP

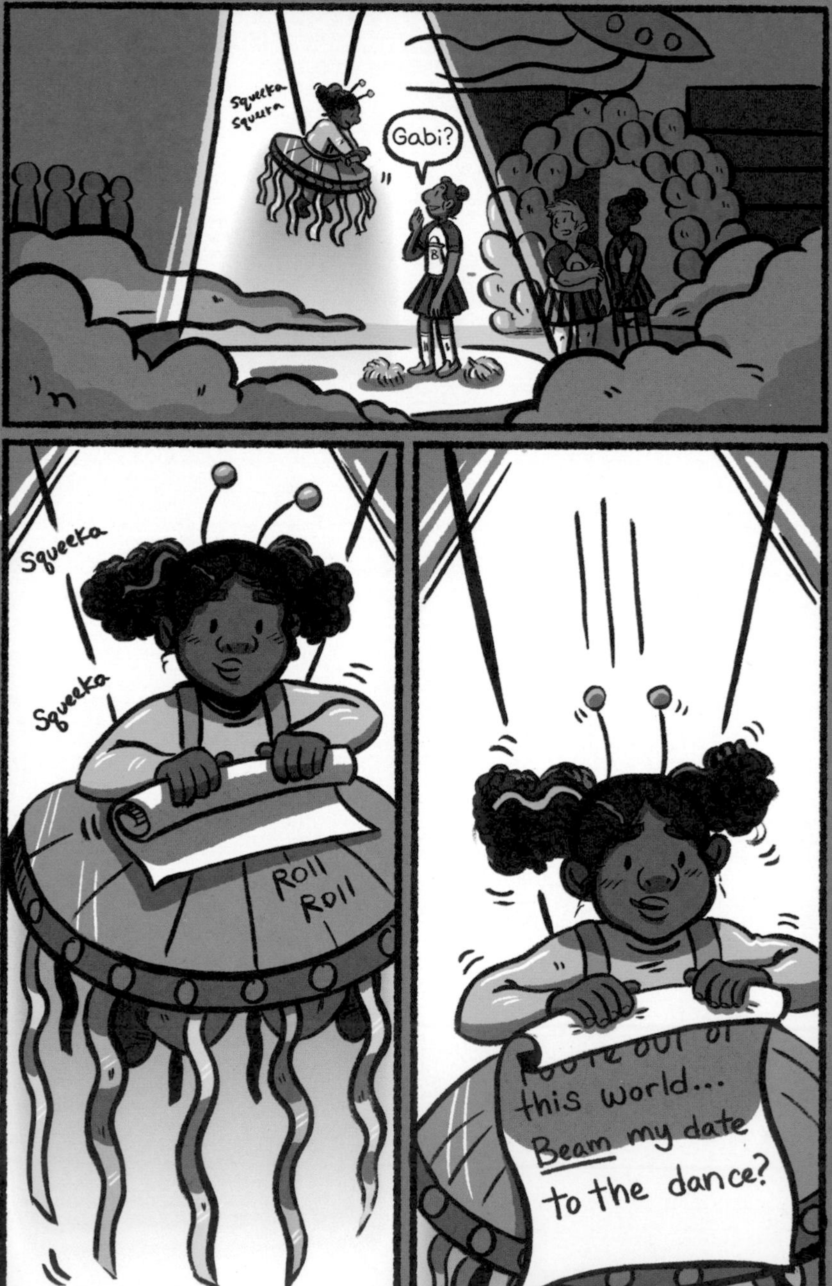

Squeeka
Squeeka
Gabi?
Squeeka
Squeeka
Roll
Roll
this world...
Beam my date
to the dance?
Roll Roll

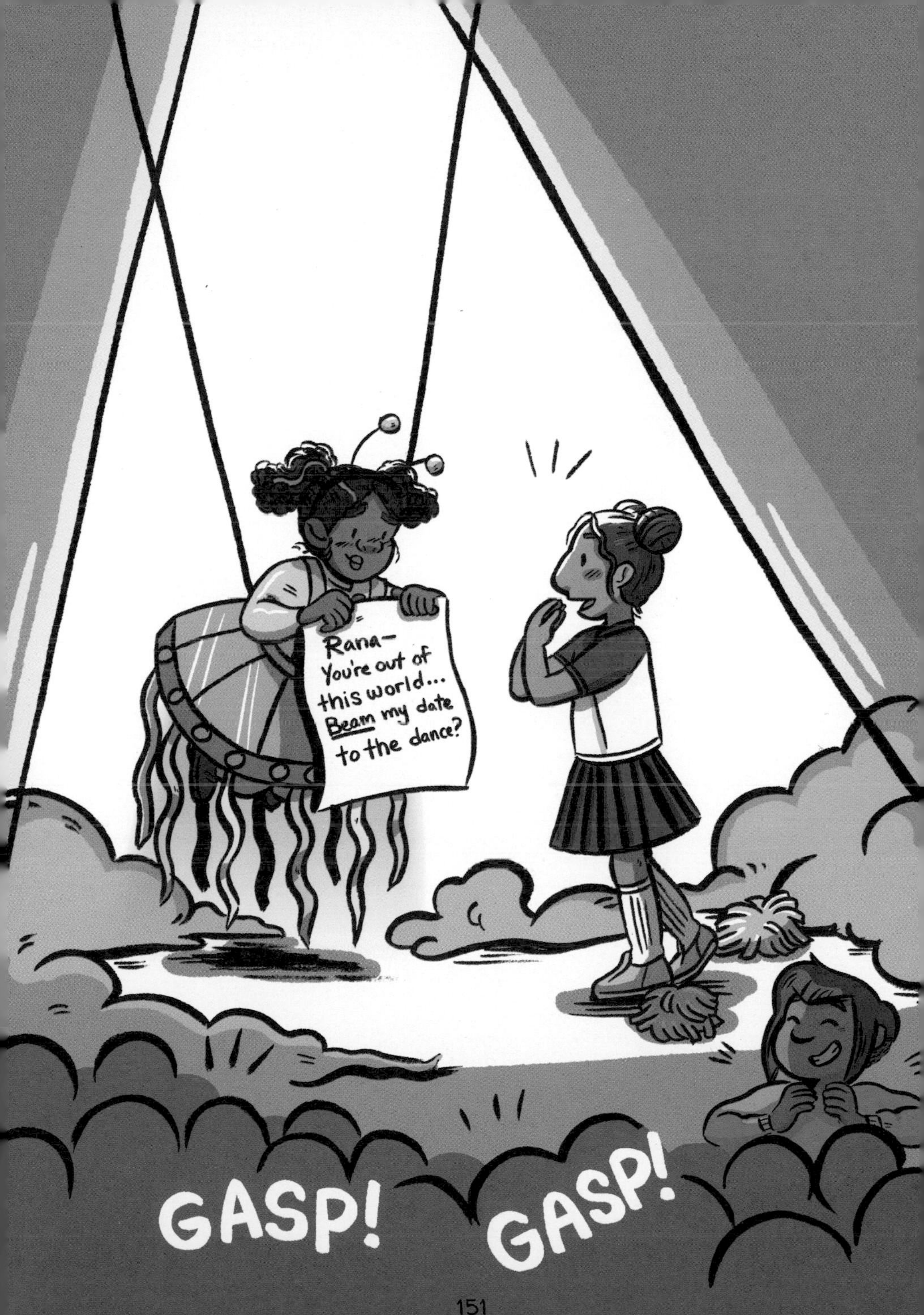
Rana-
You're out of this world...
Beam my date to the dance?
GASP!
GASP!

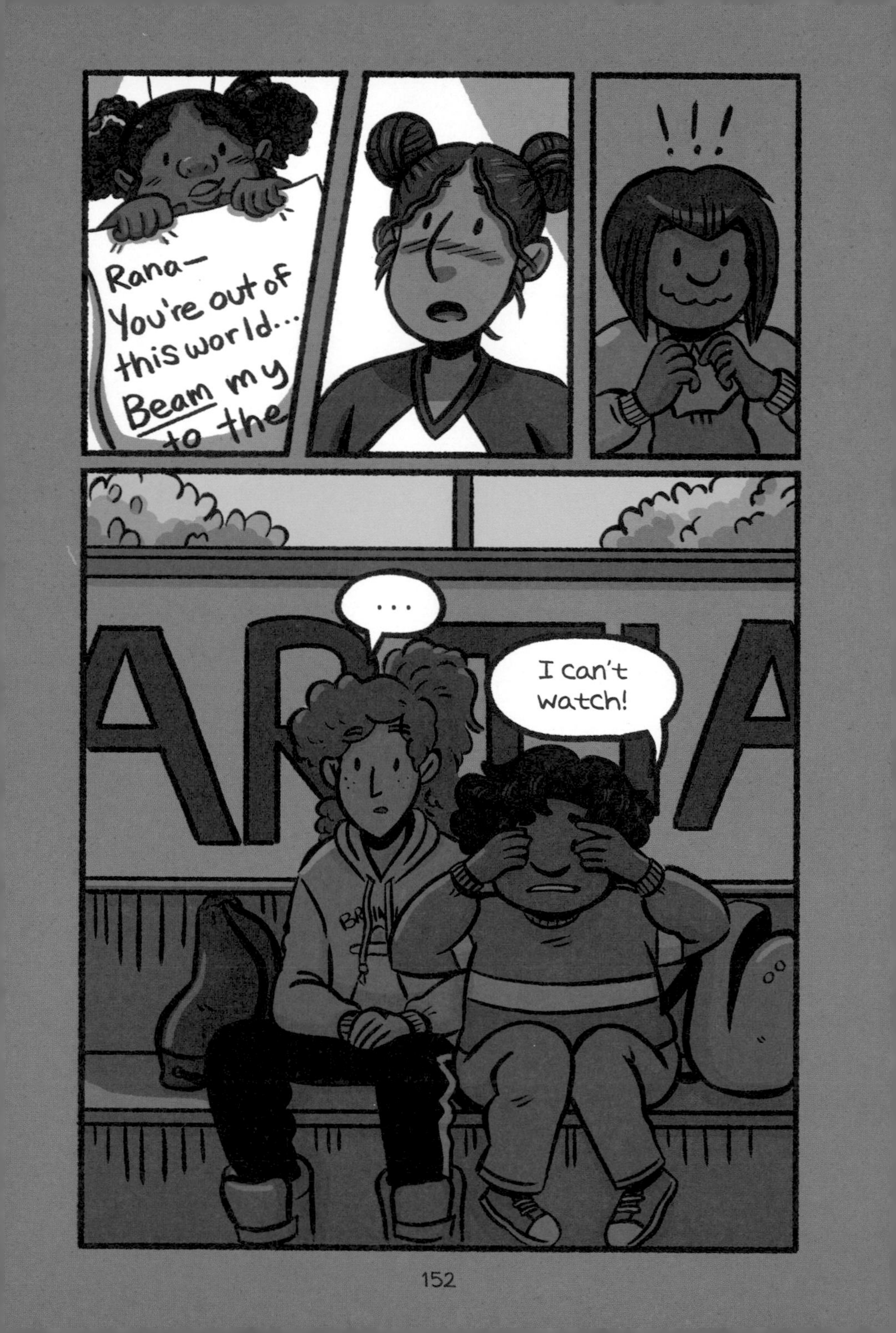
Rana—
You're out of
this world...
this world...
Beam my
to the
!!!
...
I can't watch!

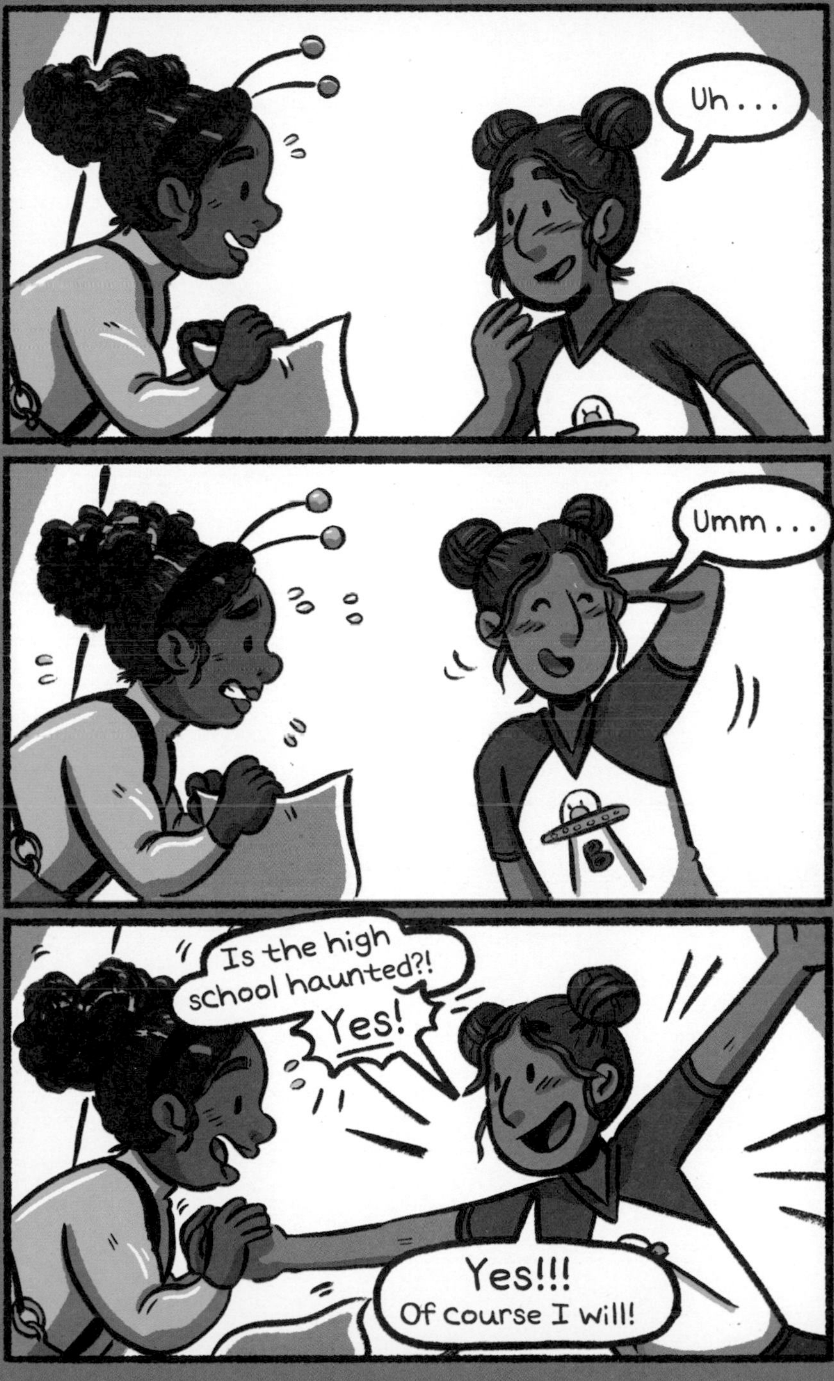
Uh . . .
Umm . . .
Is the high school haunted?!
Yes!
Yes!!!
Of course I will!

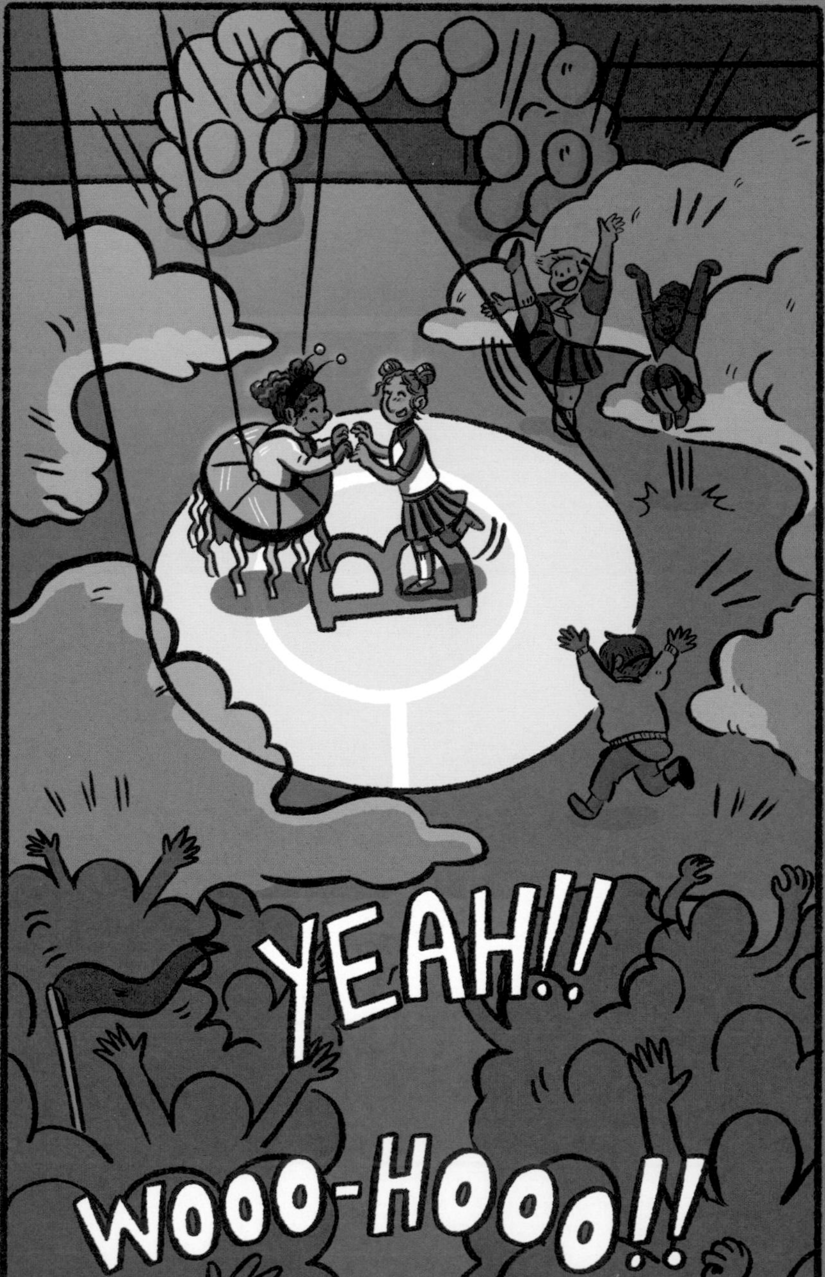
YEAH!!
WOOO-HOOO!!

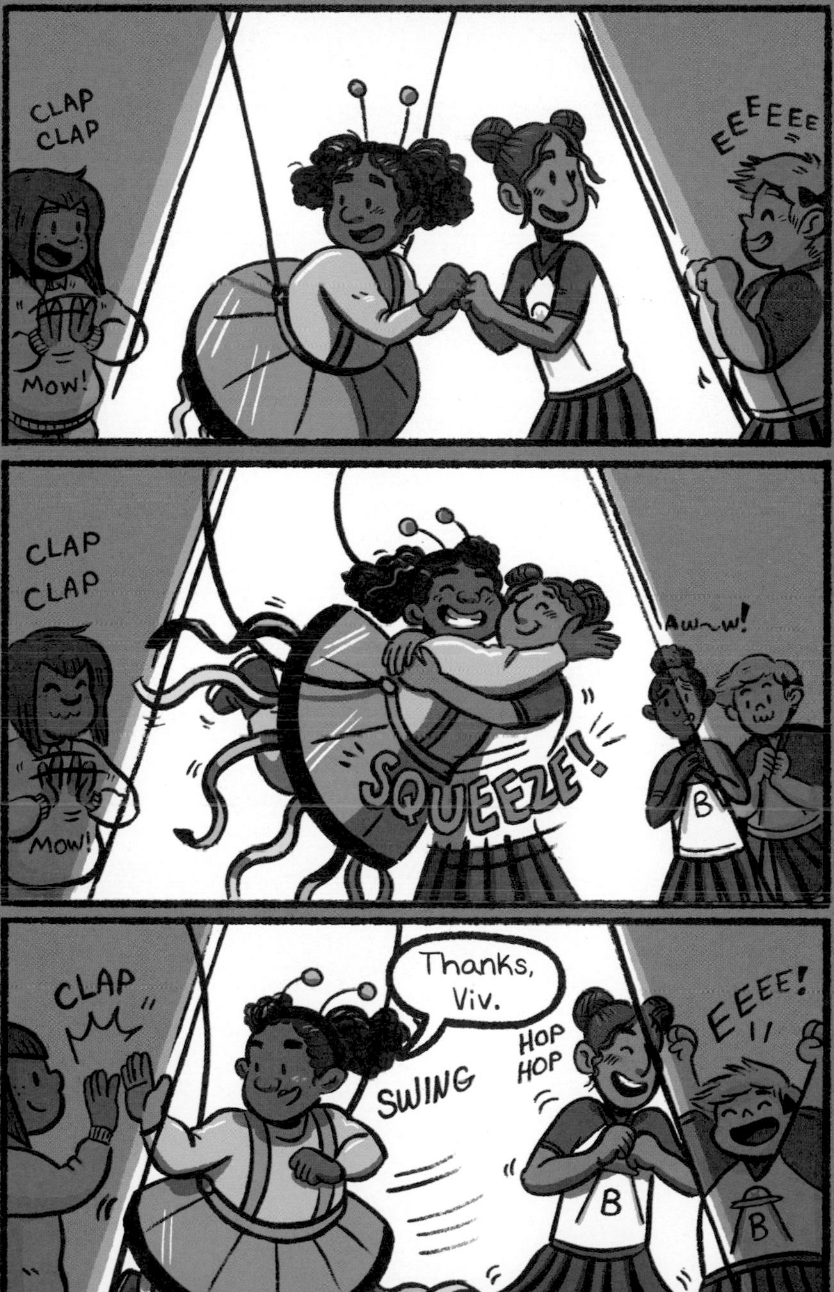
CLAP
CLAP
MOW!
EEEEEE
CLAP
CLAP
MOW!
SQUEEZE!
AW~W!
CLAP
Thanks, Viv.
SWING
HOP
HOP
EEEE!

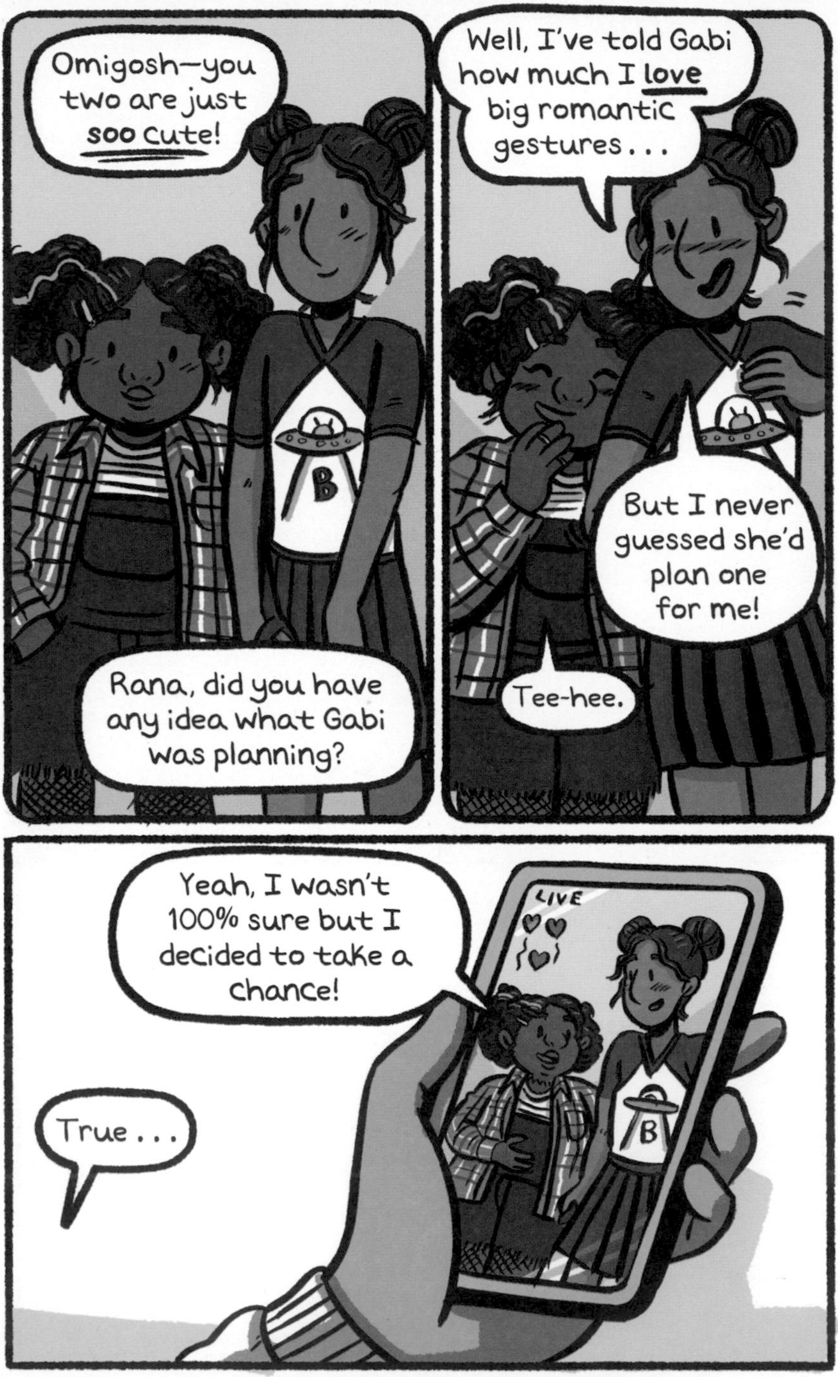
Omigosh—you two are just soo cute!
Rana, did you have any idea what Gabi was planning?
Well, I've told Gabi how much I love big romantic gestures . . .
But I never guessed she'd plan one for me!
Tee-hee.
Yeah, I wasn't 100% sure but I decided to take a chance!
LIVE
True . . .

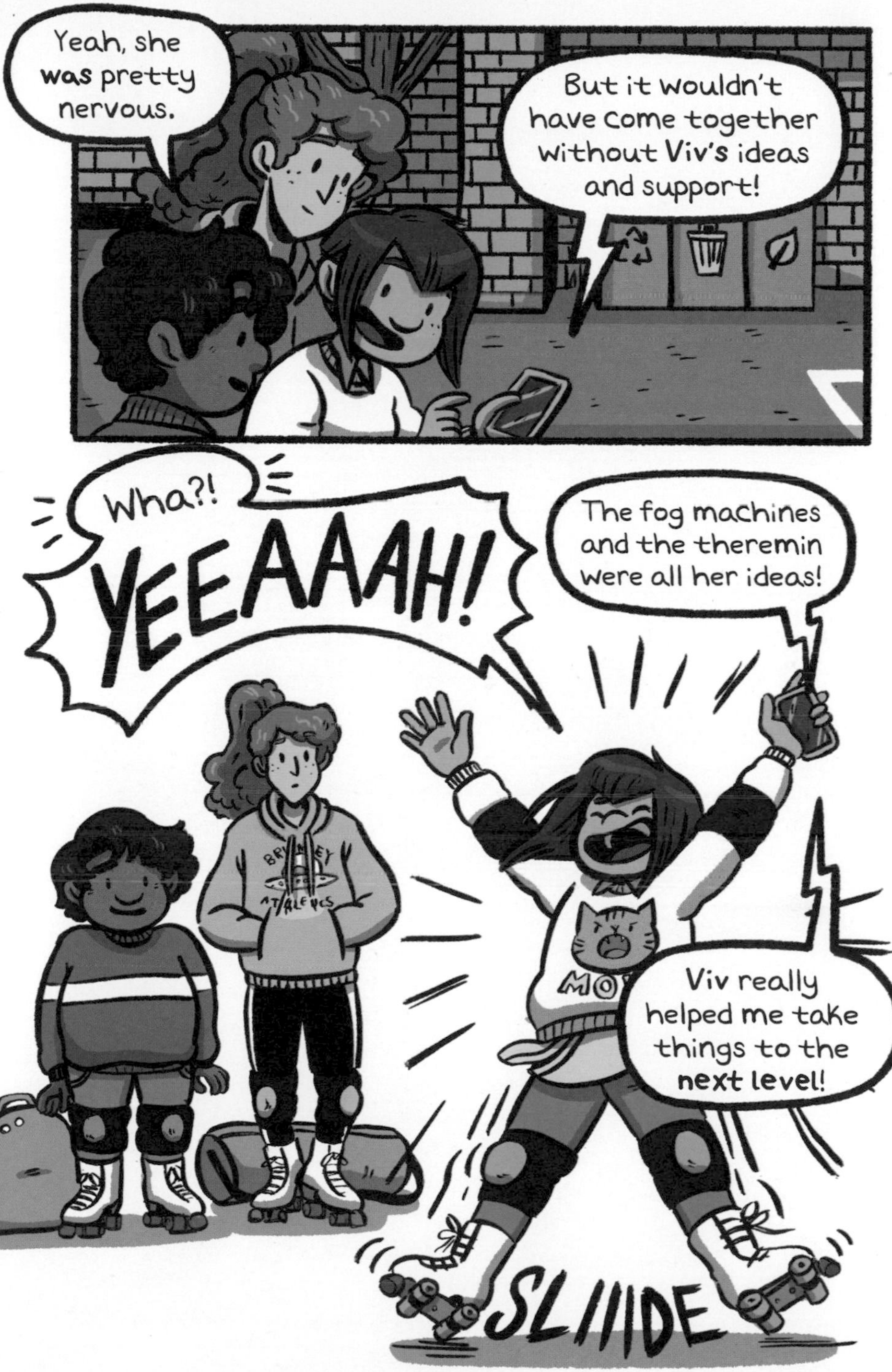
Yeah, she **was** pretty nervous.
But it wouldn't have come together without Viv's ideas and support!
Wha?!
YEEAAAH!
The fog machines and the theremin were all her ideas!
Viv really helped me take things to the **next level**!
SLIIDE

Finally!
wobble
Thank you, Gabi!
MOW!
She had so many good ideas! And we worked together well!
Wobble
I'm so glad she sees it too!
The harness rig in the costume was really cool!
DING!
I got the idea from your great Tengu Con cosplay last year!

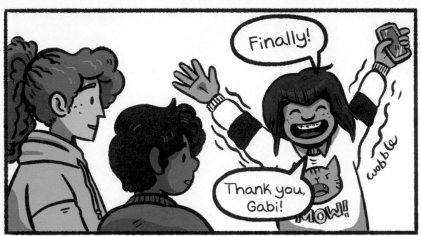

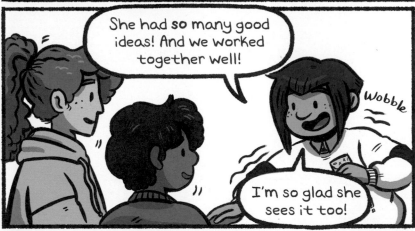

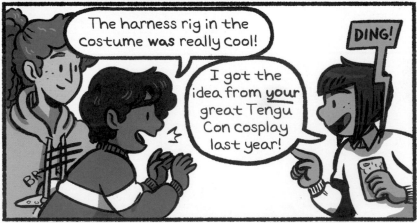

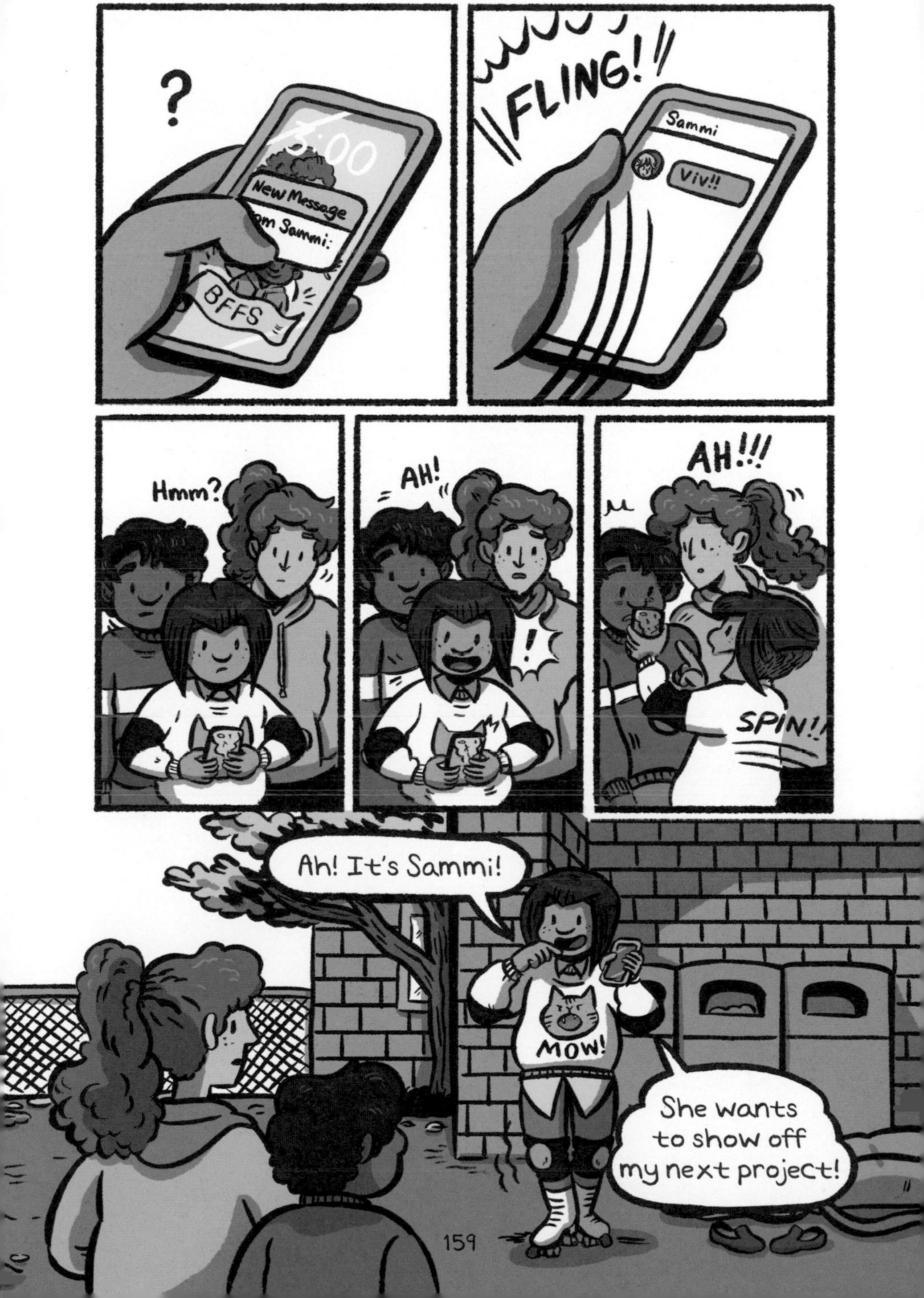
?
3:00
New Message
om Sammi:
BFFS
FLING!
Sammi
Viv!!
Hmm?
AH!
!
AH!!!
SPIN!!
Ah! It's Sammi!
MOW!
She wants to show off my next project!

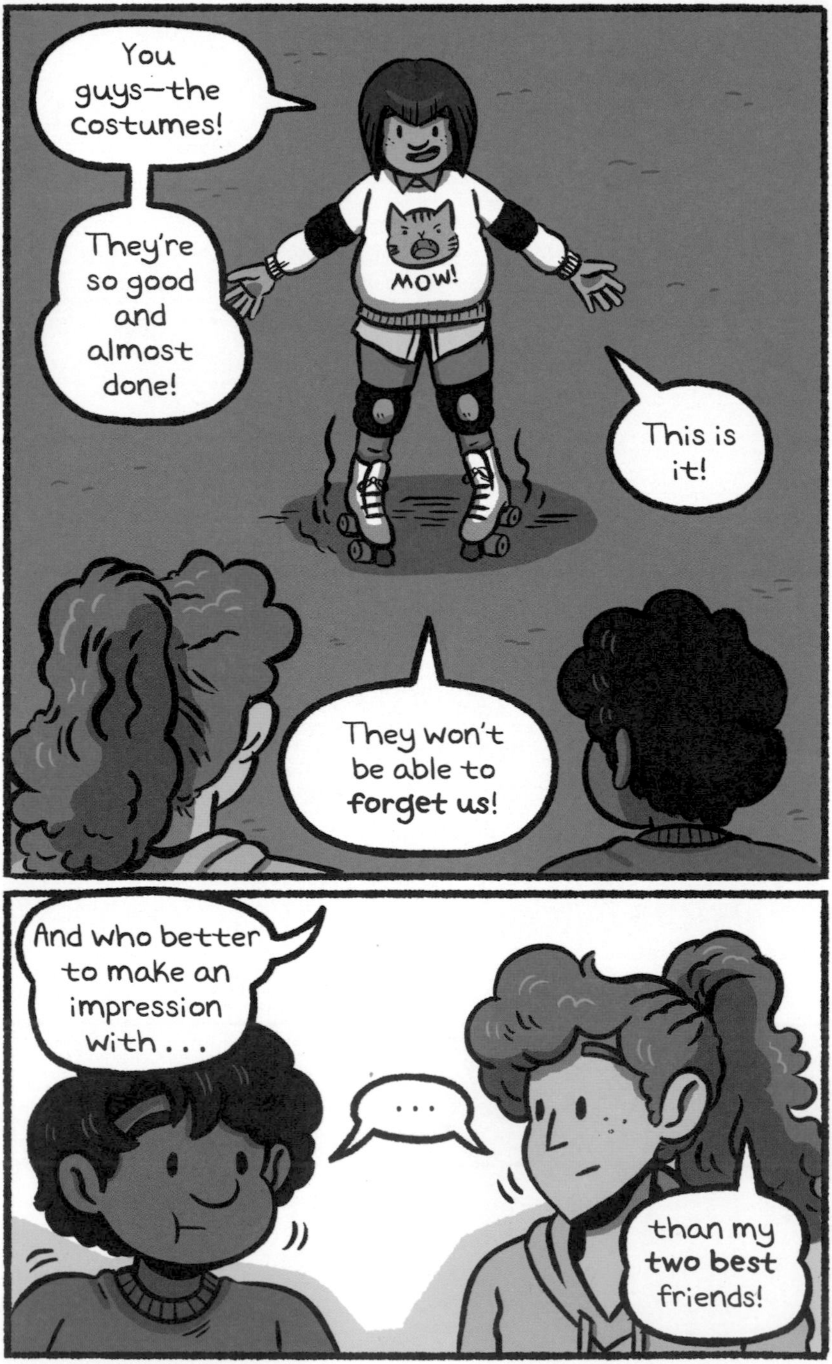
You guys—the costumes!
They're so good and almost done!
MOW!
This is it!
They won't be able to **forget us**!
And who better to make an impression with . . .
. . .
than my **two best** friends!

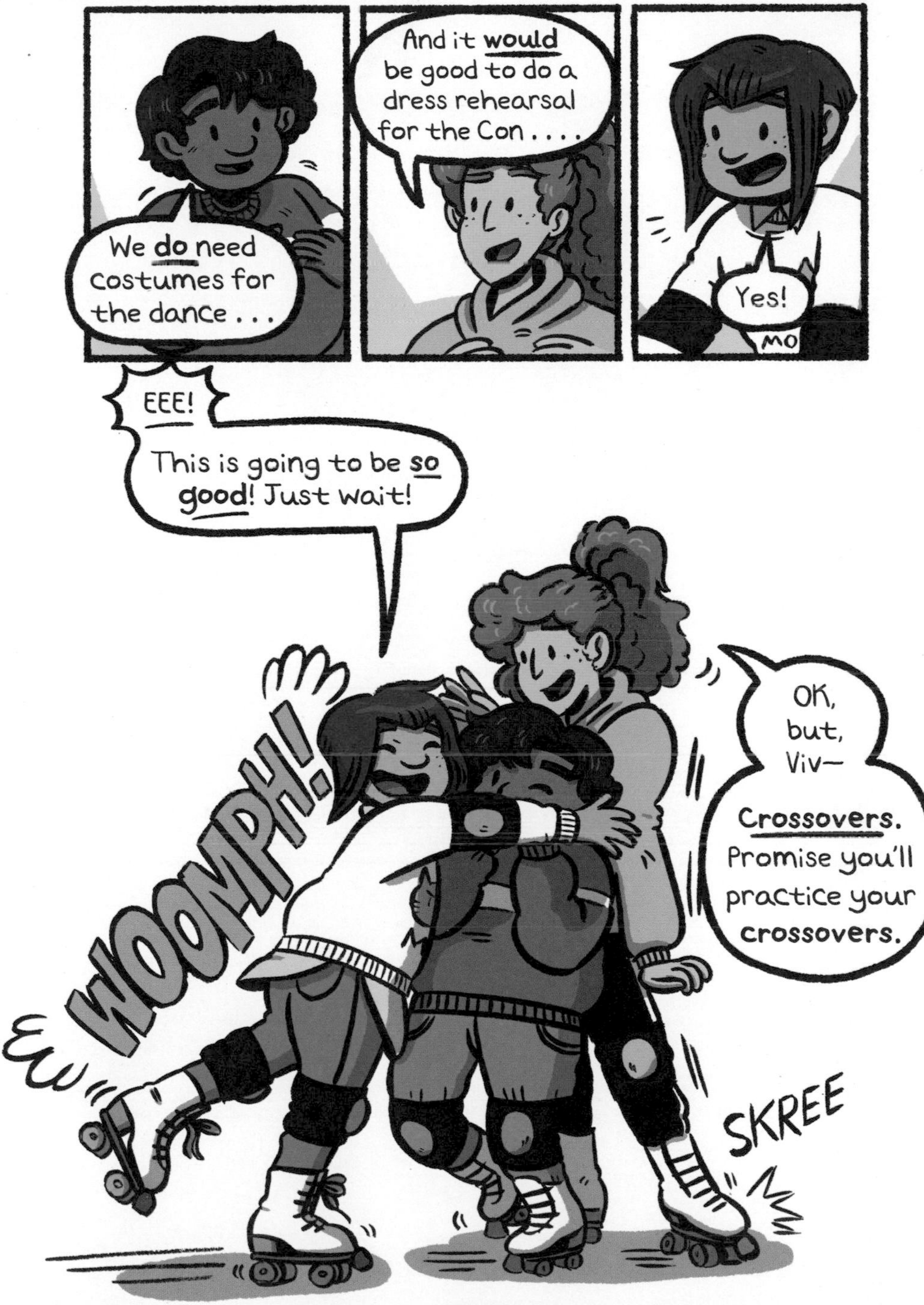
We do need costumes for the dance . . .
And it would be good to do a dress rehearsal for the Con . . . .
Yes!
MO
EEE!
This is going to be so good! Just wait!
WOOMPH!
OK, but, Viv—
Crossovers. Promise you'll practice your crossovers.
SKREE

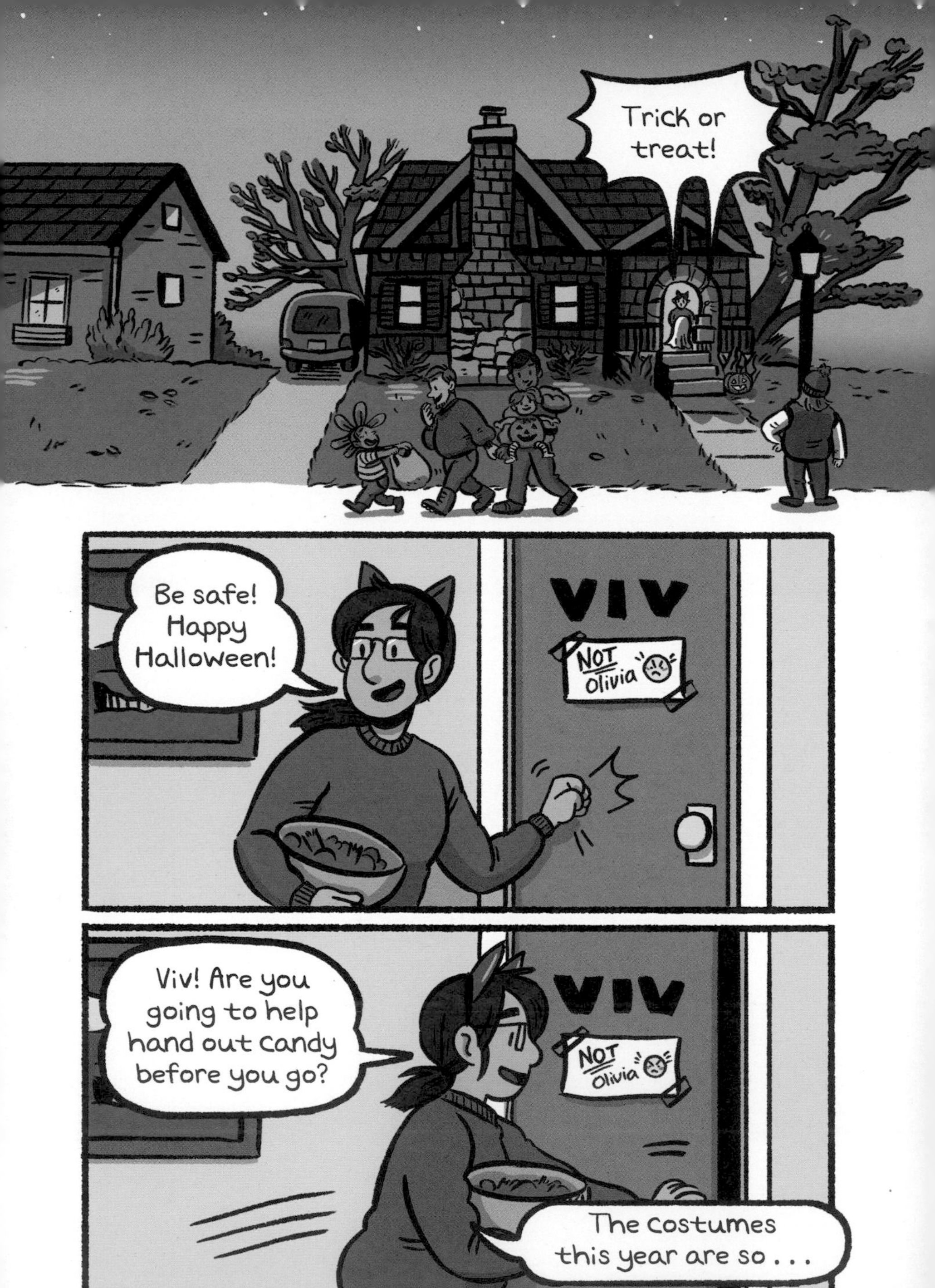

Trick or treat!
Be safe! Happy Halloween!
VIV
NOT Olivia
Viv! Are you going to help hand out candy before you go?
VIV
NOT Olivia
The costumes this year are so . . .

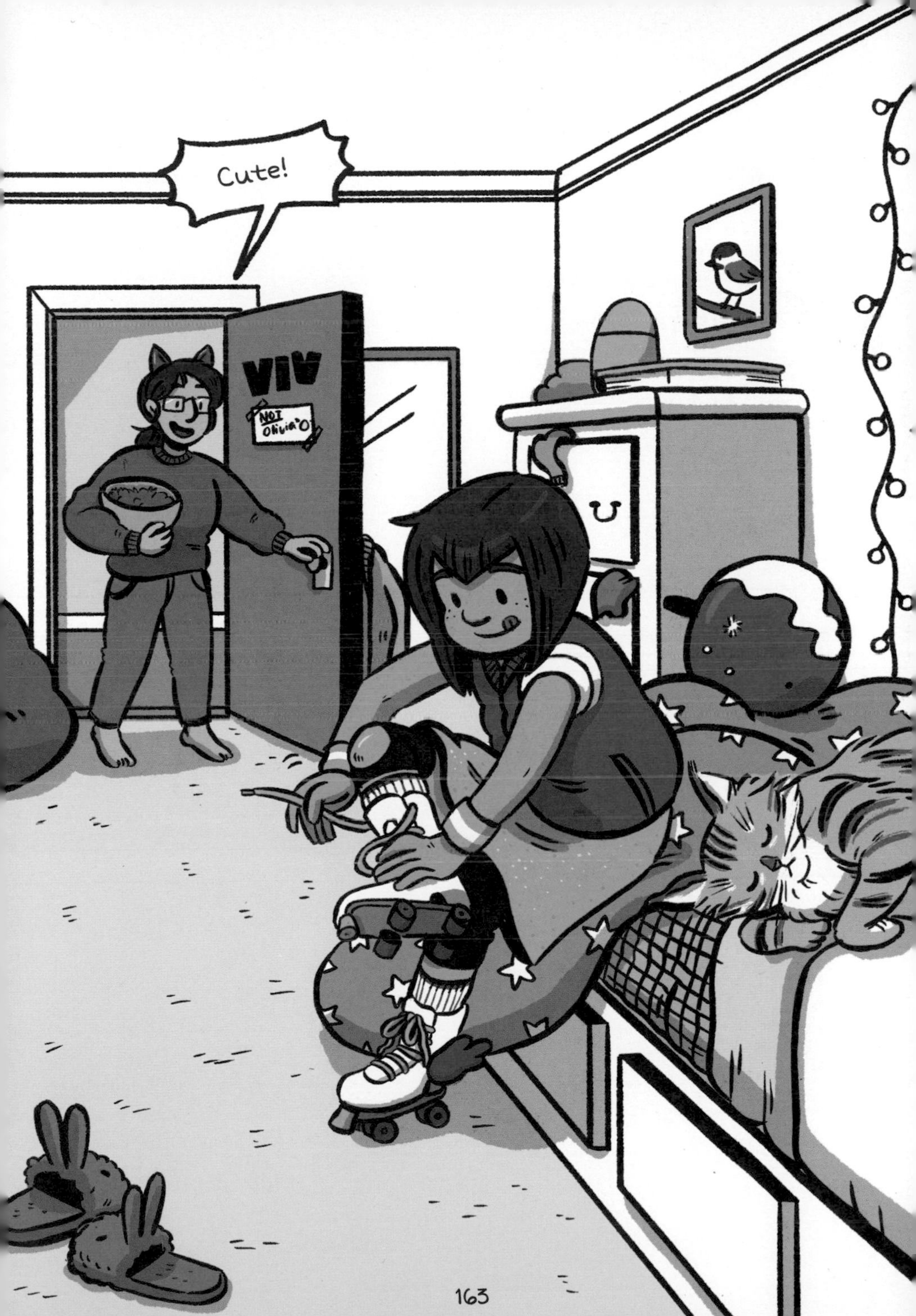
Cute!
VIV
NO! Olivia

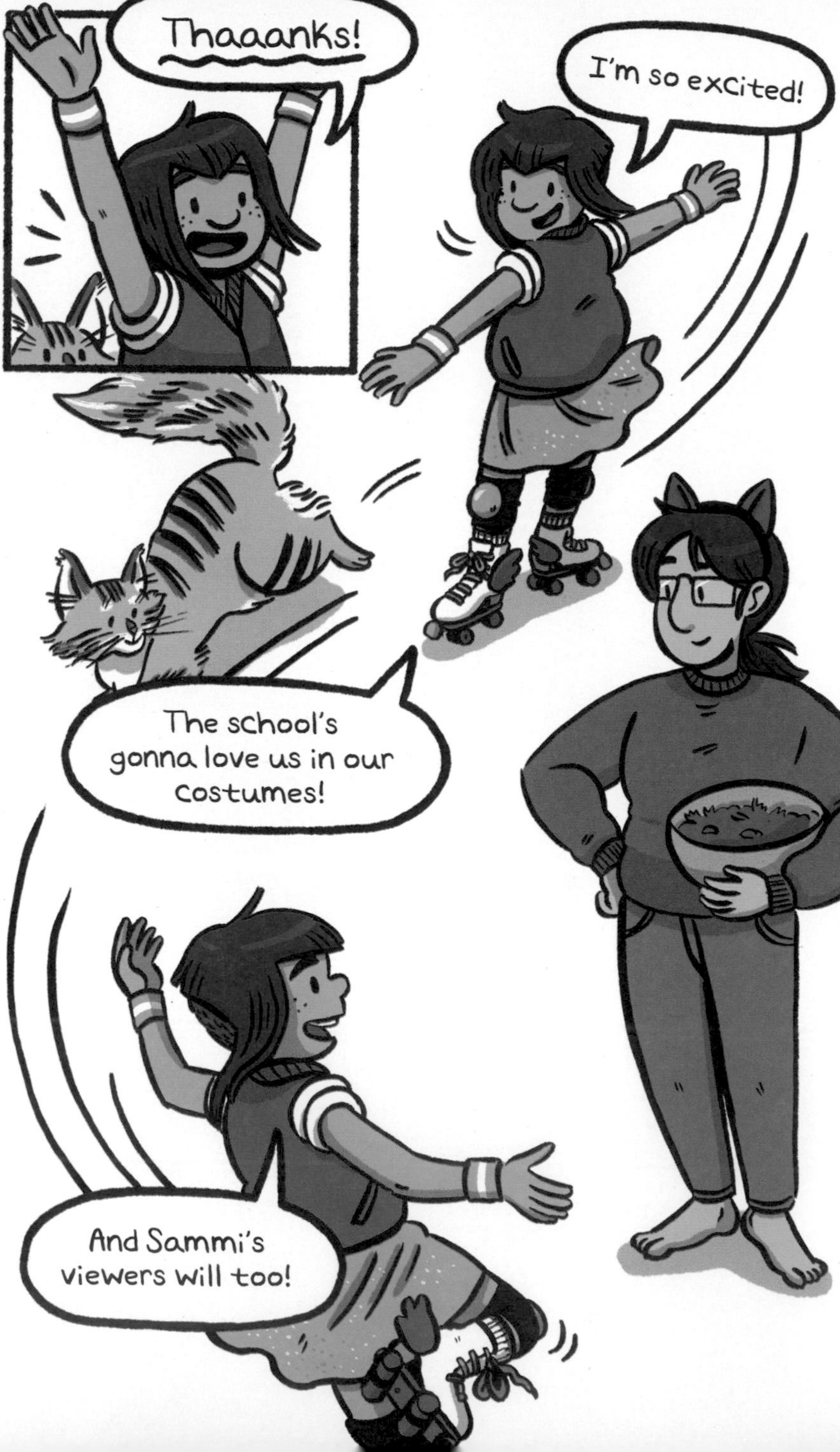

Thaaaanks!
I'm so excited!
The school's gonna love us in our costumes!
And Sammi's viewers will too!

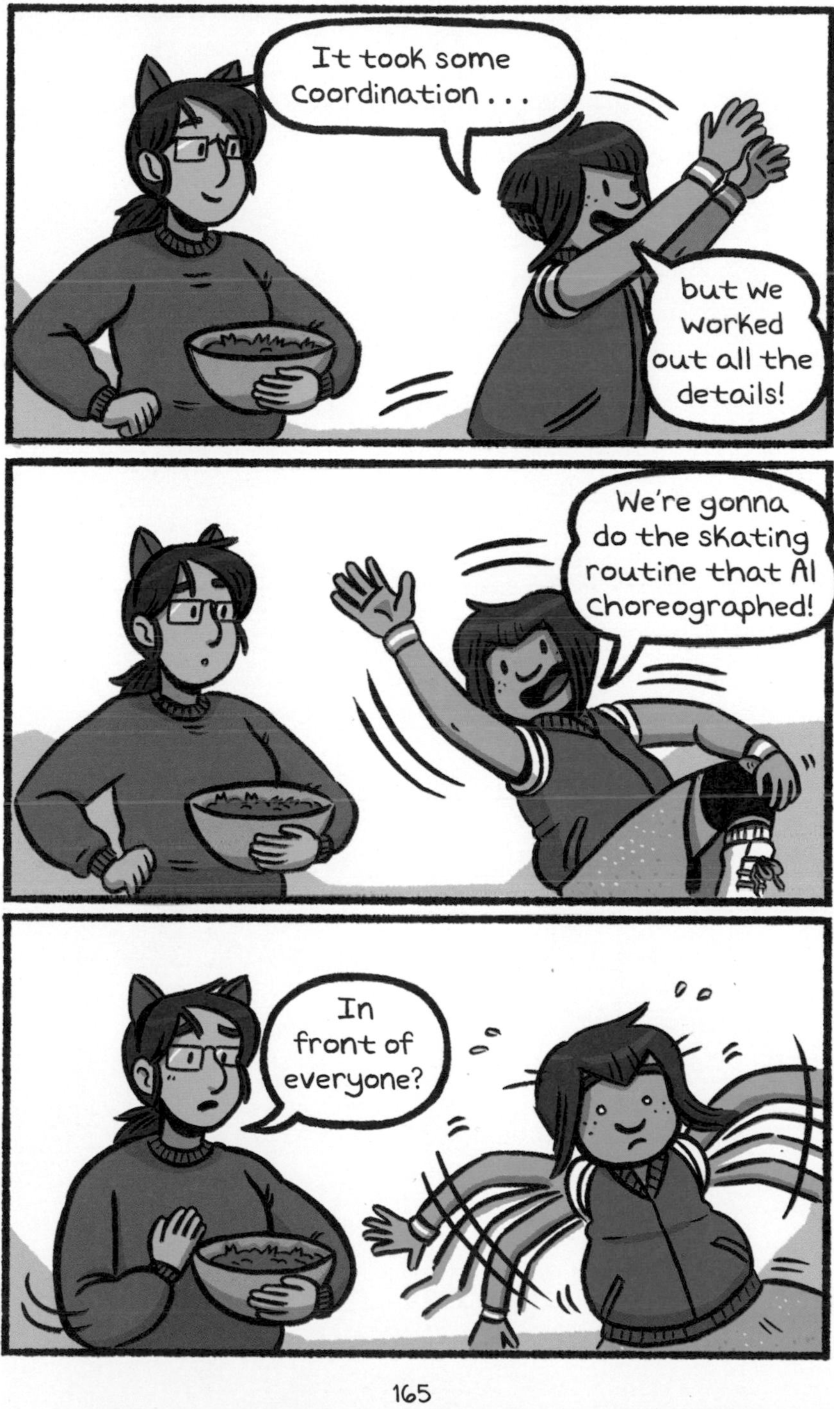

It took some coordination . . .
but we worked out all the details!
We're gonna do the skating routine that Al choreographed!
In front of everyone?

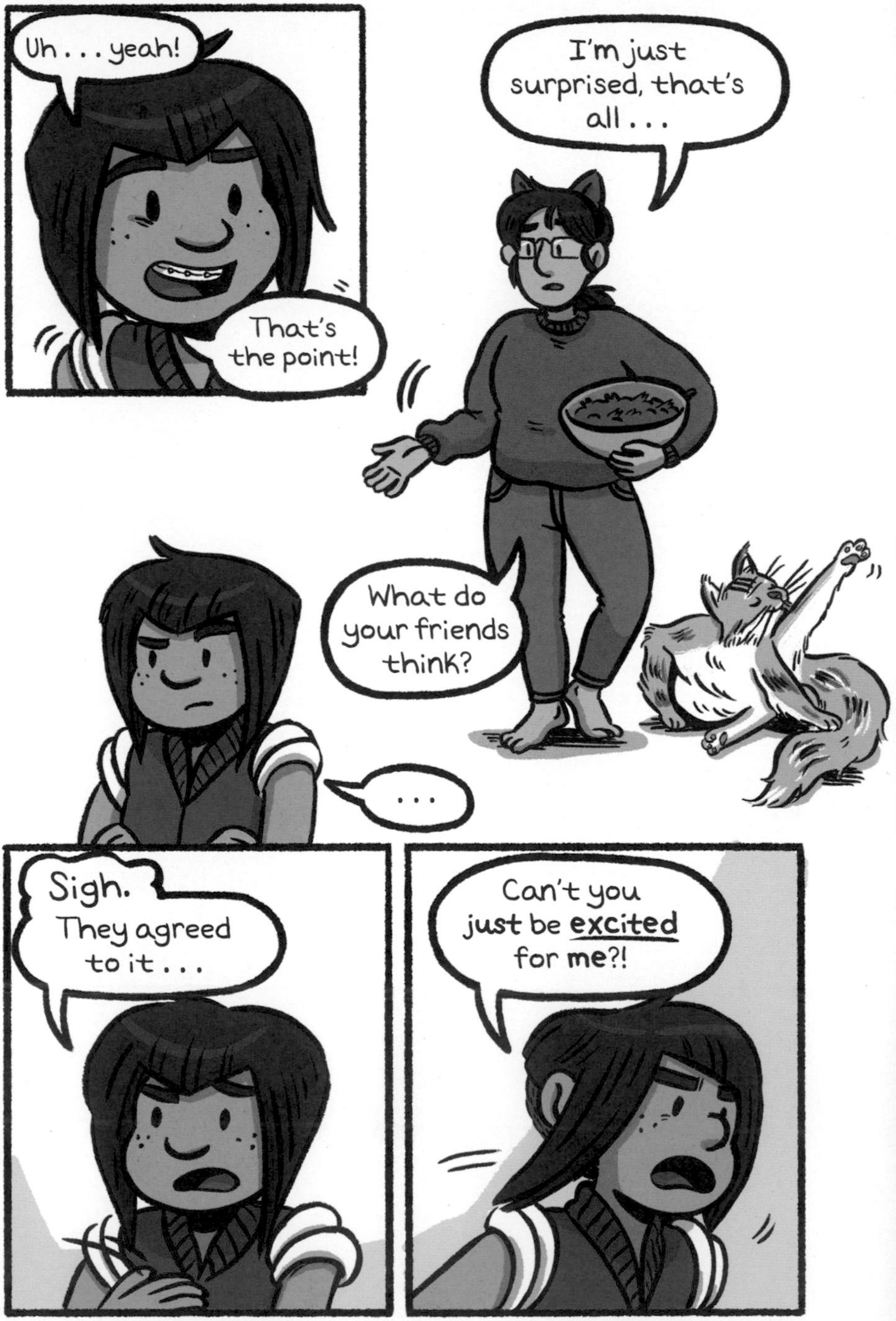
Uh . . . yeah!
That's the point!
I'm just surprised, that's all . . .
What do your friends think?
. . .
Sigh. They agreed to it . . .
Can't you just be excited for me?!

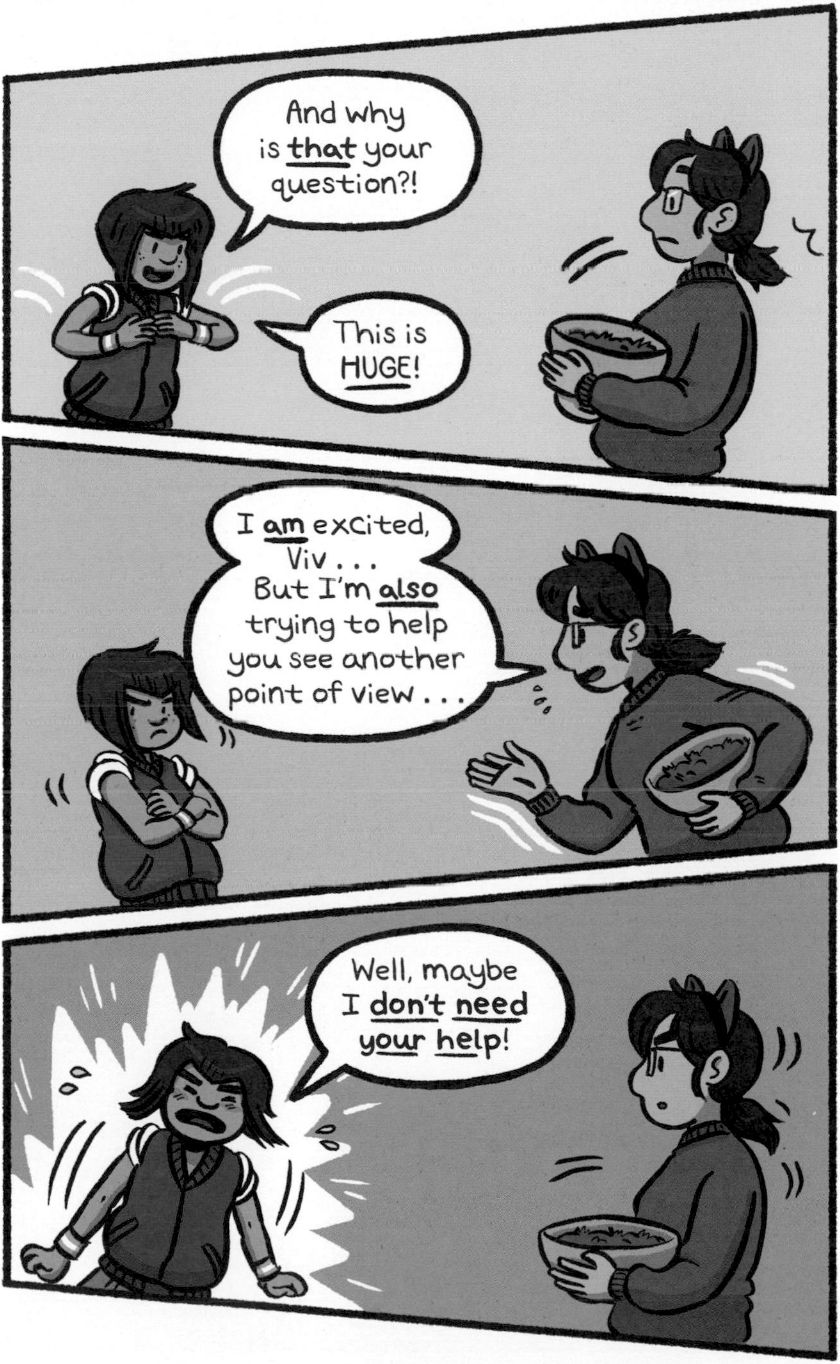
And why is that your question?!
This is HUGE!
I am excited, Viv . . . But I'm also trying to help you see another point of view . . .
Well, maybe I don't need your help!

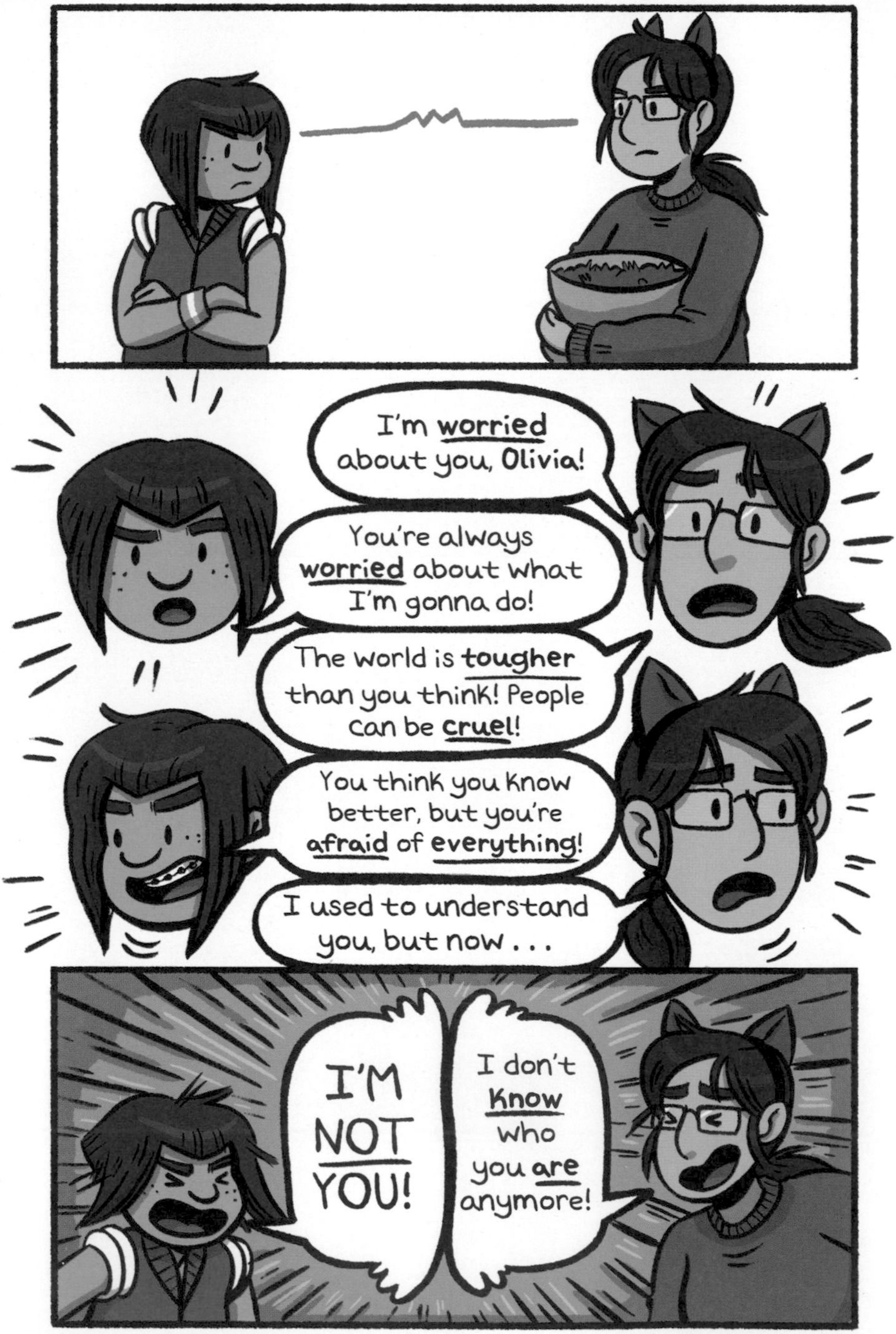
I'm worried about you, Olivia!
You're always worried about what I'm gonna do!
The world is tougher than you think! People can be cruel!
You think you know better, but you're afraid of everything!
I used to understand you, but now . . .
I'M NOT YOU!
I don't know who you are anymore!

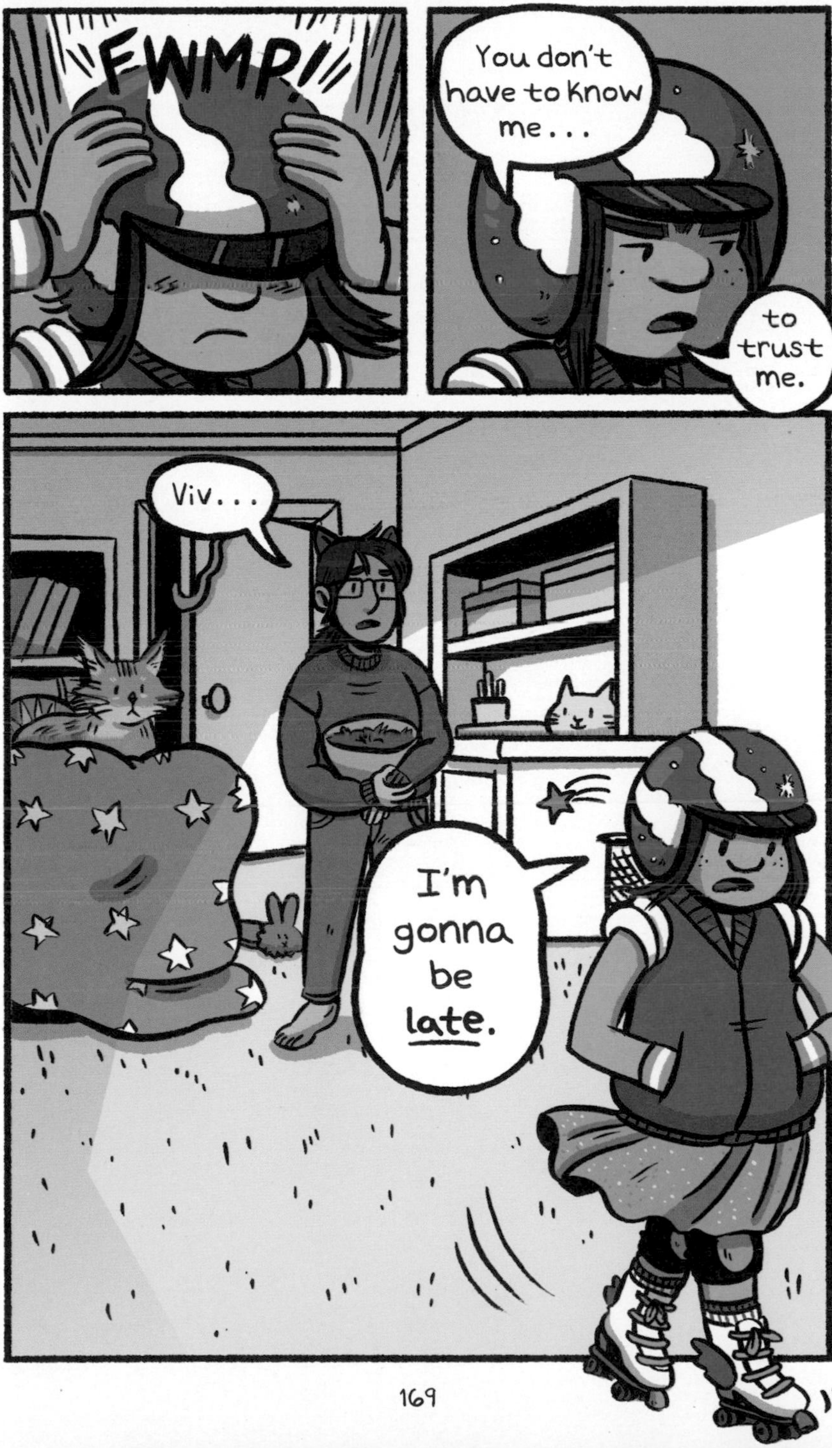
FWMP!
You don't have to know me...
to trust me.
Viv...
I'm gonna be late.

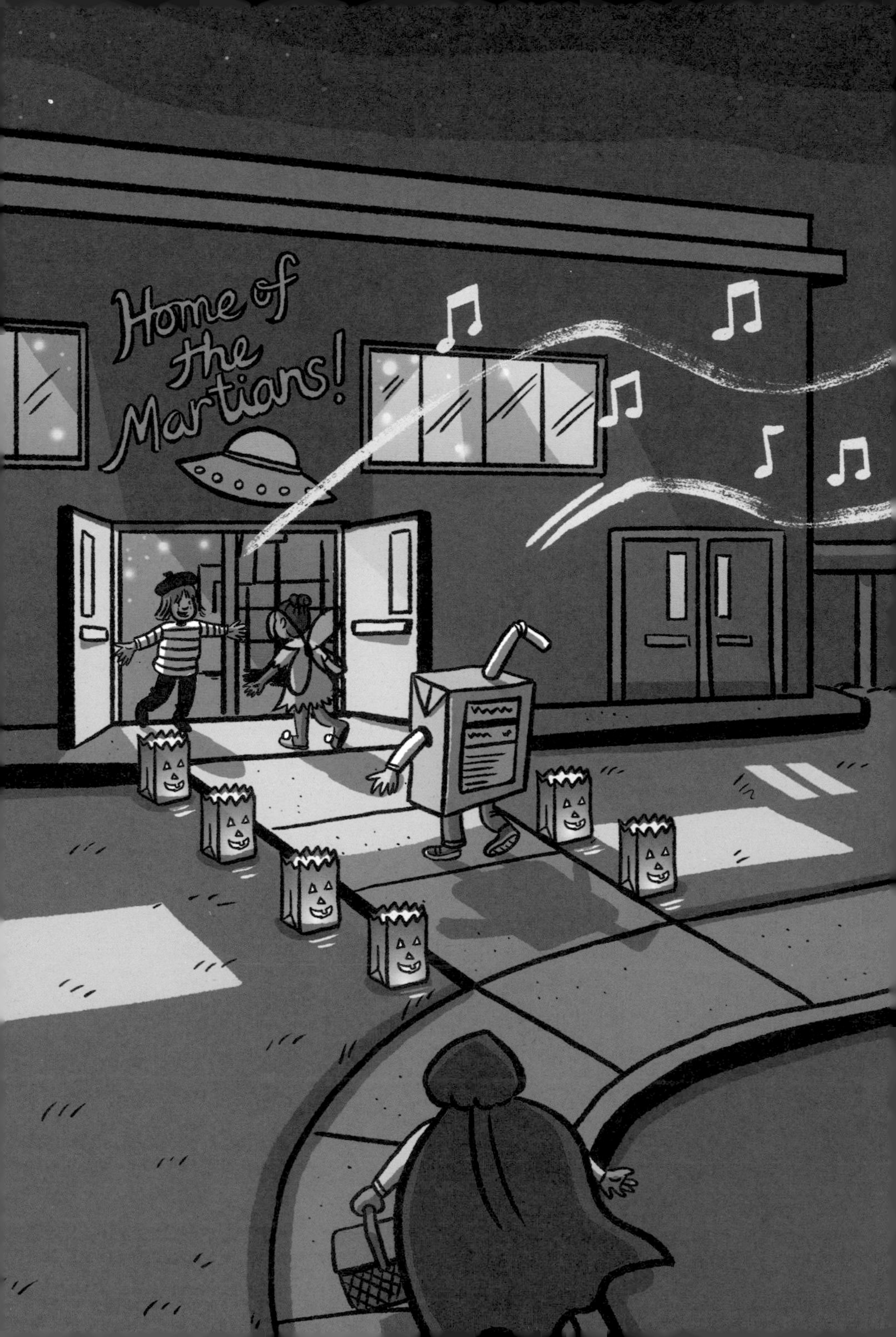
Home of the Martians!

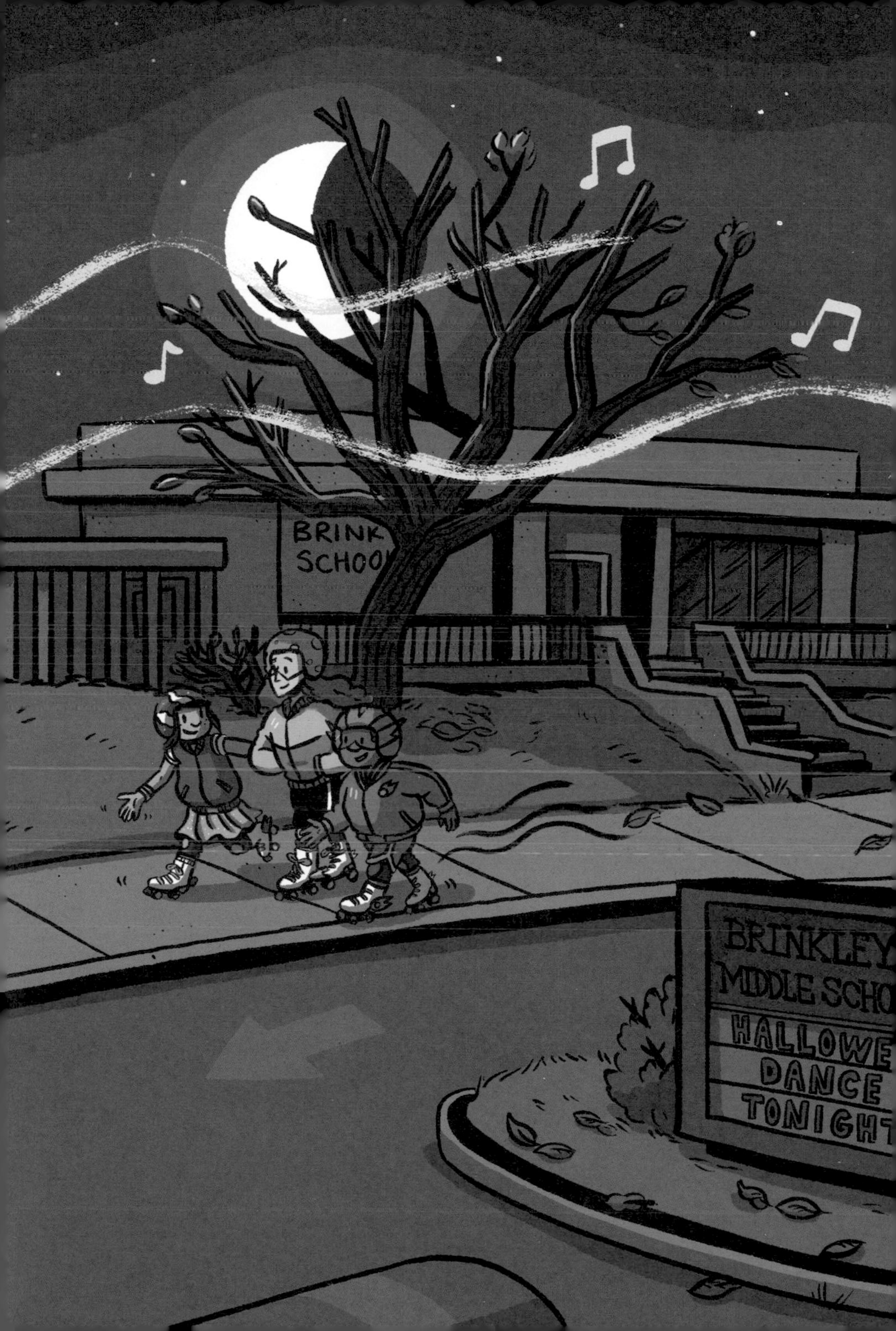
BRINK
SCHOO
BRINKLEY
MIDDLE SCHO
HALLOWE
DANCE
TONIGHT

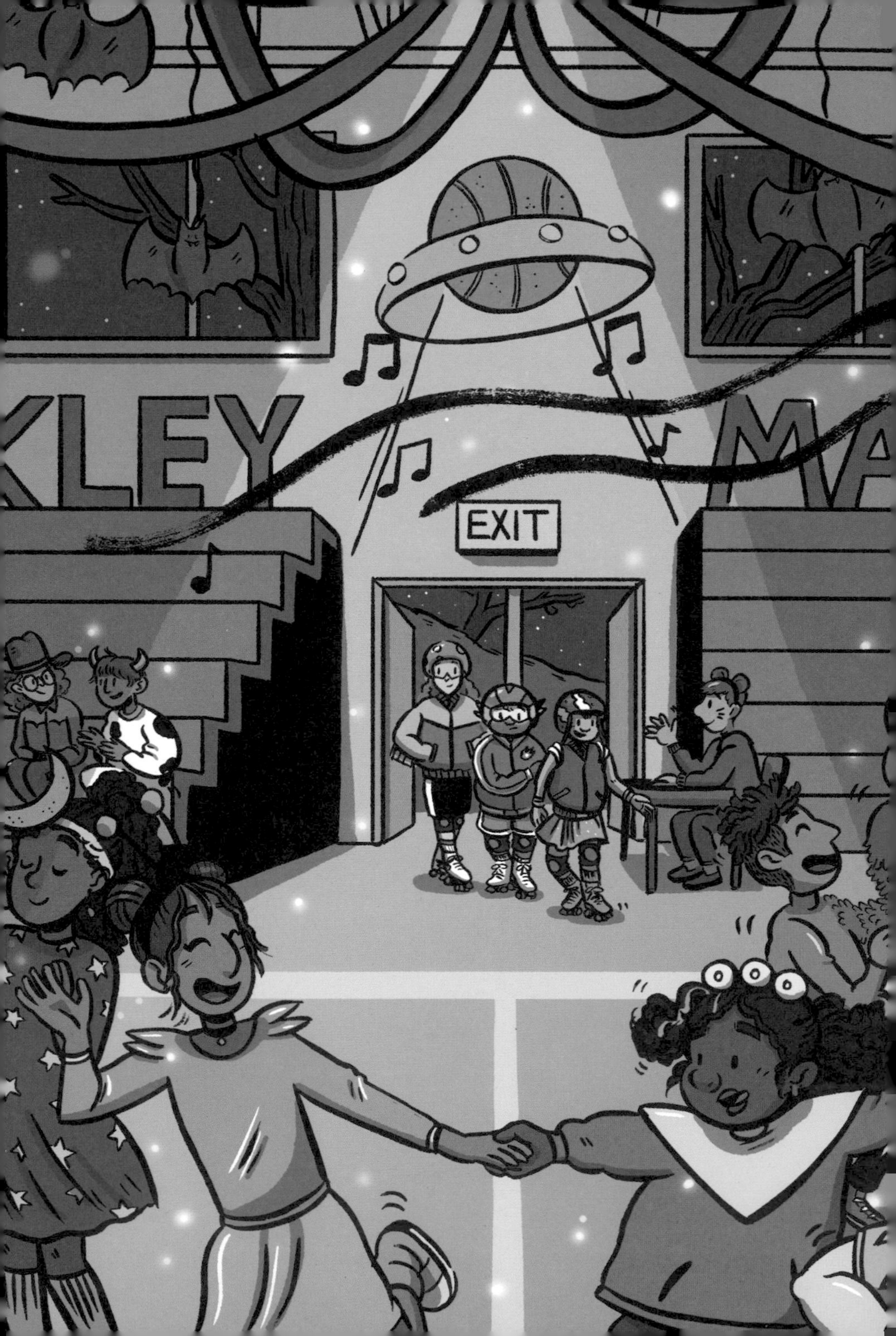

KLEY
MA
EXIT

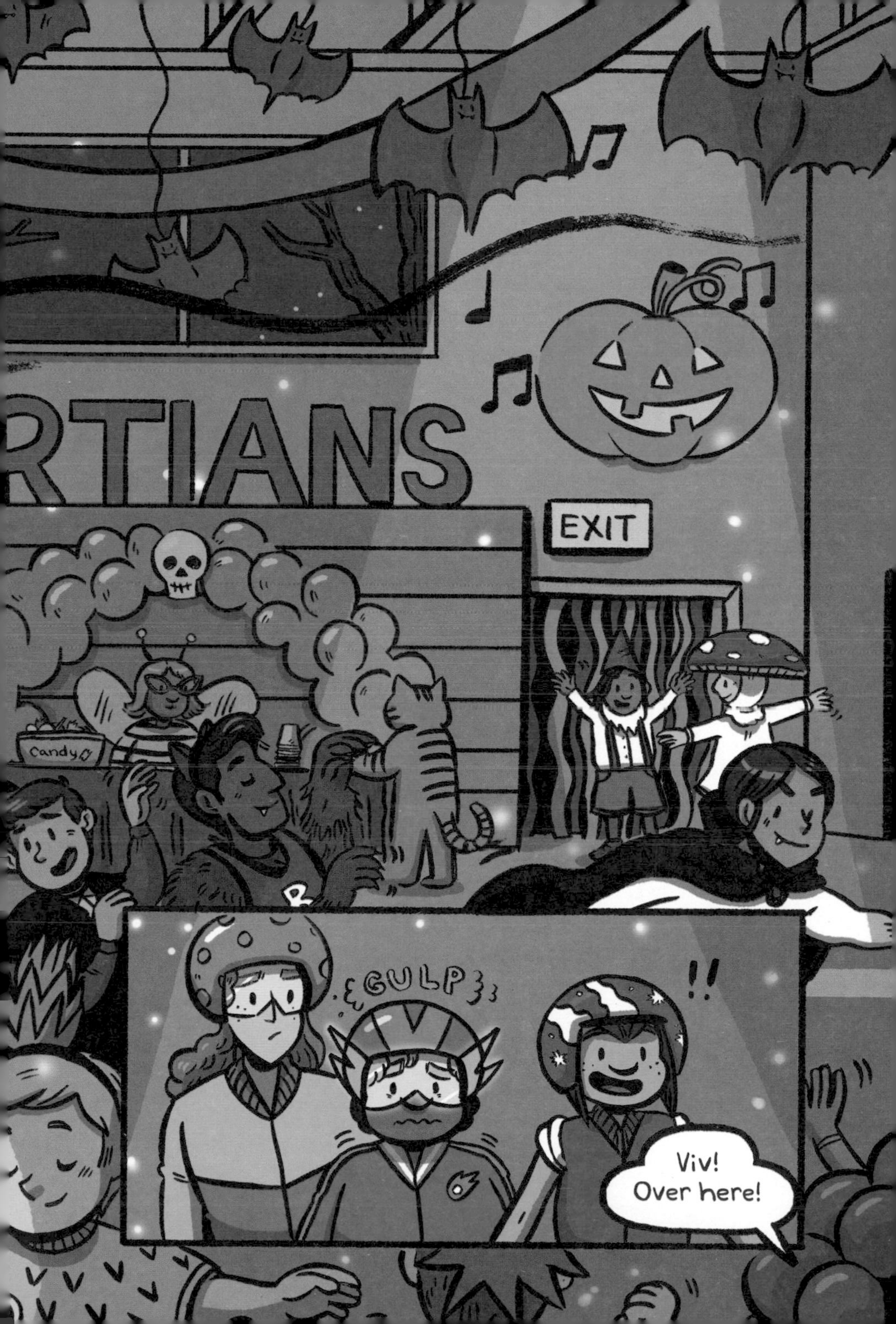
RTIANS
EXIT
Candy
GULP
!!
Viv!
Over here!

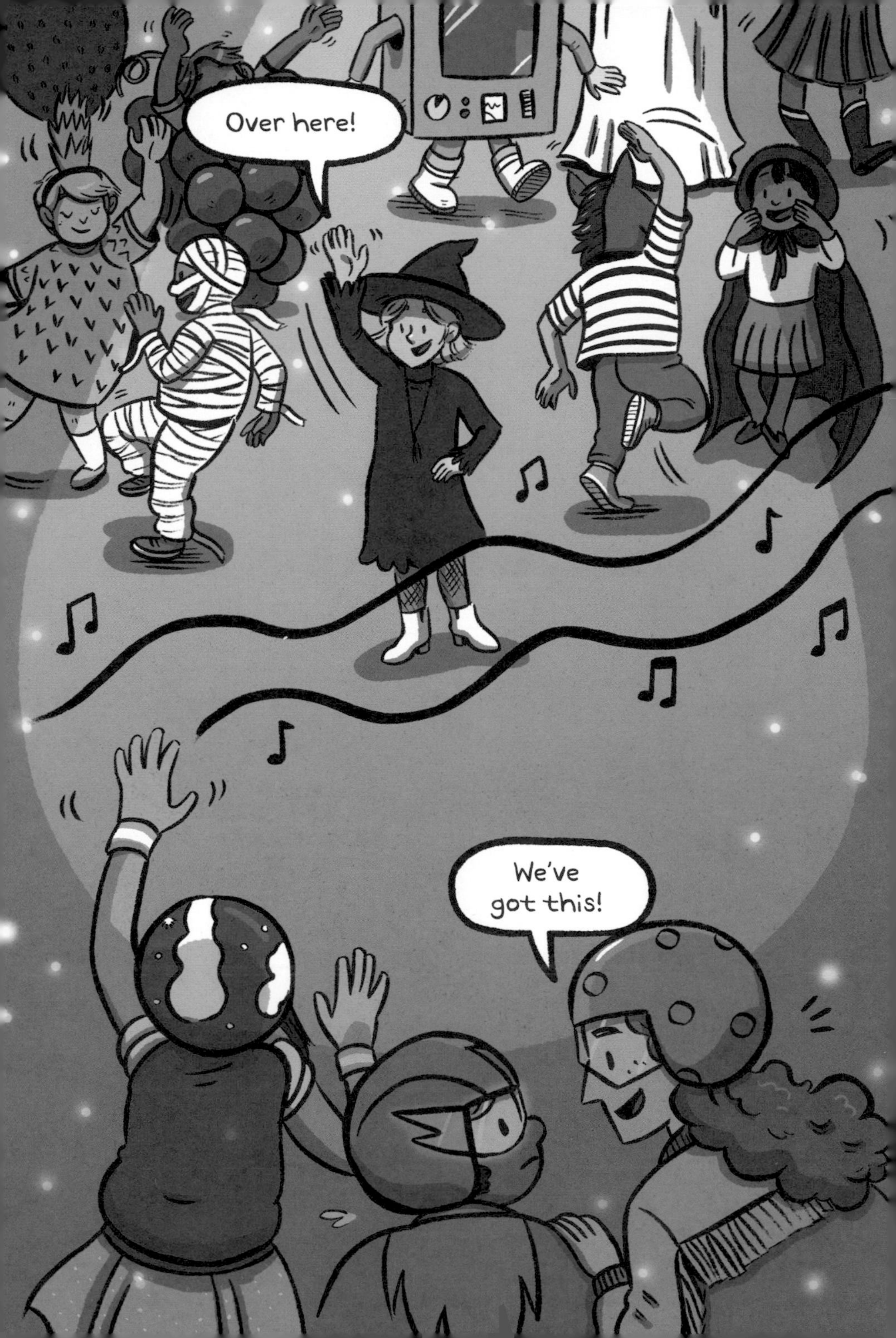
Over here!
We've got this!

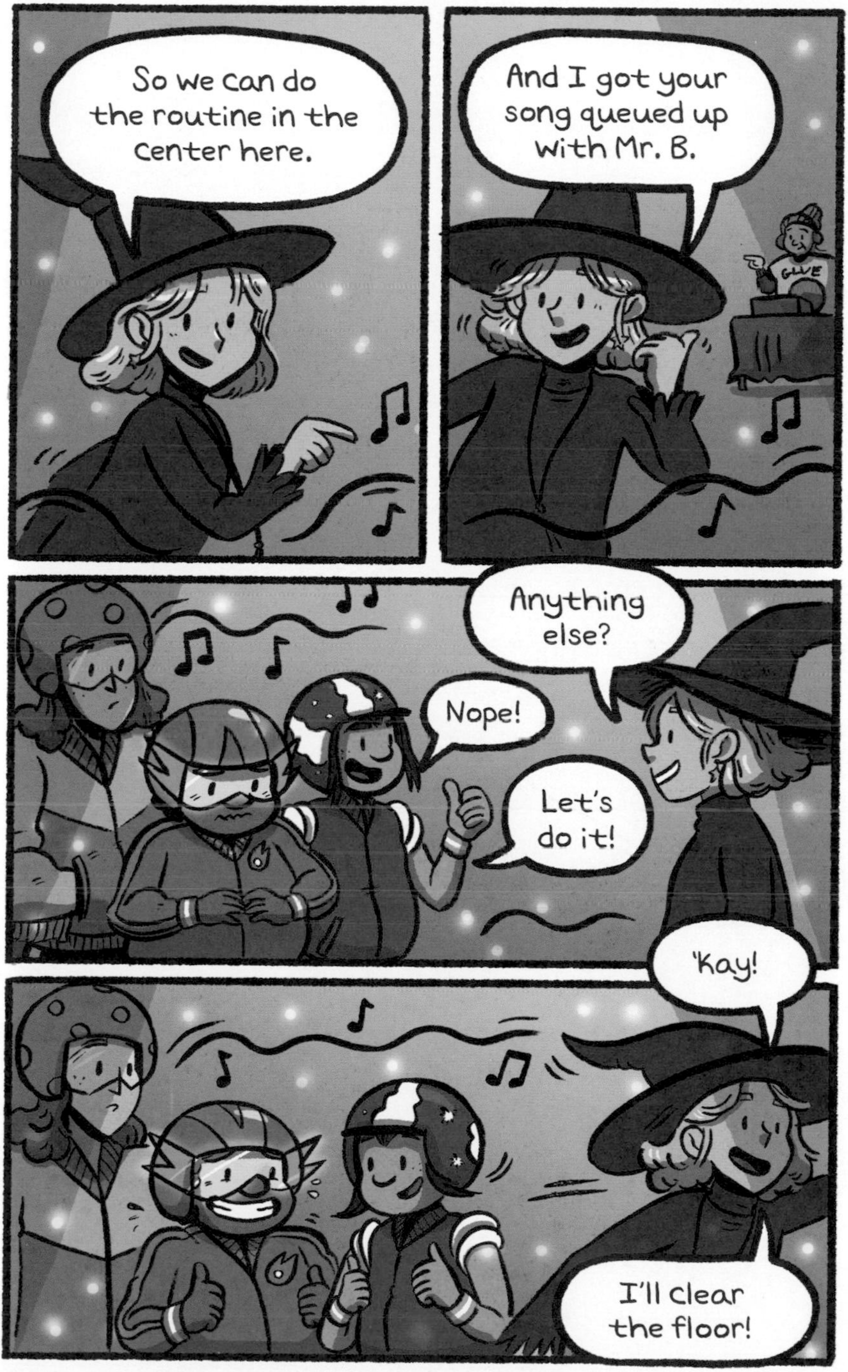
So we can do the routine in the center here.
And I got your song queued up with Mr. B.
GLUE
Anything else?
Nope!
Let's do it!
'Kay!
I'll clear the floor!

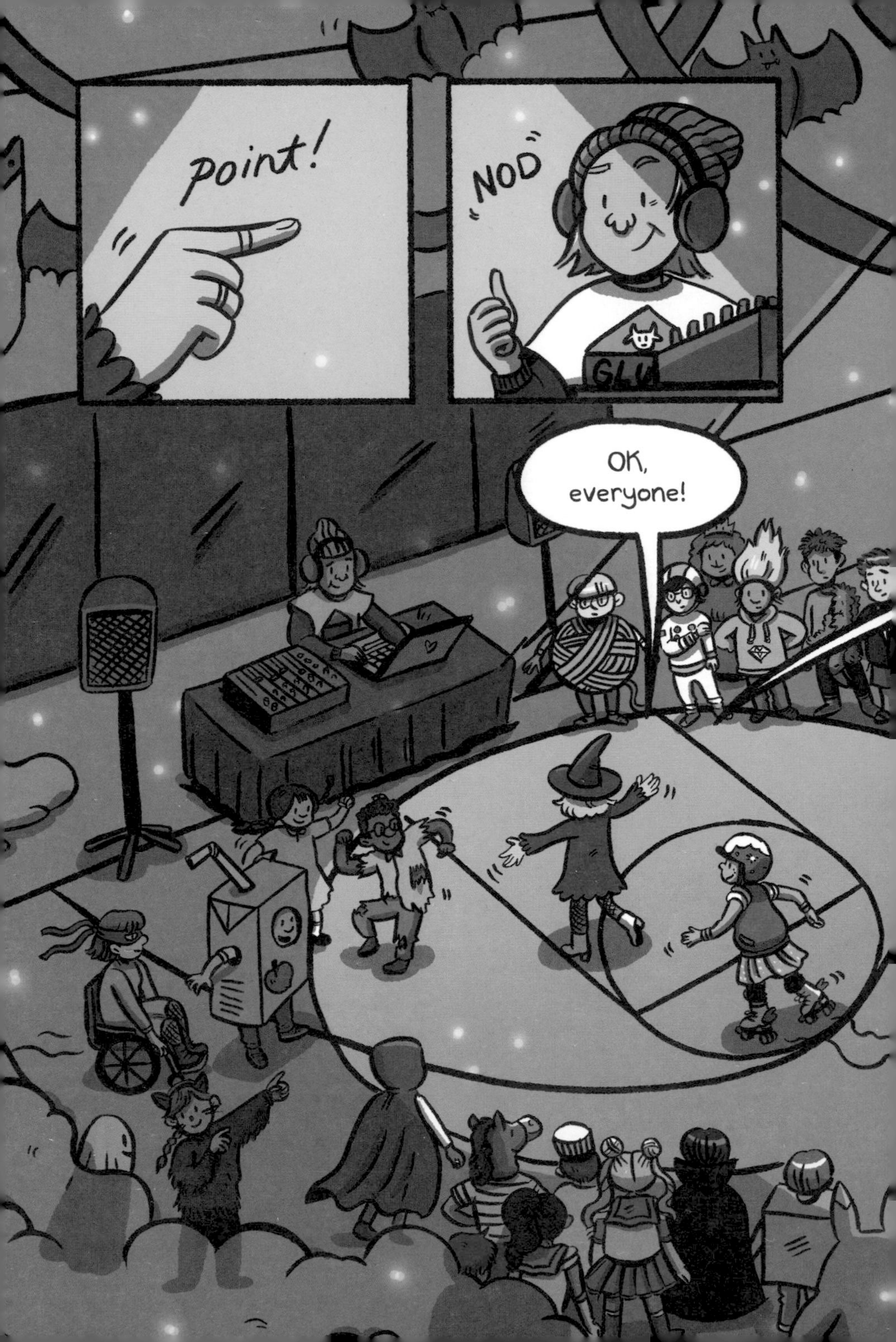
point!
NOD
GLU
OK, everyone!

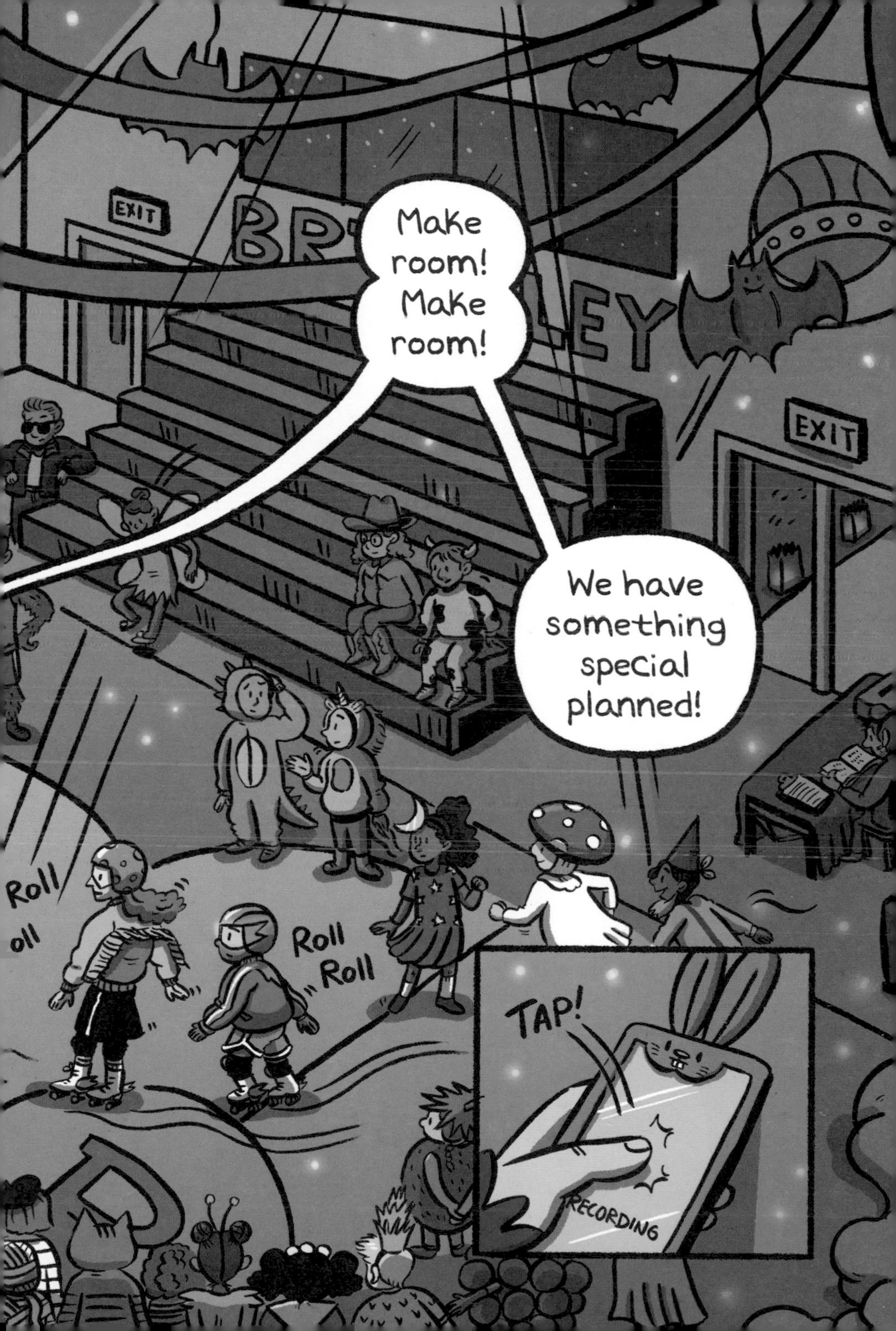
EXIT
BR
LEY
Make room! Make room!
EXIT
We have something special planned!
Roll
oll
Roll
Roll
TAP!
RECORDING

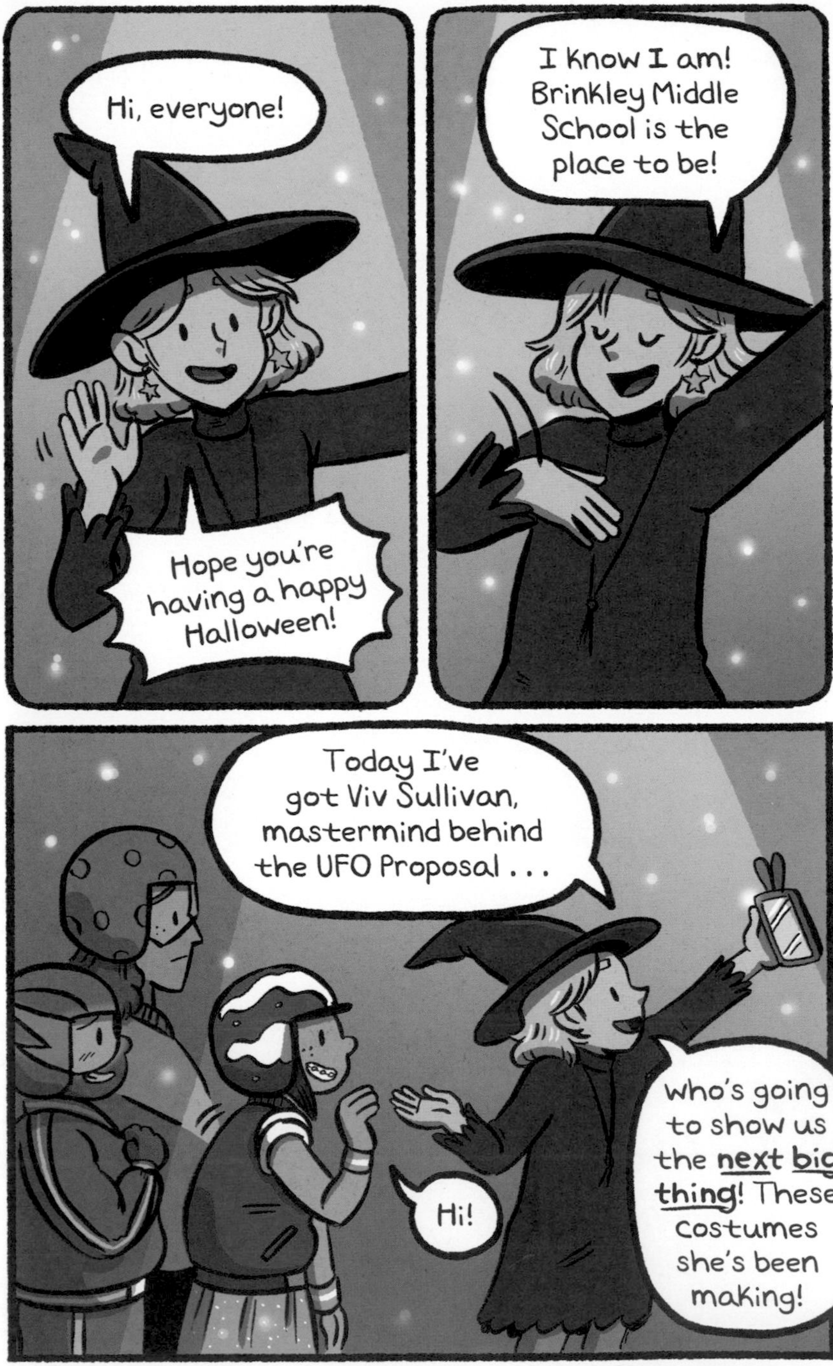
Hi, everyone!
Hope you're having a happy Halloween!
I know I am! Brinkley Middle School is the place to be!
Today I've got Viv Sullivan, mastermind behind the UFO Proposal . . .
who's going to show us the next big thing! These costumes she's been making!
Hi!

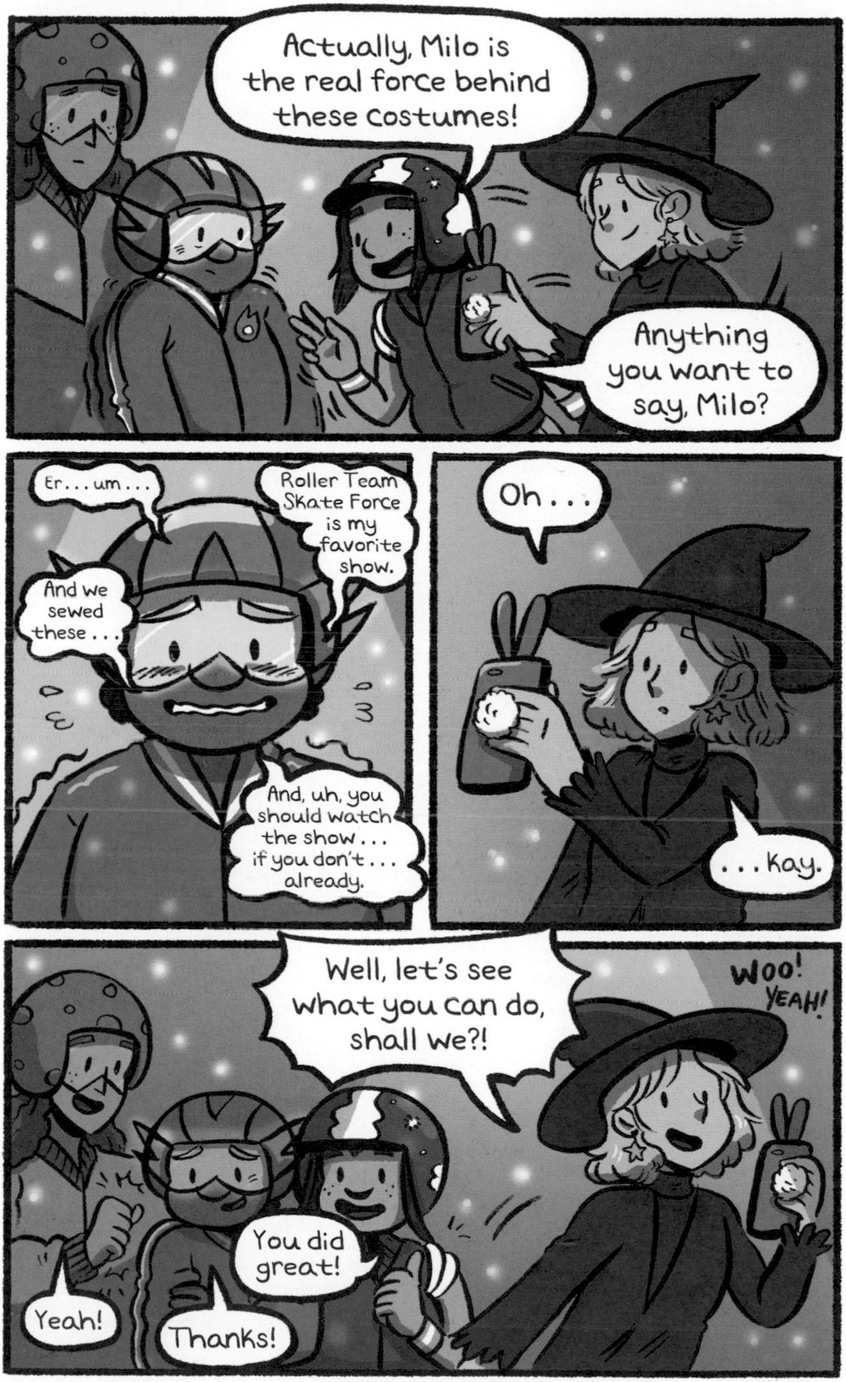
Actually, Milo is the real force behind these costumes!
Anything you want to say, Milo?
Er... um...
Roller Team Skate Force is my favorite show.
And we sewed these...
And, uh, you should watch the show... if you don't... already.
Oh...
...Kay.
Well, let's see what you can do, shall we?!
WOO! YEAH!
You did great!
Yeah!
Thanks!

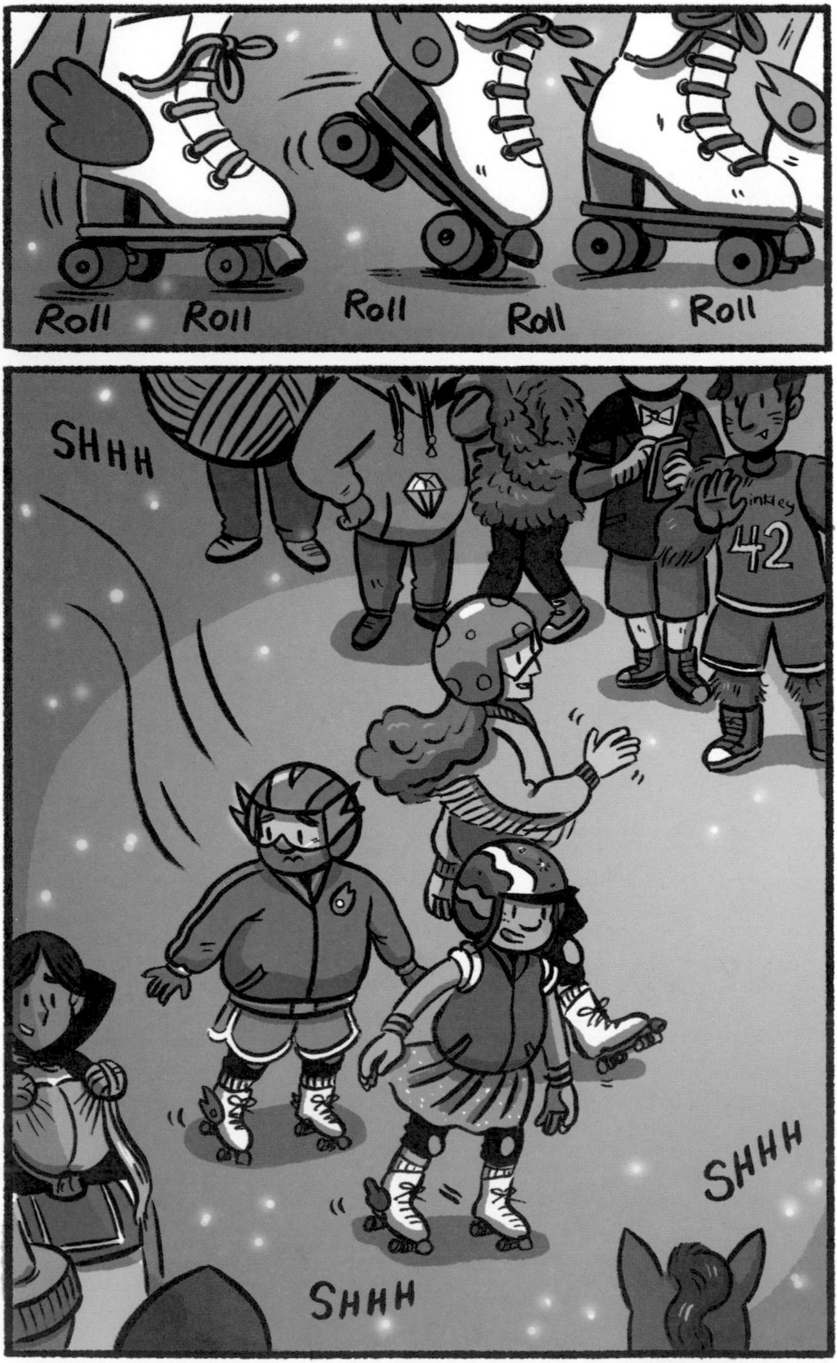
Roll
Roll
Roll
Roll
Roll
SHHH
42
SHHH
SHHH

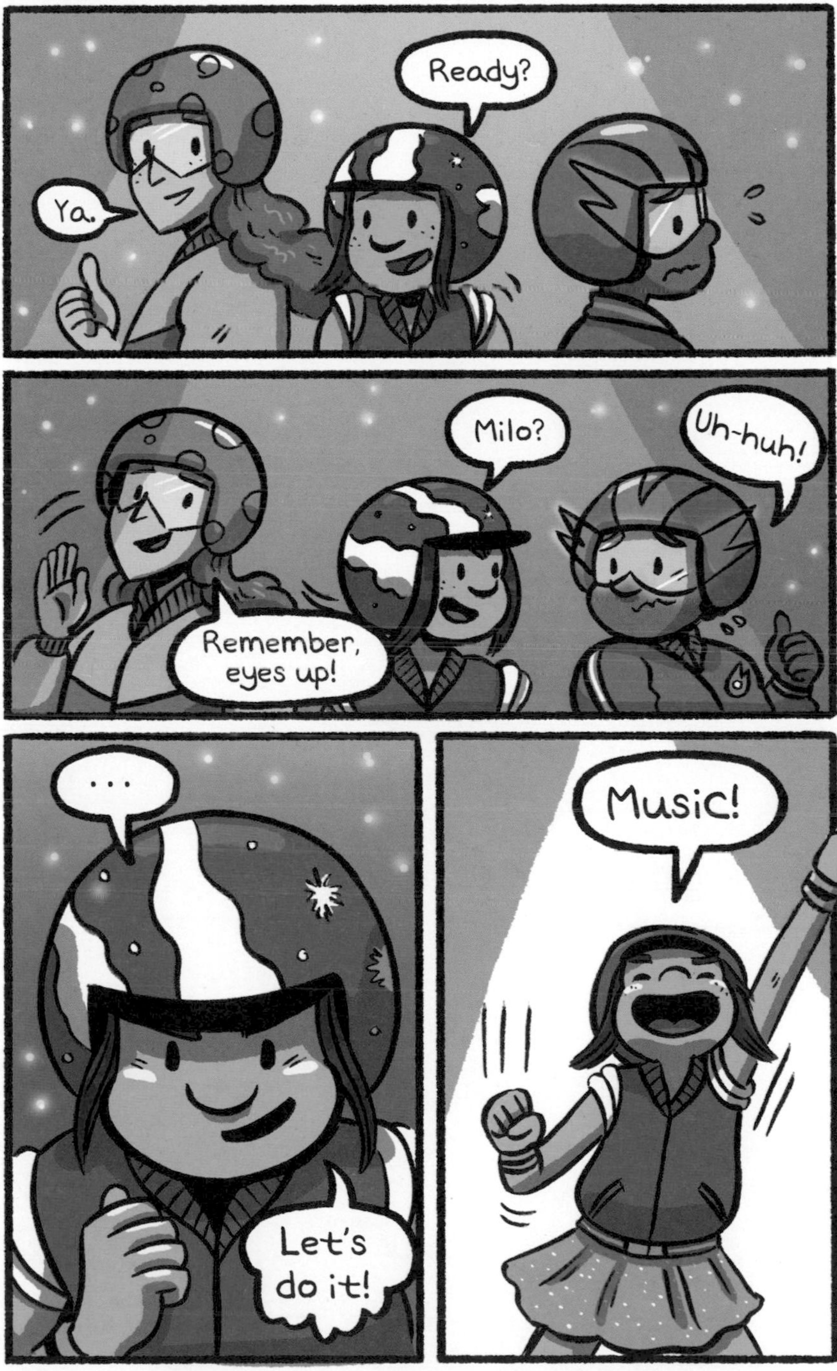
Ready?
Ya.
Milo?
Uh-huh!
Remember, eyes up!
...
Let's do it!
Music!

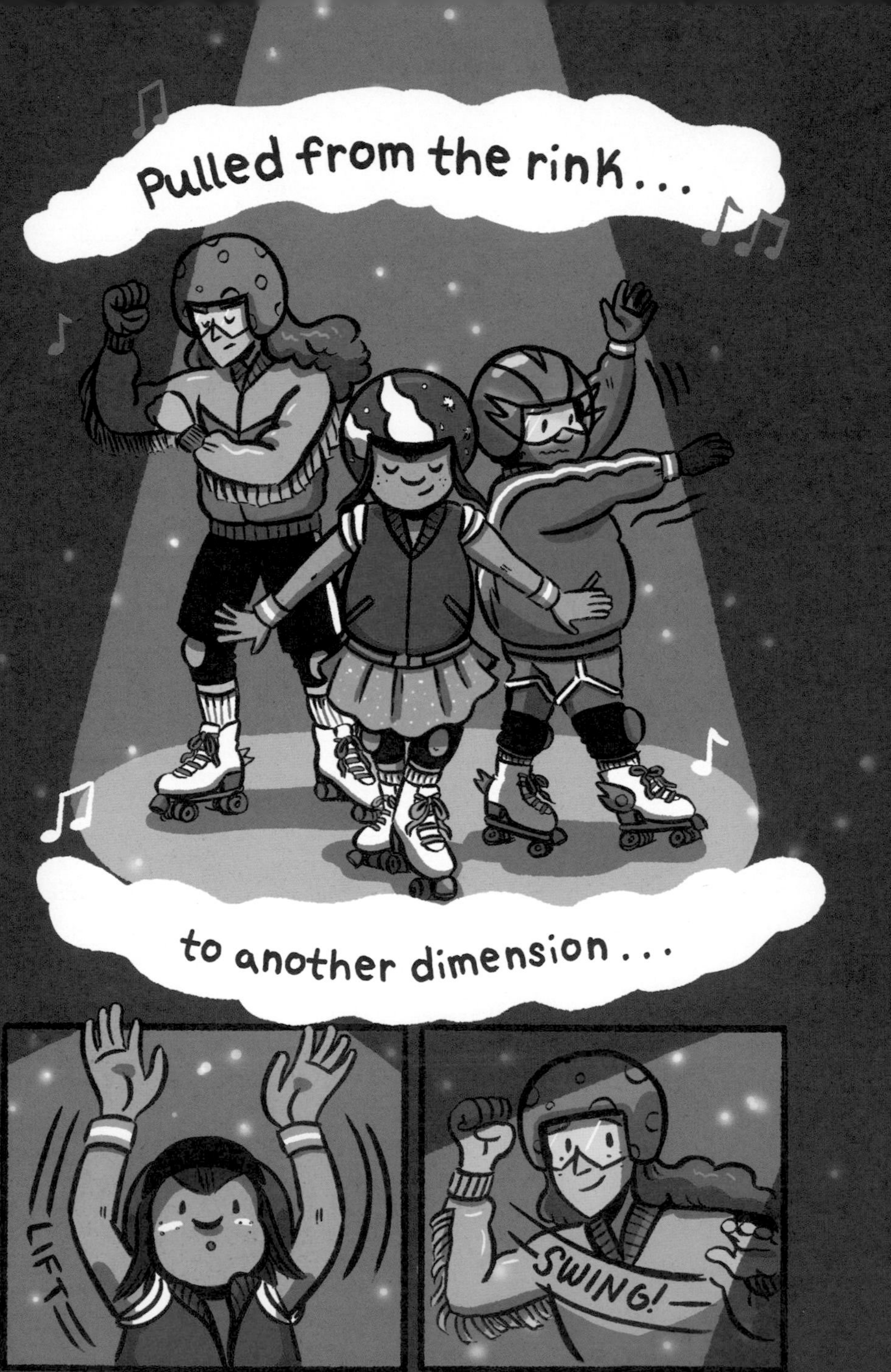
Pulled from the rink...
to another dimension...
LIFT
SWING!

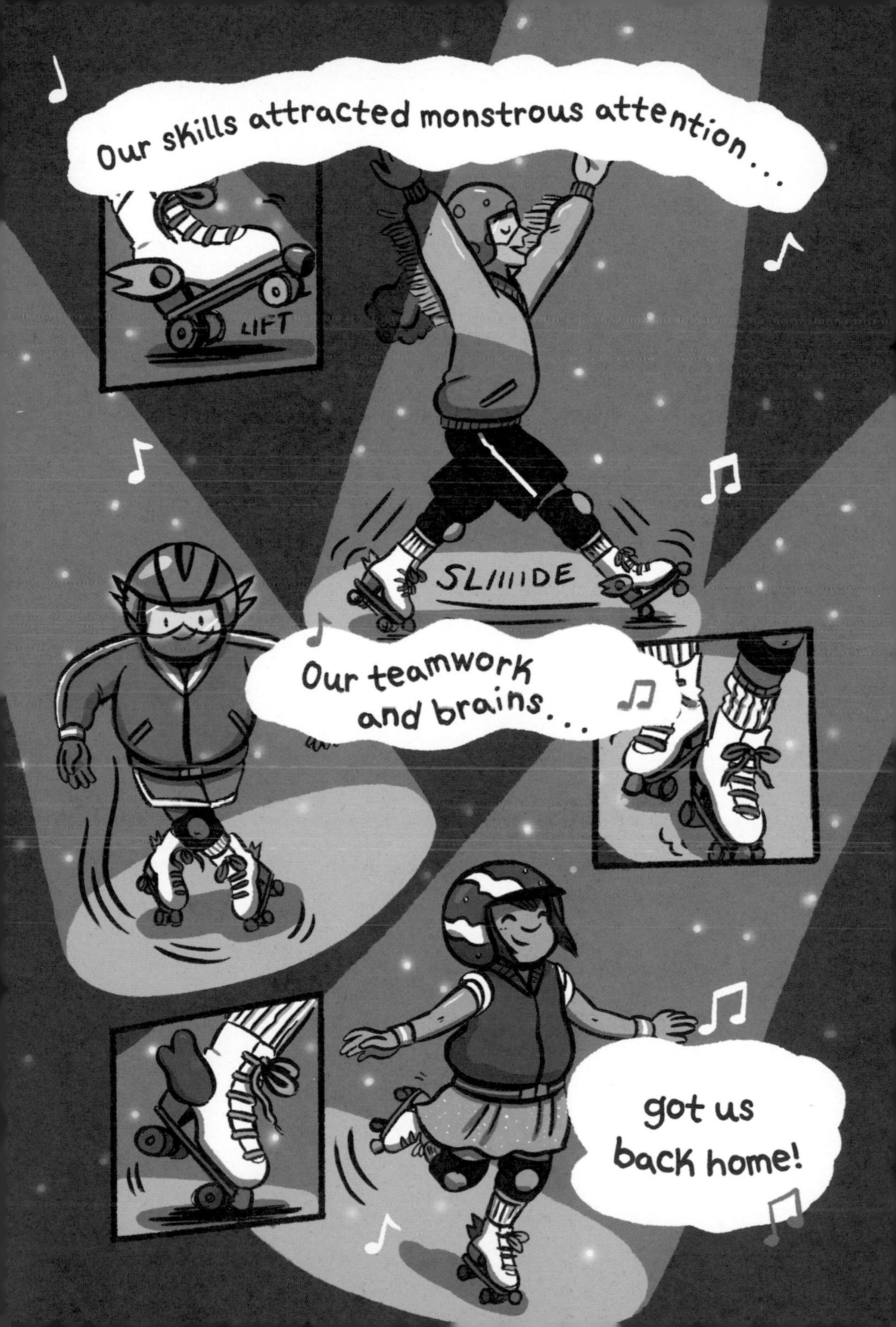
Our skills attracted monstrous attention...
LIFT
SLIIIIDE
Our teamwork and brains...
got us back home!

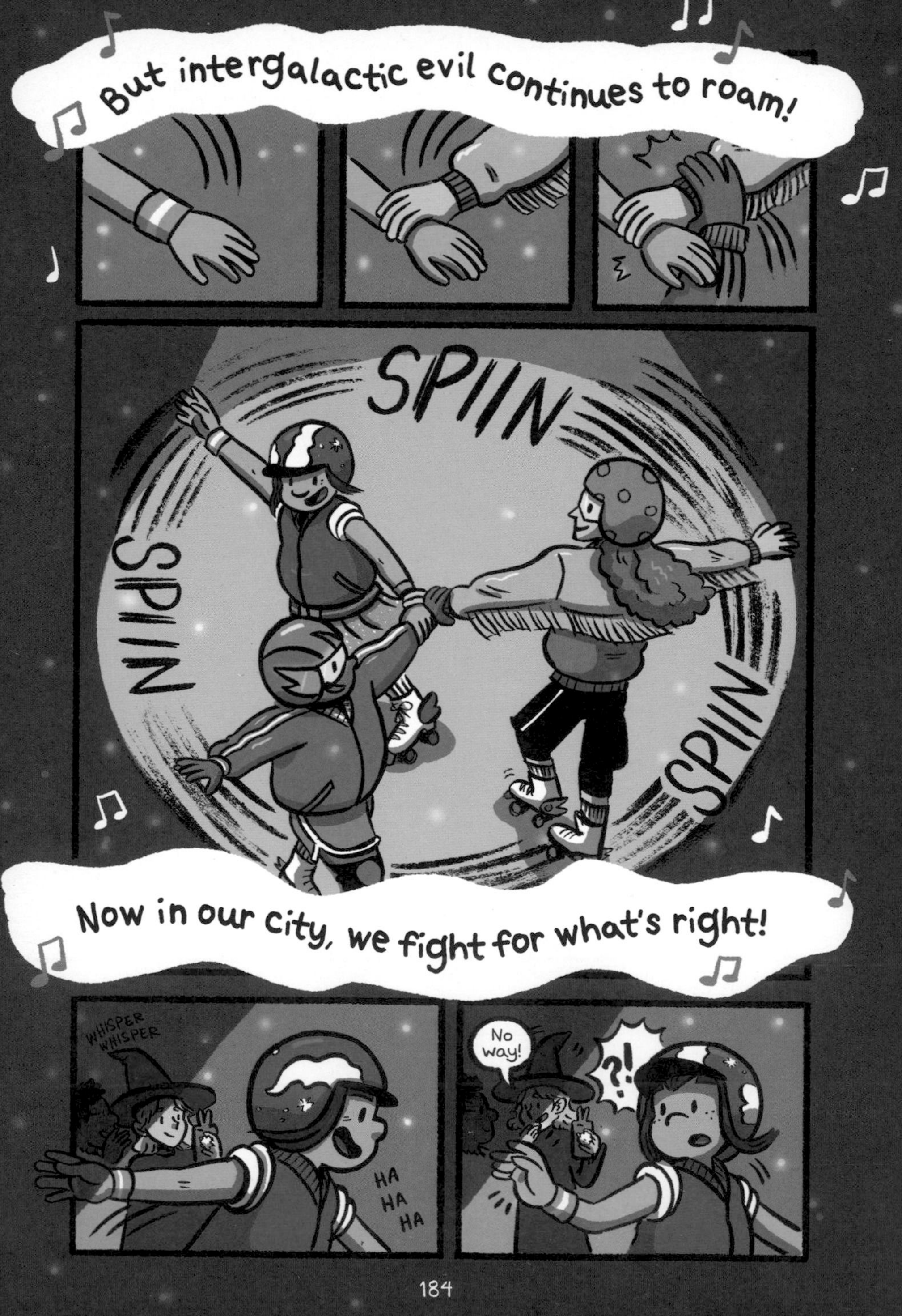
But intergalactic evil continues to roam!
SPIN
SPIN
SPIN
Now in our city, we fight for what's right!
WHISPER WHISPER
HA HA HA
No way!
?!

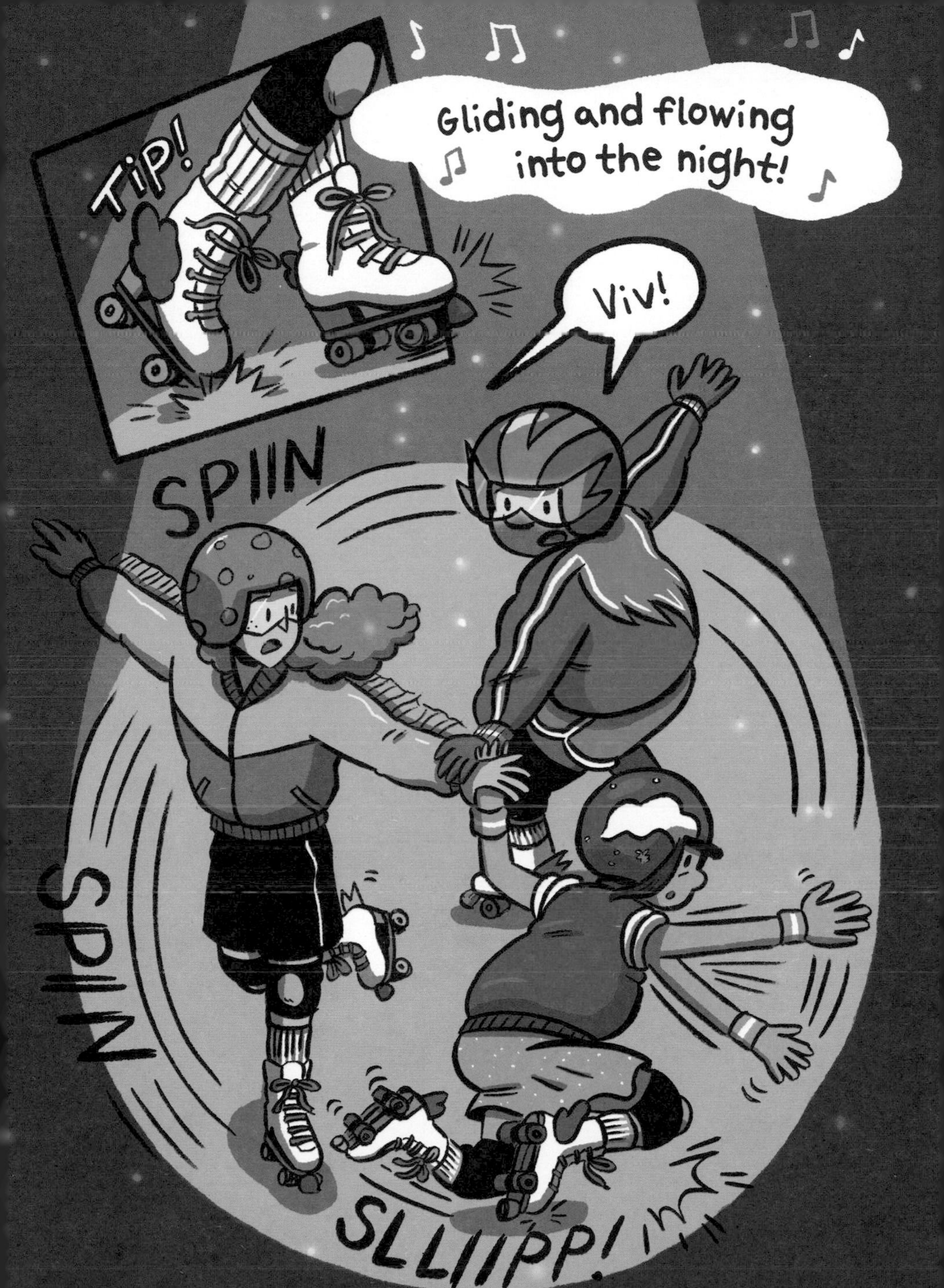
TIP!
Gliding and flowing into the night!
Viv!
SPIIN
SPIIN
SLLIIPP!

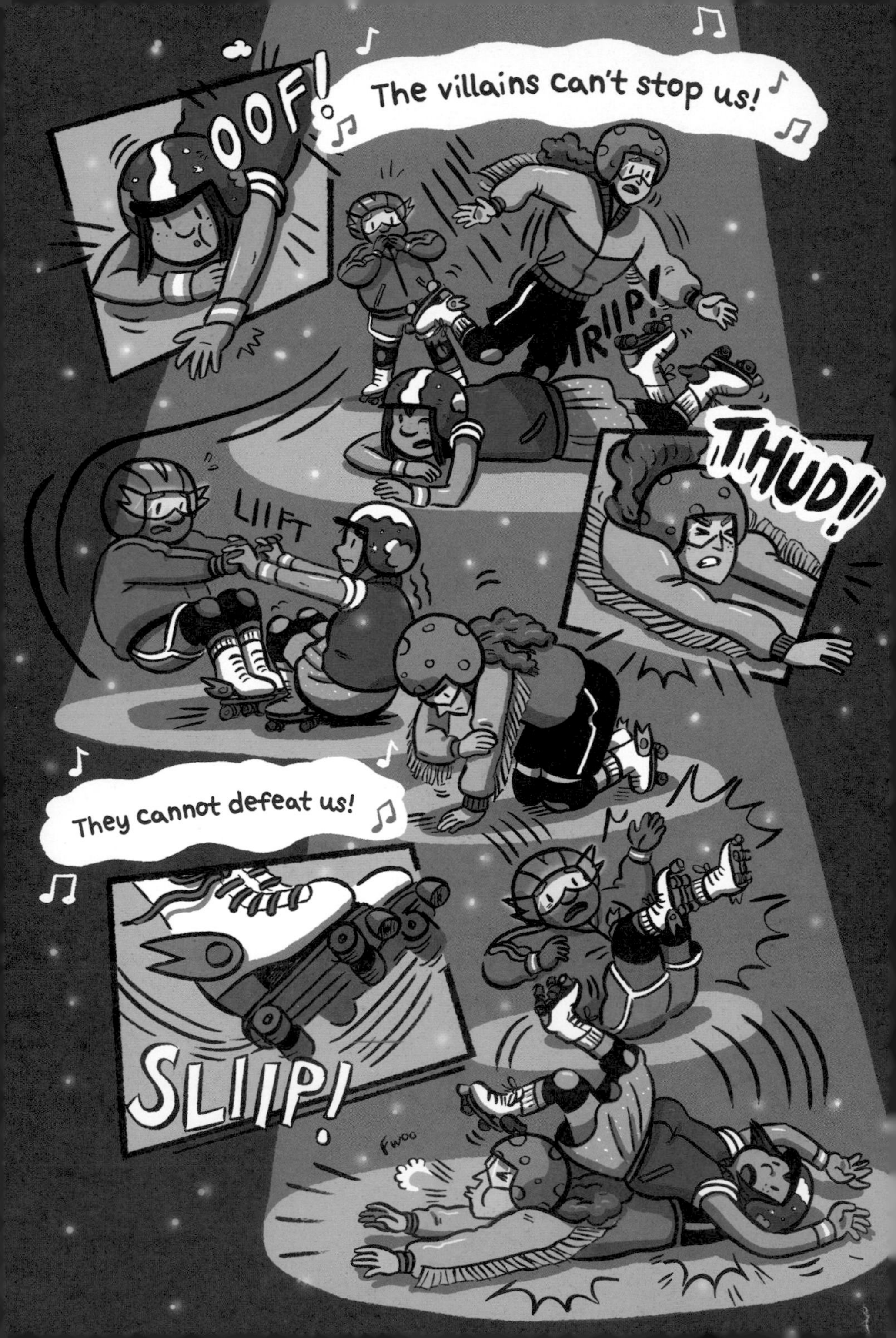

OOF!
The villains can't stop us!
RIIP!
THUD!
LIIFT
They cannot defeat us!
SLIIP!
FWOO

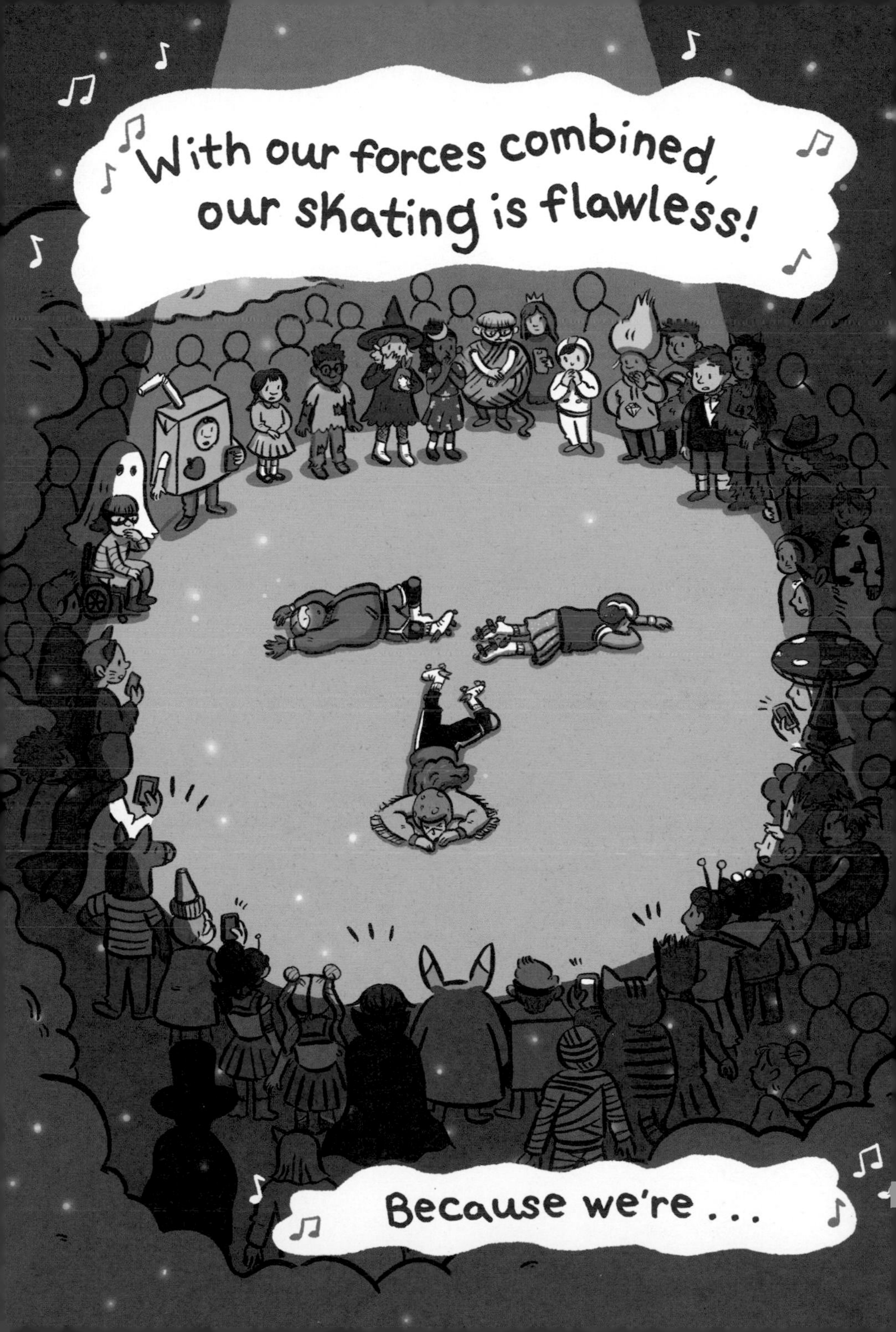
With our forces combined, our skating is flawless!
Because we're . . .

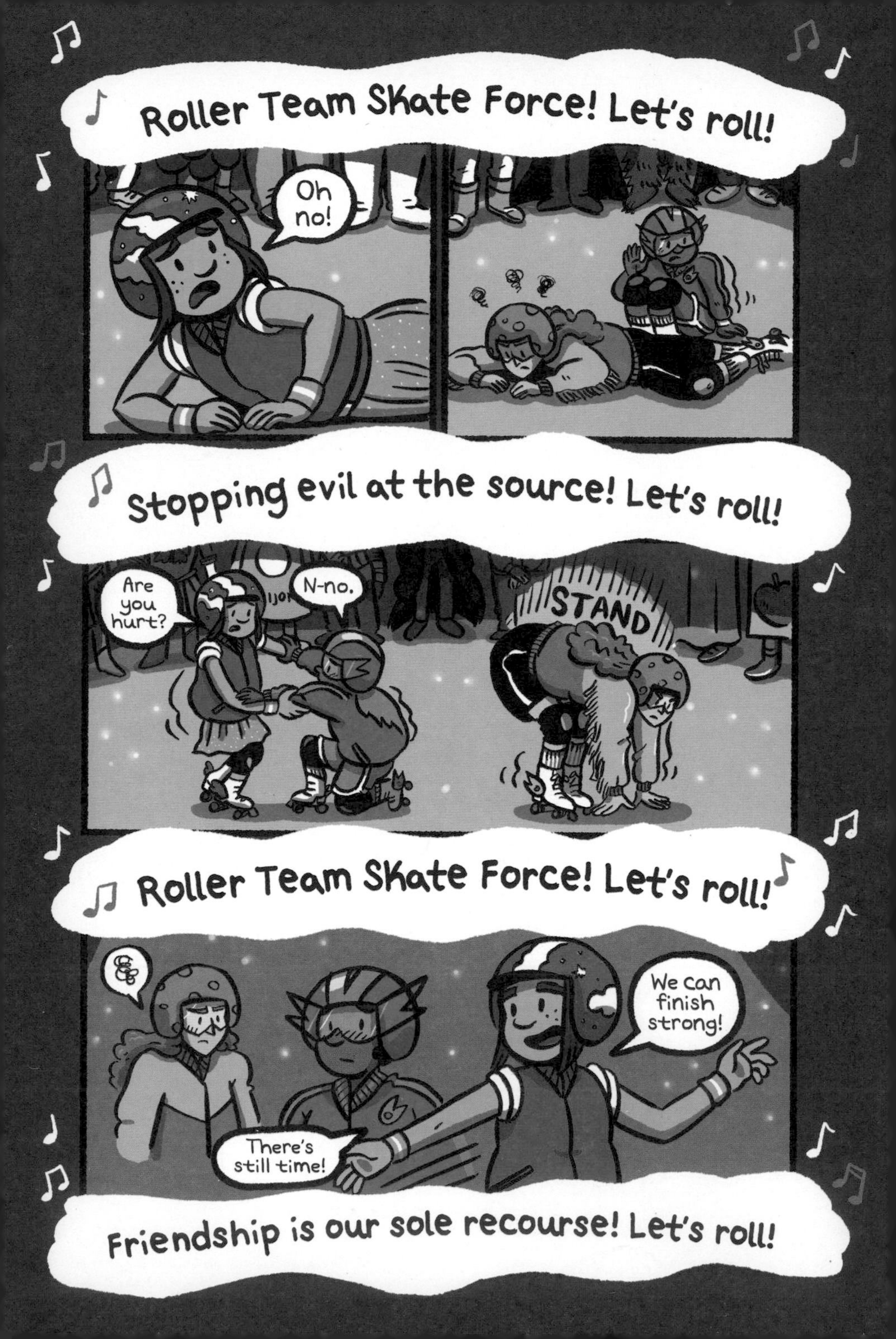
Roller Team Skate Force! Let's roll!
Oh no!
Stopping evil at the source! Let's roll!
Are you hurt?
N-no.
STAND
Roller Team Skate Force! Let's roll!
We can finish strong!
There's still time!
Friendship is our sole recourse! Let's roll!

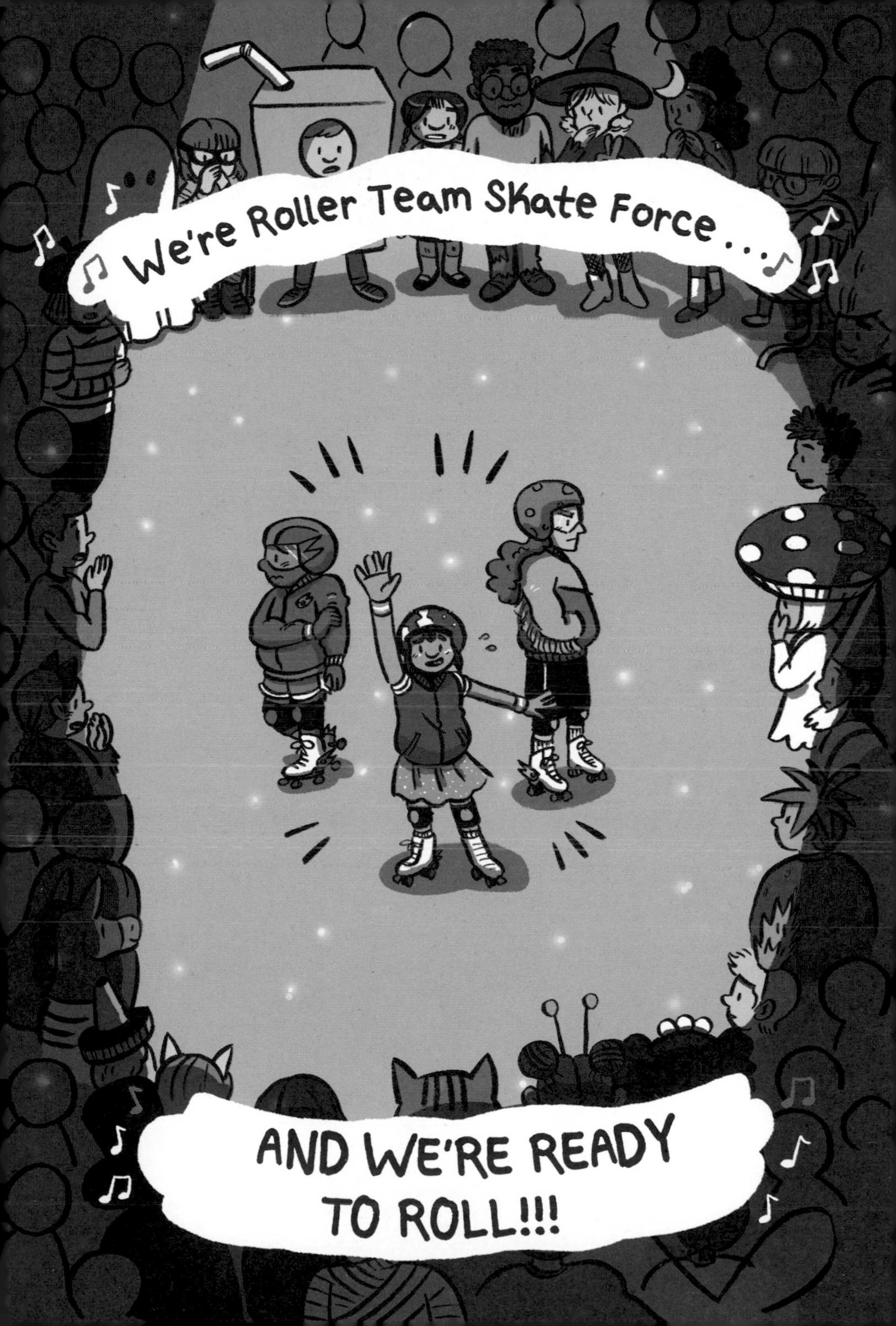
We're Roller Team Skate Force . . .
AND WE'RE READY TO ROLL!!!

...
HEE HEE
Uh.
GASP!
Wow!
TURN
CLAP
That was major!
CLAP
CLAP
CLAP
HA!
whisper
Let's give 'em a hand, everyone!

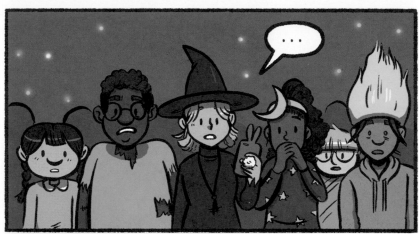

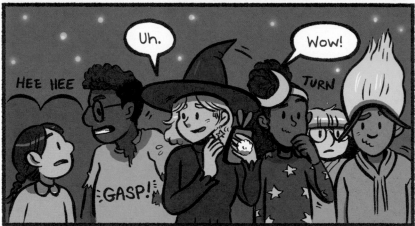

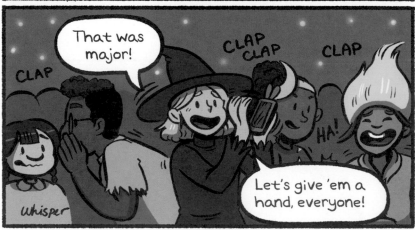

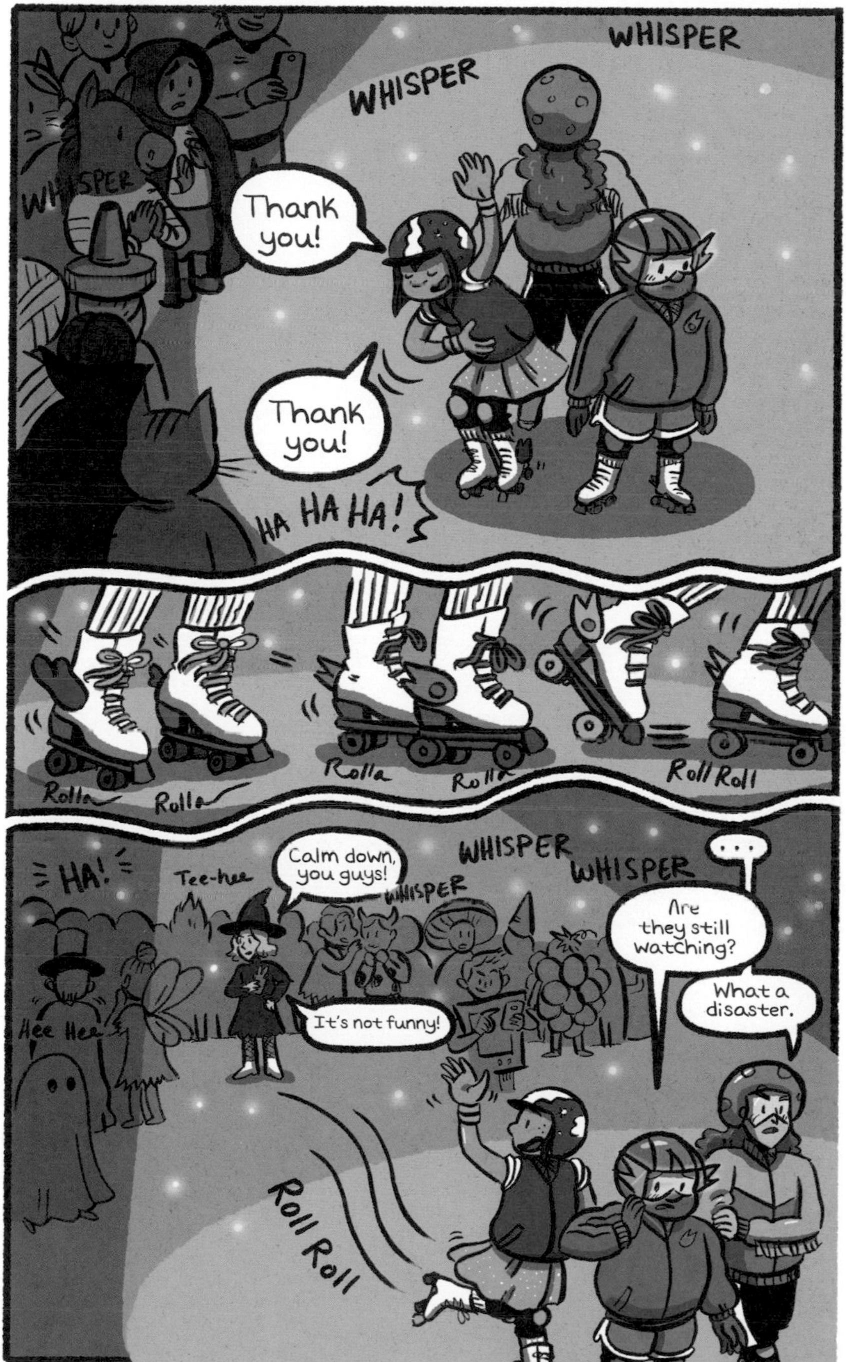
WHISPER
WHISPER
WHISPER
Thank you!
Thank you!
HA HA HA!
Rolla
Rolla
Rolla
Rolla
Roll Roll
HA!
Tee-hee
Calm down, you guys!
WHISPER
WHISPER
WHISPER
...
Are they still watching?
What a disaster.
It's not funny!
Hee Hee
Roll Roll

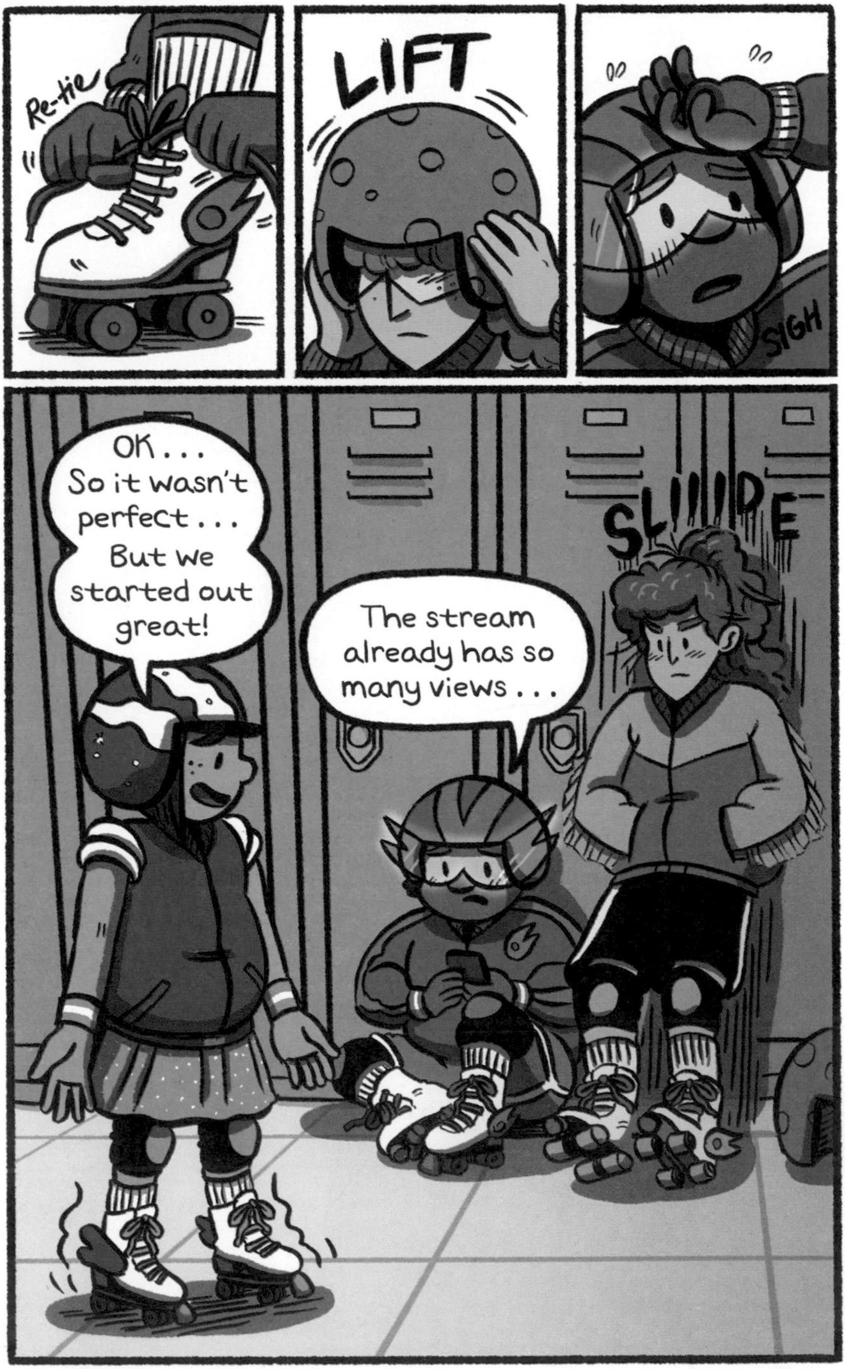
Re-tie
LIFT
SIGH
OK . . . So it wasn't perfect . . . But we started out great!
SLIIIDE
The stream already has so many views . . .

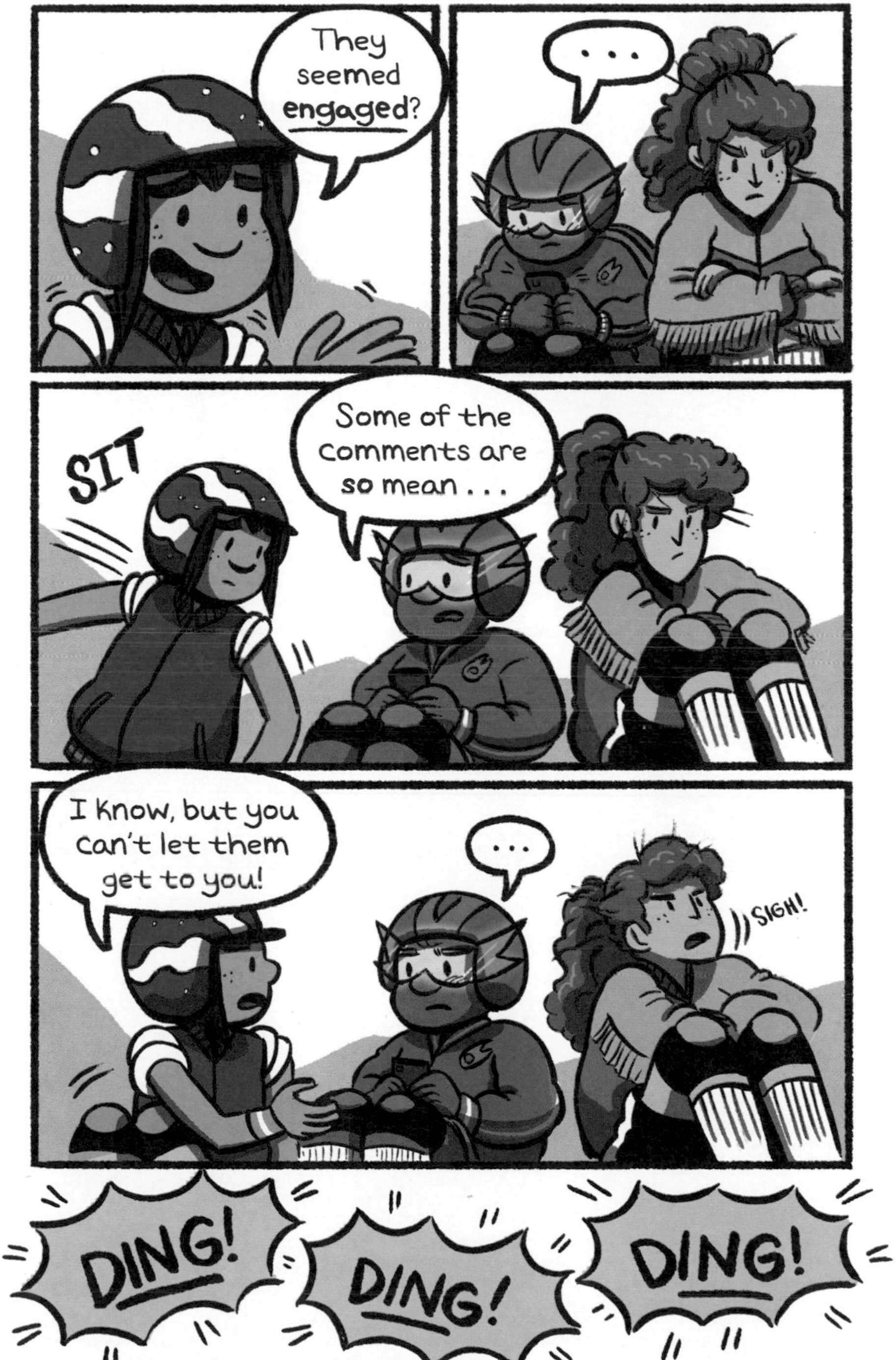

They seemed engaged?
. . .
SIT
Some of the comments are so mean . . .
I know, but you can't let them get to you!
. . .
SIGH!
DING!
DING!
DING!

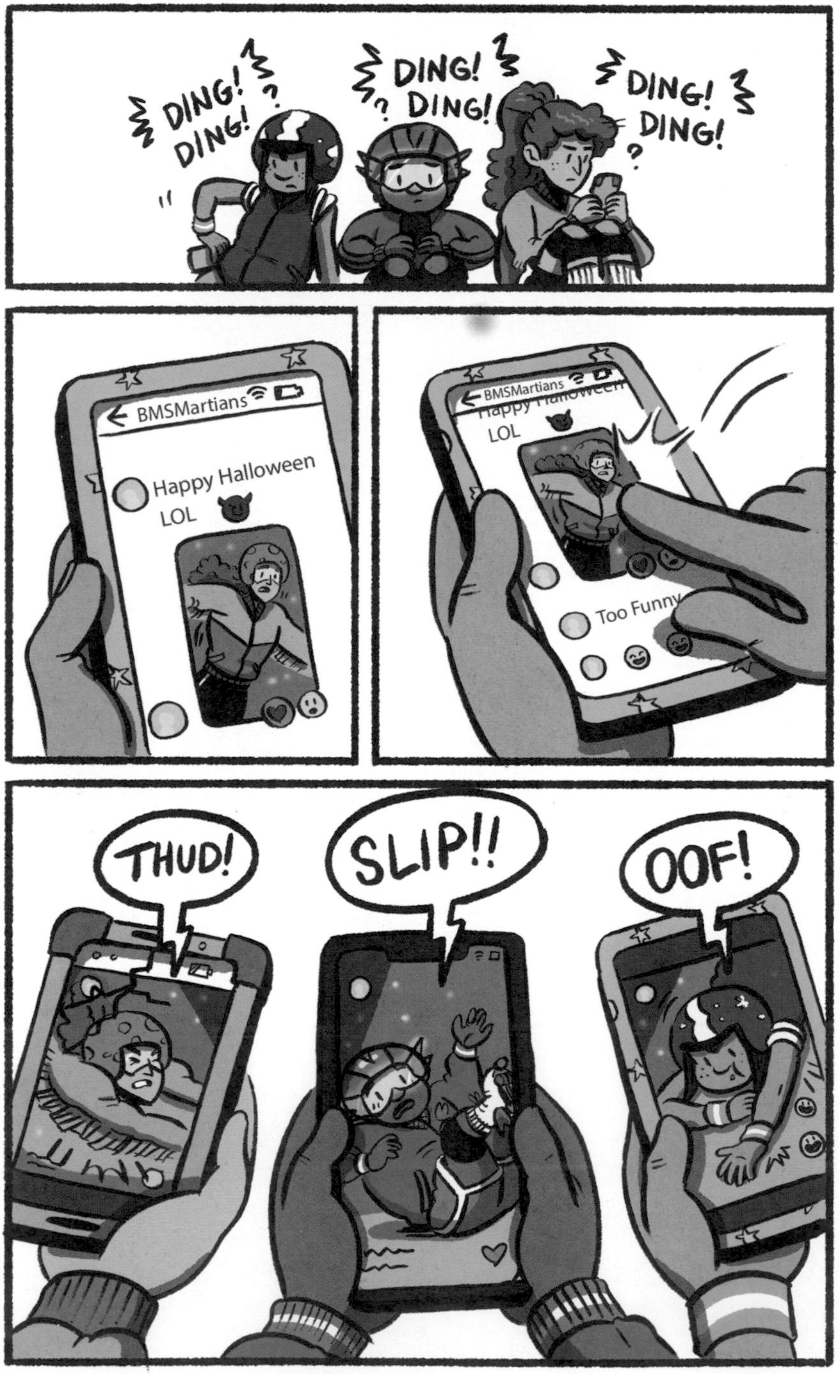
DING! DING!
DING! DING!
DING! DING!
BMSMartians
Happy Halloween LOL
BMSMartians
Happy Halloween LOL
Too Funny
THUD!
SLIP!!
OOF!

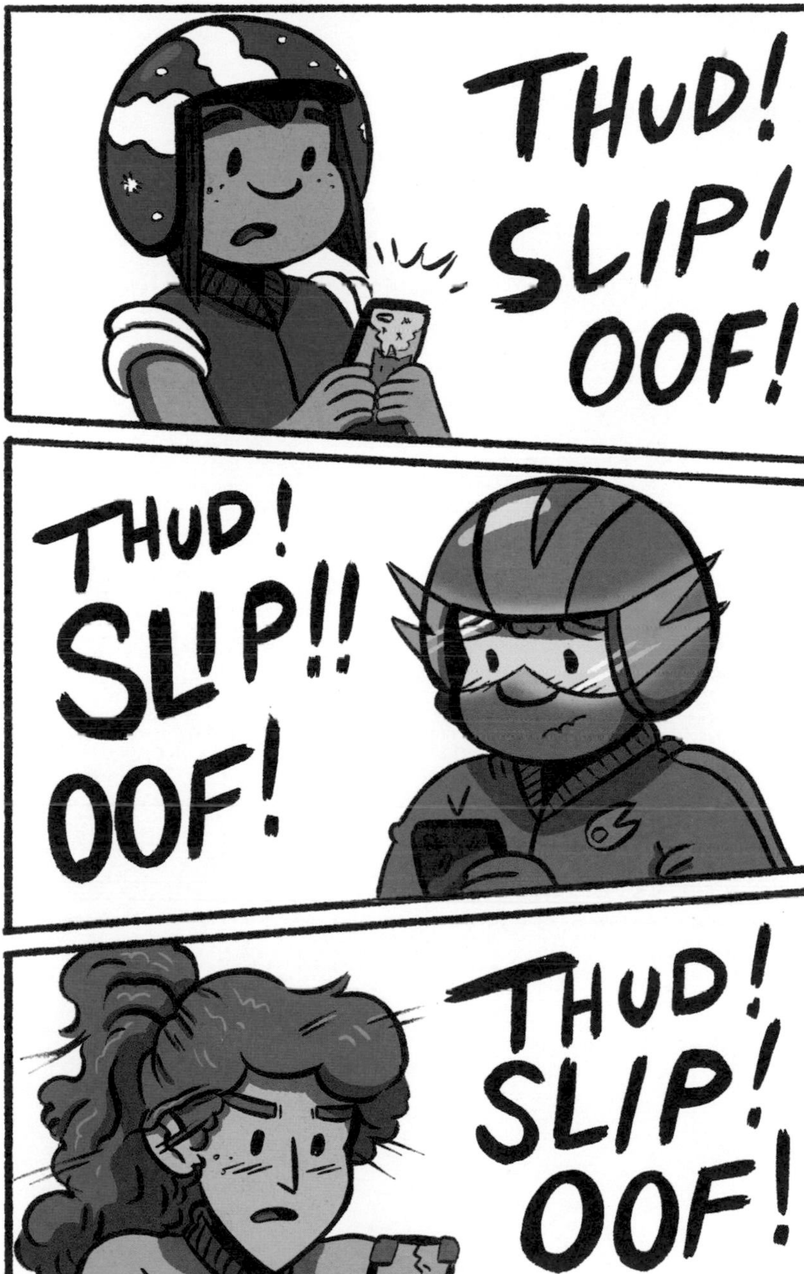
THUD!
SLIP!
OOF!
THUD!
SLIP!!
OOF!
THUD!
SLIP!
OOF!

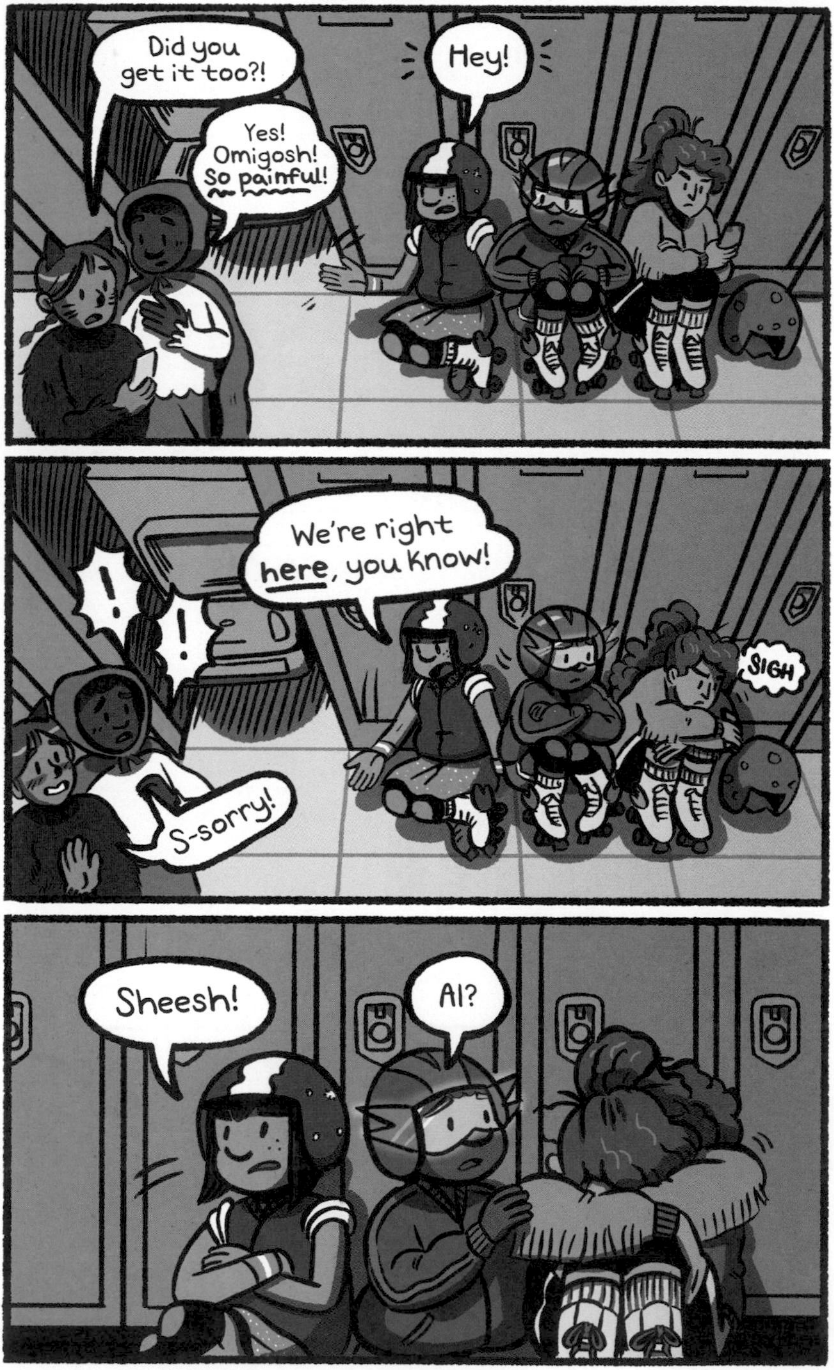
Did you get it too?!
Yes! Omigosh! So painful!
Hey!
We're right here, you know!
!
!
SIGH
S-sorry!
Sheesh!
Al?

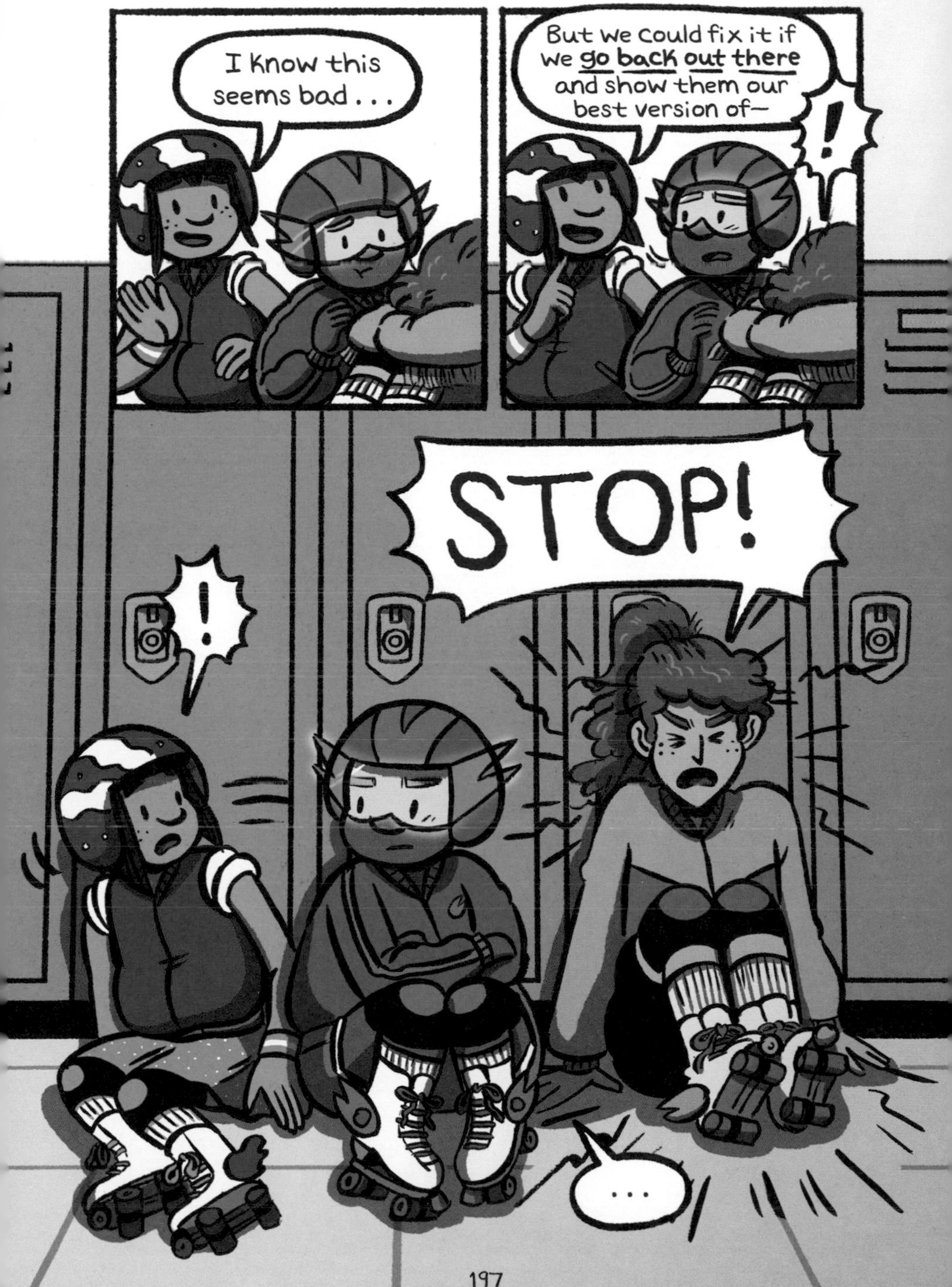
I know this seems bad . . .
But we could fix it if we **go back out there** and show them our best version of—
!
STOP!
!
. . .

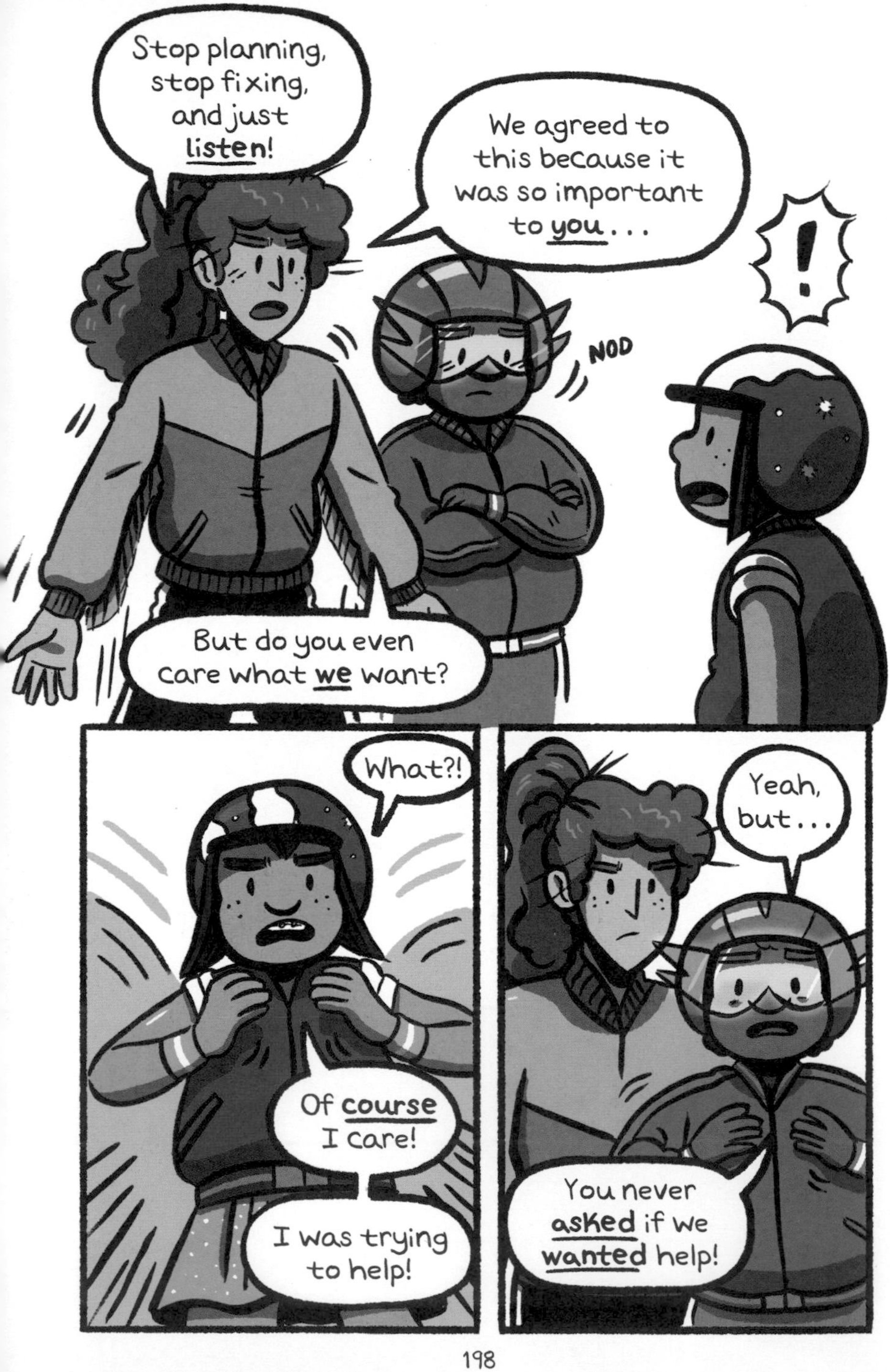
Stop planning, stop fixing, and just listen!
We agreed to this because it was so important to you...
!
NOD
But do you even care what we want?
What?!
Of course I care!
I was trying to help!
Yeah, but...
You never asked if we wanted help!

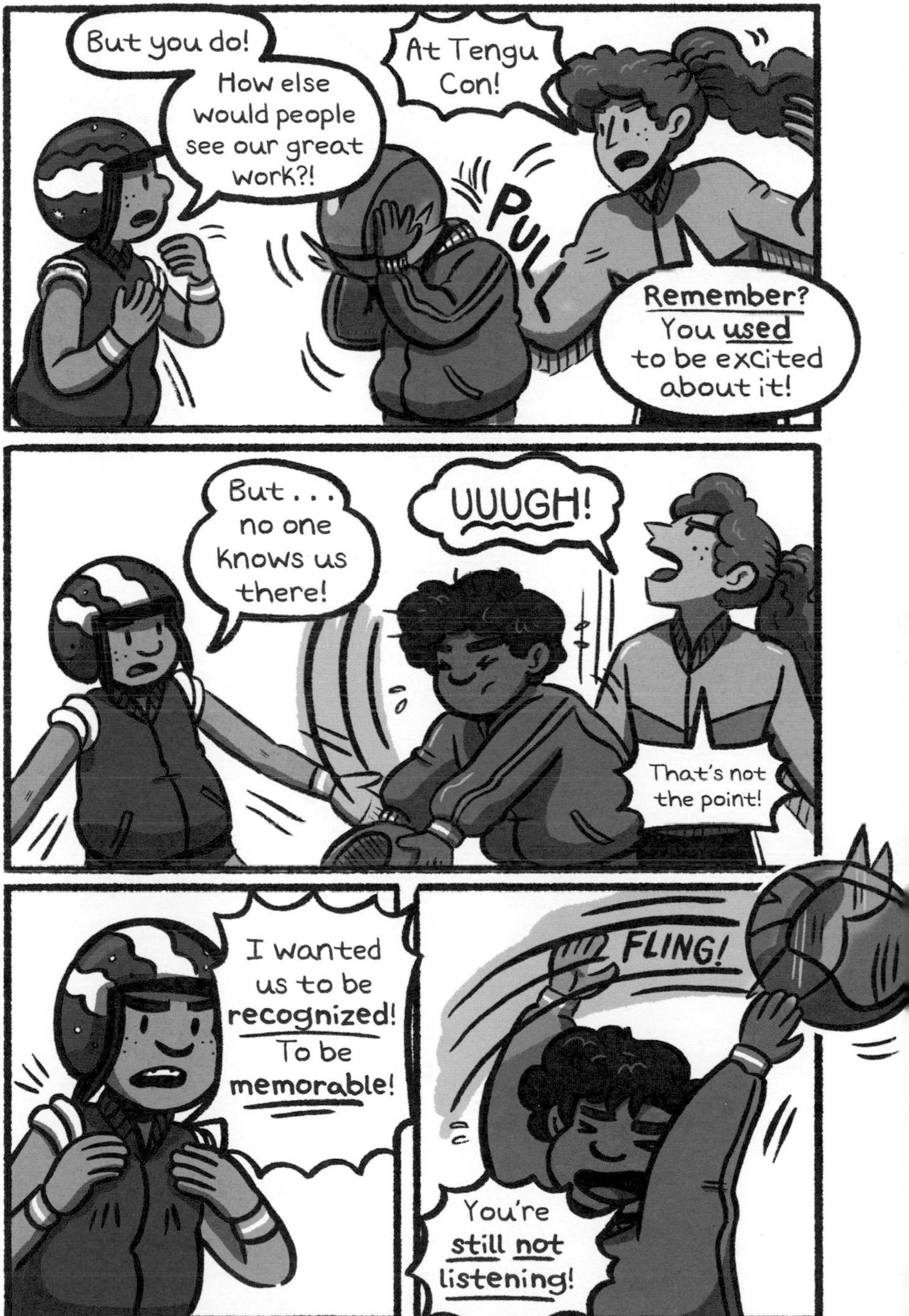

But you do!
How else would people see our great work?!
At Tengu Con!
PULL
Remember? You used to be excited about it!
But . . . no one knows us there!
UUUGH!
That's not the point!
I wanted us to be recognized! To be memorable!
FLING!
You're still not listening!

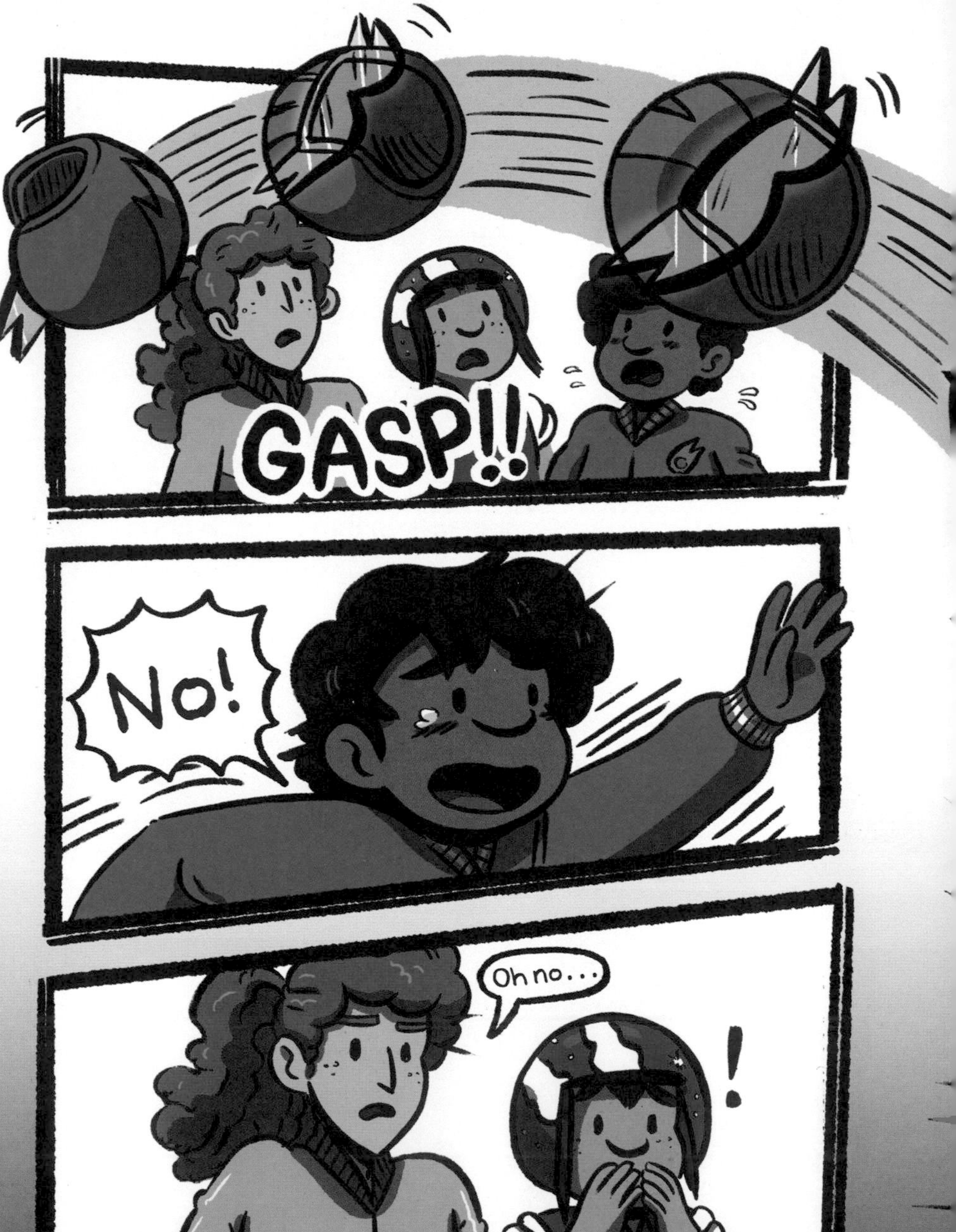
GASP!!!
No!
Oh no...
!

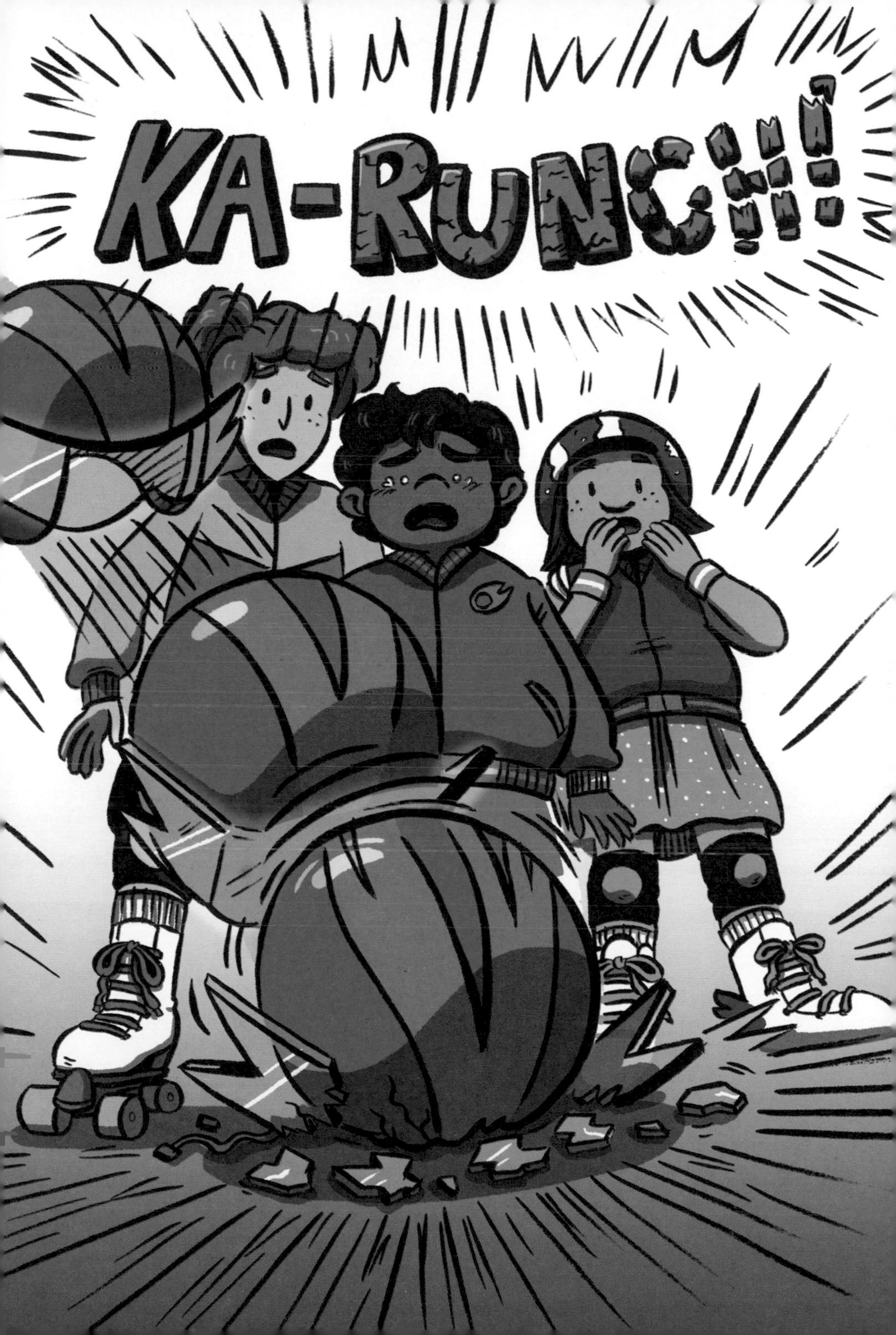
KA-RUNCH!!!

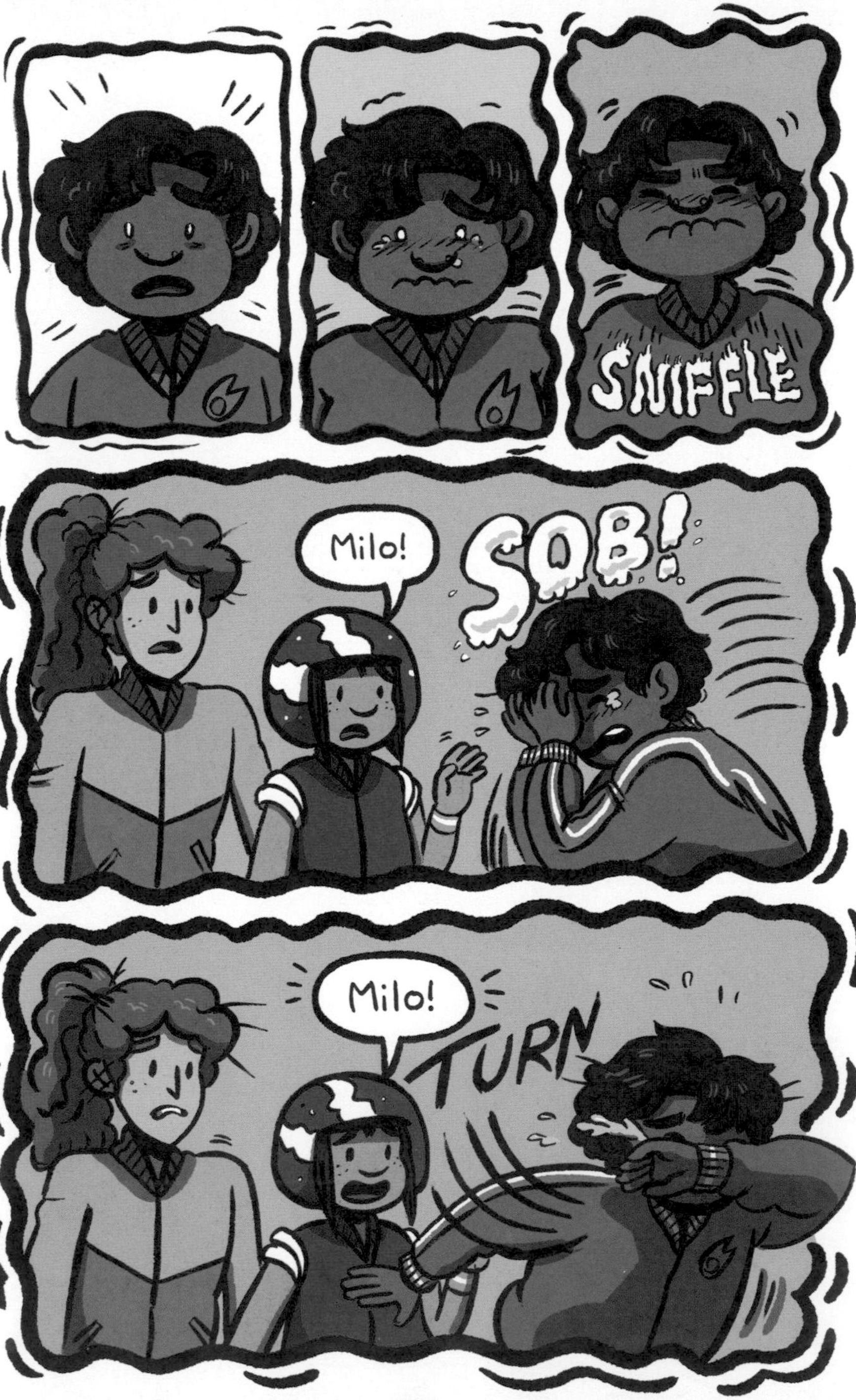
SNIFFLE
Milo!
SOB!
Milo!
TURN

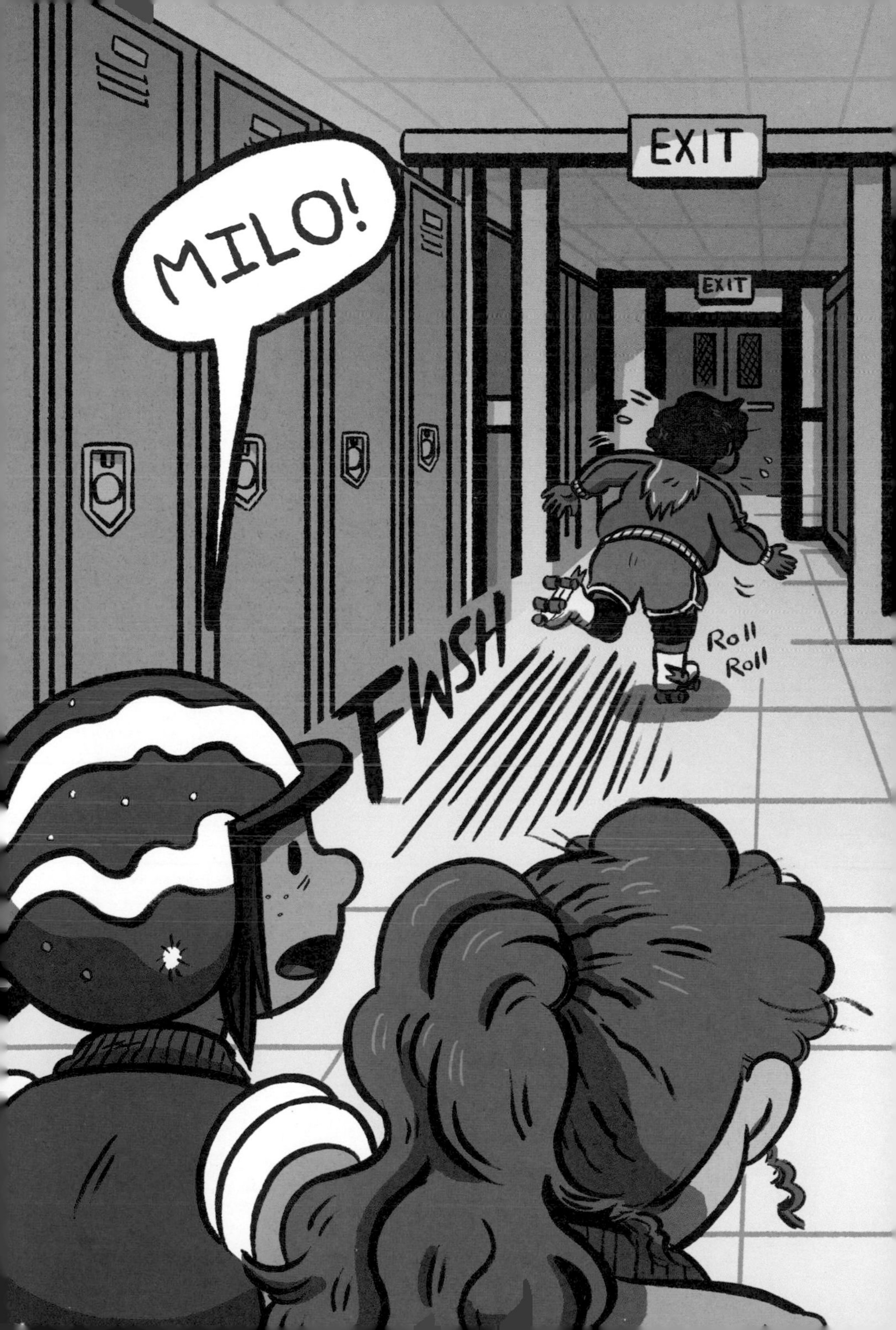
MILO!
EXIT
EXIT
FWSH
Roll
Roll

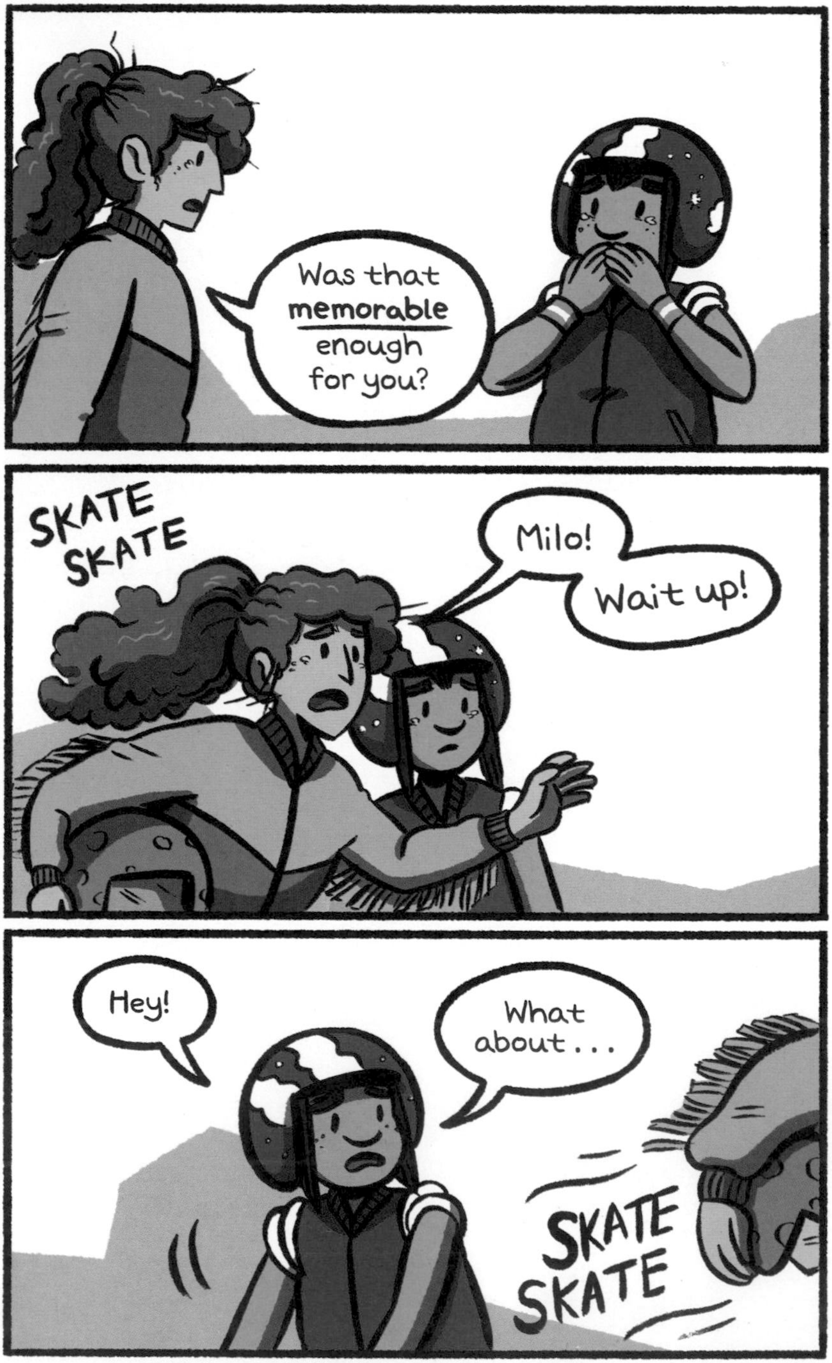
Was that memorable enough for you?
SKATE SKATE
Milo!
Wait up!
Hey!
What about . . .
SKATE SKATE

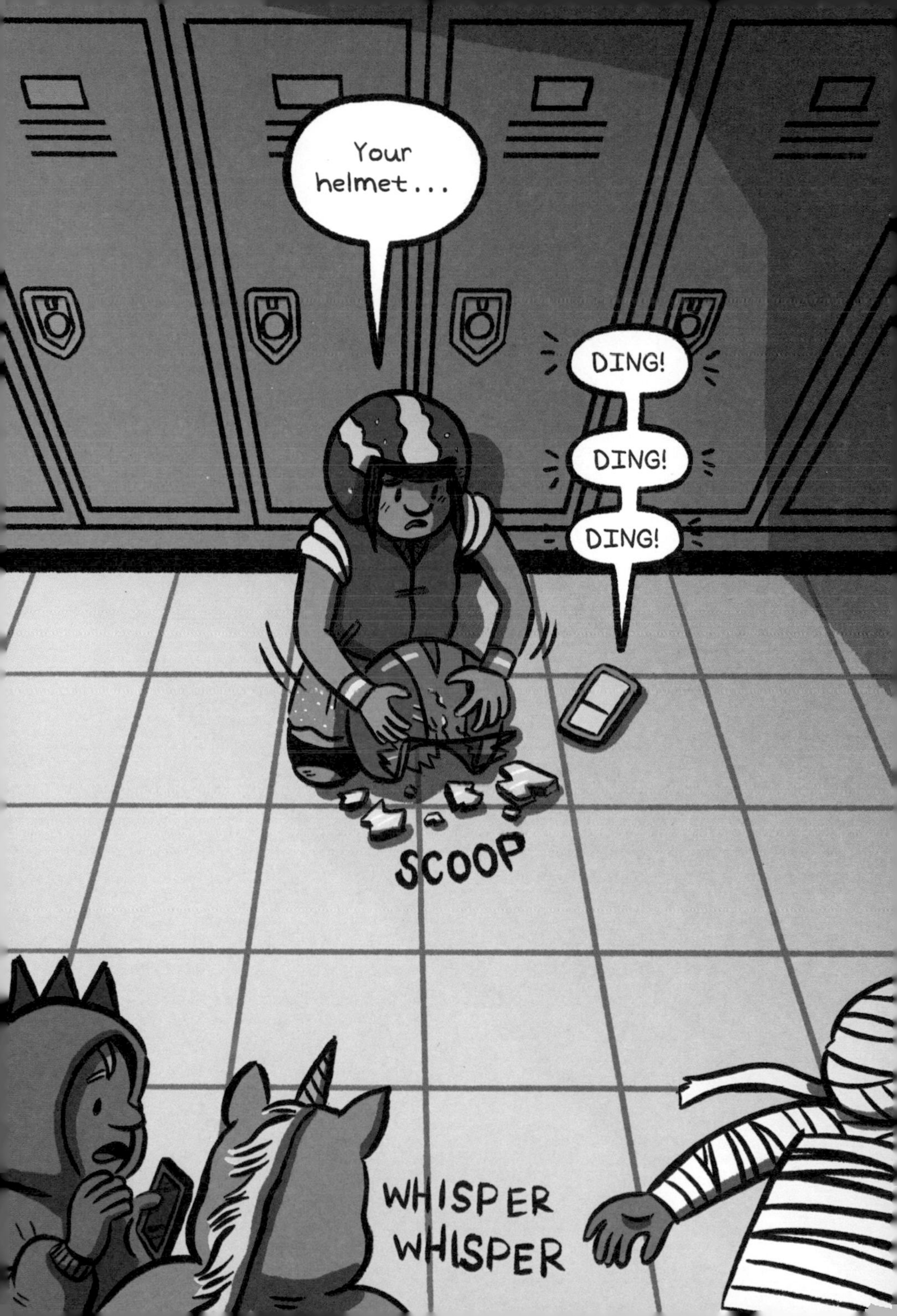
Your helmet...
DING!
DING!
DING!
SCOOP
WHISPER
WHISPER

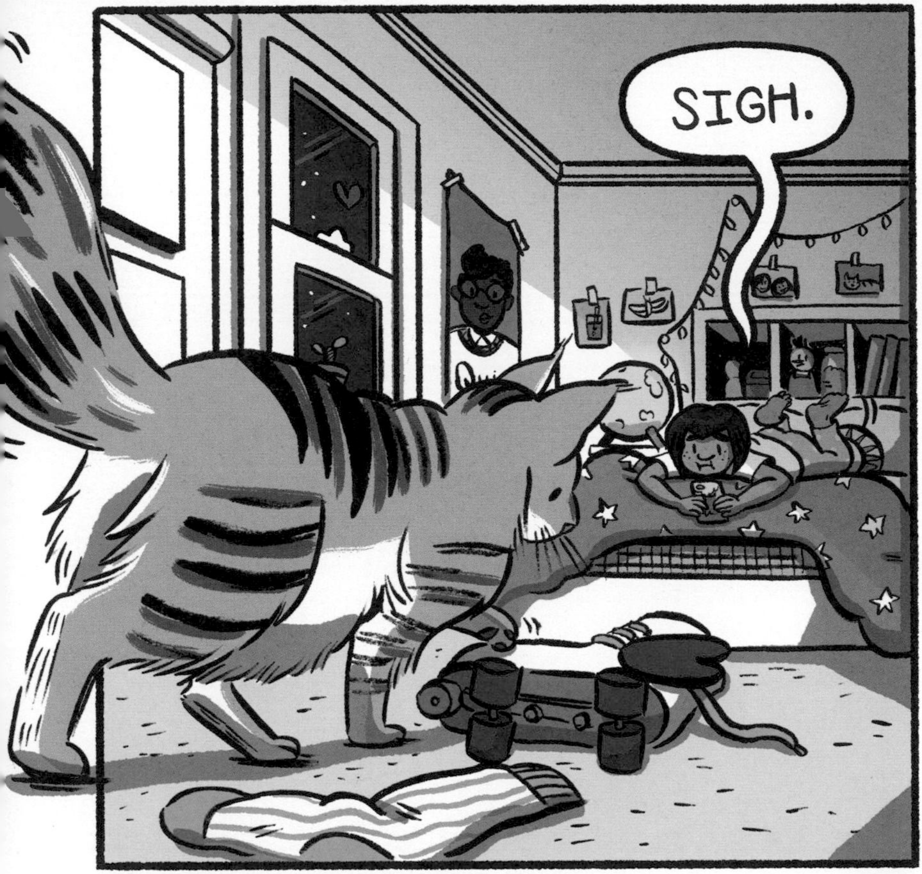
SIGH.

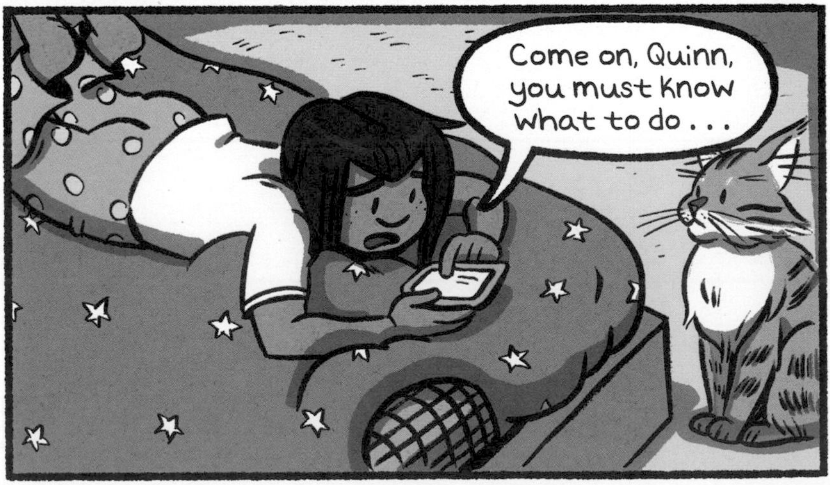
Come on, Quinn, you must know what to do . . .

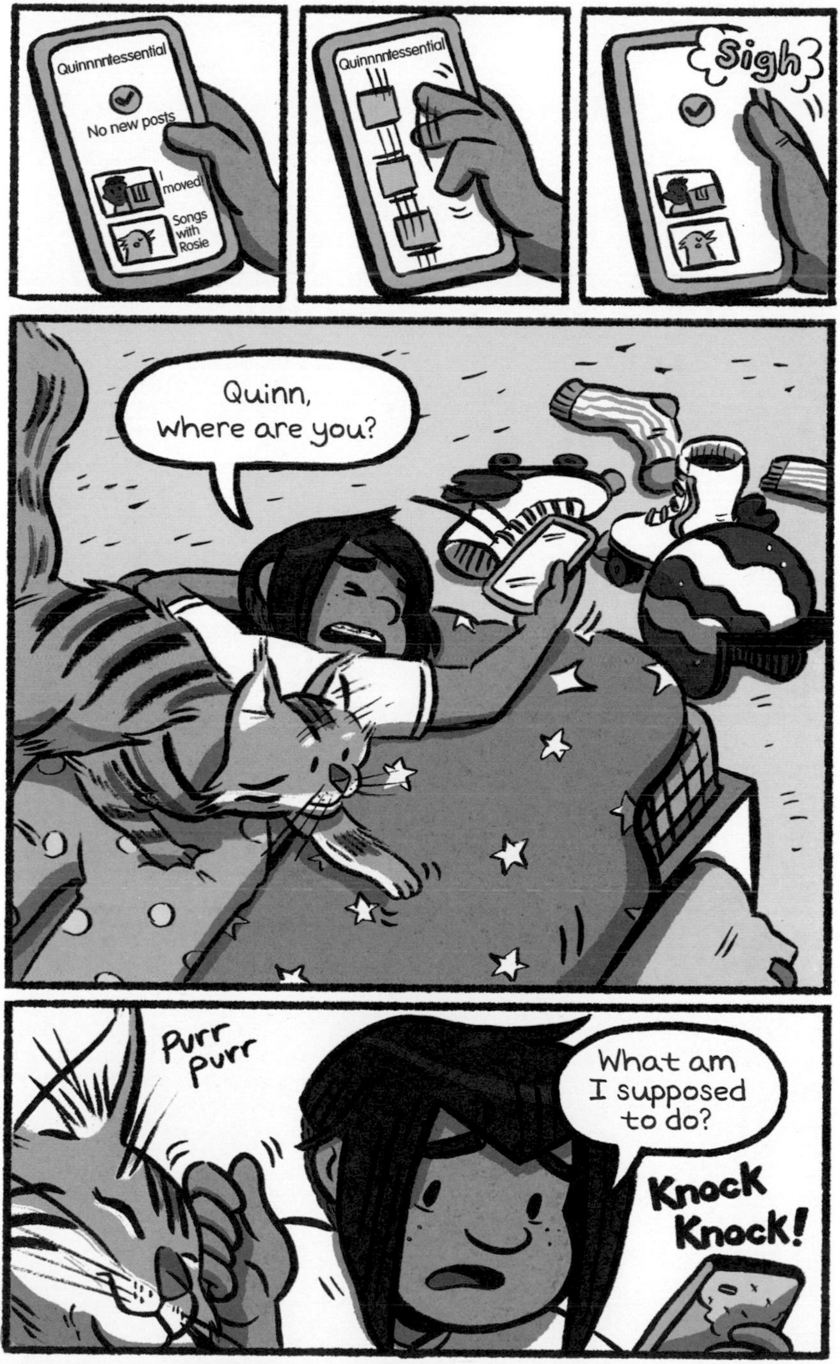
Quinnnntessential
No new posts
I moved!
Songs with Rosie
Quinnnntessential
Sigh
Quinn, Where are you?
Purr purr
What am I supposed to do?
Knock Knock!

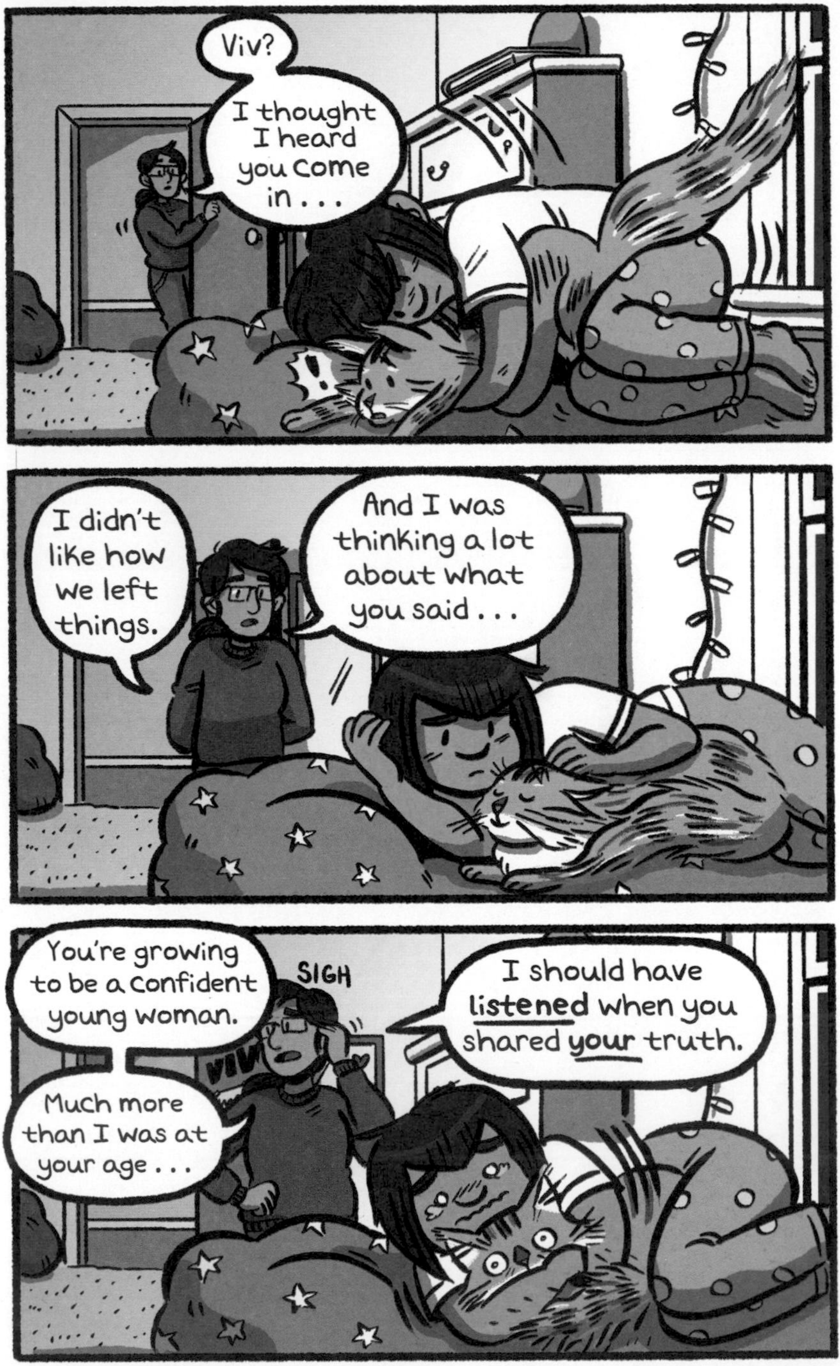
Viv?
I thought I heard you come in . . .
I didn't like how we left things.
And I was thinking a lot about what you said . . .
You're growing to be a confident young woman.
Much more than I was at your age . . .
SIGH
I should have listened when you shared your truth.
VIV

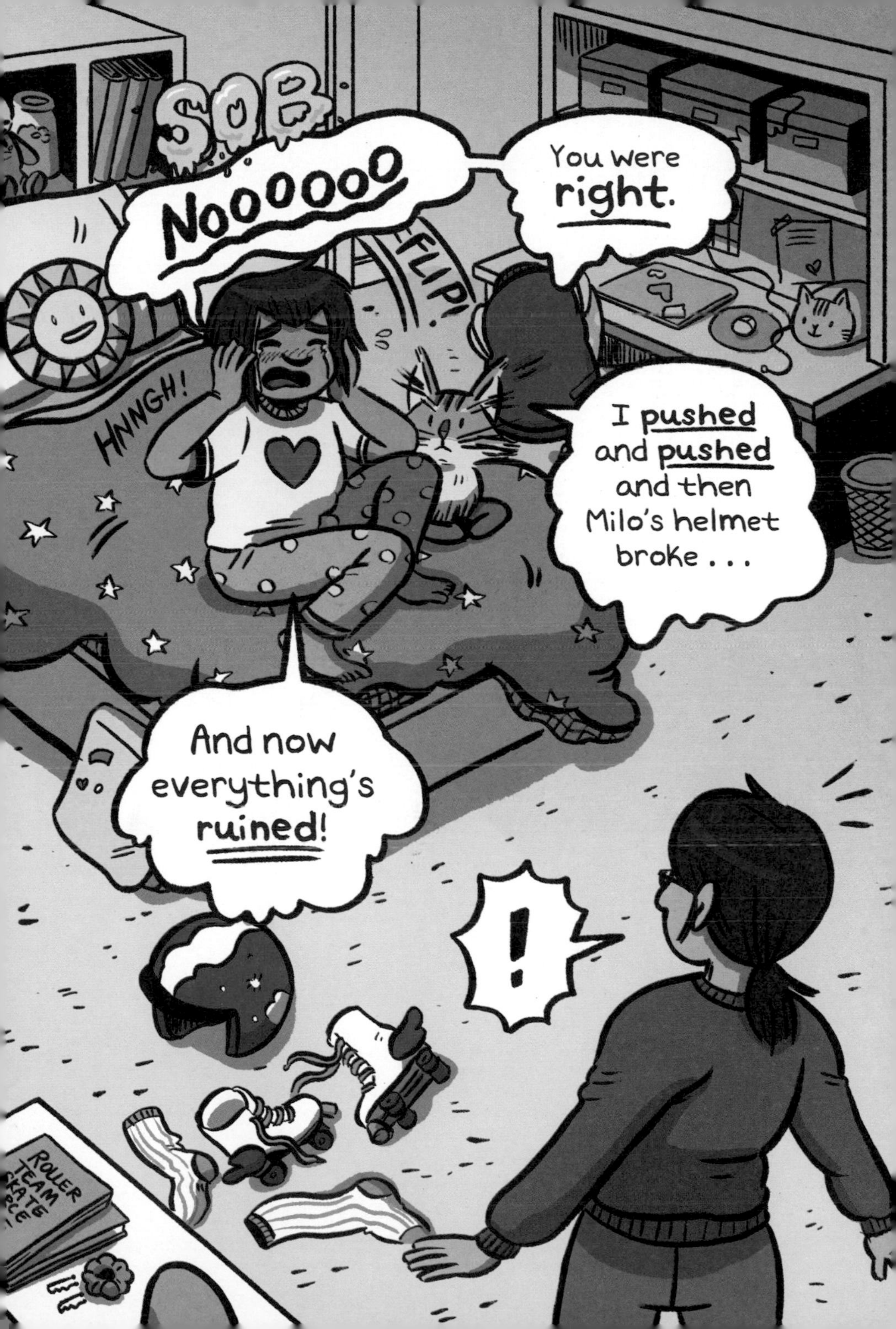

SOB
NOOOOOO
You were right.
FLIP!
HNNGH!
I pushed and pushed and then Milo's helmet broke . . .
And now everything's ruined!
!
ROLLER TEAM SKATE

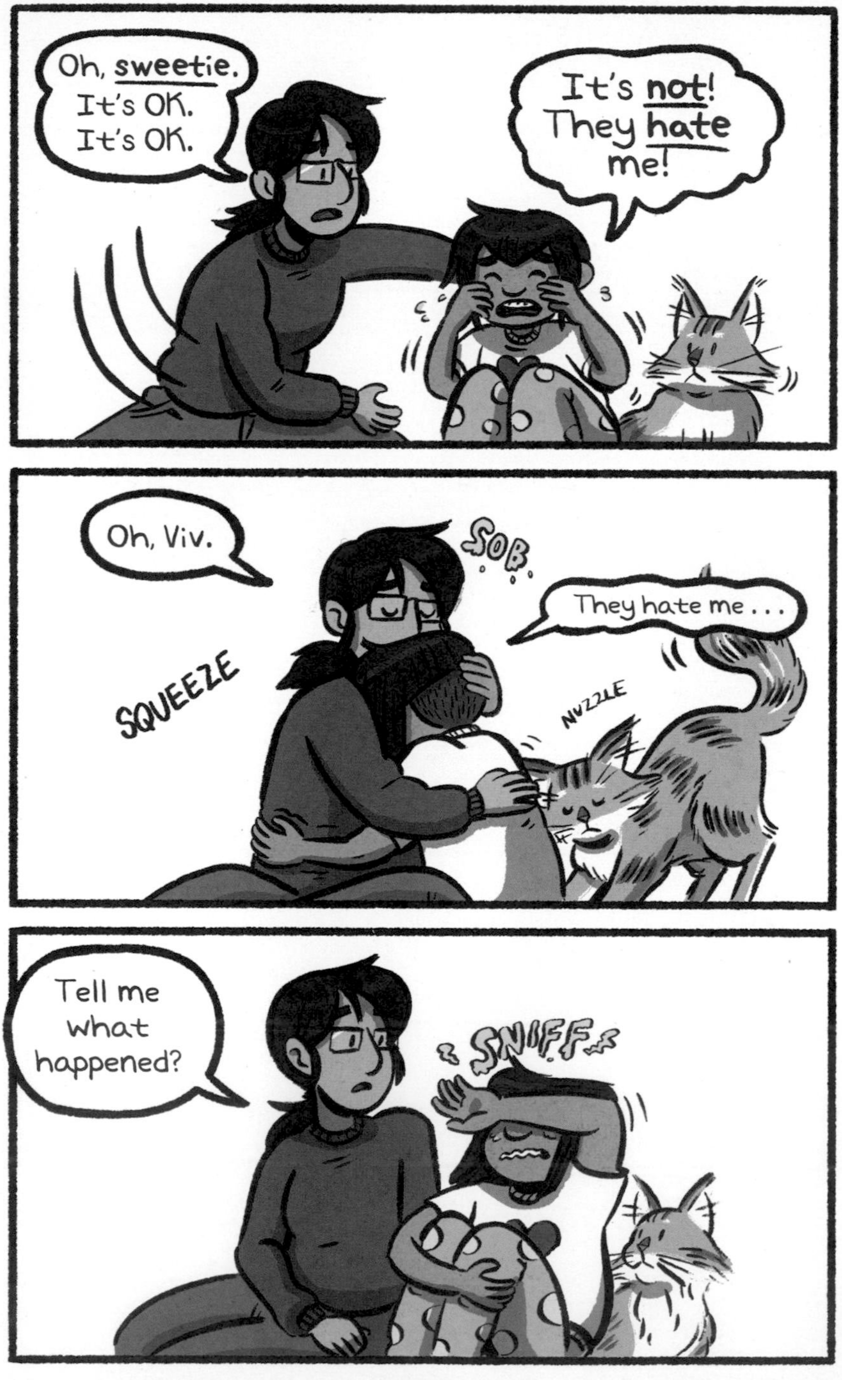
Oh, sweetie. It's OK. It's OK.
It's not! They hate me!
Oh, Viv.
SOB
They hate me . . .
SQUEEZE
NUZZLE
Tell me what happened?
SNIFF

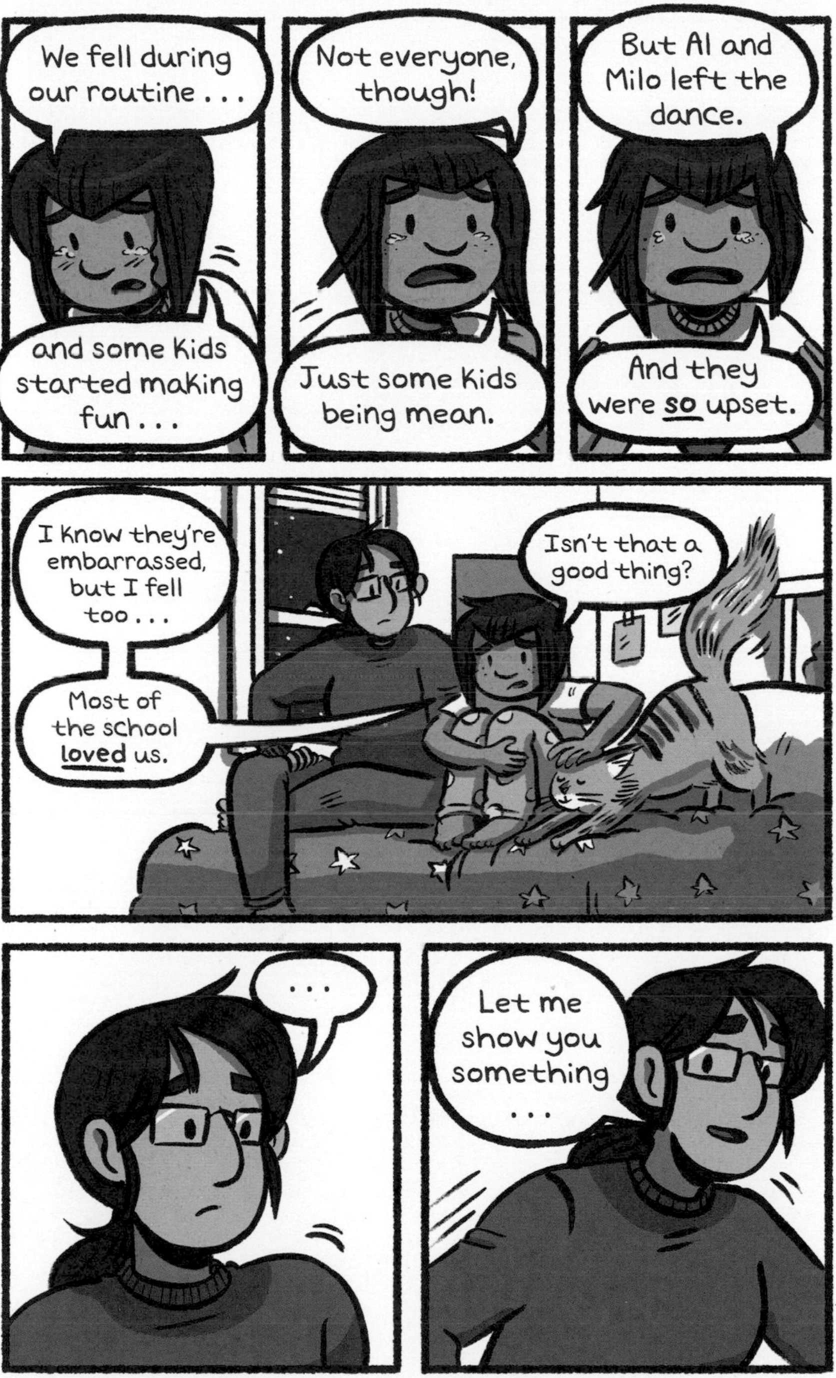
We fell during our routine . . .
and some kids started making fun . . .
Not everyone, though!
Just some kids being mean.
But Al and Milo left the dance.
And they were so upset.
I know they're embarrassed, but I fell too . . .
Most of the school loved us.
Isn't that a good thing?
. . .
Let me show you something . . .

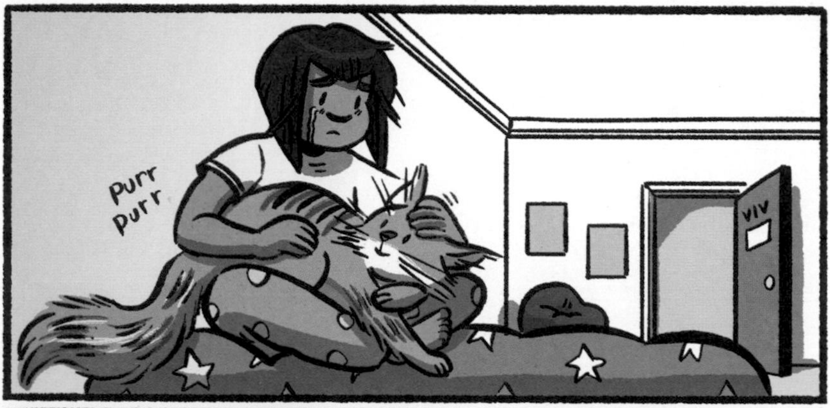
purr
purr
VIV

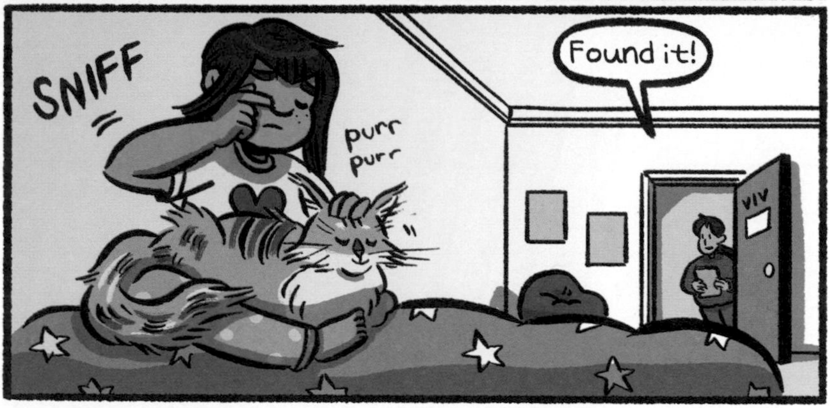
SNIFF
purr
purr
Found it!
VIV

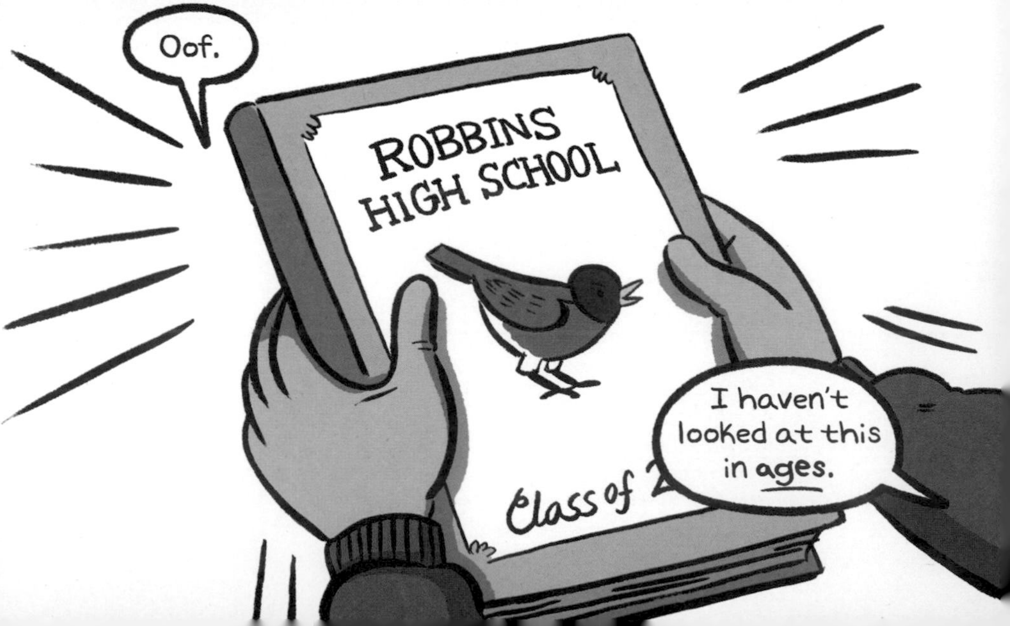
Oof.
ROBBINS
HIGH SCHOOL
Class of 2
I haven't looked at this in ages.

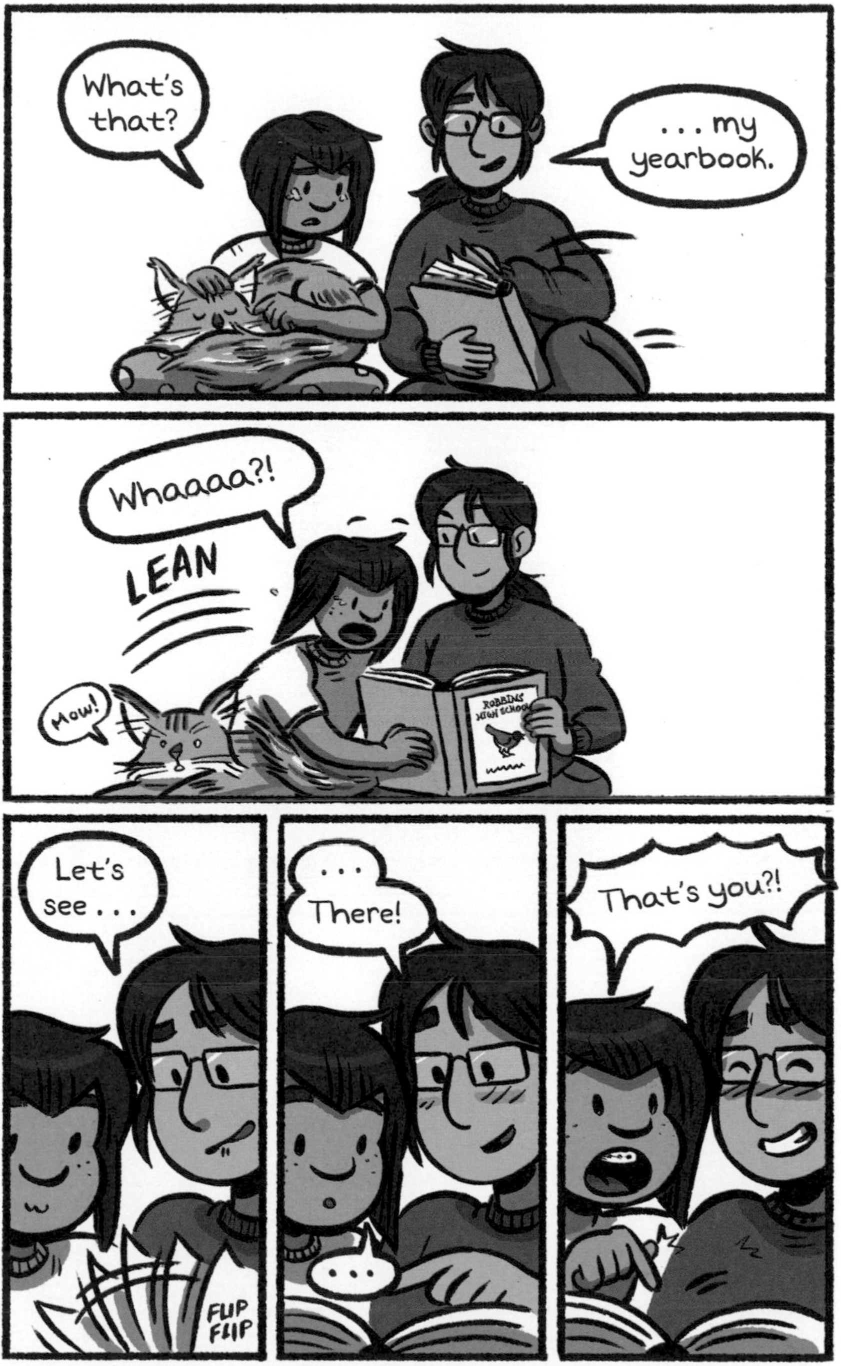
What's that?
. . . my yearbook.
Whaaaa?!
LEAN
Mow!
ROBBINS HIGH SCHOOL
Let's see . . .
FLIP FLIP
. . .
There!
. . .
That's you?!

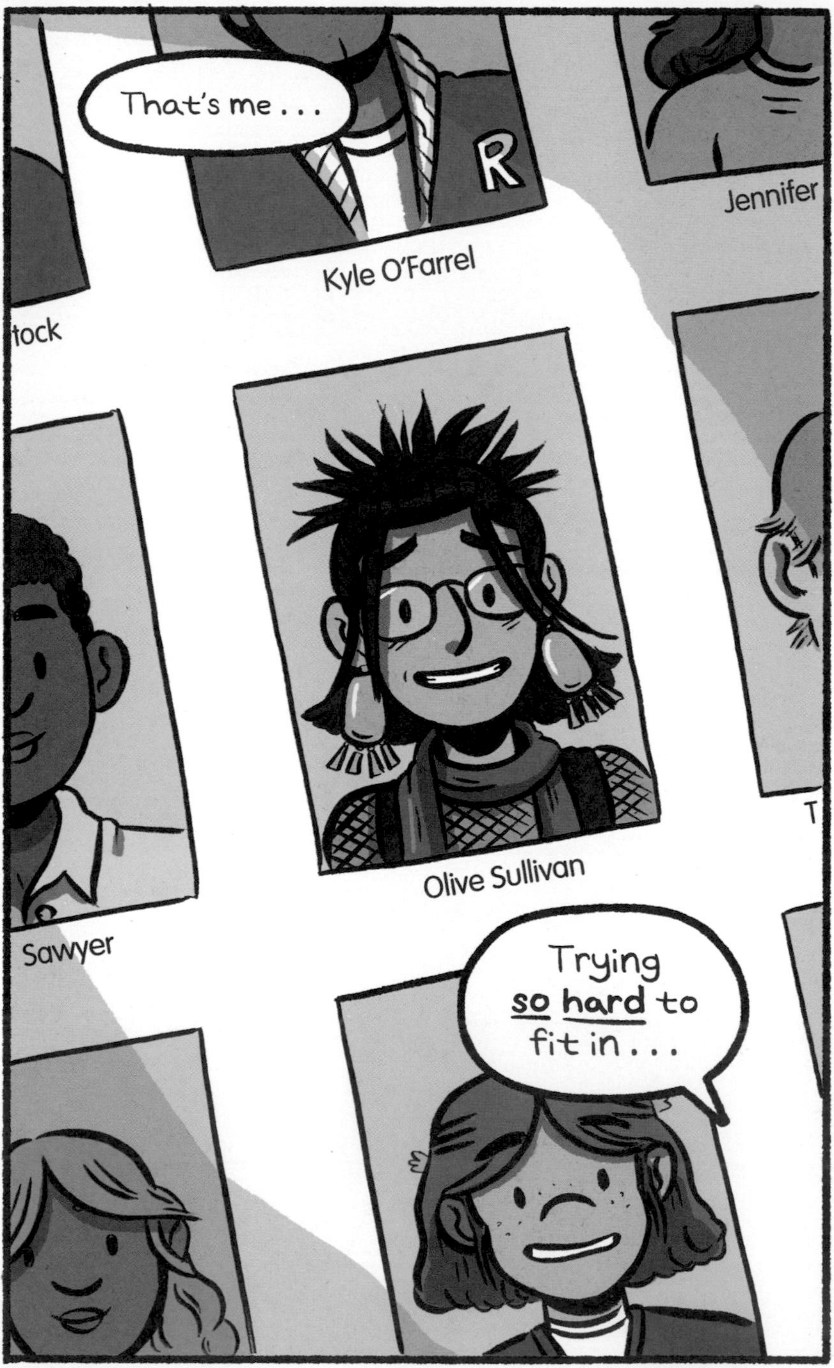
That's me . . .
R
Kyle O'Farrel
Jennifer
tock
Olive Sullivan
T
Sawyer
Trying so hard to fit in . . .

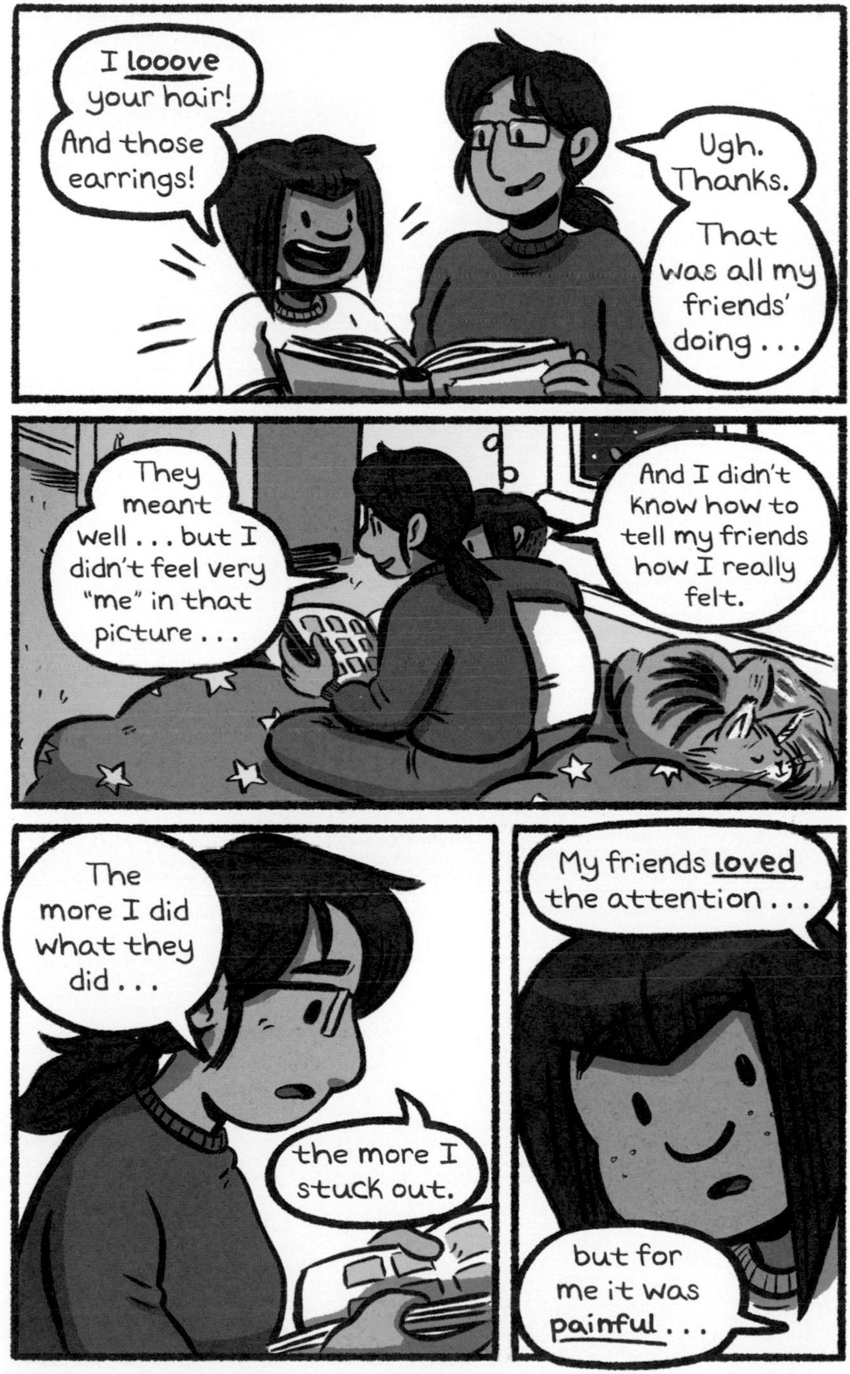
I **looove** your hair!
And those earrings!
Ugh. Thanks.
That was all my friends' doing . . .
They meant well . . . but I didn't feel very "me" in that picture . . .
And I didn't know how to tell my friends how I really felt.
The more I did what they did . . .
the more I stuck out.
My friends **loved** the attention . . .
but for me it was **painful** . . .

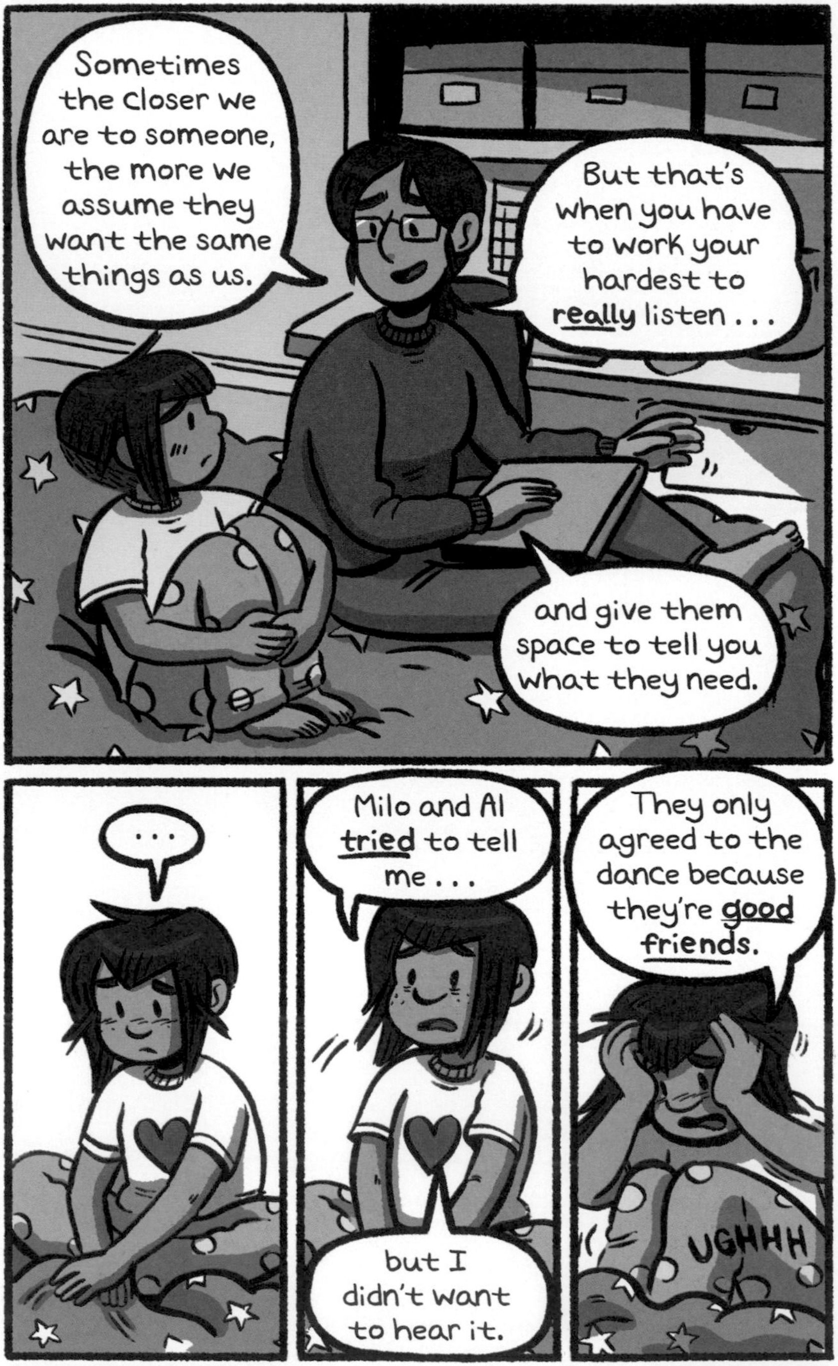

Sometimes the closer we are to someone, the more we assume they want the same things as us.
But that's when you have to work your hardest to really listen . . .
and give them space to tell you what they need.
. . .
Milo and Al tried to tell me . . .
but I didn't want to hear it.
They only agreed to the dance because they're good friends.
UGHHH

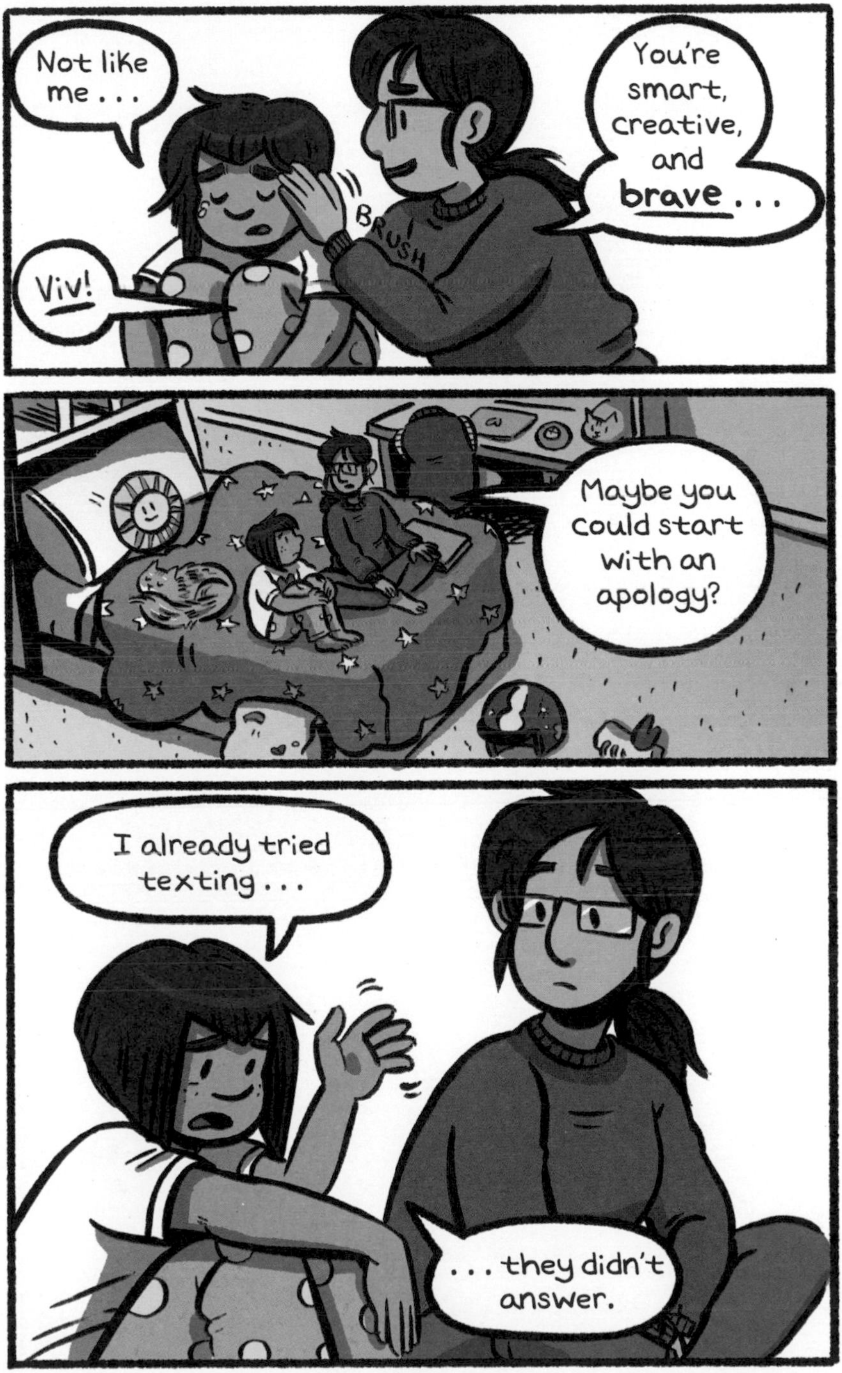
Not like me . . .
You're smart, creative, and brave . . .
BRUSH
Viv!
Maybe you could start with an apology?
I already tried texting . . .
. . . they didn't answer.

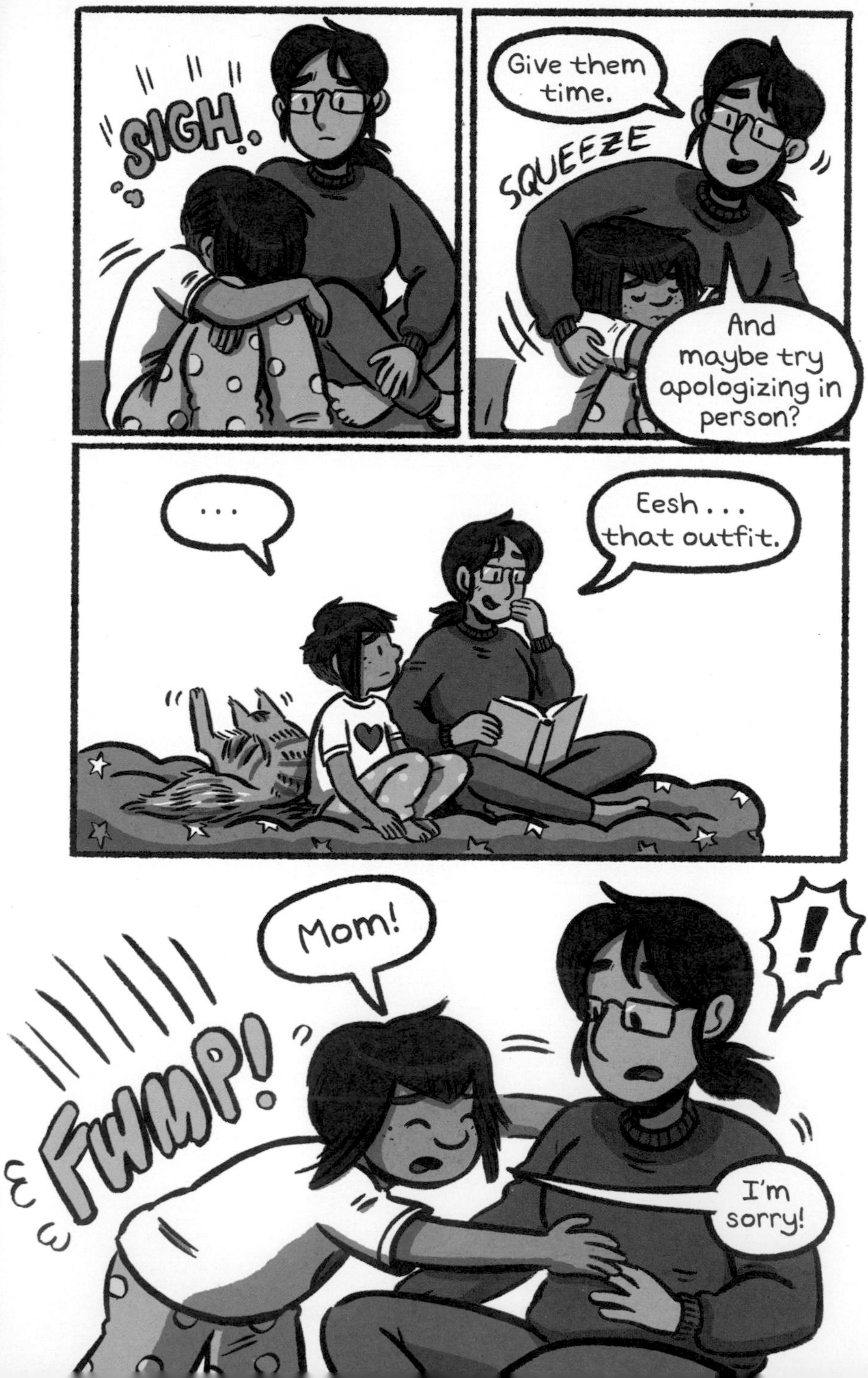
SIGH
Give them time.
SQUEEZE
And maybe try apologizing in person?
...
Eesh . . . that outfit.
Mom!
!
FWMP!
I'm sorry!

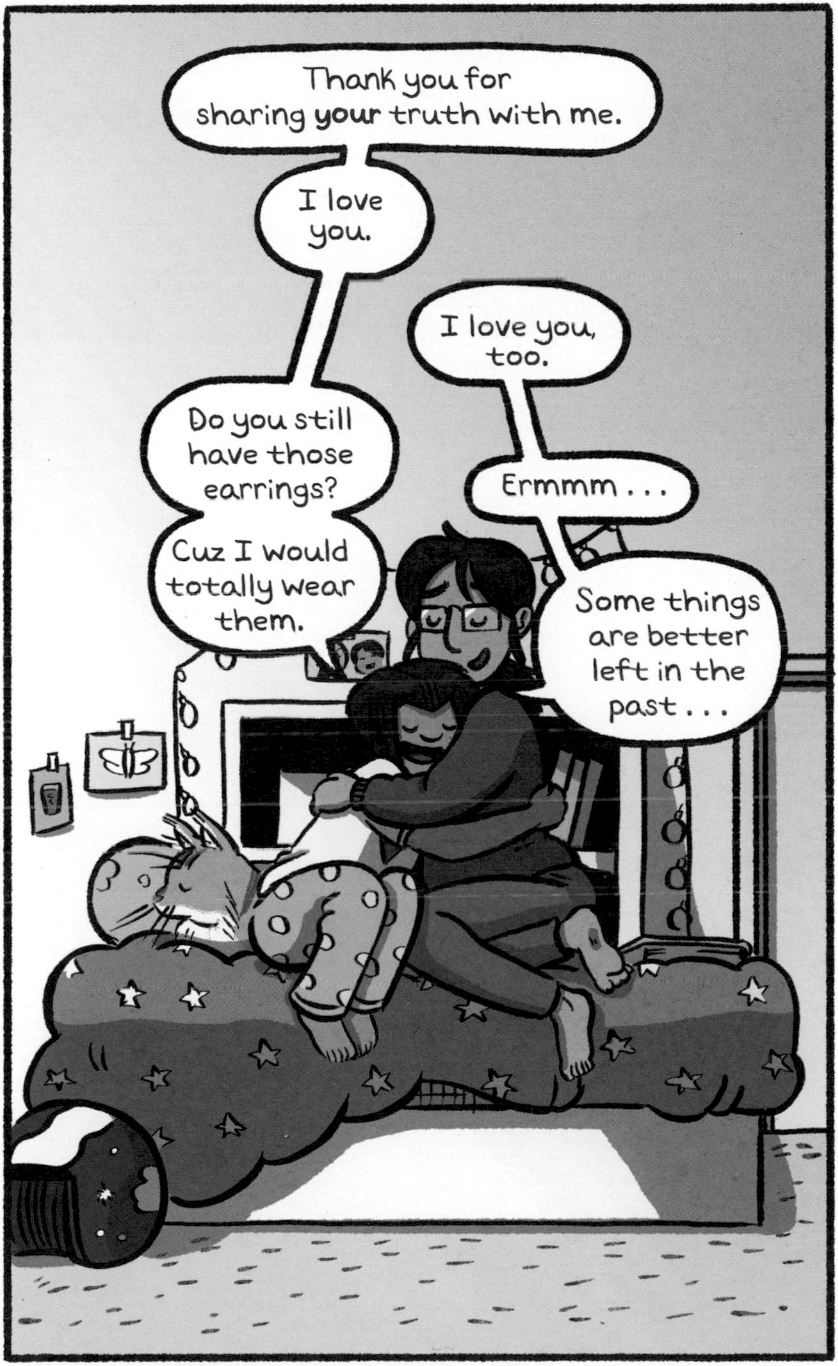
Thank you for sharing your truth with me.
I love you.
Do you still have those earrings?
Cuz I would totally wear them.
I love you, too.
Ermmm . . .
Some things are better left in the past . . .

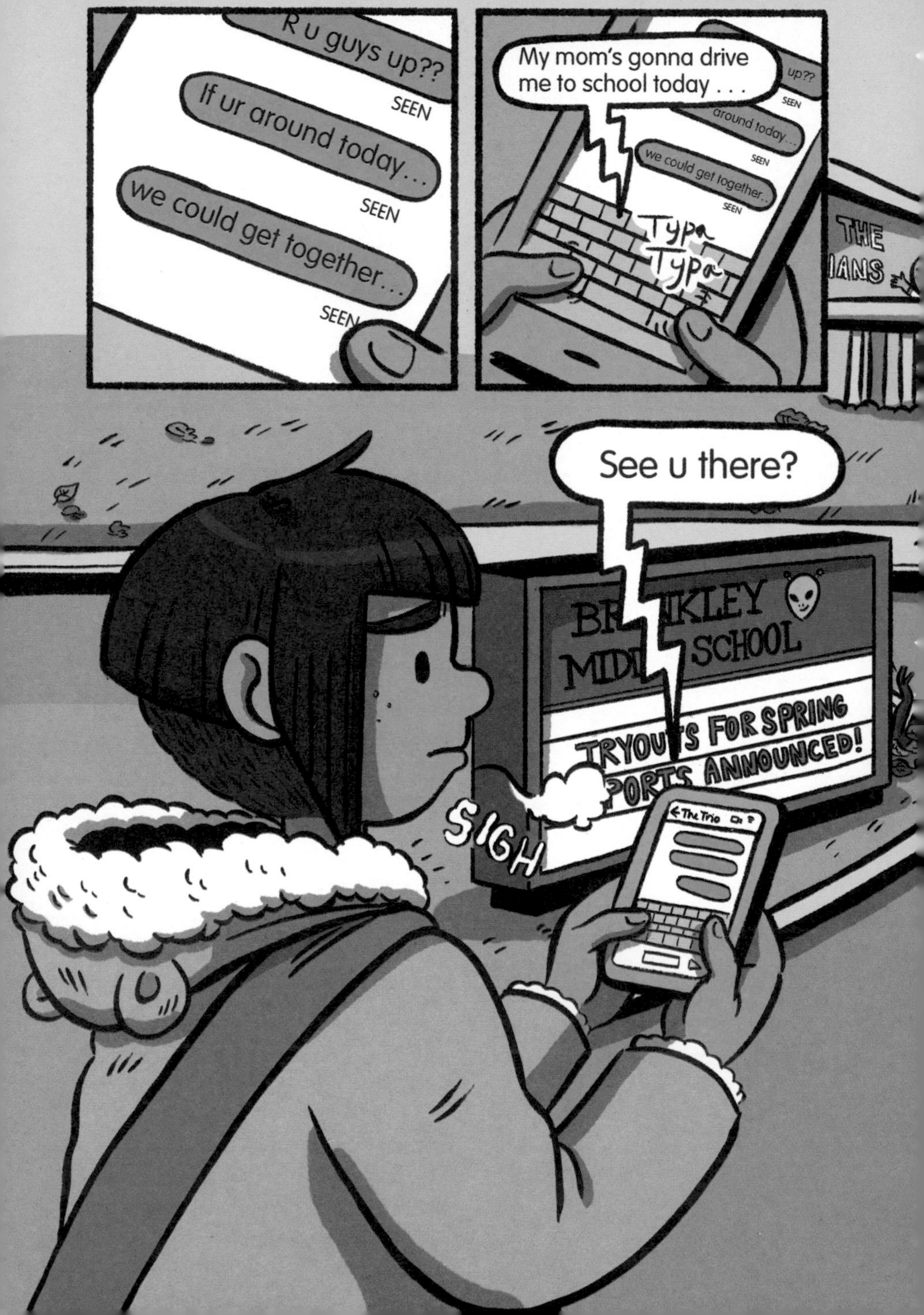
R u guys up??
SEEN
If ur around today…
SEEN
we could get together…
SEEN
My mom's gonna drive me to school today . . .
Typa Typa
See u there?
SIGH
The Trio

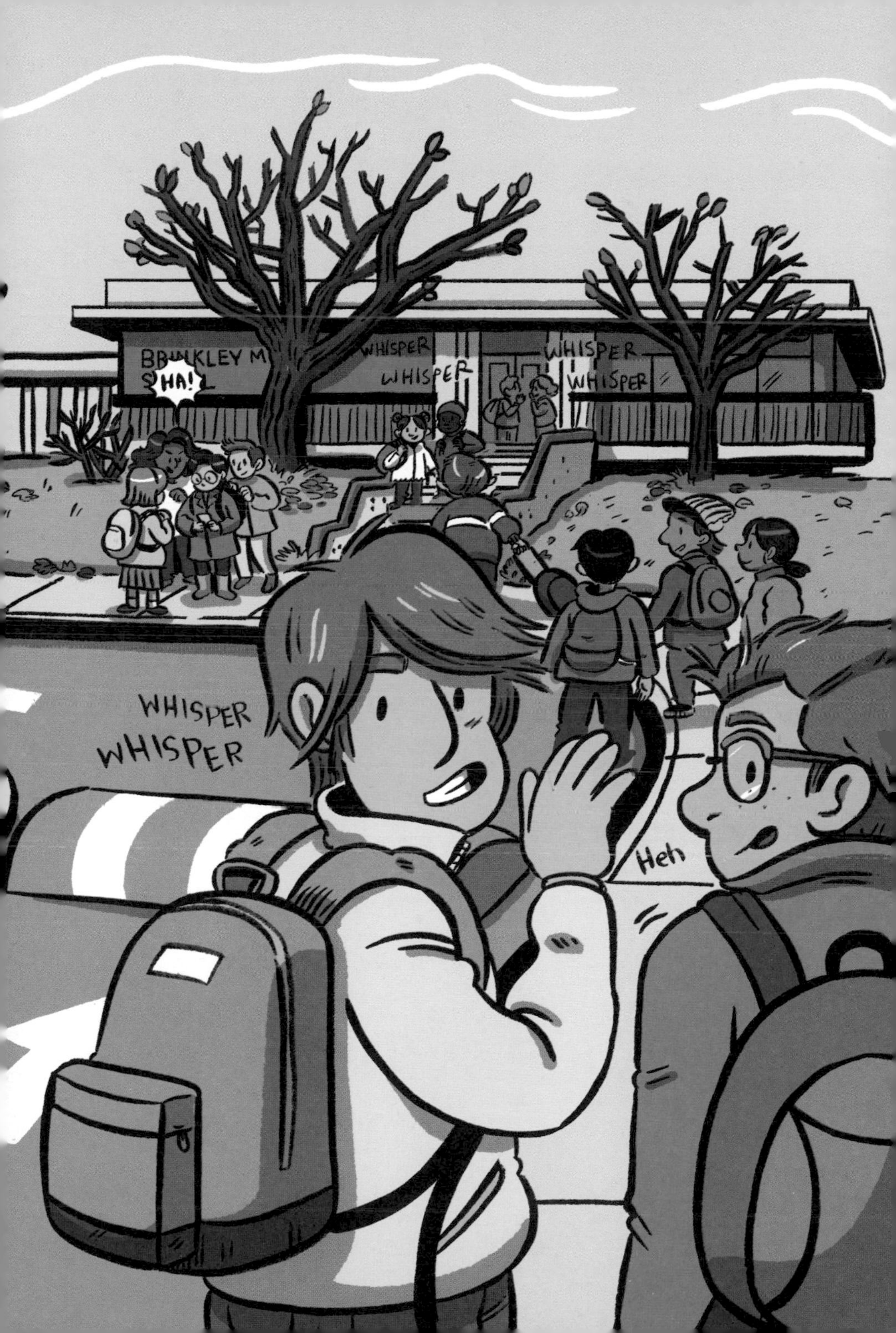
HA!
WHISPER
WHISPER
WHISPER
WHISPER
WHISPER
WHISPER
Heh

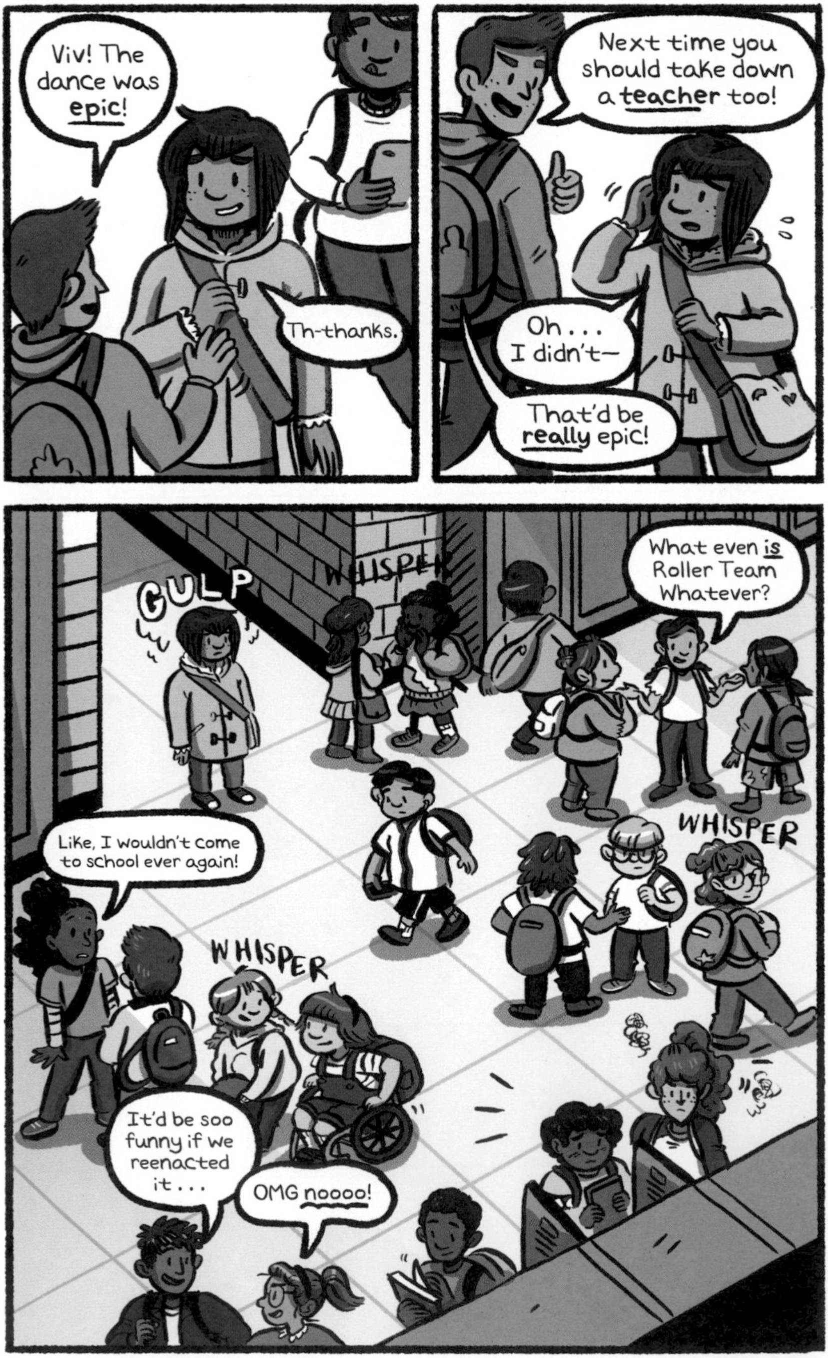

Viv! The dance was epic!
Th-thanks.
Next time you should take down a teacher too!
Oh . . . I didn't—
That'd be really epic!
GULP
WHISPER
What even is Roller Team Whatever?
Like, I wouldn't come to school ever again!
WHISPER
WHISPER
It'd be soo funny if we reenacted it . . .
OMG noooo!

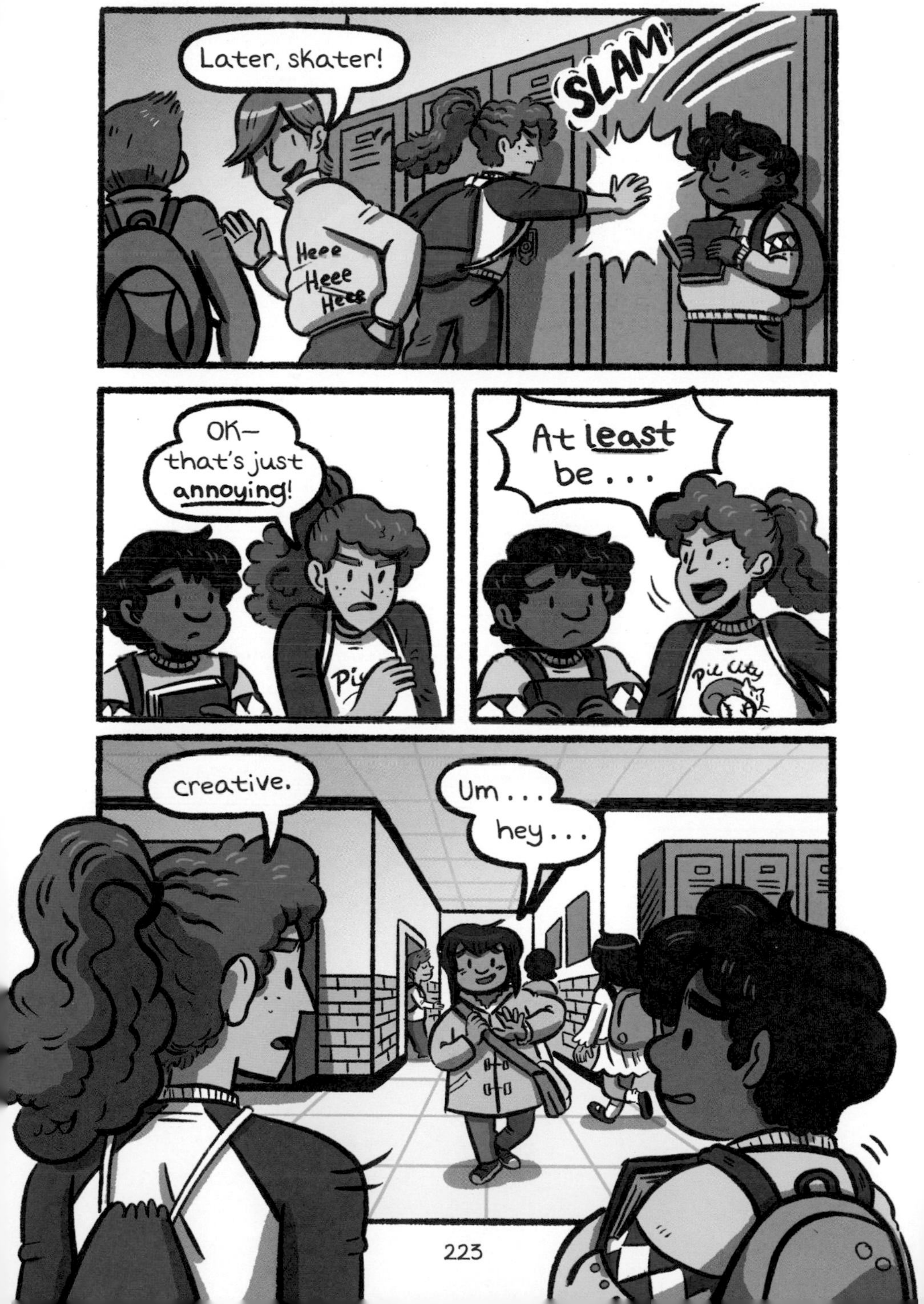

Later, skater!
SLAM!
Heee
Heee
Heee
OK— that's just **annoying**!
At **least** be . . .
creative.
Um . . . hey . . .

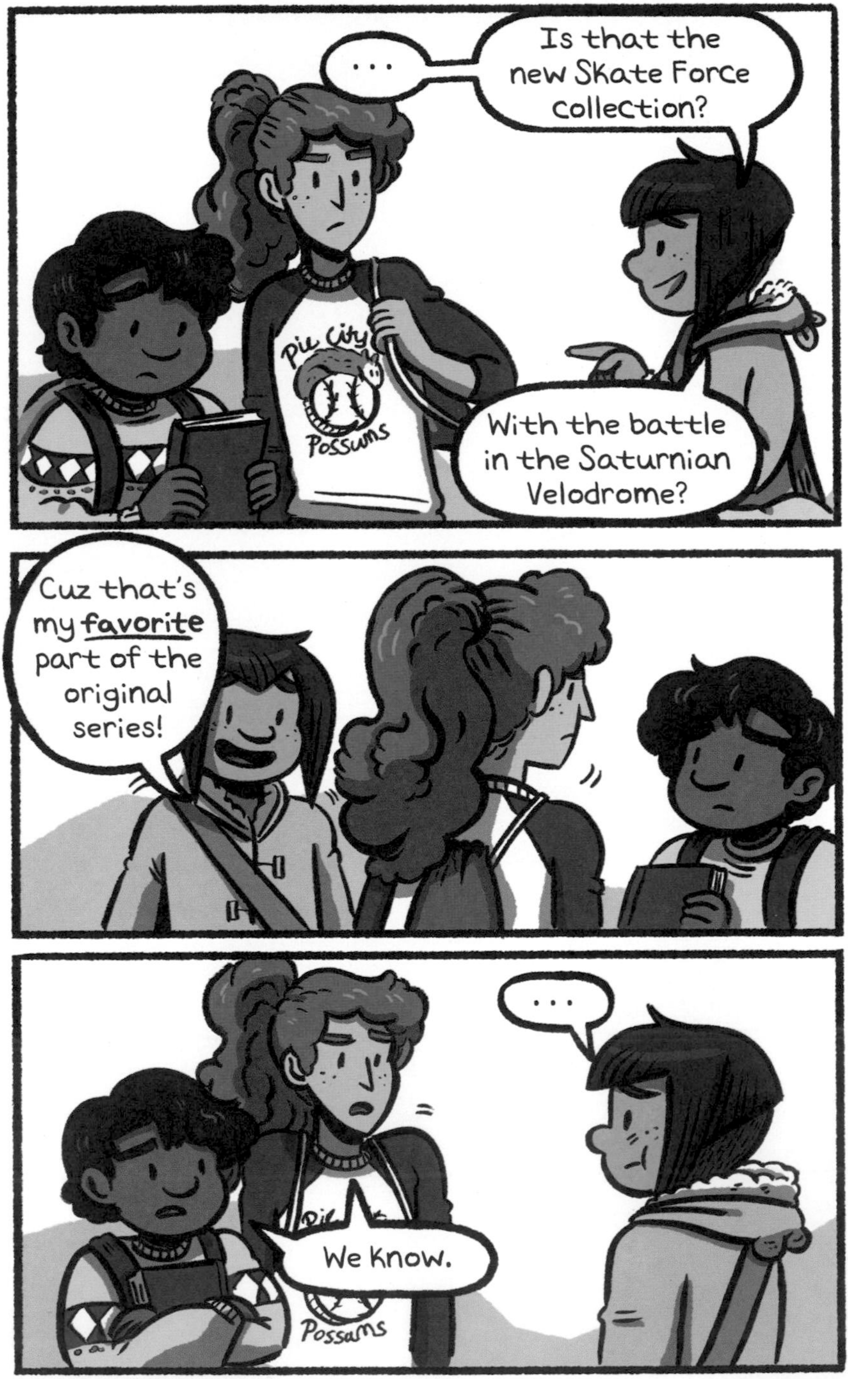
...
Is that the new Skate Force collection?
Pie City Possums
With the battle in the Saturnian Velodrome?
Cuz that's my **favorite** part of the original series!
...
We know.
Possums

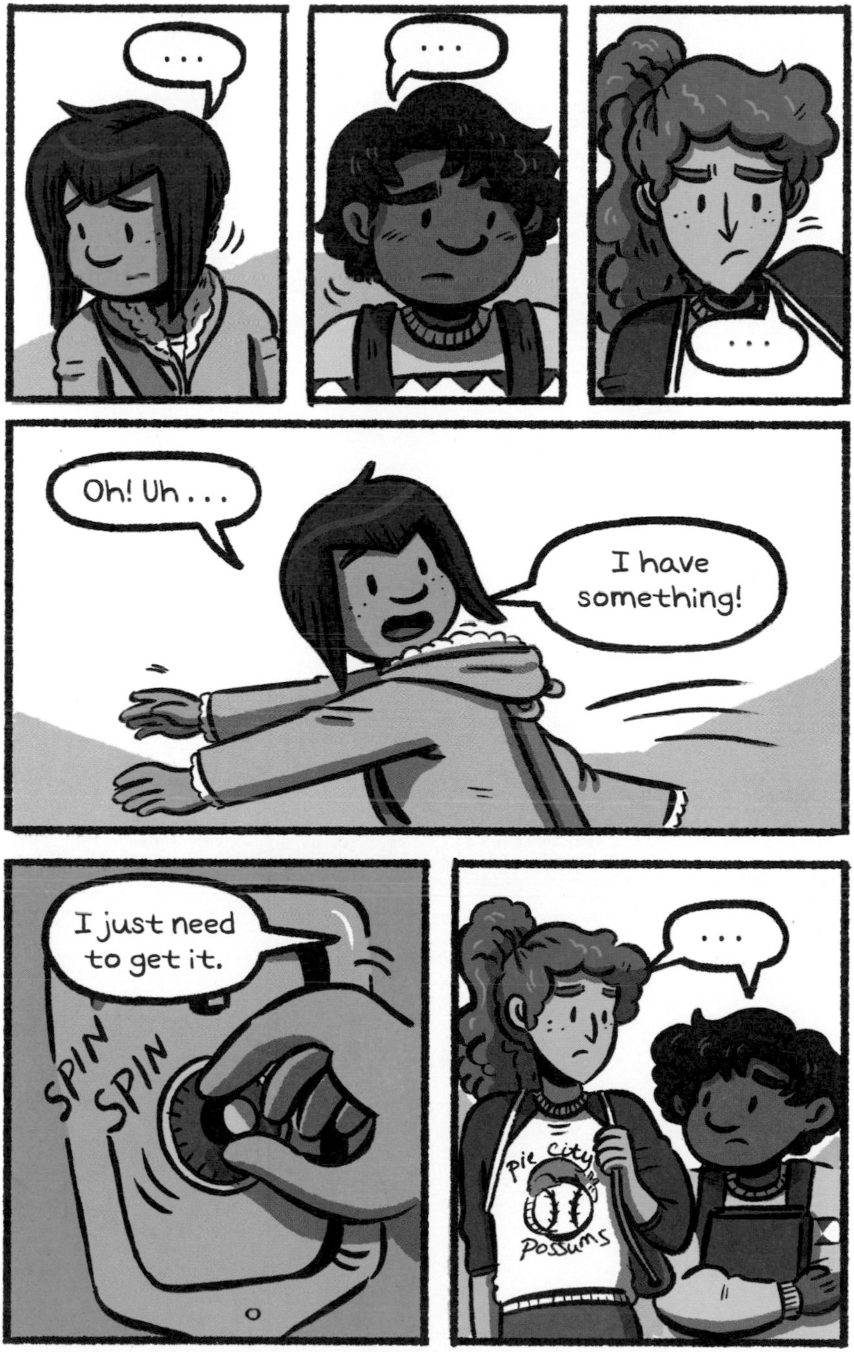
. . .
. . .
. . .
Oh! Uh . . .
I have something!
I just need to get it.
SPIN
SPIN
. . .
Pie City
Possums

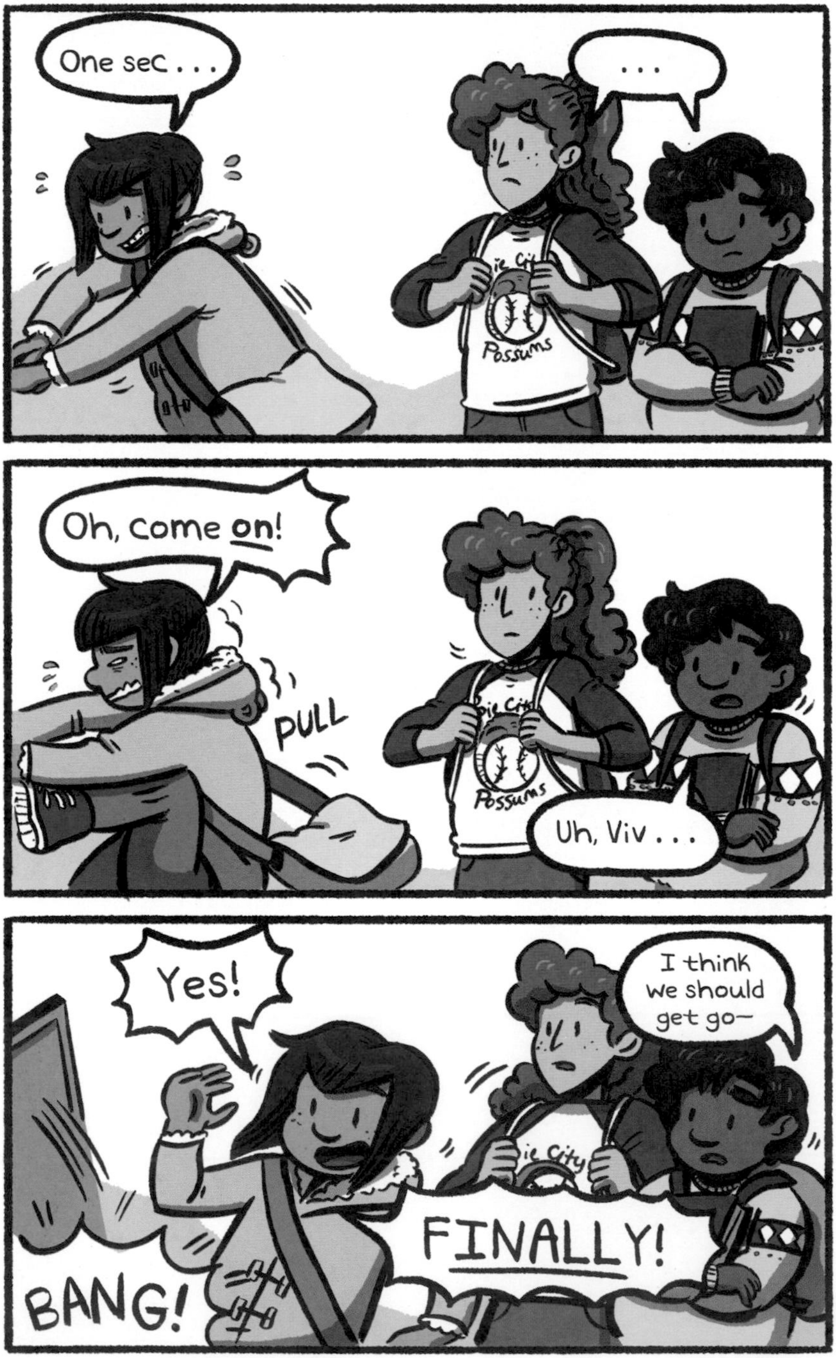
One sec . . .
. . .
Oh, come on!
PULL
Uh, Viv . . .
Yes!
I think we should get go—
BANG!
FINALLY!

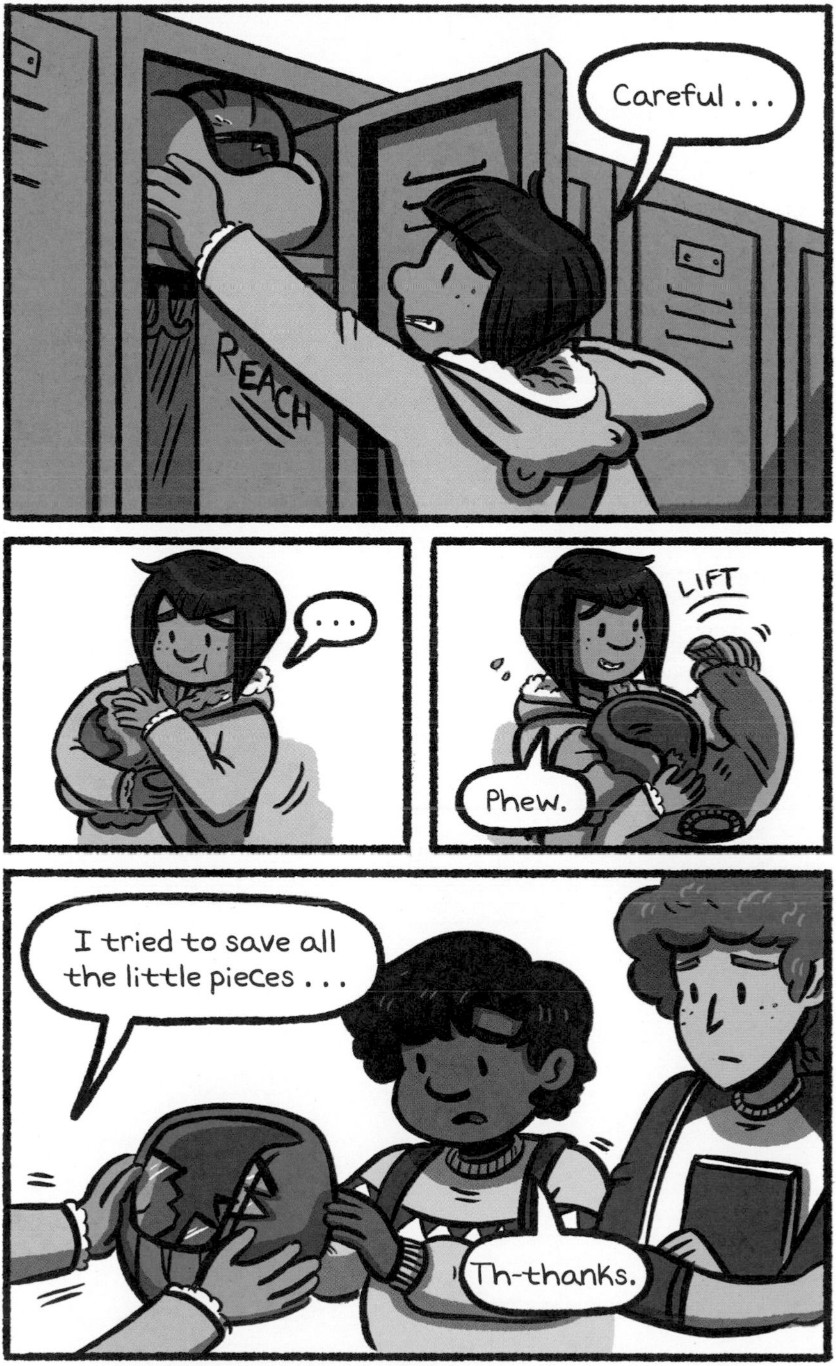
Careful . . .
REACH
. . .
LIFT
Phew.
I tried to save all the little pieces . . .
Th-thanks.

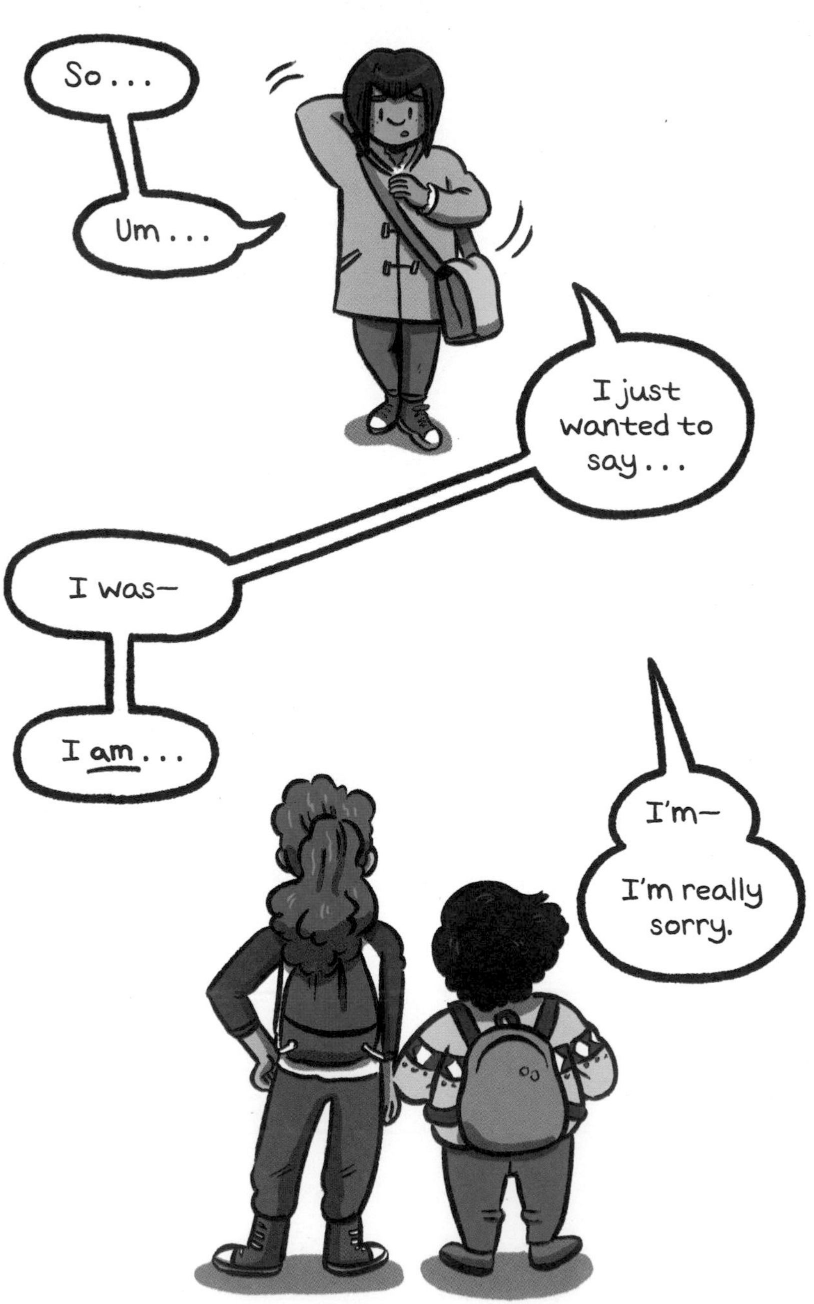
So . . .
Um . . .
I just wanted to say . . .
I was–
I am . . .
I'm–
I'm really sorry.

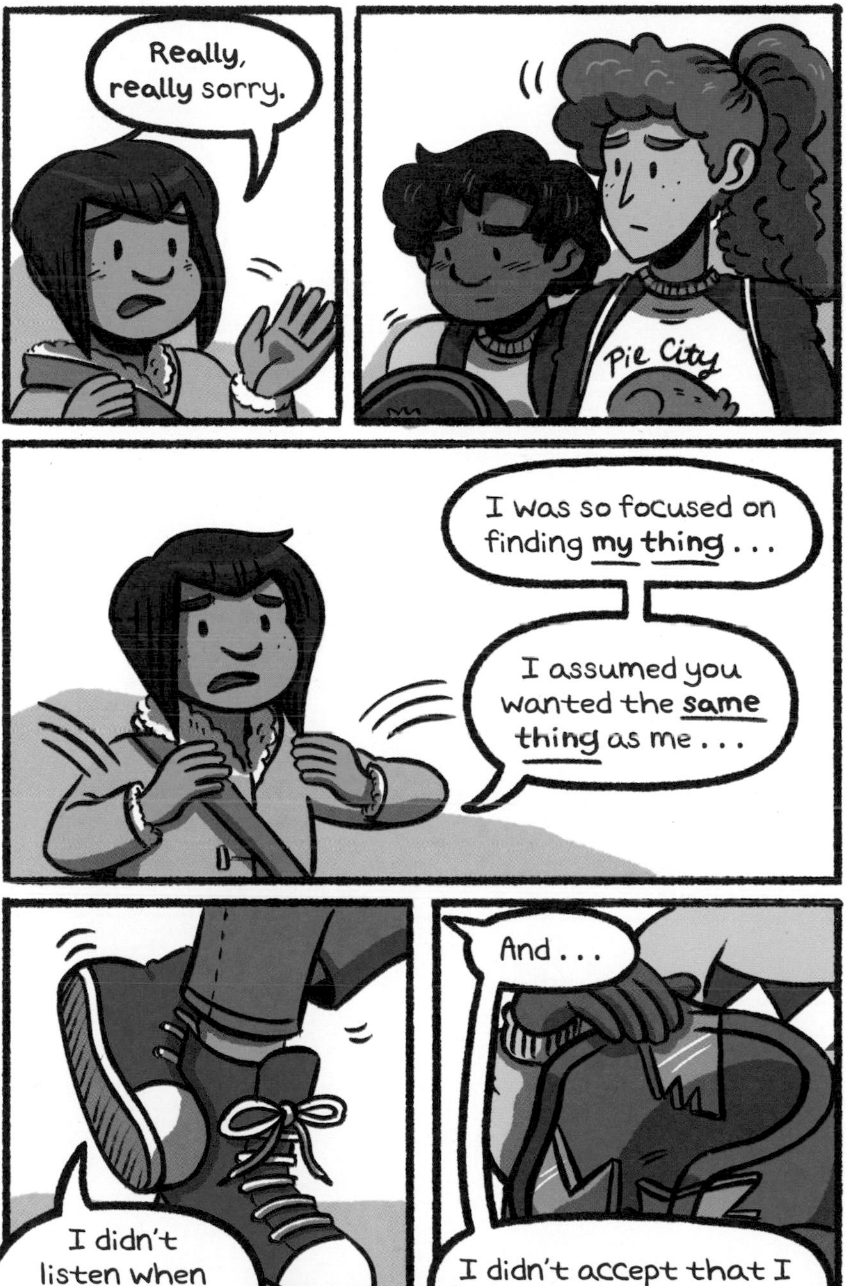
Really, really sorry.
I was so focused on finding my thing . . .
I assumed you wanted the same thing as me . . .
I didn't listen when you told me otherwise . . .
And . . .
I didn't accept that I was pushing too hard.

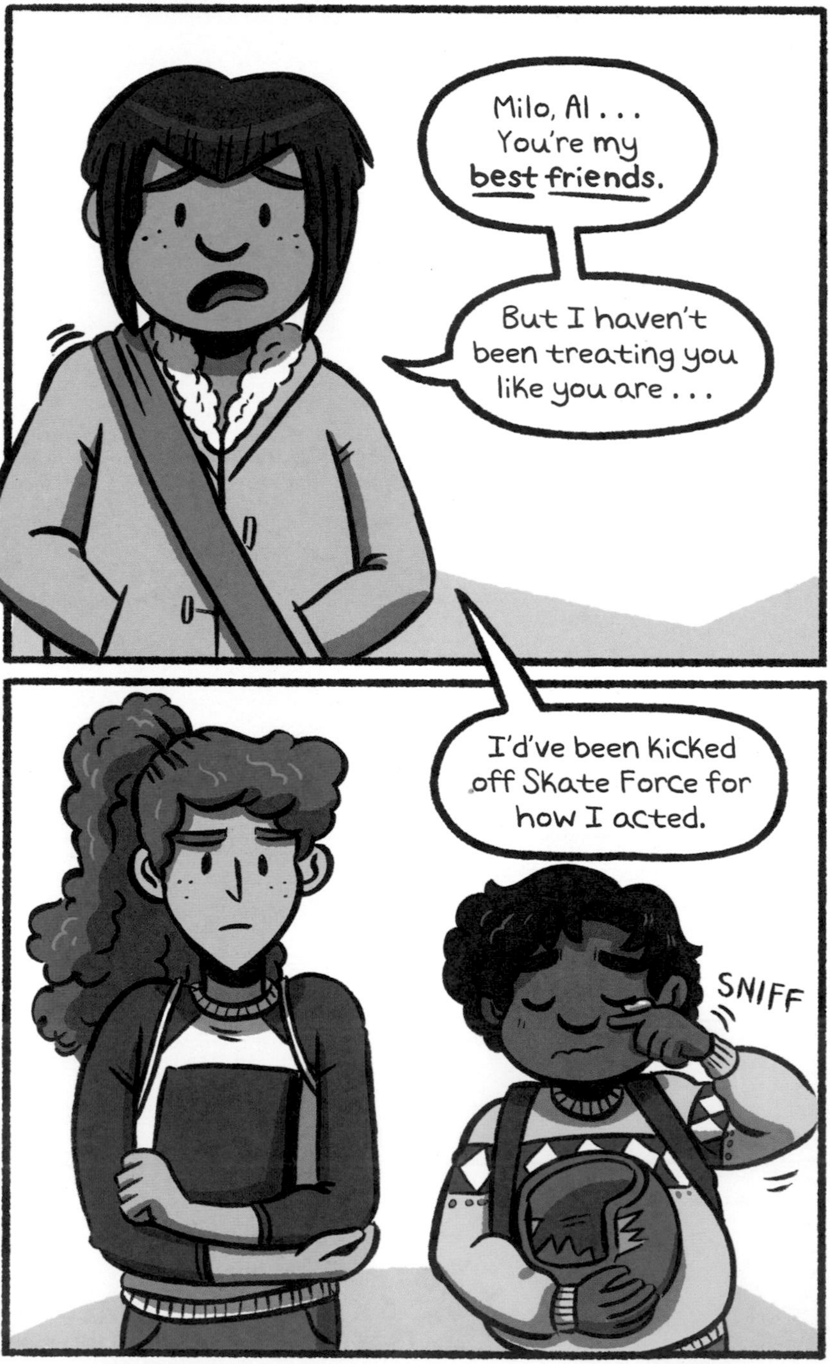
Milo, Al . . . You're my best friends.
But I haven't been treating you like you are . . .
I'd've been kicked off Skate Force for how I acted.
SNIFF

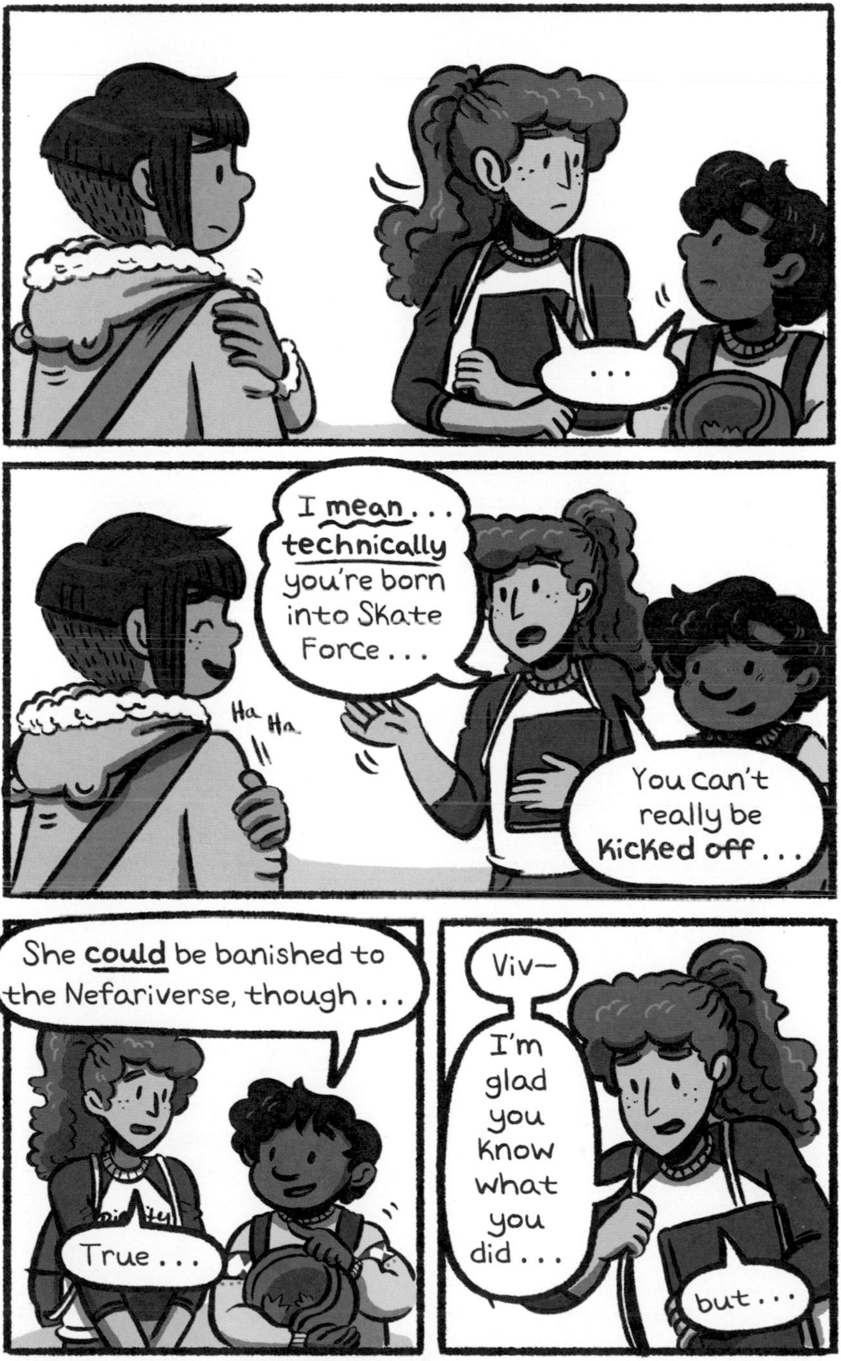
...
I mean . . . technically you're born into Skate Force . . .
Ha Ha
You can't really be Kicked off . . .
She could be banished to the Nefariverse, though . . .
True . . .
Viv—
I'm glad you know what you did . . .
but . . .

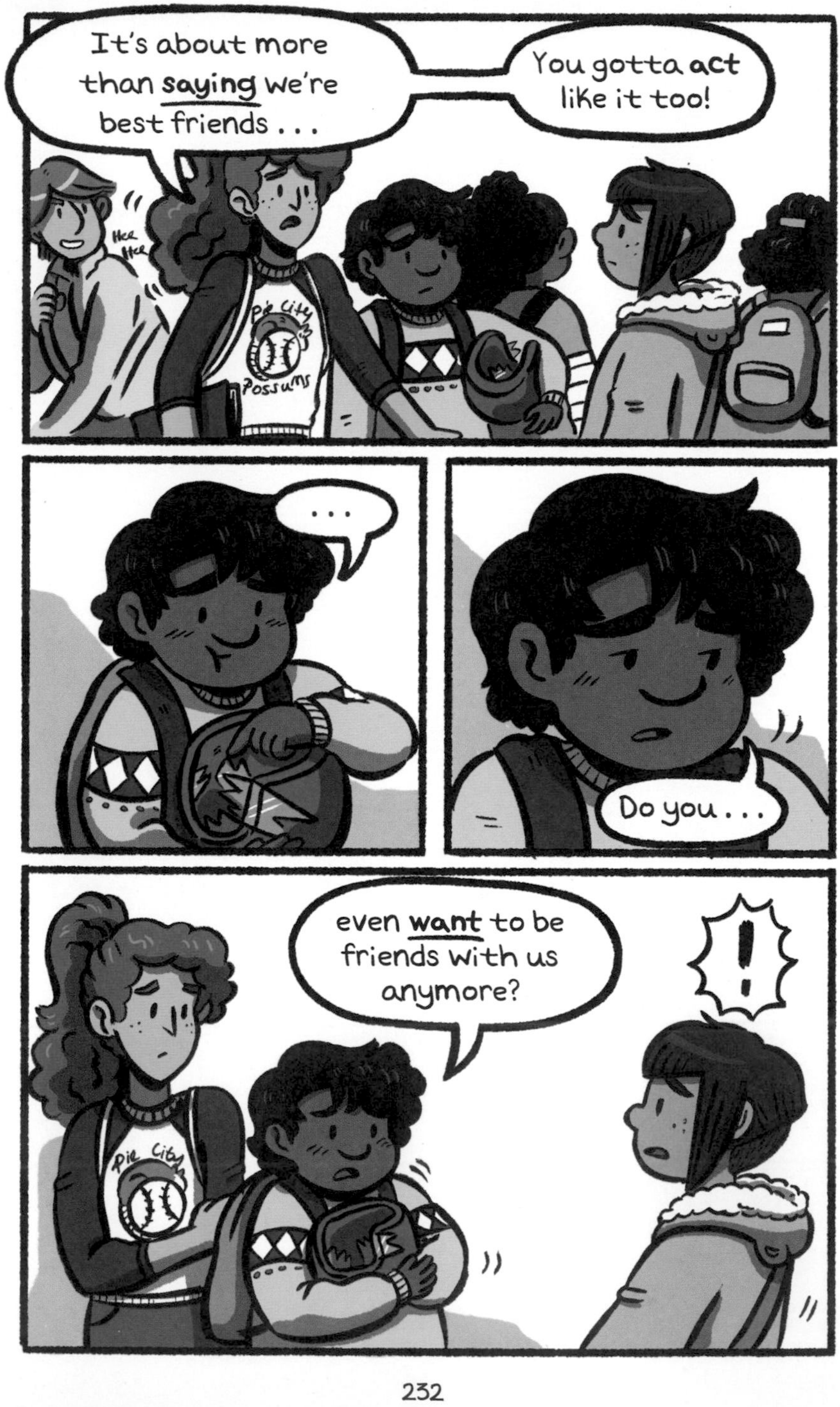
It's about more than saying we're best friends . . .
You gotta act like it too!
Hee Hee
. . .
Do you . . .
even want to be friends with us anymore?
!

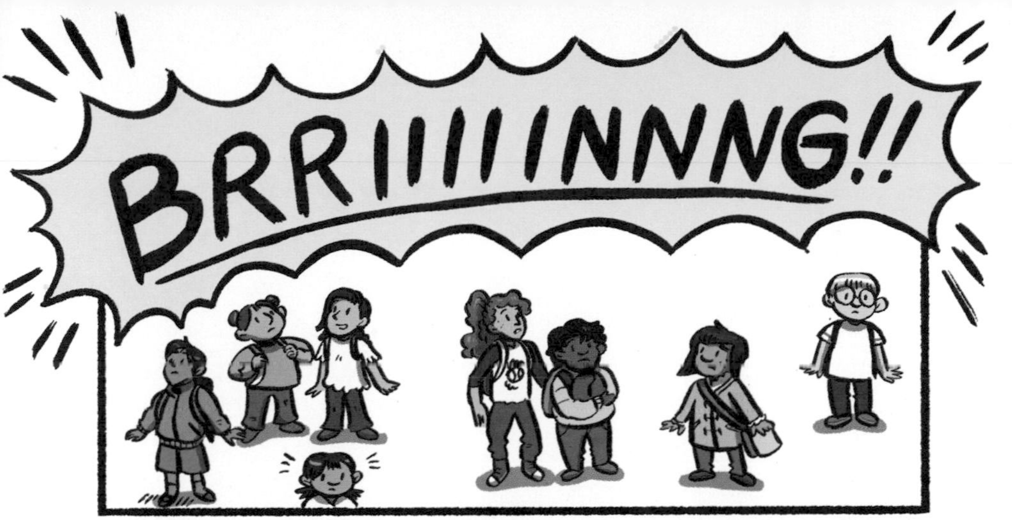
BRRIIIIINNNG!!

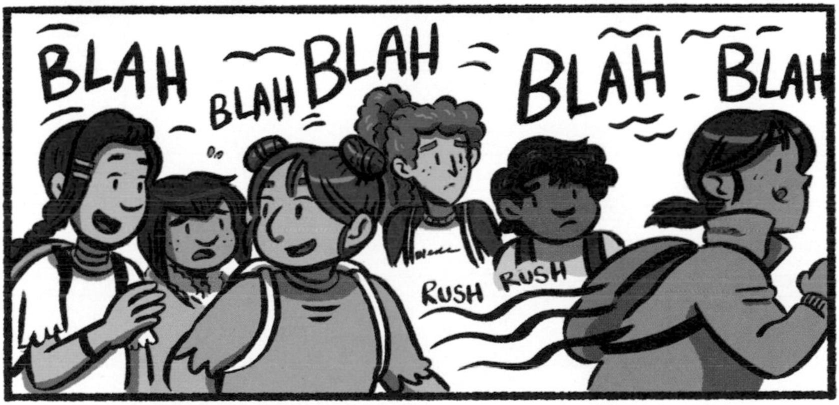
BLAH
BLAH
BLAH
BLAH
BLAH
RUSH
RUSH

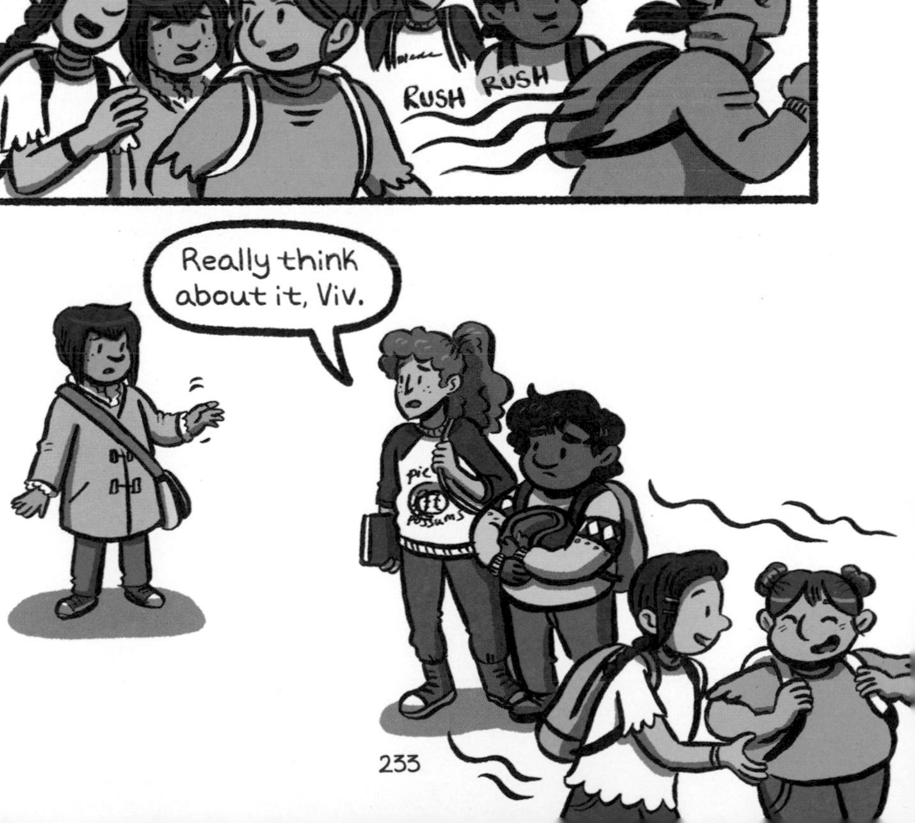
Really think about it, Viv.

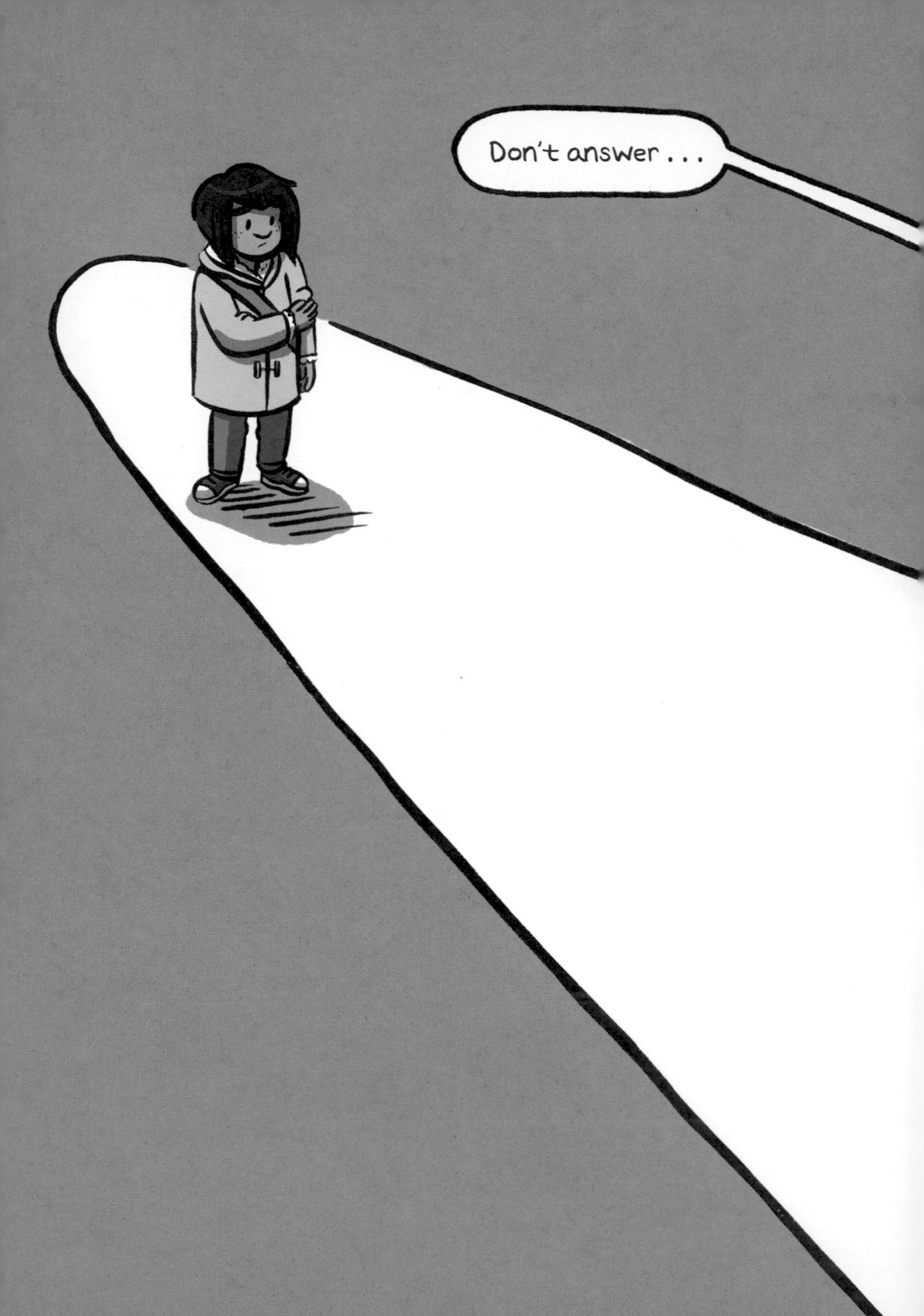
Don't answer . . .

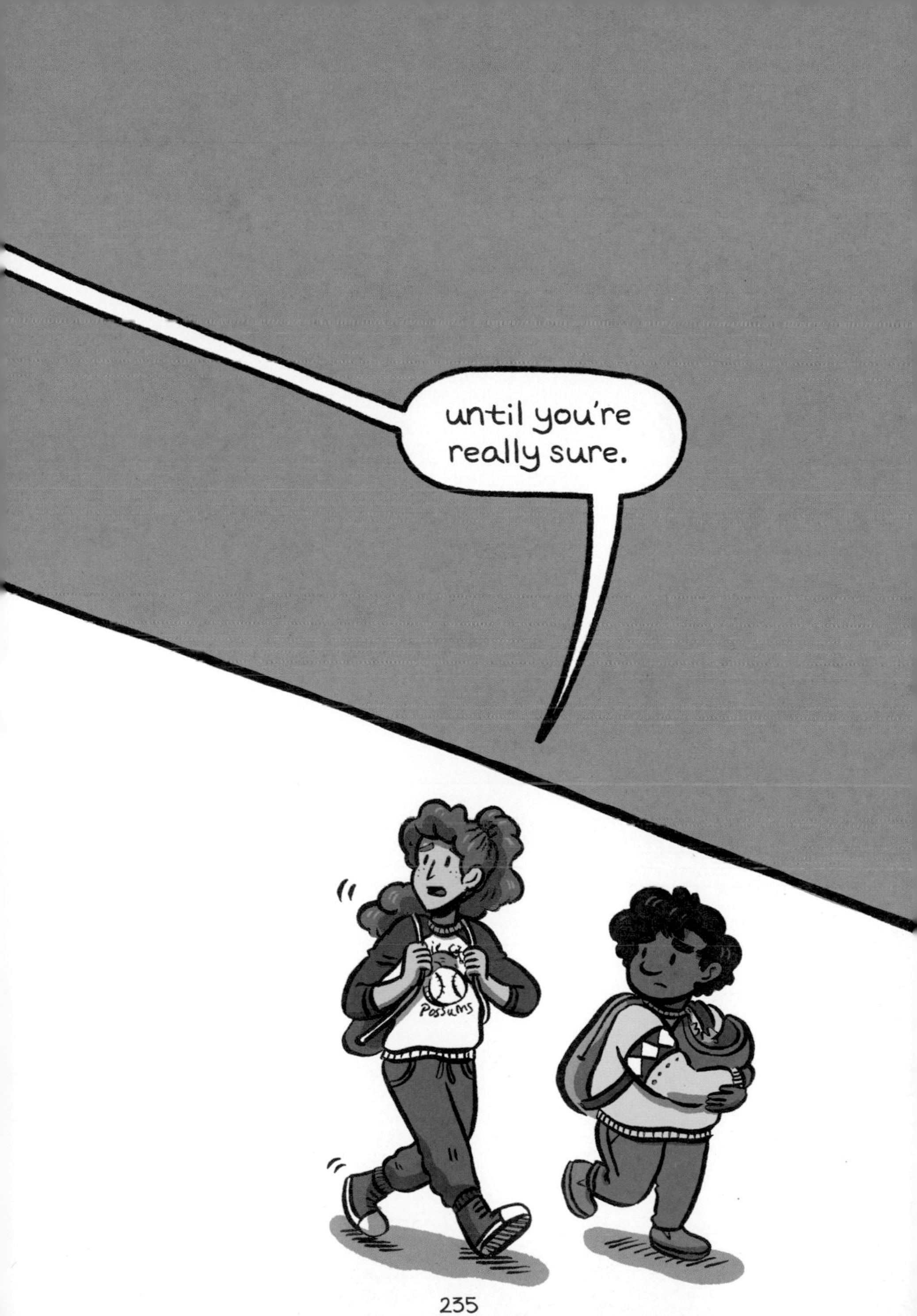
until you're really sure.
Possums

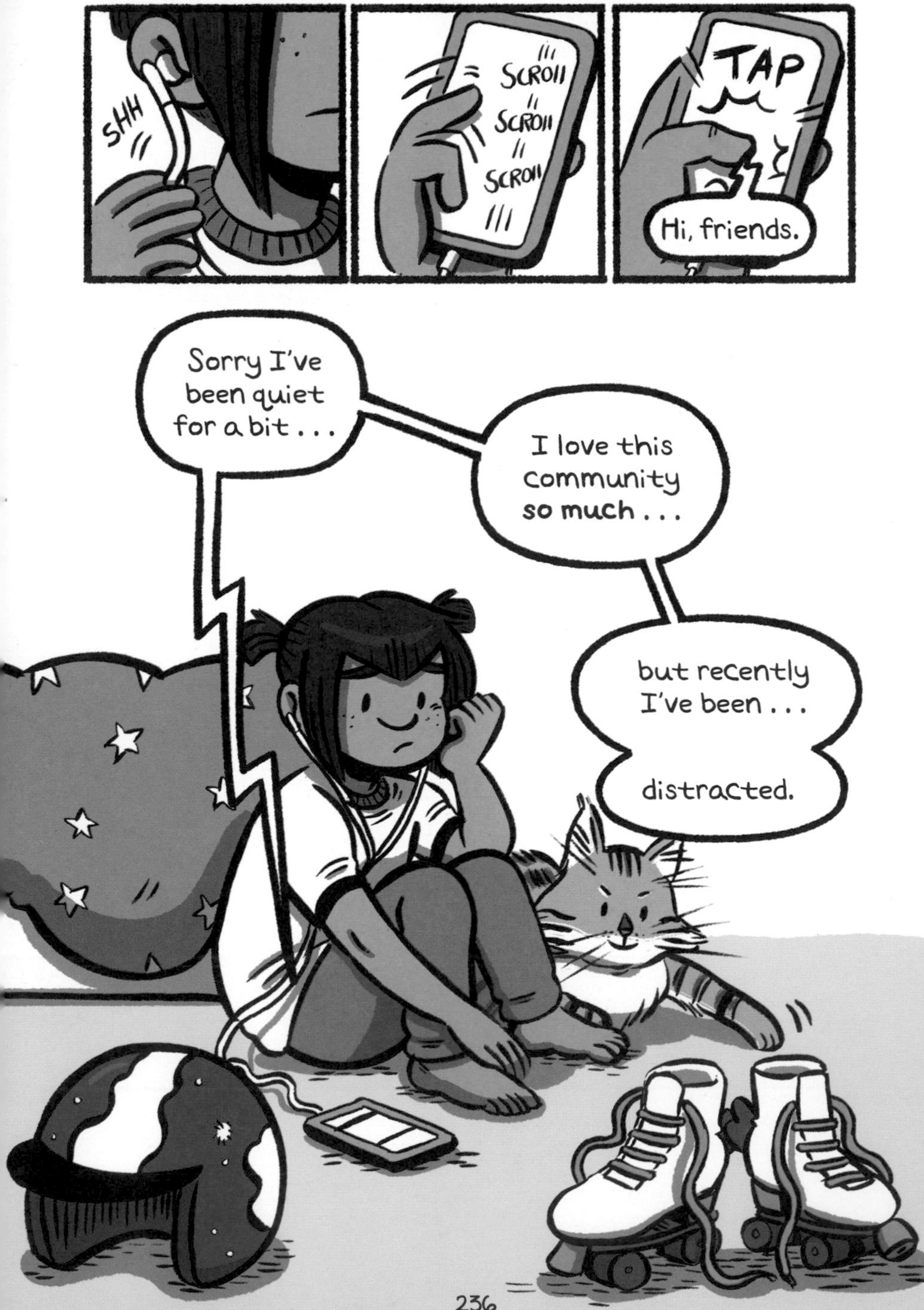
SHH
SCROll
SCROll
SCROll
TAP
Hi, friends.
Sorry I've been quiet for a bit . . .
I love this community so much . . .
but recently I've been . . .
distracted.

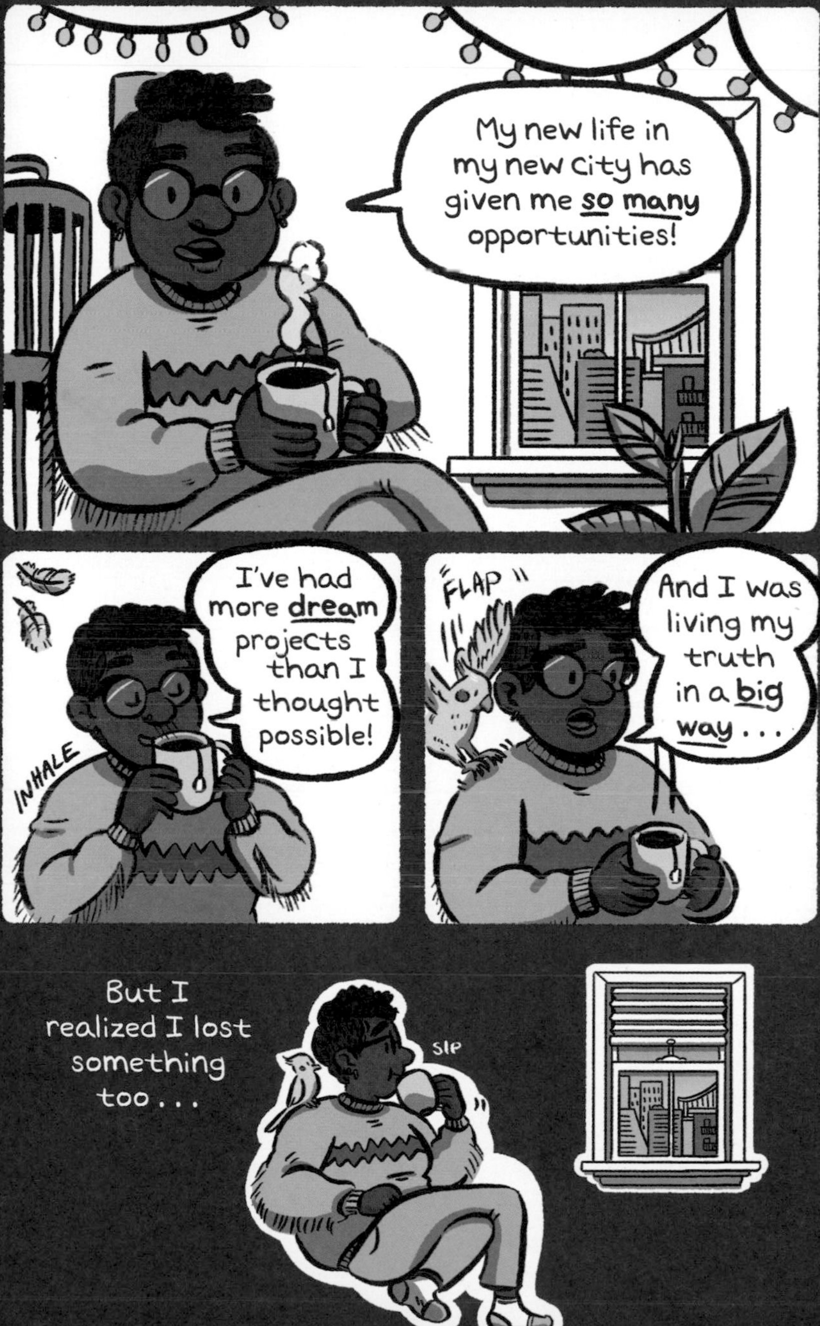
My new life in my new city has given me so many opportunities!
I've had more dream projects than I thought possible!
INHALE
FLAP
And I was living my truth in a big way . . .
But I realized I lost something too . . .
SIP

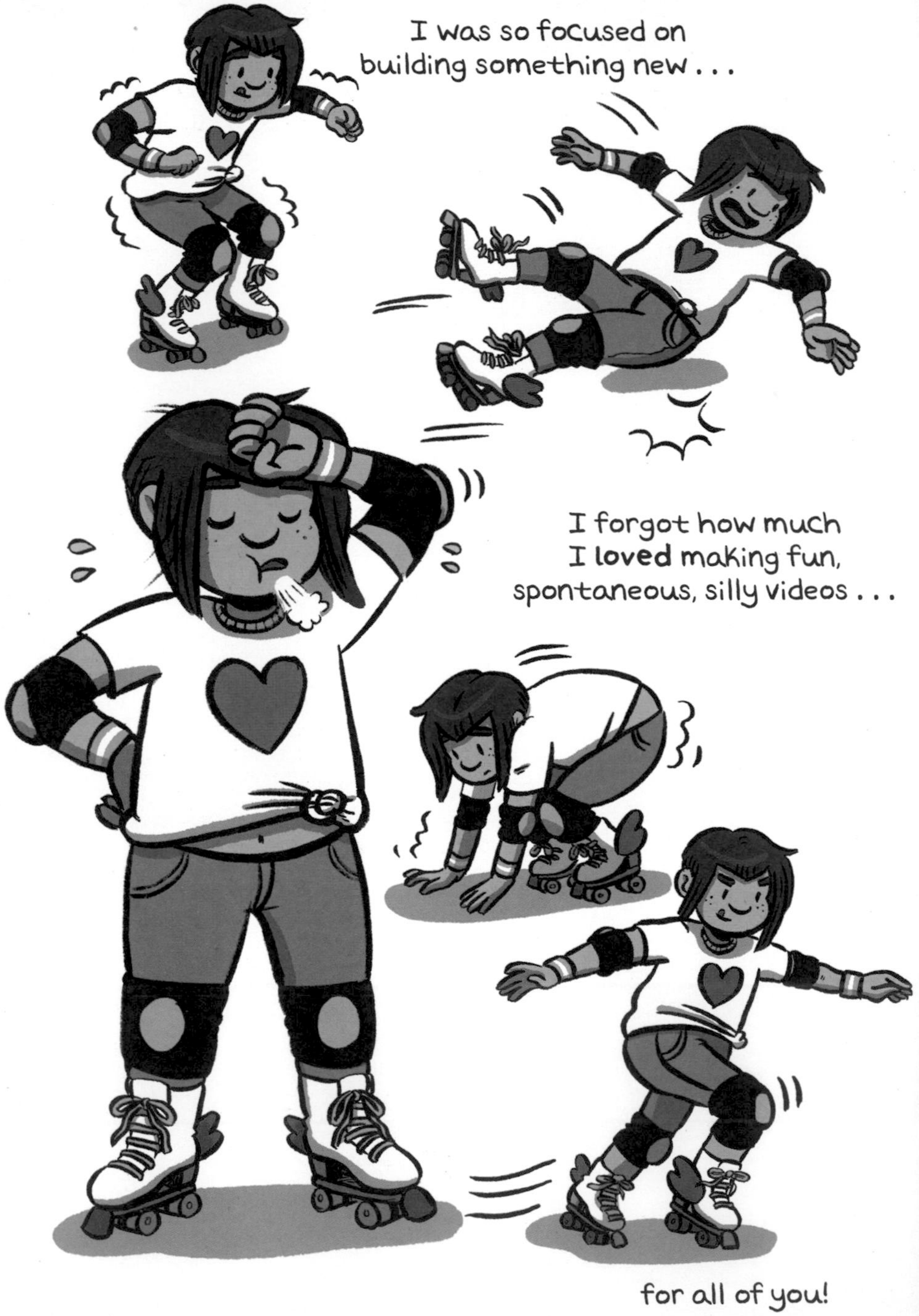
I was so focused on building something new . . .
I forgot how much I **loved** making fun, spontaneous, silly videos . . .
for all of you!

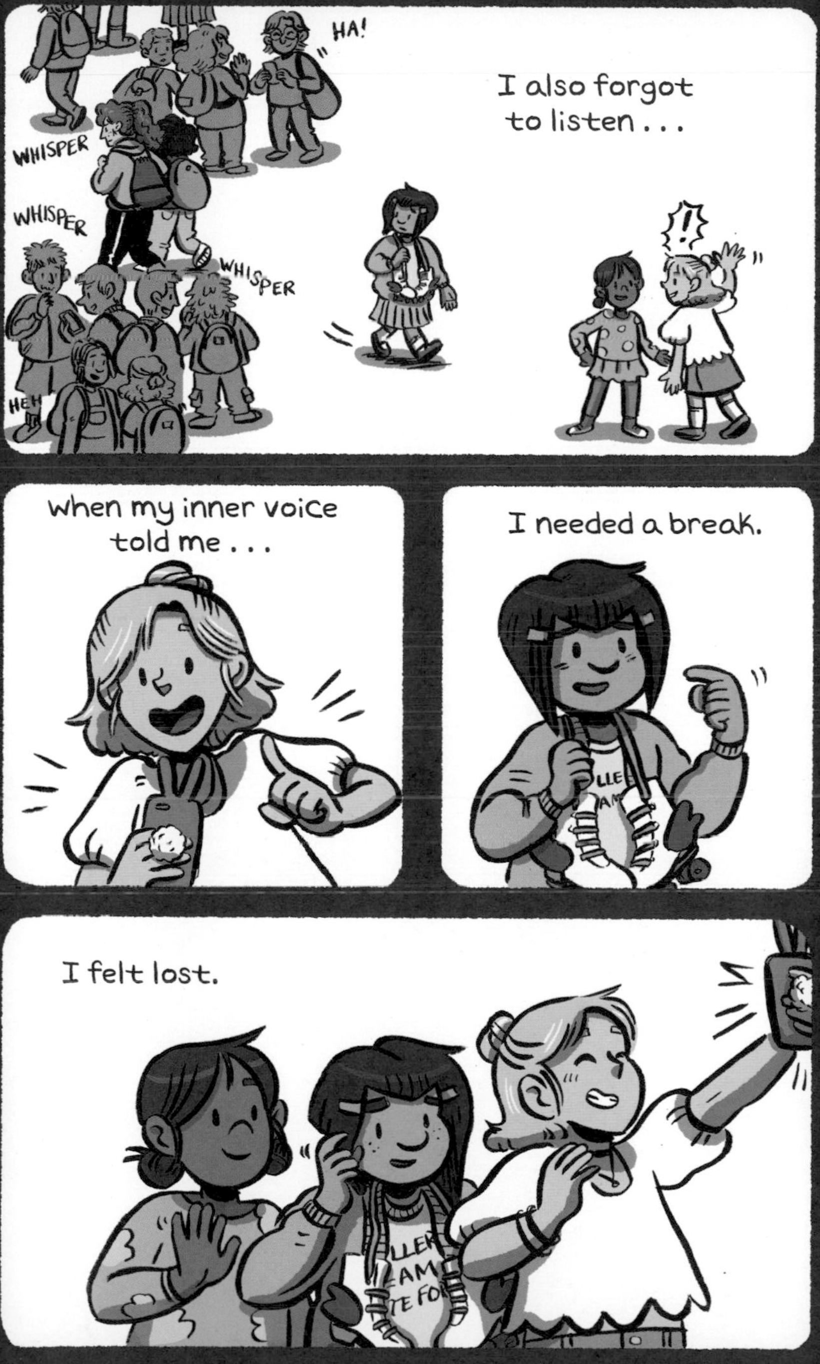
HA!
I also forgot to listen . . .
WHISPER
WHISPER
WHISPER
HEH
!
When my inner voice told me . . .
I needed a break.
I felt lost.

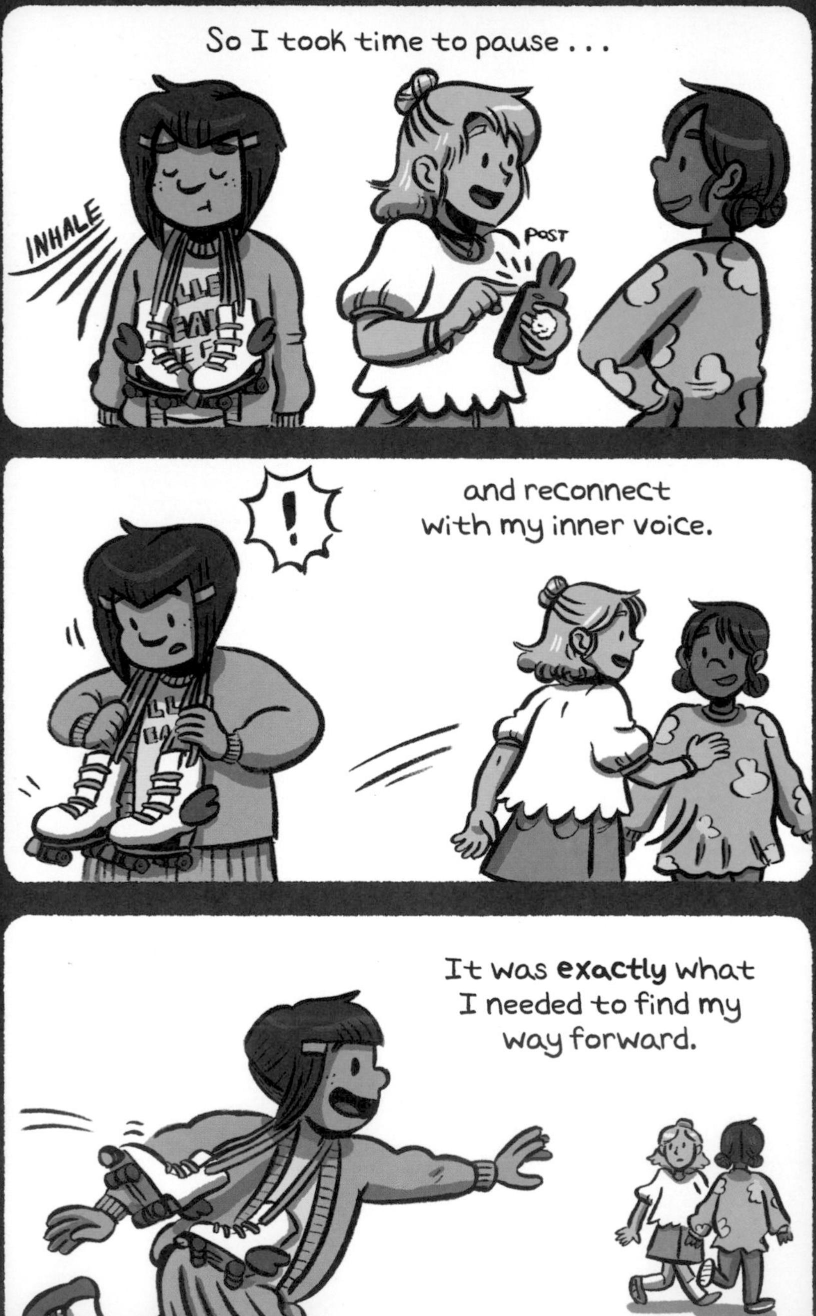
So I took time to pause . . .
INHALE
POST
!
and reconnect
with my inner voice.
It was **exactly** what
I needed to find my
way forward.

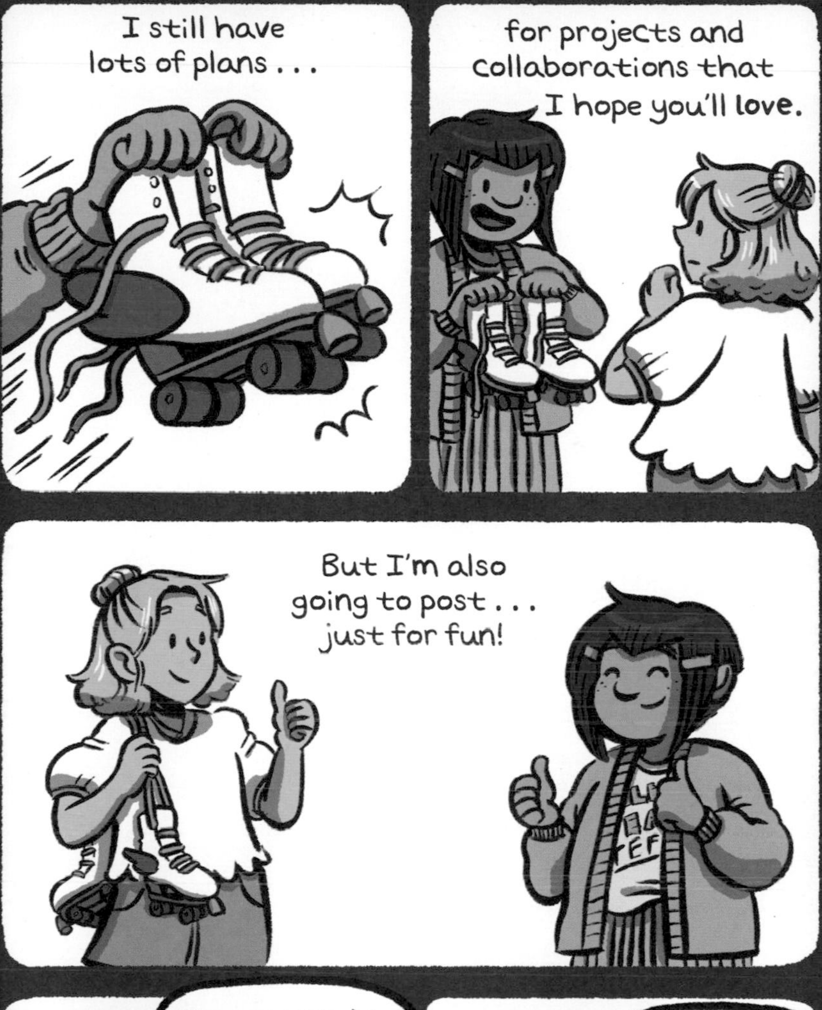
I still have lots of plans . . .
for projects and collaborations that I hope you'll **love.**
But I'm also going to post . . . just for fun!
I'm so excited to grow and change and embrace new versions of myself . . .
While honoring the parts . . .
that have always been there.

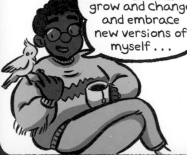

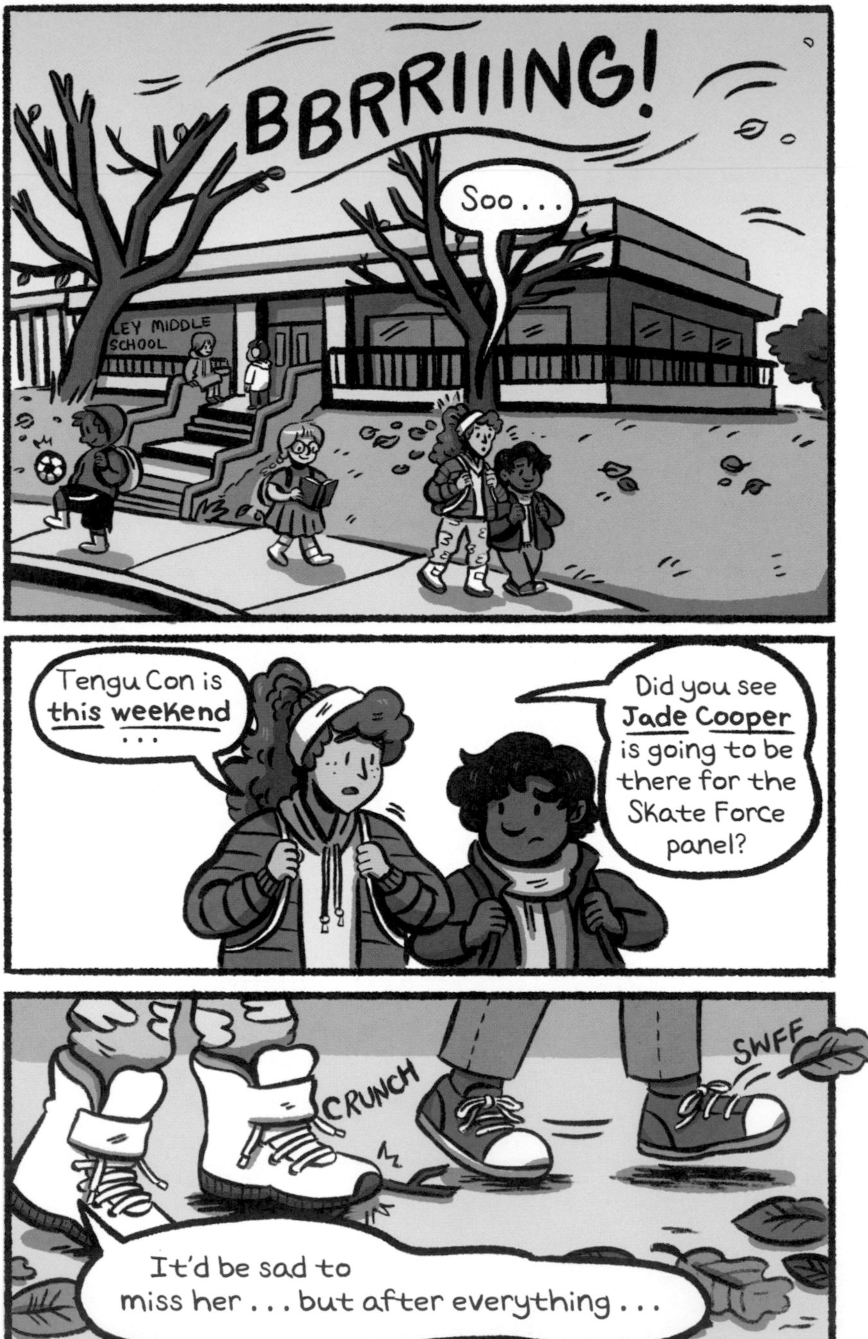
BBRRIIING!
LEY MIDDLE SCHOOL
Soo . . .
Tengu Con is this weekend . . .
Did you see Jade Cooper is going to be there for the Skate Force panel?
CRUNCH
SWFF
It'd be sad to miss her . . . but after everything . . .

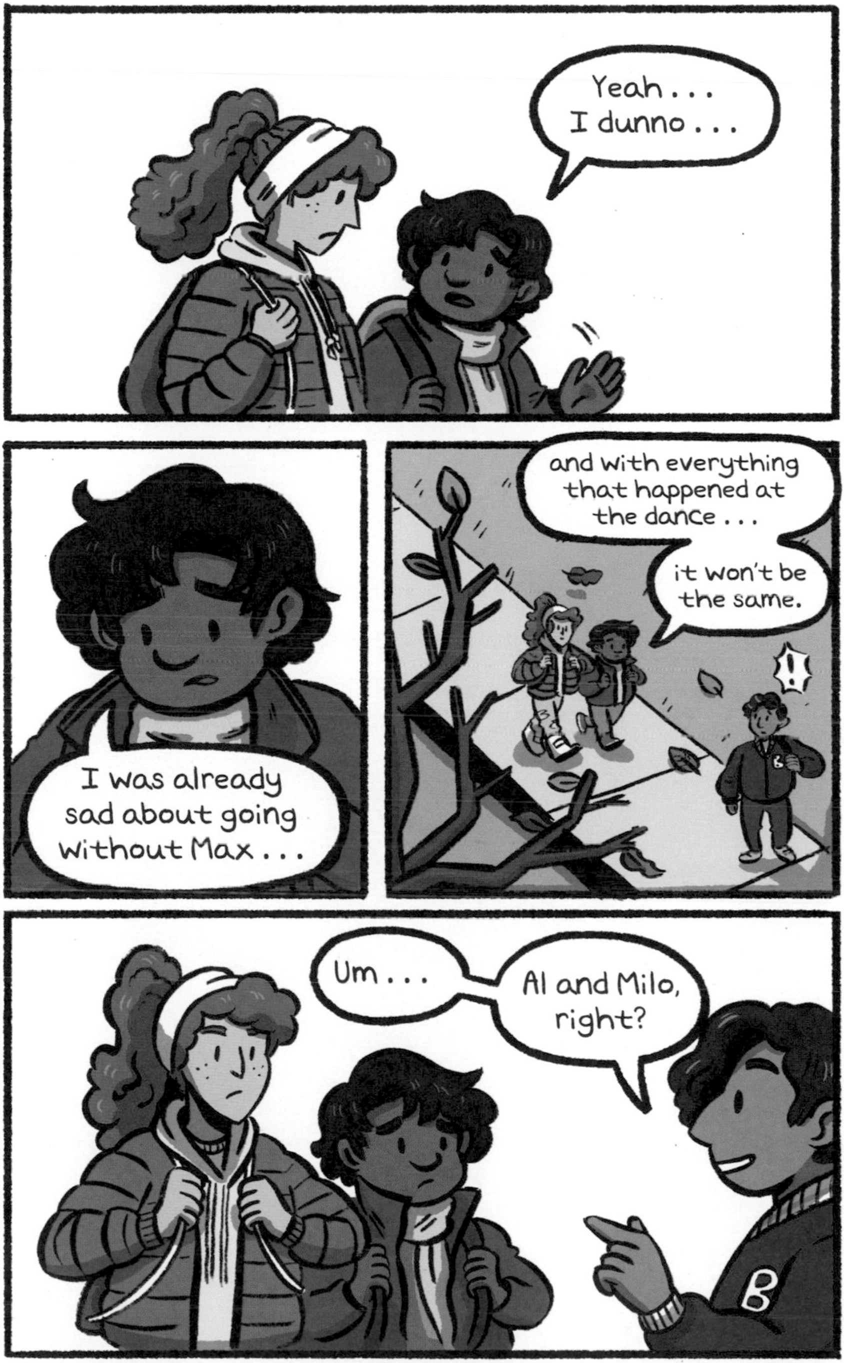
Yeah . . .
I dunno . . .
I was already
sad about going
without Max . . .
and with everything
that happened at
the dance . . .
it won't be
the same.
!
Um . . .
Al and Milo,
right?

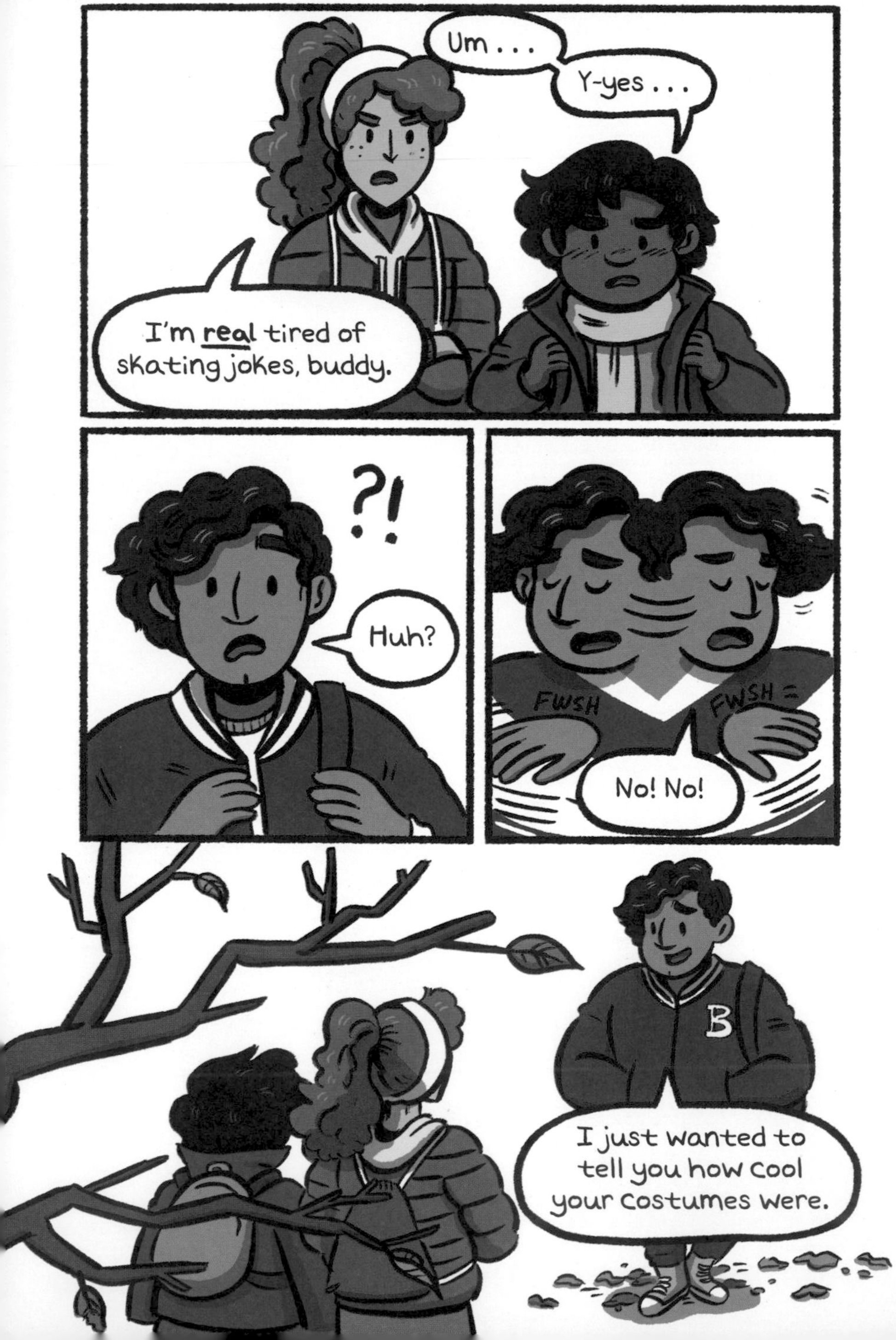
Um . . .
Y-yes . . .
I'm real tired of skating jokes, buddy.
?!
Huh?
FWSH
FWSH
No! No!
I just wanted to tell you how cool your costumes were.
B

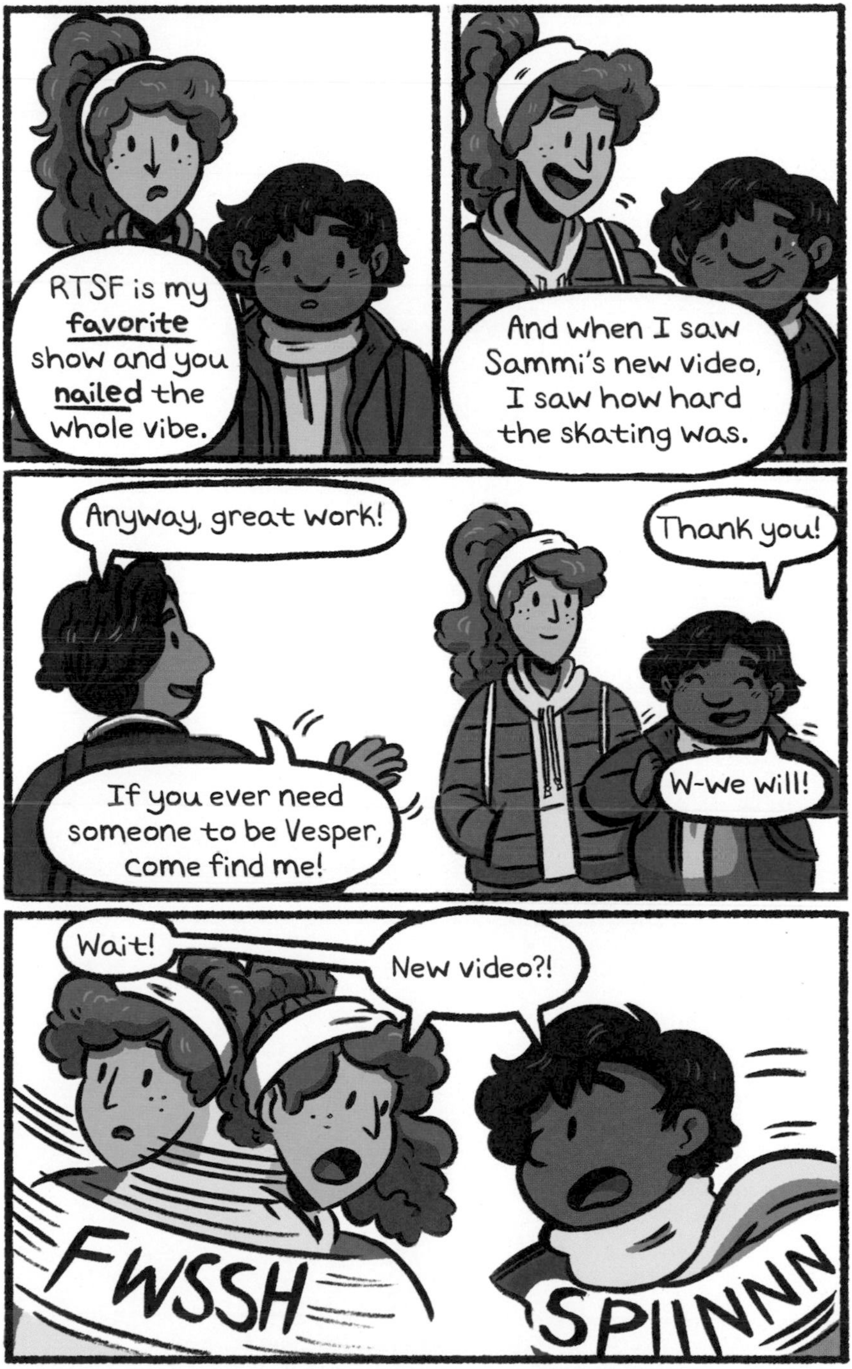
RTSF is my favorite show and you nailed the whole vibe.
And when I saw Sammi's new video, I saw how hard the skating was.
Anyway, great work!
If you ever need someone to be Vesper, come find me!
Thank you!
W-we will!
Wait!
New video?!
FWSSH
SPIINNN

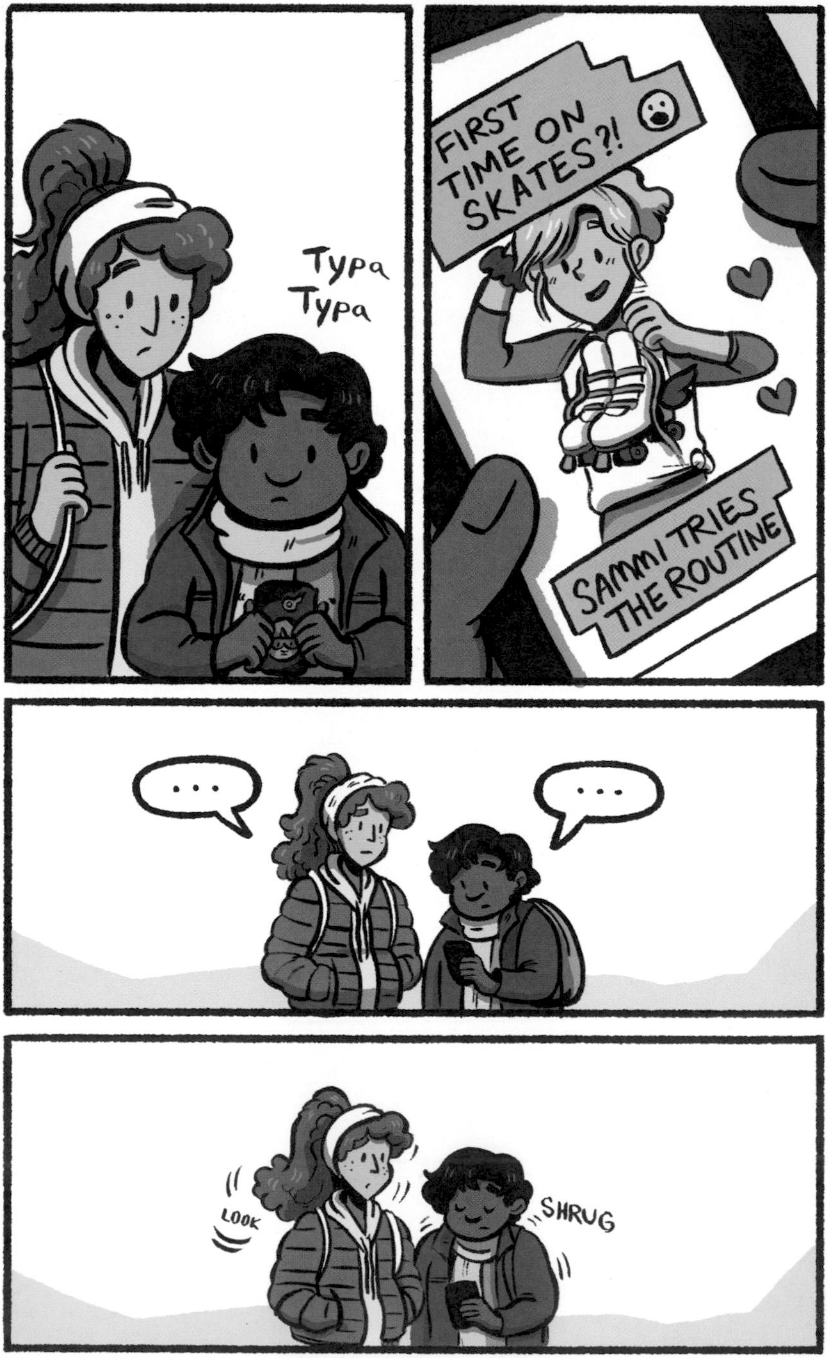
Typa
Typa
FIRST TIME ON SKATES?!
SAMMI TRIES THE ROUTINE
...
...
LOOK
SHRUG

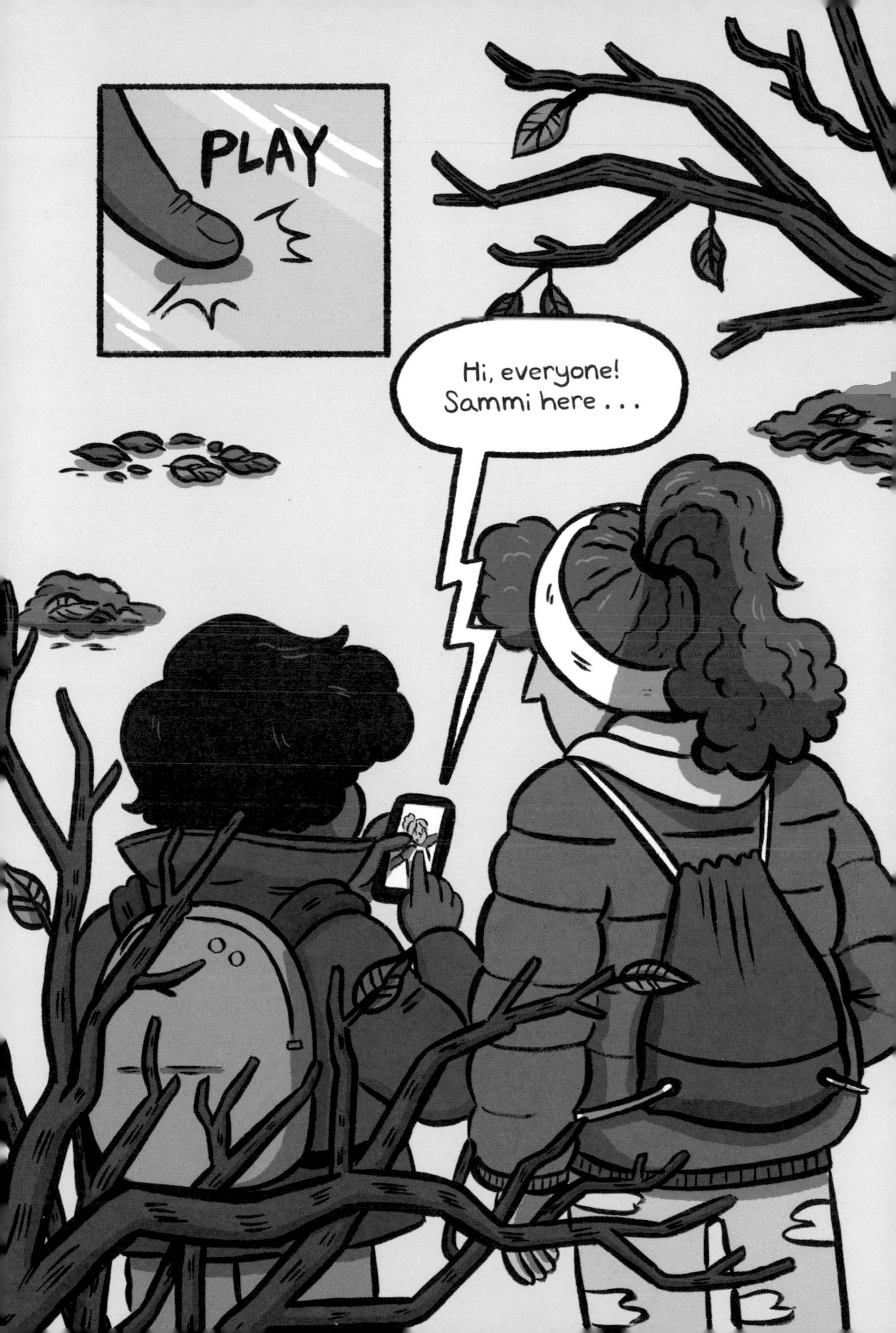
PLAY
Hi, everyone! Sammi here . . .

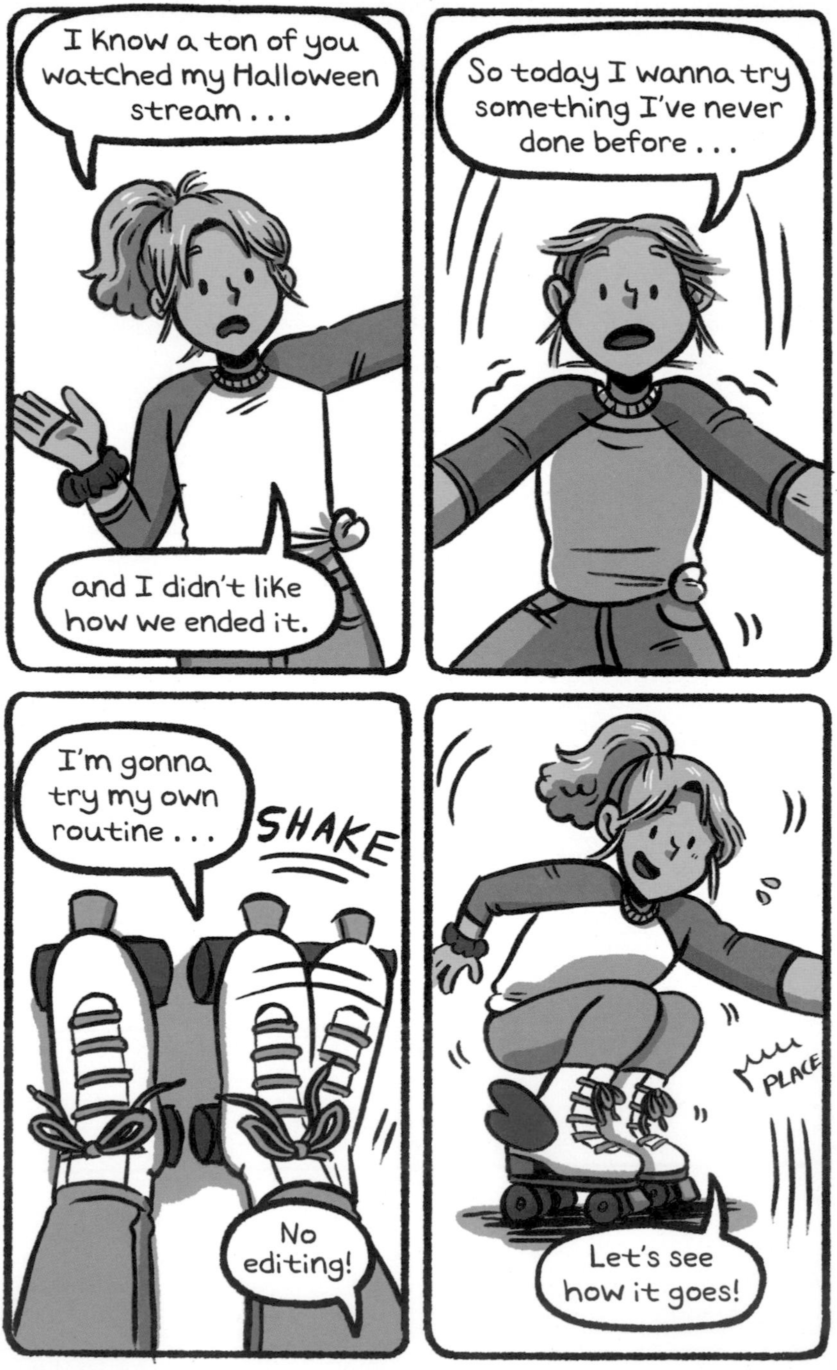
I know a ton of you watched my Halloween stream . . .
and I didn't like how we ended it.
So today I wanna try something I've never done before . . .
I'm gonna try my own routine . . .
SHAKE
No editing!
PLACE
Let's see how it goes!

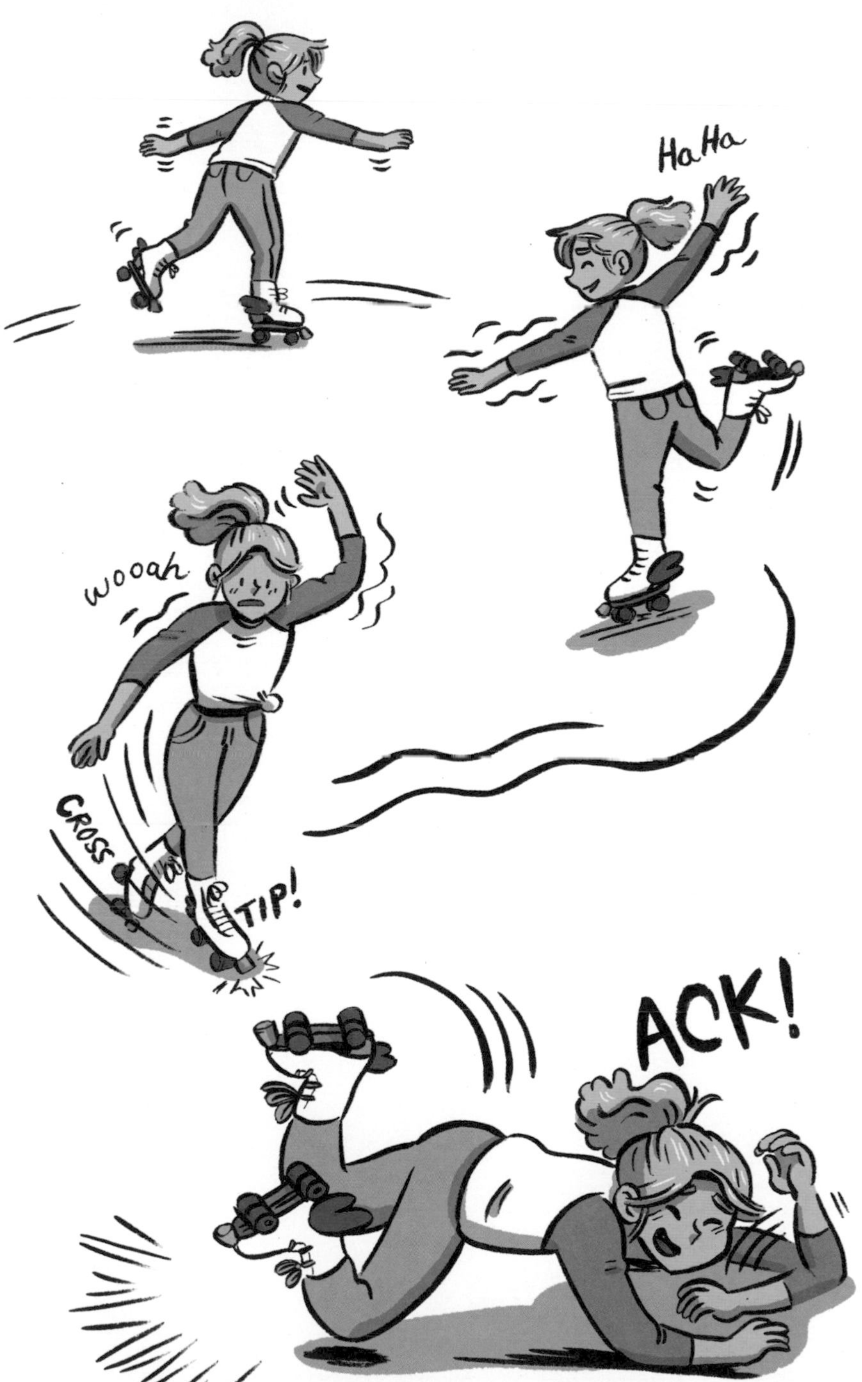
HaHa
wooah
CROSS
TIP!
ACK!

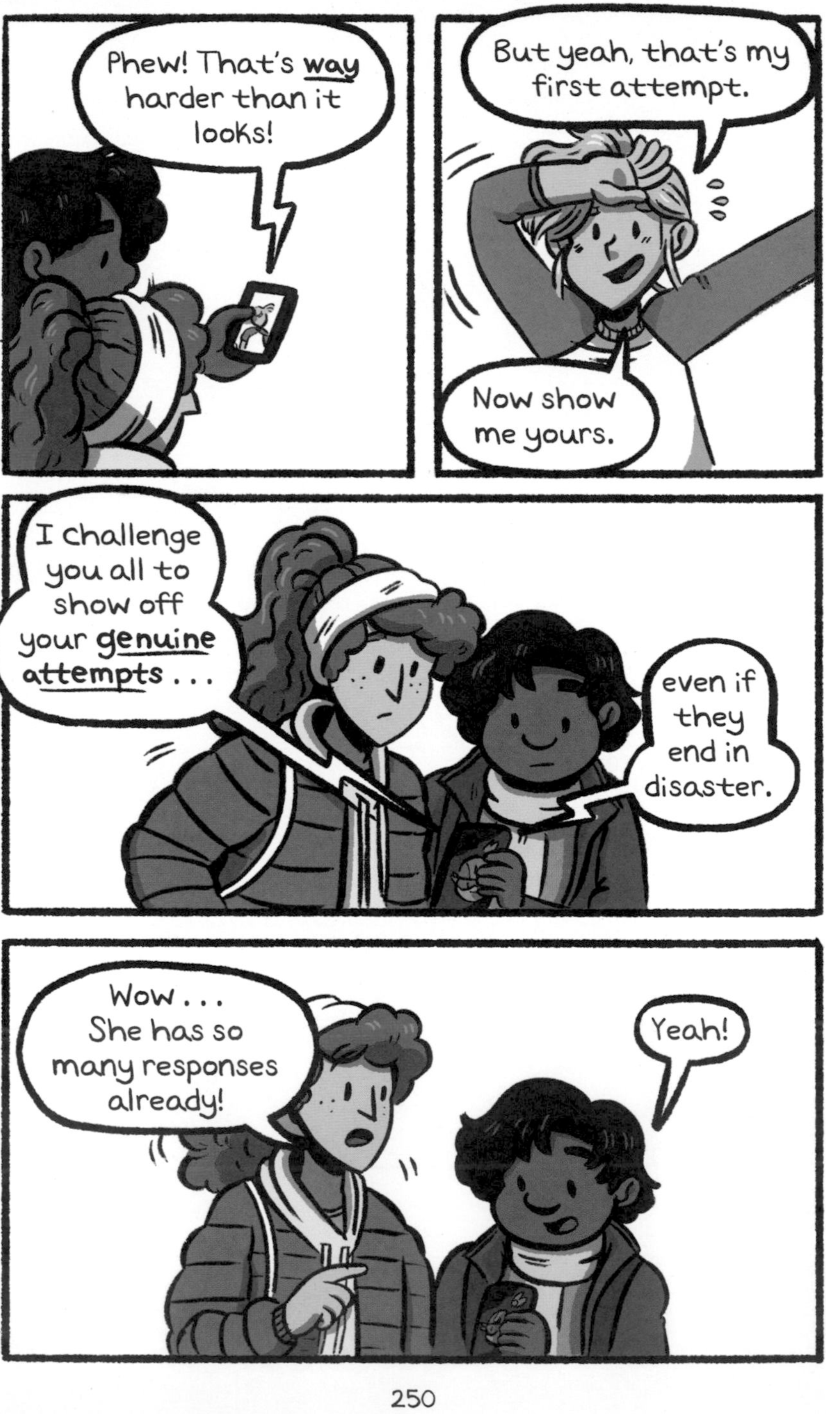
Phew! That's **way** harder than it looks!
But yeah, that's my first attempt.
Now show me yours.
I challenge you all to show off your **genuine attempts** . . .
even if they end in disaster.
Wow . . . She has so many responses already!
Yeah!

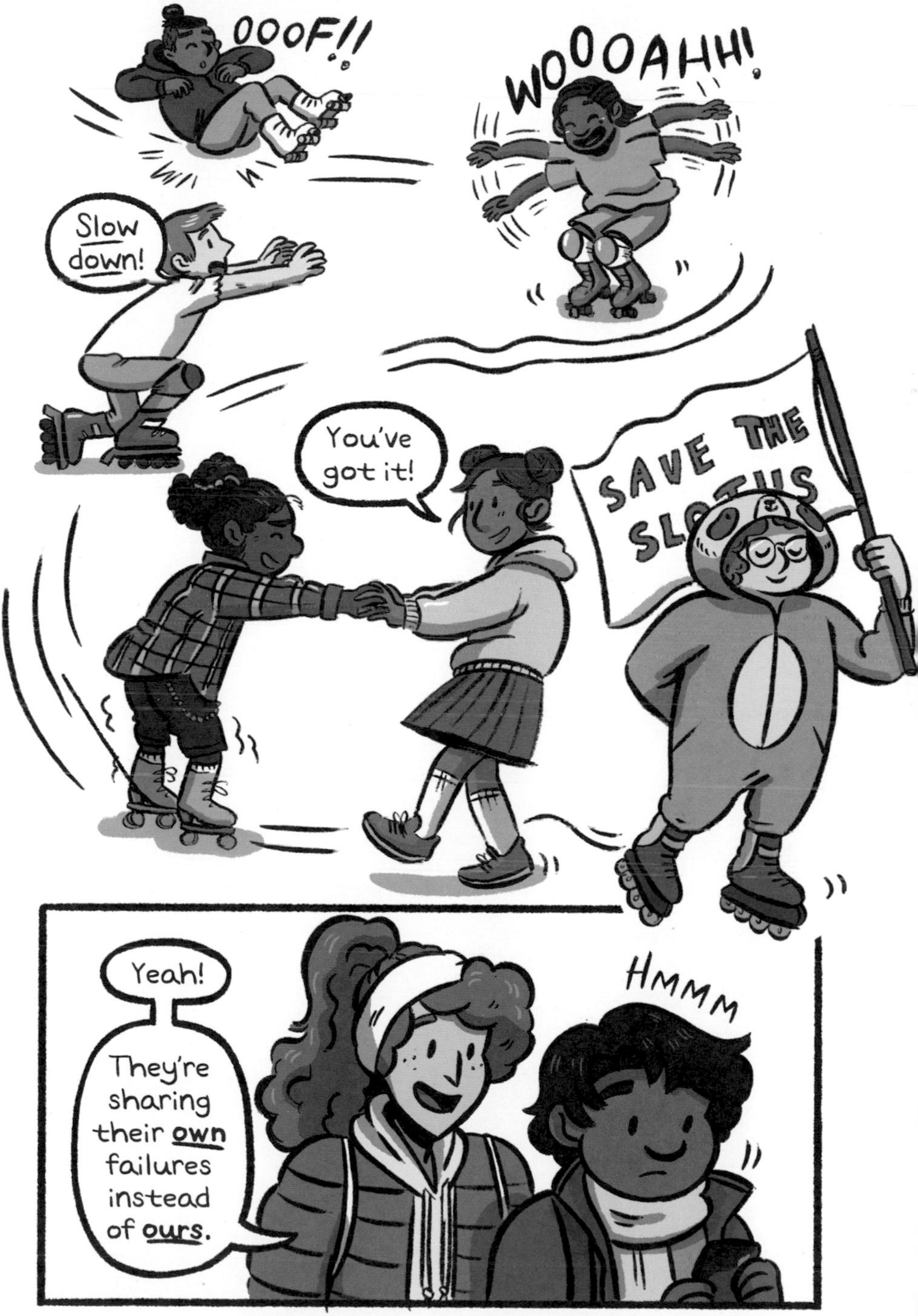
OOOF!!
WOOOAHH!
Slow down!
You've got it!
SAVE THE
SLO
Yeah!
They're sharing their **own** failures instead of **ours**.
HMMM

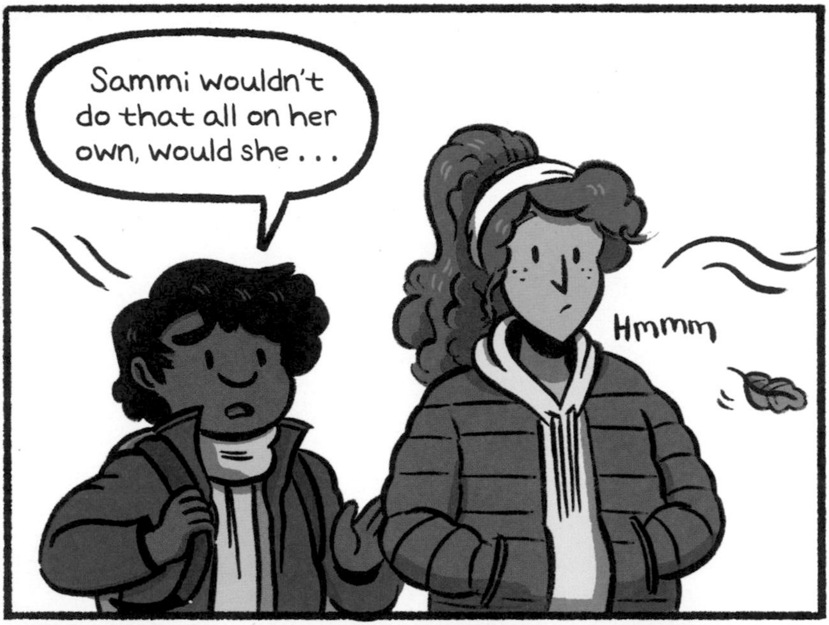
Sammi wouldn't do that all on her own, would she . . .
Hmmm

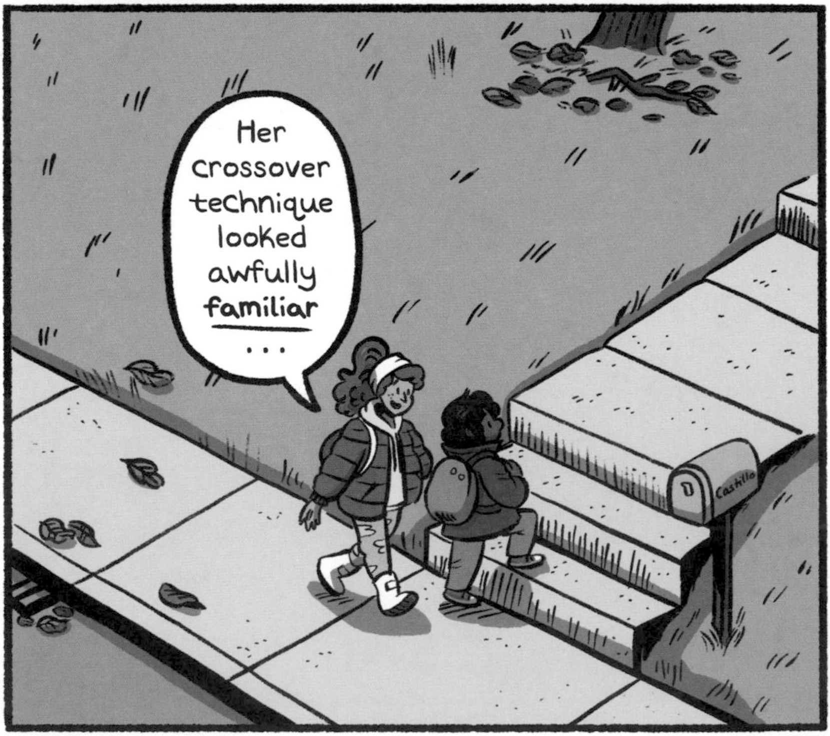
Her crossover technique looked awfully **familiar** . . .

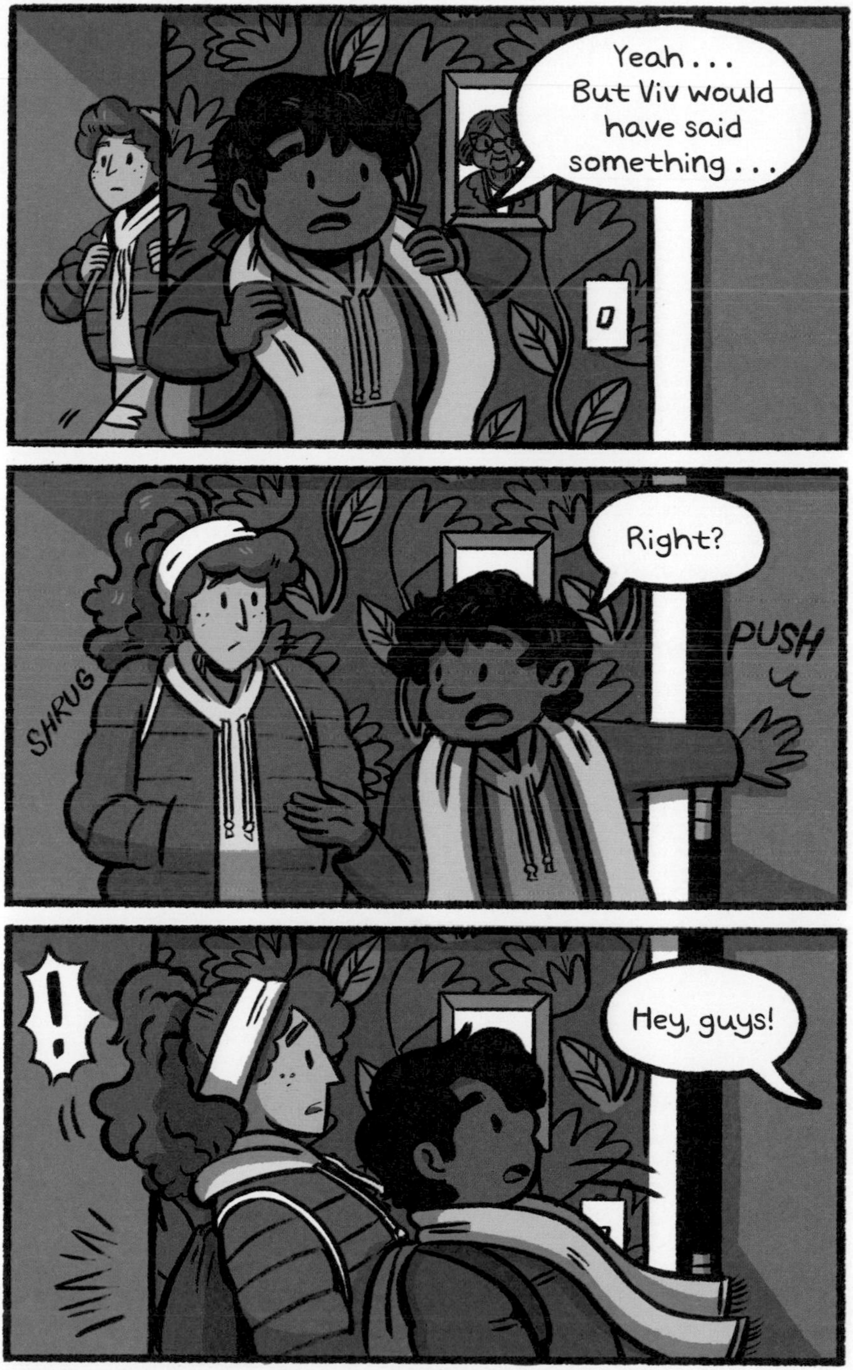
Yeah . . . But Viv would have said something . . .
Right?
SHRUG
PUSH
!
Hey, guys!

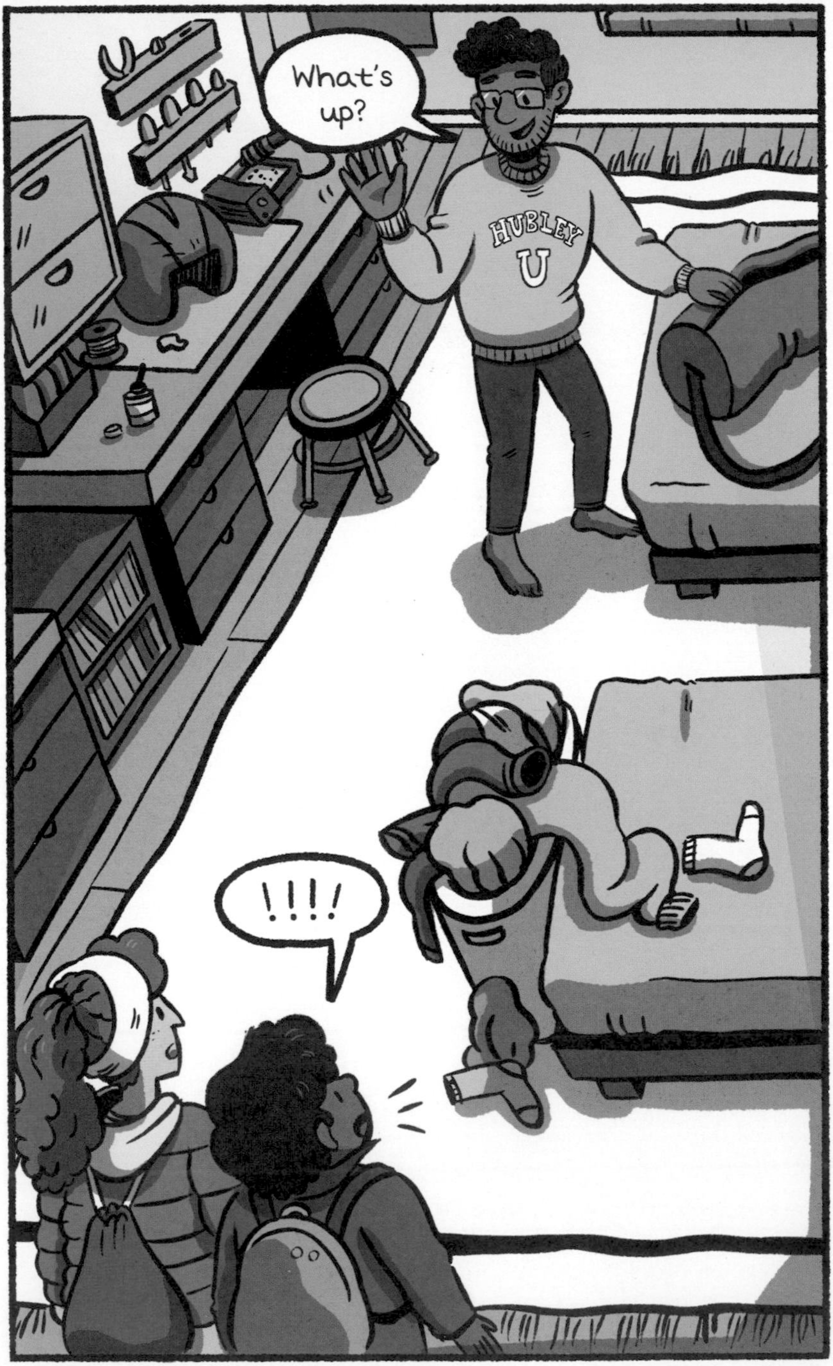
What's up?
HUBLEY U
!!!!

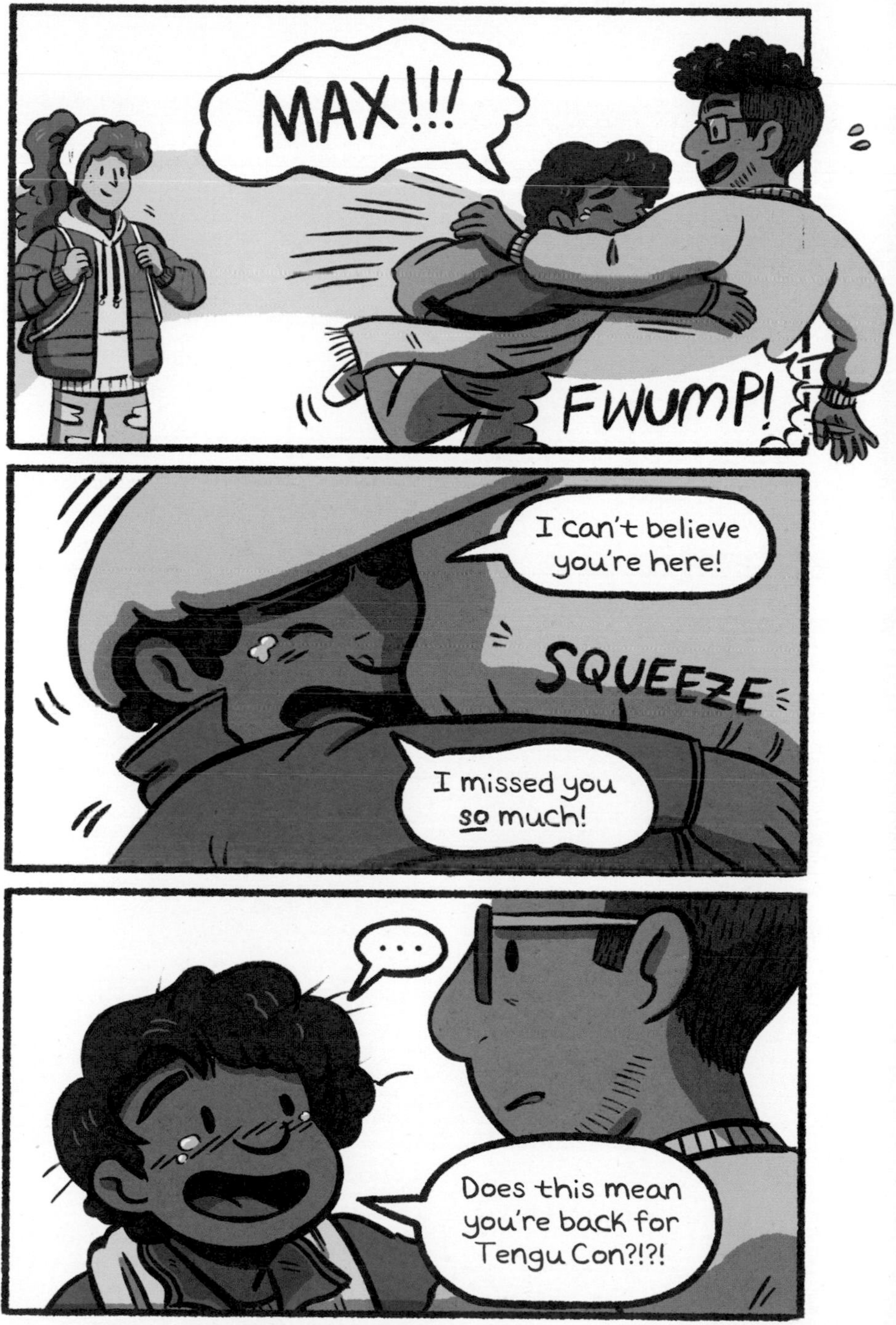
MAX!!!
FWUMP!
I can't believe you're here!
SQUEEZE
I missed you so much!
...
Does this mean you're back for Tengu Con?!?!

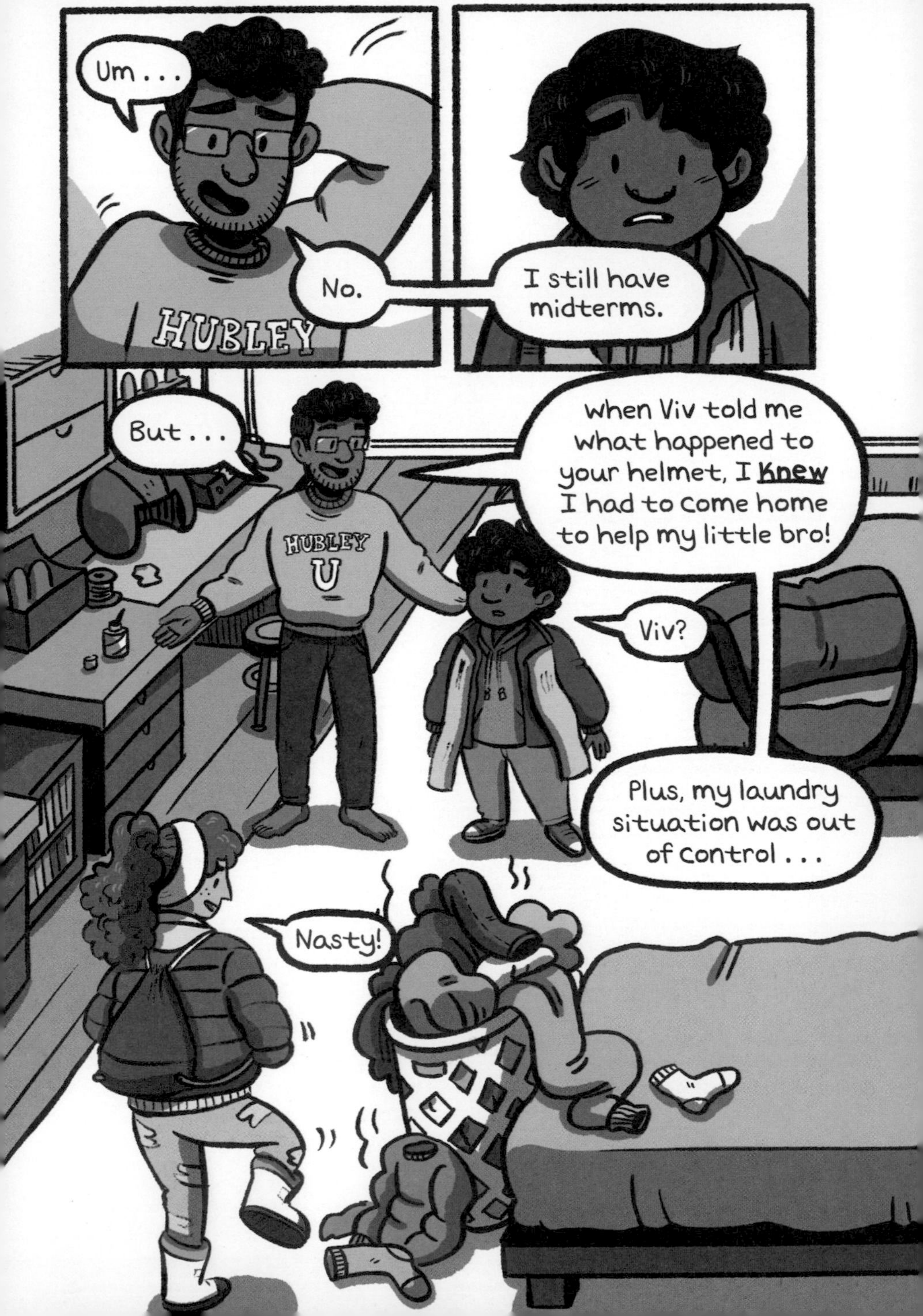
Um . . .
No.
I still have midterms.
But . . .
When Viv told me what happened to your helmet, I Knew I had to come home to help my little bro!
Viv?
Plus, my laundry situation was out of control . . .
Nasty!
HUBLEY U

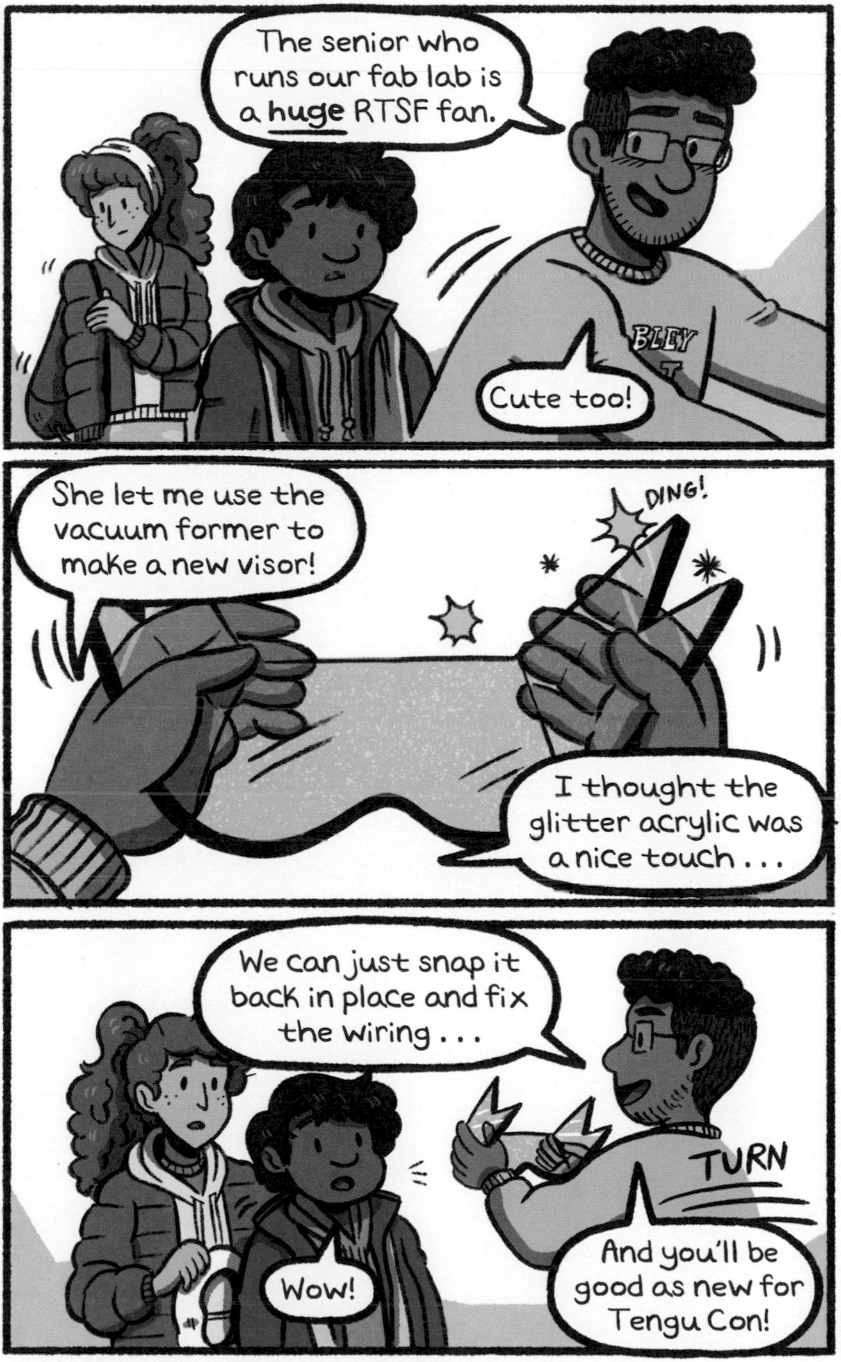
The senior who runs our fab lab is a huge RTSF fan.
BLEY
Cute too!
She let me use the vacuum former to make a new visor!
DING!
I thought the glitter acrylic was a nice touch . . .
We can just snap it back in place and fix the wiring . . .
TURN
Wow!
And you'll be good as new for Tengu Con!

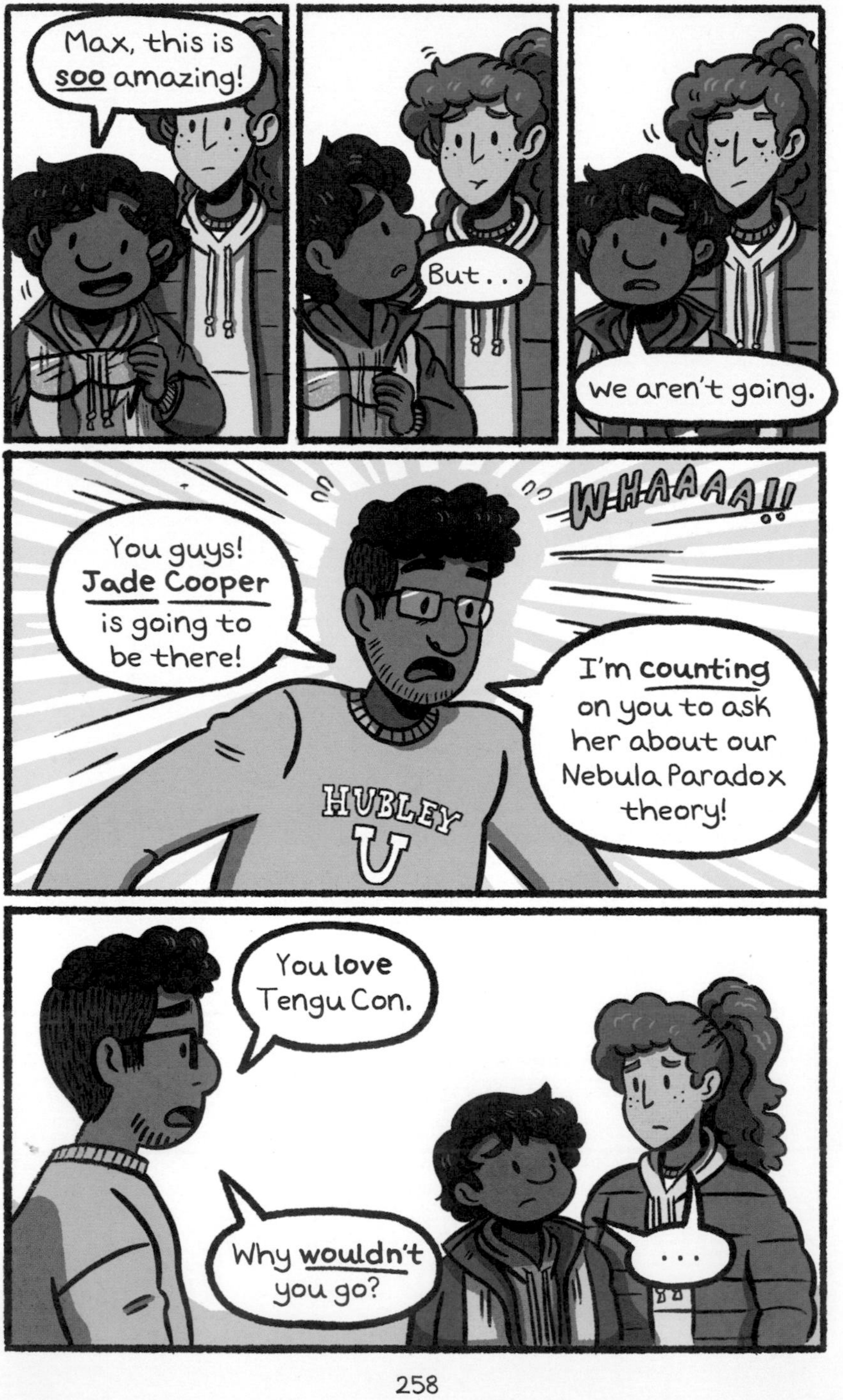
Max, this is soo amazing!
But...
We aren't going.
WHAAAAA!!
You guys! Jade Cooper is going to be there!
I'm counting on you to ask her about our Nebula Paradox theory!
HUBLEY U
You love Tengu Con.
Why wouldn't you go?
...

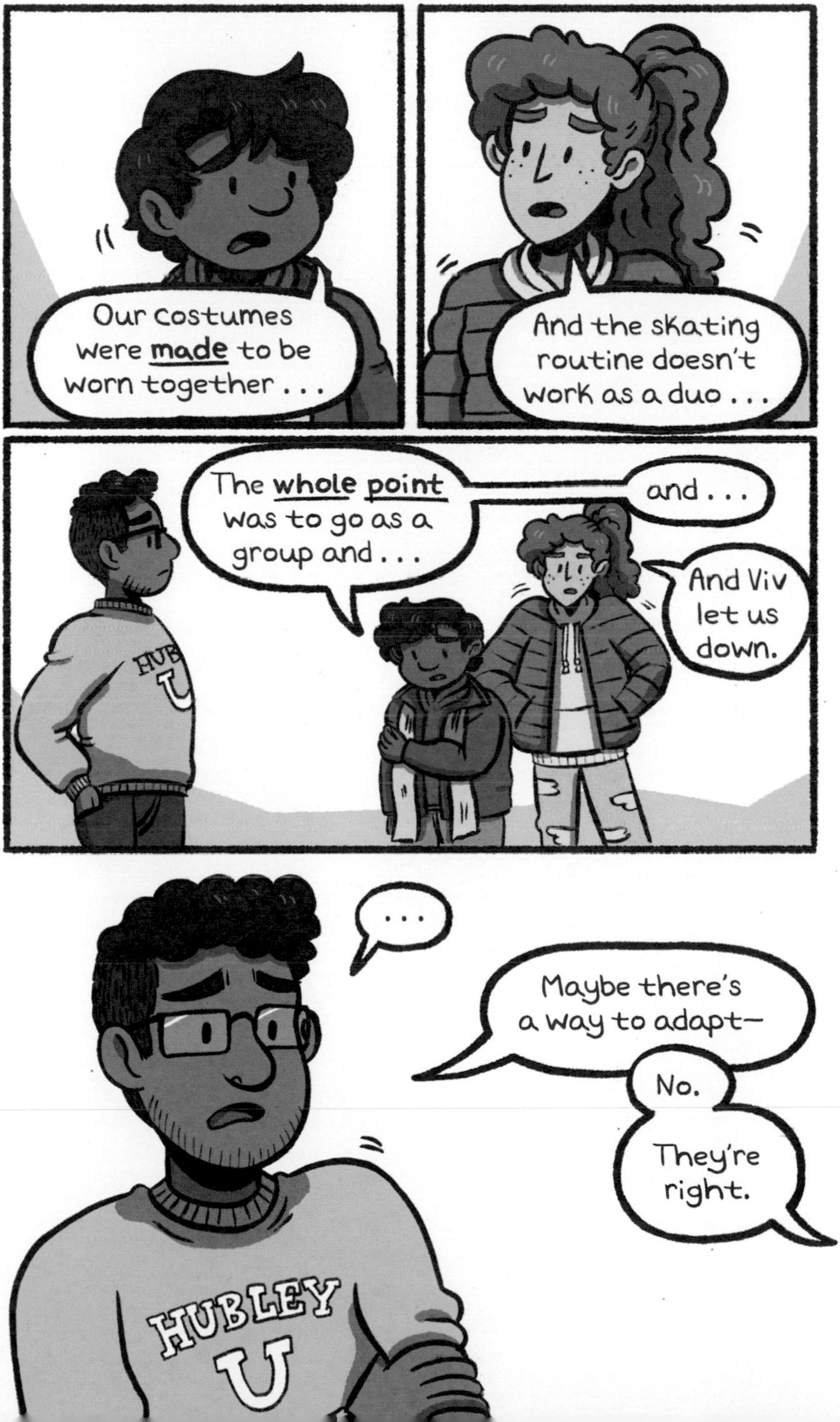
Our costumes were made to be worn together . . .
And the skating routine doesn't work as a duo . . .
The whole point was to go as a group and . . .
and . . .
And Viv let us down.
HUBLEY U
. . .
Maybe there's a way to adapt—
No.
They're right.
HUBLEY U

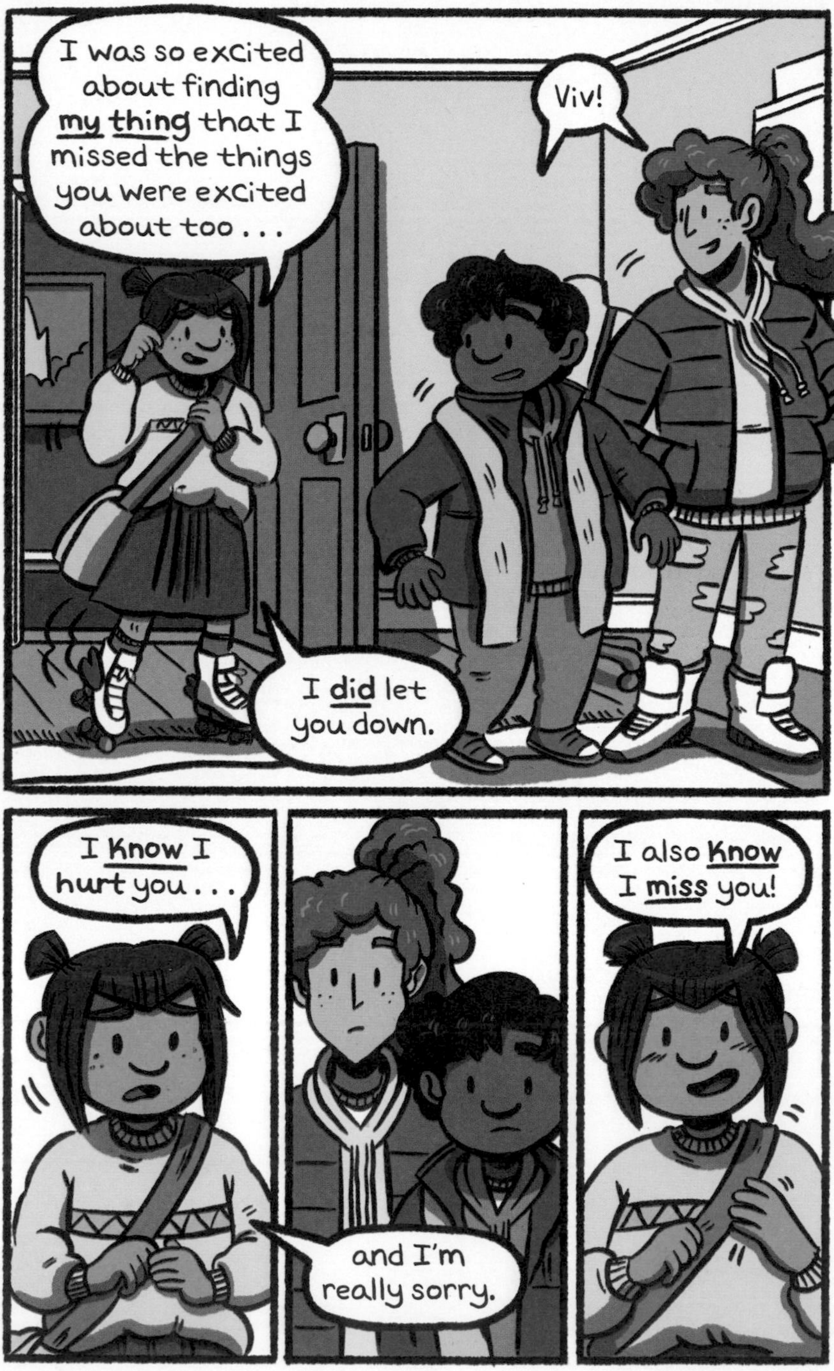
I was so excited about finding my thing that I missed the things you were excited about too . . .
Viv!
I did let you down.
I know I hurt you . . .
and I'm really sorry.
I also know I miss you!

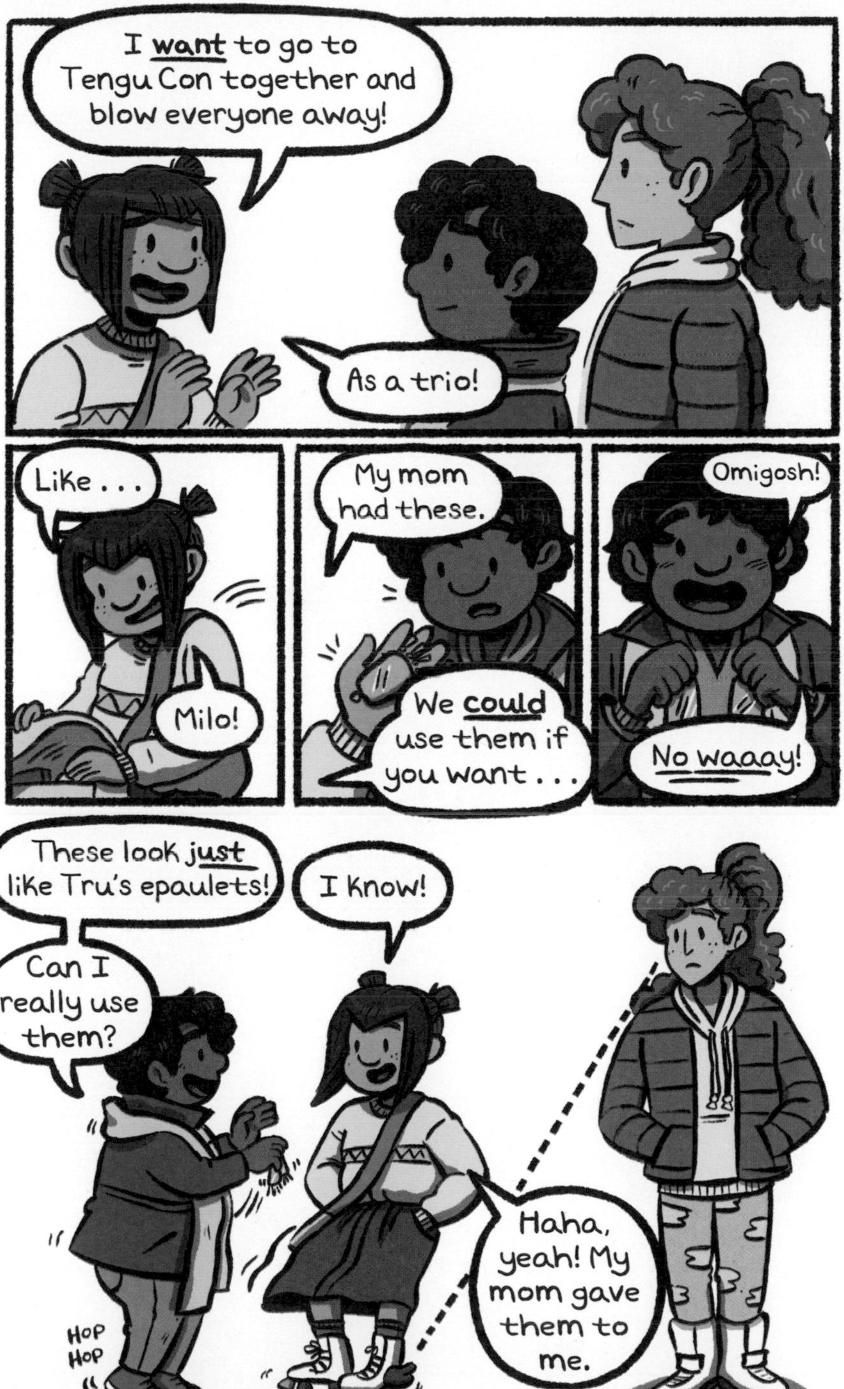
I want to go to Tengu Con together and blow everyone away!
As a trio!
Like . . .
Milo!
My mom had these.
We could use them if you want . . .
Omigosh!
No waaay!
These look just like Tru's epaulets!
I know!
Can I really use them?
HOP HOP
Haha, yeah! My mom gave them to me.

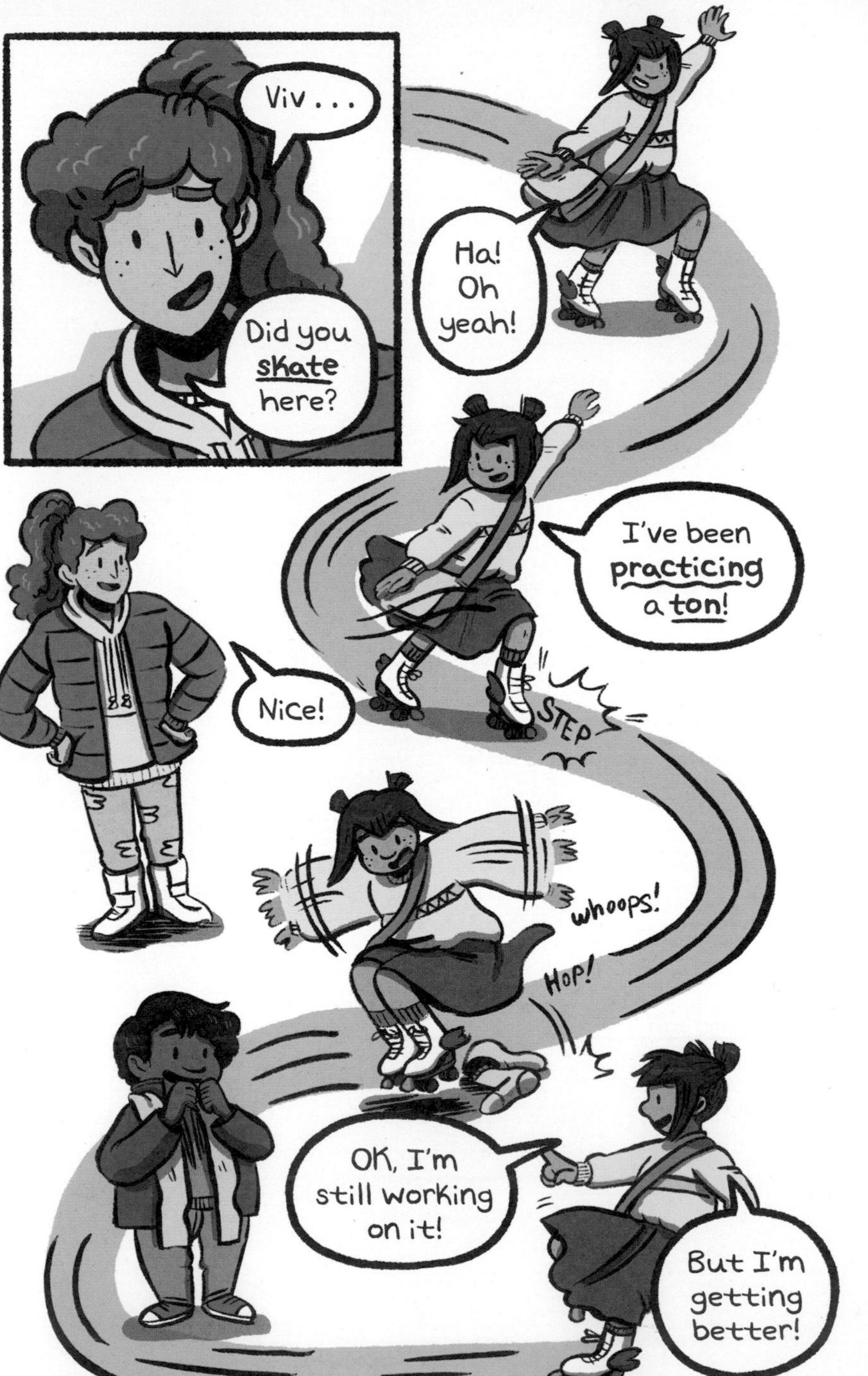
Viv . . .
Did you skate here?
Ha! Oh yeah!
I've been practicing a ton!
Nice!
STEP
whoops!
HOP!
OK, I'm still working on it!
But I'm getting better!

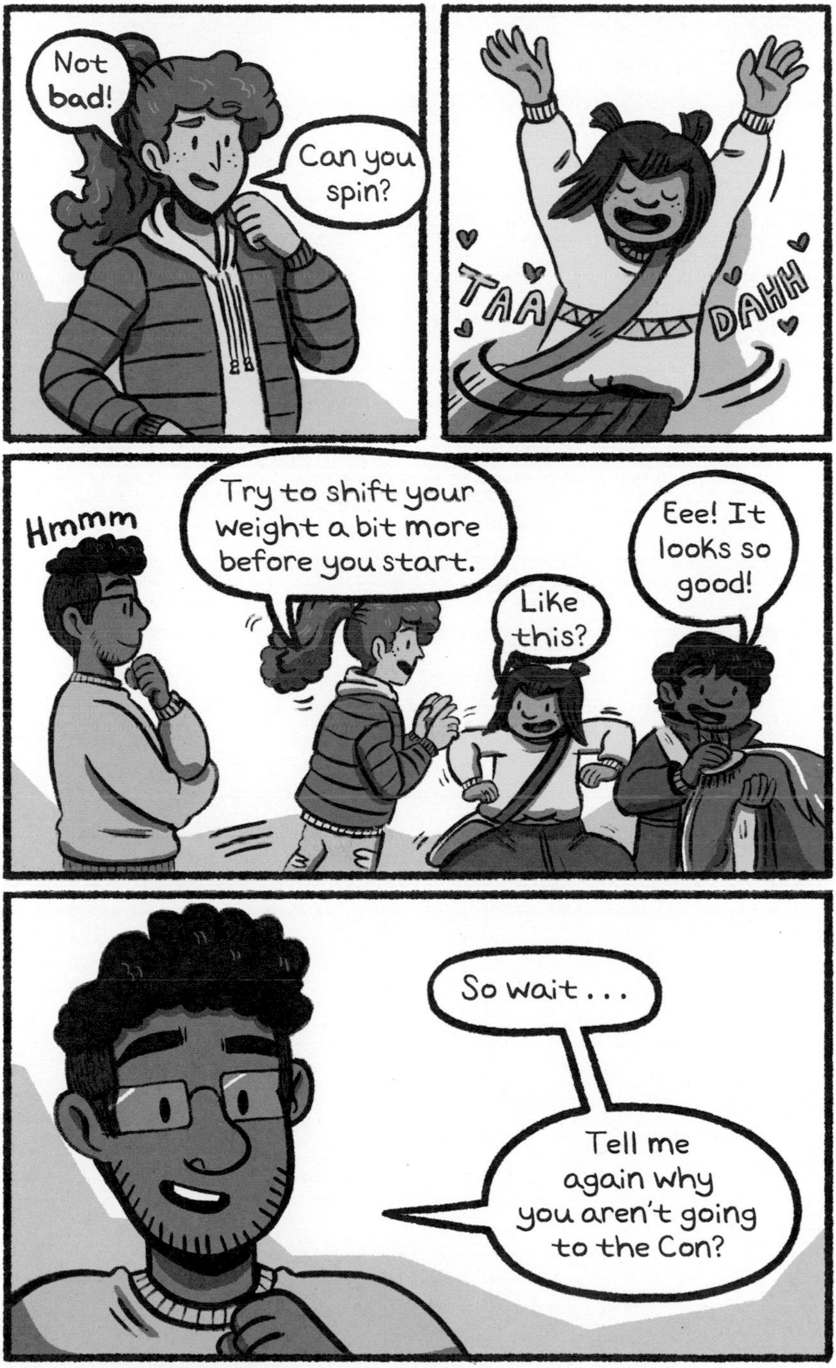
Not bad!
Can you spin?
TAA
DAHH
Hmmm
Try to shift your weight a bit more before you start.
Like this?
Eee! It looks so good!
So wait . . .
Tell me again why you aren't going to the Con?

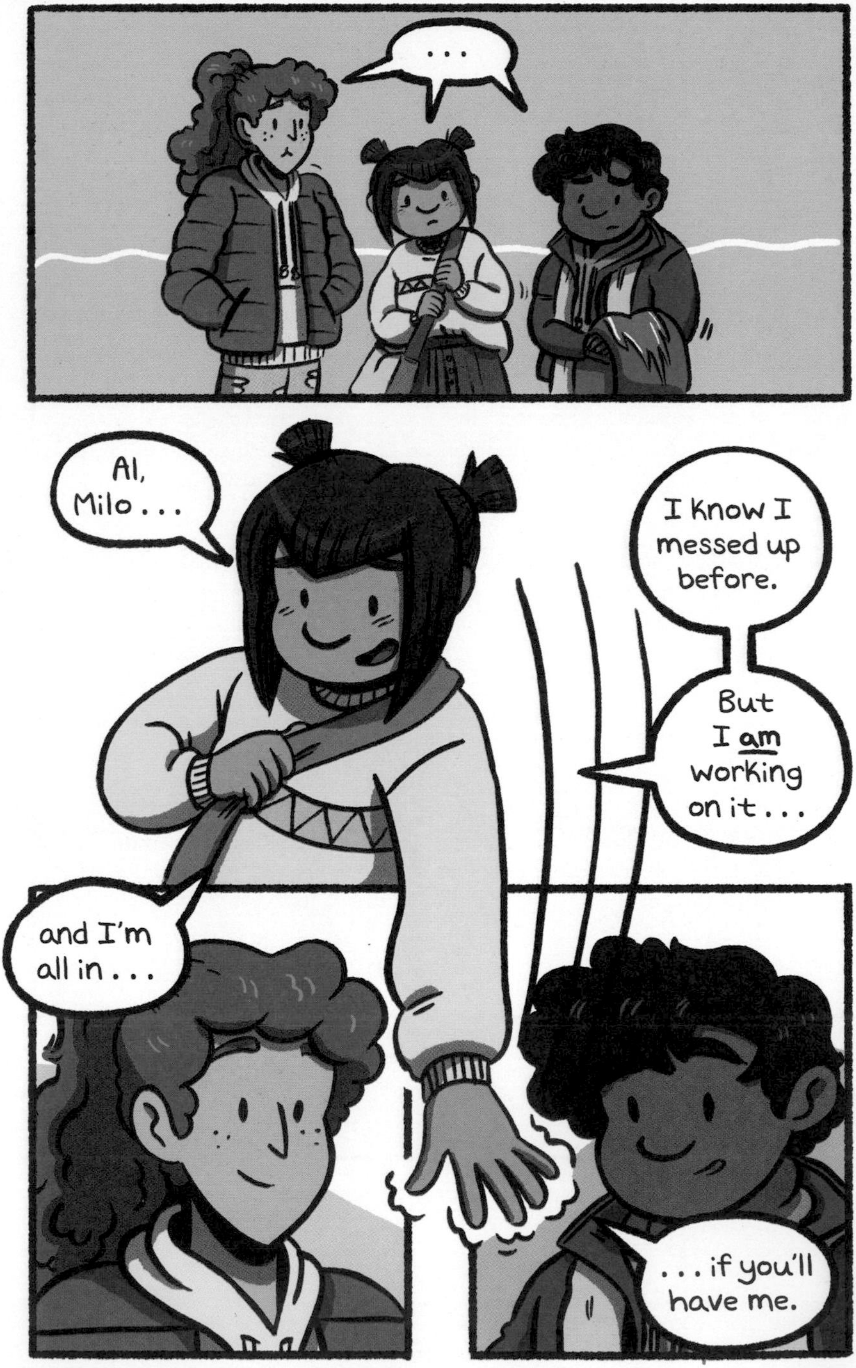
. . .
Al, Milo . . .
I know I messed up before.
But I am working on it . . .
and I'm all in . . .
. . . if you'll have me.

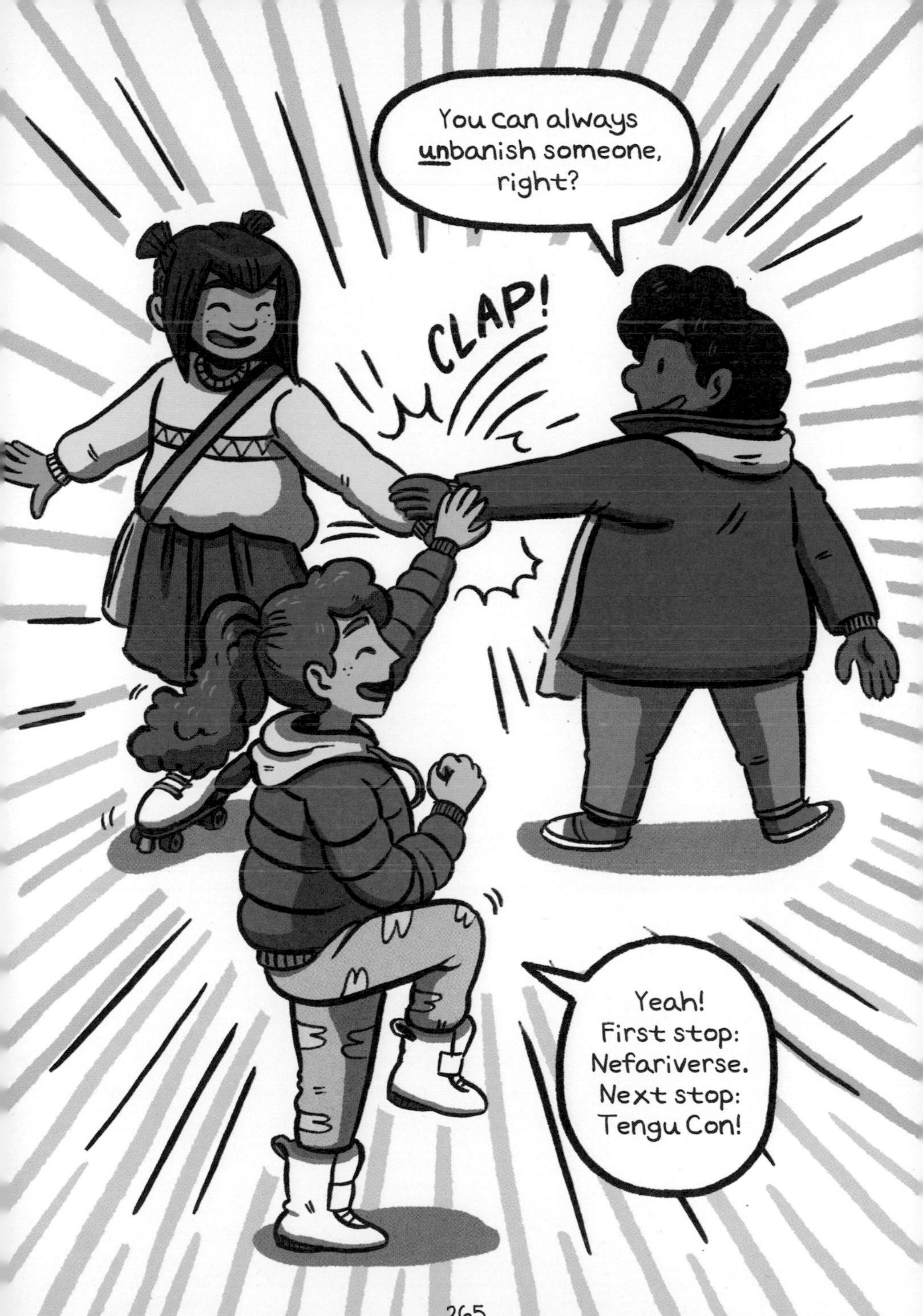
You can always unbanish someone, right?
CLAP!
Yeah! First stop: Nefariverse. Next stop: Tengu Con!

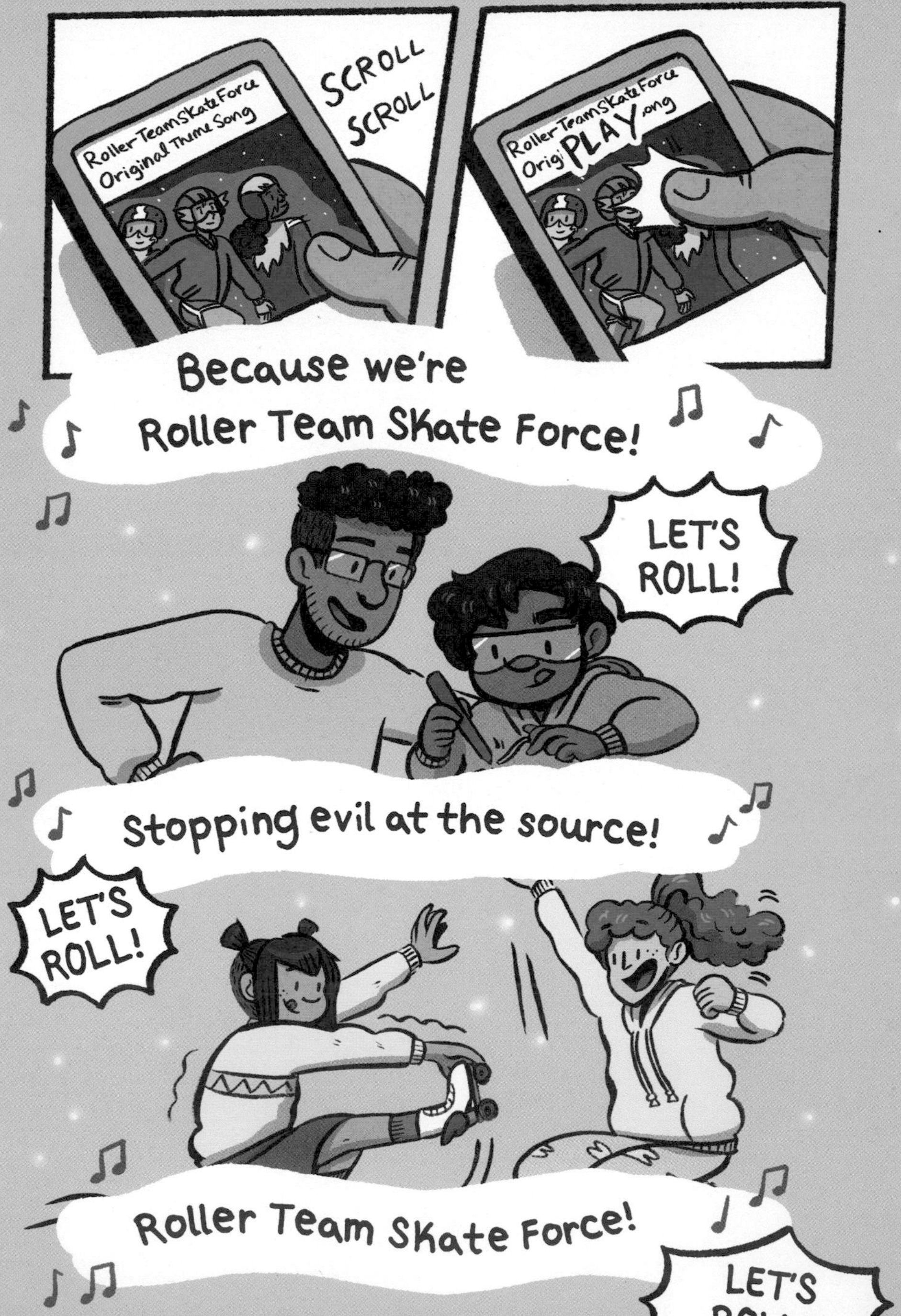
Roller Team Skate Force Original Theme Song
SCROLL SCROLL
Roller Team Skate Force Origi PLAY ong
Because we're Roller Team Skate Force!
LET'S ROLL!
Stopping evil at the source!
LET'S ROLL!
Roller Team Skate Force!
LET'S ROLL!

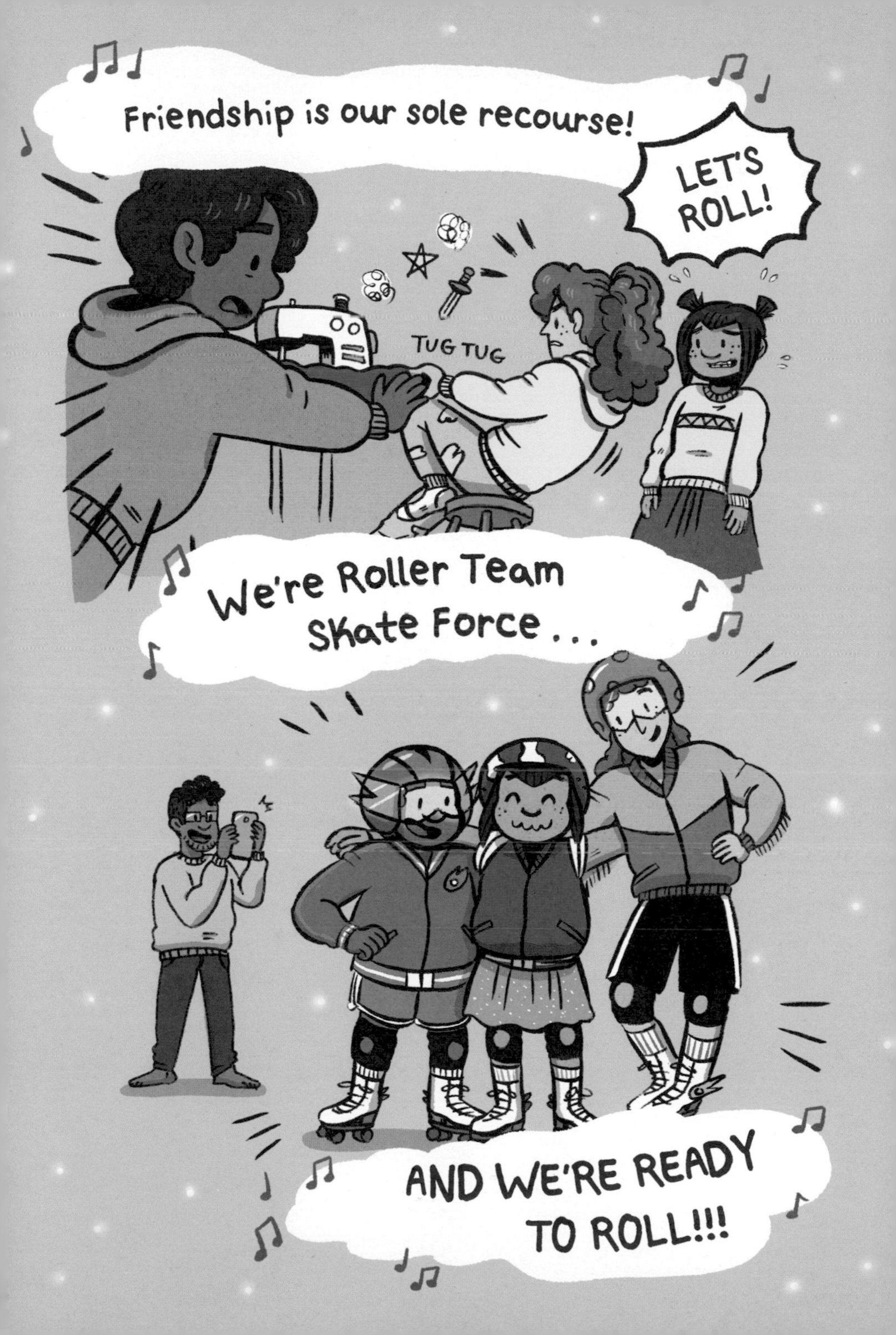
Friendship is our sole recourse!
LET'S ROLL!
TUG TUG
We're Roller Team Skate Force...
AND WE'RE READY TO ROLL!!!

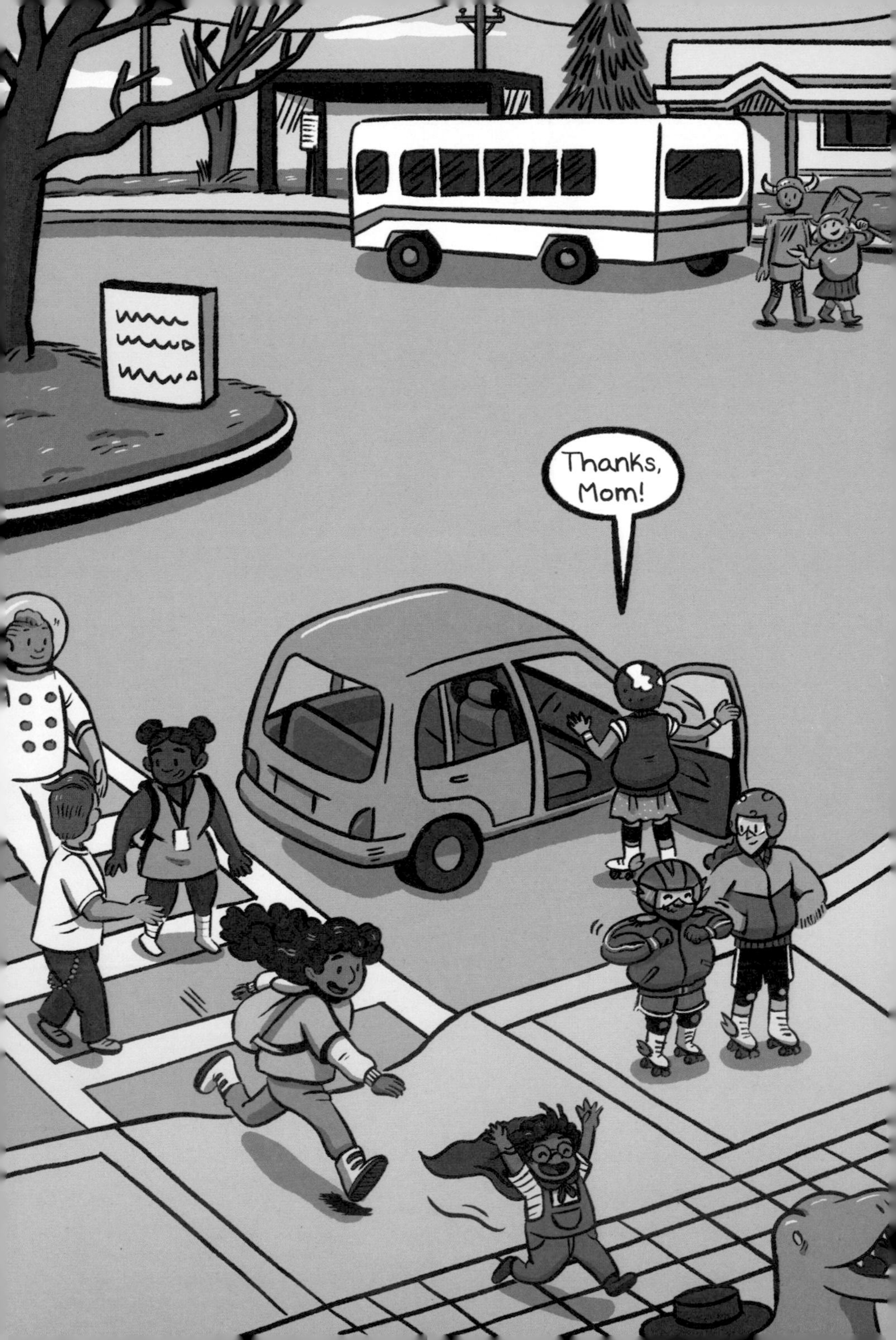
Thanks, Mom!

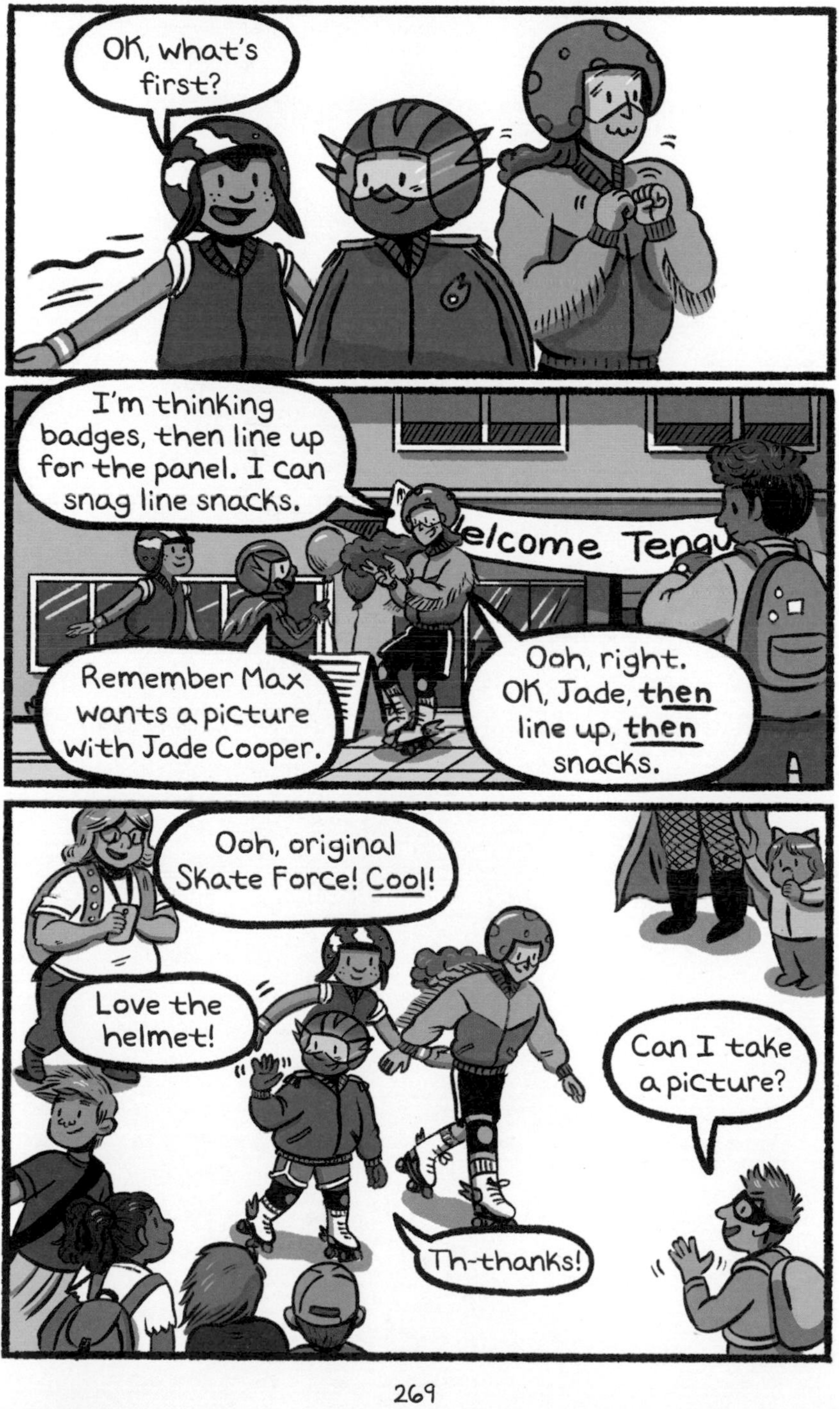
OK, what's first?
I'm thinking badges, then line up for the panel. I can snag line snacks.
elcome Tengu
Remember Max wants a picture with Jade Cooper.
Ooh, right. OK, Jade, then line up, then snacks.
Ooh, original Skate Force! Cool!
Love the helmet!
Can I take a picture?
Th-thanks!

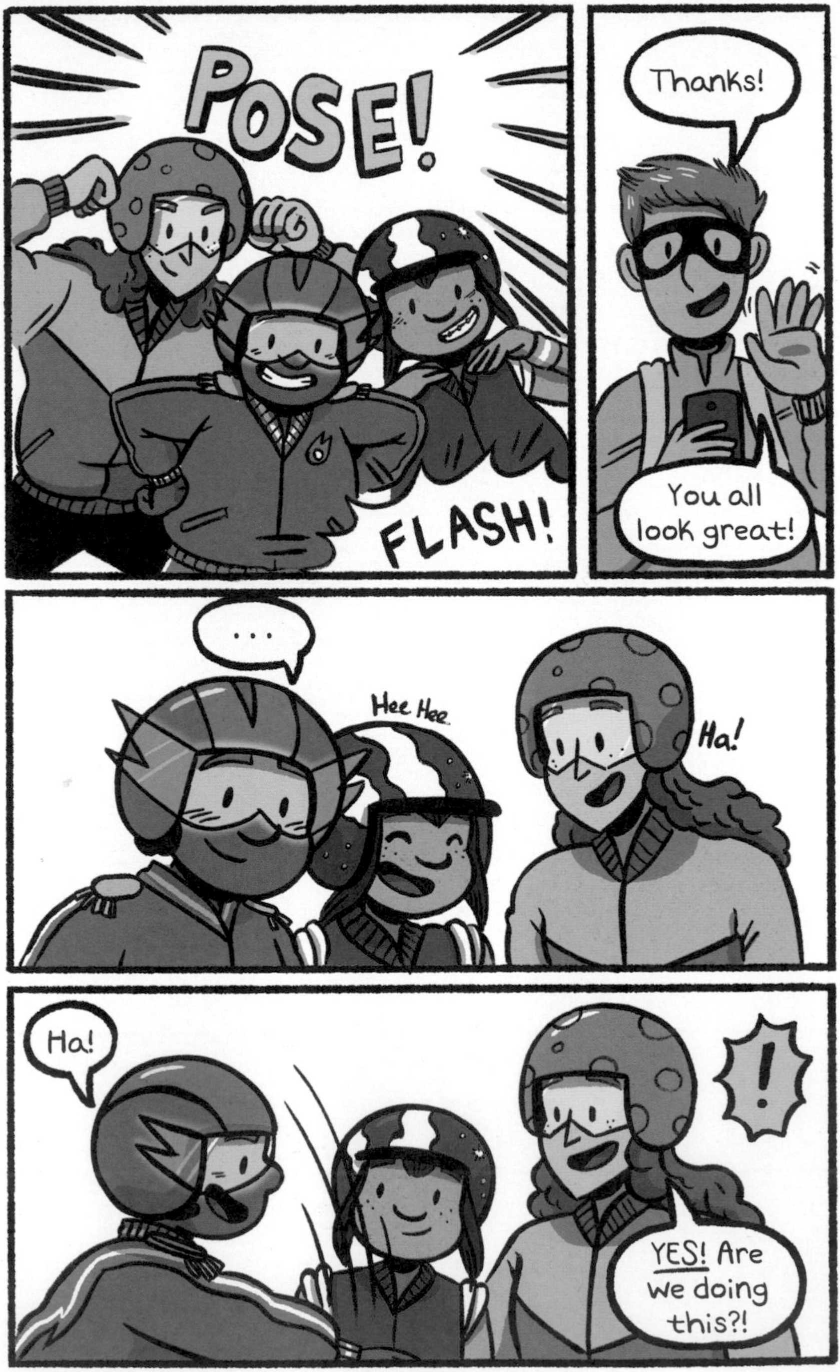
POSE!
FLASH!
Thanks!
You all look great!
...
Hee Hee
Ha!
Ha!
!
YES! Are we doing this?!

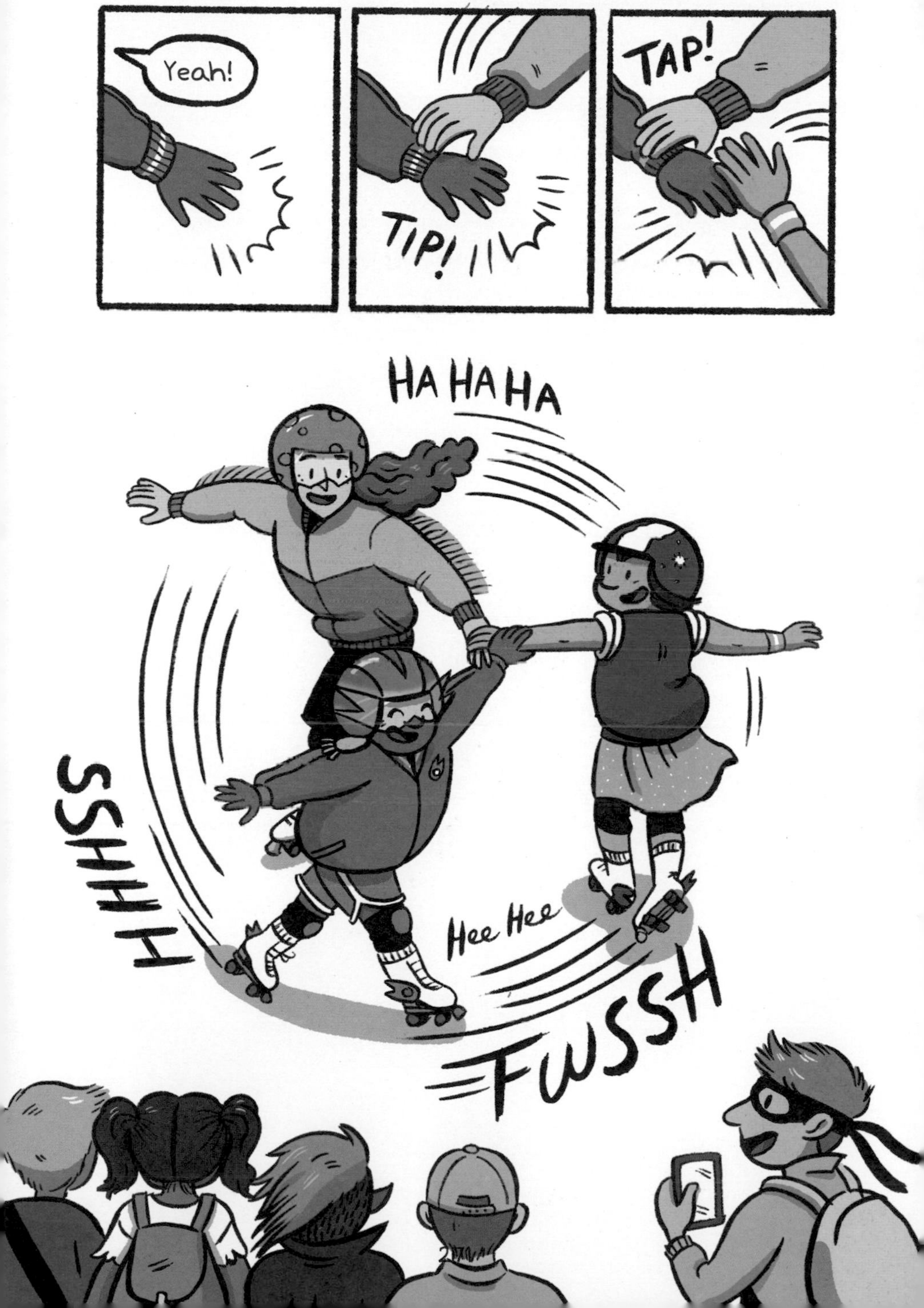
Yeah!
TIP!
TAP!
HA HA HA
HHHISS
Hee Hee
FWSSH

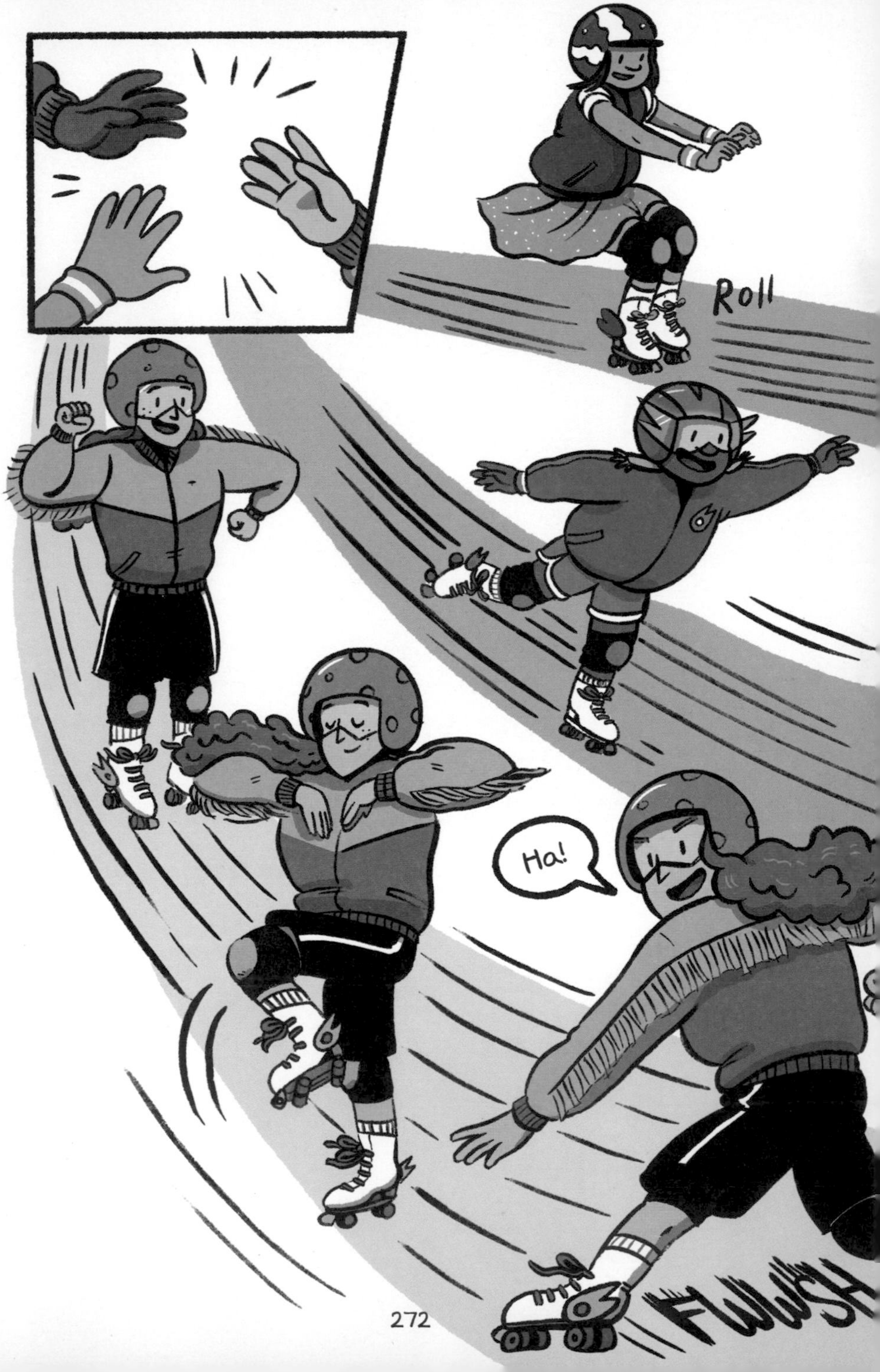
Roll
Ha!
FWUSH

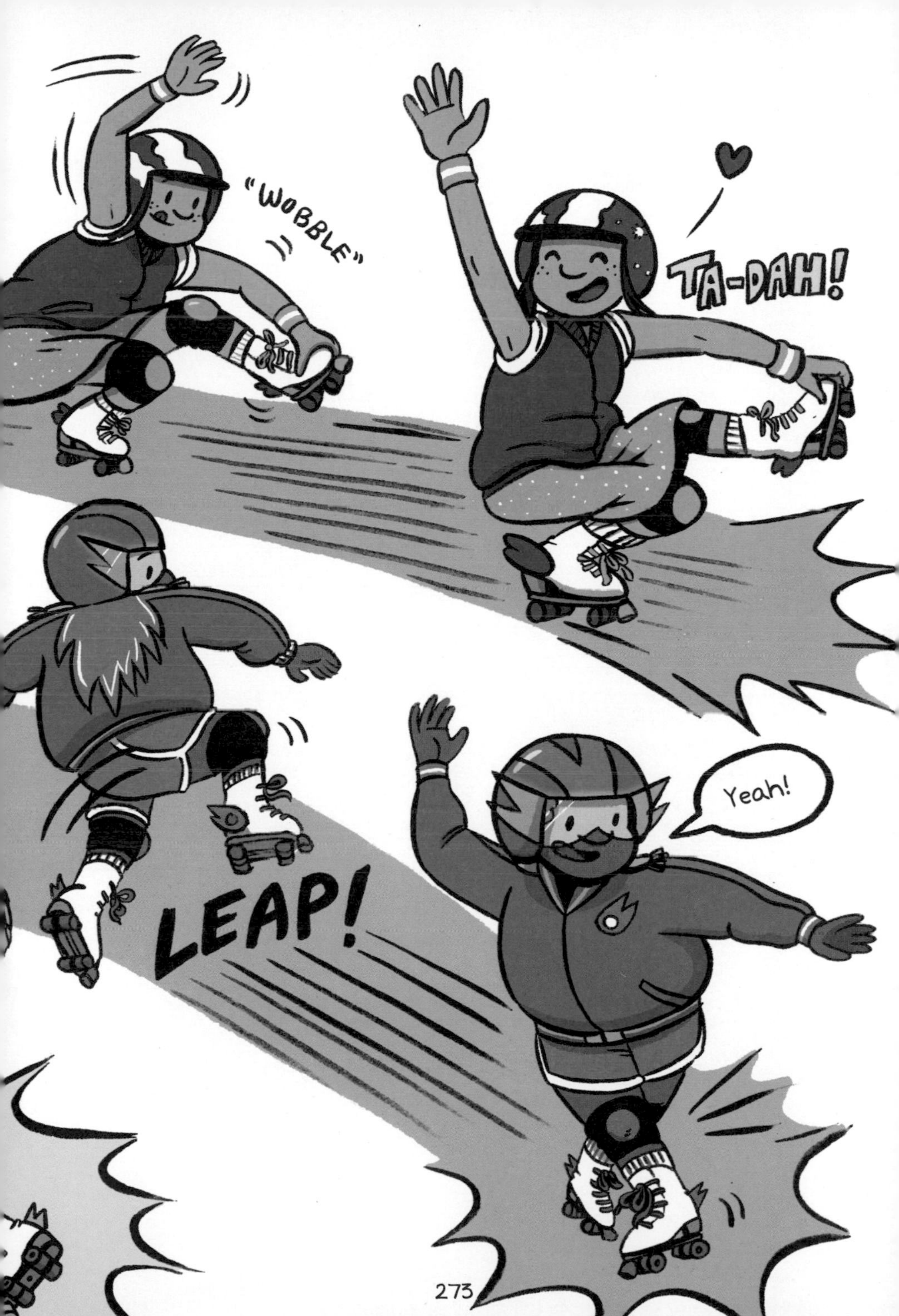
"WOBBLE"
TA-DAH!
LEAP!
Yeah!

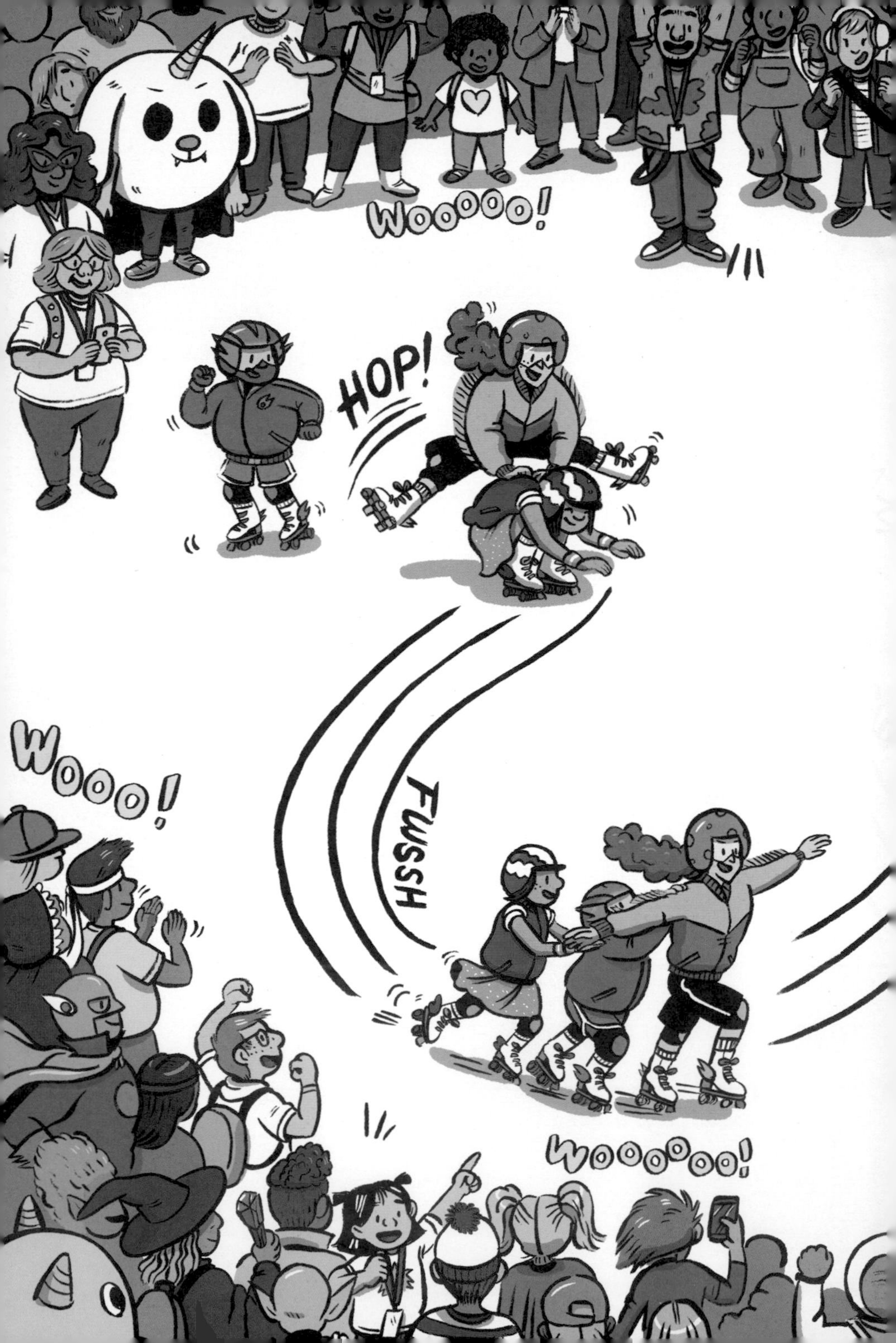
WOOOOO!
HOP!
WOOO!
FWSSH
WOOOOOO!

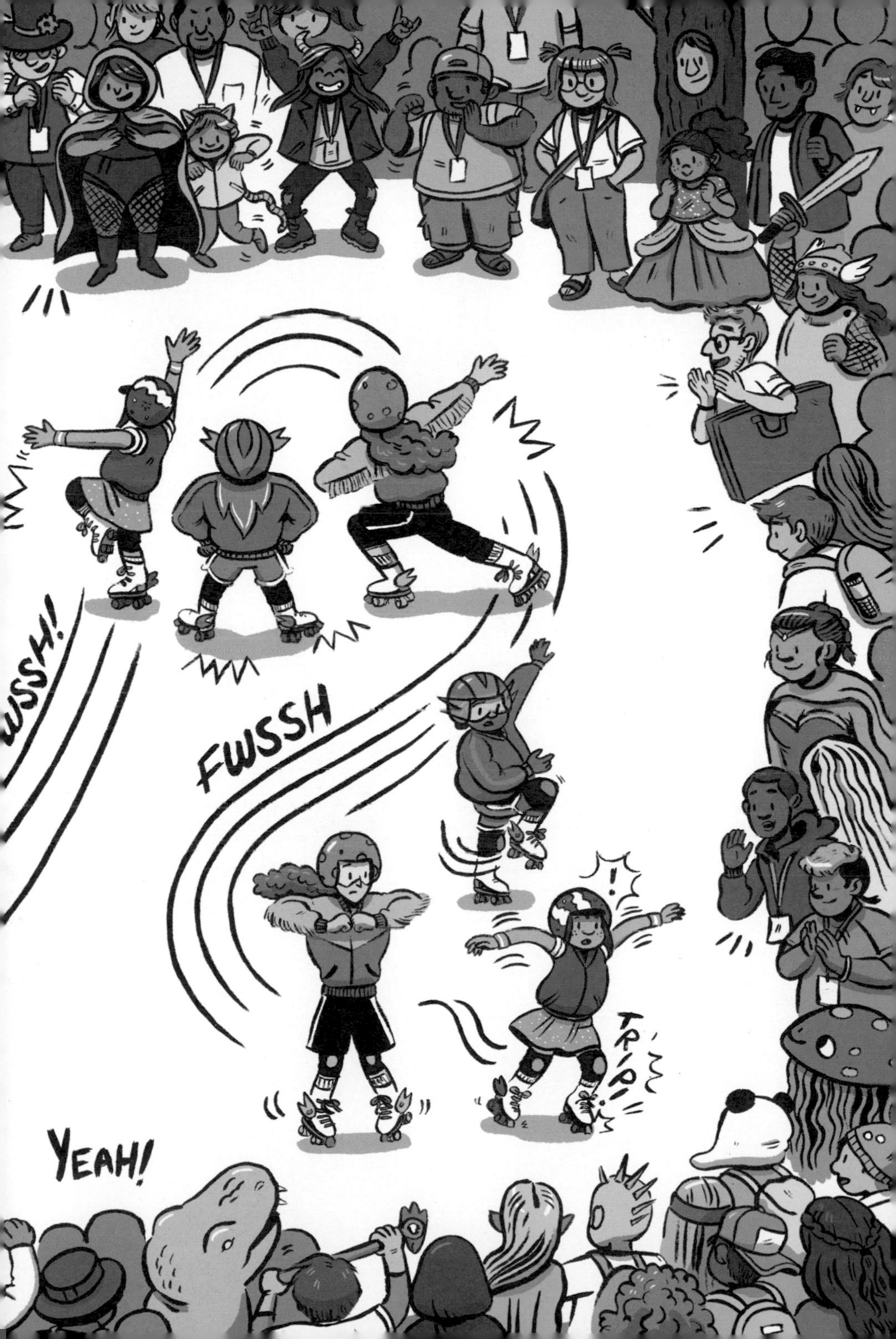
WSSH!
FWSSH
TRIP!
YEAH!

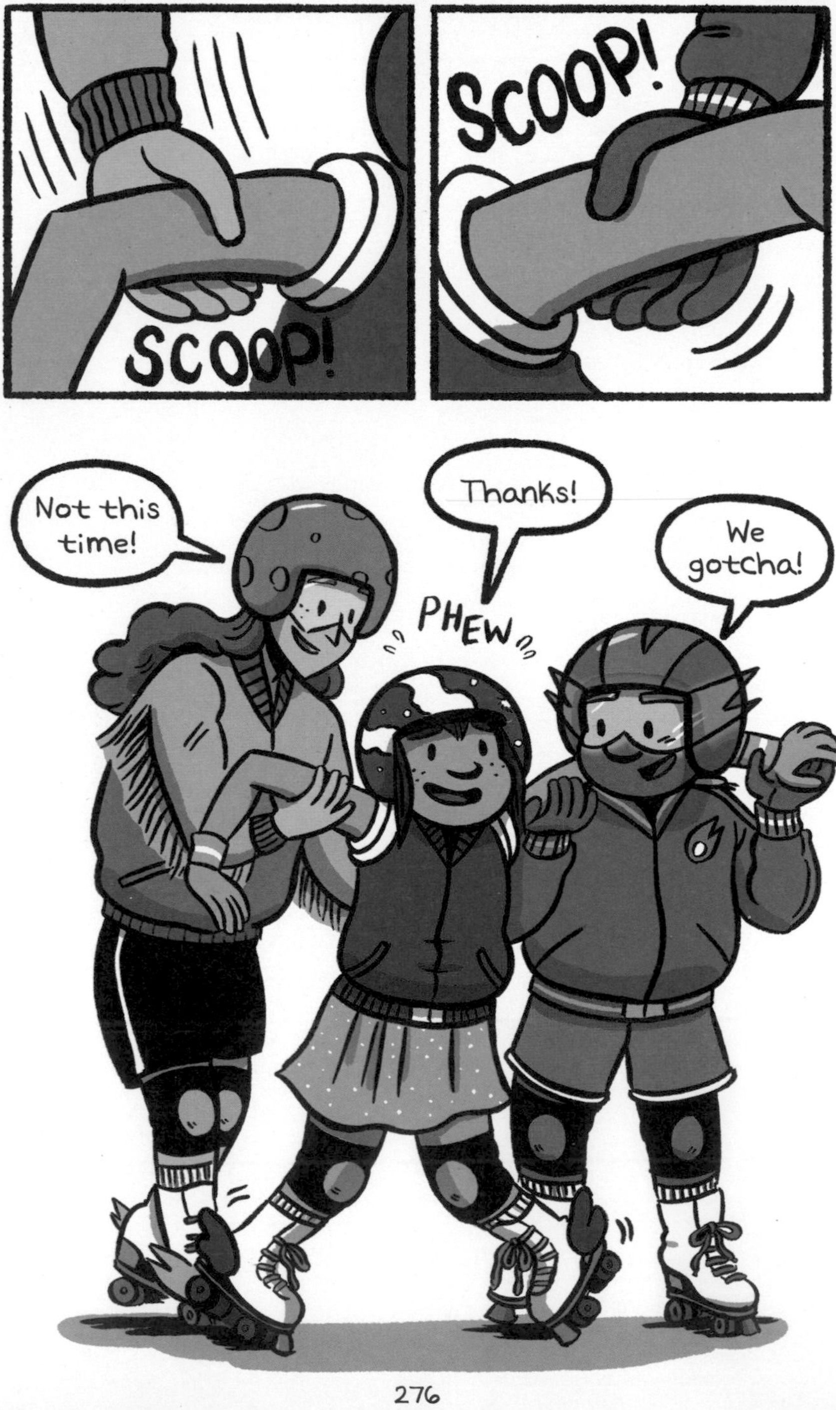
SCOOP!
SCOOP!
Not this time!
Thanks!
PHEW
We gotcha!

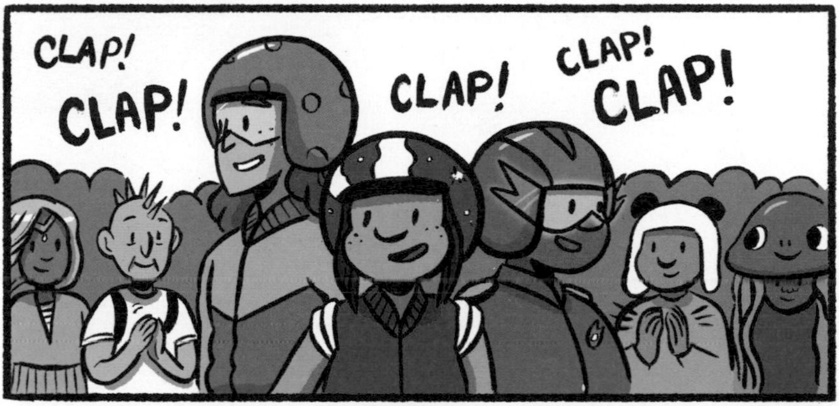
CLAP!
CLAP!
CLAP!
CLAP!
CLAP!

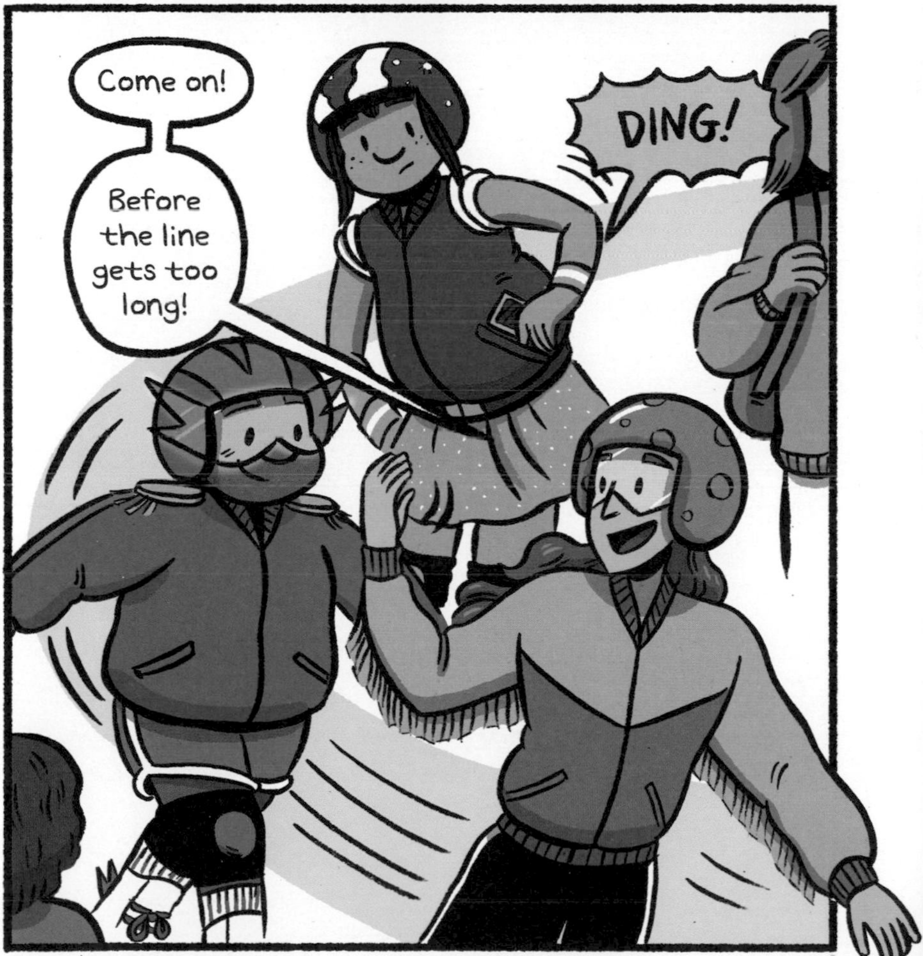
Come on!
Before the line gets too long!
DING!

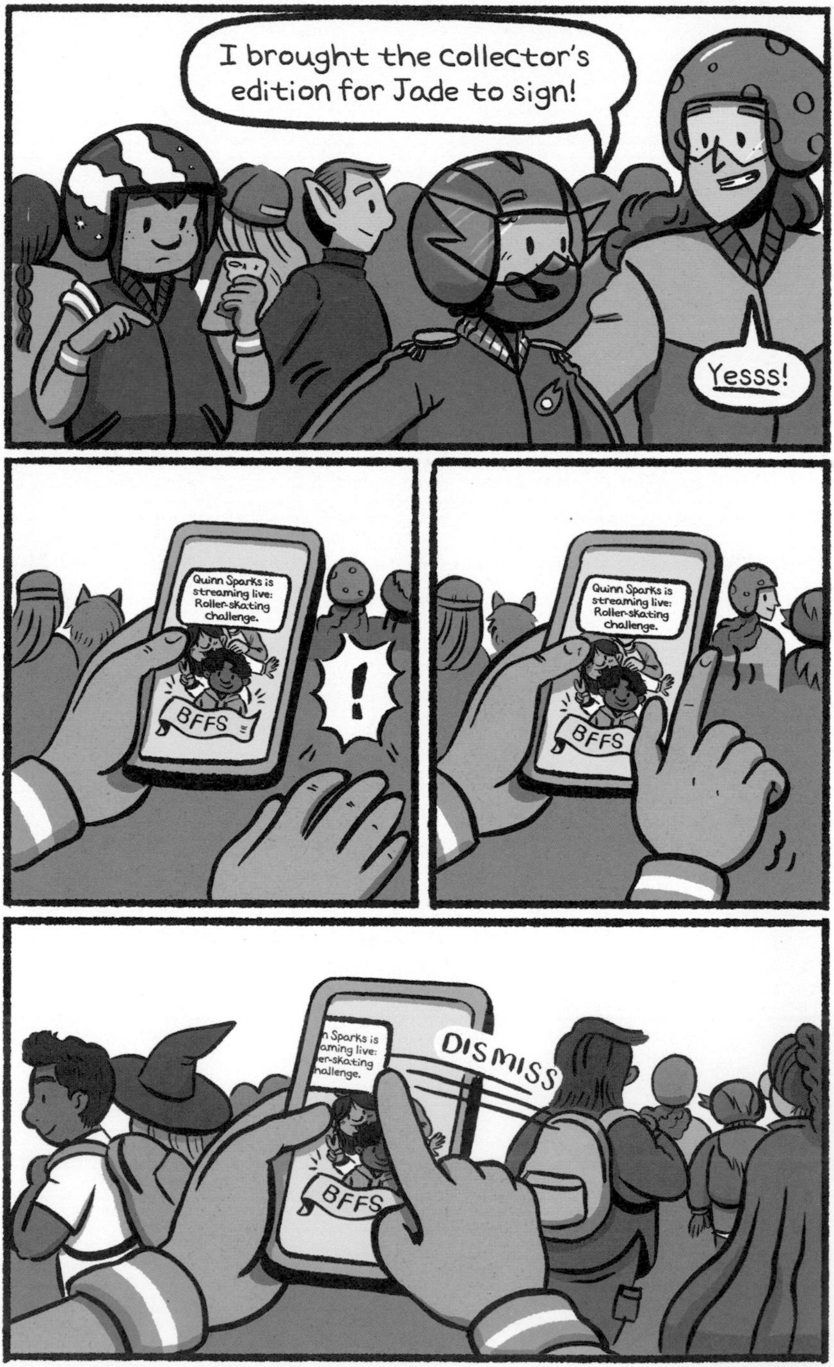
I brought the collector's edition for Jade to sign!
Yesss!
Quinn Sparks is streaming live: Roller-skating challenge.
BFFS
!
Quinn Sparks is streaming live: Roller-skating challenge.
BFFS
BFFS
DISMISS

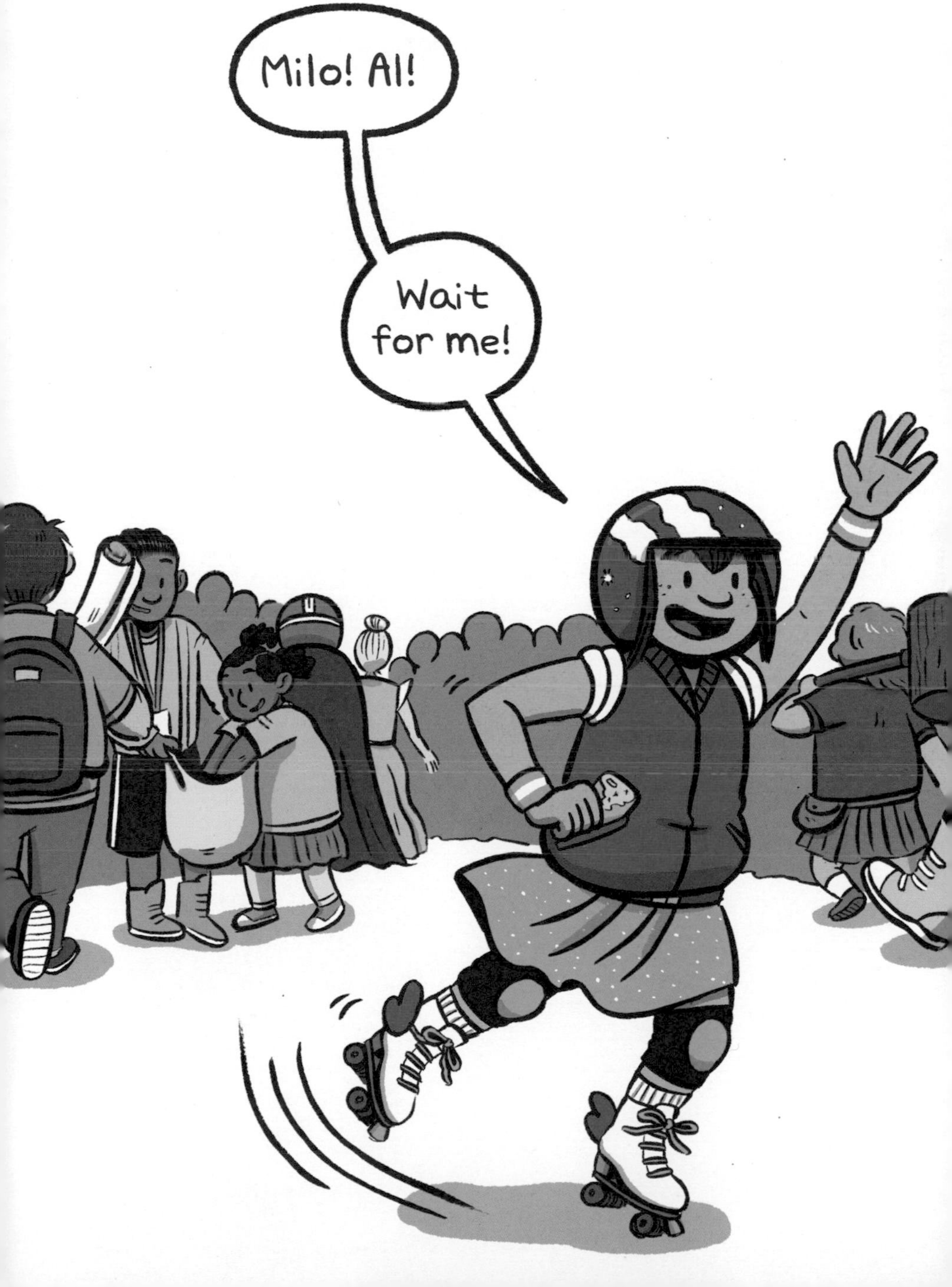
Milo! Al!
Wait for me!

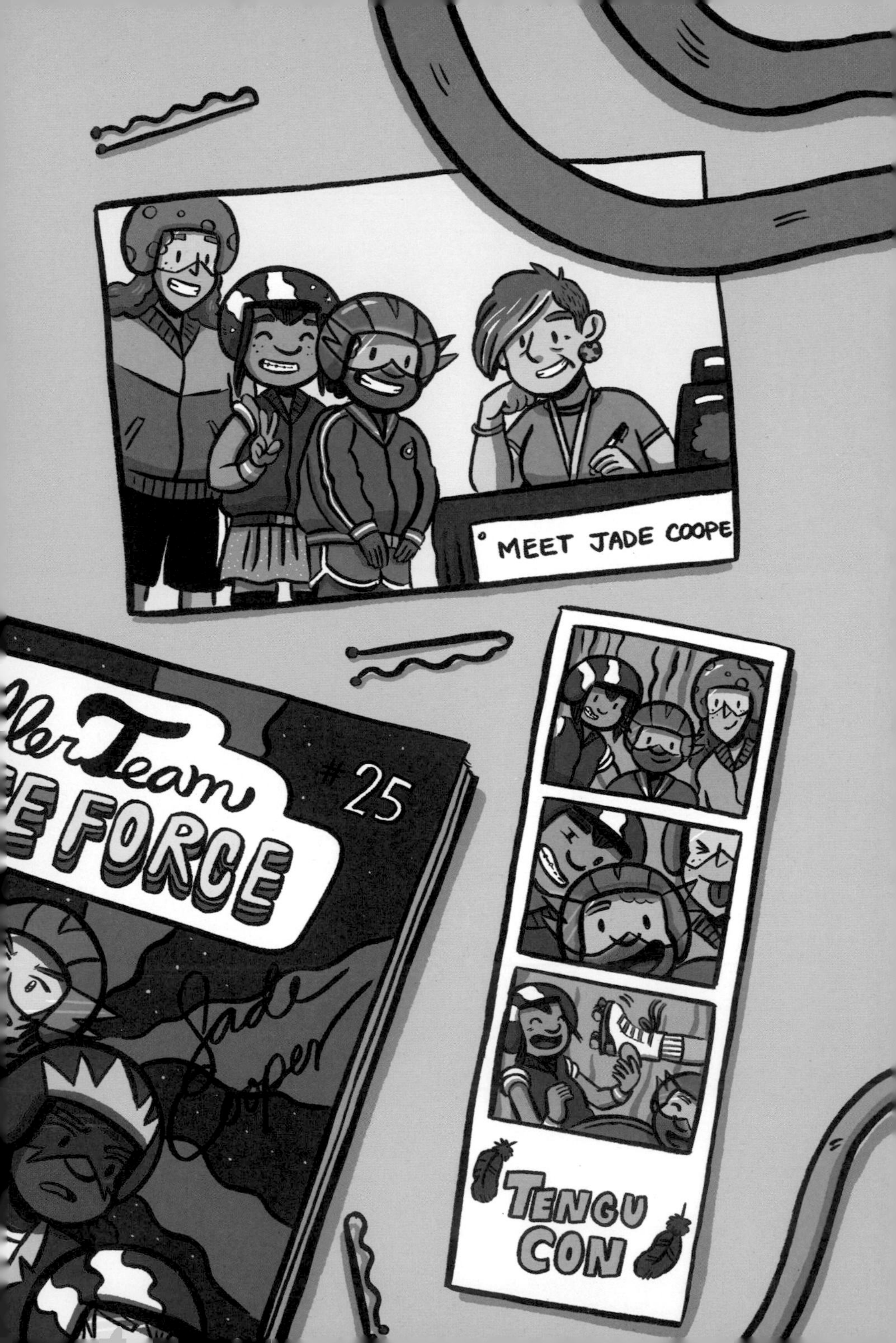

MEET JADE COOPE
#25
E FORCE
Jade Cooper
TENGU CON

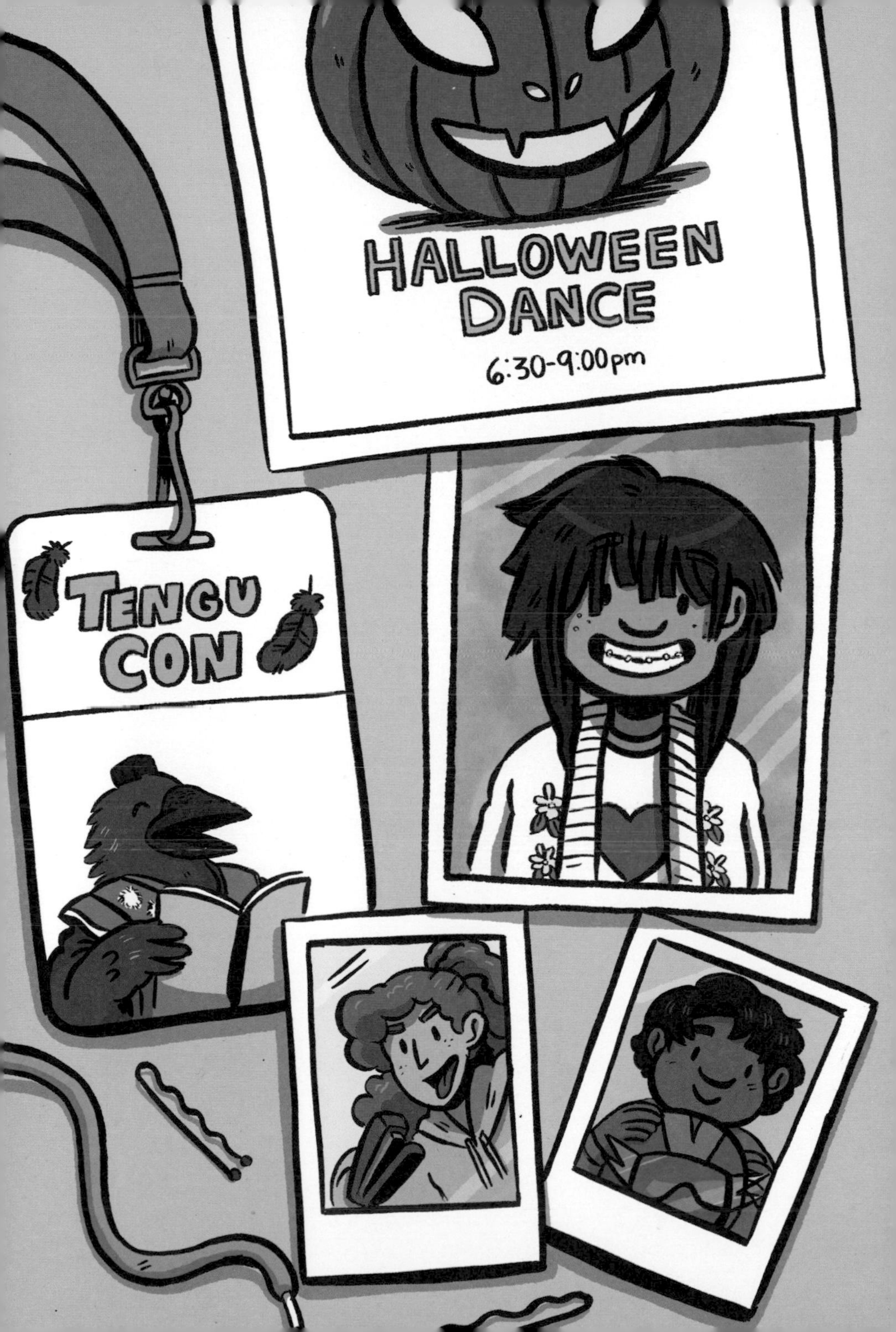
HALLOWEEN
DANCE
6:30-9:00pm
TENGU
CON

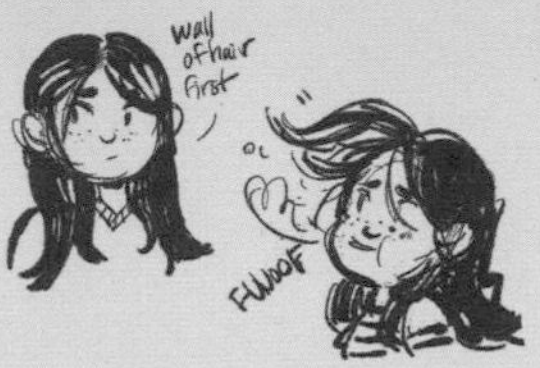
wall of hair first
FWOOF

AUTHOR'S NOTE

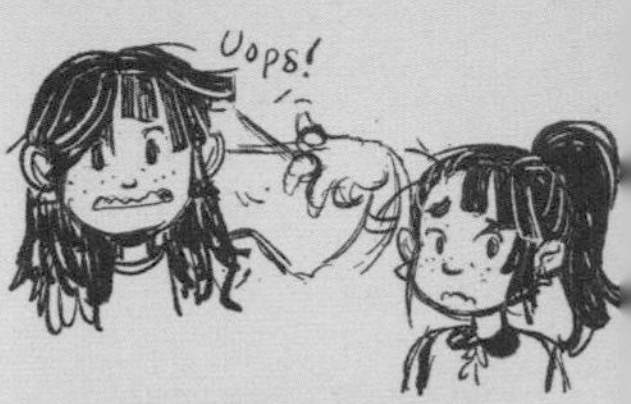
Uops!

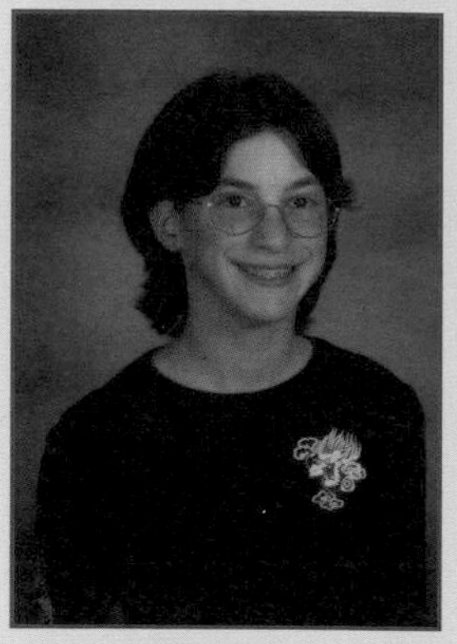

I was a kid who always loved to draw. Like Viv, Milo, and Al, I was inspired to create art and costumes fueled by the stories I loved. I could fill sketchbooks with original characters, but I always stopped short when it came to giving them their own stories. I thought of myself as someone who drew but didn't write, and at some point "didn't" changed to "can't." Whenever I thought about trying, I would get overwhelmed: How would I even know how to *start*? How would I even know what to *say*?

The idea for *Picture Day* came from an exercise I designed when I decided it was time to work through my feeling of "can't" and find my voice as a writer.

For an entire month, I wrote one sentence every day. Each sentence was from a random moment in a new story. Because it was a small task (just one sentence!), it felt achievable. At the end of the month, I had started 31 of my own stories! I printed out all my story pieces and placed them inside a tiny treasure chest.

During the next month, I did something fun and familiar: I drew the pictures! Each day I pulled a slip of paper out of the chest and drew a picture to go with it. I never knew what I was going to draw until prompted by the sentence—and figuring out the story as I drew was exhilarating. I was developing characters, building worlds. I was writing!

During that month, one of the story slices I created was this:

"Just a minute Mom" cried Dawn, "I'm almost ready to go..."

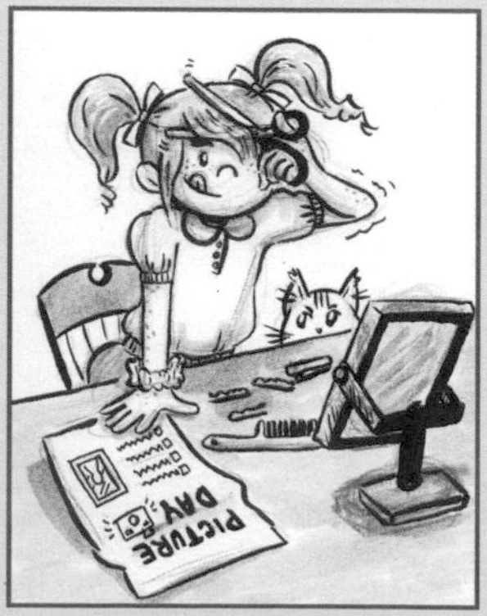
PICTURE DAY

When I drew this picture, I didn't know the character's name. All I knew was that she was about to cut off her hair on school picture day . . . and her mom didn't know about it! After asking myself a series of questions (What inspires her to make the cut? How do her friends feel about it? How does her *mom* feel about it?), I started to learn more. When I got stuck, I asked new questions and doodled to find the answers. Eventually, that one sketch became the beginning of *Picture Day*.

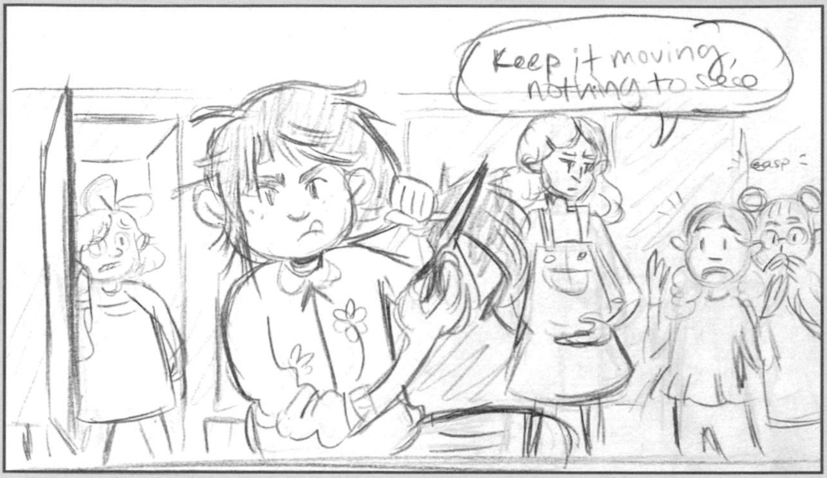
Keep it moving, nothing to see

I learned that my writing process required structure but with room for exploration. I needed a curious and open mind, and I needed to cultivate kindness toward my creations as they were developing.

It took a lot of time and confidence to find my voice as a writer, but I couldn't be happier that I finally took the leap.

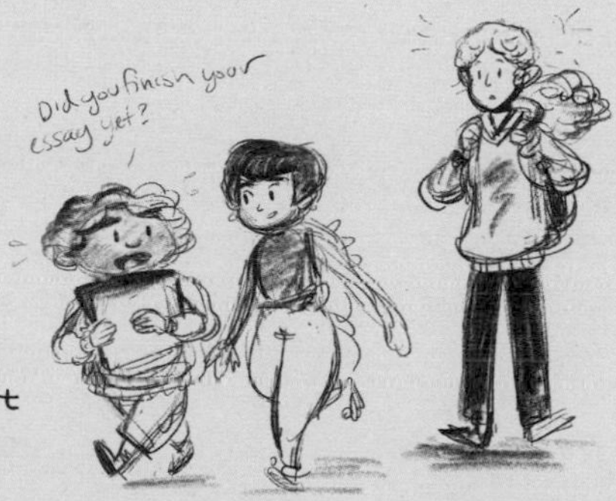
Did you finish your essay yet?

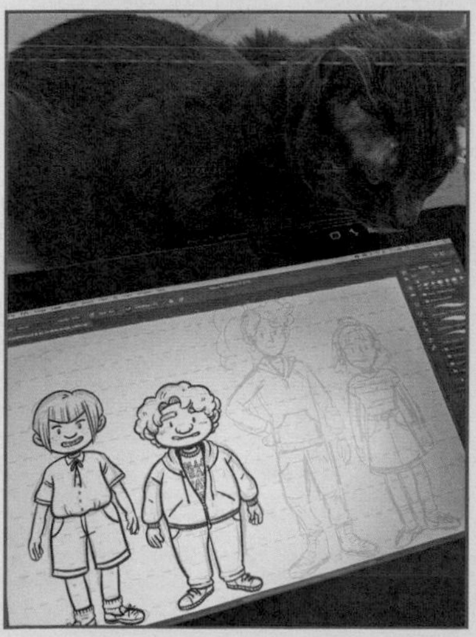

So if you are someone who thinks of themselves as a person who "can't" do something you really want to do, I hope this inspires you to start. Little by little, and with kindness toward yourself. I can't wait to see what you come up with.

—Sarah

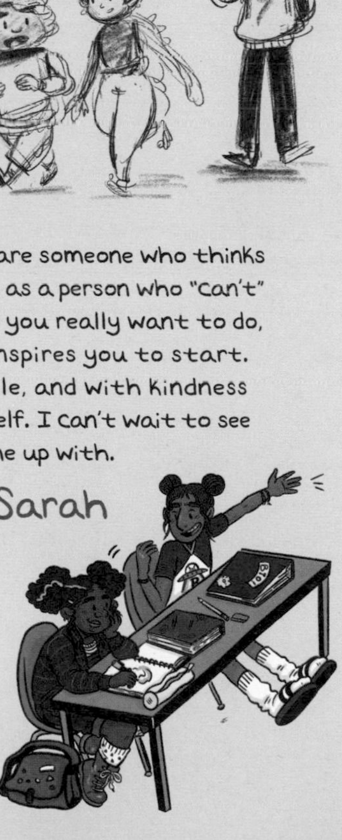

ACKNOWLEDGMENTS

Marisa DiNovis, I couldn't have asked for a more thoughtful and careful editor for this series! Thank you for never backing down from the hard questions that took my work to the next level. I always look forward to our collaborative chats. April Ward, your design work is top-notch. Thank you for making my art come to life! Jake Eldred, thank you for making my scheduling-spreadsheet dreams come true! To the rest of the Knopf and PRH team, thank you for your hard work, dedication, and enthusiasm in getting this book and series out into the world. An extra-special thanks for trusting me to lead you through extemporaneous creative activities!

Molly O'Neill, I'm so lucky to have you as my agent. You've coached me through finding my voice as a writer, and you are an unwavering champion of my work. Thank you for always being eager to hop on a call to brainstorm or answer my many questions about the publishing world. You are an integral part of my creative journey.

Thank you to my early readers, Jen de Oliveira and Elsa Vernon. Jen, you've known these characters and loved them as long as I have! Thank you for the comics/coffee chats, your careful feedback, and your friendship. I'm so glad that our books get to exist in the world together! Elsa, I'm so happy that we live in the same city again for all the reasons! Thank you for swooping in and giving me a crucial note that saved my ending.

To my Lumos Labbies community: I'm so thankful to have this wonderful group of people still in my life. Special thanks to Tyler Hinman, Ivy Ngo, Brendan Milos, Adrian Herbez, Gus Gutierrez, Matt Keefer, Bryan Young, Eli Delventhal, Shelby MacLeod, David Beavers, Aaron Kaluszka, and Bill Nega for brainstorming help with the RTSF theme song and Gabi's dance proposal puns.

Thank you to the entire team at Little Woodfords in Portland, Maine. This book was fueled by your cappuccinos and friendly conversations.

Mom, Dad, and Carrie: Thank you for instilling in me a love of reading and a love of comics, and for always enthusiastically encouraging my creative endeavors, no matter how strange (see: clicky pants). Leslie: Thank you for taking us in and giving me a space for my ideas to flourish after Luci's untimely demise.

Adam: This book truly wouldn't exist without your love and support. Thank you for everything from brainstorming plot points to building technical tools, from acting as my camera crew to cooking elaborate meals that nourish my soul. I love you and am grateful every day for such a loving partner and collaborator.

☆ Olivia C

Viv! Remember when you cut your hair!? —Ruby

Rana Latif

I had a good time getting to know u this year! Math club ♡'s u!

—Olivia N

Olivia V

I know we'll be FRIENDS FOREVER! XO JB